Tales of Weird Menace

ROBERT E. HOWARD

Introduction by Don Herron
Edited by Rob Roehm and Paul Herman

THE

Robert E. Howard

FOUNDATION PRESS

For Glenn Lord (1931-2011), preserver of Howard's typescripts and manuscripts, godfather of Howard studies, and the greatest fan that ever lived.

ISBN 978-1-955446-25-9 (Paperback)
ISBN 978-1-955446-24-2 (Hardcover)
ISBN 978-1-955446-40-2 (eBook)

Published by the REH Foundation Press, LLC by arrangement with Robert E. Howard Properties Inc.

https://rehfoundation.org
https://rehfpress.com

Cover illustration copyright © 2025, Mark Wheatley.

https://markwheatleygallery.com

Book prepared for publication by Ståle Gismervik, Savage Studios.

Version 2.0 - Ultimate Edition.

Acknowledgments

All of the Howard stories, poems and portions thereof contained in *Tales of Weird Menace* come from Howard's original typescripts, manuscripts, and carbons, when possible. Virtually all of the typescripts were scanned from the Glenn Lord collection, now at the University of Texas, Austin; the Robert E. Howard collection at Texas A&M University; or the typescript collection at Cross Plains Library.

Other sources include: For "Skull-Face," about ¾ from original typescript, and ¼ from first publication in Weird Tales; and "The Story Thus Far" is from first publication in Weird Tales.

CHANGES FROM THE FIRST EDITION:
"Moon of Zambebwei" and "The Noseless Horror": Text switched from first publication to typescript.

"The Night Was Damp" (untitled) and "Yellow Laughter"; Both switched from Glenn Lord's retyped versions to the original typescripts.

"Taverel Manor": 15-page draft replaced with a 24-page draft.

Newly added to this edition: "Sons of Hate" synopses 2 and 3, "Black Hound of Death" synopsis, and "Moon of Zambebwei" synopsis.

Contents

Acknowledgments iii

Lines of Succession vii
    introduction by Don Herron

Tales of Weird Menace

Skull-Face 3

The Noseless Horror 99

The Brazen Peacock 115

Black John's Vengeance 135

Talons in the Dark 149

The Hand of the Black Goddess 167

Sons of Hate 203

Moon of Zambebwei 245

Black Hound of Death 277

The Devils of Dark Lake 305

Guests of the Hoodoo Room 331

Black Wind Blowing 379

Miscellanea

Taverel Manor 405
    (unfinished)

The Return of the Sorcerer 431
    (unfinished)

"From the black, bandit-haunted mountains . . ." 441
    (untitled and unfinished)

The Red Stone 443
    (unfinished)

"The night was damp..." 445
    (untitled and unfinished)

The Ivory Camel 451
    (unfinished)

Yellow Laughter 457
    (fragment)

The Jade God 459
    (unfinished)

Spectres in the Dark 465
    (unfinished)

The Spell of Damballah 479
    (unfinished)

"James Norris..." 485
    (untitled synopsis)

Sons of Hate 487
    (partial synopsis 1)

Sons of Hate 489
    (partial synopsis 2)

Sons of Hate 491
    (partial synopsis 3)

The Devils of Dark Lake 493
    (untitled synopsis)

The House of Om 499
    (synopsis)

The Black Hound of Death 511
    (synopsis)

Moon of Zambebwei 513
    (untitled synopsis)

"The Story Thus Far..." 517
    (Skull-Face)

Lines of Succession

introduction by Don Herron

Closing in on forty years, off and on, as a published Robert E. Howard critic, I began to wonder recently how I got started on that road. Along the way I detoured into other avenues— major explorations into Dashiell Hammett and the hard-boiled detective crew, plus the literary world of San Francisco, Charles Willeford, Philip K. Dick—with occasional treks up meandering footpaths, such as chasing down the stock lists, brochures and other ephemera the publisher August Derleth issued relentlessly while promoting Arkham House Books and his other activities. Arkham ephemera, epigrams tossed off by Clark Ashton Smith, *The Maltese Falcon*, authentic Conan stories written by Howard versus the insipid imitations from his so-called "posthumous collaborators"—somehow I've covered a lot of ground, and ended up after all this time in the company of writers who write books-about-books.

If you asked about influences even a couple of years ago, I would have mentioned the great Chicago bookman Vincent Starrett first and foremost.

Author of *Penny Wise and Book Foolish*, *Books Alive* and many other excursions into the landscape of books and literature, Starrett was the champ at evoking the pleasures of reading and collecting, master of a smooth style he no doubt developed in tribute to his own idol, the Welsh mystical writer Arthur Machen. To be able to make the words flow with such seeming effortlessness—yes, that would be nice, indeed!

Yet Starrett was pretty much useless as a down-and-dirty critic. He was the kind of guy who goes out of his way to avoid controversy—you would not have heard about how absolutely lousy the stories added into the Lancer paperback editions of Conan by L.

Sprague de Camp and Lin Carter were from Vincent Starrett as you did from me in "Conan vs. Conantics." And as a teenager in Tennessee I made the notes for that essay and contemplated many of the ideas about Robert E. Howard I would cover later, all several years before I encountered Starrett's charming volumes.

In a completely negative way, I suppose L. Sprague de Camp provided early inspiration. My introduction to Howard came in the form of the 1967 Lancer paperback *Conan the Warrior*, picked new off the spinner rack—"Red Nails" and "Beyond the Black River" in one package made me a Howard fan for life. I grabbed other Lancer paperbacks as I saw them, but the more introductions by de Camp I read for the Conan series, the more irritated I became. . . . Really, this mediocre hack felt that he was equal to adding to Howard's dazzling run of adventures featuring the Cimmerian? The constant put-downs of the young writer as crazy, careless—my response was "Conan vs. Conantics" in 1976, but that was not the sum of what I wanted to write about Howard and his work.

By the time I edited *The Dark Barbarian* in 1984 I had plenty of models to work from, Starrett among them. But where as a kid in Tennessee could I have gotten even the glimmer of the concept that you could do a whole book about a favorite author, especially a writer like Howard? I must have known that books had been written about someone like Ernest Hemingway, but I didn't want to do books about Hemingway— I had something to say about the prolific pulp fictioneer from Cross Plains, Texas.

I realized that the answer to this mystery was right under my nose as soon as I saw that Howard's short novel *Skull-Face* anchors this collection.

Oh, yeah. . . *Lupoff*. . . .

I cannot imagine that a Howard fan of my generation could hear the title *Skull-Face* and not think instantly of Richard A. Lupoff's *Edgar Rice Burroughs: Master of Adventure* and his surprising assessment of that work—how the young Texan managed to out-Fu Fu-Manchu! The first edition of that book-length study of the creator of Tarzan and John Carter of Mars appeared in hardcover in 1965 from Canaveral Press, but it would be several more years before I began adding hardbacks to my own collection. The edition I read, along with everyone else, blazed into print in paperback from Ace Books in 1968, that bright red cover by Frank Frazetta recycled from an earlier Ace paperback of Burroughs' *The Beasts of Tarzan*. And of course it was a Frazetta painting that had drawn my eye to *Conan the Warrior* the year before—Frazetta, a cornerstone figure for that era.

In addition to profiling the many series launched by the prolific Burroughs, Lupoff looked at the extent of his influence and the many imitations that sprang up using Tarzan as a model. "These illegitimate descendants of Tarzan do raise a serious question concerning the matter of successor authors," he wrote. "After having read a number of stories of various sorts by successor authors, over a period of years, I had prior to the past few months concluded that their products were universally inferior to the original. To the extent that a successor author maintained fidelity to the original his work was superfluous. To the extent that it varied from the original, it tended to fracture the structure of imagination created by the original author. Either way, the successor's work would suffer." Then Lupoff got to Robert E. Howard:

> I have come across one exception to this principle. It is *Skull-Face*, the title of the 1946 collection of Howard stories. *Skull-Face* was serialized in *Weird Tales* in 1929. . . a pastiche of the Fu Manchu stories of Sax Rohmer. Skull-Face is Dr. Fu just as clearly as he can be, portrayed as well as Rohmer ever portrayed him. Howard's hero, the American Stephen Costigan, is far superior in conception and presentation to any of the men Rohmer ever put up against Fu. To the extent that Howard maintains fidelity to the original, his work is superior.
>
> To the extent that Howard does not rely upon Rohmer, he goes beyond Rohmer, extending rather than destroying the structure of the original author's work. Rohmer had never fully explained the origin of Fu, although he often hinted an Egyptian identity of incredible

antiquity. Howard carries back beyond Egypt, makes Skull-Face a survivor of sunken Atlantis, and brings the whole audacious thing off perfectly!

Yes. You could do literary criticism on Howard. You could do entire books on writers very much like Howard. That moment in *Master of Adventure* was exactly what I needed to see as a teenager to spur on dreams of doing criticism of the Texan of my own. And as a statement from 1965, it ranks in the forefront of modern reappraisals—recognizing that Howard was far more talented a writer than the mere pulp hack many commentators had dismissively portrayed him as being, if they mentioned his name at all.

Howard submitted *Skull-Face* to *Weird Tales* in 1928 when he was in the thick of creating his cycles of stories about King Kull and Solomon Kane, although it seems likely he wrote it as an attempt to break out of the pulp jungle and into the world of books—he also completed the autobiographical novel *Post Oaks and Sand Roughs*, inspired by Jack London's *Martin Eden*, late that same year and sent it off to a now unknown publisher. While it is possible he wrote *Skull-Face* with the idea of seeing it appear in *Weird Tales*, he would not have thought that *Post Oaks* had any chance of placing in those pages. In 1934 he pounded out the Conan novel *The Hour of the Dragon* on his Underwood for the British publisher Pawling & Ness Ltd., and only when that firm went into receivership did he use *Weird Tales* as a salvage market for the homeless manuscript. The same scenario probably played out with *Skull-Face* earlier, after it was rejected by other, unknown presses.

The wild Howardian reinvention of Fu-Manchu proved popular with at least one *Weird Tales* reader—when August Derleth assembled the first major collection of Howard's work for 1946 publication from Arkham House, he titled the massive omnibus *Skull-Face and Others*. Apparently the young Texan contemplated doing more with that potential series, since it is known that in 1931 he abandoned plans for a sequel.

And of course Howard was doing a revamp of British writer Sax Rohmer, a flat-out peddle-to-the-metal revamp. Rohmer—penname of Arthur Henry Sarsfield Ward—was among Howard's favorite writers, with no less than eight books by Rohmer surviving from Howard's personal library, including *The Insidious Dr. Fu-Manchu*, *The Return of Fu-Manchu*, *The Hand of Fu-Manchu*, *The Green Eyes of Bast*, and *The Quest of the Sacred Slipper*. Howard even tossed off quick parodies of Rohmer, such as "The Sappious Few Menchu" in a 1925 letter to his pal Tevis Clyde Smith.

Rohmer created the insidious Devil Doctor in 1912, but was by no means the first hand in the Yellow Peril genre. M. P. Shiel featured Dr. Yen How in his 1898 serial adventure *The Yellow Danger*, which Shiel scholar John D. Squires notes was "probably the first Yellow Peril novel to approach best seller status in England." As Yen How plotted nefarious plots, Rohmer, born in 1883, was only fifteen years old. Still, who would argue that the creator of Fu-Manchu took the concept and made it his own?

The influence of Rohmer pervades Howard, as does the touch of Jack London, Howard's absolute favorite writer—nine titles by London are known to have been held in the Texan's collection. Edgar Rice Burroughs, too, is another writer whose shadow appears throughout Howard's work—he had at least twelve books by Burroughs on the shelves in Cross Plains. Yet as Lupoff observed in *Master of Adventure*, "I hesitate to call Robert E. Howard's Conan the Cimmerian an imitation of Tarzan; the influence of Burroughs on Howard was great but Howard's imagination was so powerful that any Tarzan in Conan tends to be submerged in the latter's roaring, brawling, drinking, wenching personality. . . . Like Tarzan he is periodically imprisoned, makes good his escape, defies cruel monarchs, is a demon fighter."

All writers are born from their influences—the brilliant crime fiction of Raymond Chandler stands on the bedrock of the stories and novels Dashiell Hammett and other writers sold to the pulp *Black Mask* in the 1920s. When Chandler found himself out of a regular job during the Great Depression, he decided to give the hard-boiled detective tale a shot, placing his first try in the December 1933 issue of *Black Mask*. Later Chandler would compose the classic defense of the hard-boiled genre in the essay "The Simple Art of Murder," where he calls Hammett the "ace performer" in that field and states, "There has been so much of this sort of thing that if a character in a detective story says, 'Yeah,' the author is automatically a Hammett imitator."

The great writers soon come into their own, like Howard without question when he created Conan in 1932, or Chandler no later than 1939 when he created the classic Private Eye named Philip Marlowe for the novel *The Big Sleep*.

One fascinating detail of Howard's career is that he did not seem to regard *Skull-Face* as a mystery or crime novel, something he would lay claim to in that line. As he wrote to his fellow *Weird Tales* contributor H. P. Lovecraft in a letter sent around September or October 1933, "Lately I've been trying to write detective yarns, something entirely new for me, and haven't had much success—in fact none, so far, except for a short yarn, 'Talons in the Dark,' written in San Antonio last spring, and which Kline, as my agent, sold to a magazine called *Strange Detective Stories*." Entirely new? The admixture and crossover of elements from Yellow Peril, detective or weird menace makes it all an interesting stew, but I guess *Skull-Face* was *Skull-Face*.

And by the way—Howard's correspondent H. P. Lovecraft himself stands on the bedrock of Edgar Allan Poe and Lord Dunsany, with other contemporary influences such as Arthur Machen—and also touches of Edgar Rice Burroughs. But he too certainly came into his own by the time he wrote "The Call of Cthulhu" in 1926.

Howard had even worse luck selling this loose set of stories than he did with his detective series about Steve Harrison. "Talons in the Dark" saw print under the title "Black Talons" in the December 1933 issue of *Strange Detective*. "Black Wind Blowing" appeared in *Thrilling Mystery* for June 1936, the same month the young writer ended his own life. He had sent "Black Hound of Death" to his agent in August 1934, but it would not hit print until the November

1936 issue of *Weird Tales*. The others remained unsold—"Guests of the Hoodoo Room" was rejected by *Thrilling Adventures* in January 1936—and the usual pileup of fragmentary starts and drafts for more such stories went into his manuscript trunk.

Personally, I've never had much fondness for either Yellow Peril or so-called weird menace stories—give me Bruce Lee or Chow Yun-Fat over Fu-Manchu any day! Despite having a number of pals who are rabid Sax Rohmer fans, I never could build an interest in the Fu-Manchu series, not after reading *Skull-Face*. Howard was modern, headlong. Rohmer was dated, staid—it's amazing that his heroes ever managed to escape a deathtrap.

If anything, I find the whole Yellow Peril genre most interesting as a pop culture response to real world events, the various Oriental masterminds deeply fictionalized reflections of the wandering Chinese revolutionary Dr. Sun Yat-sen, born in 1866 and dead in 1925. When M. P. Shiel wrote *The Yellow Danger* in installments for magazines, he tossed breaking news into the plot, and there's not the slightest doubt his arch-villain derives from Sun. And of course the good doctor spent time in San Francisco—as well as the London known to Fu-Manchu, and other points around the globe—and remains an important facet of that city's history. I'll always remember showing the penultimate M. P. Shiel fan John D. Squires around town and walking through the park in St. Mary's Square which features a two-story sculpture of Dr. Sun Yat-sen by the artist Benny Bufano. When Squires saw the towering figure recognition spread across his face, and he exclaimed, *"Dr. Yen How!"*

From a start as a kid in Tennessee I too have gone out into the world, if not as dramatically as Sun Yat-sen, and met many writers, fellow scholars and fans. I suppose that's why it took me so long to realize that Dick Lupoff helped set me on my way. I've known Lupoff for at least three decades, since we both live in the San Francisco Bay Area. Sometimes years pass without seeing him, and then we sit together on a panel during a convention. Sometimes I bump into him every few weeks. He has become another writer I know, more so than the guy whose thumbnail critique of *Skull-Face* lit some spark in my imagination back in 1968.

As for the sparks touched off by Sax Rohmer to add to the volcanic furnace that was the imagination of Robert E. Howard, at last we have a book—a very fat book—in tribute to that primary influence on the writer who would create his own genre of fiction in Sword-and-Sorcery, and in barely a decade as a professional writer turn out enough stories to fill many, many fat books—and inspire quite a few books-about-books.

Tales of Weird Menace

Skull-Face

1. The Face in the Mist

"We are no other than a moving row
Of magic shadow-shapes that come and go."
—Khayyam.

The horror first took concrete form amid that most un-concrete of all things—a hashish dream. I was off on a timeless, spaceless journey through the strange lands that belong to this state of being—a million miles away from earth and all things earthly—yet I became cognizant that something was reaching across the unknown voids, something that tore ruthlessly at the separating curtains of my illusions and intruded itself into my visions.

I did not exactly return to ordinary waking life, yet I was conscious of a seeing and a recognizing that was unpleasant and seemed out of keeping with the dream I was at that time enjoying. To one who has never known the delights of hashish, my explanation must seem chaotic and impossible. Still, I was aware of a rending of mists and then the Face intruded itself into my sight. I thought at first it was merely a skull; then I saw that it was a hideous yellow instead of white, and was endowed with some horrid form of life. Eyes glimmered deep in the sockets and the jaws moved as if in speech. The body, except for the high, thin shoulders, was vague and indistinct, but the hands which floated in the mists before and below the skull were horribly vivid and filled me with crawling fears. They were like the hands of a mummy, long, lean and yellow, with knobby joints and cruel curving talons.

Then, to complete the vague horror which was swiftly taking possession of me, a voice spoke—imagine a man so long dead that his vocal organ had grown rusty and unaccustomed to speech. This was the thought which struck me and made my flesh crawl as I listened.

"A strong brute and one who might be useful somehow. See that he is given all the hashish he requires."

Then the face began to recede, even as I sensed that I was the subject of conversation, and the mists billowed and began to close again. Yet for a single instant a scene stood out with startling clarity. I gasped—or sought to. For over the high, strange shoulder of the apparition another face stood out clearly for an instant, as if the owner peered at me. Red lips, half-parted, long dark eyelashes, shading vivid eyes, a shimmery cloud of hair. Over the shoulder of Horror, breathtaking beauty for an instant looked at me.

2. The Hashish Slave

"Up through Earth's center, through the Seventh Gate,
I rose, and on the throne of Saturn sate—"
—Khayyam.

My dream of the skull face was borne over that usually uncrossable gap that lies between hashish enchantment and humdrum reality. I sat cross-legged on a mat in Yun Shatu's Temple of Dreams and gathered the fading forces of my decaying brain to the task of remembering events and faces.

This last dream was so entirely different from any I had ever had before, that my waning interest was roused to the point of inquiring as to its origin. When I first began to experiment with hashish, I sought to find a physical or psychic basis for the wild flights of illusion pertaining thereto, but of late I had been content to enjoy without seeking cause and effect.

Whence this unaccountable sensation of familiarity in regard to that vision? I took my throbbing head between my hands and laboriously sought a clue. A living dead man and a girl of rare beauty who had looked over his shoulder. Then I remembered.

Back in the fogs of days and nights which veil a hashish addict's living and memory, my money had given out. It seemed years or possibly centuries, but my stagnant reason told me that it had probably been only a few days. At any rate, I had presented myself at Yun Shatu's sordid dive as usual and had been thrown out by the great negro Hassim when it was learned I had no more money.

My universe crashing to pieces about me, and my nerves humming like taut piano wires for the vital need that was mine, I crouched in the gutter and gibbered bestially, till Hassim swaggered out and stilled my yammerings with a blow that felled me, half-stunned.

Then as I presently rose, staggeringly and with no thought save of the river which flowed with a cool murmur so near me—as I rose, a light hand was laid like the touch of a rose on my arm. I turned with a frightened start, and stood spellbound before the vision of loveliness which met my gaze. Dark eyes limpid with pity surveyed me and the little hand on my ragged sleeve drew me toward the door of the Dream Temple. I shrank back, but a low voice, soft and musical, urged me, and filled with a trust that was strange, I shambled along with my beautiful guide.

At the door Hassim met us, cruel hands lifted and a dark scowl on his apelike brow, but as I cowered there, expecting a blow, he halted before the girl's upraised hand and her word of command which had taken on an imperious note.

I did not understand what she said, but I saw dimly, as in a fog, that she gave the black man money, and she led me to a couch where she had me recline and arranged the cushions as if I were king of Egypt instead of a ragged, dirty renegade who lived only for hashish. Her slim hand was cool on my brow for a moment and then she was gone and Yussef Ali came bearing the stuff for which my very soul shrieked—and soon I was wandering again through those strange and exotic countries that only a hashish slave knows.

Now as I sat on the mat and pondered the dream of the skull face I wondered more. Since the unknown girl had led me back into the dive, I had come and gone as before, when I had plenty of money to pay Yun Shatu. Someone certainly was paying him for me, and while my subconscious mind had told me it was the girl, my rusty brain had failed to entirely grasp the fact, or to wonder why. What need of wondering? So someone paid and the vivid-hued dreams continued, what cared I? But now I wondered. For the girl who had protected me from Hassim and had bought the hashish for me was the same girl I had seen in the skull face dream.

Oh, the beauty of her face and hands. Through the soddeness of my degradation the lure of her struck like a knife piercing my heart. Stangely revived the memories of the days when I was a man like other men—not yet a sullen, cringing slave of dreams. Far and dim they were, shimmery islands in the mist of years—and what a dark sea lay between!

I looked at my ragged sleeve and the dirty, clawlike hand pro-truding from it—I gazed through the hanging smoke which fogged the sordid room, at the low bunks along the wall whereon lay the blankly staring dreamers—slaves, like me, of hashish or of opium. I gazed at the slippered Chinamen gliding softly to and fro bearing pipes or roasting balls of concentrated purgatory over tiny flickering fires. I gazed at Hassim standing, arms folded beside the door like a great statue of black basalt.

And I shuddered and hid my face in my hands because with the faint dawning of returning manhood, I knew that this last and most cruel dream was futile—I had crossed an ocean over which I could never return, had voluntarily cut myself off from the world of normal men or women. Naught remained now but to drown this dream as I had drowned all my others—swiftly and with hope that I should soon attain that Ultimate Ocean which lies beyond all dreams.

So these fleeting moments of lucidity, of longing, that tear aside the veils of all dope slaves—unexplainable, without hope of attainment.

So I went back to my empty dreams, to my phantasmagoria of illusions; but sometimes, like a sword cleaving a mist, through the high lands and the lowlands and seas of my visions floated, like half-forgotten music, the sheen of dark eyes and shimmery hair.

You ask how I, Stephen Costigan, American and a man of some attainments and culture, came to lie in a filthy dive of London's Limehouse? The answer is simple—no jaded debauchee, I, seeking new sensations in the mysteries of the Orient. I answer—Argonne! Heavens, what deeps and heights of horror lurk in that one word alone! Shell shock—shell torn. Endless days and nights without end and roaring red Hell over No Man's Land where I lay shot and bayoneted to shreds of gory flesh. My body recovered, how I know not; my mind never did.

And the leaping fire and shifting shadows in my tortured brain drove me down and down, along the stairs of degradation, uncaring until at last I found surcease in Yun Shatu's Temple of Dreams. There, where I slew my red dreams in other dreams—the dreams of hashish whereby a man may descend to the lower pits of the reddest Hells or soar into those unnamable heights where the stars are diamond pinpoints beneath his feet.

Not the visions of the sot, the beast, were mine. I attained the unattainable, stood face to face with the unknown and in cosmic calmness knew the unguessable. And was content after a fashion, until the sight of burnished hair and scarlet lips swept away my dream-built universe and left me shuddering among its ruins.

3. *The Master of Doom*

"And he who flung you down upon this board,
He knows about it all—he knows! He knows!"
—Khayyam.

A hand shook me roughly as I emerged languidly from my latest debauch.

"The Master wishes you! Up, swine!"

Hassim it was who shook me and who spoke.

"To Hell with the Master," I answered, for I feared and hated Hassim.

"Up with you or you get no more hashish," was the brutal response, and I rose in trembling haste.

I followed the huge black man and he led the way to the rear of the building, stepping in and out among the wretched dreamers on the floor.

"Muster all hands on deck!" droned a sailor in a bunk. "All hands!"

Hassim flung open the door at the rear and motioned me to enter. I had never before passed through that door and had supposed it led into Yun Shatu's private quarters. But it was furnished only with a cot, a bronze idol of some sort before which incense burned, and a heavy table.

Hassim gave me a sinister glance and seized the table as if to spin it about. It turned as if it stood on a revolving platform and a section of the floor turned with it, revealing a hidden doorway in the floor. Steps led downward in the darkness.

Hassim lighted a candle and with a brusque gesture invited me to descend. I did so, with the sluggish obedience of the dope addict and he followed, closing the door above us by means of an iron lever fastened to the underside of the floor. In the semi-darkness we went down the rickety steps, some nine or ten I should guess, and then came upon a narrow corridor.

Here Hassim again took the lead, holding the candle high in front of him. I could scarcely see the sides of this cave-like passageway but knew that it was not wide. The flickering light showed it to be bare of any sort of furnishings save for a number of strange-looking chests which lined the walls—receptacles containing opium and other dope, I thought.

A continuous scurrying and the occasional glint of small red eyes haunted the shadows, betraying the presence of vast numbers of the great rats which infest the Thames waterfront of that section.

Then more steps loomed out of the dark in front of us as the corridor came to an abrupt end. Hassim led the way up them and at the top knocked four times against what seemed the underside of a floor. A hidden door opened and a flood of soft, illusive light streamed through.

Hassim hustled me up roughly and I stood blinking in such a setting as I had never seen in my wildest flights of vision. I stood in a jungle of palm trees through which wriggled a million vivid-hued dragons! Then as my startled eyes became accustomed to the light, I saw that I had not been suddenly transferred to some other planet, as I had at first thought. The palm trees were there, and the dragons, but the trees were artificial and stood in great pots and the dragons writhed across heavy tapestries which hid the walls.

The room itself was a monstrous affair—inhumanly large, it seemed to me. A thick smoke, yellowish and tropical in suggestion, seemed to hang over all, veiling the ceiling and baffling upward glances. This smoke, I saw, emanated from an altar in front of the wall to my left. I started. Through the saffron billowing fog two eyes, hideously large and vivid, glittered at me. The vague outlines of some bestial idol took indistinct shape. I flung an uneasy glance about, marking the oriental divans and couches and the bizarre furnishings, and then my eyes halted and rested on a lacquer screen just in front of me.

I could not pierce it and no sound came from beyond it, yet I felt eyes searing into my consciousness through it, eyes that burned through my very soul. A strange aura of evil flowed from that strange screen with its weird carvings and unholy decorations.

Hassim salaamed profoundly before it and then, without speaking, stepped back and folded his arms, statue-like.

A voice suddenly broke the heavy and oppressive silence.

"You who are a swine, would you like to be a man again?"

I started. The tone was inhuman, cold—more, there was a suggestion of long disuse of the vocal organs—the voice I had heard in my dream!

"Yes," I replied, trance-like, "I would like to be a man again."

Silence reigned for a space, then the voice came again with a sinister whispering undertone at the back of its sound, like bats flying through a cavern.

"I shall make you a man again because I am a friend to all broken men. Not for a price shall I do it, nor for gratitude. And I give you a sign to seal my promise and my vow. Thrust your hand through the screen."

At these strange and almost unintelligible words, I stood perplexed and then as the unseen voice repeated the last command, I stepped forward and thrust my hand through a slit which opened silently in the screen. I felt my wrist seized in an iron grip and something seven times colder than ice touched the inside of my hand. Then my wrist was released, and drawing forth my hand, I saw a strange symbol traced in blue close to the base of my thumb—a thing like a scorpion.

The voice spoke again in a sibilant language I did not understand, and Hassim stepped forward deferentially. He reached about the screen and then turned to me, holding a goblet of some amber-colored liquid which he proffered me with an ironical bow. I took it hesitatingly.

"Drink and fear not," said the unseen voice. "It is only an Egyptian wine with the qualities of life-giving."

So I raised the goblet and emptied it; the taste was not unpleasant, and even as I handed the beaker to Hassim again, I seemed to feel new life and vigor whip along my jaded veins.

"Remain at Yun Shatu's house," said the voice. "You will be given food and a bed until you are strong enough to work for yourself. You will use no hashish nor will you require any. Go!"

As in a daze, I followed Hassim back through the hidden door, down the steps, along the dark corridor and up through the other door that let us into the Temple of Dreams.

As we stepped from the rear chamber into the main room of the dreamers, I turned to the negro wonderingly.

"Master? Master of what? Of Life?"

Hassim laughed, fiercely and sardonically.

"Master of Doom!"

4. The Spider and the Fly

"—There was a veil through which I might not see;
There was a door to which I found no key."
                                        —Khayyam.

I sat on Yun Shatu's cushions and pondered with a clearness of mind new and strange to me. As for that, all my sensations were new and strange. I felt as if I had wakened from a monstrously long sleep, and though my thoughts were sluggish, I felt as though the cobwebs which had clogged them for so long had been partially brushed away.

I drew my hand across my brow, noting how it trembled. I was weak and shaky and felt the stirrings of hunger—not for dope but for food. What had been in the draft I had quenched in the chamber of mystery? And why had the "Master" chosen me, out of all the other wretches at Yun Shatu's, for regeneration?

And who was this Master? Somehow the word sounded vaguely familiar—I sought laboriously to remember. Yes—I had heard it, lying half-waking in the bunks or on the floor—whispered sibilantly by Yun Shatu or by Hassim or by Yussef Ali, the Moor. Muttered in their low-voiced conversations and mingled always with words I could not understand. Was not Yun Shatu, then, master of the

Temple of Dreams? I had thought and the other addicts thought that the withered Chinaman held undisputed sway over this drab kingdom and that Hassim and Yussef Ali were his servants. And the four China boys who roasted opium with Yun Shatu and Yar Khan the Afghan and Santiago the Haitian and Ganra Singh, the renegade Sikh—all in the pay of Yun Shatu, we supposed—bound to the opium lord by bonds of gold or fear.

For Yun Shatu was a power in London's Chinatown and I had heard that his tentacles reached across the seas into high places of mighty and mysterious tongs. Was that Yun Shatu behind the lacquer screen? No; I knew the Chinaman's voice and besides I had seen him puttering about in the front of the Temple just as I went through the back door.

Another thought came to me. Often, lying half-torpid, in the late hours of night or in the early grayness of dawn, I had seen men and women steal into the Temple, whose dress and bearing were strangely out of place and incongruous. Tall, erect men, often in evening dress, with their hats drawn low about their brows, and fine ladies, veiled, in silks and furs. Never two of them came together but always they came separately and, hiding their features, hurried to the rear door where they entered and presently came forth again, hours later sometimes. Knowing that the lust for dope finds resting place in high positions sometimes, I had never wondered overmuch, supposing that these were wealthy men and women of society who had fallen victims to the craving, and that somewhere in the back of the building there was a private chamber for such. Yet now I wondered—sometimes these persons had remained only a few moments—was it always opium for which they came, or did they, too, traverse that strange corridor and converse with the One behind the screen?

My mind dallied with the idea of a great specialist to which came all classes of people to find surcease from the dope habit. Yet it was strange that such a one should select a dope joint from which to work—strange too that the owner of that house should apparently look on him with so much reverence.

I gave it up as my head began to hurt with the unwonted effort of thinking and shouted for food. Yussef Ali brought it to me on a tray, and with a promptness which was surprizing. More, he salaamed as he departed, leaving me to ruminate on the strange shift of my status in the Temple of Dreams.

I ate, wondering what the One of the screen wanted with me. Not for an instant did I suppose that his actions had been prompted by the reasons he pretended; the life of the underworld had taught me that none of its denizens leaned toward philanthropy. And underworld the chamber of mystery had been, in spite of its elaborate and bizarre nature. And where could it be located? How far had I walked along the corridor? I shrugged my shoulders, wondering if it were not all a hashish-induced dream—then my eye fell upon my hand—and the scorpion traced thereon.

"Muster all hands!" droned the sailor in the bunk. "All hands!"

To tell in detail of the next few days would be boresome to any who have not tasted the dire slavery of dope. I waited for the craving to strike me again—waited with sure sardonic hopelessness. All day, all night—another day—then the miracle was forced upon my doubting brain. Contrary to all theories and supposed facts of science and common sense the craving had left me as suddenly and completely as a bad dream! At first I could not credit my senses but believed myself to be still in the grip of a dope nightmare. But it was true. From the time I quaffed the goblet in the room of mystery, I felt not the slightest desire for the stuff which had been life itself to me. This, I felt vaguely, was somehow unholy and certainly opposed to all rules of Nature. If the dread being behind the screen had discovered the secret of breaking hashish's terrible power, what other monstrous secrets had he discovered and what unthinkable dominance was his? The suggestion of evil crawled serpentlike through my mind.

I remained at Yun Shatu's house, lounging in a bunk or on cushions spread upon the floor, eating and drinking at will, but now that I was becoming a normal man again, the atmosphere became most revolting to me and the sight of the wretches writhing in their dreams reminded me unpleasantly of what I myself had been, and it repelled—nauseated me.

So one day when no one was watching me, I rose and went out on the street and walked along the waterfront. The air, burdened as it was with smoke and foul scents, filled my lungs with strange freshness and aroused new vigor in what had once been a powerful frame. I took new interest in the sounds of men living and working, and the sight of a vessel being unloaded at one of the wharfs actually thrilled me. The force of longshoremen was short, and shortly I found myself heaving and lifting and carrying, and though my sweat coursed down my brow and my limbs trembled at the effort, I exulted in the thought that at last I was able to labor for myself again, no matter how low or drab the work might be.

As I returned to the door of Yun Shatu's that evening—hideously weary but with the renewed feeling of manhood that comes of honest toil—Hassim met me at the door.

"You been where?" he demanded roughly.

"I've been working on the docks," I answered shortly.

"You don't need to work on docks," he snarled. "The Master got work for you."

He led the way and again I traversed the dark stairs and the corridor under the earth. This time my faculties were alert and I decided that the passageway could not be over thirty or forty feet in length. Again I stood before the lacquer screen and again I heard the inhuman voice of living death.

"I can give you work," said the voice. "Are you willing to work for me?"

I quickly assented. After all, in spite of the fear which the voice inspired, I was deeply indebted to the owner.

"Good. Take these."

As I started toward the screen a sharp command halted me and Hassim stepped forward and reaching behind took what was offered. This was a bundle of pictures and papers, apparently.

"Study these," said the One behind the screen, "and learn all you can about the man portrayed thereby. Yun Shatu will give you money; buy yourself such clothes as seamen wear and take a room at the front of the Temple. At the end of two days, Hassim will bring you to me again. Go!"

The last impression I had, as the hidden door closed above me, was that the eyes of the idol, blinking through the everlasting smoke, leered mockingly at me.

The front of the Temple of Dreams consisted of rooms for rent, masking the true purpose of the building under the guise of a waterfront boardinghouse. The police had made several visits to Yun Shatu but had never gotten any incriminating evidence against him.

So in one of these rooms I took up my abode and set to work studying the material given me.

The pictures were all of one man, a large man, not unlike me in build and general facial outline, except that he wore a heavy beard and was inclined to blondness whereas I am dark. The name, as written on the accompanying papers, was Major Fairlan Morley, Special Commissioner to Natal and the Transvaal. This office and title were new to me and I wondered at the connection between an African commissioner and an opium house on the Thames waterfront.

The papers consisted of extensive data evidently copied from authentic sources and all dealing with Major Morley, and a number of private documents considerably illuminating on the major's private life.

An exhaustive description was given of the man's personal appearance and habits, some of which seemed very trivial to me. I wondered what the purpose could be, and how the One behind the screen had come in possession of papers of such intimate nature.

I could find no clue in answer to this question but bent all my energies to the task set out for me. I owed a deep debt of gratitude to the unknown man who required this of me and I was determined to repay him to the best of my ability. Nothing, at this time, suggested a snare to me.

5. *The Man on the Couch*

"What dam of lances sent thee forth
to jest at dawn with Death?"
—Kipling.

At the expiration of two days, Hassim beckoned me as I stood in the opium room. I advanced with a springy resilient tread, secure in the confidence that I had culled the Morley papers of all their worth. I was a new man; my mental swiftness and physical readiness surprized me—sometimes it seemed unnatural.

Hassim eyed me through narrowed lids and motioned me to follow, as usual. As we crossed the room, my gaze fell upon a man who lay on a couch close to the wall, smoking opium. There was nothing at all suspicious about his ragged, unkempt clothes, his dirty, bearded face or the blank stare, but my eyes, sharpened to an abnormal point, seemed to sense a certain incongruity in the clean-cut limbs which not even the slouchy garments could efface.

Hassim spoke impatiently and I turned away. We entered the rear room, and as he shut the door and turned to the table, it moved of itself and a figure bulked up through the hidden doorway. The Sikh, Ganra Singh, a lean sinister-eyed giant, emerged and proceeded to the door opening into the opium room, where he halted until we should have descended and closed the secret doorway.

Again I stood amid the billowing yellow smoke and listened to the hidden voice.

"Do you think you know enough about Major Morley to successfully impersonate him?"

Startled, I answered, "No doubt I could, unless I met someone who was intimate with him."

"I will take care of that. Follow me closely. Tomorrow you sail on the first boat for Calais. There you will meet an agent of mine who will accost you the instant you step upon the wharfs, and give you further instructions. You will sail second class and avoid all conversation with strangers or anyone. Take the papers with you.

The agent will aid you in making up and your masquerade will start in Calais. That is all. Go!"

I departed, my wonder growing. All this rigmarole evidently had a meaning, but one which I could not fathom. Back in the opium room Hassim bade me be seated on some cushions to await his return. To my question he snarled that he was going forth as he had been ordered, to buy me a ticket on the Channel boat. He departed and I sat down, leaning my back against the wall. As I ruminated, it seemed suddenly that eyes were fixed on me so intensely as to disturb my sub-mind. I glanced up quickly but no one seemed to be looking at me. The smoke drifted through the hot atmosphere as usual; Yussef Ali and the Chinese glided back and forth tending to the wants of the sleepers.

Suddenly the door to the rear room opened and a strange and hideous figure came haltingly out. Not all of they who found entrance to Yun Shatu's back room were aristocrats and society members. This was one of the exceptions, and one whom I remembered as having often entered and emerged therefrom. A tall, gaunt figure, shapeless in ragged wrappings and nondescript garments, face entirely hidden. Better that the face be hidden, I thought, for without doubt the wrapping concealed a grisly sight. The man was a leper, who had somehow managed to escape the attention of the public guardians and who was occasionally seen haunting the lower and more mysterious regions of East End. A mystery, even to the lowest denizens of Limehouse.

Suddenly my supersensitive mind was aware of a swift tension in the air. The leper hobbled out the door, closed it behind him. My eyes instinctively sought the couch whereon lay the man who had aroused my suspicions earlier in the day. I could have sworn that cold steely eyes gleamed menacingly before they flickered shut. I crossed to the couch in one stride and bent over the prostrate man. Something about his face seemed unnatural—a healthy bronze seemed to underlie the pallor of complexion.

"Yun Shatu!" I shouted. "A spy is in the house!"

Things happened then with bewildering speed. The man on the couch with one tigerish movement leaped erect and a revolver gleamed in his hand. One sinewy arm flung me aside as I sought to grapple with him and a sharp decisive voice sounded over the babble which broke forth:

"You there! Halt! Halt!"

The pistol in the stranger's hand was leveled at the leper, who was making for the door in long strides!

All about was confusion; Yun Shatu was shrieking volubly in Chinese and the four China boys and Yussef Ali were rushing in from all sides, knives glittering in their hands.

All this I saw with unnatural clearness even as I marked the stranger's face. As the flying leper gave no evidence of halting, I saw the eyes harden to steely points of determination, sighting along the pistol barrel—the features set with the grim purpose of the slayer. The leper was almost to the outer door, but death would strike him down ere he could reach it.

And then, just as the finger of the stranger tightened on the trigger, I hurled myself forward and my right fist crashed against his chin. He went down as though struck by a trip-hammer, the revolver exploding harmlessly in the air.

For in that instant, with the blinding flare of light that sometimes comes to one, I knew that the leper was none other than the Man Behind the Screen!

I bent over the fallen man, who though not entirely senseless had been rendered temporarily helpless by that terrific blow. He was struggling dazedly to rise but I shoved him roughly down again and seizing the false beard he wore, tore it away. A lean bronzed face was revealed, the strong lines of which not even the artificial dirt and greasepaint could alter.

Yussef Ali leaned above him now, dagger in hand, eyes slits of murder. The brown sinewy hand went up—I caught the wrist.

"Not so fast, you black devil! What are you about to do?"

"This is John Gordon," he hissed, "the Master's greatest foe! He must die, curse you!"

John Gordon! The name was familiar somehow, and yet I did not seem to connect it with the London police nor account for the man's presence in Yun Shatu's dope joint. However on one point I was determined.

"You don't kill him, at any rate. Up with you!" This last to Gordon, who with my aid staggered up, still very dizzy.

"That punch would have dropped a bull," I said in wonderment. "I didn't know I had it in me."

The false leper had vanished. Yun Shatu stood gazing at me as immobile as an idol, hands in his wide sleeves, and Yussef Ali stood back, muttering murderously and thumbing his dagger edge, as I led Gordon out of the opium room and through the innocent-appearing bar which lay between that room and the street.

Out in the street I said to him: "I have no idea as to who you are or what you are doing here, but you see what an unhealthy place it is for you. Hereafter be advised by me and stay away."

His only answer was a searching glance, and then he turned and walked swiftly though somewhat unsteadily up the street.

6. *The Dream Girl*

"I have reached these lands but newly
From an ultimate dim Thule."
—Poe.

Outside my room sounded a light footstep. The doorknob turned cautiously and slowly; the door opened. I sprang erect with a gasp. Red lips, half-parted, dark eyes like limpid seas of wonder, a mass of shimmering hair—framed in my drab doorway stood the girl of my dreams!

She entered and, half-turning with a sinuous motion, closed the door. I sprang forward, my hands outstretched, then halted as she put a finger to her lips.

"You must not talk loudly," she almost whispered. *"He* did not say I could not come, yet—"

Her voice was soft and musical, with just a touch of a foreign accent which I found delightful. As for the girl herself, every intonation, every movement proclaimed the Orient. She was a fragrant breath from the East. From her night-black hair, piled high above her alabaster forehead, to her little feet, encased in high-heeled pointed slippers, she portrayed the highest ideal of Asiatic loveliness—an effect which was heightened rather than lessened by the English blouse and skirt which she wore.

"You are beautiful!" I said dazedly. "Who are you?"

"I am Zuleika," she answered with a shy smile. "I—I am glad you like me. I am glad you no longer dream hashish dreams."

Strange that so small a thing should set my heart to leaping wildly!

"I owe it all to you, Zuleika," I said huskily. "Had not I dreamed of you every hour since you first lifted me from the gutter, I had lacked the power of even hoping to be freed from my curse."

She blushed prettily and intertwined her white fingers as if in nervousness.

"You leave England tomorrow?" she said suddenly.

"Yes. Hassim has not returned with my ticket—" I hesitated suddenly, remembering the command of silence.

"Yes, I know, I know!" she whispered swiftly, her eyes widening. "And John Gordon has been here! He saw you!"

"Yes!"

She came close to me with a quick lithe movement.

"You are to impersonate some man! Listen, while you are doing this, you must not ever let Gordon see you! He would know you, no matter what your disguise! He is a terrible man!"

"I don't understand," I said, completely bewildered. "How did the Master break me of my hashish craving? Who is this Gordon and why did he come here? Why does the Master go disguised as a leper—and who is he? Above all, why am I to impersonate a man I never saw or heard of?"

"I cannot—I dare not tell you!" she whispered, her face paling. "I—"

Somewhere in the house sounded the faint tones of a Chinese gong. The girl started like a frightened gazelle.

"I must go! *He* summons me!"

She opened the door, darted through—halted a moment to electrify me with her passionate exclamation: "Oh, be careful, be very careful, sahib!"

Then she was gone.

7. *The Man of the Skull!*

"What the hammer? What the chain?
In what furnace was thy brain?
What the anvil? What dread grasp
Dare its deadly terrors clasp?"
—Blake.

A while after my beautiful and mysterious visitor had left, I sat in meditation. I believed that I had at last stumbled onto an explanation of a part of the enigma, at any rate. This was the conclusion I had reached: Yun Shatu, the opium lord, was simply the agent or servant of some organization or individual whose work was on a far larger scale than merely supplying dope addicts in the Temple of Dreams. This man, or these men, needed co-workers among all classes of people; in other words, I was being let in with a group of opium smugglers on a gigantic scale. Gordon no doubt had been investigating the case, and his presence alone showed that it was no ordinary one, for I knew that he held a high position with the English government, though just what, I did not know.

Opium or not, I determined to carry out my obligation to the Master. My moral sense had been blunted by the dark ways I had traveled, and the thought of a despicable crime did not enter into my thoughts. I was indeed hardened. More, the mere debt of gratitude was increased a thousand-fold by the thought of the girl. To the Master I owed it that I was able to stand up on my feet and look into her clear eyes as a man should. So if he wished my services as a smuggler of dope, he should have them. No doubt I was to impersonate some man so high in governmental esteem that the usual actions of the customs officers would be deemed unnecessary—was I to bring some rare dream-producer into England?

These thoughts were in my mind as I went downstairs, but ever back of them hovered other and more alluring suppositions—what was the reason for the girl, here in this vile dive—a rose in a garbage heap—and who was she?

As I entered the outer bar, Hassim came in, his brows set in a dark scowl of anger—and, I believed, fear. He carried a newspaper in his hand, folded.

"I told you to wait in opium room," he snarled.

"You were gone so long that I went up to my room. Have you the ticket?"

He merely grunted and pushed on past me into the opium room and, standing at the door, I saw him cross the floor and disappear into the rear room. I stood there, my bewilderment increasing. For as Hassim had brushed past me, I had noted an item on the face of the paper, against which his black thumb was tightly pressed as if to mark that special column of news.

And with the unnatural celerity of action and judgment which seemed to be mine those days, I had in that fleeting instant read:

"African Special Commissioner Found Murdered!

The body of Major Fairlan Morley was yesterday discovered in a rotting ship's hold at Bordeaux—"

No more I saw of the details, but that alone was enough to make me think! The affair seemed to be taking on an ugly aspect. Yet—

Another day passed. To my inquiries, Hassim snarled that the plans had been changed and I was not to go to France. Then, late in the evening, he came to bid me once more to the room of mystery.

I stood before the lacquer screen, the yellow smoke acrid in my nostrils, the woven dragons writhing along the tapestries, the palm trees rearing thick and oppressive.

"A change has come in our plans," said the hidden voice. "You will not sail as was decided before. But I have other work that you may do. Mayhap this will be more to your type of usefulness, for I admit you have somewhat disappointed me in regard to subtlety. You interfered the other day in such manner as will no doubt cause me great inconvenience in the future."

I said nothing, but a feeling of resentment began to stir in me.

"Even after the assurance of one of my most trusted servants," the toneless voice continued, with no mark of any emotion save a slightly rising note, "you insisted on releasing my most deadly enemy. Be more circumspect in the future."

"I saved your life!" I said angrily.

"And for that reason alone I overlook your mistake—this time!"

A slow fury suddenly surged up in me.

"This time! Make the best of it this time, for I assure you there will be no next time. I owe you a greater debt than I can ever hope to pay, but that does not make me your slave. I have saved your life—the debt is as near paid as a man can pay it. Go your way and I go mine!"

A low, hideous laugh answered me, like a reptilian hiss.

"You fool! You will pay with your whole life's toil! You say you are not my slave? I say you are—just as black Hassim there beside you is my slave—just as the girl Zuleika is my slave, who has bewitched you with her beauty."

These words sent a wave of hot blood to my brain and I was conscious of a flood of fury which completely engulfed my reason for a second. Just as all my moods and senses seemed sharpened and exaggerated those days, so now this burst of rage transcended every moment of anger I had ever had before.

"Hell's fiends!" I shrieked. "You devil—who are you and what is your hold on me? I'll see you or die!"

Hassim sprang at me, but I hurled him backward and with one stride reached the screen and flung it aside with an incredible effort of strength. Then I shrank back, hands outflung, shrieking. A tall, gaunt figure stood before me, a figure arrayed grotesquely in a silk brocaded gown which fell to the floor.

From the sleeves of this gown protruded hands which filled me with crawling horror—long, predatory hands, with thin bony fingers and curved talons—withered skin of a parchment brownish yellow, like the hands of a man long dead.

The hands—but, oh God, the face! A skull to which no vestige of flesh seemed to remain but on which taut brownish-yellow skin grew fast, etching out every detail of that terrible death's-head. The forehead was high and in a way magnificent, but the head was curiously narrow through the temples, and from under penthouse brows great eyes glimmered like pools of yellow fire. The nose was high bridged and very thin—the mouth a mere colorless gash between thin, cruel lips. A long bony neck supported this frightful vision and completed the effect of a reptilian demon from some medieval Hell.

I was face to face with the skull-faced man of my dreams!

8. Black Wisdom

"By thought a crawling ruin,
　　By life a leaping mire,
By a broken heart in the breast of the world
　　And the end of the world's desire."
　　　　　　　　　　　　—Chesterton.

The terrible spectacle drove for the instant all thoughts of rebellion from my mind. My very blood froze in my veins and I stood motionless. I heard Hassim laugh grimly behind me. The eyes in the cadaverous face blazed fiendishly at me and I blanched from the concentrated Satanic fury in them.

Then the horror laughed sibilantly.

"I do you a great honor, Mr. Costigan; among a very few, even of my own servants, you may say that you saw my face and lived. I think you will be more useful to me living than dead."

I was silent, completely unnerved. It was difficult to believe that this man lived, for his appearance certainly belied the thought. He seemed horribly like a mummy. Yet his lips moved when he spoke and his eyes flamed with hideous life.

"You will do as I say," he said abruptly, and his voice had taken on a note of command. "You doubtless know, or know of, Sir Haldred Frenton?"

"Yes."

Every man of culture in Europe and America was familiar with the travel books of Sir Haldred Frenton, author and soldier of fortune.

"You will go to Sir Haldred's estate tonight—"

"Yes?"

"And kill him!"

I staggered, literally. This order was incredible—unspeakable! I had sunk low—low enough to smuggle opium, but to deliberately murder a man I had never seen—a man noted for his kindly deeds! That was too monstrous even to contemplate.

"You do not refuse?"

The tone was as loathly and as mocking as the hiss of a serpent.

"Refuse!" I screamed, finding my voice at last. "Refuse? You incarnate devil! Of course I refuse! You—"

Something in the cold assurance of his manner halted me—froze me into apprehensive silence.

"You fool!" he said calmly. "I broke the hashish chains—do you know how? Four minutes from now you will know and curse the day you were born! Have you not thought it strange, the swiftness of brain, the resilience of body—the brain that should be rusty and slow, the body that should be weak and sluggish from years of abuse? That blow that felled John Gordon—have you not wondered at its might? The ease with which you mastered Major Morley's records—have you not wondered at that?

"You fool, you are bound to me by chains of steel and blood and fire! I have kept you alive and sane—I alone. Each day the lifesaving elixir has been given you in your wine. You could not live and keep your reason without it. And I and only I know its secret!"

He glanced at a queer timepiece which stood on a table at his elbow.

"This time I had Yun Shatu leave the elixir out—I anticipated rebellion. The time is near—ha, it strikes!"

Something else he said, but I did not hear. I did not see nor did I feel in the human sense of the word. I was writhing at his feet, screaming and gibbering in the flames of such Hells as men have never dreamed of.

Aye, I knew now! He had simply given me a dope so much stronger that it drowned the hashish. My unnatural ability was explainable now—I had simply been acting under the stimulus of something which combined all the Hells in its make-up, which stimulated, something like heroin, but whose effect was unnoticed by the victim. What it was, I had no idea, nor did I believe anyone knew save that Hellish being who stood watching me with grim amusement. But it had held my brain together, instilling into my system a need for it, and now my frightful craving tore my soul asunder.

Never, in my moments of worst shellshock or my moments of hashish craving, have I ever experienced anything like that. I burned with the heat of a thousand Hells and froze with an iciness that was colder than any ice, a hundred times. I swept down to the deepest pits of torture and up to the highest crags of torment—a million yelling devils hemmed me in, shrieking and stabbing. Bone by bone, vein by vein, cell by cell, I felt my body disintegrate and fly in bloody atoms all over the universe—and each separate cell was an entire system of quivering, screaming nerves. And they gathered from far voids and reunited again with a greater torment.

Through the fiery bloody mists I heard my own voice scream-ing, a monotonous yammering. Then with distended eyes I saw a golden goblet, held by a clawlike hand, swim into view—a goblet filled with an amber liquid.

With a bestial screech I seized it with both hands, being dimly aware that the metal stem gave beneath my fingers, and brought the brim to my lips. I drank in frenzied haste, the liquid slopping down onto my breast.

9. Kathulos of Egypt

"Night shall be thrice night over you,
And Heaven an iron cope."
—Chesterton.

The Skull-faced One stood watching me critically as I sat panting on a couch, completely exhausted. He held in his hand the goblet and surveyed the golden stem which was crushed out of all shape. This my maniac fingers had done in the instant of drinking.

"Superhuman strength, even for a man in your condition," he said with a sort of creaky pedantry. "I doubt if even Hassim here could equal it—are you ready for your instructions now?"

I nodded, wordless. Already the Hellish strength of the elixir was flowing through my veins, renewing my burnt-out force. I wondered how long a man could live as I lived being constantly burned out and artificially rebuilt.

"You will be given a disguise and will go alone to the Frenton estate. No one suspects any design against Sir Haldred and your entrance into the estate and the house itself should be a matter of comparative ease. You will not don the disguise—which will be of rather unique nature—until you are ready to enter the estate. You will then proceed to Sir Haldred's room and kill him, breaking his neck with your bare hands—this is essential—"

The voice droned on, giving its ghastly orders in a frightfully casual and matter-of-fact way—the cold sweat beaded my brow.

"You will then leave the estate, taking care to leave the imprint of your hand somewhere plainly visible, and the automobile which will be waiting for you at some safe place nearby will bring you back here, you having first removed the disguise. I have, in case of later complications, any amount of men who will swear that you spent the entire night in the Temple of Dreams and never left it. But here must be no detection! Go warily and perform your task surely, for you know the alternative."

I did not return to the opium house but was taken through winding corridors hung with heavy tapestries, to a small room containing only an Oriental couch. Hassim gave me to understand that I was to remain there until after nightfall and then left me. The door was closed but I made no effort to discover if it was locked. The Skull-faced Master held me with stronger shackles than locks and bolts.

Seated upon the couch in the bizarre setting of a chamber which might have been a room in an Indian zenana, I faced fact squarely and fought out my battle. There was still in me some trace of manhood left—more than the fiend had reckoned, and added to this was black despair and desperation. I chose and determined on the only course I had to follow.

Suddenly the door opened softly. Some intuition told me who to expect, nor was I disappointed. Zuleika stood, a glorious vision before me—a vision which mocked me, made blacker my despair and yet thrilled me with wild yearning and reasonless joy.

She bore a tray of food which she set beside me and then she seated herself on the couch, her large eyes fixed upon my face. A flower in a serpent den she was, and the beauty of her took hold of my heart.

"Steephen!" she whispered, and I thrilled as she spoke my name for the first time.

Her luminous eyes suddenly shone with tears and she laid her little hand on my arm. I seized it in both my rough hands.

"They have set you a task which you fear and hate!" she faltered.

"Aye," I almost laughed, "but I'll fool them yet! Zuleika, tell me—what is the meaning of all this?"

She glanced fearfully around her.

"I do not know all"—she hesitated—"your plight is all my fault but I—I hoped—Steephen, I have watched you every time you came to Yun Shatu's for months. You did not see me but I saw you, and I saw in you, not the broken sot your rags proclaimed, but a wounded soul. A soul bruised terribly on the ramparts of life. And from my heart I pitied you.

"Then when Hassim abused you that day—" again tears started to her eyes—"I could not bear it and I knew how you suffered for want of hashish. So I paid Yun Shatu and going to the Master I—I—oh, you will hate me for this!" she sobbed.

"No—no—never—"

"I told him that you were a man who might be of use to him and begged him to have Yun Shatu supply you with what you needed. He had already noticed you, for his is the eye of the slaver and all the world is his slave market! So he bade Yun Shatu do as I asked—and now—better if you had remained as you were, my friend."

"No! No!" I exclaimed. "I have known a few days of regeneration, even if it was false! I have stood before you as a man, and that is worth all else!"

And all that I felt for her must have looked forth from my eyes for she dropped hers and flushed. Ask me not how love comes to a man; but I knew that I loved Zuleika—had loved this mysterious Oriental girl since first I saw her—and somehow I felt that she, in a measure, returned my affection. This realization made blacker and more barren the road I had chosen yet—for pure love must ever strengthen a man—it nerved me to what I must do.

"Zuleika," I said, speaking hurriedly, "time flies and there are things I must learn—tell me—who are you and why do you remain in this den of Hades?"

"I am Zuleika—that is all I know. I am Circassian by blood and birth; when I was very little I was captured in a Turkish raid and raised in a Stamboul harem; while I was yet too young to marry, my master gave me as a present to—to *Him.*"

"And who is he—this skull-faced man?"

"He is Kathulos of Egypt—that is all I know. My master."

"An Egyptian? Then what is he doing in London—why all this mystery?"

She intertwined her fingers nervously.

"Steephen, please speak lower; always there is someone listening everywhere. I do not know who the Master is or why he is here or why he does these things. I swear by Allah! If I knew I would tell you. Sometimes distinguished-looking men come here to the room where the Master receives them—not the room where you saw him—and he makes me dance before them and afterward flirt with them a little. And always I must repeat exactly what they say to me. That is what I must always do—in Turkey, in the Barbary States, in Egypt, in France and in England. The Master taught me French and English and educated me in many ways himself. He is the greatest sorcerer in all the world and knows all ancient magic and everything."

"Zuleika," I said, "my race is soon run, but let me get you out of this—come with me and I swear I'll get you away from this fiend!"

She shuddered and hid her face.

"No, no, I cannot!"

"Zuleika," I asked gently, "what hold has he over you, child—dope also?"

"No, no!" she whimpered. "I do not know—I do not know—but I cannot—I never can escape him!"

I sat, baffled for a few moments; then I asked, "Zuleika, where are we right now?"

"This building is a deserted storehouse back of the Temple of Dreams."

"I thought so; what is in the chests in the tunnel?"

"I do not know."

Then suddenly she began weeping softly. "You too, a slave, like me—you who are so strong and clean—oh Steephen, I cannot bear it!"

I smiled. "Lean closer, Zuleika, and I will tell you how I am going to fool this Kathulos."

She glanced apprehensively at the door.

"You must speak low. I will lie in your arms and while you pretend to caress me, whisper your words to me."

She glided into my embrace and there on the dragon-worked couch in that house of horror I first knew the glory of Zuleika's slender form nestling in my arms—of Zuleika's soft cheek pressing my breast. The fragrance of her was in my nostrils, her hair in my eyes, and my senses reeled—then with my lips hidden by her silky hair I whispered, swiftly.

"I am going first to warn Sir Haldred Frenton—then to find John Gordon and tell him of this den. I will lead the police here and you must watch closely and be ready to hide from *Him*—until we can break through and kill or capture him. Then you will be free."

"But you!" she gasped, paling. "You must have the elixir, and only he—"

"I have a way of outdoing him, child," I answered.

She went pitifully white and her woman's intuition sprang at the right conclusion.

"You are going to kill yourself!"

And much as it hurt me to see her emotion, I yet felt a torturing thrill that she should feel so on my account. Her arms tightened about my neck.

"Don't, Steephen!" she begged. "It is better to live, even—"

"No, not at that price. Better to go out clean while I have the manhood left."

She stared at me wildly for an instant, then, pressing her red lips suddenly to mine, she sprang up and fled from the room. Strange, strange are the ways of love. Two stranded ships on the shores of life, we had drifted inevitably together, and though no word of love had passed between us, we knew each other's hearts—through grime and rags, and through the accouterments of the slave, we knew each other's hearts—and from the first, loved as naturally and as purely as it was intended from the beginning of Time.

The beginning of life now and the end for me, for as soon as I had completed my task, ere I felt again the torments of my curse, love and life and beauty and torture should be blotted out together in the stark finality of a pistol ball scattering my rotting brain. Better a clean death than—

The door opened again and Yussef Ali entered.

"The hour arrives for departure," he said briefly. "Rise and follow."

I had no idea, of course, as to the time. No window opened from the room I occupied—I had seen no outer window whatever. The rooms were lighted by tapers in censers swinging from the ceiling. As I rose the slim young Moor slanted a sinister glance in my direction.

"This lies between you and I," he said sibilantly. "Servants of the same master we—but this concerns ourselves alone. Keep your distance from Zuleika—the Master has promised her to me in the days of the empire."

My eyes narrowed to slits as I looked into the frowning, handsome face of the Oriental, and such hate surged up in me as I have seldom known. My fingers involuntarily opened and closed and the Moor, marking the action, stepped back, hand in his girdle.

"Not now—there is work for us both—later perhaps—" then in a sudden cold gust of hatred, "Swine—ape-man, when the Master is finished with you I shall quench my dagger in your heart!"

I laughed grimly.

"Make it soon, desert-snake, or I'll crush your spine between my hands."

10. The Dark House

"Against all man-made shackles and a man-made Hell—
Alone—at last—unaided—I rebel!"

—Mundy.

I followed Yussef Ali along the winding hallways, down the steps—Kathulos was not in the idol room—and along the tunnel. Then through the rooms of the Temple of Dreams and out into the street, where the streetlamps gleamed drearily through the fog and a slight drizzle. Across the street stood an automobile, curtains closely drawn.

"That is yours," said Hassim, who had joined us. "Saunter across natural-like. Don't act suspicious. The place may be watched. The driver knows what to do."

Then he and Yussef Ali drifted back into the bar and I took a single step toward the curb.

"Steephen!"

A voice that made my heart leap spoke my name! A white hand beckoned from the shadows of a doorway. I stepped quickly there.

"Zuleika!"

"Shhh!"

She clutched my arm, slipped something into my hand; I made out vaguely a small flask of gold.

"Hide this, quick!" came her urgent whisper. "Don't come back but go away and hide. This is full of elixir—I will try to get you some more before that is all gone. You must find a way of communicating with me."

"Yes, but how did you get this?" I asked amazedly.

"I stole it from the Master! Now please, I must go before he misses me."

And she sprang back into the doorway and vanished. I stood undecided. I was sure that she had risked nothing less than her life in doing this and I was torn by the fear of what Kathulos might do to her, were the theft discovered. But to return to the house of mystery would certainly invite suspicion, and I might carry out my plan and strike back before the Skull-faced One learned of his slave's duplicity.

So I crossed the street to the automobile which waited. The driver was a negro whom I had never seen before, a lanky man of medium height. I stared hard at him, wondering how much he had seen. He gave no evidence of having seen anything, and I decided that even if he had noticed me step back into the shadows, he could not have seen what passed there nor have been able to recognize the girl.

He merely nodded as I climbed in the back seat and a moment later we were speeding away down the deserted and fog-haunted streets. A bundle beside me I concluded to be the disguise mentioned by the Egyptian.

To recapture the sensations I experienced as I rode through the rainy, misty night, would be impossible. I felt as if I were already dead and the bare and dreary streets about me were the roads of death over which my ghost had been doomed to roam forever. A torturing joy was in my heart, and bleak despair—the despair of a doomed man. Not that death itself was so repellent—a dope victim dies too many deaths to shrink from the last—but it was hard to go out just as love had entered my barren life. And I was still young.

A sardonic smile crossed my lips—they were young, too, the men who died beside me in No Man's Land. I drew back my sleeve and clenched my fist, tensing my muscles. There was no surplus weight on my frame and much of the firm flesh had wasted away, but the cords of the great biceps still stood out like knots of iron, seeming to indicate massive strength. But I knew my might was false, that in reality I was a broken husk of a man, animated only by the artificial fire of the elixir, without which a frail girl might topple me over.

The automobile came to a halt among some trees. We were on the outskirts of an exclusive suburb and the hour was past midnight. Through the trees I saw a large house looming darkly against the distant flares of night-time London.

"This is where I wait," said the negro. "No one can see the automobile from the road or from the house."

Holding a match so that its light could not be detected outside the car, I examined the "disguise" and was hard put to restrain an insane laugh. The disguise was the complete hide of a gorilla! Gathering the bundle under my arm I trudged toward the wall which surrounded the Frenton estate. A few steps and the trees where the negro hid with the car merged into one dark mass. I did not believe he could see me, but for safety's sake, I made not for the high iron gate at the front, but for the wall at the side where there was no gate.

No light showed in the house. Sir Haldred was a bachelor and I was sure that the servants were all in bed long ago. I negotiated the wall with ease and stole across the dark lawn to a side door, still carrying the grisly "disguise" under my arm. The door was locked, as I had anticipated, and I did not wish to arouse anyone until I was safely in the house, where the sound of voices would not carry to one who might have followed me. I took hold of the knob with both hands and, exerting slowly the inhuman strength that was mine, began to twist. The shaft turned in my hands and the lock within shattered suddenly, with a noise that was like the crash of a cannon in the stillness. An instant more and I was inside and had closed the door behind me.

I took a single stride in the darkness in the direction I believed the stair to be, then halted as a beam of light flashed into my face. At the side of the beam I caught the glimmer of a pistol muzzle. Beyond a lean shadowy face floated.

"Stand where you are and put up your hands!"

I lifted my hands, allowing the bundle to slip to the floor. I had heard that voice only once but I recognized it—knew instantly that the man who held that light was John Gordon.

"How many are with you?"

His voice was sharp, commanding.

"I am alone," I answered. "Take me into a room where a light cannot be seen from the outside and I'll tell you some things you want to know."

He was silent; then, bidding me take up the bundle I had dropped, he stepped to one side and motioned me to precede him into the next room. There he directed me to a stairway and at the top landing opened a door and switched on lights.

I found myself in a room whose curtains were closely drawn. During this journey Gordon's alertness had not relaxed and now he stood, still covering me with his revolver. Clad in conventional garments, he stood revealed a tall, leanly but powerfully built man, taller than I but not so heavy—with steel gray eyes and clean-cut features. Something about the man attracted me, even as I noted a bruise on his jawbone where my fist had struck in our last meeting.

"I cannot believe," he said crisply, "that this apparent clumsiness and lack of subtlety is real. Doubtless you have your own reasons for wishing me to be in a secluded room at this time, but Sir Haldred is efficiently protected even now. Stand still."

Muzzle pressed against my chest, he ran his hand over my garments for concealed weapons, seeming slightly surprised when he found none.

"Still," he murmured as if to himself, "a man who can burst an iron lock with his bare hands has scant need of weapons."

"You are wasting valuable time," I said impatiently. "I was sent here tonight to kill Sir Haldred Frenton—"

"By whom?" the question was shot at me.

"By the man who sometimes goes disguised as a leper."

He nodded, a gleam in his scintillant eyes.

"My suspicions were correct, then."

"Doubtless. Listen to me closely—do you desire the death or arrest of that man?"

Gordon laughed grimly.

"To one who wears the mark of the scorpion on his hand, my answer would be superfluous."

"Then follow my directions and your wish shall be granted."

His eyes narrowed suspiciously.

"So that was the meaning of this open entry and non-resistance," he said slowly. "Does the dope which dilates your eyeballs so warp your mind that you think to lead me into ambush?"

I pressed my hands against my temples. Time was racing and every moment was precious—how could I convince this man of my honesty?

"Listen; my name is Stephen Costigan of America. I was a frequenter of Yun Shatu's dive and a hashish addict—as you have guessed, but just now a slave of stronger dope. By virtue of this slavery, the man you know as a false leper, whom Yun Shatu and his friends call 'Master,' gained dominance over me and sent me here to murder Sir Haldred—why, God only knows. But I have gained a space of respite by coming into possession of some of this dope which I must have in order to live, and I fear and hate this Master.

"Listen to me and I swear, by all things holy and unholy, that before the sun rises the false leper shall be in your power!"

I could tell that Gordon was impressed in spite of himself.

"Speak fast!" he rapped.

Still I could sense his disbelief and a wave of futility swept over me.

"If you will not act with me," I said, "let me go and somehow I'll find a way to get to the Master and kill him. My time is short—my hours are numbered and my vengeance is yet to be realized."

"Let me hear your plan, and talk fast," Gordon answered.

"It is simple enough. I will return to the Master's lair and tell him I have accomplished that which he sent me to do. You must follow closely with your men and while I engage the Master in conversation, surround the house. Then, at the signal, break in and kill or seize him."

Gordon frowned. "Where is this house?"

"The warehouse back of Yun Shatu's has been converted into a veritable Oriental palace."

"The warehouse!" he exclaimed. "How can that be? I had thought of that first, but I have carefully examined it from without. The windows are closely barred and spiders have built webs across them. The doors are nailed fast on the outside and the seals that mark the warehouse as deserted have never been broken or disturbed in any way."

"They tunneled up from beneath," I answered. "The Temple of Dreams is directly connected with the warehouse."

"I have traversed the alley between the two buildings," said Gordon, "and the doors of the warehouse opening into that alley are, as I have said, nailed shut from without just as the owners left them. There is apparently no rear exit of any kind from the Temple of Dreams."

"A tunnel connects the buildings, with one door in the rear room of Yun Shatu's and the other in the idol room of the warehouse."

"I have been in Yun Shatu's back room and found no such door."

"The table rests upon it. You noted the heavy table in the center of the room? Had you turned it around the secret door would have opened in the floor. Now this is my plan: I will go in through the Temple of Dreams and meet the Master in the idol room. You will have men secretly stationed in front of the warehouse and others upon the other street, in front of the Temple of Dreams. Yun Shatu's building, as you know, faces the waterfront, while the warehouse, fronting the opposite direction, faces a narrow street running parallel with the river.

"At the signal let the men in this street break open the front of the warehouse and rush in, while simultaneously those in front of Yun Shatu's make an invasion through the Temple of Dreams. Let these make for the rear room, shooting without mercy any who may seek to deter them, and there open the secret door as I have said.

"There being, to the best of my knowledge, no other exit from the Master's lair, he and his servants will necessarily seek to make their escape through the tunnel. Thus we will have them on both sides."

Gordon ruminated while I studied his face with breathless interest.

"This may be only a snare," he muttered, "or an attempt to draw me away from Sir Haldred, but—"

I held my breath.

"I am a gambler by nature," he said slowly. "I am going to follow what you Americans call 'a hunch'—but God help you if you are lying to me!"

I sprang erect.

"Thank God! Now aid me with this suit, for I must be wearing it when I return to the automobile waiting for me."

His eyes narrowed as I shook out the horrible masquerade and prepared to don it.

"This shows, as always, the touch of the master hand. You were doubtless instructed to leave marks of your hands, encased in those hideous gauntlets?"

"Yes—though I have no idea why."

"I think I have—the Master is famed for leaving no real clues to mark his crimes—a great ape escaped from a neighboring zoo earlier in the evening and it seems too obvious for mere chance, in the light of this disguise. The ape would have gotten the blame of Sir Haldred's death."

The thing was easily gotten into and the illusion of reality it created was so perfect as to draw a shudder from me as I viewed myself in a mirror.

"It is now two o'clock," said Gordon. "Allowing for the time it will take you to get back to Limehouse and the time it will take me to get my men stationed—I promise you that at half past four the house will be closely surrounded."

"Good!" I impulsively grasped his hand. "There will doubtless be a girl there who is in no way implicated with the Master's evil doings, but only a victim of circumstances such as I have been. Deal gently with her."

"It shall be done. What signal shall I look for?"

"I have no way of signaling you and I doubt if any sound in the house could be heard on the street. Let your men make their raid on the stroke of five."

I turned to go.

"A man is waiting for you with a car, I take it? Is he likely to suspicion anything?"

"I have a way of finding out, and if he does," I replied grimly, "I will return alone to the Temple of Dreams."

11. Four Thirty-Four

"Doubting, dreaming dreams
no mortal ever dared to dream before."

—Poe.

The door closed softly behind me, the great dark house looming up more starkly than ever. Stooping, I crossed the wet lawn at a run, a grotesque and unholy figure, I doubt not, since any man had at a glance sworn me to be not a man but a giant ape. So craftily had the Master devised!

I clambered the wall, dropped to the earth beyond and made my way through the darkness and the drizzle to the group of trees which masked the automobile.

The negro driver leaned out of the front seat. I was breathing hard and sought in various ways to simulate the actions of a man who has just murdered in cold blood and fled the scene of his crime.

"You heard nothing, no sound, no scream?" I hissed, gripping his arm.

"No noise except a slight crash when you first went in," he answered. "You did a good job—nobody passing along the road could have suspicioned anything."

"Have you remained in the car all the time?" I asked. And when he replied that he had, I seized his ankle and ran my hand over the soles of his shoe; it was perfectly dry, as was the cuff of his trouser leg. Satisfied, I climbed into the back seat. Had he taken a step on the earth, shoe and garment would have showed it by the telltale dampness.

I ordered him to refrain from starting the engine until I had removed the ape skin, and then we sped through the night and I fell victim to doubts and uncertainties. Why should Gordon put any trust in the word of a stranger and a former ally of the Master's? Would he not put my tale down as the ravings of a dope-crazed addict, or a lie to ensnare or befool him? Still, if he had not believed me, why had he let me go?

I could but trust. At any rate, what Gordon did or did not do would scarcely affect my fortunes ultimately, even though Zuleika had furnished me with that which would merely extend the number of my days. My thought centered on her, and more than my hope of vengeance on Kathulos was the hope that Gordon might be able to save her from the clutches of the fiend. At any rate, I thought grimly, if Gordon failed me, I still had my hands and if I might lay them upon the bony frame of the Skull-faced One—

Abruptly I found myself thinking of Yussef Ali and his strange words, the import of which just occurred to me, *"The Master has promised her to me in the days of the empire!"*

The days of the empire—what could that mean?

The automobile at last drew up in front of the building which hid the Temple of Dreams—now dark and still. The ride had seemed interminable, and as I dismounted I glanced at the timepiece on the dashboard of the car. My heart leaped—it was four thirty-four, and unless my eyes tricked me I saw a movement in the shadows across the street, out of the flare of the street lamp. At this time of night it could mean only one of two things—some menial of the Master watching for my return or else Gordon had kept his word. The negro drove away and I opened the door, crossed the deserted bar and entered the opium room. The bunks and the floor were littered with the dreamers, for such places as these know nothing of day or night as normal people know, but all lay deep in sottish slumber.

The lamps glimmered through the smoke and a silence hung mist-like over all.

12. The Stroke of Five

"He saw gigantic tracks of death,
And many a shape of doom."
—Chesterton.

Two of the China boys squatted among the smudge fires, staring at me unwinkingly as I threaded my way among the recumbent bodies and made my way to the rear door. For the first time I traversed the corridor alone and found time to wonder again as to the contents of the strange chests which lined the walls.

Four raps on the underside of the floor and a moment later I stood in the idol room. I gasped in amazement—the fact that across a table from me sat Kathulos in all his horror was not the cause of my exclamation. Except for the table, the chair on which the Skull-face sat and the altar—now bare of incense—the room was perfectly bare! Drab, unlovely walls of the unused warehouse met my gaze instead of the costly tapestries I had become accustomed to. The palms, the idol, the lacquered screen—all were gone.

"Ah, Mr. Costigan, you wonder, no doubt."

The dead voice of the Master broke in on my thoughts. I was aware that he wore a mask, a simple piece of black velvet which entirely hid his face, and through the eyeholes of which, his serpent eyes glittered balefully. The long yellow fingers twined sinuously upon the table.

"You thought me to be a trusting fool, no doubt!" he rapped suddenly. "Did you think I would not have you followed? You fool, Yussef Ali was at your heels every moment!"

An instant I stood speechless, frozen by the crash of these words against my brain, then as their import sank home, I launched myself forward with a roar. At the same instant, before my clutching fingers could close on the mocking horror on the other side of the table, men rushed from every side. I whirled, and with the clarity of hate, from the swirl of savage faces I singled out Yussef Ali, and crashed my right fist against his temple with every ounce of my strength. Even as he dropped, Hassim struck me to my knees and a Chinaman flung a man net over my shoulders. I heaved erect, bursting the stout cords as if they were strings, and then a blackjack in the hands of Ganra Singh stretched me stunned and bleeding on the floor.

Lean sinewy hands seized and bound me with cords that cut cruelly into my flesh. Emerging from the mists of semi-unconsciousness, I found myself lying on the altar with the masked Kathulos towering over me like a gaunt ivory tower. About in a semicircle stood Ganra Singh, Yar Khan, Yun Shatu and several others whom I knew as frequenters of the Temple of Dreams. Beyond them—and the sight cut me to the heart—I saw Zuleika crouching in a doorway, her face white and her hands pressed against her cheeks, in an attitude of abject terror.

"I did not fully trust you," said Kathulos sibilantly, "so I sent Yussef Ali to follow you. He reached the group of trees before you and following you into the estate heard your very interesting conversation with John Gordon—for he scaled the house wall like a cat and clung to the window ledge! Your driver delayed purposely so as to give Yussef Ali plenty of time to get back—I have decided to change my abode anyway. My furnishings are already on their way to another house, and as soon as we have disposed of the traitor—you!—we shall depart also, leaving a little surprize for your friend Gordon when he arrives at five-thirty."

My heart gave a sudden leap of hope. Yussef Ali had misunderstood, and Kathulos lingered here in false security while the London detective force had already silently surrounded the house. Over my shoulder I saw Zuleika vanish from the door.

I eyed Kathulos, absolutely unaware of what he was saying. It was not long until five—if he dallied longer—then I froze as the Egyptian spoke a word and Li Kung, a gaunt, cadaverous Chinaman, stepped from the silent semicircle and drew from his sleeve a long thin dagger. My eyes sought the timepiece that still rested on the table and my heart sank. It was still ten minutes until five. My death did not matter so much, since it simply hastened the inevitable, but in my mind's eye I could see Kathulos and his murderers escaping while the police awaited the stroke of five.

The Skull-face halted in some harangue, and stood in a listening attitude. I believe his uncanny intuition warned him of danger. He spoke a quick staccato command to Li Kung and the Chinaman sprang forward, dagger lifted above my breast.

The air was suddenly supercharged with dynamic tension. The keen dagger-point hovered high above me—loud and clear sounded the skirl of a police whistle and on the heels of the sound there came a terrific crash from the front of the warehouse!

Kathulos leaped into frenzied activity. Hissing orders like a cat spitting, he sprang for the hidden door and the rest followed him. Things happened with the speed of a nightmare. Li Kung had followed the rest, but Kathulos flung a command over his shoulder and the Chinaman turned back and came rushing toward the altar where I lay, dagger high, desperation in his countenance.

A scream broke through the clamor and as I twisted desperately about to avoid the descending dagger, I caught a glimpse of Kathulos dragging Zuleika away. Then with a frenzied wrench I toppled from the altar just as Li Kung's dagger, grazing my breast, sank inches deep into the dark-stained surface and quivered there.

I had fallen on the side next to the wall and what was taking place in the room I could not see, but it seemed as if far away I could hear men screaming faintly and hideously. Then Li Kung wrenched his blade free and sprang, tigerishly, around the end of the altar. Simultaneously a revolver cracked from the doorway—the Chinaman spun clear around, the dagger flying from his hand—and he slumped to the floor.

Gordon came running from the doorway where a few moments earlier Zuleika had stood, his pistol still smoking in his hand. At his heels were three rangy, clean-cut men in plain clothes. He cut my bonds and dragged me upright.

"Quick! Where have they gone?"

The room was empty of life save for myself, Gordon and his men, though two dead men lay on the floor.

I found the secret door and after a few seconds' search located the lever which opened it. Revolvers drawn, the men grouped about me and peered nervously into the dark stairway. Not a sound came up from the total darkness.

"This is uncanny!" muttered Gordon. "I suppose the Master and his servants went this way when they left the building—as they are certainly not here now!—and Leary and his men should have stopped them either in the tunnel itself or in the rear room of Yun Shatu's. At any rate, in either event they should have communicated with us by this time."

"Look out, sir!" one of the men exclaimed suddenly, and Gordon, with an ejaculation, struck out with his pistol barrel and crushed the life from a huge snake which had crawled silently up the steps from the blackness beneath.

"Let us see into this matter," said he, straightening.

But before he could step onto the first stair, I halted him; for, flesh crawling, I began dimly to understand something of what had happened—I began to understand the silence in the tunnel, the absence of the detectives, the screams I had heard some minutes previously while I lay on the altar. Examining the lever which opened the door, I found another smaller lever—I began to believe I knew what those mysterious chests in the tunnel contained.

"Gordon," I said hoarsely, "have you an electric torch?"

One of the men produced a large one.

"Direct the light into the tunnel, but as you value your life, do not put a foot upon the steps."

The beam of light struck through the shadows, lighting the tunnel, etching out boldly a scene that will haunt my brain all the rest of my life. On the floor of the tunnel, between the chests which now gaped open, lay two men who were members of London's finest secret service. Limbs twisted and faces horribly distorted they lay, and above and about them writhed, in long glittering scaly shimmerings, scores of hideous reptiles.

The clock struck five.

13. The Blind Beggar Who Rode

"He seemed a beggar such as lags
Looking for crusts and ale."
—Chesterton.

The cold grey dawn was stealing over the river as we stood in the deserted bar of the Temple of Dreams. Gordon was questioning the two men who had remained on guard outside the building while their unfortunate companions went in to explore the tunnel.

"As soon as we heard the whistle, sir, Leary and Murken rushed the bar and broke into the opium room, while we waited here at the bar door according to orders. Right away several ragged dopers came tumbling out and we grabbed them. But no one else came out and we heard nothing from Leary and Murken; so we just waited until you came, sir."

"You saw nothing of a giant negro, or of the Chinaman Yun Shatu?"

"No, sir. After a while the patrolmen arrived and we threw a cordon around the house, but no one was seen."

Gordon shrugged his shoulders; a few cursory questions had satisfied him that the captives were harmless addicts and he had them released.

"You are sure no one else came out?"

"Yes, sir—no, wait a moment. A wretched old blind beggar did come out, all rags and dirt and with a ragged girl leading him. We stopped him but didn't hold him—a wretch like that couldn't be harmful."

"No?" Gordon jerked out. "Which way did he go?"

"The girl led him down the street to the next block and then an automobile stopped and they got in and drove off, sir."

Gordon glared at him.

"The stupidity of the London detective has rightfully become an international jest," he said acidly. "No doubt it never occurred to you as being strange that a Limehouse beggar should ride about in his own automobile."

Then impatiently waving aside the man who sought to speak further he turned to me and I saw the lines of weariness beneath his eyes.

"Mr. Costigan, if you will come to my apartment we may be able to clear up some few things."

14. The Black Empire

"Oh the new spears dipped in life-blood
  as the woman shrieked in vain!
Oh the days before the English!
  When will those days come again?'
  —Mundy.

Gordon struck a match and absently allowed it to flicker and go out in his hand. His Turkish cigarette hung unlighted between his fingers.

"This is the most logical conclusion to be reached," he was saying. "The weak link in our chain was lack of men. But curse it, one can not round up an army at two o'clock in the morning, even with the aid of Scotland Yard. I went on to Limehouse, leaving orders for a number of patrolmen to follow me as quickly as they could be gotten together, and to throw a cordon about the house.

"They arrived too late to prevent the Master's servants slipping out of side doors and windows, no doubt, as they could easily do with only Finnegan and Hansen on guard at the front of the building. However, they arrived in time to prevent the Master himself from slipping out in that way—no doubt he lingered to effect his disguise and was caught in that manner. He owes his escape to his craft and boldness and to the carelessness of Finnegan and Hansen. The girl who accompanied him—"

"She was Zuleika, without doubt."

I answered listlessly, wondering anew what shackles bound her to the Egyptian sorcerer.

"You owe your life to her," Gordon rapped, lighting another match. "We were standing in the shadows in front of the warehouse, waiting for the hour to strike, and of course ignorant as to what was going on in the house, when a girl appeared at one of the barred windows and begged us for God's sake to do something, that a man was being murdered. So we broke in at once. However, she was not to be seen when we entered."

"She returned to the room, no doubt," I muttered, "and was forced to accompany the Master. God grant he knows nothing of her trickery."

"I do not know," said Gordon, dropping the charred match stem, "whether she guessed at our true identity or whether she just made the appeal in desperation.

"However—the main point is this: evidence points to the fact that, on hearing the whistle, Leary and Murken invaded Yun Shatu's from the front at the same instant my three men and I made our attack on the warehouse front. As it took us some seconds to batter down the door, it is logical to suppose that they found the secret door and entered the tunnel before we effected an entrance into the warehouse.

"The Master, knowing our plans beforehand, and being aware that an invasion would be made through the tunnel and having long ago made preparations for such an exigency—"

An involuntary shudder shook me.

"—the Master worked the lever that opened the chests—the screams you heard as you lay upon the altar were the death shrieks of Leary and Murken. Then, leaving the Chinaman behind to finish you, the Master and the rest descended into the tunnel—incredible as it seems—and threading their way unharmed among the serpents, entered Yun Shatu's house and escaped therefrom as I have said."

"That seems impossible. Why should not the snakes turn on them?"

Gordon finally ignited his cigarette and puffed a few seconds before replying.

"The reptiles might still have been giving their full and hideous attention to the dying men—or else—I have on previous occasions been confronted with indisputable proof of the Master's dominance over beasts and reptiles of even the lowest or most dangerous orders. How he and his slaves passed unhurt among those scaly fiends must remain, at present, one of the many unsolved mysteries pertaining to that strange man."

I stirred restlessly in my chair. This brought up a point for the purpose of clearing up, which I had come to Gordon's neat but bizarre apartments.

"You have not yet told me," I said abruptly, "who this man is and what is his mission."

"As to who he is, I can only say that he is known as you name him—the Master. I have never seen him unmasked, nor do I know his real name nor his nationality."

"I can enlighten you to an extent there," I broke in. "I have seen him unmasked and have heard the name his slaves call him."

Gordon's eyes blazed and he leaned forward.

"His name," I continued, "is Kathulos and he claims to be an Egyptian."

"Kathulos!" Gordon repeated. "You say he claims to be an Egyptian—have you any reason for doubting his claim of that nationality?"

"He may be of Egypt," I answered slowly, "but he is different, somehow, from any human I ever saw or hope to see. Great age might account for some of his peculiarities, but there are certain lineal differences that my anthropological studies tell me have been present since birth—features which would be abnormal to any other man but which are perfectly normal in Kathulos. That sounds paradoxical, I admit, but to appreciate fully the horrid inhumanness of the man, you would have to see him yourself."

Gordon sat all attention while I swiftly sketched the appearance of the Egyptian as I remembered him—and that appearance was indelibly etched on my brain forever.

As I finished he nodded.

"As I have said, I never saw Kathulos except when disguised as a beggar, a leper or some such thing—when he was fairly swathed in rags. Still, I too have been impressed with a strange *difference* about him—something that is not present in other men."

Gordon tapped his knee with his fingers—a habit of his when deeply engrossed by a problem of some sort.

"You have asked as to the mission of this man," he began slowly. "I will tell you all I know."

"My position with the British government is a unique and peculiar one. I hold what might be called a roving commission—an office created solely for the purpose of suiting my special needs. As a secret service official during the war, I convinced the powers of a need of such office and of my ability to fill it.

"Somewhat over seventeen months ago I was sent to South Africa to investigate the unrest which has been growing among the natives of the interior ever since the World War and which has of late assumed alarming proportions. There I first got on the track of this man Kathulos. I found, in roundabout ways, that Africa was a seething cauldron of rebellion from Morocco to Cape Town. The old, old vow had been made again—the negroes and the Moham-medans, banded together, should drive the white men into the sea.

"This pact has been made before but always, hitherto, broken. Now, however, I sensed a giant intellect and a monstrous genius behind the veil, a genius powerful enough to accomplish this union and hold it together. Working entirely on hints and vague whispered clues, I followed the trail up through Central Africa and into Egypt. There, at last, I came upon definite evidence that such a man existed. The whispers hinted of a living dead man—a *skull-faced* man. I learned that this man was the high priest of the mysterious Scorpion society of northern Africa. He was spoken of variously as Skull-face, the Master, and the Scorpion.

"Following a trail of bribed officials and filched state secrets, I at last trailed him to Alexandria, where I had my first sight of him in a dive in the native quarter—disguised as a leper. I heard him distinctly addressed as 'Mighty Scorpion' by the natives, but he escaped me.

"All trace vanished then; the trail ran out entirely until rumors of strange happenings in London reached me and I came back to England to investigate an apparent leak in the war office.

"As I thought, the Scorpion had preceded me. This man, whose education and craft transcend anything I ever met with, is simply the leader and instigator of a world-wide movement such as the world has never seen before. He plots, in a word, the overthrow of the white races!

"His ultimate aim is a black empire, with himself as emperor of the world! And to that end he has banded together in one monstrous conspiracy the black, the brown and the yellow."

"I understand now what Yussef Ali meant when he said 'the days of the empire'," I muttered.

"Exactly," Gordon rapped with suppressed excitement. "Kathulos' power is unlimited and unguessed. Like an octopus his tentacles stretch to the high places of civilization and the far corners of the world. And his main weapon is—dope! He has flooded Europe and no doubt America with opium and hashish, and in spite of all effort it has been impossible to discover the break in the barriers through which the hellish stuff is coming. With this he ensnares and enslaves men and women.

"You have told me of the aristocratic men and women you saw coming to Yun Shatu's dive. Without doubt they were dope addicts—for, as I said, the habit lurks in high places—holders of governmental positions, no doubt, coming to trade for the stuff they craved and giving in return state secrets, inside information and promise of protection for the Master's crimes.

"Oh, he does not work haphazardly! Before ever the black flood breaks, he will be prepared; if he has his way, the governments of the white races will be honeycombs of corruption—the strongest men of the white races will be dead. The white men's secrets of war will be his. When it comes, I look for a simultaneous uprising against white supremacy, of all the colored races—races who, in the last war, learned the white men's ways of battle, and who, led by such a man as Kathulos and armed with white men's finest weapons, will be almost invincible.

"A steady stream of rifles and ammunition has been pouring into East Africa and it was not until I discovered the source that it was stopped. I found that a staid and reliable Scotch firm was smuggling these arms among the natives and I found more: the manager of this firm was an opium slave. That was enough. I saw Kathulos' hand in the matter. The manager was arrested and committed suicide in his cell—that is only one of the many situations with which I am called upon to deal.

"Again, the case of Major Fairlan Morley. He, like myself, held a very flexible commission and had been sent to the Transvaal to work upon the same case. He sent to London a number of secret papers for safekeeping. They arrived some weeks ago and were put in a bank vault. The letter accompanying them gave explicit instructions that they were to be delivered to no one but the major himself, when he called for them in person, or in event of his death, to myself.

"As soon as I learned that he had sailed from Africa I sent trusted men to Bordeaux, where he intended to make his first landing in Europe. They did not succeed in saving the major's life, but they certified his death, for they found his body in a deserted ship whose hulk was stranded on the beach. Efforts were made to keep the affair a secret but somehow it leaked into the papers with the result—"

"I begin to understand why I was to impersonate the unfortunate major," I interrupted.

"Exactly. A false beard furnished you, and your black hair dyed blond, you would have presented yourself at the bank, received the papers from the banker, who knew Major Morley just intimately enough to be deceived by your appearance, and the papers would have then fallen into the hands of the Master.

"I can only guess at the contents of those papers, for events have been taking place too swiftly for me to call for and obtain them. But they must deal with subjects closely connected with the activities of Kathulos. How he learned of them and of the provisions of the letter accompanying them, I have no idea, but as I said, London is honeycombed with his spies.

"In my search for clues, I often frequented Limehouse disguised as you first saw me. I went often to the Temple of Dreams and even once managed to enter the back room, for I suspected some sort of rendezvous in the rear of the building. The absence of any exit baffled me and I had no time to search for secret doors before I was ejected by the giant black man Hassim, who had no suspicion of my true identity. I noticed that very often the leper entered or left Yun Shatu's, and finally it was borne on me that past a shadow of doubt this supposed leper was the Scorpion himself.

"That night you discovered me on the couch in the opium room, I had come there with no especial plan in mind. Seeing Kathulos leaving, I determined to rise and follow him, but you spoiled that."

He fingered his chin and laughed grimly.

"I was an amateur boxing champion in Oxford," said he, "but Tom Cribb himself could not have withstood that blow—or have dealt it."

"I regret it as I regret few things."

"No need to apologize. You saved my life immediately afterward—I was stunned, but not too much to know that that brown devil Yussef Ali was burning to cut out my heart."

"How did you come to be at Sir Haldred Frenton's estate? And how is it that you did not raid Yun Shatu's dive?"

"I did not have the place raided because I knew somehow Kathulos would be warned and our efforts would come to naught. I was at Sir Haldred's that night because I have contrived to spend at least part of each night with him since he returned from the Congo. I anticipated an attempt upon his life when I learned from his own lips that he was preparing, from the studies he made on this trip, a treatise on the secret native societies of West Africa. He hinted that the disclosures he intended to make therein might prove sensational, to say the least. Since it is to Kathulos' advantage to destroy such men as might be able to arouse the Western world to its danger,

I knew that Sir Haldred was a marked man. Indeed, two distinct attempts were made upon his life on his journey to the coast from the African interior. So I put two trusted men on guard and they are at their post even now.

"Roaming about the darkened house, I heard the noise of your entry, and, warning my men, I stole down to intercept you. At the time of our conversation, Sir Haldred was sitting in his unlighted study, a Scotland Yard man with drawn pistol on each side of him. Their vigilance no doubt accounts for Yussef Ali's failure to attempt what you were sent to do.

"Something in your manner convinced me in spite of yourself," he meditated. "I will admit I had some bad moments of doubt as I waited in the darkness that precedes dawn, outside the warehouse."

Gordon rose suddenly and going to a strong box which stood in a corner of the room, drew thence a thick envelope.

"Although Kathulos has checkmated me at almost every move," he said, "I have not been entirely idle. Noting the frequenters of Yun Shatu's, I have compiled a partial list of the Egyptian's right-hand men, and their records. What you have told me has enabled me to complete that list. As we know, his henchmen are scattered all over the world, and there are possibly hundreds of them here in London. However, this is a list of those I believe to be in his closest council, now with him in England. He told you himself that few even of his followers ever saw him unmasked."

We bent together over the list, which contained the following names: "Yun Shatu, Hongkong Chinese, suspected opium smuggler—keeper of Temple of Dreams—resident of Limehouse seven years. Hassim, ex-Senegalese chief—wanted in French Congo for murder. Santiago, negro—fled from Haiti under suspicion of voodoo worship atrocities. Yar Khan, Afridi, record unknown. Yussef Ali, Moor, slave-dealer in Morocco—suspected of being a German spy in the World War—an instigator of the Fellaheen Rebellion on the upper Nile. Ganra Singh, Lahore, India, Sikh—smuggler of arms into Afghanistan—took an active part in the Lahore and Delhi riots—suspected of murder on two occasions—a dangerous man.

Stephen Costigan, American—resident in England since the war—hashish addict—man of remarkable strength. Li Kung, northern China, opium smuggler."

Lines were drawn significantly through three names—mine, Li Kung's and Yussef Ali's. Nothing was written next to mine, but following Li Kung's name was scrawled briefly in Gordon's rambling characters: "Shot by John Gordon during the raid on Yun Shatu's." And following the name of Yussef Ali: "Killed by Stephen Costigan during the Yun Shatu raid."

I laughed mirthlessly. Black empire or not, Yussef Ali would never hold Zuleika in his arms, for he had never risen from where I felled him.

"I know not," said Gordon somberly as he folded the list and replaced it in the envelope, "what power Kathulos has that draws together black men and yellow men to serve him—that unites world-old foes. Hindoo, Moslem and pagan are among his followers. And back in the mists of the East where mysterious and gigantic forces are at work, this uniting is culminating on a monstrous scale."

He glanced at his watch.

"It is nearly ten. Make yourself at home here, Mr. Costigan, while I visit Scotland Yard and see if any clue has been found as to Kathulos' new quarters. I believe that the webs are closing on him, and with your aid I promise you we will have the gang located within a week at most."

15. The Mark of the Tulwar

"The fed wolf curls by his drowsy mate
In a tight-trod earth; but the lean wolves wait."
—Mundy.

I sat alone in John Gordon's apartments and laughed mirthlessly. In spite of the elixir's stimulus, the strain of the previous night, with its loss of sleep and its heartrending actions, was telling on me. My mind was a chaotic whirl wherein the faces of Gordon, Kathulos and Zuleika shifted with numbing swiftness. All the mass of information Gordon had given to me seemed jumbled and incoherent.

Through this state of being, one fact stood out boldly. I must find the latest hiding place of the Egyptian and get Zuleika out of his hands—if indeed she still lived.

A week, Gordon had said—I laughed again—a week and I would be beyond aiding anyone. I had found the proper amount of elixir to use—knew the minimum amount my system required—and knew that I could make the flask last me four days at most. Four days! Four days in which to comb the ratholes of Limehouse and Chinatown—four days in which to ferret out, somewhere in the mazes of East End, the lair of Kathulos.

I burned with impatience to begin, but nature rebelled, and staggering to a couch, I fell upon it and was asleep instantly.

Then someone was shaking me.

"Wake up, Mr. Costigan!"

I sat up, blinking. Gordon stood over me, his face haggard.

"There's devil's work done, Costigan! The Scorpion has struck again!"

I sprang up, still half-asleep and only partly realizing what he was saying. He helped me into my coat, thrust my hat at me, and then his firm grip on my arm was propelling me out of his door and down the stairs. The streetlights were blazing; I had slept an incredible time.

"A logical victim!" I was aware that my companion was saying. "He should have notified me the instant of his arrival!"

"I don't understand—" I began dazedly.

We were at the curb now and Gordon hailed a taxi, giving the address of a small and unassuming hotel in a staid and prim section of the city.

"The Baron Rokoff," he rapped as we whirled along at reckless speed, "a Russian freelance, connected with the war office. He returned from Mongolia yesterday and apparently went into hiding. Undoubtedly he had learned something vital in regard to the slow waking of the East. He had not yet communicated with us, and I had no idea that he was in England until just now."

"And you learned—"

"The baron was found in his room, his dead body mutilated in a frightful manner!"

The respectable and conventional hotel which the doomed baron had chosen for his hiding place was in a state of mild uproar, suppressed by the police. The management had attempted to keep the matter quiet, but somehow the guests had learned of the atrocity and many were leaving in haste—or preparing to, as the police were holding all for investigation.

The baron's room, which was on the top floor, was in a state to defy description. Not even in the Great War have I seen a more complete shambles. Nothing had been touched; all remained just as the chambermaid had found it a half-hour since. Tables and chairs lay shattered on the floor, and the furniture, floor and walls were spattered with blood. The baron, a tall, muscular man in life, lay in the middle of the room, a fearful spectacle. His skull had been cleft to the brows, a deep gash under his left armpit had shorn through his ribs, and his left arm hung by a shred of flesh. The cold bearded face was set in a look of indescribable horror.

"Some heavy, curved weapon must have been used," said Gordon, "something like a saber, wielded with terrific force. See where a chance blow sank inches deep into the windowsill. And again, the thick back of this heavy chair has been split like a shingle. A saber, surely."

"A tulwar," I muttered, somberly. "Do you not recognize the handiwork of the Central Asian butcher? Yar Khan has been here."

"The Afghan! He came across the roofs, of course, and descended to the window ledge by means of a knotted rope made fast to something on the edge of the roof. About one-thirty the maid, passing through the corridor, heard a terrific commotion in the baron's room—smashing of chairs and a sudden short shriek which died abruptly into a ghastly gurgle and then ceased—to the sound of heavy blows, curiously muffled, such as a sword might make when driven deep into human flesh.

"She called the manager and they tried the door and, finding it locked, and receiving no answer to their shouts, opened it with the desk key. Only the corpse was there, but the window was open. This is strangely unlike Kathulos' usual procedure. It lacks subtlety. Often his victims have appeared to have died from natural causes. I scarcely understand."

"I see little difference in the outcome," I answered. "There is nothing that can be done to apprehend the murderer as it is."

"True," Gordon scowled. "We know who did it but there is no proof—not even a fingerprint. Even if we knew where the Afghan is hiding and arrested him, we could prove nothing—there would be a score of men to swear alibis for him. The baron returned only yesterday. Kathulos probably did not know of his arrival until tonight. He knew that on the morrow Rokoff would make known his presence to me and impart what he learned in Northern Asia. The Egyptian knew he must strike quickly, and lacking time to prepare a safer and more elaborate form of murder, he sent the Afridi with his tulwar. There is nothing we can do, at least not until we discover the Scorpion's hiding place; what the baron had learned in Mongolia, we shall never know, but that it dealt with the plans and aspirations of Kathulos, we may be sure."

We went down the stairs again and out on the street, accompanied by one of the Scotland Yard men, Hansen. Gordon suggested that we walk back to his apartment and I greeted the opportunity to let the cool night air blow some of the cobwebs out of my mazed brain.

As we walked along the deserted streets, Gordon suddenly cursed savagely.

"This is a veritable labyrinth we are following, leading nowhere! Here, in the very heart of civilization's metropolis, the direct enemy of that civilization commits crimes of the most outrageous nature and goes free! We are children, wandering in the night, struggling with an unseen evil—dealing with an incarnate devil, of whose true identity we know nothing and whose true ambitions we can only guess.

"Never have we managed to arrest one of the Egyptian's direct henchmen, and the few dupes and tools of his we have apprehended have died mysteriously before they could tell us anything. Again I repeat: what strange power has Kathulos that dominates these men of different creeds and races? The men in London with him are, of course, mostly renegades, slaves of dope, but his tentacles stretch all over the East. Some dominance is his: the power that sent the Chinaman, Li Kung, back to kill you, in the face of certain death; that sent Yar Khan the Moslem over the roofs of London to do murder; that holds Zuleika the Circassian in unseen bonds of slavery.

"Of course we know," he continued after a brooding silence, "that the East has secret societies which are behind and above all considerations of creeds. There are cults in Africa and the Orient whose origin dates back to Ophir and the fall of Atlantis. This man must be a power in some or possibly all of these societies. Why, outside the Jews, I know of no Oriental race which is so cordially despised by the other Eastern races, as the Egyptians! Yet here we have a man, an Egyptian by his own word, controlling the lives and destinies of orthodox Moslems, Hindoos, Shintos and devil-worshippers. It's unnatural.

"Have you ever"—he turned to me abruptly—"heard the ocean mentioned in connection with Kathulos?"

"Never."

"There is a widespread superstition in northern Africa, based on a very ancient legend, that the great leader of the colored races would come out of the sea! And I once heard a Berber speak of the Scorpion as 'The Son of the Ocean'."

"That is a term of respect among that tribe, is it not?"

"Yes; still I wonder sometimes."

16. The Mummy Who Laughed

"Laughing as littered skulls that lie
  After lost battles turn to the sky
    An everlasting laugh."
                                        —Chesterton.

"A shop open this late," Gordon remarked suddenly.

A fog had descended on London and along the quiet street we were traversing the lights glimmered with the peculiar reddish haze characteristic of such atmospheric conditions. Our footfalls echoed drearily. Even in the heart of a great city there are always sections which seem overlooked and forgotten. Such a street was this. Not even a policeman was in sight.

The shop which had attracted Gordon's attention was just in front of us, on the same side of the street. There was no sign over the door, merely some sort of emblem something like a dragon. Light flowed from the open doorway and the small shop windows on each side. As it was neither a café nor the entrance to a hotel we found ourselves idly speculating over its reason for being open. Ordinarily, I suppose, neither of us would have given the matter a thought, but our nerves were so keyed up that we found ourselves instinctively suspicious of anything out of the ordinary. Then something occurred which was distinctly out of the ordinary.

A very tall, very thin man, considerably stooped, suddenly loomed up out of the fog in front of us, and beyond the shop. I had only a glance of him—an impression of incredible gauntness, of worn, wrinkled garments, a high silk hat drawn close over the brows, a face entirely hidden by a muffler; then he turned aside and entered the shop. A cold wind whispered down the street, twisting the fog into wispy ghosts, but the coldness that came upon me transcended the wind's.

"Gordon!" I exclaimed in a fierce, low voice; "my senses are no longer reliable or else Kathulos himself has just gone into that house!"

Gordon's eyes blazed. We were now close to the shop, and lengthening his strides into a run he hurled himself into the door, the detective and I close upon his heels.

A weird assortment of merchandise met our eyes. Antique weapons covered the walls, and the floor was piled high with curious things. Maori idols shouldered Chinese josses, and suits of medieval armor bulked darkly against stacks of rare Oriental rugs and Latin-made shawls. The place was an antique shop. Of the figure who had aroused our interest we saw nothing.

An old man clad bizarrely in red fez, brocaded jacket and Turkish slippers came from the back of the shop; he was a Levantine of some sort.

"You wish something, sirs?"

"You keep open rather late," Gordon said abruptly, his eyes traveling swiftly over the shop for some secret hiding place that might conceal the object of our search.

"Yes, sir. My customers number many eccentric professors and students who keep very irregular hours. Often the night boats unload special pieces for me and very often I have customers later than this. I remain open all night, sir."

"We are merely looking around," Gordon returned, and in an aside to Hansen: "Go to the back and stop anyone who tries to leave that way."

Hansen nodded and strolled casually to the rear of the shop. The back door was clearly visible to our view, through a vista of antique furniture and tarnished hangings strung up for exhibition. We had followed the Scorpion—if he it was—so closely that I did not believe he would have had time to traverse the full length of the shop and make his exit without our having seen him as we came in. For our eyes had been on the rear door ever since we had entered.

Gordon and I browsed around casually among the curios, handling and discussing some of them but I have no idea as to their nature. The Levantine had seated himself cross-legged on a Moorish mat close to the center of the shop and apparently took only a polite interest in our explorations.

After a time Gordon whispered to me: "There is no advantage in keeping up this pretense. We have looked everywhere the Scorpion might be hiding, in the ordinary manner. I will make known my identity and authority and we will search the entire building openly."

Even as he spoke a truck drew up outside the door and two burly negroes entered. The Levantine seemed to have expected them, for he merely waved them toward the back of the shop and they responded with a grunt of understanding.

Gordon and I watched them closely as they made their way to a large mummy case which stood upright against the wall not far from the back. They lowered this to a level position and then started for the door, carrying it carefully between them.

"Halt!" Gordon stepped forward, raising his hand authoritatively.

"I represent Scotland Yard," he said swiftly, "and have sanction for anything I choose to do. Set that mummy down; nothing leaves this shop until we have thoroughly searched it."

The negroes obeyed without a word and my friend turned to the Levantine, who, apparently not perturbed or even interested, sat smoking a Turkish water pipe.

"Who was that tall man who entered just before we did, and where did he go?"

"No one entered before you, sir. Or, if anyone did, I was at the back of the shop and did not see him. You are certainly at liberty to search my shop, sir."

And search it we did, with the combined craft of a secret service expert and a denizen of the underworld—while Hansen stood stolidly at his post, the two negroes standing over the carved mummy case watched us impassively and the Levantine sitting like a sphinx on his mat, puffing a fog of smoke into the air. The whole thing had a distinct effect of unreality.

At last, baffled, we returned to the mummy case, which was certainly long enough to conceal even a man of Kathulos' height. The thing did not appear to be sealed as is the usual custom, and Gordon opened it without difficulty. A formless shape, swathed in moldering wrappings, met our eyes. Gordon parted some of the wrappings and revealed an inch or so of withered, brownish, leathery arm. He shuddered involuntarily as he touched it, as a man will do at the touch of a reptile or some inhumanly cold thing. Taking a small metal idol from a stand nearby, he rapped on the shrunken breast and the arm. Each gave out a solid thumping, like some sort of wood.

Gordon shrugged his shoulders. "Dead for two thousand years anyway and I don't suppose I should risk destroying a valuable mummy simply to prove what we know to be true."

He closed the case again.

"The mummy may have crumbled some, even from this much exposure, but perhaps it did not."

This last was addressed to the Levantine who replied merely by a courteous gesture of his hand, and the negroes once more lifted the case and carried it to the truck, where they loaded it on, and a moment later mummy, truck and negroes had vanished in the fog.

Gordon still nosed about the shop, but I stood stock-still in the center of the floor. To my chaotic and dope-ridden brain I attributed it, but the sensation had been mine, that through the wrappings of the mummy's face, great eyes had burned into mine, eyes like pools of yellow fire, that seared my soul and froze me where I stood. And as the case had been carried through the door, I knew that the lifeless thing in it, dead, God only knows how many centuries, was *laughing*, hideously and silently.

17. The Dead Man from the Sea

"The blind gods roar and rave and dream
   Of all cities under the sea."
                              —Chesterton.

Gordon puffed savagely at his Turkish cigarette, staring abstractedly and unseeingly at Hansen, who sat opposite him.

"I suppose we must chalk up another failure against ourselves. That Levantine, Kamonos, is evidently a creature of the Egyptian's and the walls and floors of his shop are probably honeycombed with secret panels and doors which would baffle a magician."

Hansen made some answer but I said nothing. Since our return to Gordon's apartment, I had been conscious of a feeling of intense languor and sluggishness which not even my condition could account for. I knew that my system was full of the elixir—but my mind seemed strangely slow and hard of comprehension in direct contrast with the average state of my mentality when stimulated by the hellish dope.

This condition was slowly leaving me, like mist floating from the surface of a lake, and I felt as if I were waking gradually from a long and unnaturally sound sleep.

Gordon was saying: "I would give a good deal to know if Kamonos is really one of Kathulos' slaves or if the Scorpion managed to make his escape through some natural exit as we entered."

"Kamonos is his servant, true enough," I found myself saying slowly, as if searching for the proper words. "As we left, I saw his gaze light upon the scorpion which is traced on my hand. His eyes narrowed, and as we were leaving he contrived to brush close against me—and to whisper in a quick low voice: 'Soho, 48.'"

Gordon came erect like a loosened steel bow.

"Indeed!" he rapped. "Why did you not tell me at the time?"

"I don't know."

My friend eyed me sharply.

"I noticed you seemed like a man intoxicated all the way from the shop," said he. "I attributed it to some aftermath of hashish. But no. Kathulos is undoubtedly a masterful disciple of Mesmer—his power over venomous reptiles shows that, and I am beginning to believe it is the real source of his power over humans.

"Somehow, the Master caught you off your guard in that shop and partly asserted his dominance over your mind. From what hidden nook he sent his thought waves to shatter your brain, I do not know, but Kathulos was somewhere in that shop, I am sure."

"He was. He was in the mummy case."

"The mummy case!" Gordon exclaimed rather impatiently. "That is impossible! The mummy quite filled it and not even such a thin being as the Master could have found room there."

I shrugged my shoulders, unable to argue the point but somehow sure of the truth of my statement.

"Kamonos," Gordon continued, "doubtless is not a member of the inner circle and does not know of your change of allegiance. Seeing the mark of the scorpion, he undoubtedly supposed you to be a spy of the Master's. The whole thing may be a plot to ensnare us, but I feel that the man was sincere—Soho 48 can be nothing less than the Scorpion's new rendezvous."

I too felt that Gordon was right, though a suspicion lurked in my mind.

"I secured the papers of Major Morley yesterday," he continued, "and while you slept, I went over them. Mostly they but corroborated what I already knew—touched on the unrest of the natives and repeated the theory that one vast genius was behind all. But there was one matter which interested me greatly and which I think will interest you also."

From his strong box he took a manuscript written in the close, neat characters of the unfortunate major, and in a monotonous droning voice which betrayed little of his intense excitement he read the following nightmarish narrative:

"This matter I consider worth jotting down—as to whether it has any bearing on the case at hand, further developments will show.

At Alexandria, where I spent some weeks seeking further clues as to
the identity of the man known as the Scorpion, I made the acquaintance, through my friend Ahmed Shah, of the noted Egyptologist
Professor Ezra Schuyler of New York. He verified the statement made
by various laymen, concerning the legend of the 'ocean-man.' This
myth, handed down from generation to generation, stretches back
into the very mists of antiquity and is, briefly, that some day a man
shall come up out of the sea and shall lead the people of Egypt to
victory over all others. This legend has spread over the continent so
that now all black races consider that it deals with the coming of
a universal emperor. Professor Schuyler gave it as his opinion that
the myth was somehow connected with the lost Atlantis, which, he
maintains, was located between the African and South American
continents and to whose inhabitants the ancestors of the Egyptians
were tributary. The reasons for his connection are too lengthy and
vague to note here, but following the line of his theory he told me
a strange and fantastic tale. He said that a close friend of his, Von
Lorfmon of Germany, a sort of freelance scientist, now dead, was
sailing off the coast of Senegal some years ago, for the purpose of
investigating and classifying the rare specimens of sea life found
there. He was using for his purpose a small trading-vessel, manned
by a crew of Moors, Greeks and negroes.

"Some days out of sight of land, something floating was sighted,
and this object, being grappled and brought aboard, proved to be *a
mummy case of a most curious kind.* Professor Schuyler explained to
me the features whereby it differed from the ordinary Egyptian style,
but from his rather technical account I merely got the impression
that it was a strangely shaped affair carved with characters neither
cuneiform nor hieroglyphic. The case was heavily lacquered, being
watertight and airtight, and Von Lorfmon had considerable difficulty
in opening it. However, he managed to do so without damaging the
case, and a most unusual mummy was revealed. Schuyler said that he
never saw either the mummy or the case, but that from descriptions
given him by the Greek skipper who was present at the opening of

the case, the mummy differed as much from the ordinary man as the case differed from the conventional type.

"Examination proved that the subject had not undergone the usual procedure of mummification. All parts were intact just as in life, but the whole form was shrunk and hardened to a wood-like consistency. Cloth wrappings swathed the thing and they crumbled to dust and vanished the instant air was let in upon them.

"Von Lorfmon was impressed by the effect upon the crew. The Greeks showed no interest beyond that which would ordinarily be shown by any man, but the Moors, and even more the negroes, seemed to be rendered temporarily insane! As the case was hoisted on board, they all fell prostrate on the deck and raised a sort of worshipful chant, and it was necessary to use force in order to exclude them from the cabin wherein the mummy was exposed. A number of fights broke out between them and the Greek element of the crew, and the skipper and Von Lorfmon thought best to put back to the nearest port in all haste. The skipper attributed it to the natural aversion of seamen toward having a corpse on board, but Von Lorfmon seemed to sense a deeper meaning.

"They made port in Lagos, and that very night Von Lorfmon was murdered in his stateroom and the mummy and its case vanished. All the Moor and negro sailors deserted ship the same night. Schuyler said—and here the matter took on a most sinister and mysterious aspect—that immediately afterward this widespread unrest among the natives began to smolder and take tangible form; he connected it in some manner with the old legend.

"An aura of mystery, also, hung over Von Lorfmon's death. He had taken the mummy into his stateroom, and anticipating an attack from the fanatical crew, had carefully barred and bolted door and portholes. The skipper, a reliable man, swore that it was virtually impossible to effect an entrance from without. And what signs were present pointed to the fact that the locks had been worked from *within*. The scientist was killed by a dagger which formed part of his collection and which was left in his breast.

"As I have said, immediately afterward the African cauldron began to seethe. Schuyler said that in his opinion the natives considered the ancient prophecy fulfilled. The mummy was *the man from the sea*.

"Schuyler gave as his opinion that the thing was the work of Atlanteans and that the man in the mummy case was a native of lost Atlantis. How the case came to float up through the fathoms of water which cover the forgotten land, he does not venture to offer a theory. He is sure that somewhere in the ghost-ridden mazes of the African jungles the mummy has been enthroned as a god, and, inspired by the dead thing, the black warriors are gathering for a wholesale massacre. He believes, also, that some crafty Moslem is the direct moving power of the threatened rebellion."

Gordon ceased and looked up at me.

"Mummies seem to weave a weird dance through the warp of the tale," he said. "The German scientist took several pictures of the mummy with his camera, and it was after seeing these—which strangely enough were not stolen along with the thing—that Major Morley began to think himself on the brink of some monstrous discovery. His diary reflects his state of mind and becomes incoherent—his condition seems to have bordered on insanity. What did he learn to unbalance him so? Do you suppose that the mesmeric spells of Kathulos were used against him?"

"These pictures—" I began.

"They fell into Schuyler's hands and he gave one to Morley. I found it among the manuscripts."

He handed the thing to me, watching me narrowly. I stared, then rose unsteadily and poured myself a tumbler of wine.

"'Not a dead idol in a voodoo hut," I said shakily, "but a monster animated by fearsome life, roaming the world for victims. Morley had seen the Master—that is why his brain crumbled. Gordon, as I hope to live again, *that face is the face of Kathulos!*"

Gordon stared wordlessly at me.

"The Master hand, Gordon," I laughed. A certain grim enjoyment penetrated the mists of my horror, at the sight of the steel-nerved Englishman struck speechless, doubtless for the first time in his life.

He moistened his lips and said in a scarcely recognizable voice, "Then, in God's name, Costigan, nothing is stable or certain, and mankind hovers at the brink of untold abysses of nameless horror. If that dead monster found by Von Lorfmon be in truth the Scorpion, brought to life in some hideous fashion, what can mortal effort do against him?"

"The mummy at Kamonos'—" I began.

"Aye, the man whose flesh, hardened by a thousand years of non-existence—that must have been Kathulos himself! He would have just had time to strip, wrap himself in the linens and step into the case before we entered. You remember that the case, leaning upright against the wall, stood partly concealed by a large Burmese idol, which obstructed our view and doubtless gave him time to accomplish his purpose. My God, Costigan, with what horror of the prehistoric world are we dealing?"

"I have heard of Hindoo fakirs who could induce a condition closely resembling death," I began. "Is it not possible that Kathulos, a shrewd and crafty Oriental, could have placed himself in this state and his followers have placed the case in the ocean where it was sure to be found? And might not he have been in this shape tonight at Kamonos'?"

Gordon shook his head.

"No. I have seen these fakirs. None of them ever feigned death to the extent of becoming shriveled and hard—in a word, dried up. Morley, narrating in another place the description of the mummy-case as jotted down by Von Lorfmon and passed on to Schuyler, mentions the fact that large portions of seaweed adhered to it—seaweed of a kind found only at great depths, on the bottom of the ocean. The wood, too, was of a kind which Von Lorfmon failed to recognize or to classify, in spite of the fact that he was one of the greatest living authorities on flora. And his notes again and again emphasize the enormous *age* of the thing. He admitted that there was no way of telling how old the mummy was, but his hints intimate that he believed it to be, not thousands of years old, but millions of years!

"No. We must face the facts. Since you are positive that the picture of the mummy is the picture of Kathulos—and there is little room for fraud—one of two things is practically certain: the Scorpion was never dead but ages ago was placed in that mummy case and his life preserved in some manner, or else—he was dead and has been brought to life! Either of these theories, viewed in the cold light of reason, is absolutely untenable. Are we all insane?"

"Had you ever walked the road to hashish land," I said somberly, "you could believe anything to be true. Had you ever gazed into the terrible reptilian eyes of Kathulos the sorcerer, you would not doubt that he was both dead and alive."

Gordon gazed out the window, his fine face haggard in the gray light which had begun to steal through them.

"At any rate," said he, "there are two places which I intend exploring thoroughly before the sun rises again—Kamonos' antique shop and Soho 48."

18. The Grip of the Scorpion

"While from a proud tower in the town
Death looks gigantically down."
                                        —Poe.

Hansen snored on the bed as I paced the room. Another day had passed over London and again the streetlamps glimmered through the fog. Their lights affected me strangely. They seemed to beat, solid waves of energy, against my brain. They twisted the fog into strange sinister shapes. Footlights of the stage that is the streets of London, how many grisly scenes had they lighted? I pressed my hands hard against my throbbing temples, striving to bring my thoughts back from the chaotic labyrinth where they wandered.

Gordon I had not seen since dawn. Following the clue of "Soho 48" he had gone forth to arrange a raid upon the place and he thought it best that I should remain under cover. He anticipated an attempt upon my life, and again he feared that if I went searching among the dives I formerly frequented it would arouse suspicion.

Hansen snored on. I seated myself and began to study the Turkish shoes which clothed my feet. Zuleika had worn Turkish slippers—how she floated through my waking dreams, gilding prosaic things with her witchery! Her face smiled at me from the fog; her eyes shone from the flickering lamps; her phantom footfalls re-echoed through the misty chambers of my skull.

They beat an endless tattoo, luring and haunting till it seemed that these echoes found echoes in the hallway outside the room where I stood, soft and stealthy. A sudden rap at the door and I started.

Hansen slept on as I crossed the room and flung the door swiftly open. A swirling wisp of fog had invaded the corridor, and through it, like a silver veil, I saw her—Zuleika stood before me with her shimmering hair and her red lips parted and her great dark eyes.

Like a speechless fool I stood and she glanced quickly down the hallway and then stepped inside and closed the door.

"Gordon!" she whispered in a thrilling undertone. "Your friend! The Scorpion has him!"

Hansen had awakened and now sat gaping stupidly at the strange scene which met his eyes.

Zuleika did not heed him.

"And oh, Steephen!" she cried, and tears shone in her eyes, "I have tried so hard to secure some more elixir but I could not."

"Never mind that," I finally found my speech. "Tell me about Gordon."

"He went back to Kamonos' alone, and Hassim and Ganra Singh took him captive and brought him to the Master's house. Tonight assemble a great host of the people of the Scorpion for the sacrifice."

"Sacrifice!" A grisly thrill of horror coursed down my spine. Was there no limit to the ghastliness of this business?

"Quick, Zuleika, where is this house of the Master's?"

"Soho, 48. You must summon the police and send many men to surround it, but you must not go yourself—"

Hansen sprang up quivering for action, but I turned to him. My brain was clear now, or seemed to be, and racing unnaturally.

"Wait!" I turned back to Zuleika. "When is this sacrifice to take place?"

"At the rising of the moon."

"That is only a few hours before dawn. Time to save him, but if we raid the house they'll kill him before we can reach them. And God only knows how many diabolical things guard all approaches."

"I do not know," Zuleika whimpered. "I must go now, or the Master will kill me."

Something gave way in my brain at that; something like a flood of wild and terrible exultation swept over me.

"The Master will kill no one!" I shouted, flinging my arms on high. "Before ever the east turns red for dawn, the Master dies! By all things holy and unholy I swear it!"

Hansen stared wildly at me and Zuleika shrank back as I turned on her. To my dope-inspired brain had come a sudden burst of light, true and unerring. I knew Kathulos was a mesmerist—that he understood fully the secret of dominating another's mind and soul. And I knew that at last I had hit upon the reason of his power over the girl. Mesmerism! As a snake fascinates and draws to him a bird, so the Master held Zuleika to him with unseen shackles. So absolute was his rule over her that it held even when she was out of his sight, working over great distances.

There was but one thing which would break that hold: the magnetic power of some other person whose control was stronger with her than Kathulos'. I laid my hands on her slim little shoulders and made her face me.

"Zuleika," I said commandingly, "here you are safe; you shall not return to Kathulos. There is no need of it. Now you are free."

But I knew I had failed before I ever started. Her eyes held a look of amazed, unreasoning fear and she twisted timidly in my grasp.

"Steephen, please let me go!" she begged. "I must—I must!"

I drew her over to the bed and asked Hansen for his handcuffs. He handed them to me, wonderingly, and I fastened one cuff to the bedpost and the other to her slim wrist. The girl whimpered but made no resistance, her limpid eyes seeking mine in mute appeal.

It cut me to the quick to enforce my will upon her in this apparently brutal manner but I steeled myself.

"Zuleika," I said tenderly, "you are now my prisoner. The Scorpion can not blame you for not returning to him when you are unable to do so—and before dawn you shall be free of his rule entirely."

I turned to Hansen and spoke in a tone which admitted of no argument.

"Remain here, just without the door, until I return. On no account allow any strangers to enter—that is, anyone whom you do not personally know. And I charge you, on your honor as a man, do not release this girl, no matter what she may say. If neither I nor Gordon have returned by ten o'clock tomorrow, take her to this address—that family once was friends of mine and will take care of a homeless girl. I am going to Scotland Yard."

"Steephen," Zuleika wailed, "you are going to the Master's lair! You will be killed! Send the police, do not go!"

I bent, drew her into my arms, felt her lips against mine, then tore myself away. The fog plucked at me with ghostly fingers, cold as the hands of dead men, as I raced down the street. I had no plan, but one was forming in my mind—beginning to seethe in the stimulated cauldron that was my brain. I halted at the sight of a policeman pacing his beat, and beckoning him to me, scribbled a terse note on a piece of paper torn from a notebook and handed it to him.

"Get this to Scotland Yard; it's a matter of life and death and it has to do with the business of John Gordon."

At that name, a gloved hand came up in swift assent, but his assurance of haste died out behind me as I renewed my flight. The note stated briefly that Gordon was a prisoner at Soho 48 and advised an immediate raid in force—advised, nay, in Gordon's name, commanded it.

My reason for my actions was simple; I knew that the first noise of the raid sealed John Gordon's doom. Somehow I first must reach him and protect or free him before the police arrived.

The time seemed endless, but at last the grim gaunt outlines of the house that was Soho 48 rose up before me, a giant ghost in the fog. The hour grew late; few people dared the mists and the dampness as I came to a halt in the street before this forbidding building. No lights showed from the windows, either upstairs or down. It seemed deserted. But the lair of the scorpion often seems deserted until the silent death strikes suddenly.

Here I halted and a wild thought struck me. One way or another, the drama would be over by dawn. Tonight was the climax of my career, the ultimate top of life. Tonight I was the strongest link in the strange chain of events. Tomorrow it would not matter whether I lived or died. I drew the flask of elixir from my pocket and gazed at it. Enough for two more days if properly eked out. Two more days of life! Or—I needed stimulation as I never needed it before; the task in front of me was one no mere human could hope to accomplish. If I drank the entire remainder of the elixir, I had no idea as to the duration of its effect, but it would last the night through. And my legs were shaky; my mind had curious periods of utter vacuity—weakness of brain and body assailed me. I raised the flask and with one draft drained it.

For an instant I thought it was death. Never had I taken such an amount.

Sky and world reeled and I felt as if I would fly into a million vibrating fragments, like the bursting of a globe of brittle steel. Like fire, like hellfire the elixir raced along my veins and I was a giant! A monster! A superman!

Turning, I strode to the menacing, shadowy doorway. I had no plan; I felt the need of none. As a drunken man walks blithely into danger, I strode to the lair of the Scorpion, magnificently aware of my superiority, imperially confident of my stimulation and sure as the unchanging stars that the way would open before me.

Oh, there never was a superman like that who knocked commandingly on the door of Soho 48 that night in the rain and the fog!

I knocked four times, the old signal that we slaves had used to be admitted into the idol room at Yun Shatu's. An aperture opened in the center of the door and slanted eyes looked warily out. They slightly widened as the owner recognized me, then narrowed wickedly.

"You fool!" I said angrily. "Don't you see the mark?"

I held my hand to the aperture.

"Don't you recognize me? Let me in, curse you."

I think the very boldness of the trick made for its success. Surely by now all the Scorpion's slaves knew of Stephen Costigan's rebellion, knew that he was marked for death. And the very fact that I came there, inviting doom, confused the doorman.

The door opened and I entered. The man who had admitted me was a tall, lank Chinaman I had known as a servant at Kathulos. He closed the door behind me and I saw we stood in a sort of vestibule, lighted by a dim lamp whose glow could not be seen from the street for the reason that the windows were heavily curtained. The Chinaman glowered at me undecided. I looked at him, tensed. Then suspicion flared in his eyes and his hand flew to his sleeve. But at the instant I was on him and his lean neck broke like a rotten bough between my hands.

I eased his corpse to the thickly carpeted floor and listened. No sound broke the silence. Stepping as stealthily as a wolf, fingers spread like talons, I stole into the next room. This was furnished in Oriental style, with couches and rugs and gold-worked drapery, but was empty of human life. I crossed it and went into the next one. Light flowed softly from the censers which were swung from the ceiling, and the Eastern rugs deadened the sound of my footfalls; I seemed to be moving through a castle of enchantment.

Every moment I expected a rush of silent assassins from the doorways or from behind the curtains or screens with their writhing dragons. Utter silence reigned. Room after room I explored and at last halted at the foot of the stairs. The inevitable censer shed an uncertain light, but most of the stairs were veiled in shadows. What horrors awaited me above?

But fear and the elixir are strangers and I mounted that stair of lurking terror as boldly as I had entered that house of terror. The upper rooms I found to be much like those below and with them they had this fact in common: they were empty of human life. I sought an attic but there seemed no door letting into one. Returning to the first floor, I made a search for an entrance into the basement, but again my efforts were fruitless. The amazing truth was borne in upon me: except for myself and that dead man who lay sprawled so grotesquely in the outer vestibule, there were no men in that house, dead or living.

I could not understand it. Had the house been bare of furniture I should have reached the natural conclusion that Kathulos had fled—but no signs of flight met my eye. This was unnatural—uncanny. I stood in the great shadowy library and pondered. No, I had made no mistake in the houses. Even if the broken corpse in the vestibule were not there to furnish mute testimony, everything in the room pointed toward the presence of the Master. There were the artificial palms, the lacquered screen, the tapestries, even the idol, though now no incense smoke rose before it. About the walls ranged long shelves of books, bound in strange and costly fashion—books in every language in the world, I found from a swift examination, and on every subject—outré and bizarre, most of them.

Remembering the secret passage in the Temple of Dreams, I investigated the heavy mahogany table which stood in the center of the room. But nothing resulted. A sudden blaze of fury surged up in me, primitive and unreasoning. I snatched a statuette from the table and dashed it against the shelf-covered wall. The noise of its breaking would surely bring the gang from their hiding places. But the result was much more startling than that!

The statuette struck the edge of a shelf and instantly the whole section of shelves with their load of books swung silently outward revealing a narrow doorway! As in the other secret door, a row of steps led downward. At another time I would have shuddered at the thought of descending, with the horrors of that other tunnel fresh in my mind, but inflamed as I was by the elixir, I strode forward without an instant's hesitancy.

Since there was no one in the house, they must be somewhere in the tunnel or in whatever lair to which the tunnel led. I stepped through the doorway, leaving the door open; the police might find it that way and follow me, though somehow I felt as if mine would be a lone hand from start to grim finish.

I went down a considerable distance and then the stair debouched into a level corridor some twenty feet wide—a remarkable thing. In spite of the width, the ceiling was rather low and from it hung small, curiously shaped lamps which flung a dim light. I stalked hurriedly along the corridor like old Death seeking victims, and as I went I noted the work of the thing. The floor was of great broad flags and the walls seemed to be of huge blocks of evenly set stone. This passage was clearly no work of modern days; the slaves of Kathulos never tunneled there. Some secret way of medieval times, I thought—and after all, who knows what catacombs lie below London, whose secrets are greater and darker than those of Babylon and Rome?

On and on I went, and now I knew that I must be far below the earth. The air was dank and heavy, and cold moisture dripped from the stones of walls and ceiling. From time to time I saw smaller passages leading away in the darkness but I determined to keep to the larger main one.

A ferocious impatience gripped me. I seemed to have been walking for hours and still only dank damp walls and bare flags and guttering lamps met my eyes. I kept a close watch for sinister-appearing chests or the like—saw no such things.

Then as I was about to burst into savage curses, another stair loomed up in the shadows in front of me.

19. Dark Fury

"The ringed wolf glared the circle round
  Through baleful, blue-lit eye,
Not unforgetful of his debt.
Quoth he, 'I'll do some damage yet
  Or ere my turn to die!'"
                                                —Mundy.

Like a lean wolf I glided up the stairs. Some twenty feet up there
was a sort of landing from which other corridors diverged, much
like the lower one by which I had come. The thought came to me
that the earth below London must be honeycombed with such secret
passages, one above the other.

Some feet above this landing the steps halted at a door, and
here I hesitated, uncertain as to whether I should chance knocking
or not. Even as I meditated, the door began to open. I shrank back
against the wall, flattening myself out as much as possible. The door
swung wide and a Moor came through. Only a glimpse I had of the
room beyond, out of the corner of my eye, but my unnaturally alert
senses registered the fact that the room was empty.

And on the instant, before he could turn, I smote the Moor a
single deathly blow behind the angle of the jawbone and he toppled
headlong down the stairs, to lie in a crumpled heap on the landing,
his limbs tossed grotesquely about.

My left hand caught the door as it started to slam shut and in
an instant I was through and standing in the room beyond. As I had
thought, there were no occupants of this room. I crossed it swiftly
and entered the next. These rooms were furnished in a manner before
which the furnishings of the Soho house paled into insignificance.
Barbaric, terrible, unholy—these words alone convey some slight
idea of the ghastly sights which met my eyes. Skulls, bones and
complete skeletons formed much of the decorations, if such they
were. Mummies leered from their cases and mounted reptiles ranged
the walls. Between these sinister relics hung African shields of hide

and bamboo, crossed with assagais and war daggers. Here and there reared obscene idols, black and horrific.

And in between and scattered about among these evidences of savagery and barbarism were vases, screens, rugs and hangings of the highest Oriental workmanship; a strange and incongruous effect.

I had passed through two of these rooms without seeing a human, when I came to stairs leading upward. Up these I went, several flights, until I came to a door in a ceiling. I wondered if I were still under the earth. Surely the first stairs had let into a house of some sort. I raised the door cautiously. Starlight met my eyes and I drew myself warily up and out. There I halted. A broad flat roof stretched away on all sides and beyond its rim on all sides glimmered the lights of London. Just what building I was on, I had no idea, but that it was a tall one I could tell, for I seemed to be above most of the lights I saw. Then I saw that I was not alone.

Over against the shadows of the ledge that ran around the roof's edge, a great menacing form bulked in the starlight. A pair of eyes glinted at me with a light not wholly sane—the starlight glanced silver from a curving length of steel. Yar Khan the Afghan killer fronted me in the silent shadows.

A fierce wild exultation surged over me. Now I could begin to pay the debt I owed Kathulos and all his hellish band! The dope fired my veins and sent waves of inhuman power and dark fury through me. A spring and I was on my feet in a silent, deathly rush.

Yar Khan was a giant, taller and bulkier than I. He held a tulwar, and from the instant I saw him I knew that he was full of the dope to the use of which he was addicted—heroin.

As I came in he swung his heavy weapon high in the air, but ere he could strike I seized his sword wrist in an iron grip and with my free hand drove smashing blows into his midriff.

Of that hideous battle, fought in silence above the sleeping city with only the stars to see, I remember little. I remember tumbling back and forth, locked in a death embrace. I remember the stiff beard rasping my flesh as his dope-fired eyes gazed wildly into mine. I remember the taste of hot blood in my mouth, the tang of fearful exultation in my soul, the onrushing and upsurging of inhuman strength and fury.

God, what a sight for a human eye, had anyone looked upon that grim roof where two human leopards, dope maniacs, tore each other to pieces!

I remember his arm breaking like rotten wood in my grip and the tulwar falling from his useless hand. Handicapped by a broken arm, the end was inevitable, and with one wild uproaring flood of might, I rushed him to the edge of the roof and bent him backward far out over the ledge. An instant we struggled there; then I tore loose his hold and hurled him over, and one single shriek came up as he hurtled into the darkness below.

I stood upright, arms hurled up toward the stars, a terrible statue of primordial triumph. And down my breast trickled streams of blood from the long wounds left by the Afghan's frantic nails, on neck and face.

Then I turned with the craft of the maniac. Had no one heard the sound of that battle? My eyes were on the door through which I had come, but a noise made me turn, and for the first time I noticed a small affair like a tower jutting up from the roof. There was no window there but a door, and even as I looked that door opened and a huge black form framed itself in the light that streamed from within. Hassim!

He stepped out on the roof, closed the door, his shoulders hunched and neck outthrust as he glanced this way and that—I struck him senseless to the roof with one hate-driven smash. I crouched over him, waiting some sign of returning consciousness, then away in the sky, close to the horizon, I saw a faint red tint. The rising of the moon!

Where in God's name was Gordon? Even as I stood undecided, a strange noise reached me. It was curiously like the droning of many bees.

Striding in the direction from which it seemed to come, I crossed the roof and leaned over the ledge. A sight nightmarish and incredible met my eyes.

Some twenty feet below the level of the roof on which I stood, there was another roof, of the same size and clearly a part of the same building. On one side it was bounded by the wall, on the other three sides a parapet several feet high took the place of a ledge.

A great throng of people stood, sat and squatted, close packed on the roof—and without exception they were *negroes!* There were hundreds of them, and it was their low-voiced conversation which I had heard. But what held my gaze was that upon which their eyes were fixed.

About the center of the roof rose a sort of teocalli some ten feet high, almost exactly like those found in Mexico and on which the priests of the Aztecs sacrificed human victims. This, allowing for its infinitely smaller scale, was an exact type of those sacrificial pyramids. On the flat top of it was an altar, curiously carved, and beside it stood a lank, dusky form whom even the ghastly mask he wore could not disguise to my gaze—Santiago, the Haiti voodoo fetish man. On the altar lay John Gordon, stripped to the waist and bound hand and foot, but conscious.

I reeled back from the roof edge, rent in twain by indecision. Even the stimulus of the elixir was not equal to this. Then a sound brought me about to see Hassim struggling dizzily to his knees. I reached him with two long strides and ruthlessly smashed him down again. Then I noticed a queer sort of contrivance dangling from his girdle. I bent and examined it. It was a mask similar to that worn by Santiago. Then my mind leaped swift and sudden to a wild desperate plan—which to my dope-ridden brain seemed not at all wild or desperate. I stepped softly to the tower and, opening the door, peered inward. I saw no one who might need to be silenced, but I saw a long silken robe hanging upon a peg in the wall. The luck of the dope fiend! I snatched it and closed the door again. Hassim showed no signs of consciousness but I gave him another smash on the chin to make sure and, seizing his mask, hurried to the ledge.

A low guttural chant floated up to me, jangling, barbaric, with an undertone of maniacal bloodlust. The negroes, men and women, were swaying back and forth to the wild rhythm of their death chant. On the teocalli Santiago stood like a statue of black basalt, facing the east, dagger held high—a wild and terrible sight, naked as he was save for a wide silken girdle and that inhuman mask on his face. The moon thrust a red rim above the eastern horizon and a faint breeze stirred the great black plumes which nodded above the voodoo man's mask. The chant of the worshipers dropped to a low, sinister whisper.

I hurriedly slipped on the death mask, gathered the robe close about me and prepared for the descent. I was prepared to drop the full distance, being sure in the superb confidence of my insanity that I would land unhurt, but as I climbed over the ledge I found a steel ladder leading down. Evidently Hassim, one of the voodoo priests, intended descending this way. So down I went, and in haste, for I knew that the instant the moon's lower rim cleared the city's skyline, that motionless dagger would descend into Gordon's breast.

Gathering the robe close about me so as to conceal my white skin, I stepped down upon the roof and strode forward through rows of black worshipers who shrank aside to let me through. To the foot of the teocalli I stalked and up the stair that ran about it, until I stood beside the death altar and marked the dark red stains upon it. Gordon lay on his back, his eyes open, his face rather drawn and haggard, but his gaze dauntless and unflinching.

Santiago's eyes blazed at me through the slits of his mask, but I read no suspicion in his gaze until I reached forward and took the dagger from his hand. He was too astonished to resist, and the black throng fell suddenly silent. That he saw my hand was not that of a negro it is certain, but he was simply struck speechless with astonishment. Moving swiftly I cut Gordon's bonds and hauled him erect. Then Santiago with a shriek leaped upon me—shrieked again and, arms flung high, pitched headlong from the teocalli with his own dagger hilt deep in his breast.

Then the black worshipers were on us with a screech and a roar—leaping on the steps of the teocalli like black leopards in the moonlight, knives flashing, eyes gleaming whitely.

I tore mask and robe from me and answered Gordon's exclamation with a wild laugh. I had hoped that by virtue of my disguise I might get us both safely away but now I was content to die there at his side.

He tore a great metal ornament from the altar, and as the attackers came he wielded this. A moment we held them at bay and then they flowed over us like a black wave. This to me was Valhalla! Knives stung me and blackjacks smashed against me, but I laughed and drove my iron fists in straight, steam-hammer smashes that shattered flesh and bone. I saw Gordon's crude weapon rise and fall, and each time a man went down. Skulls shattered and blood splashed and the dark fury swept over me. Nightmare faces swirled about me and I was on my knees; up again and the faces crumpled before my blows. Through far mists I seemed to hear a hideous familiar voice raised in imperious command.

Gordon was swept away from me but from the sounds I knew that the work of death still went on. The stars reeled through fogs of blood, but Hell's exaltation was on me and I reveled in the dark tide of fury until a darker, deeper tide of fury swept over me and I knew no more.

20. Ancient Horror

"Here now in his triumph where all things falter,
    Stretched out on the spoils that his own hand spread,
As a God self-slain on his own strange altar,
    Death lies dead."
                                                —Swinburne.

Slowly I drifted back into life—slowly, slowly. A mist held me and in the mist I saw a Skull—

I lay in a steel cage like a captive wolf, and the bars were too strong, I saw, even for my strength. The cage seemed to be set in a sort of niche in the wall and I was looking into a large room. This room was under the earth, for the floor was of stone flags and the walls and ceiling were composed of gigantic blocks of the same material. Shelves ranged the walls, covered with weird appliances, apparently of a scientific nature, and more were on the great table that stood in the center of the room. Beside this sat Kathulos.

The Sorcerer was clad in a snaky yellow robe, and those hideous hands and that terrible head were more pronouncedly reptilian than ever. He turned his great yellow eyes toward me, like pools of livid fire, and his parchment-thin lips moved in what probably passed for a smile.

I staggered erect and gripped the bars, cursing.

"Gordon, curse you, where is Gordon?"

Kathulos took a test tube from the table, eyed it closely and emptied it into another.

"Ah, my friend awakes," he murmured in his voice—the voice of a living dead man.

He thrust his hands into his long sleeves and turned fully to me.

"I think in you," he said distinctly, "I have created a Franken-stein monster. I made of you a superhuman creature to serve my wishes and you broke from me. You are the bane of my might, worse than Gordon even. You have killed valuable servants and interfered with my plans. However, your evil comes to an end tonight. Your friend Gordon broke away but he is being hunted through the tunnels and cannot escape.

"You," he continued with the sincere interest of the scientist, "are a most interesting subject. Your brain must be formed differently from any other man that ever lived. I will make a close study of it and add it to my laboratory. How a man, with the apparent need of the elixir in his system, has managed to go on for two days still stimulated by the last draft is more than I can understand."

My heart leaped. With all his wisdom, little Zuleika had tricked him and he evidently did not know that she had filched a flask of the lifegiving stuff from him.

"The last draft you had from me," he went on, "was sufficient only for some eight hours. I repeat, it has me puzzled. Can you offer any suggestion?"

I snarled wordlessly. He sighed.

"As always the barbarian. Truly the proverb speaks: 'Jest with the wounded tiger and warm the adder in your bosom before you seek to lift the savage from his savagery.'"

He meditated awhile in silence. I watched him uneasily. There was about him a vague and curious difference—his long fingers emerging from the sleeves drummed on the chair arms and some hidden exultation strummed at the back of his voice, lending it unaccustomed vibrancy.

"And you might have been a king of the new regime," he said suddenly. "Aye, the new—new and inhumanly old!"

I shuddered as his dry cackling laugh rasped out.

He bent his head as if listening. From far off seemed to come a hum of guttural voices. His lips writhed in a smile.

"My black children," he murmured. "They tear my enemy Gordon to pieces in the tunnels. They, Mr. Costigan, are my real henchmen and it was for their edification tonight that I laid John Gordon on the sacrificial stone. I would have preferred to have made some experiments with him, based on certain scientific theories, but my children must be humored. Later under my tutelage they will outgrow their childish superstitions and throw aside their foolish customs, but now they must be led gently by the hand.

"How do you like these under-the-earth corridors, Mr. Costigan?" he switched suddenly. "You thought of them—what? No doubt that the white savages of your Middle Ages built them? Faugh! These tunnels are older than your world! They were brought into being by mighty kings, too many eons ago for your mind to grasp, when an imperial city towered where now this crude village of London stands. All trace of that metropolis has crumbled to dust and vanished, but these corridors were built by more than human skill—ha ha! Of all the teeming thousands who move daily above them, none knows of their existence save my servants—and not all of them. Zuleika, for instance, does not know of them, for of late I have begun to doubt her loyalty and shall doubtless soon make of her an example."

At that I hurled myself blindly against the side of the cage, a red wave of hate and fury tossing me in its grip. I seized the bars and strained until the veins stood out on my forehead and the muscles bulged and crackled in my arms and shoulders. And the bars bent before my onslaught—a little but no more, and finally the power flowed from my limbs and I sank down trembling and weakened. Kathulos watched me imperturbably.

"The bars hold," he announced with something almost like relief in his tone. "Frankly, I prefer to be on the opposite side of them. You are a human ape if there was ever one."

He laughed suddenly and wildly.

"But why do you seek to oppose me?" he shrieked unexpectedly. "Why defy me, who am Kathulos, the Sorcerer, great even in the days of the old empire? Today, invincible! A magician, a scientist, among ignorant savages! Ha ha!"

I shuddered, and sudden blinding light broke in on me. Kathulos himself was an addict, and was fired by the stuff of his choice! What hellish concoction was strong enough, terrible enough to thrill the Master and inflame him, I do not know, nor do I wish to know. Of all the uncanny knowledge that was his, I, knowing the man as I did, count this the most weird and grisly.

"You, you paltry fool!" he was ranting, his face lit supernaturally. "Know you who I am? Kathulos of Egypt! Bah! They knew me in the old days! I reigned in the dim misty sea lands ages and ages before the sea rose and engulfed the land. I died, not as men die; the magic draft of life everlasting was ours! I drank deep and slept. Long I slept in my lacquered case! My flesh withered and grew hard; my blood dried in my veins. I became as one dead. But still within me burned the spirit of life, sleeping but anticipating the awakening. The great cities crumbled to dust. The sea drank the land. The tall shrines and the lofty spires sank beneath the green waves. All this I knew as I slept, as a man knows in dreams. Kathulos of Egypt? Faugh! *Kathulos of Atlantis!*"

I uttered a sudden involuntary cry. This was too grisly for sanity. "Aye, the magician, the sorcerer.

"And down the long years of savagery, through which the barbaric races struggled to rise without their masters, the legend came of the day of empire, when one of the Old Race would rise up from the sea. Aye, and lead to victory the black people who were our slaves in the old days.

"These brown and yellow people, what care I for them? The blacks were the slaves of my race, and I am their god today. They will obey me. The yellow and the brown peoples are fools—I make them my tools and the day will come when my black warriors will turn on them and slay at my word. And you, you white barbarians, whose ape-ancestors forever defied my race and me, your doom is at hand! And when I mount my universal throne, the only whites shall be white slaves!

"The day came as prophesied, when my case, breaking free from the halls where it lay—where it had lain when Atlantis was still sovereign of the world—where it had since her empery sank into the green fathoms—when my case, I say, was smitten by the deep sea tides and moved and stirred, and thrust aside the clinging seaweed that masks temples and minarets, and came floating up past the lofty sapphire and golden spires, up through the green waters, to float upon the lazy waves of the sea.

"Then came a white fool carrying out the destiny of which he was not aware. The men on his ship, true believers, knew that the time had come. And I—the air entered my nostrils and I awoke from the long, long sleep. I stirred and moved and lived. And rising in the night, I slew the fool that had lifted me from the ocean, and my servants made obeisance to me and took me into Africa, where I abode awhile and learned new languages and new ways of a new world and became strong.

"The wisdom of your dreary world—ha ha! I who delved deeper in the mysteries of the old than any man dared go! All that men know today, I know, and the knowledge beside that which I have brought down the centuries is as a grain of sand beside a mountain!

You should know something of that knowledge! By it I lifted you from one Hell to plunge you into a greater! You fool, here at my hand is that which would lift you from this! Aye, would strike from you the chains whereby I have bound you!"

He snatched up a golden vial and shook it before my gaze. I eyed it as men dying in the desert must eye the distant mirages. Kathulos fingered it meditatively. His unnatural excitement seemed to have passed suddenly, and when he spoke again it was in the passionless, measured tones of the scientist.

"That would indeed be an experiment worthwhile—to free you of the elixir habit and see if your dope-riddled body would sustain life. Nine times out of ten the victim, with the need and stimulus removed, would die—but you are such a giant of a brute—"

He sighed and set the vial down.

"The dreamer opposes the man of destiny. My time is not my own or I should choose to spend my life pent in my laboratories, carrying out my experiments. But now, as in the days of the old empire when kings sought my counsel, I must work and labor for the good of the race at large. Aye, I must toil and sow the seed of glory against the full coming of the imperial days when the seas give up all their living dead."

I shuddered. Kathulos laughed wildly again. His fingers began to drum his chair arms and his face gleamed with the unnatural light once more. The red visions had begun to seethe in his skull again.

"Under the green seas they lie, the ancient masters, in their lacquered cases, dead as men reckon death, but only sleeping. Sleeping through the long ages as hours, awaiting the day of awakening! The old masters, the wise men, who foresaw the day when the sea would gulp the land, and who made ready. Made ready that they might rise again in the barbaric days to come. As did I. Sleeping they lie, ancient kings and grim wizards, who died as men die, before Atlantis sank. Who, sleeping, sank with her but who shall arise again!

"Mine the glory! I rose first. And I sought out the site of old cities, on shores that did not sink. Vanished, long vanished. The barbarian tide swept over them thousands of years ago as the green waters swept over their elder sister of the deeps. On some the deserts stretch bare. Over some, as here, young barbarian cities rise."

He halted suddenly. His eyes sought one of the dark openings that marked a corridor. I think his strange intuition warned him of some impending danger but I do not believe that he had any inkling of how dramatically our scene would be interrupted.

As he looked, swift footsteps sounded and a man appeared suddenly in the doorway—a man disheveled, tattered and bloody. *John Gordon!* Kathulos sprang erect with a cry, and Gordon, gasping as from superhuman exertion, brought down the revolver he held in his hand and fired point blank. Kathulos staggered, clapping his hand to his breast, and then, groping wildly, reeled to the wall and fell against it. A doorway opened and he reeled through, but as Gordon leaped fiercely across the chamber, a blank stone surface met his gaze, which yielded not to his savage hammerings.

He whirled and ran drunkenly to the table where lay a bunch of keys the Master had dropped there.

"The vial!" I shrieked. "Take the vial!" And he thrust it into his pocket.

Back along the corridor through which he had come sounded a faint clamor growing swiftly like a wolf pack in full cry. A few precious seconds spent with fumbling for the right key, then the cage door swung open and I sprang out. A sight for the gods we were, the two of us! Slashed, bruised and cut, our garments hanging in tatters—my wounds had ceased to bleed, but now as I moved they began again, and from the stiffness of my hands I knew that my knuckles were shattered. As for Gordon, he was fairly drenched in blood from crown to foot.

We made off down a passage in the opposite direction from the menacing noise, which I knew to be the black servants of the Master in full pursuit of us. Neither of us was in much shape for running, but we did our best. Where we were going I had no idea. My superhuman strength had deserted me and I was going now on willpower alone. We switched off into another corridor and we had not gone twenty steps until, looking back, I saw the first of the black devils round the corner.

A desperate effort increased our lead a trifle. But they had seen us, were in full view now, and a yell of fury broke from them to be succeeded by a more sinister silence as they bent all efforts to overhauling us.

There a short distance in front of us we saw a stair loom suddenly in the gloom. If we might reach that—then we saw something else.

Against the ceiling, between us and the stairs, hung a huge thing like an iron grill, with great spikes along the bottom—a portcullis. And even as we looked, without halting in our panting strides, it began to move.

"They're lowering the portcullis!" Gordon croaked, his blood-streaked face a mask of exhaustion and will.

Now the blacks were only ten feet behind us—now the huge grate, gaining momentum, with a creak of rusty, unused mechanism, rushed downward. A final spurt, a gasping straining nightmare of effort—and Gordon, sweeping us both along in a wild burst of pure nerve-strength, hurled us under and through, and the grate crashed behind us!

A moment we lay gasping, not heeding the frenzied horde who raved and screamed on the other side of the grate. So close had that final leap been, that the great spikes in their descent had torn shreds from our clothing.

The blacks were thrusting at us with daggers through the bars, but we were out of reach and it seemed to me that I was content to lie there and die of exhaustion. But Gordon weaved unsteadily erect and hauled me with him.

"Got to get out," he croaked. "Got to warn—Scotland Yard—honeycombs in heart of London—high explosives—arms—ammunition."

We blundered up the steps, and in front of us I seemed to hear a sound of metal grating against metal. The stairs ended abruptly, on a landing that terminated in a blank wall. Gordon hammered against this and the inevitable secret doorway opened. Light streamed in, through the bars of a sort of grill. Men in the uniform of London police were sawing at these with hacksaws, and even as they greeted us, an opening was made through which we crawled.

"You're hurt, sir!" one of the men took Gordon's arm.

My companion shook him off.

"There's no time to lose! Out of here, as quick as we can go!"

I saw that we were in a basement of some sort. We hastened up the steps and out into the early dawn which was turning the east scarlet. Over the tops of smaller houses I saw in the distance a great gaunt building on the roof of which, I felt instinctively, that wild drama had been enacted the night before.

"That building was leased some months ago by a mysterious Chinaman," said Gordon, following my gaze. "Office building originally—the neighborhood deteriorated and the building stood vacant for some time. The new tenant added several stories to it but left it apparently empty. Had my eye on it for some time."

This was told in Gordon's jerky swift manner as we started hurriedly along the sidewalk. I listened mechanically, like a man in a trance. My vitality was ebbing fast and I knew that I was going to crumple at any moment.

"The people living in the vicinity had been reporting strange sights and noises. The man who owned the basement we just left heard queer sounds emanating from the wall of the basement and called the police. About that time I was racing back and forth among those cursed corridors like a hunted rat and I heard the police banging on the wall. I found the secret door and opened it but found it barred by a grating. It was while I was telling the astounded policemen to procure a hacksaw that the pursuing negroes, whom I had eluded for the moment, came into sight and I was forced to shut the door and run for it again. By pure luck I found you and by pure luck managed to find the way back to the door.

"Now we must get to Scotland Yard. If we strike swiftly, we may capture the entire band of devils. Whether I killed Kathulos or not I do not know, or if he can be killed by mortal weapons. But to the best of my knowledge all of them are now in those subterranean corridors and—"

At that moment the world shook! A brain-shattering roar seemed to break the sky with its incredible detonation; houses tottered and crashed to ruins, a mighty pillar of smoke and flame burst from the earth and on its wings great masses of debris soared skyward. A black fog of smoke and dust and falling timbers enveloped the world, a prolonged thunder seemed to rumble up from the center of the earth as of walls and ceilings falling, and amid the uproar and the screaming I sank down and knew no more.

21. The Breaking of the Chain

"And like a soul belated,
In heaven and hell unmated,
By cloud and mist abated,
    Comes out of darkness morn."
                              —Swinburne.

There is little need to linger on the scenes of horror of that terrible London morning. The world is familiar with and knows most of the details attendant to the great explosion which wiped out a tenth of that great city with a resultant loss of lives and property. For such a happening some reason must need be given; the tale of the deserted building got out, and many wild stories were circulated. Finally, to still the rumors, the report was unofficially given out that this building had been the rendezvous and secret stronghold of a gang of international anarchists, who had stored its basement full of high explosives and who had supposedly ignited these accidentally. In a way there was a good deal to this tale, as you know, but the threat that had lurked there far transcended any anarchist.

All this was told to me, for when I sank unconscious, Gordon, attributing my condition to exhaustion and a need of the hashish to the use of which he thought I was addicted, lifted me and with the aid of the stunned policemen got me to his rooms before returning to the scene of the explosion. At his rooms he found Hansen, and Zuleika handcuffed to the bed as I had left her. He released her and left her to tend to me, for all London was in a terrible turmoil and he was needed elsewhere.

When I came to myself at last, I looked up into her starry eyes and I lay quiet, smiling up at her. She sank down upon my bosom, nestling my head in her arms and covering my face with her kisses.

"Steephen!" she sobbed over and over, as her tears splashed hot on my face.

I was scarcely strong enough to put my arms about her but I managed it, and we lay there for a space, in silence except for the girl's hard, racking sobs.

"Zuleika, I love you," I murmured.

"And I love you, Steephen," she sobbed. "Oh, it is so hard to part now—but I'm going with you, Steephen; I can't live without you!"

"My dear child," said John Gordon, entering the room suddenly, "Costigan's not going to die. We will let him have enough hashish to tide him along, and when he is stronger we will take him off the habit slowly."

"You don't understand, sahib; it is not hashish Steephen must have. It is something which only the Master knew, and now that he is dead or is fled, Steephen cannot get it and must die."

Gordon shot a quick, uncertain glance at me. His fine face was drawn and haggard, his clothes sooty and torn from his work among the debris of the explosion.

"She's right, Gordon," I said languidly. "I'm dying. Kathulos killed the hashish craving with a concoction he called the elixir. I've been keeping myself alive on some of the stuff that Zuleika stole from him and gave me, but I drank it all last night."

I was aware of no craving of any kind, no physical or mental discomfort even. All my mechanism was slowing down fast; I had passed the stage where the need of the elixir would tear and rend me. I felt only a great lassitude and a desire to sleep. And I knew that the moment I closed my eyes, I would die.

"A strange dope, that elixir," I said with growing languor. "It burns and freezes and then at last the craving kills easily and without torment."

"Costigan, curse it!" said Gordon desperately, "you can't go like this! That vial I took from the Egyptian's table—what is in it?"

"The Master swore it would free me of my curse and probably kill me also," I muttered. "I'd forgotten about it. Let me have it; it can no more than kill me and I'm dying now."

"Yes, quick, let me have it!" exclaimed Zuleika fiercely, springing to Gordon's side, her hands passionately outstretched. She returned with the vial which he took from his pocket, and knelt beside me, holding it to my lips, while she murmured to me gently and soothingly in her own language.

I drank, draining the vial, but feeling little interest in the whole matter. My outlook was purely impersonal, at such a low ebb was my life, and I cannot even remember how the stuff tasted. I only remember feeling a curious sluggish fire burn faintly along my veins, and the last thing I saw was Zuleika crouching over me, her great eyes fixed with a burning intensity on me. Her tense little hand rested inside her blouse, and remembering her vow to take her own life if I died I tried to lift a hand and disarm her, tried to tell Gordon to take away the dagger she had hidden in her garments. But speech and action failed me and I drifted away into a curious sea of unconsciousness.

Of that period I remember nothing. No sensation fired my sleeping brain to such an extent as to bridge the gulf over which I drifted. They say I lay like a dead man for hours, scarcely breathing, while Zuleika hovered over me, never leaving my side an instant, and fighting like a tigress when anyone tried to coax her away to rest. Her chain was broken.

As I had carried the vision of her into that dim land of nothingness, so her dear eyes were the first thing which greeted my returning consciousness. I was aware of a greater weakness than I thought possible for a man to feel, as if I had been an invalid for months, but the life in me, faint though it was, was sound and normal, caused by no artificial stimulation. I smiled up at my girl and murmured weakly:

"Throw away your dagger, little Zuleika; I'm going to live."

She screamed and fell on her knees beside me, weeping and laughing at the same time. Women are strange beings, of mixed and powerful emotions, truly.

Gordon entered and grasped the hand which I could not lift from the bed.

"You're a case for an ordinary human physician now, Costigan," he said. "Even a layman like myself can tell that. For the first time since I've known you, the look in your eyes is entirely sane. You look like a man who has had a complete nervous breakdown, and needs about a year of rest and quiet. Great heavens, man, you've been through enough, outside your dope experience, to last you a lifetime."

"Tell me first," said I: "Was Kathulos killed in the explosion?"

"I don't know," answered Gordon somberly. "Apparently the entire system of subterranean passages was destroyed. I know my last bullet—the last bullet that was in the revolver which I wrested from one of my attackers—found its mark in the Master's body, but whether he died from the wound, or whether a bullet can hurt him, I do not know. And whether in his death agonies he ignited the tons and tons of high explosives which were stored in the corridors, or whether the negroes did it unintentionally, we shall never know.

"My God, Costigan, did you ever see such a honeycomb? And we know not how many miles in either direction the passages reached. Even now Scotland Yard men are combing the subways and basements of the town for secret openings. All known openings, such as the one through which we came and the one in Soho 48, were blocked by falling walls. The office building was simply blown to atoms."

"What about the men who raided Soho 48?"

"The door in the library wall had been closed. They found the Chinaman you killed, but searched the house without avail. Lucky for them, too, else they had doubtless been in the tunnels when the explosion came, and perished with the hundreds of negroes who must have died then."

"Every negro in London must have been there."

"I dare say. Most of them are voodoo worshipers at heart and the power the Master wielded was incredible. They died, but what of him? Was he blown to atoms by the stuff which he had secretly stored, or crushed when the stone walls crumbled and the ceilings came thundering down?"

"There is no way to search among those subterranean ruins, I suppose?"

"None whatever. When the walls caved in, the tons of earth upheld by the ceilings also came crashing down, filling the corridors with dirt and broken stone, blocking them forever. And on the surface of the earth, the houses which the vibration shook down were heaped high in utter ruins. What happened in those terrible corridors must remain forever a mystery."

My tale draws to a close. The months that followed passed uneventfully, except for the growing happiness which to me was paradise, but which would bore you were I to relate it. But one day Gordon and I again discussed the mysterious happenings that had had their being under the grim hand of the Master.

"Since that day," said Gordon, "the world has been quiet. Africa has subsided and the East seems to have returned to her ancient sleep. There can be but one answer—living or dead, Kathulos was destroyed that morning when his world crashed about him."

"Gordon," said I, "what is the answer to that greatest of all mysteries?"

My friend shrugged his shoulders.

"I have come to believe that mankind eternally hovers on the brinks of secret oceans of which it knows nothing. Races have lived and vanished before our race rose out of the slime of the primitive, and it is likely still others will live upon the earth after ours has vanished. Scientists have long upheld the theory that the Atlanteans possessed a higher civilization than our own, and on very different lines. Certainly Kathulos himself was proof that our boasted culture and knowledge were as nothing beside that of whatever fearful civilization produced him.

"His dealings with you alone have puzzled all the scientific world, for none of them has been able to explain how he could remove the hashish craving, stimulate you with a drug so infinitely more powerful, and then produce another drug which entirely effaced the effects of the other."

"I have him to thank for two things," I said slowly; "the regaining of my lost manhood—and Zuleika. Kathulos, then, is dead, as far as any mortal thing can die. But what of those others—those 'ancient masters' who still sleep in the sea?"

Gordon shuddered.

"As I said, perhaps mankind loiters on the brink of unthinkable chasms of horror. But a fleet of gunboats is even now patrolling the oceans unobtrusively, with orders to destroy instantly any strange case that may be found floating—to destroy it and its contents. And if my word has any weight with the English government and the nations of the world, the seas will be so patrolled until doomsday shall let down the curtain on the races of today."

"At night I dream of them, sometimes," I muttered, "sleeping in their lacquered cases, which drip with strange seaweed, far down among the green surges—where unholy spires and strange towers rise in the dark ocean."

"We have been face to face with an ancient horror," said Gordon somberly, "with a fear too dark and mysterious for the human brain to cope with. Fortune has been with us; she may not again favor the sons of men. It is best that we be ever on our guard. The universe was not made for humanity alone; life takes strange phases and it is the first instinct of nature for the different species to destroy each other. No doubt we seemed as horrible to the Master as he did to us. We have scarcely tapped the chest of secrets which Nature has stored, and I shudder to think of what that chest may hold for the human race."

"That's true," said I, inwardly rejoicing at the vigor which was beginning to course through my wasted veins, "but men will meet obstacles as they come, as men have always risen to meet them. Now, I am beginning to know the full worth of life and love, and not all the devils from all the abysses can hold me."

Gordon smiled.

"You have it coming to you, old comrade. The best thing is to forget all that dark interlude, for in that course lies light and happiness."

The Noseless Horror

Abysses of unknown terror lie veiled by the mists which separate man's everyday life from the uncharted and unguessed realms of the supernatural. The majority of people live and die in blissful ignorance of these realms—I say blissful, for the rending of the veil between the worlds of reality and of the occult is often a hideous experience. Once have I seen the veil so rent, and the incidents attendant thereto were burned so deeply into my brain that my dreams are haunted to this day.

The terrible affair was ushered in by an invitation to visit the estate of Sir Thomas Cameron, the noted Egyptologist and explorer. I accepted, for the man was always an interesting study, though I disliked his brutal manner and ruthless character. Owing to my association with various papers of a scientific nature, we had been frequently thrown together for several years, and I gathered that Sir Thomas considered me one of his few friends. I was accompanied on this visit by John Gordon, a wealthy sportsman to whom also an invitation had been extended.

The sun was setting as we came to the gate of the estate and the desolate and gloomy landscape depressed me and filled me with nameless forebodings. Some miles away could be faintly seen the village at which we had detrained and between this, and on all sides, the barren moors lay stark and sullen. No other human habitation could be seen and the only sign of life was some large fen bird flapping its lonely way inland. A cold wind whispered out of the east, laden with the bitter salt tang of the sea; and I shivered.

"Strike the bell," said Gordon, his impatience betraying the fact that the repellent atmosphere was affecting him, also. "We can't stand here all night."

But at that moment the gate swung open. Let it be understood that the manor house was surrounded by a high wall which entirely enclosed the estate. It was at the front gate that we stood. As it opened, we looked down a long driveway flanked by dense trees, but our attention at the present was riveted on the bizarre figure which stood to one side to let us pass. The gate was opened by a tall man in Oriental dress. He stood like a statue, arms folded, head inclined in a manner respectful but stately. The darkness of his skin enhanced the scintillant quality of his glittering eyes, and he would have been handsome save for a hideous disfiguration which at once robbed his features of comeliness and lent them a sinister and evil aspect. He was noseless.

While Gordon and I stood silent, struck speechless by this apparition, the Oriental—a Sikh of India, by his turban—bowed and said in almost perfect English: "The master awaits you in his study, sahibs."

We dismissed the lad who had brought us from the village, and as his cartwheels rattled away in the distance, we started up the shadowed driveway, followed by the Indian with our bags. The sun had set as we waited at the gate, and night fell with surprizing suddenness, the sky being heavily veiled by gray misty clouds. The wind sighed drearily through the trees on each side of the driveway and the great house loomed up in front of us, silent and dark except for a light in a single window. In the semi-darkness I heard the easy pad-pad of the Oriental's slippered feet behind us and the impression was so like a great panther stealing upon his victim that a shudder shook me.

Then we had reached the door and were being ushered into a broad, dimly lighted hallway, where Sir Thomas came striding forth to greet us.

"Good evening, my friends," his great voice boomed through the echoing house. "I have been expecting you! Have you dined? Yes? Then come into my study; I am preparing a treatise upon my latest discoveries and wish to have your advice on certain points. Ganra Singh!"

This last to the Sikh who stood motionless by. Sir Thomas spoke a few words to him in Hindustani, and with another bow, the noseless one lifted our bags and left the hall.

"I've given you a couple of rooms in the right wing," said Sir Thomas, leading the way to the stairs. "My study is in this wing—right above this hall—and I often work there all night."

The study proved to be a spacious room, littered with scientific books and papers, and queer trophies from all lands. Sir Thomas seated himself in a vast armchair and motioned us to make ourselves comfortable. He was a tall, heavily built man in early middle life, with an aggressive chin masked by a thick blond beard, and keen, hard eyes that smoldered with pent energy.

"I want your help as I've said," he began abruptly. "But we won't go into that tonight; plenty of time tomorrow and both of you must be rather fatigued."

"You live a long way from anywhere," answered Gordon. "What possessed you to buy and repair this old down-at-the-heels estate, Cameron?"

"I like solitude," Sir Thomas answered. "Here I am not pestered with small-brained people who buzz about one like mosquitoes about a buffalo. I do not encourage visitors here and I have absolutely no means of communicating with the outside world. When I am in England I am assured of quiet in which to pursue my work here. I have not even any servants; Ganra Singh does all the work necessary."

"That noseless Sikh? Who is he?"

"He is Ganra Singh. That's all I know about him. I met up with him in Egypt and have an idea that he fled India on account of some crime. But that doesn't matter; he's been faithful to me. He says that he served in the Anglo-Indian army and lost his nose from the sweep of an Afghan tulwar in a border raid."

"I don't like his looks," said Gordon bluntly. "You have a great deal of valuable trophies in this house; how can you be sure of trusting a man of whom you know so little?"

"Enough of that," Sir Thomas waved the matter aside with an impatient gesture. "Ganra Singh is all right; I never make mistakes in reading character. Let us talk of other things. I have not told you of my latest researches. "

He talked and we listened. It was easy to read in his voice the determination and ruthless driving power which made him one of the world's foremost explorers and research men, as he told us of hardships endured and obstacles overcome. He had some sensational discoveries to disclose to the world he said, and he added that the most important of his findings consisted of a most unusual mummy.

"I found it in a hitherto undiscovered temple far in the dark hinterlands of Upper Egypt, the exact location of which you shall learn tomorrow when we consult my notes together. I look to see it revolutionize history, for while I have not made a thorough examination of it, I have at least found that it is like no other mummy yet discovered. Differing from the usual process of mummifying, there is no mutilation at all. The mummy is a complete body with all parts intact just as the subject was in life. Allowing for the fact that the features are dried and distorted with the incredible passage of time, one might imagine that he is looking upon a very ancient man who recently died, before disintegration has set in. The leathery lids are drawn down firmly over the eye sockets, and I am sure when I raise those lids I shall find the eyeballs intact beneath.

"I tell you, it is epoch making and overthrows all preconceived ideas! If life could by some manner be breathed into that withered mummy, it would be as able to speak, walk, and breathe as any man; for, as I said, its parts are as intact as if the man had died yesterday. You know the usual process—the disemboweling and so on—by which corpses are made mummies. But no such things have been done to this one. What would my colleagues not give to have been the finder! All Egyptologists will die from pure envy! Attempts have already been made to steal it—I tell you, many a research worker would cut my heart out for it!"

"I think you overvalue your find, and undervalue the moral senses of your co-workers," said Gordon bluntly.

Sir Thomas sneered.

"A flock of vultures, sir," he exclaimed with a savage laugh. "Wolves! Jackals! Sneaking about seeking to steal the credit from a better man! The laity have no real conception of the rivalry that exists in the class of their betters. It's each man for himself—let everyone look to his own laurels and to the devil with the weaker. Thus far I've more than held my own."

"Even allowing this to be true," retorted Gordon, "you have scant right to condemn your rivals' tactics in the light of your own actions."

Sir Thomas glared at his outspoken friend so furiously that I half-expected him to commit bodily assault upon him; then the explorer's mood changed, and he laughed mockingly and uproariously.

"The affair of Gustave Von Honmann is still on your mind, doubtless. I find myself the object of scathing denunciations wherever I go since that unfortunate incident. It is, I assure you, a matter of complete indifference to me. I have never desired the mob's plaudits and I ignore its accusations. Von Honmann was a fool and deserved his fate. As you know, we were both searching for the hidden city of Gomar, the finding of which added so much to the scientific world. I contrived to let a false map fall into his hands and sent him away on a wild goose chase into Central Africa."

"You literally sent him to his death," Gordon pointed out. "I admit that Von Honmann was something of a beast, but it was a rotten thing to do, Cameron. You knew that all the chances in the world were against him escaping death at the hands of the wild tribesmen into whose lands you sent him."

"You can't make me angry," answered Cameron imperturbably. "That's what I like about you, Gordon; you're not afraid to speak out your mind. But let's forget Von Honmann; he's gone the way of all fools. The one camp follower who escaped the general massacre and made his way back to civilization's outpost said that Von Honmann, when he saw the game was up, realized the fraud and died swearing to avenge himself on me, living or dead, but that has never worried me. A man is living and dangerous or dead and harmless; that's all. But it's growing late and doubtless you are sleepy; I'll have Ganra Singh show you to your rooms. As for myself, I shall doubtless spend the rest of the night arranging the notes of my trip for tomorrow's work."

Ganra Singh appeared at the door like a giant phantom and we said good night to our host and followed the Oriental. Let me here say that the house was built in shape like a double-ended L. There were two stories and between the two wings was a sort of court upon which the lower rooms opened. Gordon and I had been assigned two bedrooms on the first floor in the left wing, which let into this court. There was a door between them, and as I was preparing to retire, Gordon entered.

"Strange sort of a chap, isn't he?" nodding across the court at the light which shone in the study window. "A good deal of a brute, but a great brain, marvelous brain."

I opened the door which let into the court for a breath of fresh air. The atmosphere in these rooms was crisp and sharp, but musky as if from unuse.

"He certainly doesn't have many visitors." The only light visible, besides those in our two rooms, was that in the upstairs study across the court.

"No." Silence fell for a space, then Gordon spoke abruptly, "Did you hear how Von Honmann died?"

"No."

"He fell into the hands of a strange and terrible tribe who claim descent from the early Egyptians. They are past masters at the hellish art of torture. The camp follower who escaped said that Von Honmann was killed slowly and fiendishly, in a manner which left him unmutilated, but shrunk and withered him until he was unrecognizable. Then he was sealed into a chest and placed in a fetish hut for a horrible relic and trophy."

My shoulders twitched involuntarily. "Frightful!"

Gordon rose, tossed away his cigarette, and turned toward his room.

"Getting late, good night—*what was that?*"

Across the court had come a faint crash as if a chair or table had been upset. As we stood, frozen by a sudden vague premonition of horror, a scream shuddered out across the night.

"Help! Help! Gordon! Slade! Oh God!"

Together we rushed out into the court. The voice was Sir Thomas', and came from his study in the left wing. As we raced across the court, the sounds of a terrible struggle came clearly to us and again Sir Thomas cried out like a man in his death agony: "He's got me! Oh God, he's got me—"

"Who is it, Cameron?" shouted Gordon desperately.

"Ganra Singh—" suddenly the straining voice broke short and a wild gibbering came dimly to us as we rushed into the first door of the lower left wing and charged up the stairs. It seemed an Eternity before we stood at the door of the study, beyond which still came a bestial yammering. We flung open the door and halted, aghast.

Sir Thomas Cameron lay writhing in a growing pool of gore, but it was not the dagger sunk deep into his breast which held us in our tracks like men struck dead, but the hideous and evident insanity of his face. His eyes flared redly, fixed on nothing, and they were the eyes of a man who is staring into Purgatory. A ceaseless gibbering burst from his lips and then into his yammering was woven human words: "—Noseless—the noseless one—" Then a rush of blood burst from his lips, and he dropped on his face.

We bent over him and eyed each other in horror.

"Stone dead," muttered Gordon. "But what killed him?"

"Ganra Singh—" I began, then both of us whirled. Ganra Singh stood silently in the doorway, his expressionless features giving no hint of his thoughts. Gordon rose, his hand sliding easily to his hip pocket.

"Ganra Singh, where have you been?"

"I was in the lower corridor, locking the house for the night. I heard my master call me. I came."

"Sir Thomas is dead. Do you have any idea as to who did the murder?"

"No, sahib. I am new to this English land; I do not know if my master had any enemies."

"Help me lift him on this couch." This was done. "Ganra Singh, you realize that we must hold you responsible for the time being."

"While you hold me, the real killer may escape."

Gordon did not reply to this. "Let me have the keys to the house."

The Sikh obeyed without a word.

Gordon then led him across the outer corridor to a small room in which he locked him, first assuring himself that the window, as was the case with all the other windows in the house, was heavily barred. Ganra Singh made no resistance; his face showed nothing of his emotions. As we shut the door we saw him standing impassively in the center of the room, arms folded, eyes following us inscrutably.

We returned to the study with its shattered chairs and tables, its red stain on the floor, and the silent form on the couch.

"There's nothing we can do until morning," said Gordon. "We can't communicate with anyone, and if we started out to walk to the village we should probably lose our way in the darkness and fog. It seems a pretty fair case against the Sikh. "

"Sir Thomas practically accused him in his last words. "

"As to that, I don't know. Cameron shouted his name when I yelled, but he might have been calling the fellow—I doubt if Sir Thomas heard me. Of course, that remark about the 'noseless one' could seem to mean no one else, but it isn't conclusive. Sir Thomas was insane when he died. "

I shuddered. "That, Gordon, is the most terrible phase of the matter. What was it that blasted Cameron's reason and made of him a screaming maniac in the last few minutes he had to live?"

Gordon shook his head. "I can't understand it. The mere fact of looking death in the eyes never shook Sir Thomas' nerve before. I tell you, Slade, I believe there's something deeper here than meets the eye. This smacks of the supernatural, in spite of the fact that I was never a superstitious man. But let's look at it in a logical light.

"This study comprises the whole of the upper left wing, being separated from the back rooms by a corridor which runs the whole length of the house. The only door of the study opens into that corridor. We crossed the court, entered a lower room of the left wing, went into the hall into which we were first admitted, and came up the stairs into the upper corridor. The study door was shut but not locked. And through that door came whatever it was that shattered Sir Thomas Cameron's brain before it murdered him. And the man—or thing—left the same way, for it is evident that nothing is concealed in the study and the bars on the windows prohibit escape in that manner. Had we been a few moments quicker we might have seen the slayer leaving. The victim was still grappling with the fiend when I shouted, but between that instant and the moment we came into the upper corridor, there was time for the slayer, moving swiftly, to accomplish his design and leave the room. Doubtless he concealed himself in one of the rooms across the hall and either slipped out while we were bending over Sir Thomas and made his escape—or, if it were Ganra Singh, came boldly into the study."

"Ganra Singh came after us, according to his story. He should have seen anyone trying to escape from the rooms. "

"The killer might have heard him coming and waited until he was in the study before emerging. Oh, understand, I believe the Sikh is the murderer, but we wish to be fair and look at the matter from every angle. Let's see that dagger."

It was a thin-bladed, wicked-looking Egyptian weapon, which I remembered having seen lying on Sir Thomas' table.

"It seems as if Ganra Singh's clothes would have been in disarray and his hands bloody," I suggested. "He scarcely had time to cleanse himself and arrange his garments."

"At any rate," Gordon answered, "the fingerprints of the killer should be upon this dagger hilt. I have been careful not to obliterate any such traces, and I will lay the weapon on the couch here for the examination of a Bertillon expert. I am not adept in such matters myself. And in the meanwhile I think I'll go over the room, after the accepted manner of detectives, to look for any possible clues."

"And I'll take a turn through the house. Ganra Singh may really be innocent, and the murderer lurking somewhere in the building."

"Better be careful. If there is such a being, remember that it is a desperate man, quite ready and willing to do murder."

I took up a heavy blackthorn and went out into the corridor. I forgot to say that all these corridors were dimly lighted, and the curtains drawn so closely that the whole house appeared to be dark from the outside. As I shut the door behind me, I felt more strongly than ever the oppressive silence of the house. The vaguely illumined corridor seemed a stage for grim and bloody deeds. Heavy velvet hangings masked unseen doorways and as a stray whisper of wind whipped them about, I started, and the lines from Poe flitted through my brain:

"And the silken, sad uncertain rustling of each purple curtain Thrilled me, filled with fantastic terrors never felt before."

I strode to the landing of the stair, and after another glance at the silent corridors and the blank doors, I descended. I had decided that if any man had hidden in the upper story, he would have descended to the lower floor by this time, if indeed he had not already left the house. I struck a light in the lower reception hall and went into the next room. The whole of the main building between the wings, I found, was composed of Sir Thomas' private museum, a really gigantic room, filled with idols, mummy cases, stone and clay pillars, papyrus scrolls, and like objects. I wasted little time here, however, for as I entered my eyes fell upon something I knew to be out of place in some manner. It was a mummy case, very different from the other cases, and it was open! I knew instinctively that it had contained the mummy of which Sir Thomas had boasted that evening, but now it was empty. The mummy was gone.

Thinking of his words regarding the jealousy of his rivals, I turned hastily and made for the hall and the stair. As I did so, I thought I heard somewhere in the house a faint crashing. I had no desire, however, to further explore the building alone and armed only with a club. I wished to return and tell Gordon that we were probably opposed to a gang of international thieves. I had started back toward the hall when I perceived a staircase leading directly from the museum room, and it I mounted, coming into the upper corridor near the right wing.

Again the long dim corridor ran away in front of me, with its blank mysterious doors and dark hangings. I must traverse the greater part of it in order to reach the study at the other end, and a foolish shiver shook me as I visualized hideous creatures lurking behind those closed doors. Then I shook myself. Whatever had driven Sir Thomas Cameron insane, it was human, and I gripped my blackthorn more firmly and strode down the corridor.

Then after a few strides I halted suddenly, the short hairs prickling at the back of my neck, and my flesh crawling unaccountably. I sensed an unseen presence and my eyes turned as drawn by a magnet to some heavy tapestries which masked a doorway. There was no wind in the rooms, but *the hangings moved slightly!* I started, straining my eyes on the heavy dark fabric until it seemed the intensity of my gaze would burn through it, and I was aware, instinctively, that other eyes glared back. Then my eyes strayed to the wall beside the hidden doorway. Some freak of the vague light threw a dark formless shadow there, and as I looked, it slowly assumed shape—a hideous distorted goblin image, grotesquely manlike, *and noseless!*

My nerve broke suddenly. That distorted figure might be merely the twisted shadow of a man who stood behind the hangings, but it was burned into my brain that, man, beast, or demon, those dark tapestries hid a shape of terrible and soul-shattering threat. A brooding horror lurked in the shadows and there in that silent darkened corridor with its vague flickering lights and that stark shadow hovering within my gaze, I came as near to insanity as I have ever come—it was not so much what met my eyes and senses but the phantoms conjured up in my brain, the terrible dim images that rose at the back of my skull and gibbered at me. For I knew that for the moment the commonplace human world was far away and that I was face to face with some horror from another sphere.

I turned and hurried down the corridor, my futile blackthorn shaking in my grasp, and the cold sweat forming in great beads upon my brow. I reached the study and entered, closing the door behind me. My eyes turned instinctively to the couch with its grim burden. Gordon leaned over some papers on a table, and he turned as I entered, his eyes alight with some suppressed excitement.

"Slade, I've found a map here drawn by Cameron, and according to it, he found that mummy on the borders of the land where Von Honmann was murdered—"

"The mummy's gone," I said.

"Gone? By Jupiter! Maybe that explains it! A gang of scientific thieves! Likely Ganra Singh is in with them—let's go talk to him."

Gordon strode across the corridor, I following. My nerve was still shaken and I had no use to discuss my recent experience. I must get back some of my courage before I could bring myself to put the fear I had felt into words. Gordon knocked at the door. Silence reigned. He turned the key in the lock, swung the door open, and swore. The room was empty! A door opening into another room parallel to the corridor showed how the prey had escaped. The lock had been fairly torn off.

"That was that noise I heard!" Gordon exclaimed. "Fool that I was, I was so engrossed in Sir Thomas' notes that I paid no attention, thinking it was but the noise of your opening or closing a door! I'm a failure as a detective. If I had been on my guard I might have arrived on the scene before the prisoner made his getaway."

"Lucky for you, you didn't," I answered shakily. "Gordon, let's get out of here! Ganra Singh was lurking behind the hangings as I came up the corridor—I saw the shadow of his noseless face—and I tell you, the man's not human. He's an evil spirit! An inhuman goblin! Do you think a man could unhinge Sir Thomas' reason—a human being? No, no, no! He's a demon in human form—and I'm not so sure that the form's human!"

Gordon's face was shadowed. "Nonsense! A hideous and unexplained crime has been perpetrated here tonight, but I will not believe that it cannot be explained in natural terms—listen!"

Somewhere down the corridor a door had opened and shut. Gordon leaped to the door, sprang through the passageway. Down the corridor something like a dark flying shadow whipped through a doorway, flinging the hangings away. Gordon fired blindly, then raced down the corridor. I followed, cursing his recklessness, but fired by his example to a kind of foolhardy bravery. I had no doubt but that the end of that wild chase would be a death grapple with the inhuman Indian, and the shattered door lock was ample proof of his prowess, even without the gory form which lay in the silent study. But when a man like Gordon leads, what can one do but follow?

Down the corridor we sped, through the door where we had seen the thing vanish, through the dark room beyond, and into the next. The sounds of flight in front of us told us that we were pressing close upon our prey. The memory of that chase through darkened rooms is a vague and hazy dream—a wild and chaotic nightmare. I do not remember the rooms and passages which we traversed. I only know that I followed Gordon blindly and halted only when he stopped in front of a tapestry-hung doorway beyond which a red glow was apparent. I was mazed, breathless. My sense of direction was completely gone. I had no idea as to what part of the house we were in, or why that crimson glow pulsed beyond the hangings.

"This is Ganra Singh's room," said Gordon. "Sir Thomas mentioned it in his conversation. It is the extreme upper room of the right wing. Further he cannot go, for this is the only door to the room and the windows are barred. Within that room stands at bay the man—or whatever—which killed Sir Thomas Cameron!"

"Then in God's name let us rush in upon him before we have time to reconsider and our nerve breaks!" I urged, and shouldering past Gordon, I hurled the curtains aside . . .

The red glow at least was explained. A great fire leaped and flickered in the huge fireplace, lending a red radiance to the room. And there at bay stood a nightmarish and hellish form—*the missing mummy!*

My dazed eyes took in at one glance the wrinkled leathery skin, the sunken cheeks, the flaring and withered nostrils from which the nose had decayed away—the hideous eyes were open now, and they burned with a ghastly and demoniac life. A single glimpse was all I had for in an instant the long lean thing came lurching headlong at me, a heavy ornament of some sort clutched in its lank and taloned hand. I struck once with the blackthorn and felt the skull give way, but it never halted—for who can slay the dead?—and the next instant I was down, writhing and dazed, with a shattered shoulder bone, lying where the sweep of that dried arm had dropped me.

I saw Gordon at short range fire four shots pointblank into the frightful form, and then it had grappled with him, and as I struggled futilely to regain my feet and re-enter the battle, my athletic friend, held helpless in those inhuman arms, was bent back across a table until it seemed his spine would give way.

It was Ganra Singh who saved us. The great Sikh came suddenly through the hangings like an Arctic blast and plunged into the fray like a wounded bull elephant. With a strength I have never seen equaled and which even the living-dead man could not resist, he tore the animated mummy from its prey and hurled it across the room. Borne on the crest of that irresistible onslaught, the mummy was flung backward until the great fireplace was at its back. Then with one last volcanic effort, the avenger crashed it headlong into the fire, beat it down, stamped it into the flames until they caught at the writhing limbs, and the frightful form crumbled and disintegrated among them with an intolerable scent of decayed and burning flesh.

Then Gordon, who had stood watching like a man in a dream, Gordon, the iron-nerved lion hunter who had braved a thousand perils, now crumpled forward on his face suddenly, in a dead faint!

Later we talked the affair over, while Ganra Singh bandaged my hurts with hands as light of touch and gentle as those of a woman.

"I think," I said weakly, "and I will admit that my view is untenable in the light of reason, but then any explanation must be incredible and improbable, that the people who made this mummy centuries and possibly thousands of years ago knew the art of preserving life—that by some means this man was simply put to sleep and slept in a deathlike manner all these years, just as Hindu fakirs appear to lie in death for days and weeks at a time. When the proper time came, then the creature awoke and started on its—or his—hideous course."

"What do you think, Ganra Singh?"

"Sahib," said the great Sikh courteously, "who am I to speak of hidden things? Many things are unknown to man. After the sahib had locked me into the room, I bethought me that whoever slew my master might escape while I stood helpless, and desiring to go elsewhere, I plucked away the lock with as much silence as I could and went forth searching among the darkened rooms. At last I heard sounds in my own bedroom and going there, found the sahibs fighting with the living-dead man. It was fortunate that before all this occurred I had built a great fire in my room so as to last all night, for I am unused to this cold country. I know that fire is the enemy of all evil things, the Great Cleanser, and so thrust the Evil One into the flame. I am glad to have avenged my master and aided the sahibs."

"Aided!" Gordon grinned. "If you hadn't showed up just when you did our bally ships would have been sunk. Ganra Singh, I've already apologized for my suspicions; you're a real man.

"No, Slade," his face grew serious, "I think you are wrong. In the first place, the mummy isn't thousands of years old. It's scarcely ten years old! As I find by reading his secret notes, Sir Thomas didn't find it in a lost temple in Upper Egypt, he found it in a fetish hut in Central Africa. He couldn't explain its presence there, and so said he found it in the hinterlands of Egypt. He being an Egyptologist, it sounded better too. But he really thought it was very ancient, and as we know, he was right about the unusual process of mummification. The tribesmen who sealed that mummy into its case knew more about such things than the ancient Egyptians, evidently. But it wouldn't have lasted over twenty years anyway, I'm sure. Then Sir Thomas came along and stole it from the tribesmen—the same tribe, by the way, who murdered Von Honmann.

"No, your theory is wrong, I feel—yet—you have heard of the occult theory which states that a spirit, earthbound through hate or love, can only do material good or evil when animating a material body? The occultists say, reasonably enough, that to bridge the gulf which lies between the two worlds of life and death, the spirit or ghost must inhabit and animate a fleshly form—preferably its own former habitation. This mummy had died as men die, but I believe that the hate it felt in life was sufficient to span the void of death, to cause the dead and withered body to move and act and do murder.

"Now, if this be true, there is no limit to the horror to which mankind may be heir. If this be true, men may be hovering forever on the brink of unthought oceans of supernatural terror, parted from the next world by a thin veil which may be rent—as we have just seen it rent. I would like to believe otherwise—but Slade—

"As Ganra Singh hurled the struggling mummy into the fire, I watched—the sunken features expanded in the heat for a fleeting instant, just as a toy balloon when inflated, and for one brief second took on a human and familiar likeness. *Slade, that face was the face of Gustave von Honmann!*"

The Brazen Peacock

The grisly and fantastic adventure began suddenly enough. I was sitting writing quietly in my room when the door burst open and my Arab servant Ali rushed in, breathless, eyes starting from his head. Close at his heels came a man I thought long dead.

"Girtmann!" I was on my feet in amazement. "What in heaven's name—!"

With a motion for silence he turned and, looking carefully out the door, closed and locked it with a sigh of relief. For a moment he breathed heavily as if winded and I looked him over curiously. The years had not changed him—his short, broad figure still evinced dynamic physical power and the strongly carved face with its jutting jaw and hooked nose and arrogant eyes still reflected the stubborn determination and ruthless self-assurance of the man. But now those cold eyes were shadowed and lines of strain made the features seem almost haggard. There was a nervous tension about his whole aspect that told me he had been through a terrific grind of some sort.

"What's up?" I asked, some of his evident nervousness vaguely imparting itself to me.

"Beware of him, sahib," burst forth Ali. "Have no dealings with the devil-hunted, lest the demons smell you out likewise! I say to you, sahib—"

"Wait!" Girtmann raised his hand; I saw that he held a peculiar-looking bundle under his other arm. He came close to me and gripped my arm with a strange passion, his eyes burning into mine. He was shaken in the clutch of some terrific excitement and I looked at him in amazement. Was this Erich Girtmann whose name was a byword for steely nerves and cynical self-control?

"You owe me your life," he was saying, speaking so hurriedly that the words tripped over each other. "I dragged you out of Lagos Bay when the sharks were ripping the shirt off of you—you've got to help me—you've got to hide me! I don't intend to lose the game after playing it this far! I'll split the proceeds with you, if you wish, but you've got to help me!"

"If you'll pull yourself together and tell me what you want," I said, "I'll be in a better position to help you. Of course, I'll do what I can for you, but you better tell me what sort of a jam you're in so I'll know how to go about it."

"Fair enough," he panted. "A drink first—Gad, that heathen of yours runs like an antelope—a pretty sight we must have made galloping through the alleys—courting publicity, and that's the last thing I want—but I didn't dare let him get out of my sight or I'd have never found you—couldn't go around all over the town looking for you, not after I spied that brown-faced devil, anyhow."

I mixed him a whiskey-and-soda and offered to take his bundle while he drank but he shook his head violently, hugging the strangely shaped packet almost fiercely. Meanwhile Ali had retired to the other side of the room in sullen silence, glaring at Girtmann in a most truculently suspicious manner.

"I thought you were dead," said I. "The rumor got about a year ago that you were killed by Bedouin bandits in the wild hill country somewhere near the Djebel Druse. Naturally, seeing you here in Djibouti was something of a surprize."

"That wasn't me the native *gendarmes* found stripped and muti-lated," he grunted. "It was a Dutch adventurer named Stalenaus. And it wasn't Bedouins who killed him—it was Druses who thought they were getting me. The Dutchman looked quite a bit like me though, and I saw my opportunity to fade out of the picture. That night Erich Girtmann died—temporarily—and a humble Druse peddler took his place. I fooled the Druses themselves—and others!" He laughed rather wildly.

"That's why I'm in Djibouti tonight, fleeing for my life," he continued. "I'm playing a desperate game, with monstrous stakes—my life against a fortune that would shame the riches of King Solomon!"

His eyes were blazing and from his wild talk I concluded that he had had a touch of the sun.

"Look here!" he cried, smiting the bundle, which gave out a metallic clink. "What do you think I have here? You'd never guess! It's wealth beyond all dreams of avarice! Gold that was taken from the mines of Ophir in the days of Solomon! Jewels that shone on the crowns of Assyria's kings! Here's riches, power, the lordship of the world!"

I stole an uneasy glance at Ali, but he merely looked back in a gloomy and pessimistic manner as if to hint that it was my own fault.

Girtmann began to undo the leather wrappings.

"I'll show you," he said hastily. "Put your boy at that outer window—I don't want anybody climbing up the wall and looking over the sill—"

The man was evidently mad, but I motioned Ali to humor him. Girtmann tore off the last wrapping and triumphantly held up to my gaze a bizarre and fantastic object. I heard Ali give a strangled cry of pure horror, but I saw nothing shocking about the object. It was an image of brass, carved in the shape of a peacock, not very large, and worked with exquisite skill; pure gold was inlaid along the wings and the tip of the spreading tail. The claws were spread as if to grip some support.

Girtmann's face was distorted with his strange gloating triumph.

"Look at it!" he exclaimed. "Glut your eyes on it! You are the first white man who has looked on it, besides myself!"

I extended a hand to examine it more closely, but Ali cried out fiercely and, leaping forward, struck my hand down.

"Because you are doomed, there is no need that you should drag my master into your own ruin," he shouted at Girtmann. "Touch it not, sahib, as you value your soul. It is death for a Christian or a Moslem to lay hand on that accursed thing! Allah defend us, it is Melek Taus himself this fool has stolen!"

"Melek Taus!" recognition burst upon me and I stood aghast. "Great God, Girtmann, do you mean to tell me that this thing is the veritable brazen peacock worshipped by those unspeakable devil-worshippers, the Yezidees?"

"The same!" he was momentarily drunk with vanity and exultation. "Melek Taus, that all the Moslem world and all the Christians of the Orient fear and hate. You've heard, then, of the Yezidees?"

"I've heard many wild tales," I answered. "Who, in the East, hasn't heard them? I've heard of that sect which worships the veritable Devil, Satan, or to give him their name, Shaitan. The legends say that seven towers link Mount Lalesh with Manchuria. These towers are the earthly abiding place of Shaitan, and gleams of light flash back and forth between them, weaving spells of evil for the sons of men. I have heard that their stronghold is in the hill town of Sheikh-Adi, beyond Mosul, and that they worship this brazen image as the symbol of Shaitan, and to it they offer up human sacrifices in great caverns below the temple."

Girtmann nodded. "True. A few Americans, Englishmen and Frenchmen have been to Baadri and seen the castle of the Mir Beg, the Black Pope of all the Yezidees, scowling down on the village a hundred yards below. A few have even been to Sheikh-Adi and have seen the temple which is built into the solid stone of the mountainside. But what of the real temple, which lies below?"

He laughed again in savage triumph and I heard Ali call on Allah under his breath.

"My supposed murder gave the opportunity I looked for," continued Girtmann. "I had long been seeking a means to enter the secret citadel of the devil-worshippers; now that Erich Girtmann was supposedly dead, no one would be looking for him in the disguise of a Druse peddler. As a humble Druse of no rank I could more readily gain admittance into the towns of the Yezidees for the Druses are not devil-worshippers, yet neither are they Christian or Moslem, as you know.

"So I came to Baadri driving a donkey laden with European-made trinkets, and there I stayed for weeks, before venturing on to Sheikh-Adi. I acted the part of a harmless, garrulous and kindly fool. The Yezidees despised me but had no suspicions about me. Then at last I went on to Sheikh-Adi which lies only an hour's ride from Baadri. The trail winds up through wild and rocky hills and gorges, until it halts at the fantastic town that clings to the slope of Mount Lalesh the Accursed. In one of the hundreds of empty stone huts, erected for the shelter of pilgrims, I took up my abode. At first I made no attempt to even enter the outer temple. When I finally did so, it was with a great appearance of trepidation and reverence, and to the amusement of the Yezidees, I fled screaming at the sight of the great black stone serpent which stands on its tail in the inner courtyard near the doorway.

"It is said they worship this serpent, and I have seen them perform strange rites before it, but it is not the symbol of the Dark Master they adore—that is Melek Taus, the brazen peacock, into which, their legend says, Shaitan himself long ago entered. For months I abode in Sheikh-Adi. It is a strange place and a strange people. All ideas and principles which seem right and normal to us, there are reversed. Light and the lords of light are abominable to them, to whom evil and the gods of darkness are friends and masters. A Yezidee may not speak the name of Shaitan—so it is commanded in the Black Book of their creed, the scroll dictated long ago by Satan to Sheikh-Adi, founder of the cult. If you speak the name of Shaitan before a Yezidee, he is bound to kill you, or failing that, to kill himself.

"You must not wear a blue garment or ornament, since blue is a color inimical to Shaitan. And so on, and so on. You may speak freely of Melek Taus, however, since that is the name by which Shaitan permits himself to be discussed by his worshippers. As for the Seven Towers of Evil, I cannot say, but I have seen one of them. It is a tall, slim white tower rising above the rest of the city, and when the sun strikes it, it shoots long gleams of light in all directions. But they are merely the reflection of the sun on a great golden ball on the top of the tower, though I do not doubt that the Yezidees use this by some means as a signal tower.

"Well, by carefully masking my fierce interest behind the naive curiosity of an ignorant peddler, I managed to convince myself that the temple was merely a blind—a mask to conceal the true place of worship which must lie in the subterranean corridors below. But how to reach these tunnels without being apprehended was my problem and for months I racked my mind in vain. There was always a number of priests guarding the temple and, while they did not object to my occasional awed scrutiny of the place, I dared not show that I even suspected the existence of any lower temple or shrine.

"On certain nights a great drum throbbed and thundered in the hills and the Yezidees would file through the temple doors, a silent, expectant throng. Then the outer doors would be guarded until dawn by armed warriors and no sound would come from within the temple save the steady pulsing of a drum that sounded as if it was beaten far underground, and an occasional ghastly scream. On such nights the aliens of Sheikh-Adi, such as myself, were sternly ordered, on pain of frightful torture and death, to keep to their huts.

"But at last the chance came. In the spring the Yezidees have a festival in the open, which anyone can look upon. It is called the Feast of the Tower and it is grisly enough, God knows. A white bull, bedecked with flowers, is brought to the Tower of Evil and there a vein is opened in his throat and he is led around and around the Tower until he drops and dies from weakness, and the blood spurting from his throat has dyed the base of the Tower crimson all about. All the Yezidees attend this festival and this time the temple was left unguarded. I had made my plans. I had announced my intention to depart and had loaded my few belongings on my mule. My peddler's pack was on my back as I came to gape open-mouthed at the festival of the Feast. While all were intent on the gory spectacle, I slipped away to the temple. It lay unguarded.

"I hastened through the great archway into the courtyard which gave upon the temple entrance. I went down the flight of stone steps, through the gateway and into the Courtyard of the Serpent. I passed the great stone snake which gleams black as evil and went into the great stone room that was the main temple. Lighted wicks, floating in oil, illuminated the place. A row of stone columns divided the great hall into two equal parts. There was no altar, no shrine. The room was bare. One of the walls was the sheer cliff against which the temple was built and in this wall was a door. It was not locked; stairs led down to a chamber wherein was the mausoleum of Sheikh-Adi. Another door opened from this chamber. Again I went down a flight of stone steps and this time I came into a great natural cavern—a gigantic thing, whose vaulted roof I could barely make out in the darkness. I heard a sound as of a river flowing swiftly and went forward cautiously, feeling my way with my tiny electric torch. After walking some time in the darkness which my slender shaft of light barely pierced, I suddenly rounded a corner and came face to face—with the real temple of the Devil-worshippers!

"The cavern widened out into a perfectly colossal cave, lighted by torches as thick as a man's thigh, flaring in niches cut into the stone. Before me a crimson and horrific altar loomed, a grisly, horrible thing, of some sort of red stone, stained darkly and flanked with rows of grinning skulls laid out in curious designs. Somewhere back in the darkness of that great shadowy cavern, beyond the flickering light of the torches, a mysterious, subterranean river plunged and gurgled. Altogether it was a hideous place, and I shuddered to think what my fate would be if caught there.

"But I saw what I had come for. With its claws gripping a golden bar set into the stone of the altar stood—Melek Taus! I sprang forward and, seizing the image, wrenched it quickly from its roost—and as I did, with a grating and grinding of hinges and bolts, a section of the floor slid back behind the altar, revealing a crypt beneath! Gazing through the bars which guarded the chamber, I caught my breath. The flickering torchlight gleamed on the wealth of Araby and the Indies! My starting eyes beheld great heaps of shimmering golden coins that must have dated back to the days of Alexander the Great—flaming gems, diamonds, rubies, emeralds, sapphires, topazes, all heaped in careless confusion—the treasure of the Yezidees!

"I dared not take time to solve the mystery of the bars. I had been in the vaults longer than I should have been already. I seized the bar from which I had torn the peacock and pulled on it; the section of the floor slid back in place. Then putting Melek Taus in my peddler's pack, I hastened back the way I had come. I was not an instant too soon. As I emerged into the upper temple, I heard a priest entering. The festival of the Feast was over.

"The priest came down the hall, but the row of columns was between us. I slipped along in the dim gloom, keeping the columns between us, and gained the outer courtyard without being seen. But there I was accosted by a lesser priest who asked me suspiciously what I was doing loitering about the temple. He had seen me at the Feast of the Tower. I answered that I was preparing to leave Sheikh-Adi and had come to say farewell to the head priest and offer him a poor peddler's blessings for the kindness he had shown me.

"This seemed to satisfy the priest, but a bad mistake of mine aroused his suspicions. As I left the temple, to hide my nervousness—and I defy anyone to pass through such an experience and not be a little nervous!—I lit a cigarette, then thoughtlessly cast down the burning match and trod on it to extinguish it. Instantly I saw the priest's eyes narrow with sudden doubt. I cursed myself. Fire is sacred to Melek Taus and it is forbidden to spit in a flame or to tread on a flame. No Oriental would have made that mistake in Sheikh-Adi—even a Moslem would have had his wits about him and refrained from infuriating the Yezidees.

"I hastened on down the hill, and let a number of Yezidees see me untie my donkey from in front of my door, then seem to change my mind, tie him again and enter my hut. That saved my life, for I know that shortly afterward the priest came seeking me and was told I was still in my hut—was not my laden donkey tied in front of the door? So the priest waited a bit until I should come out, wishing to trap me and not alarm me, by showing his suspicion, and by that time I was far away. Going into my hut I slipped out through a crevice in the rear which let into a thick clump of bushes.

Wriggling through, I slipped down the slope, stole a horse I found and rode like mad.

"They were not many hours behind me when I rode into Mosul—my horse dropped dead at the outskirts of the city. At Mosul I changed my disguise—I became a staid and respectable Turkish merchant. And I made a bold leap—left Mosul in the night and made straight across country for Damascus—a desperate move considering the turbulent state of the country. But thanks to my disguise I made it. But somehow my hunters got on my track and they hunted me to the very gates of Damascus—but I didn't know it then. At Damascus I changed again—back into my normal being. Erich Girtmann came to life. I believed that this move would baffle my pursuers completely. I did not then know the full extent of the Yezidee nature—the tireless, relentless hate that keeps them like bloodhounds on the trail of an enemy—God, there was a Buddhist priest who eluded them for thirty years, but in the end—

"Well, on the verge of my departure from Damascus I found that I had not fooled my enemies—by changing back into my real personality I had but betrayed to them the true identity of the man they pursued—and that must have fanned the flames of their fury, for Erich Girtmann is not well loved in Syria. But I went into hiding—I have friends in Damascus. I baffled them after all. They could not find me. But a certain Damascene merchant, a friend of mine, brought me word that a Yezidee answering the description of the minor priest Yurzed had been seen lurking about the wharfs in Beirut. They expected me to hasten to the nearest western port, and since they could not find me in Damascus, they intended waiting for me—but I crossed them; I felt sure that they had all other ports guarded—Haifa, Yaffa, El Arish and Said—and I fled to Jerusalem. There I rested a spell, until some second sense warned me that my foes were again close at hand. And I saw a Yezidee peering at me in the bazaar. That night I fled again; disguised as a Bedouin I raced southward on a racing camel.

"My enemies were hard at my heels. God—the grinding grill of that fearful hunt! I rode day and night without ceasing—once they were so near I could hear the grunting of their camels. But I eluded them, more by luck than skill, and finally came to a little village on the shore of the Red Sea. There I once more became Erich Girtmann and went as a passenger on a vile-smelling Arab dhow which cruised about the Sea on shady business.

"This morning I landed and came ashore at Djibouti. I didn't know you were here, John Mulcahy, until I saw Ali. Then while I was talking to him—God! I saw the scarred face of Yurzed among the crowded bazaar! I don't believe he saw me—my one bit of luck— but after he had passed, I was fool enough to whisper his name and nature to your idiotic Arab and the fool turned the color of ashes and started sprinting along the back alleys—I had to keep up with him, because I had to find you—but I'm betting it attracted the attention of people who will tell my enemies."

"I'll help you all I'm able," I said. "But what do you mean to do?"

"Get in hiding," he exclaimed fiercely. "Somewhere where they can't find me—not even those human bloodhounds! Then I'll enter into negotiations with them—never mind how! I have friends in the East—I have their idol—they'll pay high to get it back—and pay high they shall! The ransom of Melek Taus will be every coin, every silver ingot, every pinch of gold dust, every jewel I saw in that crypt below the altar!"

"Girtmann, you're mad!" I exclaimed sharply. "They'll never pay that sum!"

"They'll pay," his eyes burned with ferocious avarice. "This brazen thing is their god—they must get it back, regardless of all cost. Oh, they'll try to kill me first, just as they've tried ever since the day I stole the idol. But I'll outwit them. I'm the shrewder and I'll prove it."

"Well," I said slowly, "to my mind it's rather a rotten thing to do, in the first place. Admitting the hideous infamy of the cult, still if you use that superstition to acquire you a fortune, you're no better than one of the members, to my mind."

"I didn't ask for your opinion," he grunted. "I take what I want, and I let nothing stand in my way—cult, creed, or principle. You were always a fool, John Mulcahy, a weakling in spite of your iron body. Well, you can round out a mediocre life in poverty if you wish—not Erich Girtmann. I'm not interested in what you think of me. What I want to know is, are you going to help me out of this jam?"

"Yes, I am," I answered shortly. "After all, you're a white man—at least your hide is white—and I owe you a debt. I usually pay my obligations. What do you want me to do?"

"Get me some clothes—some garments of your Arab will do," he said swiftly. "I'll disguise myself again—slip out of the hotel tonight by the servant's entrance. Send your Arab to get me a horse and have it waiting outside the city. I'll ride to that ruined fortress that lies a mile outside the city. I'll hide there."

"What!" I exclaimed. "That's madness! They'll find you and butcher you. Stay in my apartments. Here in the midst of the city, with Ali and I to keep watch, you'll have a chance."

He shook his head. "You don't know these devils. They can kill a man and never wake his bedfellow. They can strike down a man in the midst of an army. No—they'll be looking for me in the city. I'll fool them again. They'll never think of looking for me in the old fort. I'll slip out there tonight and hide. You'll have to get food out to me every now and then—but you'll have to be careful, because they'll likely be watching this hotel, in case they managed to track me here. It won't be long—the British steamer *Nagpur* is overdue. You must arrange for a passage—get it in your own name and have your things at the docks—in the last minute we'll switch and I'll slip aboard. We'll fool those devils yet! You understand you're taking a risk too—but I'll repay you well. Once I squeeze the treasure out of them, I'll see that you get a fat slice of it."

"I don't want your treasure," I answered shortly. "You couldn't hire me to do this—I'm doing it simply because you saved my life once—and I pay my debts."

He merely grunted. When I turned to tell Ali to get some of his garments, the Arab started to remonstrate, then made a gesture of true Moslem fatalism and obeyed without a word. Arrayed in flowing turboush, turban and sandals, Girtmann looked like a true Arab—an effect heightened by his hooked nose and hard black eyes. Years of travelling in the East had schooled him in his part and even Ali grunted in grudging admiration. If Girtmann had played the Druse as well as he played the Arab, no wonder he had fooled even those masters of subtlety on Mount Lalesh.

He and Ali watched closely from a small window before he glided out through the servant's entrance and vanished like a white-clad ghost in the alleys. He took with him the peacock, a supply of food and wine, and a heavy automatic pistol in a shoulder holster.

"No doubt he has gotten clean away," Ali growled to me. "The Devil watches over such rogues, even though he has stolen the Devil's demon-bird. It is you and I, sahib, who will be like to get our throats cut. The Yezidees will track him here, if they have not already done so. I was seen with him in the bazaar. We are doomed, sahib! The Devil-worshippers will come seeking him and will slay us instead. Have you not heard tales of them?"

And he regaled me with story after story, all dealing on the diabolism and atrocities of the Yezidees, some logical enough and some so extravagant of fancy that I could not control my laughter, to Ali's infinite disgust.

The next night the question arose as to food for Girtmann, and Ali and I argued over who should take it to him.

"You were seen with him," said I. "The natural thing for the Yezidees to do would be to follow you; on the other hand, I have not been seen in connection with him and I had better take the food to him."

"Rest assured those devils have connected us both with him," answered Ali pessimistically. "You are subtle as a bull elephant and stealthy as an army. I will hide my face and slip out the servant's door as did he."

So he did and returned with the word that Girtmann was safely ensconced in the old crumbling fortress, "among the rats and lizards," and believed he had finally given his implacable enemies the slip. As for me, I was beginning to believe most of his terror emanated from his own guilty conscience. I had not seen a Yezidee, nor any sign of one. Doubtless Girtmann only thought he recognized a priest of that fearsome cult in the bazaar.

But Ali shook his head gloomily. "They watch us," he answered. "Thrice have I seen a shadow flitting among the alleys outside this hotel; they will not show themselves till they are ready to strike—and then they will strike silently. I evaded them—I think they believe Girtmann to be still in your apartments, but in their own good time they will cut our throats—and they will hunt down Girtmann and slay him, too."

That steamer continued to be overdue. Again Ali stole forth to carry food and wine to Girtmann. He slipped out just after dusk, and close upon midnight I heard a stealthy, sandaled step in the corridor. A key turned in the lock and a figure entered; I recognized the flowing turboush and the turban end which concealed all the face except the blazing eyes. Those eyes—something unfamiliar about them struck me—and that figure—Ali was not that tall! And then stark unreasoning terror gripped me as the man flung aside the turban end and laughed, hideously and soundlessly, in my face. It was not so much physical terror of the lean vulture-like stranger who stood before me in Ali's garments, but the whole thing seemed so unreal it smacked of sorcery.

Still laughing in frightful, silent mockery and triumph, the Yezidee drew from beneath his robes a heavy pistol which he leveled at my heart. His left hand groped among his garments. And I awoke from the trance of horror which gripped me, and hurled myself on him, staking all on the desperate chance that he would not dare fire lest the shot arouse the people of the hotel. I was right. Instead of pulling the trigger, he lifted the weapon and struck at me savagely with the barrel. A stunning blow, had it landed solidly—as it was it staggered me and filled my vision with points of flying light.

But the next instant I had gripped him like a grizzly and he could not break my hold. It was a knife he gripped in his left hand and he dropped the pistol and devoted all his attention to driving the long cruel blade into my heart. We tumbled about on the floor, fighting silently except for our labored breathing. He was lean and hard as a wolf, as tall as I though not so heavy, and possessed of steel-spring thews. Once he almost got a gouging thumb in my eye and again he sank his fanglike teeth into my arm so the blood started.

We reeled upright, somehow, still close-clinched, and he drove his knee to my groin. Maddened by the pain I wrenched savagely at his wrist and felt the bone snap between my fingers. He groaned and momentarily relaxed and in that instant I tore loose and crashed my right fist to his jaw with every ounce of my beef behind it. He dropped like a log and lay without twitching.

Without another glance at him, but gasping for breath, I caught up my helmet, buckled on a heavy pistol and took up a double-barreled ten-bore shotgun. I was in the game, up to the hilt, and I was resolved to play it out, whatever hand Fate dealt me. As I went out the door I glanced at the Yezidee and saw that he was regaining consciousness.

Down in the compound I awoke an amazed and volubly resentful servant who sleepily brought out and saddled my horse. In a few minutes more I was riding recklessly through the narrow winding streets. Djibouti lay silent beneath the stars; my steed's drumming hoofs waked eerie echoes. Of plans I had but one—to ride as swiftly as I could to the deserted fortress. That both Girtmann and Ali were dead, I felt certain, and a slow relentless wrath burned in me. I owed a debt to Girtmann; a greater debt to Ali. If Girtmann had saved my life once, Ali had saved me half a dozen times—from Bedouin bullets, Taureg scimitars, Matabele spears—he was more than a servant; he was a tried and trusty friend; and now he had fallen victim to a foul brood of demon-worshippers, aiding a man whom he hated, but aided because the man claimed friendship to me. I cursed as I rode and the veins throbbed in my temples. If I could not rescue, I could revenge, by Satan!

The silent town fell away behind me and now across the scrub-strewn waste I saw loom the dark and mysterious pile of stone that was the ruined fortress. A relic of Arab rule it was, and once commanded the city of Djibouti with its frowning cannon whose flaring muzzles were piously inscribed with Koranic verses.

A few hundred yards from the ruin I dismounted and tied my horse in a dense thicket, stealing forward on foot. Dense clouds masked the moon and it was very dark. I groped forward and finally came into the ancient courtyard, or compound, feeling under my feet the cracked slabs through which dense weeds and vines pushed up. All was silent. The moon showed a hint of breaking through and I hastened into the shadow of a moldering wall. A crumbling stairway showed near at hand and up it I went, hugging the shadows. The moon came out clear now and flung the black shadows into bold relief. I came into a corridor, dusty and bat haunted, eerily lighted by the moonbeams which flowed through the long fallen roof. I stole along it, feeling uncomfortably as if I were stalking blindly into a trap, when ahead of me I saw a tiny gleam of light. I remembered Ali saying that there were chambers in the old fortress almost intact, in spite of the ravages of time. I stole forward. The light emanated from a small crevice in the wall. Cautiously I placed my eye thereto.

I was looking into one of the more intact chambers. It was dusty and ancient and showed signs that owls had nested, and jackals laired there, but the walls were solid and the roof not altogether fallen down. It was lighted by a candle stuck on the wall and ten men were in the room. I saw Girtmann first; he was bound hand and foot, a rope about his body holding him upright to a ring set in the wall; he was apparently unharmed, but his eyes blazed like a mad animal's in the candlelight, with fear, rage and hate; he was like a trapped wolf. Flung carelessly on the floor, likewise bound and naked save for his loincloth, was Ali; blood was dried on a wound in his scalp, but he was conscious. The other eight were Yezidees. No doubt about that. They were tall, lean, rangy, with evil, vulture-like faces.

One, a scarred-faced devil I knew must be Yurzed, was speaking in Kurdish: "You are doomed, man; you have laid the hands of sacrilege on Melek Taus and not all the hosts of God could save you. But you will save yourself much torture if you will tell us where you have hidden Melek Taus."

"You dare not kill me," snarled Girtmann, "for then you would lose your idol forever. Only I know where it is hidden."

I had no time to waste listening to the conversation. I saw the chamber had two doors and a window; the doors were in the end walls, and the window in the wall opposite the crevice through which I gazed. I believed that the door to the left opened upon a landing and a stair, and perhaps the door to the right did also. At any rate, I stole quickly down the corridor, seeking a door or chamber that could let me into the other chamber.

I gained a courtyard again—an inner courtyard, dark as a well; above I saw a faint gleam of light that marked the chamber I wished to reach, shining through the silks that had been hung across the broken window. I stole past the crumbling stairway without attempting to mount it. I felt that it was well guarded. I would enter the building on the opposite side of the court and was sure I would find a stair that would let me into the upper corridors. I wanted to come upon the Yezidees from the unguarded door.

As I stole past the stairs I glanced up and halted short, tensed, thinking to have glimpsed a sudden sinister movement in the shadows halfway up the broken stairs. I strained my eyes, but the stairway, hanging to the overshadowing walls, was a well of darkness. I passed on swiftly. And now I was halfway across the courtyard, and a sudden stealthy sound made me whirl, electrified.

The moon was out and in its light I saw a horrific shape, apparently poised in midair; in full mid-leap I saw him, the lean figure, the loose garments spread like the wings of a gigantic bat, the hideous face contorted with passion and bloodlust, the gleaming knife held high in a dusky hand—all this I caught in one flashing, horrified glimpse, even as I acted instinctively. There was no time for conscious thought; even as I whirled I fired from the hip, and the blast caught and crumpled the leaping Yezidee in midair, literally blowing him from the very muzzle.

The crash of the heavy shotgun reverberated through the ruined fortress terrifically, waking cataclysmic echoes, and a fierce shout sounded from above. Light streamed suddenly from the window as the silks were thrust aside and I could visualize savage eyes peering out and down. But even while the echoes of my shot were thundering through the ruins, I had leaped into the shadows of the wall and crouched there, unseen by the watchers from above. The moon was hidden again and I doubted if even the keen eyes of the devil-worshippers could recognize the shattered shape which lay, like a bundle of tattered clothes, at the foot of the wall.

The silks fell back in place and, straining my ears, I heard the unmistakable sound of men moving above. And I took a desperate chance. It was evident that the Yezidees were stealing down to investigate the shot. Those remaining in the torture chamber would be triply on guard, doubtless watching both doors. I laid down my shotgun and began climbing the wall. It would have been an impossible feat except for the fact that the crumbling of the wall had left deep crevices in it, and jutting stones. As I mounted I twisted my head about to see shadowy figures glide from the well of the stair. My flesh crawled and my hair bristled to think how helpless I would be, clinging like a spider on the wall, if they spied me. But they had sighted the shot-riddled body of the man I had killed and they clustered about him, as I could see dimly. Then I reached the window and drew myself up to the ledge.

Most of the bars had long fallen out; I looked through the silks and my heart leaped. Only one Yezidee remained guarding the room—a big, sombre devil with a pistol in one hand and a scimitar in the other. He was paying no attention to the window—in fact he had his back to it. His gaze flickered from one door to the other. Holding my breath I drew myself over the sill—and as I was half-over, he whirled and his beastlike eyes blazed.

Our shots crashed at the same instant and it was pure luck that saved me, because there was no time to aim. His bullet cut a lock of hair from my head and, through the smoke of our fire, I saw him sway and crumple limply. The next instant I was in the chamber and bending over Ali.

"Sahib!" he stammered wildly. "Allaho akbar! I knew—I knew you would come—"

Working frenziedly with one eye on the doors, I freed him and he sprang up and caught up the scimitar of the fallen Yezidee; that he was weak and stiff from his bonds and from loss of blood was evident, but his eyes flashed with murderous anger. I freed Girtmann and gave him the pistol the Yezidee had used. He spoke no word of thanks, but he grinned fiercely and without mirth: "They'll never get the peacock, the yellow-skinned dogs!"

Outside the silence was sinister, breathless.

"What happened, Ali?" I asked swiftly.

"I walked into a trap," he answered. "I saw naught, heard naught, but as I entered the shadows of the fortress, a shadow rose from the darkness and struck me senseless. When I came to my senses I was bound and stripped, and lay on the chamber floor—"

"They'd got me, too," growled Girtmann. "Caught me with a trick as old in the East as Egypt—I heard a racket in the courtyard and was fool enough to look out the window; one of them was on the roof and he threw a noose over my head and choked me unconscious. How did you get here? They dressed one of their murderers in Ali's clothes and sent him to get you."

"Never mind," I answered, "we've got to get out of here. They're planning some deviltry and this room isn't one we can defend against a rush. We've got to take a chance of slipping out. Out in the open, away from these ruins, we've a fighting chance. Here, we're caught like rats in a trap."

"Wait!" Girtmann sprang to the ring in the wall and twisted it powerfully; with a creak of rusty bolts a portion of the wall slid away, disclosing a dull glint of brass. Girtmann took from the secret niche the brazen peacock.

"The fools," he grunted, "had me tied to the very key of the puzzle and didn't know it. I discovered that niche the first night I was hiding here. All right, let's go."

"Wait," I cautioned him. "If we try to go down those stairs, they'll pick us off in the dark. I'll scout a bit through this other door; I don't believe they can reach us from the courtyard by that direction. Girtmann, you watch the stair and Ali, keep your attention on that window."

I went through the door, coming into a wide, dusty chamber; through this I went and into a corridor; I groped my way along in the dark, cocked revolver held in front of me, and my skin crawling in anticipation of a sudden and silent knife thrust. Then I came into the moonlight and swore. I had come to the end of the corridor. Through the fallen roof and shattered walls the vagrant moon, now clear, shone brightly, and no stair led down.

Somewhere back along the corridor I knew there must be a door or chamber letting into the parallel corridor into which I had first come. There were two choices—either make our way into that other corridor and down the crumbling stair I had first ascended, or essay to climb down the wall at the end of this corridor—a task I could see at a glance would be much more difficult than climbing the courtyard wall. I froze suddenly as a hideous scream split the silence, and hard on its fearsome echoes came the clash of steel and the fierce yells of fighting men.

I whirled and raced recklessly back the way I had come, leaping into the chamber. A blood-curdling sight met my eyes. Girtmann lay sprawled in a pool of blood on the floor and but a glance was needed to tell that he was dead; from his throat protruded the ivory hilt of a thin, wicked dagger. And backed against the wall was Ali, fighting in wild beast desperation for his life against a group of lean, snarling devils led by a tall, scarred swordsman—Yurzed. Ali's scimitar leaped and flickered like a living thing, but it was evident that only a matter of seconds lay between him and extinction; he could not long keep at bay those licking, dancing blades. Fools, we had forgotten the broken roof; through it the Yezidees had come.

I drew my revolver, then sudden inspiration struck me. On the floor, at the very edge of the grisly pool whose slowly widening tide dabbled its wings in crimson, lay the brazen peacock. With a swift stride I reached it and placed the muzzles of the gun within a few inches of it. If I pulled the trigger, the blast at that range would shatter the frail image into a thousand bits. The Yezidees whirled and stood frozen, while Ali fell back against the window sill, panting and gasping.

"One move and I blast your god into bits of metal," I said grimly. "I will bargain for our lives—our lives against Melek Taus."

"You cannot live," said Yurzed. "You have committed the sacrilege unspeakable."

"The sahib has not touched your accursed idol," said Ali. "Nor have I; only he—" pointing at the corpse on the floor. "And he has paid the penalty."

"Then give us Melek Taus and we will go in peace," said Yurzed.

"I'd prefer to see you hanged for murder," I growled. "How can I trust you?"

"I swear not to harm either of you, now or later," said the priest, raising his hand with a certain impressiveness. "I swear by the wings of Melek Taus, by the Seven Towers of Evil, by the beard of Sheikh-Adi, by the sceptre of the Mir Beg, by the Serpent of Wisdom, by the Nameless Name of all Names."

Ali flung down his scimitar: "Be at ease, sahib," he said. "No spawn of Hell dare break that oath. Take up your demon-bird, dogs, and begone."

And Yurzed, sheathing his scimitar, reverentially took up the brazen thing and wrapped it in his long cloak. Then, salaaming to us, the Devil-worshippers went noiselessly into the night. No sound came back to mark their going; it was as if they had come from night and nowhere like a band of specters. And like phantoms they vanished.

Black John's Vengeance

Night hung over the river like a sullen threat, pregnant with doom. I crouched in the straggling bushes and shivered in the dampness. Somewhere in the great dark house in front of me, a gong sounded faintly—once. Eight times that gong had sounded since I had hidden there. I had counted the notes mechanically. I watched the great shadowed bulk of the house grimly. House of mystery it was—the house of the mysterious Yotai Yun, the Chinese merchant prince— and what unsavory business went on within its brooding walls no white man knew. Bill Lannon had wondered—ex-secret service man of the British Empire, and swift to revert to old ways. He had made secret investigations of his own—had spoken to me vaguely of grim things hidden behind the walls of Yotai Yun's house—had hinted to me and to Eric Brand of mysterious gatherings, deep plots and a terrible Hooded Monk of some dark cult who promised a yellow empire.

Eric Brand, lean, reckless-eyed adventurer, had laughed at Lannon, but I had not. I knew the lad was like a hunting hound on the trail of something sinister and mysterious. He had told us one night—the three of us sitting in the European Clubroom and sipping our whiskey-and-sodas, that he meant to slip into Yotai Yun's house that night to learn what was going on there. They found his body next morning, rolling limply in the wash of the Yangtze's filthy yellow tide—with a thin dagger hilt-deep between his shoulders.

Bill Lannon was my friend. That was why I was crouching in the thin bushes in the hours past midnight, watching the house of Yotai Yun, where it loomed just beyond the ragged outskirts of Hankow. And I wondered what Bill Lannon had found before they butchered him and flung him to the fishes—was it piracy, smuggling, or sedition on a huge scale that was being plotted in that dark house? That Yotai Yun dealt in shady commerce and crooked river business, all knew—but none had ever been able to pin anything on him.

Through the mist loomed suddenly a tall, shuffling figure—a native, wrapped in shapeless garments. He made his way toward a squalid, deserted looking fishing hut that perched on the bank of the river, perhaps fifty yards from the wall that surrounded the great house. I stiffened suddenly. Eight men had gone into that hut while I lay watching; none had come out. Once or twice I had thought to see a glimmer of light within the hut, but to all outward appearances it was absolutely vacant. And each time, soon after the native had disappeared in the hut, the gong had sounded from somewhere within the Dragon-house. Eight men had gone into the hut; eight times the gong had sounded in the house. What was the connection between that sordid, ruined fisher's hut and the palacelike dwelling of Yotai Yun?

The native approached the ruined door and I rose from my covert and followed him swiftly and recklessly. Had he turned he could not have failed to have seen me. But he went in without a backward look, pulling the sagging door to behind him. I stole to the wall and peered through a crack. All was utter darkness within the hut, but presently a match was struck and I saw the native crouching in the middle of the floor. I looked for the eight men who had preceded him; the hut was empty, but for that one native! He moved some rags aside on the floor and struck on the floor with his knuckles—three times—then paused—struck thrice more— paused—then struck three more times.

The match had gone out, but a sudden thin square of light formed in the hut floor; it widened as a trap door was thrust up and a villainous yellow face was framed in the aperture. No words were exchanged; the doorkeeper merely nodded and withdrew and the newcomer clambered down into the trap. As he did his features were clearly limned and I recognized him—a well known river-pirate, long wanted by the authorities for robbery and murder. He vanished and the trap door slipped back in place again. Now I began to sense the connection. Evidently that secret door let into a tunnel which connected the hut with the Dragon-house. The gong was used to announce the coming of the men who used that mode of entry. Why, I was determined to learn.

I entered the hut swiftly and stealthily and, feeling with my hands in the darkness, located the contour of the trapdoor, and knocked as the Chinaman had done. Almost instantly the trapdoor began to rise and I crouched quickly behind it. Again the wicked yellow face appeared, and beady eyes darted about as the owner failed to discover me where I crouched behind his head. He half-emerged from the door—and before he could turn and locate me, I caught his throat in a grip that strangled the yell in his gullet, and crashed my right fist behind his ear. He sagged in my grasp, out cold.

I dragged him out of the aperture, and bound and gagged him with strips torn from his garments. Then I laid him in a dingy corner of the hut and hid him under some dirty rags that I found on the floor. The hut was faintly illuminated by the light from the open trap. Then I drew my pistol, an automatic .45, and cautiously descended the trap, closing the secret door behind me. Where I was going, what I was to do, I had no idea; but I knew that the trail of vengeance led somehow straight to Yotai Yun, and that was the trail I had sworn to follow to the bitter end.

Stone steps led down into a narrow, stone-walled tunnel that ran straight, as near as I could tell, for the Dragon-house. It was fairly well lighted with lanterns hung at regular intervals, and I went along it swiftly but warily, gun ready. But I saw no one and after a time I believed I was directly under the great house; and then the tunnel ended in a stout wooden door. I tried it cautiously, my nerves on edge, not knowing what might lie on the other side. It gave under my fingers and swung inward, disclosing a wide chamber, with floor, walls and ceiling of stone. A rough table and some chairs, suggestive of European manners, adorned the otherwise bare chamber, but it was empty of humans.

I entered, closing the door behind me. Across the room in front of me I saw a stone stairway leading up, and beside the foot of the stair, a small door. I had started up the stair when I heard a sudden murmur of voices above me and the trap door at the top of the stairs began to open. I hastily sprang from the stairs and jerked at the small door. It opened and I slipped in, not a second too soon. Someone was descending the stair and I heard the staccato babble of Oriental conversation.

I had no idea what sort of a place I had gotten into. It was as dark as the inside of a cat. As I groped about, expecting to fall into a pit or get a sudden knife in the back, I found myself wondering what Eric Brand would say if my body was found floating in the Yangtze the next day. He had predicted that end for Bill Lannon, warning him, in his cynical way, to avoid meddling in Oriental affairs. I never liked Brand as Lannon had liked him, and had never made a confidant of him; that supercilious, sophisticated clubman was too listless in his attitude toward life, for me. His attitude toward human values differed from mine; he affected to despise all human effort and ambitions and emotions; well, I'm but a rough sailorman, uncultured and untaught in sophist ways, and my cult is an eye for an eye, a tooth for a tooth. And that's why I was stalking Yotai Yun that night in the silence and the mist.

By feeling along I found I was in a very narrow corridor and soon I felt what was evidently a narrow stone stair, leading up. So up I groped in the utter darkness and presently came into what I felt was another chamber, though I could see nothing and dared not strike a match. I barked my shin on a case of some sort and stumbled onto a stack of objects that brought my heart into my mouth by their sudden rattle. But nothing happened and I began to feel about. Gad, the place was a regular armory! My fingers made out stacks of rifles, cases of holstered pistols, dismantled machine guns, and cases that I knew were filled with ammunition. Revolution and uprising it could mean, no less, and I sweated in the dark as I thought of the innocent Europeans, Americans and peaceful Chinese who slept in Hankow ignorant of the peril looming over them.

I groped until I found a door, about opposite, I judged, from the place I entered. There was a catch on it, but it was on the inside and I manipulated it with ease, stepping through the door into a sort of narrow corridor. A dim sort of light filtered in from somewhere and I knew what kind of a place it was—one of those secret corridors running through a wall—China's honeycombed with such, as is all the Orient, where masters spy continually on their servants and their household. I stole along until a mutter of conversation reached me from outside the corridor and I halted and began to hunt for the peephole I knew should be there. I found it quickly enough and peered through it.

I was looking into a large and ornately furnished chamber, whose walls were hung with velvet tapestries worked in dragons, gods and demons, and which was lighted by candles which shed a weird golden glow over all. On silken cushions and divans sat a strange and motley crew—respectable merchants and minor government officials jowl-and-jowl with wild, evil-visaged raggamuffins who had all the earmarks of cutthroats. I recognized the river pirate who had preceded me into the tunnel and realized the reason for the secret entrance. Through that tunnel came outlaws and criminals who might cast suspicion on the Dragon-house if they came in openly. Evidently the others, the officials and the traders, had come in openly. Altogether there were about forty of them, all Orientals—Chinese, mainly, but I saw a few Eurasians and Malays.

All were seated, watching a dais at the other end of the room. On that dais sat Yotai Yun, lean, sardonic, hawk-like, and beside him sat a tall, black-robed figure, whose features were hidden in a black mask—the Hooded Lama! He was no myth then, but a savage reality. I looked at him closely; from his hood glimmered two piercing, magnetic eyes. Evil exuded from him like an aura. I shuddered involuntarily. Then he rose to his full gaunt height and began to speak, and his audience hung breathless on his words. His resonant voice filled the room, his gestures were imposing, commanding. Shudders of abhorrence shook me as I listened to the blasphemous utterances that poured, in stately Chinese, from his hidden lips. It was revolution he was preaching, rapine and red war! Death to all foreign devils and to all Orientals who stood in their way!

Prophet of an old and evil religion he was, of a devil-worshipping cult, the very existence of which is not dreamed of by most white men. Old, evilly old it was, and long had it lurked in the brooding black mountains of the East. Genghis Khan had bowed before its priests, and Tamerlane, and centuries before them, Attila. Now that terrible cult, which had slumbered for so many thousands of years in the wastes of Mongolia, was rousing from its slumber, was shaking its foul mane and gazing about for victims, was stretching forth tentacles to grasp the heart of China.

And it was the part of its followers to pave the way for the new empire, said the Hooded Lama. Let them forget the false teachings of Confucius and Buddha, and the gods of Tibet and Lhassa, who had allowed their people to come under the yoke of the white-skinned devils. Let them rise under the leadership of the prophet the Old Ones had sent them and the great Cthulhu would sweep them all to victory. Just as Genghis Khan had trampled the world beneath his horse hoofs, so would they trample the white devils and found a new, yellow empire that should outlast a million years.

His voice rose to a blood-frenzied scream—murder, rapine, death, hate, plunder, bloodshed! He caught up his listeners in the torrent of his own madness and they leaped and howled like mad dogs. Then he changed his mood swiftly, and became cunning, crafty. The time was not yet, he said; much remained to be done: more converts were to be gained, more sedition was to be planted, more secret work to be done. The red madness faded from the eyes of his listeners to be replaced by the thoughts he had implanted in their minds—craft, patience like a hunting wolf's, ferocious guile.

I listened in horror, realizing the extent to which this insanity might reach. China is always a powder keg, ready for a match. This unknown priest had power, persuasion, personality. Many an Oriental empire has been founded on less. I felt weak as I visualized the red events attendant on a sudden, determined uprising—all China relaxed, unsuspecting, peaceful. Blood would run in the streets; a sudden, unexpected attack in force would wipe out the government troops. Hordes of malcontents and bandits would join the revolutionaries. Foreigners would be slaughtered wholesale.

The rebellion would fail, of course. The nations of the world would send their armies to protect their citizens and their interests. The revolt would be crushed in blood and slaughter, and Yotai Yun and the Black Lama would leave their heads on Peking Tower. But before that many would die, Chinese and white people. The thought of the damage to lives and property turned me sick.

Now suddenly a native rushed in, eyes blazing—evidently the man I had heard descend into the tunnel from the house. Behind him, face contorted in rage and fear, came the man who had guarded the trapdoor in the hut. They spoke rapidly to Yotai Yun and his eyes glinted in a way that made the doorkeeper blanch. But the merchant prince showed no perturbation. He spoke quickly to the Lama who nodded and sat down, and Yotai Yun rose and said tranquilly:

"Lords and honorable friends, there is a spy in the house; these unworthy ones have just reported; who it is, we cannot say, but his shift will be short. Go now, without haste but without delay, each the same way he came. Later you shall be sent for again."

I turned cold all over for I knew who the spy was! The Orientals rose hurriedly and went with no more ado. In a remarkably short time the room was vacant except for Yotai Yun, the Lama who stood like a black image, and the servants who quaked before them. To them Yotai Yun spoke: "You—" to the first one, "gather the servants and search the house; find this spy as you value your life!" The servant bowed low and left the room and Yotai Yun turned to the trapdoor keeper.

"You," he said with concentrated venom, "have failed me. You whom I selected for that difficult task because of your former courage and sagacity. Bah!"

The wretched servant was shaking like a leaf.

"But Master, I have never failed before—"

"One failure is too many, dog," said Yotai Yun in a toneless voice. "I discharge you from my service!"

And whipping a small revolver from his robes, he fired point-blank. The servant fell without a groan, blood trickling from his temple. Yotai Yun clapped his hands and two big coolies entered. At a gesture from their master, they lifted the body and carried it stolidly from the room.

The Lama, who had stood motionless throughout, evincing no interest whatever, spoke to Yotai Yun and they went through a curtain-hung doorway and vanished. Believing them to have gone into an adjoining chamber, I went swiftly along the corridor until I came to the next peephole. I peered through into the room. Sure enough, there sat Yotai Yun and the Black Lama, white-man fashion, at a lacquered table, drinking rice wine from amber cups thin as eggshells. I could tell nothing of the Lama's face; he raised his mask only just enough to bring the cup to his lips. They were speaking in low tones and I pressed close to the wall straining my ears. That Yotai Yun's slipper-footed servants were gliding through rooms and corridors, knives in their hands and murder in their hearts, I knew, but one part of the house seemed as safe as another, and I lingered, eavesdropping.

"You have wrought well, my friend," Yotai Yun was saying. "Your tongue makes men drunk and maddens them. You almost convince me that your mad scheme will succeed."

"That it will succeed I know," answered the Lama, and I thrilled with a sudden sense of vague familiarity—I had heard that voice somewhere—but where?

"We will succeed," continued the Masked Monk, "because the people are fat and restless—ripe for revolt. But we must work cautiously. Time—it will take time. The men who came here tonight represent the horde which waits in semi-ignorance and expectancy. Each of those men is a sedition spreader—a talker of revolt. We must be wary. Let anything happen unexpectedly—let the leaders lose faith in us, or let even one of us lose his life, and the revolt dies before it is fully born."

"We must not take too long," grunted Yotai Yun. "The coils of the government are closing about me—I feel them, though I cannot see them. The authorities have too many spies—my businesses have grown too big to keep hidden altogether. If I dared I would make a break, as the Yankees say—but I could not leave Hankow without being seized, arrested and held on suspicion. They already suspect much of my smuggling and gunrunning—an attempt at flight would crystallize their suspicions. Otherwise you had not persuaded me so easily to join you."

"Safety for you and wealth for us both," said the Black Lama, filling his goblet. "When the revolt breaks the government will have its hands too full to bother about smuggling—and we will have the whole screeching horde of cutthroats behind us. Easy to watch which way the feather falls; if the revolt becomes popular with the masses and spreads all over China—well, that yellow empire I have been ranting about may prove to be no pipedream. If not—if we see that the revolt is about to be crushed, it will be an easy matter to loot Hankow in the midst of the fighting and slip away downriver, or across country."

"I wonder at your daring and ruthlessness, Masked One," said Yotai Yun slowly. "You play a dangerous game—did your dupes know, for instance, that you are not even a Mongolian, they would tear you to pieces. And the real priests of Yog-Sothoth—do you not fear their vengeance when they learn—as they eventually must—that you have been posing as one of their infernal cult?"

"Danger is the breath of life to me," answered the imposter with a wild laugh. "I have lost all my illusions; without the breathtaking touch-and-go of risk and adventure, I should perish of boredom. No—I do not fear the Mongolian devil-worshippers. Only one man is like to hinder us; one man that we must put out of the way—Black John O'Donnell."

Yotai Yun nodded. "A great black bear of a man, fierce and unforgiving. But he has no craft. Why fear him?"

"I don't fear him. But he has the craft of the bear you name him, and the ferocious patience of the brute. He does not forget and his is a one-track mind that, having once taken up a trail, follows it to the bitter end, through Hell and high water. That fool Lannon was his friend; and Lannon told him enough to make him suspect that you, at least, had a hand in his friend's murder. I tell you, we must kill Black John or he will find a way to kill both of us. In fact, I would not be at all surprized if he were not the 'spy' who has found entrance into the Dragon House tonight."

Yotai Yun gave a startled exclamation and half-rose, drawing his pistol. The Lama laughed sardonically. "Don't be afraid. Have you no confidence in your servants? They will rout him out, wherever he's hiding; you said yourself that he has no subtlety; the secrets of this house are not known to him—"

I was pressing close to the peephole, shaken with red rage, but even in my anger, I was alert enough to hear a sudden stealthy sound behind me. It was just enough to save my life. I wheeled suddenly, in time to see, in the dim light, a glittering blade lifted above me, clenched in a yellow hand, and below that hand a slit-eyed, yellow face, contorted into a devil's mask.

As I turned the dagger hissed toward my heart, but by blind chance I caught his wrist in my left hand, and with my clenched right I smashed him hard under the heart. He gasped and staggered, then hurled himself bodily upon me. He was a big man, big as I was, and strong as a bull—an ex-wrestler, I think. We clenched and tore on hard-braced feet; he could not break the grip I had on his knife hand, and I could not free my right fist so as to crash home a knock out blow. Sweat stood out on his yellow forehead and his breath hissed between his parted lips. I was gasping myself from the struggle, but I felt him weakening—I put forward all my effort in a sudden explosive wrench and heave—his weakening legs gave way suddenly and we crashed together into the thin partition— crashed clear through it in a cloud of plaster and a splintering of light wood, and landed on the floor outside with a terrific impact. The Chinaman was on the bottom and his head had gotten twisted down somehow—I heard his neck snap like a rotten branch as we crashed on the floor.

I looked up into the muzzles of two pistols. Raising my hands slowly above my head I rose sullenly and stood, with my feet wide-braced, my head sunk on my broad breast, glaring at my captors from beneath my heavy brows. My terrible hate beat through my soul in deep red surges as I looked on the men who murdered Bill Lannon, and only the thought of the pistol under my left arm kept me from leaping upon them, guns and all, with my bare hands.

"By Buddha," murmured Yotai Yun, his slant eyes widened, "it is the black bear, after all! Lord Lama, you were right."

The Lama laughed sardonically. "Black John O'Donnell it is, right enough! He was not slow in taking the trail. I think he has killed your servant—who was fool enough to come to grips with the bear! But summon your men and we'll soon have this obstacle out of our way."

"You damned swine," I growled. "You killed Bill Lannon—and you hold the upper hand at the moment; but the game's not played out yet, by thunder!"

"Not quite, but almost," answered the Lama, as Yotai Yun clapped his hands. "It but remains a quick dagger-thrust and the splash of a corpse in the river—and the big black bear will bite no more!"

Seven or eight big Chinese entered—hard-faced, wicked-eyed men, with daggers and bludgeons in their hands. Yotai Yun nodded toward me.

"Dispose of him," he said, as if he were speaking of a hog or a beef.

They approached me and I backed slowly away, hands still high. Yotai Yun and the Lama still had their guns trained on me, and the servants were closing in in a sort of half-circle, herding me toward an outer door. I gathered that they intended butchering me in some other part of the house. I backed slowly toward the door; a sidelong glance showed that it was open. The Lama and Yotai Yun stood side by side, and Yotai Yun was laughing at me. A big Chinese caught me roughly by the shirtfront with one hand, pricking me with a knife he held in the other. And like a flash I moved.

I've taken many a man by surprize; no one expects me to be half as quick as I am, because of my bulk. I swept the Chinaman off his feet and, with the same motion, hurled him bodily against Yotai Yun and the Lama. The three went down in a heap, Yotai Yun firing as he fell. The bullet snapped past my ear, but I was already leaping for the door. The whole pack was howling and hacking at my heels, but I was through the door by a flashing fraction of a second the quicker, and I slammed it in their faces, bracing myself to hold it against their frenzied efforts until I could slam in place the bolt I found on the other side.

Then I turned quickly. The door was splintering swiftly under the assaults of my pursuers and I knew it would stand only for a moment or so. I heard the furious voices of Yotai Yun and the Lama urging their minions on. I was standing in a wide chamber, much like that I had just left, and on the opposite side there was a closed door. The walls were hung with heavy tapestries, as in the other rooms. I crossed the room swiftly and hurled the door open. Into what sort of chamber or corridor it let, I did not stop to see. I was not seeking escape, but vengeance. Drawing my pistol I concealed myself behind the hangings on the wall, just as the door crashed inward. The horde flooded through howling like mad dogs and brandishing their blades. Seeing the other door open, they leaped to the natural conclusion that I had escaped by that route, and rushing across the room, crowded through the doorway. I heard the sound of their flying feet dwindle away down some corridor. Behind them came Yotai Yun and the Lama, half-running, but left behind by their followers' mad dash. I grinned wolfishly; all was coming about as I had hoped.

The two had reached the outer door when I leaped from the hangings and growled: "Turn, you swine, and take it from the front!"

Taken by sudden surprise though they were, they whirled firing. I heard the spat of their bullets and I felt their impact, but my gun too was blazing and the Black Lama dropped like an empty sack and lay still. Yotai Yun reeled back as though struck by an invisible hammer, clutched at the hangings with a bloody hand, fired his last shot pointblank and, as my third bullet tore through his body, slumped to the floor and lay twitching.

I knew I had plenty of lead in me; at that range there could be little missing. My left leg felt numb from the thigh down, my left arm and shoulder were rapidly growing stiff, and blood was trickling down my breast. And I could hear the Chinese coming back along the corridor, shouting and clashing their weapons. They had heard the shots and turned back. And I had to meet them, crippled and with a half-empty gun. But I grinned with savage mirth. I had accomplished my design; my foes lay stark before my feet and Bill Lannon was avenged. I'd paid that debt and had no regrets. Sooner or later, a man must die anyway.

The yellow pack came howling through the door and I gripped the tapestries to steady myself and emptied my gun into the thick of them. The foremost went down in a windrow and the rest drew back, aghast. I could hear them whispering and jabbering outside the chamber; I could hear the slap pad of slippered feet and the rattle of blades. Weakness began to steal over me and my left arm felt dead. I shook my head to clear it and the red drops spattered.

"Come in and have it over, you yellow devils!" I roared, fearing that if they did not rush me quick, my weakness would bowl me over and I would be butchered like a sheep without a chance to strike a blow.

Then suddenly the room was flooded with men from the other door. One of them approached me and I struck at him viciously with my empty gun before I saw he wore the uniform of the Chinese constabulary.

"Easy, my friend," he said soothingly. "We are friends—do you not know me?"

"Oh, it's you, Kang Yao," I said dizzily. "Sorry—blood in my eyes; let me sit down."

He guided my blundering steps to a divan. Looking about I saw the room was full of native police and soldiers. They had herded up Yotai Yun's servants, who stood about, manacled and with sullen resignation. Kang Yao bent over the two plotters. The Black Lama had been hit only once, but he was stone dead. Yotai Yun had three bullets through him, but he was still conscious.

His eyes roved to the still form of his partner in crime and a sardonic smile twisted his pallid lips.

"One man can overthrow an unborn empire," he whispered. "We laughed at the black bear—but the black bear has bitten us both—and—vengeance—ends—the—dreams—of—empire—"

The blood surged from his lips and he died.

"Let me see to your wounds, honorable friend," said Kang Yao, with characteristic Oriental courtesy. "You are bleeding in many places."

"I'm hit in the leg, arm, shoulder and breast-muscles," I grunted. "But nothing serious. But tell me—how did you come here?"

"This one," Kang Yao gestured toward a man in the clothes of a servant. He was the tunnel keeper and blood was clotted thickly on his temple.

"Yotai Yun shot him," said Kang Yao, "and had him thrown in the river. But the bullet had merely cut a deep groove through his scalp, and the plunge into the water revived him. He got ashore, and thirsting for revenge on his cruel lord, came swiftly to the police and gasped out a tale of plotting and sedition that brought us quickly to the Dragon House. Without, we heard the shots, and burst in quickly. But who lies here in the guise of a Mongolian lama?"

"Rip off his mask," I said. "I'd like to know, myself."

Kang Yao bent and tore off the mask. A startled exclamation escaped him; the skin beneath the mask was neither yellow nor brown. The Black Lama was a white man—Eric Brand!

Talons in the Dark

Joel Brill slapped shut the book he had been scanning, and gave vent to his dissatisfaction in language more appropriate for the deck of a whaling ship than for the library of the exclusive Corinthian Club. Buckley, seated in an alcove nearby, grinned quietly. Buckley looked more like a college professor than a detective, and perhaps it was less because of a studious nature than a desire to play the part he looked, that caused him to loaf around the library of the Corinthian.

"It must be something unusual to drag you out of your lair at this time of the day," he remarked. "This is the first time I ever saw you in the evening. I thought you spent your evenings secluded in your rooms, pouring over musty tomes in the interests of that museum you're connected with."

"I do, ordinarily." Brill looked as little like a scientist as Buckley looked like a dick. He was squarely built, with thick shoulders and the jaw and fists of a prize fighter; low browed, with a mane of tousled black hair contrasting with his cold blue eyes.

"You've been shoving your nose into books here since six o'clock," asserted Buckley.

"I've been trying to get some information for the directors of the museum," answered Brill. "Look!" He pointed an accusing finger at the rows of lavishly bound volumes. "Books till it would sicken a dog—and not a blasted one can tell me the reason for a certain ceremonial dance practiced by a certain tribe on the West African Coast."

"A lot of the members have knocked around a bit," suggested Buckley. "Why not ask them?"

"I'm going to." Brill took down a phone from its hook.

"There's John Galt—" began Buckley.

"Too hard to locate. He flits about like a mosquito with the St. Vitus. I'll try Jim Reynolds." He twirled the dial.

"Thought you'd done some exploring in the tropics yourself," remarked Buckley.

"Not worthy of the name. I hung around that God-forsaken hellhole of the West African Coast for a few months until I came down with malaria—Hello!"

A suave voice, too perfectly accented, came along the wire.

"Oh, is that you, Yut Wuen? I want to speak to Mr. Reynolds." Polite surprize tinged the meticulous tone.

"Why, Mr. Reynolds went out in response to your call an hour ago, Mr. Brill."

"What's that?" demanded Brill. "Went where?"

"Why, surely you remember, Mr. Brill." A faint uneasiness seemed to edge the Chinaman's voice. "At about nine o'clock you called, and I answered the phone. You said you wished to speak to Mr. Reynolds. Mr. Reynolds talked to you, then told me to have his car brought around to the side entrance. He said that you had requested him to meet you at the cottage on White Lake shore."

"Nonsense!" exclaimed Brill. "This is the first time I've phoned Reynolds for weeks! You've mistaken somebody else for me."

There was no reply, but a polite stubbornness seemed to flow over the wire. Brill replaced the phone and turned to Buckley, who was leaning forward with aroused interest.

"Something fishy here," scowled Brill. "Yut Wuen, Jim's Chinese servant, said *I* called, an hour ago, and Jim went out to meet me. Buckley, you've been here all evening. *Did* I call up anybody? I'm so infernally absent-minded—"

"No, you didn't," emphatically answered the detective. "I've been sitting right here close to the phone ever since six o'clock. Nobody's used it. And you haven't left the library during that time. I'm so accustomed to spying on people, I do it unconsciously."

"Well, say," said Brill, uneasily, "suppose you and I drive over to White Lake. If this is a joke, Jim may be over there waiting for me to show up."

As the city lights fell behind them, and houses gave way to clumps of trees and bushes, velvet black in the starlight, Buckley said: "Do you think Yut Wuen made a mistake?"

"What else could it be?" answered Brill, irritably.

"Somebody might have been playing a joke, as you suggested. Why should anybody impersonate you to Reynolds?"

"How should I know? But I'm about the only acquaintance he'd bestir himself for, at this time of night. He's reserved, suspicious of people. Hasn't many friends. I happen to be one of the few."

"Something of a traveler, isn't he?"

"There's no corner of the world with which he isn't familiar."

"How'd he make his money?" Buckley asked, abruptly.

"I've never asked him. But he has plenty of it."

The clumps on each side of the road grew denser, and scattered pinpoints of light that marked isolated farmhouses faded out behind them. The road tilted gradually as they climbed higher and higher into the wild hill region which, an hour's drive from the city, locked the broad crystalline sheet of silver that men called White Lake. Now ahead of them a glint shivered among the trees, and topping a wooded crest, they saw the lake spread out below them, reflecting the stars in myriad flecks of silver. The road meandered along the curving shore.

"Where's Reynolds' lodge?" inquired Buckley.

Brill pointed. "See that thick clump of shadows within a few yards of the water's edge? It's the only cottage on this side of the lake. The others are three or four miles away. None of them occupied, this time of the year. There's a car drawn up in front of the cottage."

"No light in the shack," grunted Buckley, pulling up beside the long low roadster that stood before the narrow stoop. The building reared dark and silent before them, blocked against the rippling silver sheen behind it.

"Hey, Jim!" called Brill. "Jim Reynolds!"

No answer. Only a vague echo shuddering down from the blackly wooded hills.

"Devil of a place at night," muttered Buckley, peering at the dense shadows that bordered the lake. "We might be a thousand miles from civilization."

Brill slid out of the car. "Reynolds must be here—unless he's gone for a midnight boat ride."

Their steps echoed loudly and emptily on the tiny stoop. Brill banged the door and shouted. Somewhere back in the woods a night bird lifted a drowsy note. There was no other answer.

Buckley shook the door. It was locked from the inside.

"I don't like this," he growled. "Car in front of the cottage—door locked on the inside—nobody answering it. I believe I'll break the door in—"

"No need." Brill fumbled in his pocket. "I'll use my key."

"How comes it you have a key to Reynolds' shack?" demanded Buckley.

"It was his own idea. I spent some time with him up here last summer, and he insisted on giving me a key, so I could use the cottage any time I wanted to. Turn on your flash, will you? I can't find the lock. All right, I've got it. Hey, Jim! Are you here?"

Buckley's flash played over chairs and card tables, coming to rest on a closed door in the opposite wall. They entered and Buckley heard Brill fumbling about with an arm elevated. A faint click followed and Brill swore.

"The juice is off. There's a line running out from town to supply the cottage owners with electricity, but it must be dead. As long as we're in here, let's go through the house. Reynolds may be sleeping somewhere—"

He broke off with a sharp intake of breath. Buckley had opened the door that led to the bedroom. His flash played on the interior—on a broken chair, a smashed table—a crumpled shape that lay in the midst of a dark widening pool.

"Good God, it's Reynolds!"

Buckley's gun glinted in his hand as he played the flash around the room, sifting the shadows for lurking shapes of menace; it rested on a bolted rear door, rested longer on an open window, the screen of which hung in tatters.

"We've got to have more light," he grunted. "Where's the switch? Maybe a fuse has blown."

"Outside, near that window." Stumblingly Brill led the way out of the house and around to the window. Buckley flashed his light, grunted.

"The switch has been pulled!" He pushed it back in place, and light flooded the cottage. The light streaming through the windows seemed to emphasize the blackness of the whispering woods around them. Buckley glared into the shadows, seemed to shiver. Brill had not spoken; he shook as with an ague.

Back in the house they bent over the man who lay in the middle of the red-splashed floor.

Jim Reynolds had been a stocky, strongly built man of middle age. His skin was brown and weather-beaten, hinting of tropic suns. His features were masked with blood; his head lolled back, disclosing an awful wound beneath his chin.

"His throat's been cut!" stammered Brill. Buckley shook his head.

"Not cut, torn. Good God, it looks like a big cat had ripped him."

The whole throat had literally been torn out; muscles, arteries, windpipe and the great jugular vein had been severed; the bones of the vertebrae showed beneath.

"He's so bloody I wouldn't have recognized him," muttered the detective. "How did you know him so quickly? The instant we saw him, you cried out that it was Reynolds."

"I recognized his garments and his build," answered the other. "But what in God's name killed him?"

Buckley straightened and looked about. "Where does that door lead to?"

"To the kitchen, but it's locked on this side."

"And the outer door of the front room was locked on the inside," muttered Buckley. "Doesn't take a genius to see how the murderer got in—and he—or *it*—went out the same way."

"What do you mean, *it?*"

"Does that look like the work of a human being?" Buckley pointed to the dead man's mangled throat. Brill winced.

"I've seen black boys mauled by the big cats on the West Coast—"

"And whatever tore Reynolds' gullet out, tore that window screen. It wasn't cut with a knife."

"Do you suppose a panther, from the hills—" began Brill.

"A panther smart enough to throw the electric switch before he slid through the window?" scoffed Buckley.

"We don't know the killer threw the switch."

"Was Reynolds fooling around in the dark, then? No; when I pushed the switch back in place, the light came on in here. That shows it had been on; the button hadn't been pushed back. Whoever killed Reynolds had a reason for wanting to work in the dark. Maybe this was it!" The detective indicated, with a square-shod toe, a stubby chunk of blue steel that lay not far from the body.

"From what I hear about Reynolds, he was quick enough on the trigger." Buckley slipped on a glove, carefully lifted the gun, and scanned the chamber. His gaze, roving about the room again, halted at the window, and with a single long stride, he reached it and bent over the sill.

"One shot's been fired from this gun. The bullet's in the windowsill. At least, one bullet is, and it's logical to suppose it's the one from the empty chamber of Reynolds' gun. Here's the way I reconstruct the crime: *something* sneaked up to the shack, threw the switch, and came busting through the window. Reynolds shot once in the dark and missed, and then the killer got in his work. I'll take this gun to headquarters; don't expect to find any fingerprints except Reynolds', though. We'll examine the light switch, too, though maybe my dumb pawing erased any fingerprints that might have been there. Say, it's a good thing you have an iron-clad alibi."

Brill started violently. "What the hell do you mean?"

"Why, there's the Chinaman to swear you called Reynolds to his death."

"Why the devil should I do such a thing?" hotly demanded the scientist.

"Well," answered Buckley, "I know you were in the library of the club all evening. That's an unshakable alibi—I suppose."

*   *   *   *   *

Brill was tired as he locked the door of his garage and turned toward the house which rose dark and silent among the trees. He found himself wishing that his sister, with whom he was staying, had not left town for the weekend with her husband and children. Dark empty houses were vaguely repellent to him after the happenings of the night before.

He sighed wearily as he trudged toward the house, under the dense shadows of the trees that lined the driveway. It had been a morbid, and harrying day. Tag ends of thoughts and worries flitted through his mind. Uneasily he remembered Buckley's cryptic remark: "Either Yut Wuen is lying about that telephone call, or—" The detective had left the sentence unfinished, casting a glance at Brill that was as inscrutable as his speech. Nobody believed the Chinaman was deliberately lying. His devotion to his master was well known—a devotion shared by the other servants of the dead man. Police suspicion had failed to connect them in any way with the crime. Apparently none of them had left Reynolds' town house during the day or the night of the murder. Nor had the murder-cottage given up any clues. No tracks had been found on the hard earth, no fingerprints on the gun other than the dead man's, nor any except Buckley's on the light switch. If Buckley had had any luck in trying to trace the mysterious phone call, he had divulged nothing.

Brill remembered, with a twinge of nervousness, the way in which they had looked at him, those inscrutable Orientals. Their features had been immobile, but in their dark eyes had gleamed suspicion and a threat. He had seen it in the eyes of Yut Wuen, the stocky yellow man; of Ali, the Egyptian, a lean, sinewy statue of bronze; of Jugra Singh, the tall, broad-shouldered, turbaned Sikh. They had not spoken their thoughts; but their eyes had followed him, hot and burning, like beasts of prey.

Brill turned from the meandering driveway to cut across the lawn. As he passed under the black shadow of the trees, something sudden, clinging and smothering, enveloped his head, and steely arms locked fiercely about him. His reaction was as instinctive and violent as that of a trapped leopard. He exploded into a galvanized burst of frantic action, a bucking heave that tore the stifling cloak from his head, and freed his arms from the arms that pinioned him. But another pair of arms hung like grim Fate to his legs, and figures surged in on him from the darkness. He could not tell the nature of his assailants; they were like denser, moving shadows in the blackness.

Staggering, fighting for balance, he lashed out blindly, felt the jolt of a solid hit shoot up his arm, and saw one of the shadows sway and pitch backward. His other arm was caught in a savage grasp and twisted up behind his back so violently that he felt as if the tendons were being ripped from their roots. Hot breath hissed in his ear, and bending his head forward, he jerked it backward again with all the power of his thick neck muscles. He felt the back of his skull crash into something softer—a man's face. There was a groan, and the crippling grip on his imprisoned arm relaxed. With a desperate wrench he tore away, but the arms that clung to his legs tripped him. He pitched headlong, spreading his arms to break his fall, and even before his fingers touched the ground, something exploded in his brain, showering a suddenly starless night of blackness with red sparks that were engulfed abruptly in formless oblivion.

Joel Brill's first conscious thought was that he was being tossed about in an open boat on a stormy sea. Then as his dazed mind cleared, he realized that he was lying in an automobile which was speeding along an uneven road. His head throbbed; he was bound hand and foot, and blanketed in some kind of a cloak. He could see nothing; could hear nothing but the purr of the racing motor.

Bewilderment clouded his mind as be sought for a clue to the identity of the kidnappers. Then a sudden suspicion brought out the cold sweat on his skin.

The car lurched to a halt. Powerful hands lifted him, cloak and all, and he felt himself being carried over a short stretch of level ground, and apparently up a step or so. A key grated in a lock, a door rasped on its hinges. Those carrying him advanced; there was a click, and light shone through the folds of the cloth over Brill's head. He felt himself being lowered onto what felt like a bed. Then the cloth was ripped away, and he blinked in the glare of the light. A cold premonitory shudder passed over him.

He was lying on the bed in the room in which James Reynolds had died. And about him stood, arms folded, three grim and silent shapes: Yut Wuen, Ali the Egyptian, and Jugra Singh. There was dried blood on the Chinaman's yellow face, and his lip was cut. A dark blue bruise showed on Jugra Singh's jaw.

"The *sahib* awakes," said the Sikh, in his perfect English.

"What the devil's the idea, Jugra?" demanded Brill, trying to struggle to a sitting posture. "What do you mean by this? Take these ropes off me—" His voice trailed away, a shaky resonance of futility as he read the meaning in the hot dark eyes that regarded him.

"In this room our master met his doom," said Ali.

"*You* called him forth," said Yut Wuen.

"But I didn't!" raged Brill, jerking wildly at the cords which cut into his flesh. "Damn it, I knew nothing about it!"

"Your voice came over the wire and our master followed it to his death," said Jugra Singh.

A panic of helplessness swept over Joel Brill. He felt like a man beating at an insurmountable wall—the wall of inexorable Oriental fatalism, of conviction unchangeable. If even Buckley believed that somehow he, Joel Brill, was connected with Reynolds' death, how was he to convince these immutable Orientals? He fought down an impulse to hysteria.

"The detective, Buckley, was with me all evening," he said, in a voice unnatural from his efforts at control. "He has told you that he did not see me touch a phone; nor did I leave his sight. I could not have killed my friend, your master, because while he was being killed, I was either in the library of the Corinthian Club, or driving from there with Buckley."

"How it was done, we do not know," answered the Sikh, tranquilly. "The ways of the *sahibs* are beyond us. But we *know* that somehow, in some manner, you caused our master's death. And we have brought you here to expiate your crime."

"You mean to murder me?" demanded Brill, his flesh crawling.

"If a *sahib* judge sentenced you, and a *sahib* hangman dropped you through a black trap, white men would call it execution. So it is execution we work upon you, not murder."

Brill opened his mouth, then closed it, realizing the utter futility of argument. The whole affair was like a fantastic nightmare from which he would presently awaken.

Ali came forward with something, the sight of which shook Brill with a nameless foreboding. It was a wire cage, in which a great gaunt rat squealed and bit at the wires. Yut Wuen laid upon a card table a copper bowl, furnished with a slot on each side of the rim, to one of which was made fast a long leather strap. Brill turned suddenly sick.

"These are the tools of execution, *sahib,*" said Jugra Singh somberly. "That bowl shall be laid on your naked belly, the strap drawn about your body and made fast so that the bowl shall not slip. Inside the bowl the rat will be imprisoned. He is ravenous with hunger, wild with fear and rage. For a while he will only run about the bowl, treading on your flesh. But with irons hot from the fire, we shall gradually heat the bowl, until, driven by pain, the rat begins to gnaw his way *out*. He cannot gnaw through copper; he *can* gnaw through flesh—through flesh and muscles and intestines and bones, *sahib.*"

Brill wet his lips three times before he found voice to speak.

"You'll hang for this!" he gasped in a voice he did not himself recognize.

"If it be the will of Allah," assented Ali calmly. "This is your fate; what ours is, no man can say. It is the will of Allah that you die with a rat in your bowels. If it is Allah's will, we shall die on the gallows. Only Allah knows."

Brill made no reply. Some vestige of pride still remained to him. He set his jaw hard, feeling that if he opened his mouth to speak, to reason, to argue, he would collapse into shameful shrieks and entreaties. One was as useless as the other, against the abysmal fatalism of the Orient.

Ali set the cage with its grisly occupant on the table beside the copper bowl—without warning the light went out.

In the darkness Brill's heart began to pound suffocatingly. The Orientals stood still, patiently, expecting the light to come on again. But Brill instinctively felt that the stage was set for some drama darker and more hideous than that which menaced him. Silence reigned; somewhere off in the woods a night bird lifted a drowsy note. There was a faint scratching sound, somewhere—

"The electric torch," muttered a ghostly voice which Brill recognized as Jugra Singh's. "I laid it on the card table. Wait!"

He heard the Sikh fumbling in the dark; but he was watching the window, a square of dim, star-flecked sky blocked out of blackness. And as Brill watched, he saw something dark and bulky rear up in that square. Etched against the stars he saw a misshapen head, vague monstrous shoulders.

A scream sounded from inside the room, the crash of a wildly thrown missile. On the instant there was a scrambling sound, and the object blotted out the square of starlight, then vanished from it. *It was inside the room.*

Brill, lying frozen in his cords, heard all hell and bedlam break loose in that dark room. Screams, shouts, strident cries of agony mingled with the smashing of furniture, the impact of blows, and a hideous, worrying, tearing sound that made Brill's flesh crawl. Once the battling pack staggered past the window, but Brill made out only a dim writhing of limbs, the pale glint of steel, and the terrible blaze of a pair of eyes he knew belonged to none of his three captors.

Somewhere a man was moaning horribly, his gasps growing weaker and weaker. There was a last convulsion of movement, the groaning impact of a heavy body; then the starlight in the window was for an instant blotted out again, and silence reigned once more in the cottage on the lakeshore; silence broken only by the death gasps in the dark, and the labored panting of a wounded man.

Brill heard someone stumbling and floundering in the darkness, and it was from this one that the racking panting was emanating. A circle of light flashed on, and in it Brill saw the blood-smeared face of Jugra Singh. The Sikh's turban was gone, his eyes were glassy and staring; bloody foam bubbled at the corners of his mouth.

The light wandered erratically away, dancing crazily about the walls. Brill heard the Sikh blundering across the room, moving like a drunken man, or like one wounded unto death. The flash shone full in the scientist's face, blinding him. Fingers tugged awkwardly at his cords, a knife edge was dragged across them, slicing skin as well as hemp. Brill set his teeth against the agony of returning circulation and sat up, chaffing his numb wrists.

Jugra Singh sank to the floor. The flash thumped beside him and went out. Brill groped for him, found his shoulder. The cloth was soaked with what Brill knew was blood.

"You spoke truth, *sahib*," the Sikh whispered. "How the call came in the likeness of your voice, I do not know. But I know now what slew Reynolds, *sahib*. After all these years—but they never forget, though the broad sea lies between. Beware! The fiend may return. The gold—the gold was cursed—I told Reynolds, *sahib*—had he heeded me, he—"

A sudden welling of blood drowned the laboring voice. Under Brill's hand the great body stiffened and twisted in a brief convulsion, then went limp.

Groping on the floor, the scientist failed to find the flashlight. He rose and went to the window; his foot slipped in something wet; he stumbled over an object bulky and yielding. The moaning had died away. As his fingers closed on the windowsill, they encountered a splotch of warm sticky stuff. Leaning out of the window, he groped along the wall, found the switch and flooded the cottage with light.

Turning back into the room, a stifled cry escaped his lips. He had been prepared for horror, but not for what met his dilated stare.

A tornado might have raged in the cottage. Card tables and chairs were smashed to kindling wood. Blood lay in thick pools and smears on the floor, was splashed on the walls, the bed, the broken furniture.

Jugra Singh lay slumped near the bed; huddled in a corner was Yut Wuen, his yellow hands, palms upturned, limp on the floor at his sides; Ali sprawled face down in the middle of the room. All three were dead. Throats, breasts and bellies were slashed to ribbons; their garments were in strips, and among the rags hung bloody tatters of flesh. Yut Wuen had been disemboweled, and the gaping wounds of the others were like those of sheep after a mountain lion has ranged through the fold.

A blackjack still stuck in Yut Wuen's belt. Ali's dead hand clutched a knife, but it was unstained. Death had struck them before they could use their weapons. But on the floor near Jugra Singh lay a great curved dagger, and it was red to the hilt. Bloody stains led across the floor and up over the windowsill. Brill found the flash, snapped it on, and leaned out the window, playing the white beam on the ground outside. Dark, irregular splotches showed, leading off toward the dense woods.

With the flash in one hand and the Sikh's knife in the other, Brill followed those stains. At the edge of the trees he came upon a track, and the short hairs lifted on his scalp. A foot, planted in a pool of blood, had limned its imprint in crimson on the hard loam. And the foot, bare and splay, was that of a human.

That print upset vague theories of a feline or anthropoid killer, stirred nebulous thoughts at the back of his mind—dim and awful race memories of semi-human ghouls, of werewolves who walked like men and slew like beasts.

A low groan brought him to a halt, his flesh crawling. Under the black trees in the silence, that sound was pregnant with grisly probabilities. Gripping the knife firmly, he flashed the beam ahead of him. The thin light wavered, then focused on a black heap that was not part of the forest.

Brill bent over the figure and stood transfixed, transported back across the years and across the world to another wilder, grimmer woodland.

It was a naked black man that lay at his feet, his glassy eyes reflecting the waning light. His legs were short, bowed and gnarled, his arms long, his shoulders abnormally broad, his shaven head set plump between them without visible neck. That head was hideously malformed; the forehead projected almost into a peak, while the back of the skull was unnaturally flattened. White paint banded face, shoulders and breast. But it was at the creature's fingers which Brill looked longest. At first glance they seemed monstrously deformed. Then he saw that those hands were furnished with long curving steel hooks, sharp-pointed, and keen-edged on the concave side. To each finger one of these barbarous weapons was made fast, and those fingers, like the hooks clotted and smeared with blood, twitched exactly as the talons of a leopard twitch.

An icy finger played on Brill's spine; this was necromantic, impossible. He stood in a woodland grown suddenly haunted and strange, gazing down at that black shape brought so inexplicably out of imponderably alien and distant abysses of the bestially primitive.

A light step brought him round. His dimming light played on a tall figure, and Brill mumbled: "John Galt!" in no great surprise. He was so numbed by bewilderment that the strangeness of the man's presence did not occur to him.

"What in God's name is this?" demanded the tall explorer, taking the light from Brill's hand and directing it on the mangled shape. "What in Heaven's name is that?"

"A black nightmare from Africa!" Brill found his tongue at last, and speech came in a rush. "An Egbo! A leopard man! I learned of them when I was on the West Coast. He belongs to a native cult which worships the leopard. They take a male infant and subject his head to pressure, to make it deformed; and he is brought up to believe that the spirit of a leopard inhabits his body. He does the bidding of the cult's head, which mainly consists of executing the enemies of the cult. He is, in effect, a human leopard!"

"What's he doing here?" demanded Galt, in seeming incredulity.

"God knows. But he must have been the thing that killed Reynolds. He killed Reynolds' three servants tonight—would have killed me, too, I suppose, but Jugra Singh wounded him, and he evidently dragged himself away like a wild beast to die in the jungle—"

Galt seemed curiously uninterested in Brill's stammering narrative.

"Sure he's dead?" he muttered, bending closer to flash the light into the hideous face. The illumination was dim; the battery was swiftly burning out.

As Brill was about to speak, the painted face was briefly convulsed. The glazed eyes gleamed as with a last surge of life. A clawed hand stirred, lifted feebly up toward Galt. A few gutturals seeped through the blubbery lips; the fingers writhed weakly, slipped from the iron talons, which the black man lifted, as if trying to hand them to Galt. Then he shuddered, sank back and lay still. He had been stabbed under the heart, and only a beast-like vitality had carried him so far.

Galt straightened and faced Brill, turning the light on him. A beat of silence cut between them, in which the atmosphere was electric with tension.

"You understand the Ekoi dialect?" It was more an assertion than a question.

Brill's heart was pounding, a new bewilderment vying with a rising wrath. "Yes," he answered shortly.

"What did that fool say?" softly asked Galt.

Brill set his teeth and stubbornly took the plunge reason cried out against. "He said," he replied between his teeth: "'Master, take my tools to the tribe, and tell them of our vengeance; they will give you what I promised you.'"

Even as he ground out the words, his powerful body crouched, his nerves taut for the grapple. But before he could move, the black muzzle of an automatic trained on his belly.

"Too bad you had to understand that death-bed confession, Brill," said Galt coolly. "I don't want to kill you. I've kept blood off *my* hands so far through this affair. Listen, you're a poor man, like most scientists—how'd you consider cutting in on a fortune? Wouldn't that be preferable to getting a slug through your guts and being planted alongside those yellow-bellied stiffs down in Reynolds' shack for them to get the blame?"

"No man wants to die," answered Brill, his gaze fixed on the light in Galt's hand—the glow which was rapidly turning redder and dimmer.

"Good!" snapped Galt. "I'll give you the low down. Reynolds got his money in the Kameroons—stole gold from the Ekoi, which they had stored in the ju-ju hut; he killed a priest of the Egbo cult in getting away. Jugra Singh was with him. But they didn't get all the gold. And after that the Ekoi took good care to guard it so nobody could steal what was left.

"I knew this fellow, Guja, when I was in Africa. I was after the Ekoi gold then, but I never had a chance to locate it. I met Guja a few months ago, again. He'd been exiled from his tribe for some crime, had wandered to the Coast and been picked up with some more natives who were brought to America for exhibition in the World's Fair.

"Guja was mad to get back to his people, and he spilled the whole story of the gold. Told me that if he could kill Reynolds, his tribe would forgive him. He knew that Reynolds was somewhere in America, but he was helpless as a child to find him. I offered to arrange his meeting with the gold thief, if Guja would agree to give me some of the gold his tribe hoarded.

"He swore by the skull of the great leopard. I brought him secretly into these hills, and hid him up yonder in a shack the existence of which nobody suspects. It took me a wretched time to teach him just what he was to do—he'd no more brains than an ape. Night after night I went through the thing with him, until he learned the procedure: to watch in the hills until he saw a light flash in Reynolds' shack. Then steal down there, jerk the switch—and kill. These leopard men can see like cats at night.

"I called Reynolds up myself; it wasn't hard to imitate your voice. I used to do impersonations in vaudeville. While Guja was avenging his tribe on Reynolds, I was dining at a well-known night club, in full sight of all.

"I came here tonight to smuggle him out of the country. But his bloodlust must have betrayed him. When he saw the light flash on in the cottage again, it must have started a train of associations that led him once more to the cottage, to kill whoever he found there. I saw the tag-end of the business—saw him stagger away from the shack, and then you follow him.

"Now then, I've shot the works. Nobody knows I'm mixed up in this business, but you. Will you keep your mouth shut and take a share of the Ekoi gold?"

The glow went out. In the darkness, Brill, his pent-up feelings exploding at last, yelled: "Damn you, no, you murdering dog!" and sprang aside. The pistol cracked, an orange jet sliced the darkness, and the bullet fanned Brill's ear. He swung up his arm and threw the heavy knife blindly, heard it rattle futilely through the bushes. He stood frozen with a sense of having lost his desperate gamble.

But even as he tensed himself against the tearing impact of the bullet he expected, a sudden beam drilled the darkness, illuming the convulsed features of John Galt, who blinked in the glare, pistol lifted shoulder high. A voice broke the tense stillness.

"Don't move, Galt; I've got you covered."

It was the voice of Buckley. With a snarl, Galt took as desperate a chance as Brill had taken. He wheeled toward the source of the light, snapping up his automatic. But even as he did so, the detective's .45 crashed, and limned against the brief glare, Galt swayed and fell like a tall tree in a gale and pitched face first to the sward.

Bewilderedly Brill saw Buckley run forward and bend over the prostrate figure.

"Is he dead?" asked the scientist.

"Bullet went through his forearm and smashed his shoulder," grunted Buckley. "Just knocked out; he'll live to decorate the gallows. Here, help me put a tourniquet on him. I nearly got you killed; shouldn't have waited so long to make my appearance. But I wanted to hear everything he had to spill. That light going out took me by surprize."

"You—you heard—?" Brill stuttered.

"Everything. I was just coming around the bend of the lakeshore and saw a light in Reynolds' cottage, then your flash bobbing among the trees. I came sneaking through the bushes just in time to hear you give your translation of the nigger's dying words. I've been prowling around this lake all night, trying to find something I could tie to."

"You suspected Galt all the time?"

The detective grinned wryly.

"I ought to say yes, and establish myself as a super sleuth. But the fact is, I suspected *you* all the time. That's why I came up here tonight—trying to figure out your connection with the murder. That alibi of yours was so iron-clad it looked phony to me. I had a sneaking suspicion that I'd bumped into a mastermind trying to put over the 'perfect crime.' I apologize! I've been reading too many detective stories lately!"

The Hand of the Black Goddess

Kirby halted with one foot in the doorway. The setting was familiar: the drab hallway, the glass-doored offices at the far end, and at this end the stairway that led up to his own office. But the figure before him was bizarrely unfamiliar. Kirby instinctively knew that the man who stood just within the hallway was out of place in such a setting, exotically alien in spite of his conventional attire. It was not merely that his dark skin and foreign features suggested the Orient; there was an intangible *aura* of the East about him—a vague suggestion of things neither natural nor wholesome, according to a white man's traditional way of thinking.

"You are Mr. Kirby?" The voice was deep and rich as the peal of a temple bell, but there was an indefinite hint of hostility in its resonance. And a light of mockery and menace danced in the depths of the dark eyes.

"Yes, I'm Kirby." He tried to keep his unreasoning antagonism out of his voice.

"I shall not detain you. I merely wish to suggest that it is better to let Fate follow its chosen course, than to interfere with things which do not concern you."

"What do you mean?" demanded Kirby. "I never saw you before—"

"And if you are wise you will never see me again!" The tone continued suave, but the glint of menace flickered redly in the dark eyes. The man's hands were in his topcoat pockets, and might have held a weapon; but there was in his arrogant bearing a subtle implication of physical prowess not dependent upon weapons. He bulked enormous in the narrow hallway. "You will find an object in your office to lend point to my suggestion," he continued. "I need say no more. I bid you good day, Mr. Kirby."

And with a sardonic bow, such as a Westerner could never imitate, he brushed past the astonished Kirby and strode out into the street. The latter glared after him for an instant, and then turned and mounted the stair, shaking his head in bewilderment. It was a strange experience, even for a private investigator, to be halted on his own stair by a giant Oriental voicing cryptic allusions and thinly veiled threats. What it all meant he could not even guess.

Kirby reached his door, which bore on its frosted glass the words: "Kirby & Gorman, Private Detective Agency." As he turned the knob he shrugged his shoulders; he had yet to receive his first customer—

He halted short in the open doorway, a strange sensation crawling up his spine to prickle the short hair at the back of his neck.

There was a man in that office. He sprawled on his back in the middle of the floor, about midway between the door and the one desk the office boasted. There was a crimson smear on the carpet, and something stood stiffly up from his bosom—

Kirby found speech at last in an explosive imprecation. As if that awoke his reflexes, he wheeled and dashed out of the office and down the narrow stair. He went in such a hurry that he almost upset a slim feminine figure halfway down. As he crowded past muttering a half-intelligible apology, he had only a confused impression of curly dark hair, parted red lips, and expressive brown eyes. It registered on some part of his mind that the girl cried out something, but he did not halt. He raced out into the street and stood glaring up and down, baffled. He ran to the nearest corner, and repeated his procedure.

"Donovan!" he yelled. *"Donovan!"*

The big cop came on the run, sensing urgency in the call.

"Which way did he go?" demanded Kirby, before he realized that Donovan did not know what he was talking about. He elucidated: "A big, brown-skinned devil in a topcoat, with a green scarf around his neck. Did you see him? Did he come around the corner? He came out of my hallway a few minutes ago."

"I didn't notice him," grunted Donovan. "Maybe he went the other way. Anyway, with me seein' crowds of people every day and all the time, how do you expect me—"

"There's a dead man up in my office," broke in Kirby. "Murdered. I believe the fellow I'm talking about did it. I met him coming down the stair as I went up—well, he's gone now."

"We'll pick him up," grunted Donovan, heading for the hallway. He was a man of action. But as they entered the office he remarked: "A fine detective agency you're runnin'! A murder committed in your own office, and you have to call in the regular police!"

Kirby did not heed that thrust; he was staring at the corpse. The body was that of a short, stocky individual, with thin light hair and a rather keen face, adorned by a scrubby mustache. The expression on his dead grey face was not pleasant to look at. But that was not what caused Kirby to swear suddenly.

"He's been tampered with since I went out!" he exclaimed. "He's not lying in the same position at all!"

"Sure you didn't move him yourself?" demanded Donovan.

"Do you take me for a complete fool?" snapped Kirby heatedly. "I haven't touched him—look there! His pockets have been turned out! Somebody's been through him since I ran down the stair a few minutes ago. By thunder—" He halted suddenly, and did not continue.

Donovan grunted, stepped to the phone, dialed a number and spoke into the mouthpiece succinctly. Then he turned back to the corpse with an over-done professional air that would have exasperated Kirby had the detective been less engrossed in his own speculations. Kirby was not easily upset, but any man is likely to be momentarily thrown out of his stride by finding a murdered stranger in his own office.

"I've been a coroner's assistant," mused Donovan judicially, "and havin' had experience in such cases, I'd say offhand that the fellow's been dead half an hour, at least. That lets *you* out."

"What do you mean, lets me out?" demanded Kirby, sweating between exasperation and perplexity.

"Well," said Donovan, "you found him. Nobody but you saw the man you think did the killin'. Folks might think *you* done it!"

"Don't be a fool, Donovan!" exclaimed Kirby angrily. He was somewhat above medium height, built as trimly and compactly as a steel spring. His keen, mobile face reflected intelligence combined with physical co-ordination, and when exasperated—as now—his grey eyes turned to glinting steel.

"Well," grinned the cop, "I know you've been out of this joint for an hour or so. You passed the time of day with me as you went down the street for dinner, and you stopped around the corner to talk with me again as you were comin' back. This fellow was killed while you were out. There's your alibi, *Mister* Kirby."

Kirby scarcely heard him. He was stooping, not touching, but staring at the dagger which projected from the dead man's breast. It was of peculiar design. There was no guard, and the hilt was of gold, ornamented with a carven serpent which twined about it, so that its head formed the pommel. But in place of an ordinary snake's head, there was the likeness of a human skull. All the ornamental work was of gold.

"Damned exotic weapon," muttered Kirby. "Chinese? Scarcely. Indian? Yes, I think so. I wonder if the man on the stair was an Indian?"

He voiced this thought to his partner, Butch Gorman, half an hour later. The cops were gone, taking the body with them, and Kirby and Gorman were alone in the office. Outside the building darkness was gathering, and the unlighted corridor beyond the glass-paneled door was a shadowy mystery. Gorman was a tall man, strongly built, no older than Kirby. He had flaming red hair and cold blue eyes, but his complexion had been burnt bronze by wind and sun, and there was a pantherish hardness about him rarely met with among civilized men. Gorman was born in an adobe hut on the left bank of the Rio Grande, and had spent most of his life in the mountains south of that river, where a knife thrust is the customary retort to argument.

"I think he was a Hindu," Kirby was saying with conviction. "And I've got a feeling that he won't be picked up as easily as Donovan thought. I believe the knife was left in the body, either as a warning of some kind, or because the killing had some sort of a ritualistic meaning. The Hindu warned me against interfering into what wasn't my business. The man he murdered evidently came here to see us, maybe to employ us. I left the office unlocked when I went to dinner, because I knew you'd be back soon, and you're always losing your key. Anyway, there's nothing in here to steal. The Indian must have followed him in and killed him. And another thing—the man had been dead at least half an hour when Donovan and I came in. That means the Hindu killed him and instead of leaving instantly, deliberately waited to give me that warning."

"And nobody saw this Indian but you?" asked Gorman.

"No. Nobody in this building but us, you know. This was a perfect place for a murder, in this all but deserted office building. Then somebody went through the fellow's pockets while I was gone after Donovan. There wasn't a thing left to identify him. Even a tag ripped out of his hat that might have had his initials on it."

"The Indian again?" suggested Gorman.

"I don't think so. He had plenty of time to go through the corpse before I returned the first time, if he'd wanted to. No, I passed a girl on the stair as I went down after Donovan. I said nothing about it to him, because he and the other cops seem to think we're a couple of saps playing at detective work. We'll keep this clue to ourselves, and trace it down. I'm sure that girl was the one who ransacked the dead man—*listen!*"

It might have been a quick intake of breath, too slight to be caught by any senses not whetted by the nervousness of unwonted happenings. It seemed to come from a closet where generally the partners' coats and hats hung. Kirby was sitting with his back a few feet from this closet door, and his flesh crawled. In an instant he was on his feet, facing the door, an automatic glinting bluely in his hand. Gorman sprang up too, his hand flicking under his coat where reposed a weapon in which he placed more reliance than a pistol.

"Come out!" Kirby's voice was brittle with electric tension. "Come out, or I'll empty this gun through the door!"

"Oh, don't shoot!" Both men started at the timbre of the muffled voice.

Then the door opened and a trembling figure stood framed in the opening; Kirby stared.

"The girl on the stair!"

She nodded dumbly, apparently incapable of reply; there was terror in every line of her trim figure, and her wide eyes held a mute entreaty.

"What were you doing in there?" Kirby asked, not harshly. "Why should you spy on us?"

"I wasn't spying," she answered, finding her voice at last. "I've been hiding, waiting for a chance to slip out—it seems for hours!"

"Who are you?"

"My name is Gloria Corwell. Don't call the police! Please don't!"

"Suppose you sit down and pull yourself together," suggested Kirby, thrusting a chair toward her. "Do you know anything about the man who was murdered in this office?"

She hesitated and glanced from one man to the other uncertainly, then seemed to make up her mind. It was easy to see the girl was in a state of desperation.

"Yes," she said. "I knew the man. His name was William Harper. It was because I was following him that I came to your office."

Kirby and Gorman exchanged glances, and Gorman made a gesture that implied he left the matter wholly up to Kirby—as he usually did, in matters that did not involve blows of hammerlike fists or the lick of a razor-edged knife.

The girl was regaining a little of her composure. Her fingers fluttered mechanically arranging her attire, feminine fashion.

"Suppose you trust us," suggested Kirby, and there was a look about him that inspired confidence in women, as well as men.

The girl looked up, with a gleam that might have been hopefulness in her eyes. Then she rushed into hurried speech, as if the floodgates of restraint were down, stammering in her eagerness.

"You men are detectives! Harper was coming to employ you! I'll make you the same offer he was going to make—three times your regular fee!"

"Better give us the details," Kirby answered cautiously.

"I'll try!" She pressed her palms to her temples in a curiously childish gesture, and shuddered involuntarily. "I told you my name. All my family except myself are traveling in Europe, and I'm staying with my uncle, Richard Corwell, at his country estate, Corwell Manor, near Baskerton. He's a bachelor. A week ago a strange man came there—strange to me, that is, though Uncle Richard knew him, it seems. He said the man's name was Farnum. He came in the night, and since then Corwell Manor has literally been in a state of siege! Uncle Richard barricaded the house, and neither he nor Farnum has left it since. He tried to persuade me to leave that very night that Farnum arrived, and go to visit some friends, but I believed he was in danger, and I didn't trust Farnum.

"I've seen men skulking about the place, dark, foreign men, and there have been numbers of attempts to enter the house by night. Uncle's four dogs—big fierce mastiffs—have all been killed; shot with poisoned darts!"

Kirby grunted, remembering the Hindu knife; more and more this affair revealed the flavor of the Orient.

"I tried to get Uncle Richard to appeal to the police," the girl went on, "but he positively shivered at the suggestion. He refused to tell me anything, except that a band of Orientals were trying to kill Farnum, and that he was bound to protect him, and that if the police were brought into it, both Farnum and himself would be ruined.

"But last night there was an unusually determined effort to break in, and Farnum was wounded in the arm—there was fighting in the dark. So Harper, Uncle Richard's valet, and I talked it over and decided to go and get help from some private detective agency. He knew no more than I, but he was devoted to Uncle Richard. He slipped out of the house just before dawn, and at the same time I slipped out in another direction, leaving a note for Uncle Richard.

The idea was that if they got one of us, maybe the other would get through."

If she were telling the truth, thought Kirby, this girl had nerve.

"Well, I got away all right," she continued. "Of course, I didn't know whether Harper did or not. I came on to the city alone, and came straight to your agency. And as I approached I saw a man leaving the building—" She shuddered again as if the mere memory of the man were loathsome. "I have seen him lurking about Corwell Manor; Farnum knew him, and called him Khemsa. Farnum tried to shoot him and cursed like a madman every time he got a glimpse of him.

"I was startled when I saw Khemsa here, and when I met you rushing down the stair, I knew from your expression that something terrible had happened. I ran up into this office and found poor Harper lying there with a dagger in his breast—just such a dagger as was thrown through a window at my uncle. I was so shocked and terrified that all I could think of was my uncle's fear of the police. I went through Harper's pockets and took out everything that might identify him, so they couldn't trace him back to my uncle. Later the body can be identified and taken care of properly, but just now the police mustn't be brought into this affair—though why, I'm sure I don't know.

"I heard you returning with the policeman before I could get away. So I hid in the closet and have been there ever since, afraid to move. Please—you're not regular police—can't you come out to Corwell Manor and help us, without dragging the authorities into it?"

"Let's take a fling at it, Brent," urged Gorman eagerly.

Kirby opened his lips to reply—then the glass in the door crashed suddenly, and almost simultaneously he felt a sharp stinging prick over his breastbone. Through the broken glass he glimpsed a dark face and a thing that looked like a bamboo tube. Gorman had shot to his feet, his hand whipping under his coat, when inexplicably he checked, swayed, and fell stiffly back into his chair. Kirby tried to speak—to rise—to draw his gun, but he could not move. His whole body was numb, almost without feeling; he could see and hear, but his tongue was dead, his reflexes without response.

A hand reached through the broken glass and threw the bolt. Then the door opened and a man entered noiselessly—the big brown man Kirby had met in the hallway. He was dressed differently now. The topcoat was gone, for one thing, and the green scarf was no longer about his neck. He was flicking it suggestively through his fingers. He looked more Oriental than ever.

Gloria Corwell sat gripping her chair arms so the knuckles of her hands showed white. Kirby knew that she was not a victim to the curious paralysis that gripped him and Gorman; it was sheer terror that held her rigid.

"I gave you one warning today, Mr. Kirby," said the Hindu sardonically. "I thought that would be sufficient. Miss Corwell, I will admit you tricked us in escaping from your uncle's house. Harper was more subtle than we thought. We saw him leave the house, but he eluded us, and while we were searching for him, you likewise slipped away. It was an unexpected move.

"I found his trail at last, and followed him into the city, but I had no idea you were here until I saw you enter this building. You saw me, but did not know that I saw you. So I hid nearby and presently returned." He stared at her with a curious blank fixity that was horrifying; it chilled the girl. He seemed less like a man than an incarnation of ferocity.

"All in Corwell Manor have been condemned to death," he said, and his voice thrummed thickly with bloodlust. "I, Khemsa, am your executioner. As for you men, I have no particular desire to kill you. That dart in your breast, detective, and the one in your friend's arm, are steeped in an Eastern drug that produces paralysis as long as the darts remain in your flesh. Tomorrow someone will discover you, and when they are withdrawn, you will regain the use of your limbs. But let me warn you that you will be constantly watched, and that any attempt to aid Richard Corwell or Farnum will result in instant death. As for this girl, she is doomed, and you shall see how a votary of *Kali* breaks a neck with a silk scarf."

He advanced on Gloria with the step of a hunting tiger, and she cringed back in her chair, staring with dilated eyes at the scarf which flowed back and forth through his fingers like a green serpent. Kirby felt his brain reeling with his helpless fury. He could not doubt that this devilish Oriental meant to kill the girl; there was murder in his tigerish stalk, in his burning, slitted eyes. With chilling certainty he recognized the clue given in the mention of Kali, the Hindu goddess of death. This brute was a *Thug*, a member of a murder cult vowed and devoted to destruction. And must he, Kirby, sit there like a petrified block, while an abominable crime was committed under his very eyes? But he could not move a finger.

Gloria, breaking the spell of horror that gripped her, cried out and sprang from her chair. The Thug was after her with a noiseless quickness that was suggestive of a huge python. The scarf flickered toward her white neck—and then, unexpectedly, miraculously, Butch Gorman came into the game with the suddenness and violence of a typhoon. With no preliminary motion he launched himself from his chair and his clenched left smashed like a sledgehammer under the Thug's ear. The man swayed backward, his head hit the wall with a stunning crack, and as he pitched forward from the impact, Gorman's malletlike right caught him full on the jaw and stretched him his full length on the floor. He did not even quiver.

Butch glared around as if for other victims, located the girl cowering in a corner, grinned reassuringly at her, and then stepped over to Kirby and wrenched something from his shirt bosom. Instantly Kirby felt a reviving flow of life churn through his numb limbs. He worked his jaws, achieving speech, and rose unsteadily, his extremities prickling as if because of returning circulation. Butch, between thumb and forefinger, gingerly pinched a thorn-shaped sliver of dark wood.

"Sticking in your wishbone," grunted Gorman, tossing it on the floor and grinding it under his heel. "Mine stuck in my sleeve— didn't stick in my arm, just scratched the flesh. That was enough to knock me out for a few minutes, though. I could feel my power coming back, but I was mortal scared he'd kill the young lady before

I could get going. There's his blasted blowgun!" And Gorman's heel reduced the lethal tube to splinters. "What's next?"

"Let's go!" exclaimed Kirby, galvanized. "You heard him say we'd be watched. Well, I believe he was the only one spying on us; likely had some way of signaling his friends if we started toward Corwell Manor. Now's our chance to make a break while he's out. We'll make it to Corwell Manor before he can come to and get word ahead of us. No, don't tie him up. We don't want the watchman or janitor or somebody to find him tied up in our office—have to make a lot of embarrassing explanations. He'll be out for hours. I've seen you slug men before. My car's parked down the street. Let's go!"

Kirby snapped off the light, slammed the door behind them, grabbed the girl's arm, and they rushed downstairs and into the street. It was empty; not even a cop in sight. Kirby half pushed the girl into the car and sprang into the driver's seat beside her. With a foot on the running board, and a hand on the rear door, Gorman wheeled at the sound of hurried footsteps. A man loomed up out of the shadows, running toward them.

"Sahibs!" The voice was urgent, alienly accented. "Wait! Halt!"

His hand was lifted, whether or not in menace Gorman did not pause to learn; the glimpse he had of dark skin was enough. He swung for the fellow's jaw, and the man went down like a pole-axed ox. The next instant Butch was in the car, and Kirby was stepping hard on the accelerator. Down the deserted street they roared on a wilder quest than even Kirby guessed.

.2.

It was approaching midnight when they came within sight of Corwell Manor, looming darkly among the trees. Off to the southeast, a mile and a half away, a few lights indicated the village of Baskerton. There were no nearer lights, no other houses to break the solitude of shadowy woodlands. Evidently the master of Corwell Manor was not a gregarious soul.

The past mile had been traversed tensely, for they dreaded an ambush in every clump of trees. But a sleeping silence lay over the wooded land, scarcely broken by the purr of the powerful motor.

"The men watching the place can hardly know we're reinforcements," muttered Kirby. "They'll guess, though, when we turn in at the gate. We'll have to work fast, and take a chance of being blasted down."

"We'll go in through the side door." Gloria was fidgety with nervousness as she tried to peer into the shadows under the trees. "I slipped out that way. I haven't a key for the big gate in front. They'd kill us before Uncle Richard could come and let us in."

The "Manor" faced east and was surrounded by a high stone wall. The dusty road ran past the strong wrought-iron gate in the east wall. But at Gloria's directions, just as they reached the corner of the grounds, Kirby wrenched the wheel over and shot down a narrow path that followed the north wall. He knew it was a desperate chance. The instant they turned in from the main road, the men watching would know the car contained no belated travelers passing by. He instinctively hunched over the wheel, momentarily expecting a blast of lead from the bushes. Then Gloria cried out a quick command, and he halted the car with a suddenness that set the brakes screeching.

Gorman was out of the car in a second, glaring into the bushes which marched close by the path and might have concealed an army. Kirby followed him, almost jerking the girl with him. Now it was touch and go! Gloria was fumbling at a small iron-braced door in the wall, and Kirby's flesh crawled at the thought of poisoned arrows from the darkness. Pistol in hand he crouched by Gorman, straining his eyes, as they sheltered the girl with their own bodies. In the silence he heard her quick breathing, and the scrape of her key on iron. The silence was oppressive, stifling. Somewhere, far off in the woods, he heard a strange quavering cry that might have been that of a night bird. But no bird's cry ever made instinctive chills crawl up his spine like that.

Then the key turned in the lock, and an instant later all three were inside the wall, and Gloria was locking the door behind them, limp with relief.

They all turned toward the house, bulking huge above a wide lawn, thickly shadowed by trees and shrubs. Not a light showed. Kirby told Gloria to call out, to identify them to the men in the house; he feared a volley from the nervous defenders. But she shook her head silently, seemingly perturbed at the absence of lights. They followed a narrow walk among the shrubs to a side door, and there Gloria beat a quick tattoo with her slim knuckles. There was no other sound. Kirby saw her face turned toward him, a pallid oval in the starlight.

"They don't answer the door!" she whispered, clutching his hand; he could sense the wild beating of her heart. "It's so still! Oh, I'm afraid!"

Away off in the woods rose again that weird cry, and Kirby knew no bird ever lifted that call. He scanned the blank windows uneasily. Even in the starlight he could see that they were heavily barred, and shattered on the inside.

"Let's try the front," he muttered, and they hurried around the silent house which seemed to have taken on a newer aspect of mystery. They reached the wide, pillared verandah—

A low cry burst from Gloria's lips. The front door gaped, sagging on its hinges. The inner darkness was Stygian, but Kirby thought he heard something stirring—a stealthy footfall. Taking a desperate chance, he flashed a beam from his electric torch through the door. Gloria screamed poignantly.

"Uncle Richard! They've killed him!"

Just inside the door lay a man, with a great blood-clotted blue welt on his temple. Gloria broke from Kirby's restraining hand and ran to throw herself beside the prostrate form, sobbing convulsively. The men followed her and Kirby, his flesh creeping at what the darkness might be concealing, turned his beam in all directions—it halted on another body lying near the wide fireplace in a pool of clotted blood. The man's throat had been cut from ear to ear.

"Is that Farnum?" Kirby asked, dreading to show the girl the new horror, but urgently needing information.

She looked, shuddered sickly, but shook her head. "No, that's the other servant, Daley."

"Keep watch, Butch," ordered Kirby, and dropped down beside the girl. Gorman stood like a statue, breathing softly as he strained his ears and stared into the shadows. Kirby's light played on the prostrate master of the house, but it lent enough illumination to show the broad stair winding up into inky gloom, and the wide, curtained door that let into a broad hallway. The room was a large one, including the whole front part of the house. Gorman wondered what lay in the darkness beyond the range of his faculties.

As Kirby worked over the senseless man, he too was listening with painful intensity for sounds from the interior of the house. For all he knew the silent Manor was full of stealthy murderers. But he did not think so.

"They did their job and took it on the run," he muttered. "That's why we weren't molested when we drove up. Guess the noise I heard in here was made by Corwell; he seems to be regaining consciousness. But that cry—that was no bird."

Richard Corwell was beginning to groan and stir. Kirby pressed a flask to his lips, and presently the master of the Manor opened his eyes and blinked dazedly in the light of the torch. He was a slight, aristocratic-looking man of middle age.

"Kill me if you will," he muttered dizzily. "I know nothing. Farnum has told me nothing! I can not tell you where it is hidden."

"It's Gloria, Uncle Richard!" cried the girl, throwing her arms around his neck and shaking him in the intensity of her emotion. "Don't you know me? What happened?"

"Gloria?" he mumbled. "Thank God you're safe. When I found your note I didn't think I'd ever see you alive again."

"But what happened?"

"They got in. The alarms didn't work. They were battering in the door before we knew it—dark-skinned devils with red eyes like mad dogs! God!" He shuddered. "I think Farnum killed one of them. Somebody knocked me in the head." He saw the corpse then and his face went grey. "Poor Daley! Oh, the murdering swine!" Then he seemed aware of the two strangers for the first time and demanded: "Who are these men?"

"Private detectives, Uncle Richard," she answered. "They are here to help us. The Hindu, Khemsa, killed Harper in their office."

"Harper!" exclaimed Corwell, pressing his hands to his throbbing head. "Harper, Daley—and Farnum! They've got Farnum! God, they'll torture him! We must find him! He's a rogue, but we can't leave him to their mercies."

"Who are 'they'?" asked Kirby.

"Hindus! Votaries of the goddess Kali! *Thugs!*"

Kirby had found and now snapped on a small lamp whose faint gleam, he believed, would scarcely be visible through the shuttered and curtained windows. He pushed the broken door shut, propping it with a chair. The faint light made shadows lurk eerily in the corners, glinted on antique weapons and the horns of mounted trophies adorning the walls.

"Stay here, Butch," snapped Kirby. "I'm going to look through the house. I doubt if anybody's hiding here, but we've got to make sure. I'll take the lower part of the house first. Farnum's body may be here somewhere—"

"They wouldn't kill him," muttered Corwell. "They'd torture him to make him tell—"

"Tell what?" demanded Kirby, as the man halted. But Corwell was mute. Shaking his head impatiently, Kirby pushed through the satin curtains and went cautiously along the wide hallway, flashing his light ahead of him, and into the rooms on either side. He saw no one, living or dead, but as he approached the rear of the house, he came onto another open door. It was on the south side of the house, opening on the lawn. Snapping off his light he investigated and his quick fingers told him the door had neither been broken nor forced from the outside. Had the slayers left the house by this door? If so, why had they chosen this exit, instead of leaving by the same way they had entered?

Suddenly he crouched down in the deeper darkness. Out on the lawn he had glimpsed a skulking figure, moving under the branches of the trees. Like a shadow it was moving toward the house. Then he jumped at a sudden sound, startling in the stillness—the shrill peal of a bell somewhere in the house. The unknown marauder heard it, too, for he halted short, and then melted like a phantom into the bushes.

Even as Kirby identified the sound as the ringing of a police alarm, he heard something else—the slap of flying feet through the grass, and the labored breathing of a man. Then a second figure dashed out of the shrubs near the wall and ran toward the house, not furtively, but openly and with desperate haste. As he passed the shrubbery into which the other shape had vanished, it reappeared without warning—flashed from the shadows and full onto his shoulders, like a leaping panther. They merged in a writhing, voiceless tangle, and Kirby abandoned caution and raced across the lawn. His beam revealed two figures close locked. The man underneath was white. The other might have stepped out of a nightmare—a muscular, dark-skinned figure, naked but for a loin-cloth, with a horrific symbol painted on his low forehead. His eyes burned red as a panther's, and his long black hair fell about his shoulders. His dark hands gripped a silk cord, drawing it fiercely about the white man's neck. The strands sank deeper and deeper in the straining flesh, and the victim clawed at it vainly, his face purpling. Kirby brought down his automatic barrel on the strangler's skull, and the man fell sprawling backward. The other reeled up, tearing the cord away with a gasping gurgle.

Kirby turned the light on him. He saw a slender man of medium height, smaller than himself, but one who looked hard and capable as a Damascus blade. The keen, mobile face was ruthless, and the restless eyes sparkled with vital energy.

"Who are you?" demanded Kirby.

"I'll answer that when I know who you are," retorted the other.

"I'm Brent Kirby," answered the detective briefly. "I'm a private investigator, and I came here with Miss Corwell."

"Then she's told you about me. I'm Farnum. *Look out!*"

Kirby wheeled in time to see the Thug, whom he thought still senseless if not dead, roll into the deep shadow, spring up like a flash and disappear in the darkness. The crack of his automatic split the night's stillness, but he knew he had missed when the bell inside the house dinned stridently again.

"He's gone over the wall!" ejaculated Farnum. "He'll find the rest of them and bring them back! Come on!"

He ran across the lawn, with Kirby at his heels, made straight for the open side door, plunged through, slammed and locked it after them, and ran along the hall into the drawing room. Corwell and his niece stared wildly at them; there was no one else in the room, except the corpse which had been placed on a divan and covered with a rug.

"Farnum!" exclaimed Corwell. "You got away from them?"

"They never had me," returned the other with a wild laugh. "When I saw you and Daley were down, I ran out a side door and over the wall. They couldn't catch me. I led them a long way through the woods, and then doubled back—you know why. Didn't expect to find one here, but there was. Maybe he got tired running and came back to wait for the others."

"Where's Gorman?" broke in Kirby.

"He ran out of the house when he heard the shot," answered Gloria.

Kirby silently swore. One fault of Gorman's was that he would abandon any post when he thought his friend was in danger. Kirby ran out the front door and rounding the southeast corner of the house, called his partner's name. There was no reply. He advanced into the starlight, sweeping the shadowy lawn with a searching gaze, repeating his call. Nowhere did a leaf rustle, nor was there any reply. The still, mysterious night had engulfed Butch Gorman without a trace. Baffled, confused, and with an icy hand of fear at his spine, Kirby turned and hurried back into the house.

Gloria was staring pallidly out of the broken door, and Farnum and Corwell, in the drawing room, were engaged in some kind of an altercation.

"I tell you," Corwell was saying hotly, "you should not have returned here! You have already drawn down ruin on this house. Ditta Ram's devils have sworn to murder everyone in it, because we harbored you—"

Kirby interrupted bluntly.

"Look here," he said, tense with anger. "Gorman and I have been groping in the dark, not knowing what we were up against. Now he's disappeared, and I don't know where to look for him, or what step to take next. I want to know what this is all about. I'll be damned if I'm going to get my throat cut without knowing why!"

Farnum started to speak, but Corwell put him aside with a nervous gesture. The older man had a haggard, desperate look, and evidently Gloria had told him he could trust the detective.

"I'll tell you!" said Corwell. "A year ago Farnum came to me and wanted me to finance a venture in India. I'd known him in China, knew him to be a capable man, though reckless. I did not then know how utterly unscrupulous he was."

"Thanks!" murmured Farnum sardonically. He looked like a medieval soldier of fortune, with his disheveled hair, reckless eyes and a bandage on his arm.

"He was after the treasure of Akbar, emperor of India in the sixteenth century. The Great Moghul is supposed to have hidden a vast hoard which was never discovered by his successors. I financed

Farnum as a gamble, and almost forgot about him. A week ago he returned, and said he had found the treasure—"

"Let me have the pleasure, since we're spilling everything," broke in Farnum mockingly. "There was a Hindu who knew more about the treasure than I did, but not quite enough to find it. He was a Brahman who'd lost his caste. I don't know what his real name was, but he called himself Ditta Ram. He was in a prison in India, and I got him out. In doing it I had to kill a man—a white man. Ditta Ram and I agreed to combine our knowledge, find the treasure and split it, and what he told me enabled me to find it. It's hidden under an old temple near Agra—just where, I'm not saying. It's guarded by a society of Muhammadan fanatics who call themselves Sons of Akbar, headed by a man named Ahmed Shah—but I fooled *them* to a turn, and got away. I couldn't bring the gold—there's a whole crypt of it. I did bring away a fortune in jewels. Some day I'll get the gold too! Ditta Ram wasn't with me when I found the stuff, and I decided I didn't need him anymore, and I hated the idea of sharing the gems with him, so I knocked him in the head and threw him into the Jumna River. Thought sure I'd finished him, but the devil takes care of his own. Before I could get out of India I learned he was alive and on my trail with a gang of Thugs he'd managed to get control over. Those cursed Sons of Akbar were after me too, and I managed to get both gangs to fighting with each other, and during the fireworks I got away.

"I smuggled the jewels out of India, and I smuggled them into America. But I hadn't shaken Ditta Ram and his Thugs; they were right on my heels the night I came to Corwell Manor. We've been standing siege ever since. You can see why I don't want the police in on the business, and neither does Corwell; he doesn't want it known that he's partners with a smuggler and a murderer!"

Corwell winced, and Farnum laughed maliciously. The man was equally devoid of fear and morals.

"And now what?" he demanded.

"I'm going out and hunt for Gorman," said Kirby. "You people can barricade the house again, or if you want to chance it, take my car and run for it."

"We'd never get away," said the girl. "If they have Gorman, it's a sign that the house is surrounded."

"I've denned up as long as I'm going to," said Farnum. "I thought we could wear them out, but it's useless. I'm going to take my chance outside. You've wanted me to go, Corwell; well, I'm going, and I'm taking the jewels—all of them."

"It would give me the utmost pleasure to see the last of you and your infernal jewels!" exclaimed Corwell fervently. "According to the note the man Khemsa threw over the wall at the beginning of this affair, my niece and I are to be killed in any event, for protecting you, so I doubt if your belated flight will save us, but I prefer not even to die in your company!"

Farnum laughed without resentment, turned to a picture on the wall and drew it aside, revealing a small wall safe. This he manipulated and pulled open—to recoil with a searing imprecation. The safe was empty.

"The jewels!" he exclaimed furiously. "They're gone! You double-crossed me, Corwell! You took them, you lying hypocrite!"

As if beside himself he rushed at Corwell and seized the older man by the throat. The next instant he stretched his full length on the floor as Kirby's right jolted hard against his jaw. He was rising, convulsed with fury, when he checked on one knee, his expression changing. Somewhere behind the house there sounded a low cry, and the noise of a desperate struggle.

.3.

When Gorman heard the shot outside, his only thought was that Kirby was in trouble, and his reaction was instinctive. Ordering his companions to stay where they were, he rushed out of the house. Not knowing the arrangement of the building, he made his exit by way of the front door, raced down the long verandah and plunged around the southeast corner of the house. As he made the turn he saw two figures enter the side door, and even in the starlight he recognized one as Kirby. Who the other might be he had no idea, but their haste suggested flight, so he crouched low to see who was pursuing them. But nothing appeared, and it occurred to him to make a round of the house before he returned indoors. He felt confident of Kirby's ability to handle things inside. But the restless instincts handed down to him by pioneer sires were whispering to him.

He traversed the full length of the house, moving as noiselessly as the Indians his ancestors fought, and was rounding the south-western corner, when he heard the faint rasp of a bolt being drawn, inside the house. He dropped flat, and peering around the corner, saw a door partly open. A shadowy hand rested on the jamb, and a dark face peered out. He caught the gleam of the eyes in the starlight.

Then he heard Kirby shouting up toward the front part of the building, and the face and hand were quickly withdrawn, the door closed. Turning his head, he saw Kirby appear around the southeast corner, repeating his call. But Kirby could not see Gorman as the latter lay in the deep shadow by the house, and the Texan dared not answer or make a signal for fear of being discovered by the unknown lurking at the back door.

Kirby turned back and vanished around the house, and Gorman lay still and waited. Just as he was beginning to fear that the skulker had decided to try another exit, the door opened again. A broadly built man came out noiselessly, closing the door behind him. He moved away toward the south, his course carrying him parallel with the wall. And as he reached the corner, Butch launched himself from the ground, lashing out for his jaw with all his power.

The stranger was quick, for all his bulk. He uttered a startled cry as he recoiled and Gorman's fist missed his chin by a fraction of an inch. Then before Butch could recover his balance, the man was at his throat, stabbing and slashing like a madman. The very frenzy of his attack—which screamed of panic—robbed it of accuracy. The knife ripped Gorman's coat and drew blood from his neck, and then Butch caught the other's wrist with his left hand, and drove his right fist to the wrist in the man's midriff.

The fellow collapsed with a gasp, and from his garments, as he fell, tumbled something which burst open on the ground and disgorged a double handful of objects that shone in the starlight like drops of frozen fire.

"Judas!" muttered Gorman, absently mopping the blood off his neck. He bent, swept up the jewels and replaced them in the case—a curiously carved metal box—and stuck the box under his arm. There was the sound of quick footsteps in the house and he straightened, his hand closing on the hilt under his coat. The sting of steel had roused the hot blood of the Borderman, and he was about through with fist work for the night. But the door burst open to emit Kirby, gun in hand.

"That you, Butch? You're hurt! You're bleeding!"

A low laugh reassured him.

"Just a scratch. Got a prisoner, and loot, Brent." Gorman hauled the groaning captive to his feet with one hand and shoved him toward the door, bent double and holding his belly. Farnum shouldered Kirby aside in his haste.

"I told you to stay with Corwell and the girl," snapped Kirby, but Farnum ignored him. His face was thrust close to the prisoner's.

"Ditta Ram!" he snarled.

"I reckon he's been hiding in the house all the time we've been here," said Butch. "That must have been him we heard moving in the drawing room before we went in. He had these. No, you don't!"

He had displayed the jewels, jerking them away when Farnum pounced at them.

"The jewels of Akbar!" exclaimed Farnum with a savage oath. "So it wasn't Corwell! It was you who got them!"

He trembled in his passion, seeming to hesitate between attacking the Hindu or Gorman, and Kirby shoved him back into the house.

"Bring that Hindu into the drawing room, Butch," he said, locking the door behind him. "I'd have thought those Thugs that were chasing Farnum would have been back by now."

"They probably are," snarled Farnum. "But they know now that we have reinforcements, and Ditta Ram isn't out there to lead them, so they're wary. They're out there beyond the wall, I'll stake my life on it."

Ditta Ram made no resistance. He was getting his breath back, and his groans ceased. With Gorman's big fist locked in his collar he was escorted through the house into the drawing room, where Corwell and Gloria stared at him. Ditta Ram was a portly man, not much darker than Farnum. His face was marked by dissipation and excesses, but it lacked the utterly inhuman quality that had characterized Khemsa and the other Thug. They were mere bestial demons; Ditta Ram was still a man, though a criminal without scruples. There was the suggestion of a grim smile on his lips as he looked at Farnum, and the white man grinned mirthlessly back at him. They were akin in roguery, at least.

"So you stayed to cop the gems while your Thugs chased me, eh?"

"It occurred to me that the jewels were probably hidden in the house," admitted the Brahman in perfect English. "So I did not join in the pursuit. It did not take me long to find the wall safe and open it. I have had experience in that line." He glanced at his long, dexterous fingers, too nimble to be the fingers of an honest man. "You people entered the house just after I had secured the jewels. I went quietly up the stairs, and after listening awhile, descended the stair in the back part of the house and was about to take my departure when Fate, in the person of a human tiger intervened."

Kirby took the jewel-case and laid it open on the table. The gems were cut in an archaic fashion, and they burned and glowed like a heap of living fire, reflecting a thousand colors. The hunger of wolves burned in the eyes of Ditta Ram and of Farnum.

"The jewels of Akbar!" muttered the Brahman, licking his lips. "The plunder of India!"

"And we've got them—and you!" mocked Farnum, a red glint of menace flaming luridly in his eyes.

"On the contrary," answered Ditta Ram coolly. "I have you!"

"What do you mean?" demanded Kirby. "We hold you hostage. If your men attack us, we'll shoot you like a dog."

"That would only infuriate my followers," retorted Ditta Ram. "You are surrounded. The telephone wires are cut. We have broken a breach in the west wall, and can enter without setting off the burglar alarms. We have killed one of your men, and Khemsa has doubtless slain the man he trailed to the city. As soon as he returns, the Thugs will have a leader as capable as I. Do you think you can stay here forever, holding me prisoner and fighting them off?"

Kirby did not reply. Ditta Ram was their prisoner, but they were still prisoners in the house, surrounded by his followers.

"Listen!" Ditta Ram lifted a hand. From the woods outside came that same quavering weird call that Kirby had heard before.

"They are there," said the Brahman serenely. "I am your only hope; they lust for your lives. They are merely blood-mad beasts, whom only I can control. Slay me, and you remove their last restraint. But I am a human being, able to reason and compromise."

Kirby caught him up at that word.

"What is your idea of a compromise?"

"Khemsa and his men want your lives; that is part of their religion. But I wish only the jewels, and the secret of Akbar's treasure."

"You'll never get that!" snarled Farnum. "Torture couldn't wring it out of me."

"I had hoped to make the experiment," retorted Ditta Ram. "But this feud is at a deadlock. You surround me, my men surround you. If you kill me, they will kill you. On the other hand, if they attack you, I am likely to be slain by way of reprisal. I do not care to be made a martyr. You might threaten to kill me, and they might make you promises; but they would not keep them. They have no code of honor, like ordinary men. But you can trust me. Give me the jewels and release me, and I will take the Thugs and go. I do not demand the secret of the gold. Each of us must sacrifice something to strike an even balance. I take the jewels, you keep the secret of the gold."

Kirby did not at once reply.

"What about me?" demanded Farnum.

"If you stay out of India, you will not be molested. But if you ever return, it will be your life or mine!"

"Yours now!" snarled Farnum, and tearing a rapier from the wall, he lunged at the defenseless Brahman. Kirby struck up the blade and Gorman, with an oath, tore the sword from Farnum's hand and hurled the adventurer back against the wall with bone-shaking violence.

"One more move like that, Farnum," he promised, fully roused, "and I'll cripple you for life!" Their eyes clashed murderously, and then Farnum laughed mockingly, wiping a trickle of blood from his lips.

"I seem to be outvoted," he said. "But you're fools to trust that brown devil."

"How do we know you'd keep your word?" demanded Kirby.

The Brahman's eyes met his squarely. Rogue though he was, yet somewhere there was a vestige of honor left in him.

"You do not. You have only my word."

"Will you swear—" began Corwell.

There was bitterness in Ditta Ram's laugh. "What are oaths to a man who has lost his caste? If you make me swear an oath I will break it. But if I give my promise freely, I will keep my word."

"You're a bit sick of this siege, aren't you?" said Kirby slowly.

"Yes," answered the Hindu frankly. "It was not I who condemned to destruction all in this house. That was Khemsa's idea. It is part of his ghastly cult. He will object to any bargain that spares lives. But I can manage him."

Kirby turned to Corwell. "According to what Farnum says, you have a claim to half these jewels. Are you willing to give them to Ditta Ram?"

"Willing?" exclaimed Corwell, mopping the sweat from his skin. "I am eager to see the last of the accursed things!"

"And so everybody agrees to sacrifice me," gibed Farnum.

"I don't see why all the rest of us should be sacrificed for you," retorted Kirby. "If you had your desserts, you'd hang. Besides, this is to save your life as much as the rest of ours."

Farnum made a gesture that for the first time betrayed his desperation.

"Do what you like; we'll all be dead before morning anyway."

Kirby closed the jewel-case and handed it to Gorman.

"I'm going to trust you part way, Ditta Ram," he said. "You and I are going out together to talk with these Thugs."

"What!" It was a cry from Gloria and Corwell. The girl stared at him as if he had taken leave of his senses.

"Gorman will keep the jewels," said Kirby. "We'll go to the gate and you'll call out to your men that I'm not to be harmed. You'll call them to the other side of the gate and tell them—in English—to go. When I'm sure they're gone, we'll return to the house and wait until morning. Then, if they are really gone, we'll give you the jewels and let you go."

"Brent, you're crazy!" cried Gorman. "What's to prevent them from killing you and rescuing Ditta Ram? Or grabbing you for a hostage?"

Kirby continued to address the Hindu.

"If there's any hint of treachery, Gorman here will dump the jewels down the sewer. They'll be gone forever."

"No!" involuntarily exclaimed Ditta Ram, evincing more emotion than he had yet shown.

"Not if you play fair."

"But how do I know that you will?"

"You'll have to trust me," answered Kirby. "Just as I am trusting you."

"Very well," said Ditta Ram. "I trust you. I agree."

Farnum laughed with bitter mockery, his eyes dancing devilishly, as he stood with legs thrown wide, bending the gleaming rapier between his hands.

"Don't trust him! Throw the jewels down the sewer and cut his throat! Throw his body out where the Thugs can see! And then we'll all die fighting!" A gnawing madness seemed to have Farnum in its grip. The long strain was telling; the man was cracking in his own peculiar way.

Kirby did not reply, nor did he answer Gorman's angry protests. He showed his pistol to Ditta Ram, and replaced it in his coat pocket.

"I trust you just as far as you trust me. Go ahead."

They advanced out on the verandah; the starlight was not yet paling, but a hint of dawn was in the light breeze. On all sides the silence brooded, tense, enormous, as if the monstrous gods of India crouched among the trees, ready to leap and crush—Kirby forced such vagrant thoughts out of his mind. He did not look back at the doorway, where, despite orders to close and bar the portal, he knew Butch Gorman stood silently watching. And he knew the girl, too, was watching, unspeaking, over Gorman's shoulder.

As they went down the wall toward the great iron gate, Kirby felt the glare of hidden eyes upon him. Ditta Ram began calling the names of his men in a rich deep voice that carried far. There was no response. He called again, warning the unseen watchers that the white man with him was not to be harmed, telling them a bargain had been struck. There was no reply. Before they reached the gate Ditta Ram halted, turning to Kirby a face that showed tense in the starlight.

"They don't answer me! They think it is a trap! They think you are covering me with a gun in your pocket, and forcing me to say these things! Trust me! Let me go on to them alone!"

"Do you take me for a fool?" demanded Kirby.

"Listen, *sahib!*" begged Ditta Ram, reverting to semi-vernacular in his urgency. "You are in terrible danger! I understand their minds. They do not believe that I have made a bargain. They think I am doing this under compulsion of death, and at any moment they may strike you down. You are almost within dart-range of the wall, and they are there, on the other side, even though we can't see them. They will kill you and then your friend will throw the jewels down the sewer! They will be gone forever, the jewels that mean more than life to me!"

Sweat beaded the Brahman's face, and he was trembling. Kirby was impressed. After all, it was the jewels, not the pistol in his pocket, that held Ditta Ram in bondage to him.

"Go back!" begged the Hindu. "Go back, before they kill you! I will keep my promise to you. I would not keep a promise to Farnum, but you are a man of honor, and I will not lie to you. I will go to them and send them away, and then I will return to you and remain your prisoner until daybreak. You must trust me! In a moment they will loose death on you, and I cannot stay them."

Kirby made a quick decision, based on a deep knowledge of human nature.

"All right," he grunted. "But remember: if you don't put in your appearance in ten minutes, the jewels are gone forever."

"I will keep my word!" exclaimed the Brahman. Lifting his voice he called to the silent wall and the dark woods beyond. "Do not harm the white man! He is going back to the house, and must not be harmed! I am coming to you alone and unhurt."

Kirby backed up the walk toward the house, unable, in spite of himself, to turn his back on those lurking shadows. When he had covered half the distance to the verandah, Ditta Ram had opened the gate and stepped into outer darkness.

Kirby halted, wondering what kind of a fool he was, assailed by black doubt and icy fear. Behind him he could sense the tense silence that gripped the house. Down by the gate, outside the wall, there was an unintelligible muttering going on, that rose higher and higher until the different voices separated themselves and became distinct. Then, suddenly, shockingly, they were drowned in a blood-freezing scream. Kirby jumped and swore. And in through the gate, slamming it frantically behind him, a figure came reeling drunkenly. "Sahib!" the figure screamed. "Help! Help!"

"Ditta Ram!" yelped Kirby, and ran toward the shape which came staggering toward him, streaming blood. Dark figures clustered at the gate—which had locked automatically—and he poured a stream of lead through the grille. They scattered, and he reached the Brahman just as the man collapsed, turning up to him an agonized and blood-dripping face.

"Khemsa!" he mouthed hysterically. "He has turned on me—"

Kirby grabbed his collar and began dragging him back up the walk. Somewhere a police alarm pealed, and he blazed away at a dark shape that appeared momentarily above the wall. "Butch!" he yelled urgently. "*Butch!*"

Gorman was coming down the walk like a stampeding bull.

"They've knifed Ditta Ram!" yelled Kirby. "They'll be over the wall in a second! Help me get him back to the house!"

Gorman stooped, gripped the bleeding Hindu and slung him over his shoulders like a sack of wheat. Then he ran toward the verandah, carrying with ease a weight at least equal to his own. Kirby followed him, facing the wall, expecting an instant charge to follow the knifing of the Brahman.

Gorman charged on through the door and dropped Ditta Ram on a divan. Kirby slammed the broken door and jammed the chair in place, then turned back to the bewildered group.

"It's the death-grip now," he snarled. "Ditta Ram was our only hope, and they've turned on him."

He turned to the divan, and then halted, realizing that there was nothing that could be done for the Brahman. The miracle was that he was still living, with those ghastly wounds in him.

"Khemsa!" he gasped through blue lips. "He has returned, mad with hate at the men who struck him down. He accused me of treachery—of using the votaries of Kali for my own ends, and then discarding them at my pleasure. He cares nothing for jewels.

He is blood mad. He will kill—kill you all—as he has killed me. The jewels! Where are they?"

The girl, pity and horror shadowing her dark eyes, took them and placed them in his hands. The bloody fingers closed lovingly on the arabesqued case, and a travesty of a smile twisted the crimson-smeared features.

"The jewels of Akbar!" muttered the Brahman. "For them he plundered an empire. For them I bartered my soul—" And clutching them close to his bloody bosom he died.

The others stared at each other, haggardly.

"And what now, Mister Detective?" Even such a moment could not drown Farnum's barbed irony.

"Fight!" muttered Kirby. "Are there any guns here?"

"The Thugs took them all when they ransacked the house," answered Corwell.

"One gun between us, and one cartridge in it!" Kirby glanced despairingly at his automatic. "And a broken door to keep them out. Anyway, they're still outside the wall. We'll know when they come over it, because the alarms are still working." He had forgotten the Brahman's boast concerning the breached wall. "We'd better turn out that light. They'll be shooting us through the windows."

"They can't see through the shutters," said Farnum brusquely. "We'll need the light, if they break in. They see like cats in the dark. They're rotten shots, and they won't use guns unless they have to. Khemsa had a blowgun and darts—"

"I broke it," said Gorman.

"No matter. Knife and silk cord—that's their way."

"Well," said Kirby wearily, "let's look to our defenses. All the doors downstairs are locked except that broken one. They'll probably make their assault on it. Butch, go upstairs and see if you can find a place we can defend up there. If they get in the house, we ought to have another place we can fall back on."

Gorman nodded and mounted the stair. He did not seem perturbed. He had been in close places before, and under his armpit nestled a keen-pointed razor-edged answer to his enemies that had guarded his life many a time in the past.

Corwell sank down on a divan, seemingly near the end of his endurance. Farnum seemed jerky, restless, but not intimidated.

"Why can't we be stationed each at an outer door?" he demanded.

"Not enough of us," answered Kirby. "We've got to concentrate our forces in one spot, and fight it out there. God, to think that a thing like this can happen in Twentieth Century America!"

He was thinking of the girl, looking at her, pitying her from the bottom of his heart.

"It's so still!" she whispered. She was pale, but there was no hysteria in the dark eyes she lifted to his. Her hand instinctively sought his.

"You're brave," he said simply. "I wish I had half your courage. I—what's that?"

From the floor above sounded a sudden rush of feet, the impact of heavy bodies, a loud cry. Kirby took a long stride toward the stair up which Gorman had disappeared—Corwell, glancing through the heavy curtains into the darkness of the hallway, screamed: "Look out! *They're in the house!*"

And then the shadows disgorged them in a frenzied rush that seemed to spew fantastic figures out of the dark—half-naked men, dark-skinned, muscular, with long black hair sweeping their shoulders, knives in their hands and murder in their redly gleaming eyes.

In the fleeting instant that was given him Kirby remembered the hole in the west wall where men could crawl through without touching off the alarm—knew that the invaders had silently forced a door or window in the rear and attacked both floors at once. The rest was red fury and madness, an end to plot and counterplot, to stealth and intrigue. It was a crimson climax of hand-to-hand slaughter, primitive and bestial.

He fired his last bullet pointblank and saw a man go down; saw Corwell crumpled under the blow of a bludgeon. He heard the girl scream as he parried with his empty gun the slashing knife of a rabid-eyed fanatic. They were all about him; he dodged and struck instinctively. He saw Farnum run a frothing devil through the body, as the gun in his own hand crashed down on a Thug's head. Then the broken door splintered behind them. In it loomed the giant Gorman had slugged in the firm's office: Khemsa, more gigantic than ever. With a fierce cry Farnum wheeled toward him, when a knife, wielded from behind with bestial force, plunged into the adventurer's back, severing his spine.

Kirby was trying to reach the man who had Gloria bent back across his knee, strangling her slowly, grinning in awful delight. Grimly the detective fought, but his strength was waning. Hands clung to him, dragging him down. Bludgeons swung at him, and knives hacked at him. The blood roared in his temples and his limbs seemed dead. Dimly in a mist he saw Gloria writhing weakly between the merciless dark hands—Khemsa's hateful face leered at him out of the mist—he was down, unable to rise—and Butch was dead—

But Butch was not dead. The men who had quietly mounted the back stair and come along the upper corridor were ahead of those below. As Gorman stepped out of the radius of light welling up from below, a knife licked venomously at him from the shadows. He ducked before his conscious mind registered the attempt, felled the man with a poleaxe blow, and then whipped out his bowie knife, recognizing the death grapple. Another Thug was on him like a leopard, but that Thug was no quicker nor more savage than that son of the Southern Border. Butch gutted him before he could guard himself, slashed downward through the neck of the other man, who was stabbing at his legs, and then Gorman came down the stairs like a Panhandle sandstorm, knife-first—the terrible, fifteen-inch stabber of the southwestern pioneers.

A man springing up the steps to meet him was impaled on the keen point, and then Butch hit the floor feetfirst, ducking a bludgeon aimed at him, and ploughed like a bull through the screeching, stabbing mob straight at the man who was strangling Gloria. Warned by strident howls, the Thug turned, but not in time. Gorman ripped his throat wide open so the spurting blood drenched the girl's dress as she fell fainting.

A knife dug fiercely into Gorman's thigh, but he did not pause. He plunged into another writhing group, slashing, hacking and kicking, trying to reach Kirby, when a knife licking past his ear brought him around to face Khemsa. The giant Thug wore a bestial grin of bloodlust and self-confidence. But he had never faced the berserk ferocity of the old pioneer stock. His thrust cut thin air and he was down, ripped open from groin to breastbone before he realized his danger.

Gorman stooped, ducking a blow aimed at the base of his skull, grasped Kirby's collar and pulled him clear. A knife tore along his ribs, bringing a stream of blood, another slashed fiercely at his leg, and he felt the limb go suddenly numb. As he staggered, a club smashed down on his head, sending a wave of blackness like a curtain across his brain, and blinding him with a gush of blood. He shook his head stubbornly, keeping his feet, cleared a space with a devastating sweep of his dripping blade, and reeled backward, dragging Kirby with him.

He felt the wall at his back and fell against it, legs wide braced, knife lifted. The room with its dead men floated in a crimson haze, through which shadows slunk toward him. He shook the blood and fog out of his eyes, and waited, glaring from burning eyes, bloody, indomitable, a fearsome figure at bay. This, he knew, was in truth the death-grip. He alone of all his party was on his feet, and now through the fog he saw a gleam of blue steel in the hands of one of the Thugs. They dared not close with him; they had fallen back on foreign weapons at last. Butch glared full into the muzzle of the shotgun, and the blazing eyes behind it. He saw the finger crooking on the trigger, and he tried to nerve his crippled leg to leap and strike home with his red knife. But it was as if he stood on a dead thing of wood. With a savage, inarticulate cry he lurched away from the wall, falling headlong and stabbing thin air as he fell, deafened by the reverberation of the exploding shotgun. Yet even so it seemed that a fraction of an instant before the gun roared, a pistol cracked.

Marveling that he was still alive, his ears numbed by the explosion, Gorman struggled up on one arm, glaring at the figure that stretched near him. It was the Thug, still gripping the shotgun, his brains oozing from a neat round hole in his head. Smoke floated through the room in blue wisps, and he was aware that the other Thugs had vanished—there had been at least three or four of them. Outside the house he heard sounds of a brief, fierce struggle—clash of steel, the crackle of shots, and a howl that broke short in a gurgle. Then he looked up suddenly, to see a man standing almost over him—a tall, dark man in a turban, his arms folded. He looked down tranquilly, contemplatively at the prostrate white man.

"You're the man I slugged in the street below the agency office," said Gorman dazedly, and tried to struggle up, gripping his knife. But the movement caused a sick dizziness to sweep over him, blinding him, and when he recovered his senses, he found himself lying on a divan, and a strange, bearded man was stanching his wounds and bandaging them with swift, efficient fingers.

"Where's Kirby, and the girl?" demanded Butch groggily, and the stranger smiled and pointed. Gorman saw Kirby sitting on a chair nearby, looking pale and haggard, and being attended to by other dark, bearded men, and yet others were working over Corwell and Gloria who were stretched out on divans. The room looked like a shambles, with its blood and corpses.

"How is he?" That was Kirby, looking anxiously at the prostrate Gorman. He was answered by the man Butch had seen first, who now stood in the center of the room, arms folded serenely.

"He has been terribly punished, but he will live. The girl and the other man, they are not badly hurt. They will be all right when they regain consciousness."

"But who are you men?" Kirby's head was still swimming, and he was not sure just what had happened since he had come to himself to see the room full of bearded strangers.

"We are the Sons of Akbar," answered the other. "I am Ahmed Shah."

"The guardians of Akbar's treasure?" exclaimed Kirby.

Ahmed Shah bowed. "Our society has been true to its trust for three hundred years. Great is our shame that that man who lies dead there—Farnum—tricked us and stole part of the forbidden treasure. We had overtaken him before he left India, but Ditta Ram and his Thugs interfered with us, drawing doom upon themselves. Again, in America we lost all trace of him, and of the Thugs. Tonight, in the city, I chanced to see Khemsa the Strangler enter your office. I hoped he would lead me to Farnum's hiding place, for it was our duty to recover the jewels, and to see that Ditta Ram and his men did not learn the secret of the gold. But when you came forth, and I accosted you to learn what had become of Khemsa, the big man, thinking me an enemy, struck me senseless.

"When I came to myself, you had departed, I knew not whither. I went into your office, and found Khemsa lying senseless. I hid myself and awaited until he had regained his senses, and then I followed him, gathering my people as I went. We lost him in the woods, but the sound of battle guided us here."

"I don't remember all that happened," said Kirby. "I remember a shot—"

"The Thug with the shotgun fired as your friend lunged at him. But I put a bullet through his head an instant before he pulled the trigger, so the gun was harmlessly discharged into the air. My men then took care of the others who tried to flee from the house."

"It all seems tangled," muttered Kirby. The other smiled like a benevolent patriarch.

"Later you will understand," he said. "We must go now. Farnum is dead, Ditta Ram is dead and so are his Thugs, and our work is done here. We understand that you are blameless, having no share in the looting of the treasure the lord Akbar left in our keeping. Allah keep you!"

He bowed, the jewel case under his arm, and his men likewise bowed, backing out, leaving in Kirby's dizzy mind a confused impression of bobbing turbans and beards bristling in the friendliest of smiles. Then they were gone, and a hint of dawn was stealing in through the shutters.

Kirby rose and weaved his way to the divan where Gloria lay. The girl was beginning to recover her senses; her lashes trembled on her soft young cheeks, and her hands twitched. Kirby tenderly smoothed back her soft hair and said wearily to Gorman, who had struggled to a sitting posture on the divan: "Butch, has this nightmare been real, or am I nutty?"

"Strange things come out of the East," answered Gorman groggily.

"And other things come out of the West," retorted Kirby; "a man with a knife, for instance." And he glanced again at the staring figures sprawling on the stair and about the room.

Sons of Hate

"Lonesome old place after dark," commented Butch Gorman, rolling a cigarette leisurely. "The only office occupied in a whole buildin' otherwise vacant; no light out there in the hall; one dim bulb hangin' over the stair. Say a man was after either of us, he could hide down there in the lower hall, right under the stair, and drill us as we went up the steps. We'd never see him."

Gorman's remark was characteristic, denoting, not timidity, but the instincts of a man who had spent most of his life in perilous pursuits. Butch Gorman was red-headed, brawny as a bull, a product of the wastelands and the wild countries of the earth; almost too hard and sinewy for a civilized man.

His partner, Brent Kirby, was a contrast to him—slightly above medium height, slim, but compactly built, with dark hair and keenly-chiseled features, with a quickness of speech and action reflecting intense nervous energy.

"A few more clients like Colonel John A. Pembroke," said Kirby, "and maybe we can move into more elaborate quarters."

"He's due here soon, ain't he?" asked Gorman. Kirby consulted his watch.

"Should be here any minute now. He told me he'd be here at ten, sharp. It's ten now. Do you know anything about him?"

"I know him by sight and that's all. You've seen his place—big house and grounds, out beyond the edge of the city. He's lived here only three or four years, I understand. Don't know where he came from—somewhere in the East. Retired millionaire, I reckon. What did he want?"

"He only made the appointment," answered Kirby. "Phoned from his club. Gave no details, but said it was a matter of life and—what's that?"

From somewhere below them rang a strangled, desperate cry, the sound of a struggle.

Kirby was out of his chair and around the desk in an instant, but Gorman was nearer the door, and quick as a huge cat, for all his weight. He reached the door first, dashed across the unlighted corridor and plunged down the stair a pace ahead of Kirby. A small bulb dangled from the ceiling, and its light imperfectly illumined the corridor below. In that light both men saw the crumpled figure sprawled at the foot of the steps, and the muffled shape that darted through the door that opened onto the street.

"Go after him, Butch!" yelped Kirby. "I'll see how badly this fellow's hurt."

Gorman plunged after the fleeing figure, and Kirby bent over the victim who suddenly rose on his hands and knees and glared wildly around. He was a portly man, well advanced in years, with bristling iron-grey moustaches and a rubicund countenance. His top hat, crushed about his ears, showed it had borne the brunt of the attack.

"Where is he?" roared this individual in a voice of surprizing volume. "Where did the scoundrel go?"

"Out the door?" answered Kirby. "Who was he?"

"How the devil should I know?" roared the old man irascibly. "I was groping my way to the stair, along this abominably lighted hallway, when I was struck down by someone I never saw. But for my hat, I'm sure the first blow would have cracked my skull. I fell on my face and contrived to cover my head with my arms, while the villain struck at my head repeatedly—dammit, sir, I believe my arm is broken!"

"Just badly bruised, I think," decided Kirby, helping him to his feet, and inspecting the member in question. "Here's Butch."

The big redhead strode in through the door, shaking his head disgustedly. "Got away," he growled. "Ducked around the corner just as I hit the sidewalk. Disappeared—probably into an alley—before I could round the corner. Couldn't tell anything about him except that he had a long coat on, and his hat was pulled low, with a scarf or something wrapped around his face. Kept his head down as he ran. This is Colonel Pembroke?"

The visitor verified the supposition in a voice that suggested a temper in constant eruption, and added: "Let's don't stand here on this infernal stair! He may come back and shoot me through the doorway."

Kirby started up the stair and Pembroke followed, dusting and adjusting his clothing, and cursing in a steady stream. Age had not tempered his fiery disposition.

Back in the office Kirby closed the door whose frosted glass bore the title: "Kirby & Gorman, Detective Agency," and gave their visitor a chair. Gorman saw that the door was locked, and took his seat somewhat to the side, where he could watch both their guest and the door, while he rolled another cigarette.

"You have no idea as to the identity of your attacker, Colonel Pembroke?" Kirby asked.

"I have a very good idea," answered Pembroke grimly. "Look here!" He drew a folded newspaper from inside his coat and slapped it down on the desk, glaring at Kirby in his aggressive manner. Kirby took it up and unfolded it. It was the picture section of a Sunday edition of a nationally circulated daily, and was some weeks old. There was an article marked, which was illustrated by three photographs. One was a picture of a house which Kirby recognized as the Pembroke mansion, even before he read the legend beneath; one was a picture of the Colonel himself; the third was the reproduction of a curious statue—that of a cat, crouching as if asleep, her head resting on her outstretched paws.

"Is that a good likeness of myself?" demanded Pembroke.

"Why, yes," answered Kirby. "I'd say that it was."

"Exactly!" snorted Pembroke. "So good it is likely to cost me my life!"

"What do you mean?"

Pembroke leaned toward him, like a giant, bloated, purple-faced toad squatting on the edge of the chair.

"If you had been concealing the very fact of your existence for fifty years," said he, "hiding from a man whose sole aim in life was to kill you, would you like to see your picture and address spread over half the papers of the world?"

"Hardly," said Kirby. "But if you have reason for avoiding publicity, why did you give the reporter the interview?"

Pembroke's strong teeth snapped viciously on a cigar stem.

"I didn't! Do you take me for an utter fool? My empty-headed niece, Constance, is responsible. She knows nothing about my past, and she let a young upstart of a reporter talk her into giving him an old photograph of myself, and letting him take the other pictures. I wasn't even present when the young fool came out to my house 'to get a story.' Bah! With the few vague facts she could give him about my travels, and with some misinformation obtained at the public library, coupled with an unscrupulous imagination, he turned out that highly colored article about my 'adventurous career' and that infernal cat."

Kirby glanced over the article with fresh interest.

"'—Egyptian relic, carved of jade, taken from one of the pyramids,'" he read at random, skipping over the lines. "'Probably belonged to one of the Pharaohs—'"

"The fool hit it there," snarled Pembroke, chewing his cigar savagely. "It *did* belong to a Pharaoh, but it never came from a pyramid. Look here!" Fumbling in his pocket, he drew out an object and laid it on the desk. It was the original of the photograph in the paper.

Kirby took it up and scanned it with deep interest. It was jade of a peculiar deep sea-green, not over seven inches long, but carved with all the artistry of a vanished civilization. Its remarkable antiquity was evident; Kirby commented on that fact.

"Five thousand years old, if it's a day," grunted Pembroke. "Any museum or collector would pay high for it, but I prefer to keep it myself. But look here!" He drew something else from his pocket— an envelope from which he took a piece of paper, which showed to be merely the photograph of the cat, cut from a paper carrying the article under discussion. Above the cat, on the white part of the paper, was drawn a curious symbol.

"I received that this morning," said Pembroke. "I had no intimation, until then, that such an article had been published. I questioned my niece, and learned of her indiscretion. Fearing an instant attack upon my life, I hurriedly left my house and went to my club, where I remained the whole day, in an abominable state of uncertainty and apprehension. This is not a matter I care to put in the hands of the regular police, if I can help it. So I decided at last to call upon you."

Kirby studied the envelope. The address was neatly typed, and there was no return address. The postmark was dated August 3rd.

"Mailed yesterday," muttered Kirby, "and from somewhere in the city. What do you feel it portends, Colonel?"

"There is only one explanation!" cried Pembroke. "The article has been read and the pictures recognized by the man who seeks my life! That stuff is syndicated and goes all around the world."

"And you think it was this man who attacked you tonight?"

"Who else could it have been, sir? I tell you somebody has been watching and following me all day. I have felt it."

"Who knew that you were coming here?" asked Kirby.

"No one in the city. No one, in fact, but my man William, an old and trusted valet. In fact, it was at his suggestion that I turned to you. I had divulged to him some of my fears, and this afternoon I called him from the club, to learn if he had seen any suspicious characters about the estate. He reported he had not, but urged me to secure the assistance of a private detective agency, recommending your own."

"You can trust him?"

"Absolutely."

"Yet *somebody* knew you were coming here."

"I know!" exclaimed the Colonel in a sort of helpless wrath. "I tell you we are dealing with a man fiendishly clever! But let me give you all the details of this matter. First, do you know what that mark is?"

"It looks like a heraldic design, or coat of arms," answered Kirby.

"It is!" snapped Pembroke. "The arms of the Stalbridges, an old south-country family. I was born in England, and I knew the breed, even before I went to Africa. A cold, hard race, proud as Satan, and as unforgiving. For long-cherished hate and merciless vengeance, no breed equals a true-born aristocrat of the old blood."

"Well?"

"Well," snarled Pembroke, rising and pacing back and forth as if his burning thoughts would not allow him to sit still. His small eyes smoldered under his heavy brows, and there was a peculiar suggestion of ruthlessness in the way he ground out his cigar between thick, hairy fingers. The man's animal vitality was almost repellant. "You have heard of the Mahdist rebellion, in the Soudan? Well, I was at Khartoum at the time—"

"That was in 1885," said Kirby, with surprise. Pembroke was much older than he looked. The man carried his age well.

"Exactly. The Dervishes, as the Mahdi's followers were called, took and sacked the town amid horrible scenes of rapine and slaughter. But they didn't kill everybody. Among the prisoners taken were myself, and young Joseph Stalbridge, the explorer.

"Stalbridge had just returned from an expedition up towards the sources of the Nile. There he had made a most remarkable discovery—he had found the secret crypt of one of the early Pharaohs of Egypt. As you may not know, the mummies of the kings of Egypt were never really placed in the pyramids. They were too easily looted. The Egyptians' conception of immortality was based on the preservation of the physical body.

"So the pyramids were reared as a blind, and false mummies placed in them, while the real corpses of the kings were carried far out into the desert and placed in a hidden crypt, with great stores of treasure, and the slaves who constructed the crypt were then killed, to keep the place a secret.

"Well, Stalbridge discovered one of these crypts, and brought away, not only the mummy, but an enormous fortune in gold and jewels. But he kept it a secret, because times were troublous in the country then. No one knew he'd brought back anything but the mummy. He hid the treasure in a well in Khartoum.

"He told me all this during our captivity together. But he was overheard speaking of the treasure by a spy who betrayed him to the Mahdi. The Mahdi had him put to the torture, to make him tell where the stuff was hidden. The spy hadn't learned that."

Pembroke was silent for awhile, his eyes glittering unpleasantly as he unconsciously twisted his long moustache.

"I was poor," he said abruptly. "I'd worked like hell for a bare living ever since I was a ragged child in London. Stalbridge had told me where the stuff was hidden. I knew the Mahdi would kill him anyway. I made a break and escaped—beat the Dervishes to the well, got the loot out and carried it off on camels."

"And what about Stalbridge?" asked Kirby.

"When they came and found the well empty," said Pembroke, "they thought Stalbridge had lied to them. They mutilated him and left him for dead in one of the alleys in Khartoum. But he had all the stubborn stamina and toughness of the Sussex Stalbridges. He managed to crawl into an empty boat, drifted down the Nile, and eventually reached Wadi Halfa. He lived long enough to tell his story to his brother, James Stalbridge, who was an officer in the garrison at Assouan.

"Meanwhile, I reached France, turned most of my fortune into cash, and settled down to enjoy it. But in 1898, the year that the Mahdi's successor, the Khalif Abdullah, and his Dervishes were smashed at Omdurman, I received news that made me a fugitive. James Stalbridge had resigned his commission and was searching for me, to kill me!

"He blamed *me* for his brother's suffering!—had gotten the idea somehow that I betrayed him to the Madhi; and he felt that he was entitled to the treasure I'd appropriated.

"The Stalbridges knew me only as John Ravenby, a name I had adopted in Africa for my own reasons, and under which I'd lived in France. I came to America and assumed my own name, which I hadn't used since early childhood. One branch of my family had already come to America. They know nothing about my past; to this branch Constance belongs.

"I've lived in various parts of the United States ever since, avoiding publicity, and dragging every sort of a red herring across my trail. But now that's all gone for naught, thanks to that infernal reporter and my idiotic niece."

"And you think it was James Stalbridge who sent you that clipping, and who made the attack upon you?"

"Who else? The arms on the clipping are conclusive proof. Good God, sir, it's like a black horrible shadow out of the forgotten past!"

"The cat was part of the treasure?"

"Yes; it's one of the few relics taken from the crypt that I did not at once convert into cash. There is another, an emerald necklace of even greater value."

"And you wish us—?"

"To protect me!" said Pembroke. "To guard me day and night. You both look like fighters. It will come to a grapple soon; I know the Stalbridges. I don't fear an open fight, with your help. But they are devilishly clever."

"Good enough," said Kirby. "Butch will go with you now, and I'll drive out later, as soon as I attend to some matters here."

Pembroke turned and stared at Gorman's sun-burnt face and powerful frame with approval.

"All right," he grunted, rising, "let's go!"

.2.

Kirby stood on the sidewalk under the streetlamp, watching Pembroke's big car roar away southward, and wishing that he had forced a gun on Gorman. The big redhead was a Texan, but, contrary to popular conceptions, he was no gunman. In fact, he seldom would carry a gun, but depended on a razor-edged knife which he wielded with experience gained in many a bloody brawl south of the Rio Grande, where men wear steel as a natural part of their ordinary costume. Kirby felt that Butch might need a gun before that night was over.

When the car had vanished, he turned back into the hallway, where he was occupied for some minutes with an electric torch. Then he mounted the stair and entered the office, and from a row of shelves that supported a bewildering array of curious titles, he selected a bulky volume, seated himself at his desk and began to read.

Presently he lifted his head, thinking he had heard the stair creak. Before he could investigate, the phone on the desk jangled stridently. He picked it up; over the wire floated Gorman's voice.

"Say, Brent, you better beat it out here if you want to get in on the fun. Things have begun to break."

"What do you mean?" demanded Kirby.

"The Colonel's valet, William, has disappeared! Nobody here when we arrived but Miss Constance and another servant, a Cuban named Juan Perez. He's scared stiff; caught somebody tryin' to break into the house just now. Juan heaved a knife at him and he beat it. I didn't see him. The Colonel's jittery; prowlin' around with an elephant gun. Miss Constance is locked in her room upstairs. Wish she was somewhere else, but the Colonel says there's no place for her to go. You better get over here. I've got a hunch that hell's goin' to pop before daylight."

"I'll be right over," promised Kirby. He visualized his partner at the other end of the wire grinning thinly with the expectation of a battle. "Listen, Butch," he said, unconsciously lowering his voice, "is Pembroke in the room with you?"

"No, he's in his study. Why?"

"Well, I've been checking up on his story. I've got a book here written by a fellow who was at Khartoum, and later a captive of the Mahdi. He mentions Joseph Stalbridge among the white captives of the Mahdi, but doesn't say anything about a John Ravenby being a prisoner."

"And what does that prove?" demanded Gorman.

"Maybe nothing; but it suggests that Pembroke didn't give us the true facts. Anyway, I'll be over there right away."

He hung up the receiver, replaced the volume, reached for his hat—and wheeled suddenly toward the door. His hand froze, halfway to a hidden scabbard.

A figure stood framed against the darkness of the unlighted corridor—a tall, slender man, hat brim shadowing his cold, pallid features. From that shadow gleamed eyes as hard as the steel that shone bluely in his right hand.

"Stand still, Mr. Kirby!" The words were curt, clipped with an English accent. "I don't want to hurt you."

"Who the hell are you, and what do you want?" demanded Kirby.

"Never mind who I am," answered the other. "I'm quite sure you have an idea. But never mind that. I want you to call your partner, at Colonel Pembroke's house, and tell him to bring the Colonel to this office, at once."

"What for?"

"That doesn't interest you. What does interest you is the fact that you'll get a bullet through your bally guts if you don't do as I say."

"You think you could get away with that?" demanded Kirby.

"Why not? It's late; nobody in the building except ourselves; nobody on the street below, not even a bobby. Do as I tell you."

"Get Pembroke here so you can murder him?" said Kirby. "And what about Gorman and me? I suppose you'll eliminate all witnesses!"

"You'll not be hurt if you obey orders," answered the other. "You have no choice. If you refuse, I'll surely kill you. Get Gorman on that phone! I want to hear his voice, and know he's on the wire. Go ahead!"

Slowly Kirby lifted the phone and dialed the number, racking his brain for some subterfuge. Certainly he was not going to tell Gorman to bring the Colonel there to his death, though he knew that if he gave the bald command, Butch would obey him, if he had to slug Pembroke and bring him along senseless. How to warn Gorman without seeming to—the keen, cold face under the narrow hat brim was bent toward him, the muzzle of the automatic unwavering. An English gangster? A new type of criminal? Vividly Kirby recalled Pembroke's words: "A cold, hard race, proud as Satan, and as unforgiving." There was ruthlessness in those eyes of chilled steel, a predatory jut to the thin-nostrilled nose.

"Hello, Butch!" Kirby spoke into the phone, and as the answer came back over the wire, the gunman bent closer, his muzzle almost touching Kirby's coat.

"Yes, this is Butch." The answer was perfectly audible to the man with the gun. He nodded, and drew back slightly, motioning Kirby to go ahead. Kirby set his teeth; his first duty was to his client and his partner. No trick occurred to him. He'd have to do his duty as he saw it, and it wouldn't do to think about what would happen afterwards. He fought against the chill nervousness that was tensing his muscles into rigid cords, against the icy hardening of his spine. He wondered fleetingly how a bullet felt ripping through a man's body at close range, even as he opened his mouth to yell the frantic warning he felt would be his last action on earth.

Butch was inquiring as to what he wanted—his voice ceased abruptly with a dull click at the other end. Kirby stiffened convulsively. He had heard that sound before. "Butch!" he yelled into the mouthpiece, though he knew it was useless. *"Butch!"*

"What's the matter?" exclaimed the Englishman, startled at the change in Kirby's manner.

"The wire's been cut at the other end!" ejaculated Kirby, sweat starting out on his skin as his fear was suddenly transferred from himself to that lonely house in the suburbs. There was a grisly implication in the click of a severed wire.

"What?" The gunman seemed bewildered and perturbed himself. "Give me that phone!" He snatched it, and as he reached, the muzzle wavered for the first time. And Kirby, galvanized by desperation, moved like a steel spring uncoiling. The blow he struck was too quick for the eye to follow. His lightning-like fist smacked terrifically against the Englishman's jaw, and the man went down as though shot through the head, the gun exploding as if with the impact of the blow. The bullet ripped a long tear in Kirby's coat and smashed into the wall.

Kirby was on his victim so quickly it was as if both fell together. Wrenching the gun from the limp hand, he hurled it across the room, tore out a pair of handcuffs, fumbling and sweating in his haste, and clapped them on the man's wrists. He dragged the dazed Englishman to his feet, drawing his own gun as he did so.

"What—what do you—" the man was mumbling groggily, as Kirby headed for the door, fairly dragging him.

"I'm going to Pembroke's house," he gritted between his teeth. "You're coming along. Don't hinder me, if you value your hide!"

He took the dim-lit stair three steps at a time, heedless of his captive's profane protests, dashed out into the street and into the driver's seat of his touring car without checking his speed. He vaguely noted another, bigger, swifter machine stood parked at the curb nearby.

He jerked his prisoner in after him, and slammed him down in the seat.

"One move out of you," he promised, "and I'll bend my gun barrel over your head! You sit there and keep still!"

It was late; he roared down a deserted street. His foot nailed the accelerator to the floorboard, and the car groaned and vibrated with the strain of that headlong pace, but even so it seemed to Kirby in his frantic impatience that he was but crawling. Minutes were like hours until the lights of the city fell away behind him, and he saw a cluster of giant oaks looming against the sky ahead of him.

An iron-wrought gate stood open in a stone wall. He whirled into a winding driveway, flanked by towering black trees, and halted with a scream of brakes a short distance before the wide portico of the great house. Light poured through the cracks of shutters on the lower floor. If tragedy had already stalked in that isolated mansion, there was no external evidence to prove it.

Kirby glared at the shadows about him, cursing the somber oaks and shrubbery which loomed in almost jungle thickness. But he wasted no time. He swarmed out of the car and hauled his prisoner out after him. The man seemed to have fully recovered from the effects of that stunning punch.

"Here, I say," he protested, staggering against the car from Kirby's nervous violence. "No use in being so rough, you know—uh!"

Something whined venomously past Kirby's ear and thudded against bone. The Englishman grunted and went limp in the detective's hands. He slumped against the fender, tumbled to the sward. Kirby wheeled, caught a vague movement in the dense bushes, black in the starlight. From the gun in his hand a crackling stream of fire and lead spurted into the shadows.

The veranda door burst open and a bull's voice boomed above the fusillade.

"Butch!" yelled Kirby. "Hey, Butch—!" His shout was strangled in a gurgle as a steely arm hooked fiercely about his throat from behind. Another hand locked in an unbreakable grip on his right wrist, forcing his gun hand upward. A long leg was wound about one of his, completing his imprisonment. His first thought was that the Englishman had attacked him, but that fellow was down and out; Kirby's free foot, fighting for leverage, struck against his prostrate figure. The detective's slim wiry body was a straining knot of steely sinews, but the unseen assailant was more like an ape than a man.

Kirby felt his head bent unbearably back until he was looking up at the stars that peeped through the oak branches. His gun arm was being almost twisted out of the socket. An acrid body-scent was in his nostrils, an unintelligible gibberish mumbling gutturally in his ear. His brain was swimming, the stars were turning red—dimly he heard the swift, purposeful rush of feet across the grass, and then the impact of a thundering blow. He felt the terrific jolt of that blow himself, through the limbs that imprisoned him, as they gave way. There sounded the fall of a heavy body.

He reeled himself, and then other arms were grasping him— iron arms these, too, but supporting, bracing him, not strangling.

"Butch!" Gorman's face was a pale oval in the starlight.

"What the hell?"

Kirby pulled away and glared at the shadows. In the bushes he had raked with lead something was flopping convulsively; there was a gasping that died away in a gurgle—beyond that there was a padding of swift feet—

"Grab the fellow with the cuffs on!" he gasped, his chest still heaving from that savage struggle. "Never mind the other one. Bring him in! Quick! Another minute and they'll have us cut off from the house!"

Gorman did not waste time in questions. He stooped, grabbed the senseless prisoner and slung him over his shoulder like a sack of grain, and headed for the house. Kirby ran after him, gun in hand, glaring this way and that, thankful that at least the trees and bushes ended some yards from the house.

Up on the wide, pillared veranda, Kirby jerked at the door and swore to find it locked.

"Open up in there!" he yelled, his skin crawling with the fear of a bullet from the dark. "It's me, Kirby!"

"Open, Juan!" roared a familiar voice from within. There came a clicking of bolts and the door opened; light flooded the group on the veranda and something whirred out of the darkness and smashed against the opening door, falling within the threshold. Kirby rushed in, and Gorman followed. A wiry, swarthy man slammed the door and began bolting it. Colonel Pembroke was standing in the center of the room, legs wide braced, a heavy, double-barreled rifle in his hands, his eyes blazing and moustaches bristling. He changed color as he saw the man Gorman dumped down on a divan.

"What does this mean?" he exclaimed.

"The house is surrounded," snapped Kirby; "at least it's being watched." He stooped and picked up the object that had been hurled at them. It was a crudely molded lead slug, and its flattened side, where it had struck the panel, was evidence of the force with which it had been propelled. "Sling," muttered Kirby. "Couldn't be anything else—what's that?"

It was a quick rush of light feet beyond the curtained door, and a slender young girl ran into the room. She stopped short, paling when she saw the man on the divan.

"Constance!" roared Colonel Pembroke. "What are you doing down here? I told you to stay in your room!"

"I heard the shooting!" she faltered. "I was afraid—oh, what has happened?"

"Nothing that concerns you!" blustered the Colonel. "I have told you that violence might be expected as a result of your stupidity! Go back to your room!"

"Stay here if you wish, Miss Pembroke," said Kirby quietly. "It might be best to concentrate our forces in this room. Don't be frightened. We're here to protect you and your uncle. If you could get me some water—"

She hastily complied, and Kirby bent over the senseless man. The Englishman had a ragged cut on the side of his head. The missile that had knocked him senseless had struck glancingly, and Kirby felt that it was only because of that fact that the man was still alive.

"Better take a look at the doors and windows, Butch," he directed, and the big redhead nodded, and vanished through the curtains of the door that led into the wide hall. Kirby, working over his prisoner, mechanically noted that four doors led out of the great, richly furnished room. There was the door opening onto the unlighted veranda; one to the right that gave into a smaller room, a library or study; one on the left hand, and nearer the rear wall which must open directly upon the lawn; and then the wide curtained doorway which gave upon the broad hall. Heavy shutters protected the windows, and the locks on the doors looked strong.

The prisoner was rapidly regaining consciousness, and Kirby beckoned Pembroke who stood and glared down at him. From behind the Colonel, Juan Perez peered fearfully, sallow pale under his dark skin that hinted of negroid blood.

"Do you know this fellow, Colonel Pembroke?" Kirby asked.

Slowly Pembroke shook his head, plainly puzzled.

"I never saw him before in my life," he grunted.

The Englishman groaned and struggled to a sitting posture, lifting his manacled hands to his bandaged head.

"What the devil happened?" he muttered.

"One of your men tried to rescue you, evidently," answered Kirby. "He slung at me and hit you instead."

"What do you mean?" mumbled the other. "My men? I have no men."

"Then who are those fellows out there in the dark?" demanded Kirby, sarcastically.

"I don't know what you're talking about." The man lifted his head, and as he stared directly at Colonel Pembroke, the electric light fell across his face clearly for the first time.

Kirby saw the Colonel's rubicund hue pale.

"God!" he whispered. "A resemblance! A youth, where I expected an old man!" A strange frenzy seemed to seize him. "Damn you, sir!" he shouted. "You are a Stalbridge!"

There was menace and mockery in the other's cold stare.

"Richard Stalbridge, son of James Stalbridge, Lord Grimstead, at your service," he answered with a knife edge of venom in his voice.

The Colonel went livid. He staggered with a terrible oath, as though from a physical impact, then murder flamed in his eyes as he whipped up the elephant gun.

Kirby knocked it up.

"Are you mad, Pembroke?" he cried.

"Let me kill him, sir!" roared the maddened Colonel, while Constance cowered whimpering with terror in a corner; Gorman, summoned by the noise, came suddenly through the curtained door. "He's a devil, like all his family! I know the breed, I tell you! He'll murder us all before this night's over—"

"Take it easy, Colonel." As tranquilly as if he did it with his victim's consent instead of against his wrathful resistance, Gorman twisted the rifle out of Pembroke's grasp with one hand, and with the other shoved the Colonel back and down into an armchair. He had lived too long south of the Border where blood runs hot and untamed, to be disturbed by violence and displays of primitive passion.

He patted Pembroke on the shoulder, impersonally, as one might soothe a horse, tossed the rifle on a table, and resumed his pacing of the room, eyes and ears aware of what went on within, but also alert as a wolf's for any sound from without.

Pembroke and Stalbridge sat glaring at one another, the one white and cold, the other purple-faced and shaking with passion.

"I suppose you traced me by that infernal newspaper article," said the Colonel at last.

Stalbridge nodded. "I'd never seen you, so of course I didn't recognize your picture. But I did recognize that of the cat."

Pembroke shot a murderous glance at his niece, shrinking in a corner, that made her fairly tremble. Kirby frowned. The man was a brute. He looked unusually sinister as he sat there like a fat, bloated, purple toad.

"You slugged Pembroke tonight in the hall below our agency?" asked Kirby abruptly.

Stalbridge shook his head. "I know nothing about that."

"You're a liar," rasped Pembroke. "It was a typical Stalbridge trick—murderers that you all are!"

Stalbridge's laugh was not pleasant to hear.

"Murderers? Then what, in God's name, are you, John Ravenby?"

"Ravenby?" exclaimed Constance in bewilderment. She shrank back as Stalbridge turned his somber stare on her.

"You are his niece, I understand," he said. "Have you never heard the name of Ravenby?"

"Never," she faltered.

"Your uncle wore that name in Africa, fifty years ago," said Stalbridge. "He was a young man then, but well known among the adventurers of the Soudan. Do you know what was his occupation?"

She shook her head mutely.

"He was a slave trader!" said Stalbridge harshly. "A white renegade, working with filthy Arab slavers!"

Constance turned pale, and Kirby was aware of a surge of disgust. Gorman, grandson of slave owners, alone showed no particular concern. Pembroke grunted scornfully. It was as if a mask had fallen from the man, revealing him in all his elemental brutality, his arrogant disdain of their opinions.

"That wasn't the limit of his swinishness," said Stalbridge in a voice as brittle as edged obsidian. His hate was almost tangible, a withering fire that seemed to have consumed all other emotions.

"When the Mahdi rose, the slave traders joined him—and John Ravenby fought against his own color and race in the ranks of filthy black fanatics!"

"You didn't tell us that!" said Kirby.

"I doubt if even he is proud of it," said Stalbridge bitterly. "Did he tell you how he wormed his way into the confidence of my uncle, Joseph Stalbridge, a prisoner captured during the sack of Khartoum?"

"He said they were prisoners together," said Kirby shortly.

"Another lie! He knew Uncle Joseph had brought a mummy down from the sources of the Nile, and he suspected a treasure. He pretended friendship and learned enough to confirm his suspicion. Then he betrayed my uncle to the Mahdi who tortured him, until even Joseph Stalbridge's iron will gave way, and he revealed its hiding place.

"But he lived, in spite of his ghastly mutilations, and reached Assouan. The only thing stronger than the vitality of a Stalbridge is the hate of a Stalbridge." The stare he directed at Pembroke might have been forged of chilled steel.

"Until 1898," he continued, "my father was employed, with all other English officers, in putting down the rebellion. After that he was free to pursue his private vengeance. After Omdurman he questioned hundreds of natives and learned that shortly after the Mahdi's death, which occurred only a few months after the sack of Khartoum, Ravenby had stolen the loot of the Egyptian crypt, which the Mahdi had appropriated himself, out of the Mahdi's treasure house, and fled with it on camel back.

"For years my father hunted him, but he never found him. He has told me the tale a thousand times—taught me to hate the name of John Ravenby as the devil hates holy water!" He shot a glance at the scowling Pembroke which made the allusion to his Satanic majesty not inappropriate. "All my life I have dreamed of the day when I should at last find John Ravenby and pay him for all my family suffered. I was in Australia when I saw the newspaper article—"

"But you had never seen Pembroke," protested Kirby. As long as Stalbridge was in the mood to talk, it was as well to learn all he could.

"I recognized the cat. There were three of these cats in the tomb. One of them Uncle Joseph had sent down the river to my father, along with some other relics, before Khartoum was taken. The cat in the picture was identical with the cat in my father's possession. I sent the article to my father, in England, for identification of the man's photograph, and came on here."

"How long have you been here?" asked Kirby.

"I arrived the morning of the 3rd."

"You mailed that picture with the coat of arms to Colonel Pembroke?"

"Certainly. I could not be certain of my man. An innocent man might have somehow acquired the cat. But his actions on receiving my message would betray him. It did betray him. I watched this house and saw him leave and hurry to town. I followed. All day I loitered near his club. When he came out tonight, with the air of a man whose sins have caught up with him, and drove away, I followed him. I was sure I had the right man. His every action betrayed fear. I lost him for awhile in a traffic snarl, but soon saw his car parked below your detective agency. Then I knew I had the right man. An innocent man would not rush to a private detective agency merely upon receiving a coat of arms scrawled over the picture of an Egyptian cat. Only John Ravenby would understand its significance.

"When he came out and drove away with the redheaded man, Gorman, and you returned to your office, Kirby, I stole upstairs with a vague plan forming in my mind. I overheard your side of the telephone conversation, and my plan was crystallized. That it did not succeed was due to chance."

"Why didn't you shoot Pembroke as he came out of the building?" asked Kirby.

"Shoot him?" Stalbridge's laugh was appalling. "I wanted to get him in my hands—to kill him slowly, as Uncle Joseph died. I wanted to see him writhe, to hear him scream!" His white hands clenched convulsively as he ripped out the last word.

"My God, is this real?" muttered Kirby to himself. To Stalbridge he said: "Why are you telling us all this so freely?"

"Because he thinks he has us at his mercy!" roared Pembroke. "His men surround us—"

"I work alone," answered Stalbridge somberly. "I tell you this because I have no need nor desire to conceal my actions. I am not a criminal; I am a man of honor, paying a debt. As I *will* pay it, in spite of these!" There was a grim finality in his voice as he lifted the handcuffs which glinted in the light. Pembroke blenched.

"Since you admit all these things," said Kirby, "why don't you admit that it was you who slugged the Colonel?"

"Because it wasn't," answered Stalbridge. "I've told you I didn't want to kill him so easily."

Gorman wheeled suddenly at a slight sound in the study. He crossed the floor with a few long strides, jerked open the door—and faced Juan Perez, who was apparently just preparing to emerge.

"What are you doin' in there?" demanded Gorman.

"I was seeing to the locks on the doors and windows opening from the study, *señor,*" answered the Cuban.

"Oh, all right. By the way, Brent," added Gorman, "we've set the burglar alarm for every door and window on the place. Great invention, burglar alarm."

"Come here, Juan," said Kirby, and the Cuban approached respectfully. "You say a man tried to break in here tonight, before I came?"

"*Si, señor,* a white man."

"Why do you say that?" demanded Kirby. "We'd naturally take it for granted that it was a white man."

"You never got a glimpse of that fellow I knocked loose from your neck, tonight, did you, Brent?" Gorman broke in unexpectedly. "He was a nigger!"

"The devil you say!" ejaculated Kirby, and turned to Juan: "Have you seen any colored people lurking around this place?"

"No, no, *señor!*" The Cuban gesticulated vigorously. "It was a white man who tried to break in! Ask *Señor* Gorman!"

"Don't ask me," retorted Gorman. "I never saw or heard him. I heard you yell and ran back to the back part of the house, and you said you'd scared a man away from the door."

"I threw my knife at him," asserted Perez. "Perhaps it was that *hombre* there!" He pointed at Stalbridge.

"It couldn't have been him," said Kirby. "He was listening outside my office door while I was talking to Gorman. He couldn't have gotten to town *that* quick. What about this fellow William?"

"I do not know, *señor*. I knew nothing of any danger threatening *Señor* Pembroke. I spent the evening in the city, at the theater, and when I returned, *Señorita* Constance was in the house alone. Poor William had disappeared."

"What time did you get back from town?"

"A few minutes until ten. I drove there and back in my small car."

"Why, that can't be, Juan!" exclaimed Constance. "Just before you came, I thought I heard a scuffle downstairs, on the side portico. I called William and got no answer. I was afraid to go down and investigate, so I locked my door, and stayed in my room. I noticed the time then, and it was fifteen minutes past ten. It was at least fifteen minutes after that before you came. I heard your car come up the driveway, and when you entered I called down to you, and asked if it was you, don't you remember? Then we discovered that William was gone."

"One forgets these small details," admitted Juan.

"So Juan returned about ten thirty," said Kirby. "And there's no way of knowing just when William vanished."

"It occurs to me, *señor,*" said Perez timidly, "that perhaps this William is a traitor. Could it not be *he* who attacked *Señor* Pembroke, and failing in his attempt, followed him here and tried to break in?"

"I can't believe it," muttered Pembroke. "I trusted William— but, well, what are we going to do about it?"

"We're practically in a state of siege," answered Kirby. "Wires cut, men outside. We hold a hostage, unless Stalbridge is telling the truth, and those fellows out there are a different gang."

"Who else could they be, but his thugs?" roared Pembroke.

"One thing supports his claim," answered Kirby. "The cutting of the wire surprized him as much as it did me, and interfered with his plans, so it wasn't done by his order. And there's another thing."

He turned and stared at Perez searchingly for a moment, and then said: "Juan, have you been cleaning a furnace?"

The Cuban showed his surprise. "But no, *señor!* Why should one clean a furnace in the summer?"

"Nevertheless," returned Kirby, "there is soot on your shoes." Perez stooped and stared with some annoyance at the black smudges which flecked the heels and sole edges of his otherwise immaculate brown low quarters.

"Juan," said Kirby, "why did you slug Colonel Pembroke?"

.3.

Perez stared at Kirby as if the detective had lost his mind.

"You are mad, *señor!*" His voice shrilled and cracked with his vehemence.

"That's what I think!" roared Pembroke. "Why, Juan's been with me for years! If you'd devote your efforts to those devils outside—"

"Wait!" snapped Kirby. "Juan has told too many lies tonight."

"*Señor!*" The Cuban's dark eyes flashed dangerously.

"It's proven that he didn't return before ten thirty," said Kirby. "The Colonel was attacked at ten. Plenty of time for the man who did it to drive out here from the city. Something like this probably happened: Juan, learning in some way—probably from William—that the Colonel meant to consult us at ten o'clock, went into town this afternoon, changed his clothes, and waited for Pembroke in the darkness beneath the stair, in the lower hall. When Pembroke came in, he apparently tried his best to kill him, but failed, and so ran away, changed his clothing again, and returned here. "

"How do you figure all that?" demanded Pembroke.

"The man who slugged you had his face hidden in a scarf. That shows he was somebody you'd recognize. Of course, that might have been William. But look there." Again Kirby pointed at the Cuban's shoes.

"He didn't think it necessary to change his shoes. In the darkness he couldn't see that the floor was thickly powdered with soot. For months an old stove was kept stored beneath that stair, and the soot fell out of it onto the floor. The janitor's a lazy devil; he never bothers to sweep under there. Tonight, after you and Butch left, I found the tracks of a man in the soot. As he'd stood there for some time, occasionally moving slightly, the tracks weren't clear-cut or distinct; but it was evident that some soot would remain on the fellow's shoes."

"But what motive could Juan have?" protested Pembroke.

"I can't answer that. But one thing suggests itself to me. I doubt very much if he really saw anyone trying to break in tonight. Butch didn't see or hear anything, and he has the keenest eyes and ears of any man I ever knew. I think Juan was simply trying to establish his loyalty and vigilance. He said it was *a white man* he saw—said that before Butch had mentioned the negro. That constitutes a betrayal of the fact that he knew colored men were lurking about the place. None of us expected him to see anything but a white man. He was so anxious to conceal their presence, conceal his knowledge of their presence, that he betrayed that very knowledge. He wouldn't have said 'white man' if the consciousness of a black man, or men, hadn't been lurking in his mind.

"I'm forced to conclude that Juan is in league with those men outside!"

As Kirby had talked, Juan's excitement and perturbation had visibly grown. His swarthy skin had turned ashy, and his lips drew back from his gums. His hands clenched and unclenched spasmodically, making abortive gestures. Gorman had silently approached from behind, wise in the ways of Latin temperament, from his years among the Mexican mountains.

Kirby, engrossed in his unraveling of the skein, had forgotten that explosive Latin temperament, and he was caught flatfooted when Perez flashed out a knife with an incoherent cry, and stabbed murderously at his throat.

But the blow was never completed. Quick as Juan was, big Butch Gorman was quicker, with the swift sureness of a great cat. One big arm whipped around Juan's neck, jerking his head back; the other hand caught his wrist and gave it a whiplash wrench that sent the knife ringing to the floor. The Cuban screamed in feline rage, but he was like a child in the hands of the giant Texan.

"Get a lariat or somethin', Brent," advised Gorman tranquilly. "Your cuffs are on Stalbridge, and I never can remember to pack mine. We'll tie this spig up, and then I'm goin' out and gather in some more hostages. I'm tired of all this rag chewin'."

"Juan, a traitor!" ejaculated Pembroke. "One of the two men in the world I thought I could trust!"

"Trust?" Perez twisted his head to scream hate and fury at his employer. "Dog! Pig! Have I not endured your arrogance for seven years? Am I a dog to be kicked or patted at your pleasure? Bah! I spit on you!" And so he did, writhing in Gorman's grasp. And then, throwing back his head like a madman, he screamed hysterically, mere incoherent howls sandwiched with meaningless gibberings, until Gorman, annoyed, clapped a big hand over his mouth, while Kirby tied him with cords that Pembroke produced, like a man in a daze.

They laid the Cuban on the divan by Stalbridge, who stared at him indifferently. The Englishman had watched the whole episode without a change of expression, somberly, impersonally, as if he witnessed a rather dreary farce on a stage. The man's singleness of purpose, his self-centered resolution were abnormal. He must have been brought up from his cradle on a philosophy of hate, reflected Kirby.

"And what now?" wondered the Colonel.

"Prepare for anything!" snapped Kirby. "We'll go through the house and take another look at the locks—"

He broke short as a scream rang from the darkness outside. "Help! Help! Colonel Pembroke! Help! *Ahhh!*" The cry thinned to a squeal of pain.

"Who's that?" exclaimed Kirby, springing up.

"I don't know!" Pembroke was evidently puzzled. "Good God, it sounds like—"

The cry was repeated, edged with poignant agony.

"It's William!" screamed Constance. "I know his voice!"

Butch stepped to the side door and opened it a crack. "By Jupiter," he said softly. "I see him! I'm goin' after him."

And before Kirby could stop him, the reckless Borderman glided out of the door. Through this door, which he left partly open, a stream of light reached out over the lawn, and into the further edge of this light Kirby saw a figure crawling on hands and knees. The posture, no less than the agonized cries, suggested some frightful injury or grisly mutilation, and this was rendered a certainty by the gouts and splotches of crimson which dabbled the wretch's garments and dripped from his head. It was nightmarish—a bloody, mowing horror crawling into the patch of light out of Stygian blackness.

"Great God!" breathed Pembroke. "Is that William?"

Gorman had reached the wounded man; he cast a quick glance from side to side, challenging the darkness, starting to stoop—plainly to Kirby's ears came a dull, sickening crack, and Gorman's great body swayed drunkenly, and slumped to the earth. Kirby cried out chokingly and leaped toward the door, heedless of Pembroke's bellow: "Don't go out there, you fool!"

"They've got Gorman!" he yelled, white with passion. He did not weigh the frantic recklessness of his action. It simply did not occur to him that he could leave Butch lying out there wounded or dead, to the mercy of whatever devils were lurking in the darkness. He plunged through the door—and even as his feet hit the pillared stoop, the lights went out behind him. Blinded by the sudden plunge into darkness, his feet missed the step and he toppled out upon the lawn on his all-fours. Inside the darkened house he heard the reverberant crash of the elephant gun, mingled with the roaring voice of Colonel Pembroke. Constance screamed and there was a crash as of a table overturned. All this in the instant that he was scrambling to his feet. And then he heard a swift rush of feet across the grass, saw dim figures looming in the starlight, and the glint of steel.

He fired point-blank as a lifted knife caught the starlight, and saw a staring black face briefly illumined in the flash. Then something struck his spinal column, in the middle of his back, with numbing force.

It was such a blow as only an expert in the art of manhandling could deliver. Kirby did not wholly lose consciousness, but life and feeling went out of his limbs as suddenly as though they had been severed from his body. He did not even feel the impact of his fall, there was an interim of semi-consciousness, and then he was aware that the lights in the house were on again, and he saw a giant black man in bizarre garments bending over him.

.4.

Kirby stared up in amazement at the brutish, bullet-shaped head with its crisp, short, black wool, the thick lips, and the reddish, rolling eyes, the fantastic, half-European, half-Oriental garb. A negro, yes, but no such negro as was ever born on American soil. Kirby had seen his kind in Algeria, in the bazaars of Cairo.

The fellow grasped Kirby's collar with one hand, and dragged the limp detective after him as he stalked across the small porch and into the house. As he crossed the threshold he brutally kicked something that Kirby could not see, but which cried and whimpered in a manner that froze the detective's tongue to his palate with nameless horror. Then Kirby was carelessly thrown down on the rich carpet, inside the room.

The detective's brain had not been affected by that blow which deadened a nerve center and induced temporary paralysis. The scene that met his eyes in that room was etched forever on his brain.

Pembroke, the hue of his purple face threatening apoplexy, was sprawled in his great armchair, his hands tied behind him, and a black man similar to Kirby's captor, though less gigantic, standing behind him with a long, curved knife in his dusky hand. Constance, bound hand and foot, cowered in another chair, ignored by her captors. Stalbridge, still handcuffed, sat on the divan, with another black behind him, likewise brandishing a knife. There was no evidence that the Englishman had moved from his seat during the whole affair. His moody expression had not altered. Juan Perez, freed now and openly gloating over his master's plight, was one of the group. But the whole scene was dominated by the tall figure that stood broodingly in the center of the room.

This man was not black; his skin was of a light copper color, and his features were straight, as was his close-cropped hair, though most of that was hidden under a green fez. Whatever other blood might course through his veins, it was evident that the predominating strain was Arab. A long, striped cloak hung to his ankles, and sandals were on his feet. The man might have just stepped out of some *suk* of the Orient.

He was as tall as any of the giant blacks, but he was lean and wiry, though broad-shouldered. His face was striking—lean, intelligent, predatory, with glittering eyes. It was a cruel, clean-cut face, without doubt or mercy or remorse, such as a Pharaoh or a prophet of Islam might have owned. He stood with his head slightly bowed, in an attitude of somber contemplation, and in the silence nothing was heard except Constance's jerky, hysterical sobbing, and a drooling whimper from the door.

This whimpering grew louder, and presently human words were mixed with it, words that stumbled and strangled, as if on a gag of gushing blood.

"Colonel—Colonel—sir—" mowed the eerie voice. "I never meant—to—do—it—they—told me—told me to crawl toward the house—and cry for help—I never meant—never meant to betray you—but the pain—the pain—oh, for the love of God—ahhh!"

There was the sound of a blow and the inhuman slavering ceased. Constance shrieked and twisted her head away, drove her face frenziedly into the plush of her chair to shut out the sight. Even Stalbridge started convulsively, and muttered: "Oh, I say, now!"

The Arab did not lift his head, gave no sign that he had heard. He was staring at Colonel Pembroke, and the unnatural stillness was not broken. Kirby felt rough hands binding his ankles and wrists. He was beginning to feel the stir and tingle of returning sensation, but still his tongue felt dead, and he could move only his head.

He twisted his head, impelled by a horrible fascination, and stared out of the still open door. On the stoop lay a ghastly thing at the sight of which Kirby would have involuntarily cried out, had he been able—once it had been a man—Kirby wrenched his gaze away from that huddled, crimson figure with its unnamable mutilations, and stared beyond it, searching the streaming wedge of light, bracing himself against what he knew he must see. Just beyond the edge of the stoop lay a crumpled black figure, its blasted head in a pool of blood on the grass: the black Kirby had shot; and beyond that again—Kirby turned sick, and the lights and the room reeled drunkenly. Butch Gorman lay as he had fallen, face down, the light gleaming redly on the back of his head—

Kirby knew that Butch had not been struck glancingly, as was Stalbridge, by the slug that had been hurled at him from the darkness. The concussion of its impact had spoken too plainly of a direct hit. The actions of the blacks, in ignoring their victim, showed that they were certain Gorman was dead. And God, what a death! To be struck down like a blind, helpless sheep, with no chance to hit back! The very death Gorman would have most abhorred! A red haze swam before Kirby's eyes, a frantic fury that made his brain reel. But he could not move a finger, and the low, soft laughter of the great negro mocked him.

He twisted his head back toward the tableau in the room. Colonel Pembroke was staring at the tall Arab without speaking. His face was no longer purple; it was grey, and drops of sweat glistened on his skin. In his eyes was growing an awful realization, as if he slowly recognized a monstrous truth that defied sanity.

"Who are you?" The voice was no longer a bellow. It was a straining whisper.

The Arab spoke at last, and his voice was strong, emotionless, ghostly.

"Why do you ask? Have you forgotten the Bahr-el-Ghazal? Or do you dream that the men of Kordofan have forgotten you?"

Pembroke stared at him as at a ghost come to life out of the dust of the past.

"My name is Kerim Ali," said the Arab. "You do not know me, but you knew my father, in the days when he was an *emir* of Muhammad Ahmed, the Mahdi ar Rasul; his name is Achmet Kerim."

"Achmet Kerim!" whispered Pembroke, as if his lips framed the words without his conscious volition. "God!"

"Did you think he and the children of the *Saiyid* had forgotten, Ravenby *pasha?*" said the Arab. "Did you dream that men have not sought you for fifty years?—that a paper with pictures of a man and a cat would not be sent instantly to my father, who also owns a jade cat taken from an Egyptian crypt?"

"So it was to him that the Mahdi gave the third cat," whispered Pembroke. His haggard stare roved to Juan Perez. "You damned traitor!" he muttered, the veins on his temples swelling. "It was you who betrayed me!"

"Yes, you pig!" cried Perez. "It was I! These men have been hiding about the premises ever since this morning. They came shortly after you drove into town. They seized me behind the trees, and questioned me, and would have killed me, if I had not convinced them that I could aid them. You dog, I have waited for years for an opportunity to repay you for your insults. I helped *Señor* Kerim Ali lay his plan. It was I who admitted him into the house awhile ago, hid him in the study and showed him the switch that controlled the lights all over the house. It was I who gave him and his men the signal to attack; I screamed it at the top of my voice, while the redheaded swine was binding me, and you stupid fools did not understand."

Kirby saw the whole diabolical plan now. The man William had been used as a ghastly decoy to get one or both of the detectives out of the house; then the Arab, hidden in the study, had turned out the lights and in the darkness Pembroke and his niece had fallen easy prey to the dark-skinned devils. Probably one of the blacks had been in the study with Kerim Ali. But why had they not attacked Gorman and Pembroke when they drove up to the house, earlier in the night, as he and Stalbridge had been attacked?

"It was not a perfect trap," said Kerim Ali somberly. "Two of my men are dead. Had we all been at the front of the house when the black-haired detective and the other drove up, we would have trapped them. But only two were on watch there, the rest of us behind the house. Before we could reach the spot, one of my servants had been shot and the other knocked senseless."

One of the blacks involuntarily caressed a great, blood-clotted lump behind his ear.

"Yet it was a good plan," continued the Arab. "It was well that we captured the man William tonight; when my men, hiding in the darkness, hacked him with their knives and drove him toward the house, the detectives were drawn out into the darkness. That was well. I did not wish to risk my life against the big red-headed man."

That was characteristic of the breed, thought Kirby bitterly; it was not cowardice, but the craft and treachery of a cobra.

"The gun of the black-haired *kaffir* shoots straight, even in the dark," said Kerim Ali. "But I had seized you from behind, Ravenby *pasha*, before you knew I was in the room. Your shot was futile. This man—a Stalbridge, Juan tells me—did not resist as we seized his companions."

"Why should I?" returned the Englishman. "I'm a prisoner, not a friend of Pembroke's."

"You can't get away with this!" gasped the Colonel. "This is America, not Africa!"

"The hour is late, the road lonely, the house isolated," answered Kerim Ali. "Make your peace with your Christian God, you infidel dog, for tonight I shall send you to hell, as you sent the Mahdi ar Rasul to Paradise."

"A lie!" gasped Pembroke. "A cursed, foul lie! I had nothing to do with Muhammad's death."

A wild flame lit the Soudani's eyes.

"You lie, you *kaffir* dog! You poisoned him as all men know, for the loot he took from the Englishman, Stalbridge! You stole it from the *Beit-el-Maal*, the treasure-house, and fled with it on camels: gold and silver and precious stones, the ransom of a sultan! For fifty years knives in Kordofan have been sharp for you! Hell gapes, dog!"

"Then kill me and be done with it!" panted Pembroke, veins swelling and knotting like purple worms on his temples.

"Nay, not yet. I could have killed you a score of times tonight, had I wished. I could have killed you when you first drove up to the house with the big redheaded man, returning from the city. But I would not let my children cast their bullets at him, for fear of hitting you. That is why I drew them away from you, out of the house, lest in a pitched battle you might be slain by a chance shot or blow. You shall not die until you tell us the whereabouts of the rarest piece of the Mahdi's treasure, which you stole—the Necklace of Balkis, Queen of Sheba!"

"I sold it in France, long ago," gasped Pembroke.

"Again you lie! For fifty years men have sought it in vain. Had it been sold, our agents in Europe or America, Turks, Jews and Levantines, would have learned of it. Where is it?"

Pembroke was shaking as with an ague, his grey skin shining with clammy sweat. Yet his flaming eyes reflected a sort of insane obstinacy.

"I'll never tell you!" he whispered.

Constance stared about her, frightened but uncomprehending, like one in a nightmare from which she half-expects to waken. Kirby shuddered as he recalled nameless tales told of the Mahdi and his followers, and the monstrous customs of that devilish land that lies south of Egypt.

"Gobir!" snapped Kerim Ali, and the great black shut the side door and sprang forward, grinning savagely. The negro standing behind Pembroke seized the Colonel's shoulders in a brutal grasp and jerked him backward, and Gobir seized his legs; together they stretched him out helpless on his chair, and Kerim Ali drew from his robe a long brass-hilted knife whose cruel curved edge glittered bleakly in the light. Colonel Pembroke's distended eyes rolled toward that knife with awful anticipation. His lips parted, he gagged, but no speech came; one of the blacks had hooked an arm about the Colonel's thick throat so viciously that the man was half-strangled.

Constance began an incoherent appeal to Juan, who stood by with an expression mingled of vindictive pleasure and apprehension. But Stalbridge rose suddenly and stalked toward the group clustered about the armchair. His guard sprang after him, but Stalbridge said, in a voice as hard as granite: "Don't mind me; I'm not trying to rescue the swine. I just want to watch, that's all." The black halted near him, uncertainly. There was no more pity in the stare Stalbridge bent on Pembroke than there is in the glare of a hawk.

Kirby shuddered, seeing the same bleak mercilessness reflected in both the face of Stalbridge and the face of Kerim Ali. What a heritage of hate was theirs, molding their lives into vessels of vengeance for men who had died before they were born. Fanatics both, sons of hate, another phase of the horrors spawned so long ago in the Hell's broth of the Dervish rebellion.

Kerim Ali bent over Pembroke's feet with the knife in his hand. Kirby could not see what was taking place, but suddenly Pembroke bellowed like an ox in agony, writhing convulsively in the hands of his captors. Blood was streaming down on the carpet, and then Kerim Ali straightened, with a red, dripping object in his hand. He tossed it contemptuously aside—the severed first joint of a human toe.

"There are nine others," he said. "And then there are fingers, and eyes, and ears—Ravenby *pasha*, will you tell me where the Necklace of Balkis is hidden?"

"Tell him! For God's sake, tell him, Uncle John!" screamed Constance, in a voice that wavered with a knife edge of frantic madness.

For an instant the tableau held—the black, bestial faces and the hawk-like brown countenance clustered about the livid figure in the chair. Juan shrank behind them, and Stalbridge stood close, a grim, cruel smile playing over his thin lips, as if he were thinking of another man who writhed under the knives of the Soudan, long ago.

Pembroke's head jerked spasmodically on his shoulders, from side to side.

"I'll tell you," he panted. "Look behind the—"

Abruptly the lights went out. There was a scuffle, a strangled cry. There followed Kerim Ali's voice, spitting curses in Arabic, as he groped for the light button. When he found it and snapped it on again, Constance screamed once, in a voice that haunted Kirby all the rest of his life, and fainted.

Colonel Pembroke was slumped in his chair, a long, curved knife standing up between his shoulders; he was beyond torture or punishment at last.

Stalbridge was rising from the floor, as if he had been knocked down, and the others were clustered about the corpse in various attitudes of bewilderment or surprise.

Kerim Ali, wheeling from the light button on the wall, stared open mouthed for an instant. Then a flame of hell's fire blazed in his eyes; he threw high his lean arms, in a gesture more suggestive of frantic fury than any tirade of words. Thrice he strove to speak, and thrice his passion choked him.

"Who slew the dog?" he shrieked, finding his voice at last. "Who robbed me of my vengeance?" Brutally he wrenched the dagger free and glared at it. "Gobir's knife!" he yelped, and wheeling on the huge black he pointed an accusing finger at his belt. Gobir's hand flew to his scabbard, and finding it empty, the great black went ashy.

"Did you slay the *kaffir?*" asked Kerim Ali in a tone the more deadly for its restraint. "Have I not warned you to control your accursed blood lust?"

Gobir was trembling; he burst into a flood of Arabic, accompanied by wild gestures which indicated that he was explaining that someone had snatched the knife from his scabbard in the dark. Kerim Ali wheeled suddenly on Stalbridge.

"You slew him!" he raved. "He was your enemy, as well as mine! You could strike the blow, with your hands manacled in front of you!"

"That's a lie!" snapped Stalbridge. "I'd have killed him willingly if I'd had the chance. But when the lights went out, somebody knocked me down, apparently to get at Pembroke. I don't know who did it."

"You lie!" With his open hand Kerim Ali struck the Englishman a terrific blow across the face. Stalbridge staggered back, then with an oath he leaped forward, manacled hands lifted. But Gobir seized him from behind, and the next instant he was helpless on the floor, with his arms and feet bound with cords. Kerim Ali stared down at him, all the hellish fury of the fanatic burning redly in his wide eyes.

"Fool, fool to come between a son of Islam and his enemy!" he muttered. "You shall die as *he* was to die, and slowly!"

Stalbridge glared up at him with no trace of fear; capable of watching the torture of an enemy, he was capable as well of facing that same torture without flinching. But suddenly the jumbled bits of a pattern that had been revolving half-forgotten in Kirby's mind clicked into place. He found his voice just as Kerim Ali squatted beside the helpless man, caressing the red knife edge.

"Wait!" he called sharply, speaking for the first time since he was struck down. His tongue felt strange, but he could make himself understood. All looked toward him as he struggled up on to a sitting posture.

"How do you know Stalbridge killed Pembroke?" he demanded. "The light button was on the wall, within easy reach of any of you. Any one of you might have put out the lights, snatched the knife and struck the blow."

"Who would strike it, except Stalbridge?" cried Juan heatedly.

Kirby did not heed him, but addressed Kerim Ali, who stared back at him somberly.

"Stalbridge did not kill Pembroke," he said. "You want the necklace, don't you? Well, I can tell you who knows where it is!"

.5.

Kerim Ali was on his feet in an instant, looming over the bound detective like a great vulture.

"Quick!" he hissed. "Speak quickly, *kaffir!*"

"Very well." Kirby hoped the beating of his heart was not as loud as it seemed to him. "Pembroke was killed to keep him from telling where the necklace is hidden. Isn't that logical? Just as he was about to tell, someone put out the light and killed him in the dark. It might have been Gobir; it might have been Stalbridge. But I don't think it was either of them. It was a man who wished to keep the hiding place of the necklace a secret; why? There is only one reason. He wanted to steal it for himself!"

Kerim Ali said nothing, but his eyes began to burn with a wolfish light.

"This man knows the secret of the necklace," said Kirby. "It's evident that he does. Perhaps he had intended stealing it for some time, but had been afraid to. Now, however, your invasion gave him a perfect chance to make the theft look like part of an outside job, that included the murder of the Colonel. But he knew you wanted the necklace too. He knew you intended capturing the Colonel and torturing him into telling where it was hidden. He wished to prevent this, by killing the Colonel before he could tell the secret. This he had already attempted once tonight. Did you know that Juan Perez tried to kill Colonel Pembroke in the city earlier in the night?"

The Cuban shrieked and darted for the door, but Gobir was before him. Seizing the wrist that lifted a knife, the great Soudanese twisted it brutally. Perez screamed and the knife fell to the floor as a dull snap told of a broken bone. The Cuban turned ashy and sagged, whimpering in his captor's hands.

"Dog!" Kerim Ali ran at him, his dark face convulsed with passion. "Traitor! Fool that I was to trust a *kaffir* dog, even a mongrel like you! So you went into the city tonight to rob me of my vengeance! You lied when you said you but went to spy on Ravenby *pasha!* Howl, dog!"

Seizing the limp hand of the Cuban, Kerim Ali moved it back and forth on the splintered bone. Froth flew from Perez' lips, and his screams rose until it seemed they would break even the deathlike insensibility of the girl who lay huddled in the great chair. Kirby went sick. Horror had been heaped on horror that night until it was all unreal and delirious.

"Where is the necklace, dog?" Kerim Ali gritted between his teeth, which his back-drawn lip bared. "Tell me, before I twist this useless member from your yellow body!"

"In my room!" screamed the Cuban. "It is hidden in my room! I stole it yesterday from the Colonel's safe! Mercy! Ah, *Dios*, mercy!"

Kerim Ali hurled him headlong into the arms of one of the other blacks, and snapped in Arabic, which Kirby barely understood: "Gobir, remain here and watch these dogs. Achmet, go forth and collect the bodies which lie outside, and drag them into this room. When we go forth, a lighted match held to a curtain will solve our problem as far as these *kaffirs* are concerned—living or dead. Abdullah, come with me, and bring that whining cur with you. He shall give us the necklace before we cut his throat."

Achmet salaamed and glided out of the side door, closing it behind him. Kerim Ali turned toward the curtained door, then halted and stared for a moment at the pale girl who lay still senseless in the big chair.

"If she is not dead, she shall go with me," he muttered. "I can smuggle her out of the country easily enough. She shall pay her uncle's debt, since he is beyond my vengeance. Come, Abdullah."

He disappeared through the curtains, followed by Abdullah who stolidly dragged the moaning Perez with him.

Gobir squatted, staring at the man who lay bound on the floor, at the corpse in the great chair. Kirby licked dry lips, wondering if it were not a ghastly nightmare, after all. He glanced at the girl, lying so deathlike in the great chair. It was well that she had fainted. Her sanity would have stood no more. He shuddered as he remembered Kerim Ali's words. The man was capable of the outrage he contemplated, capable of dragging Constance Pembroke into the captivity of an Egyptian *harim* in revenge for a wrong of which she was innocent. What a hell's broth had been stirred down there in the black country by the mad Dervish. The Mahdi was dead and his bones rotted, but the black shadows of his reign still crawled like slimy tentacles out of the nighted past.

Kirby glanced at Stalbridge. The man was deathly pale, as if his own iron nerve was beginning to wear under the strain. After all, there was a great gulf between the Englishman and Kerim Ali. Stalbridge was merely the product of hate taught him since babyhood. He was still a white man, with a white man's way of thinking. Obviously he did not include the helpless girl in the hatred he felt for her uncle.

Faint noises came from the back of the house. Achmet did not return. Gobir sat like a great black image in the center of the room. Kirby began to watch the giant black uneasily; there was something strange and unnatural in his looks, in the furtive turning of his bullet head. A grisly light grew in his red eyes. Unconsciously he licked his thick lips, and he would not meet Kirby's stare. Suddenly from the back of the house there rang a shriek of agony, cut short in a blood-choked gurgle; Kirby knew it marked the end of Juan Perez. Gobir started convulsively to his feet, as if the animal pain in that cry struck a responsive chord in his brutish bosom.

With a long stride he reached Stalbridge, squatted behind him and pulled the Englishman's head up and back on his knees.

"Here, you black brute!" ejaculated Stalbridge wrathfully. "What the devil are you—" The words died on his lips as he met the glare of Gobir's eyes. The great negro was in the grip of primitive bloodlust that would not be denied. These men were doomed anyway—

Gripping Stalbridge's hair, he forced the Englishman's head back until his throat was fully presented. Then he sucked in his lips noisily and drew the long, curved dagger that had killed Colonel Pembroke.

Kirby lay rigid with horror, staring at a scene that might have been witnessed in a devil-hut beside the Congo. The black was drunk with the desire to see blood spurt and flesh part under the keen steel edge.

He was squatting near the study door, with his broad back to it. Now Kirby saw this door open softly. He checked the yell that started to his lips. Butch Gorman was framed in that door.

Gorman was pale under his bronze. His coat and shirt were gone; there was blood on his neck, splotches of blood on his bare shoulders and undershirt. But his step was as springy and sure as ever; and in his hand was a knife, not a curved blade like Gobir's, but the straight, fifteen-inch clipper-pointed Bowie of the Southern frontiersman. There was blood on the blade.

Gobir had not looked about from where he squatted, gloating over his victim. Noiselessly Gorman glided into the room, behind the unconscious black. Muscles rippled mightily under Gorman's skin, white in contrast with the ebon body of Gobir. The Soudanese was even bigger, a great statue of living black bronze.

With a quick stride Gorman had almost reached the broad dusky back—when Gobir turned his head, knife hovering over Stalbridge's throat. With a guttural cry he shot to his feet, wheeling as he did so. Up went the curved knife in his hand—and even as it did, there was the dull impact of a heavy blow. Gorman had struck too quick for the eye to follow him. With a choking cry the great black reeled and fell as an uprooted tree falls, and it was only when he saw the blood gushing from a great wound under his ribs that Kirby realized just exactly what had happened.

With a quick stride Gorman reached Kirby and began slashing his ropes. There was a big, blood-crusted lump on the back of Butch's head.

"Butch! My God, Butch!" gibbered Kirby. "I thought you were dead! You must have a skull like a bull!"

"I came to awhile ago," grunted Gorman. "Too dizzy to remember what it was all about. Then I saw a big nigger sneakin' towards me, so I waited till he bent over me to pick me up, and let him have it—up through the jugular. He ruined my coat and shirt with his blood. Sneaked up and peeked in through a crack in the shutters and saw you all tied up. Afraid to try the door for fear of the burglar alarm; I could tell the fort was in the hands of the enemy. Went around the house lookin', and found an outside window in the study open."

"That's the way Juan let Kerim Ali into the house," muttered Kirby. "Quick! I haven't time for explanations now! There's an Arab and another negro in the back of the house, and they'll be back here any minute. I'm sure the Arab has a gun, at least. Oh, curse it!"

He was free, but the blow he had received, together with the numbness of his limbs, from lack of proper circulation, rendered him unable to stand.

Gorman glanced at Stalbridge, evidently puzzled as to the Englishman's status.

"Cut those cords off him," snapped Kirby, groping for the key to the handcuffs. "Then hand me that rifle. I can shoot, if I can't stand!"

Gorman complied, and stepped across the room to where the elephant gun lay half-behind the open door of the study. He closed the door, bent toward the rifle—then wheeled and straightened. Between the curtains of the hall door stood Kerim Ali, a leather bag in one hand, an automatic pistol in the other. Beside him crouched the black Abdullah, knife in hand.

"Dog!" said the Arab calmly, lifting the pistol. "So the slug from the sling did not crack your infidel skull. Well, we shall see how a slug from a pistol shall—"

Gorman's hand, extended along the wall, jammed suddenly against the light button. The room was plunged in darkness, slashed by a streak of orange flame. Kirby, lying on the floor, sweated with fear for Butch, trapped in that black room with two murderers. Kirby cursed sickly; he could not help, could not move. He could only lie there and hold his breath as he listened to that grim game of life and death.

Kerim Ali laughed harshly, a disembodied voice in Stygian blackness. "Dog, you cannot escape! If you open a door to flee, I will see you against the starlight, and I shall not miss! And if you remain in this room, Abdullah's knife will find you at last!" Then followed staccato commands in Arabic, obviously addressed to Abdullah.

Then there was silence, except for the faint pad of feet, the soft rasp of garments. "Open a door and run, dog!" taunted the unseen Arab. "A bullet is kinder than Abdullah's knife—ha!" The taut stillness was broken by the sound of a blow, a gasp, a heavy fall. Kirby bit his tongue to keep from crying out. A knife had found its mark in the darkness—but which knife? Who was down, bleeding to death on the floor? Kerim Ali called: "Abdullah!" The only answer was a soft laugh out of that well of darkness, and Kirby breathed again. He knew that laugh. Kerim Ali shouted something, and now his voice was edged with panic. He fired again, and yet again, blindly, in the direction of the soft sounds that reached his ears, like the pad of a tiger stalking his prey.

The shots stabbed the blackness with red, and were followed by absolute stillness in which the night itself seemed to hold its breath. Then Kerim Ali shrieked and fired and shrieked again. His scream broke in a gurgle and something tumbled heavily to the floor.

"Butch!" yelled Kirby frantically, taut nerves snapping at last. *"Butch!"*

"All right, Brent." That cool, faintly amused voice out of the darkness was like a sedative.

There was a sound of someone groping along the wall, and the light flared on again. Butch Gorman was revealed, his thin lips smiling bleakly, his blue eyes blazing with the battle lust. In his right hand the Bowie dripped red.

Abdullah lay face down near the center of the room, a red pool oozing from under his body. Near the curtained door lay Kerim Ali, one hand still gripping the leather sack, the other the pistol that had failed him. His head was drawn back unnaturally so he stared blankly at the ceiling. He had literally been ripped open from groin to breastbone.

Gorman grinned faintly.

"They weren't the only ones that could fight in the dark," he said. "Knives in a dark room—that's an old Mexican custom; right popular in Texas, too."

Kerim Ali, master of his own particular brand of savagery, reflected Kirby, struggling to his feet, had encountered a brand with which even he could not cope. The detective, moving uncertainly, but with growing ease, found the key to the cuffs and freed Stalbridge, then hobbled over to the girl.

Gorman calmly twisted the sack from the Arab's stiff hand, and dumped the contents on the table—a long string of gleaming green jewels, curiously cut, of unmistakable antiquity, and undoubtedly worth a fortune in themselves. Stalbridge stood chafing his limbs and staring at them, and Kirby snapped: "Here, you fellows. Help me get Miss Pembroke to the car. We've got to get her into the city, to a doctor. She's insensible, and I don't want her to come to in this shambles. Bring those jewels along, Butch. They belong to her, now."

"Didn't her uncle steal them from Stalbridge's uncle?" said Butch, whose ideas of justice were elemental and somewhat primitive.

"I don't think so," answered Kirby. "From what I've heard, I gather that the necklace wasn't part of the loot. Pembroke stole that from the Mahdi. Dammit, will you help me?"

"Well," said Gorman, lifting the unconscious girl in his arms as lightly as if she had been a baby, "seein' that her uncle robbed the Stalbridges, maybe she'd like to split that necklace with this gent, and—"

Stalbridge shook his head impatiently.

"I waive my claim," he said. "I have no wish to rob a helpless girl."

And he turned and strode through the door into the dawn that was just lifting.

Moon of Zambebwei

1. The Horror in the Pines

The silence of the pine woods lay like a brooding cloak about the soul of Bristol McGrath. The black shadows seemed fixed, immovable as the weight of superstition that overhung this forgotten backcountry. Vague ancestral dreads stirred at the back of McGrath's mind; for he was born in the pine woods, and sixteen years of roaming about the world had not erased their shadows. The fearsome tales at which he had shuddered as a child whispered again in his consciousness; tales of ghosts and ghouls, of black shapes stalking the midnight glades. . . .

Cursing these childish memories, McGrath quickened his pace. The dim trail wound tortuously between dense walls of giant trees. No wonder he had been unable to hire anyone in the distant river village to drive him to the Ballville estate. The road was impassable for a vehicle, choked with rotting stumps and new growth. Ahead of him it bent sharply.

McGrath halted short, frozen to immobility. The silence had been broken at last, in such a way as to bring a chill tingling to the backs of his hands. For the sound had been the unmistakable groan of a human being in agony. Only for an instant was McGrath motionless. Then he was gliding about the bend of the trail with the noiseless slouch of a hunting panther.

A blue snub-nosed revolver had appeared as if by magic in his right hand. His left involuntarily clenched in his pocket on the bit of paper that was responsible for his presence in that grim forest. That paper was a frantic and mysterious appeal for aid; it was signed by McGrath's worst enemy, and contained the name of a woman long dead.

McGrath rounded the bend in the trail, every nerve tense and alert, expecting anything—except what he actually saw. His startled eyes hung on the grisly object for an instant, and then swept the forest walls. Nothing stirred there. A dozen feet back from the trail visibility vanished in a ghoulish twilight, where *anything* might lurk unseen. McGrath dropped to his knee beside the figure that lay in the trail before him.

It was a man, spread-eagled, hands and feet bound to four pegs driven deeply in the hard-packed earth; a black-bearded, hook-nosed, swarthy man. "Ahmed!" muttered McGrath. "Ballville's Arab servant! God!"

For it was not the binding cords that brought the glaze to the Arab's eyes. A weaker man than McGrath might have sickened at the mutilations which keen knives had wrought on the man's body. McGrath recognized the work of an expert in the art of torture. Yet a spark of life still throbbed in the tough frame of the Arab. McGrath's gray eyes grew bleaker as he noted the position of the victim's body, and his mind flew back to another, grimmer jungle, and a half-flayed black man pegged out on a path as a warning to the white man who dared invade a forbidden land.

He cut the cords, shifted the dying man to a more comfortable position. It was all he could do. He saw the delirium ebb momentarily in the bloodshot eyes, saw recognition glimmer there. Clots of bloody foam splashed the matted beard. The lips writhed soundlessly, and McGrath glimpsed the bloody stump of a severed tongue.

The black-nailed fingers began scrabbling in the dust. They shook, clawing erratically, but with purpose. McGrath bent close, tense with interest, and saw crooked lines grow under the quivering fingers. With the last effort of an iron will, the Arab was tracing a message in the characters of his own language. McGrath recognized the name: "Richard Ballville"; it was followed by "danger," and the hand waved weakly up me trail; then—and McGrath stiffened convulsively—*"Constance."* One final effort of the dragging finger traced "John De Al—" Suddenly the bloody frame was convulsed by one last sharp agony; the lean, sinewy hand knotted spasmodically and then fell limp. Ahmed ibn Suleyman was beyond vengeance or mercy.

McGrath rose, dusting his hands, aware of the tense stillness of the grim woods around him; aware of a faint rustling in their depths that was not caused by any breeze. He looked down at the mangled figure with involuntary pity, though he knew well the foulness of the Arab's heart, a black evil that had matched that of Ahmed's master, Richard Ballville. Well, it seemed that master and man had at last met their match in human fiendishness. But who, or *what?* For a hundred years the Ballvilles had ruled supreme over this backcountry, first over their wide plantations and hundreds of slaves, and later over the submissive descendants of those slaves. Richard, the last of the Ballvilles, had exercised as much authority over the pinelands as any of his autocratic ancestors. Yet from this country where men had bowed to the Ballvilles for a century, had come that frenzied cry of fear that McGrath clenched in his coat pocket.

Stillness succeeded the rustling, more sinister than any sound. McGrath knew he was watched; knew that the spot where Ahmed's body lay was the invisible deadline that had been drawn for him. He believed that he would be allowed to turn and retrace his steps unmolested to the distant village. He knew that if he continued on his way, death would strike him suddenly and unseen. Turning, he strode back the way he had come.

He made the turn and kept straight on until he had passed another crook in the trail. Then he halted, listened. All was silent. Quickly he drew the paper from his pocket, smoothed out the wrinkles and read, again, in the cramped scrawl of the man he hated most on earth:

Bristol:
    If you still love Constance Brand, for God's sake forget your hate and come to Ballville Manor as quickly as the devil can drive you.
    Richard Ballville.

That was all. It reached him by telegraph in that Far Western city where McGrath had resided since his return from Africa. He would have ignored it, but for the mention of Constance Brand. That name had sent a choking, agonizing pulse of amazement through his soul, had sent him racing toward the land of his birth by train and plane, as if, indeed, the devil were on his heels. It was the name of one he thought dead for three years; the name of the only woman Bristol McGrath had ever loved.

Replacing the telegram, he left the trail and headed westward, pushing his powerful frame between the thick-set trees. His feet made little sound on the matted pine needles. His progress was all but noiseless. Not for nothing had he spent his boyhood in the country of the big pines.

Three hundred yards from the old road he came upon that which he sought—an ancient trail paralleling the road. Choked with young growth, it was little more than a trace through the thick pines. He knew that it ran to the back of the Ballville mansion; did not believe the secret watchers would be guarding it. For how could they know he remembered it?

He hurried south along it, his ears whetted for any sound. Sight alone could not be trusted in that forest. The mansion, he knew, was not far away now. He was passing through what had once been fields, in the days of Richard's grandfather, running almost up to the spacious lawns that girdled the Manor. But for half a century they had been abandoned to the advance of the forest.

But now he glimpsed the Manor, a hint of solid bulk among the pine tops ahead of him. And almost simultaneously his heart shot into his throat as a scream of human anguish knifed the stillness. He could not tell whether it was a man or a woman who screamed, and his thought that it might be a woman winged his feet in his reckless dash toward the building that loomed starkly up just beyond the straggling fringe of trees.

The young pines had even invaded the once generous lawns. The whole place wore an aspect of decay. Behind the Manor, the barns, and outhouses which once housed slave families, were crumbling in ruin. The mansion itself seemed to totter above the litter, a creaky giant, rat gnawed and rotting, ready to collapse at any untoward event. With the stealthy tread of a tiger Bristol McGrath approached a window on the side of the house. From that window sounds were issuing that were an affront to the tree-filtered sunlight and a crawling horror to the brain.

Nerving himself for what he might see, he peered within.

2. Black Torture

He was looking into a great dusty chamber which might have served as a ballroom in antebellum days; its lofty ceiling was hung with cobwebs, its rich oak panels showed dark and stained. But there was a fire in the great fireplace—a small fire, just large enough to heat to a white glow the slender steel rods thrust into it.

But it was only later that Bristol McGrath saw the fire and the things that glowed on the hearth. His eyes were gripped like a spell on the master of the Manor; and once again he looked on a dying man.

A heavy beam had been nailed to the paneled wall, and from it jutted a rude crosspiece. From this crosspiece Richard Ballville hung by cords about his wrists. His toes barely touched the floor, tantalizingly, inviting him to stretch his frame continually in an effort to relieve the agonizing strain on his arms. The cords had cut deeply into his wrists; blood trickled down his arms; his hands were black and swollen almost to the bursting point. He was naked except for his trousers, and McGrath saw that already the white-hot irons had been horribly employed. There was reason enough for the deathly pallor of the man, the cold beads of agony upon his skin. Only his fierce vitality had allowed him thus long to survive the ghastly burns on his limbs and body.

On his breast had been burned a curious symbol—a cold hand laid itself on McGrath's spine. For he recognized that symbol, and once again his memory raced away across the world and the years to a black, grim, hideous jungle where drums bellowed in fire-shot darkness and naked priests of an abhorred cult traced a frightful symbol in quivering human flesh.

Between the fireplace and the dying man squatted a thick-set black man, clad only in ragged, muddy trousers. His back was toward the window, presenting an impressive pair of shoulders. His bullet head was set squarely between those gigantic shoulders, like that of a frog, and he appeared to be avidly watching the face of the man on the crosspiece.

Richard Ballville's bloodshot eyes were like those of a tortured animal, but they were fully sane and conscious; they blazed with desperate vitality. He lifted his head painfully and his gaze swept the room. Outside the window McGrath instinctively shrank back. He did not know whether Ballville saw him or not. The man showed no sign to betray the presence of the watcher to the bestial black who scrutinized him. Then the brute turned his head toward the fire, reaching a long apelike arm toward a glowing iron—and Ballville's eyes blazed with a fierce and urgent meaning the watcher could not mistake. McGrath did not need the agonized motion of the tortured head that accompanied the look. With a tigerish bound he was over the windowsill and in the room, even as the startled black shot erect, whirling with apish agility.

McGrath had not drawn his gun. He dared not risk a shot that might bring other foes upon him. There was a butcher knife in the belt that held up the ragged, muddy trousers. It seemed to leap like a living thing into the hand of the black as he turned. But in McGrath's hand gleamed a curved Afghan dagger that had served him well in many a bygone battle.

Knowing the advantage of instant and relentless attack, he did not pause. His feet scarcely touched the floor inside before they were hurling him at the astounded black man.

An inarticulate cry burst from the thick red lips. The eyes rolled wildly, the butcher knife went back and hissed forward with the swiftness of a striking cobra that would have disemboweled a man whose thews were less steely than those of Bristol McGrath.

But the black was involuntarily stumbling backward as he struck, and that instinctive action slowed his stroke just enough for McGrath to avoid it with a lightning-like twist of his torso. The long blade hissed under his armpit, slicing cloth and skin—and simultaneously the Afghan dagger ripped through the black, bull throat.

There was no cry, but only a choking gurgle as the man fell, spouting blood. McGrath had sprung free as a wolf springs after delivering the death-stroke. Without emotion he surveyed his handiwork. The black man was already dead, his head half-severed from his body. That slicing sidewise lunge that slew in silence, severing the throat to the spinal column, was a favorite stroke of the hairy hillmen that haunt the crags overhanging the Khyber Pass. Less than a dozen white men have ever mastered it. Bristol McGrath was one.

McGrath turned to Richard Ballville. Foam dripped on the seared, naked breast, and blood trickled from his bloodless lips. McGrath feared that Ballville had suffered the same mutilation that had rendered Ahmed speechless; but it was only suffering and shock that numbed Ballville's tongue. McGrath cut his cords and eased him down on a worn old divan nearby. Ballville's lean, muscle-corded body quivered like taut steel strings under McGrath's hands. He gagged, finding his voice.

"I knew you'd come!" he gasped, writhing at the contact of the divan against his seared flesh. "I've hated you for years, but I knew—"

McGrath's voice was harsh as the rasp of steel. "What did you mean by your mention of Constance Brand? She is dead."

A ghastly smile twisted the thin lips.

"No, she's not dead! But she soon will be, if you don't hurry. Quick! Brandy! There on the table—that beast didn't drink it all."

McGrath held the bottle to his lips; Ballville drank avidly. McGrath wondered at the man's iron nerve. That he was in ghastly agony was obvious. He should be screaming in a delirium of pain. Yet he held to sanity and spoke lucidly, though his voice was a laboring croak.

"I haven't much time," he choked. "Don't interrupt. Save your curses till later. We both loved Constance Brand. She loved you.

Three years ago she disappeared. Her garments were found on the bank of a river. Her body was never recovered. You went to Africa to drown your sorrow; I retired to the estate of my ancestors and became a recluse.

"What you didn't know—what the world didn't know—was that Constance Brand came with me! No, she didn't drown. That ruse was my idea. For three years Constance Brand has lived in this house!" He achieved a ghastly laugh. "Oh, don't look so stunned, Bristol. She didn't come of her own free will. She loved you too much. I kidnapped her, brought her here by force—Bristol!" His voice rose to a frantic shriek. "If you kill me you'll never learn where she is!" The frenzied hands that had locked on his corded throat relaxed and sanity returned to the red eyes of Bristol McGrath.

"Go on," he whispered in a voice not even he recognized.

"I couldn't help it," gasped the dying man. "She was the only woman I ever loved—oh, don't sneer, Bristol. The others didn't count. I brought her here where I was king. She couldn't escape, couldn't get word to the outside world. No one lives in this section except nigger descendants of the slaves owned by my family. My word is—*was*— their only law.

"I swear I didn't harm her. I only kept her prisoner, trying to force her to marry me. I didn't want her any other way. I was mad, but I couldn't help it. I come of a race of autocrats who took what they wanted, recognized no law but their own desires. You know that. You understand it. You come of the same breed yourself.

"Constance hates me, if that's any consolation to you, damn you. She's strong, too. I thought I could break her spirit. But I couldn't, not without the whip, and I couldn't bear to use that." He grinned hideously at the wild growl that rose unbidden to McGrath's lips. The big man's eyes were coals of fire; his hard hands knotted into iron mallets.

A spasm racked Ballville, and blood started from his lips. His grin faded and he hurried on.

"All went well until the foul fiend inspired me to send for John De Albor. I met him in Vienna, years ago. He's from East Africa—a devil in human form! He saw Constance—lusted for her as only a man of his type can. When I finally realized that, I tried to kill him. Then I found that he was stronger than I; that he'd made himself master of the niggers—*my* niggers, to whom my word had always been law. He taught them his devilish cult—"

"Voodoo," muttered McGrath involuntarily.

"No! Voodoo is infantile beside this black fiendishness. Look at the symbol on my breast, where De Albor burned it with a white-hot iron. You have been in Africa. You understand the brand of Zambebwei.

"De Albor turned my negroes against me. I tried to escape with Constance and Ahmed. My own blacks hemmed me in. I did smuggle a telegram through to the village by a man who remained faithful to me—they suspected him and tortured him until he admitted it. John De Albor brought me his head—

"Before the final break I hid Constance in a place where no one will ever find her, except you. De Albor tortured Ahmed until he told that I had sent for a friend of the girl's to aid us. Then De Albor sent his men up the road with what was left of Ahmed, as a warning to you if you came. It was this morning that they seized us; I hid Constance last night. Not even Ahmed knew where. De Albor tortured me to make me tell—" the dying man's hands clenched and a fierce passionate light blazed in his eyes. McGrath knew that not all the torments of all the hells could ever have wrung that secret from Ballville's iron lips.

"It was the least you could do," he said, his voice harsh with conflicting emotions. "I've lived in hell for three years because of you—and Constance has. You deserve to die. If you weren't dying already I'd kill you myself."

"Damn you, do you think I want your forgiveness?" gasped the dying man. "I'm glad you suffered. If Constance didn't need your help, I'd like to see you dying as I'm dying—and I'll be waiting for you in hell. But enough of this. De Albor left me awhile to go up the road and assure himself that Ahmed was dead. This beast got to swilling my brandy and decided to torture me some himself.

"Now listen—Constance is hidden in Lost Cave. No man on earth knows of its existence except you and me— not even the negroes. Long ago I put an iron door in the entrance, and I killed the man who did the work, so the secret is safe. There's no key. You've got to open it by working certain knobs." It was more and more difficult for the man to enunciate intelligibly. Sweat dripped from his face, and the cords of his arms quivered.

"Run your fingers over the edge of the door until you find three knobs that form a triangle. You can't see them; you'll have to feel. Press each one in counterclockwise motion, three times, around and around. Then pull on the bar. The door will open. Take Constance and fight your way out. If you see they're going to get you, shoot her! Don't let her fall into the hands of that black beast—"

The voice rose to a shriek, foam spattered from the livid writhing lips, and Richard Ballville heaved himself almost upright— then toppled limply back. The iron will that had animated the broken body had snapped at last, as a taut wire snaps.

McGrath looked down at the still form, his brain a maelstrom of seething emotions, then wheeled, glaring, every nerve a-tingle, his pistol springing into his hand.

3. The Black Priest

A man stood in the doorway that opened upon the great outer hall—a tall man in a strange alien garb. He wore a turban and a silk coat belted with a gay-hued girdle. Turkish slippers were on his feet. His skin was not much darker than McGrath's, his features distinctly oriental in spite of the heavy glasses he wore.

"Who the devil are you?" demanded McGrath, covering him.

"Ali ibn Suleyman, *effendi,*" answered the other in faultless Arabic. "I came to this place of devils at the urging of my brother, Ahmed ibn Suleyman, whose soul may the Prophet ease. In New Orleans the letter came to me, I hastened here. And lo, stealing through the woods, I saw black men dragging my brother's corpse to the river. I came on, seeking his master."

MeGrath mutely indicated the dead man. The Arab bowed his head in stately reverence.

"My brother loved him," he said. "I would have vengeance for my brother and my brother's master. *Effendi*, let me go with you."

"All right." McGrath was afire with impatience. He knew the fanatical clan-loyalty of the Arabs, knew that Ahmed's one decent trait had been a fierce devotion for the scoundrel he served. "Follow me."

With a last glance at the master of the Manor and the black body sprawling like a human sacrifice before him, McGrath left the chamber of torture. Just so, he reflected, one of Ballville's warrior-king ancestors might have lain in some dim past age, with a slaughtered slave at his feet to serve his spirit in the land of ghosts.

With the Arab at his heels, McGrath emerged into the girdling pines that slumbered in the still heat of noon. Faintly to his ears a distant pulse of sound was borne by a vagrant drift of breeze. It sounded like the throb of a faraway drum.

"Come on!" McGrath strode through the cluster of outhouses and plunged into the woods that rose behind them. Here, too, had once stretched the fields that built the wealth of the aristocratic Ballvilles; but for many years they had been abandoned. Paths straggled aimlessly through the ragged growth, until presently the growing denseness of the trees told the invaders that they were in forest that had never known the woodsman's ax. McGrath looked for a path. Impressions received in childhood are always enduring. Memory remains, overlaid by later things, but unerring through the years. McGrath found the path he sought, a dim trace, twisting through the trees.

They were forced to walk single-file; the branches scraped their clothing, their feet sank into the carpet of pine needles. The land trended gradually lower. Pines gave way to cypresses, choked with underbrush. Scummy pools of stagnant water glimmered under the trees. Bullfrogs croaked, mosquitoes sang with maddening insistence about them. Again the distant drum throbbed across the pinelands.

McGrath shook the sweat out of his eyes. That drum roused memories well fitted to these somber surroundings. His thoughts reverted to the hideous scar seared on Richard Ballville's naked breast. Ballville had supposed that he, McGrath, knew its meaning. But he did not. That it portended black horror and madness he knew, but its full significance he did not know. Only once before had he seen that symbol, in the horror-haunted country of Zambebwei, into which few white men had ever ventured, and from which only one white man had ever escaped alive. Bristol McGrath was that man, and he had only penetrated the fringe of that abysmal land of jungle and black swamp. He had not been able to plunge deep enough into that forbidden realm either to prove or to disprove the ghastly tales men whispered of an ancient cult surviving a prehistoric age, of the worship of a monstrosity whose mold violated an accepted law of nature. Little enough he had seen; but what he had seen had filled him with shuddering horror that sometimes returned now in crimson nightmares.

No word had passed between the men since they had left the Manor. McGrath plunged on through the vegetation that choked the path. A fat, blunt-tailed moccasin slithered from under his feet and vanished. Water could not be far away; a few more steps revealed it. They stood on the edge of a dank, slimy marsh from which rose a miasma of rotting vegetable matter. Cypresses shadowed it. The path ended at its edge. The swamp stretched away and away, lost to sight swiftly in twilight dimness.

"What now, *effendi?*" asked Ali. "Are we to swim this morass?"

"It's full of bottomless quagmires," answered McGrath. "It would be suicide for a man to plunge into it. Not even the piney woods niggers have ever tried to cross it. But there *is* a way to get to the hill that rises in the middle of it. You can just barely glimpse it, among the branches of the cypresses, see? Years ago, when Ballville and I were boys—and friends—we discovered an old, old Indian path, a secret, submerged road that led to that hill. There's a cave in the hill, and a woman is imprisoned in that cave. I'm going to it. Do you want to follow me, or to wait for me here? The path is a dangerous one."

"I will go, *effendi,*" answered the Arab.

McGrath nodded in appreciation, and began to scan the trees about him. Presently he found what he was looking for—a faint blaze on a huge cypress, an old mark, almost imperceptible. Confidently then, he stepped into the marsh beside the tree. He himself had made that mark, long ago. Scummy water rose over his shoe soles, but no higher. He stood on a flat rock, or rather on a heap of rocks, the topmost of which was just below the stagnant surface. Locating a certain gnarled cypress far out in the shadow of the marsh, he began walking directly toward it, spacing his strides carefully, each carrying him to a rock step invisible below the murky water. Ali ibn Suleyman followed him, imitating his motions.

Through the swamp they went, following the marked trees that were their guideposts. McGrath wondered anew at the motives that had impelled the ancient builders of the trail to bring these huge rocks from afar and sink them like piles into the slush. The work must have been stupendous, requiring no mean engineering skill. Why had the Indians built this broken road to Lost Island? Surely that isle and the cave in it had some religious significance to the red men; or perhaps it was their refuge against some stronger foe.

The going was slow; a misstep meant a plunge into marshy ooze, into unstable mire that might swallow a man alive. The island grew out of the trees ahead of them—a small knoll, girdled by a vegetation-choked beach. Through the foliage was visible the rocky wall that rose sheer from the beach to a height of fifty or sixty feet. It was almost like a granite block rising from a flat sandy rim. The pinnacle was almost bare of growth.

McGrath was pale, his breath coming in quick gasps. As they stepped upon the beachlike strip, Ali, with a glance of commiseration, drew a flask from his pocket.

"Drink a little brandy, *effendi,*" he urged, touching the mouth to his own lips, oriental fashion. "It will aid you."

McGrath knew that Ali thought his evident agitation was a result of exhaustion. But he was scarcely aware of his recent exertions. It was the emotions that raged within him—the thought of Constance Brand, whose beautiful form had haunted his troubled dreams for three dreary years. He gulped deeply of the liquor, scarcely tasting it, and handed back the flask.

"Come on!"

The pounding of his own heart was suffocating, drowning the distant drum, as he thrust through the choking vegetation at the foot of the cliff. On the gray rock above the green mask appeared a curious carven symbol, as he had seen it years ago, when its discovery led him and Richard Ballville to the hidden cavern. He tore aside the clinging vines and fronds, and his breath sucked in at the sight of a heavy iron door set in the narrow mouth that opened in the granite wall.

McGrath's fingers were trembling as they swept over the metal, and behind him he could hear Ali breathing heavily. Some of the white man's excitement had imparted itself to the Arab. McGrath's hands found the three knobs, forming the apices of a triangle—mere protuberances, not apparent to the sight. Controlling his jumping nerves, he pressed them as Ballville had instructed him, and felt each give slightly at the third pressure. Then, holding his breath, he grasped the bar that was welded in the middle of the door, and pulled. Smoothly, on oiled hinges, the massive portal swung open.

They looked into a wide tunnel that ended in another door, this a grille of steel bars. The tunnel was not dark; it was clean and roomy, and the ceiling had been pierced to allow light to enter, the holes covered with screens to keep out insects and reptiles. But through the grille he glimpsed something that sent him racing along the tunnel, his heart almost bursting through his ribs. Ali was close at his heels.

The grille door was not locked. It swung outward under his fingers. He stood motionless, almost stunned with the impact of his emotions.

His eyes were dazzled by a gleam of gold; a sunbeam slanted down through the pierced rock roof and struck mellow fire from the glorious profusion of golden hair that flowed over the white arm that pillowed the beautiful head on the carved oak table.

"*Constance!*" It was a cry of hunger and yearning that burst from his livid lips.

Echoing the cry, the girl started up, staring wildly, her hands at her temples, her lambent hair rippling over her shoulders. To his dizzy gaze she seemed to float in an aureole of golden light.

"Bristol! Bristol McGrath!" she echoed his call with a haunting, incredulous cry. Then she was in his arms, her white arms clutching him in a frantic embrace, as if she feared he were but a phantom that might vanish from her.

For the moment the world ceased to exist for Bristol McGrath. He might have been blind, deaf and dumb to the universe at large. His dazed brain was cognizant only of the woman in his arms, his senses drunken with the softness and fragrance of her, his soul stunned with the overwhelming realization of a dream he had thought dead and vanished for ever.

When he could think consecutively again, he shook himself like a man coming out of a trance, and stared stupidly around him. He was in a wide chamber, cut in the solid rock. Like the tunnel, it was illumined from above, and the air was fresh and clean. There were chairs, tables and a hammock, carpets on the rocky floor, cans of food and a water cooler. Ballville had not failed to provide for his captive's comfort. McGrath glanced around at the Arab, and saw him beyond the grille. Considerately he had not intruded upon their reunion.

"Three years!" the girl was sobbing. "Three years I've waited. I knew you'd come! I knew it! But we must be careful, my darling. Richard will kill you if he finds you—kill us both!"

"He's beyond killing anyone," answered McGrath. "But just the same, we've got to get out of here."

Her eyes flared with new terror.

"Yes! John De Albor! Ballville was afraid of him. That's why he locked me in here. He said he'd sent for you. I was afraid for you—"

"Ali!" McGrath called. "Come in here. We're getting out of here now, and we'd better take some water and food with us. We may have to hide in the swamps for—"

Abruptly Constance shrieked, tore herself from her lover's arms. And McGrath, frozen by the sudden, awful fear in her wide eyes, felt the dull jolting impact of a savage blow at the base of his skull. Consciousness did not leave him, but a strange paralysis gripped him. He dropped like an empty sack on the stone floor and lay there like a dead man, helplessly staring up at the scene which tinged his brain with madness—Constance struggling frenziedly in the grasp of the man he had known as Ali ibn Suleyman, now terribly transformed.

The man had thrown off his turban and glasses. And in the murky whites of his eyes, McGrath read the truth with its grisly implications—the man was not an Arab. He was a negroid mixed breed. Yet some of his blood must have been Arab, for there was a slightly Semitic cast to his countenance, and this cast, together with his oriental garb and his perfect acting of his part, had made him seem genuine. But now all this was discarded and the negroid strain was uppermost; even his voice, which had enunciated the sonorous Arabic, was now the throaty gutturals of the negro.

"You've killed him!" the girl sobbed hysterically, striving vainly to break away from the cruel fingers that prisoned her white wrists.

"He's not dead yet," laughed the octoroon. "The fool quaffed drugged brandy—a drug found only in the Zambebwei jungles. It lies inactive in the system until made effective by a sharp blow on a nerve center."

"Please do something for him!" she begged.

The fellow laughed brutally.

"Why should I? He has served his purpose. Let him lie there until the swamp insects have picked his bones. I should like to watch that—but we will be far away before nightfall." His eyes blazed with the bestial gratification of possession. The sight of this white beauty struggling in his grasp seemed to rouse all the jungle lust in the man.

McGrath's wrath and agony found expression only in his bloodshot eyes. He could not move hand nor foot.

"It was well I returned alone to the Manor," laughed the octoroon. "I stole up to the window while this fool talked with Richard Ballville. The thought came to me to let him lead me to the place where you were hidden. It had never occurred to me that there was a hiding place in the swamp. I had the Arab's coat, slippers and turban; I had thought I might use them sometime. The glasses helped, too. It was not difficult to make an Arab out of myself. This man had never seen John De Albor. I was born in East Africa and grew up a slave in the house of an Arab—before I ran away and wandered to the land of Zambebwei.

"But enough. We must go. The drum has been muttering all day. The blacks are restless. I promised them a sacrifice to Zemba. I was going to use the Arab, but by the time I had tortured out of him the information I desired, he was no longer fit for a sacrifice. Well, let them bang their silly drum. They'd like to have *you* for the Bride of Zemba, but they don't know I've found you. I have a motorboat hidden on the river five miles from here—"

"You fool!" shrieked Constance, struggling passionately. "Do you think you can carry a white girl down the river, like a slave?"

"I have a drug which will make you like a dead woman," he said. "You will lie in the bottom of the boat, covered by sacks. When I board the steamer that shall bear us from these shores, you will go into my cabin in a large, well-ventilated trunk. You will know nothing of the discomforts of the voyage. You will awake in Africa—"

He was fumbling in his shirt, necessarily releasing her with one hand. With a frenzied scream and a desperate wrench, she tore loose and sped out through the tunnel. John De Albor plunged after her, bellowing. A red haze floated before McGrath's maddened eyes. The girl would plunge to her death in the swamps, unless she remembered the guide marks—perhaps it was death she sought, in preference to the fate planned for her by the fiendish negro.

They had vanished from his sight, out of the tunnel; but suddenly Constance screamed again, with a new poignancy. To

McGrath's ears came an excited jabbering of negro gutturals. De Albor's accents were lifted in angry protest. Constance was sobbing hysterically. The voices were moving away. McGrath got a vague glimpse of a group of figures through the masking vegetation as they moved across the line of the tunnel mouth. He saw Constance being dragged along by half a dozen giant blacks, typical pineland dwellers, and after them came John De Albor, his hands eloquent in dissension. That glimpse only, through the fronds, and then the tunnel mouth gaped empty and the sound of splashing water faded away through the marsh.

4. The Black God's Hunger

In the brooding silence of the cavern Bristol McGrath lay staring blankly upward, his soul a seething hell. Fool, fool, to be taken in so easily! Yet, how could he have known? He had never seen De Albor; he had supposed he was a full-blooded negro. Ballville had called him a black beast, but he must have been referring to his soul. De Albor, but for the betraying murk of his eyes, might pass anywhere for a white man.

The presence of those black men meant but one thing: they had followed him and De Albor, had seized Constance as she rushed from the cave. De Albor's evident fear bore a hideous implication; he had said the blacks wanted to sacrifice Constance—now she was in their hands.

"God!" The word burst from McGrath's lips, startling in the stillness, startling to the speaker. He was electrified; a few moments before he had been dumb. But now he discovered he could move his lips, his tongue. Life was stealing back through his dead limbs; they stung as if with returning circulation. Frantically he encouraged that sluggish flow. Laboriously he worked his extremities, his fingers, hands, wrists and finally, with a surge of wild triumph, his arms and legs. Perhaps De Albor's hellish drug had lost some of its power through age. Perhaps McGrath's unusual stamina threw off the effects as another man could not have done.

The tunnel door had not been closed, and McGrath knew why: they did not want to shut out the insects which would soon dispose of a helpless body; already the pests were streaming through the door, a noisome horde.

McGrath rose at last, staggering drunkenly, but with his vitality surging more strongly each second. When he tottered from the cave, no living thing met his glare. Hours had passed since the negroes had departed with their prey. He strained his ears for the drum. It was silent. The stillness rose like an invisible black mist around him. Stumblingly he splashed along the rock trail that led to hard ground. Had the blacks taken their captive back to the death-haunted Manor, or deeper into the pinelands?

Their tracks were thick in the mud: half a dozen pairs of bare, splay feet, the slender prints of Constance's shoes, the marks of De Albor's Turkish slippers. He followed them with increasing difficulty as the ground grew higher and harder.

He would have missed the spot where they turned off the dim trail but for the fluttering of a bit of silk in the faint breeze. Constance had brushed against a tree trunk there, and the rough bark had shredded off a fragment of her dress. The band had been headed east, toward the Manor. At the spot where the bit of cloth hung, they had turned sharply southward. The matted pine needles showed no tracks, but disarranged vines and branches bent aside marked their progress, until McGrath, following these signs, came out upon another trail leading southward.

Here and there were marshy spots, and these showed the prints of feet, bare and shod. McGrath hastened along the trail, pistol in hand, in full possession of his faculties at last. His face was grim and pale. De Albor had not had an opportunity to disarm him after striking that treacherous blow. Both the octoroon and the blacks of the pinelands believed him to be lying helpless back in Lost Cave. That, at least, was to his advantage.

He kept straining his ears in vain for the drum he had heard earlier in the day. The silence did not reassure him. In a voodoo sacrifice drums would be thundering, but he knew he was dealing with something even more ancient and abhorrent than voodoo.

Voodoo was comparatively a young religion, after all, born in the hills of Haiti. Behind the froth of voodooism rose the grim religions of Africa, like granite cliffs glimpsed through a mask of green fronds. Voodooism was a mewling infant beside the black, immemorial colossus that had reared its terrible shape in the older land through uncounted ages. Zambebwei! The very name sent a shudder through him, symbolic of horror and fear. It was more than the name of a country and the mysterious tribe that inhabited that country; it signified something fearfully old and evil, something that had survived its natural epoch—a religion of the Night, and a deity whose name was Death and Horror.

He had seen no negro cabins. He knew these were farther to the east and south, most of them, huddling along the banks of the river and the tributary creeks. It was the instinct of the black man to build his habitation by a river, as he had built by the Congo, the Nile and the Niger since Time's first gray dawn. Zambebwei! The word beat like a throb of a tom-tom through the brain of Bristol McGrath. The soul of the black man had not changed, through the slumberous centuries. Change might come in the clangor of city streets, in the raw rhythms of Harlem; but the swamps of the Mississippi do not differ enough from the swamps of the Congo to work any great transmutation in the spirit of a race that was old before the first white king wove the thatch of his wattled hut-palace.

Following that winding path through the twilight dimness of the big pines, McGrath did not find it in his soul to marvel that black slimy tentacles from the depths of Africa had stretched across the world to breed nightmares in an alien land. Certain natural conditions produce certain effects, breed certain pestilences of body or mind, regardless of their geographical situation. The river-haunted pinelands were as abysmal in their way as were the reeking African jungles.

The trend of the trail was away from the river. The land sloped very gradually upward, and all signs of marsh vanished.

The trail widened, showing signs of frequent use. McGrath became nervous. At any moment he might meet someone. He took to the thick woods alongside the trail, and forced his way onward, each movement sounding cannon loud to his whetted ears. Sweating with nervous tension, he came presently upon a smaller path, which meandered in the general direction he wished to go. The pinelands were crisscrossed by such paths.

He followed it with greater ease and stealth, and presently, coming to a crook in it, saw it join the main trail. Near the point of junction stood a small log cabin, and between him and the cabin squatted a big black man. This man was hidden behind the bole of a huge pine beside the narrow path, and peering around it toward the cabin. Obviously he was spying on someone, and it was quickly apparent who this was, as John De Albor came to the door and stared despairingly down the wide trail. The black watcher stiffened and lifted his fingers to his mouth as if to sound a far-carrying whistle, but De Albor shrugged his shoulders helplessly and turned back into the cabin again. The negro relaxed, though he did not alter his vigilance.

What this portended, McGrath did not know, nor did he pause to speculate. At the sight of De Albor a red mist turned the sunlight to blood, in which the black body before him floated like an ebony goblin.

A panther stealing upon its kill would have made as much noise as McGrath made in his glide down the path toward the squatting black. He was aware of no personal animosity toward the man, who was but an obstacle on his path of vengeance. Intent on the cabin, the black man did not hear that stealthy approach. Oblivious to all else, he did not move or turn—until the pistol butt descended on his woolly skull with an impact that stretched him senseless among the pine needles.

McGrath crouched above his motionless victim, listening. There was no sound nearby—but suddenly, far away, there rose a long-drawn shriek that shuddered and died away. The blood congealed in McGrath's veins. Once before he had heard that sound—in the low forest-covered hills that fringe the borders of forbidden Zambebwei; his black boys had turned the color of ashes and fallen on their faces. What it was he did not know; and the explanation offered by the shuddering natives had been too monstrous to be accepted by a rational mind. They called it the voice of the god of Zambebwei.

Stung to action, McGrath rushed down the path and hurled himself against the back door of the cabin. He did not know how many blacks were inside; he did not care. He was berserk with grief and fury.

The door crashed inward under the impact. He lit on his feet inside, crouching, gun leveled hip high, lips asnarl.

But only one man faced him—John De Albor, who sprang to his feet with a startled cry. The gun dropped from McGrath's fingers. Neither lead nor steel could glut his hate now. It must be with naked hands, turning back the pages of civilization to the red dawn days of the primordial.

With a growl that was less like the cry of a man than the grunt of a charging lion, McGrath's fierce hands locked about the octoroon's throat. De Albor was borne backward by the hurtling impact, and the men crashed together over a camp cot, smashing it to ruins. And as they tumbled on the dirt floor, McGrath set himself to kill his enemy with his bare fingers.

The octoroon was a tall man, rangy and strong. But against the berserk white man he had no chance. He was hurled about like a sack of straw, battered and smashed savagely against the floor, and the iron fingers that were crushing his throat sank deeper and deeper until his tongue protruded from his gaping blue lips and his eyes were starting from his head. With death no more than a hand's breadth from the octoroon, some measure of sanity returned to McGrath.

He shook his head like a dazed bull; eased his terrible grip a trifle, and snarled: "Where is the girl? Quick, before I kill you!"

De Albor retched and fought for breath, ashen faced. "The blacks!" he gasped. "They have taken her to be the Bride of Zemba!

I could not prevent them. They demand a sacrifice. I offered them you, but they said you were paralyzed and would die anyway—they were cleverer than I thought. They followed me back to the Manor from the spot where we left the Arab in the road—followed us from the Manor to the island.

"They are out of hand—mad with bloodlust. But even I, who know black men as none else knows them, I had forgotten that not even a priest of Zambebwei can control them when the fire of worship runs in their veins. I am their priest and master—yet when I sought to save the girl, they forced me into this cabin and set a man to watch me until the sacrifice is over. You must have killed him; he would never have let you enter here."

With a chill grimness, McGrath picked up his pistol.

"You came here as Richard Ballville's friend," he said unemotionally. "To get possession of Constance Brand, you made devil worshippers out of the black people. You deserve death for that. When the European authorities that govern Africa catch a priest of Zambebwei, they hang him. You have admitted that you are a priest. Your life is forfeit on that score, too. But it is because of your hellish teachings that Constance Brand is to die, and it's for that reason that I'm going to blow out your brains."

John De Albor shriveled. "She is not dead yet," he gasped, great drops of perspiration dripping from his ashy face. "She will not die until the moon is high above the pines. It is full tonight, the Moon of Zambebwei. Don't kill me. Only I can save her. I know I failed before. But if I go to them, appear to them suddenly and without warning, they'll think it is because of supernatural powers that I was able to escape from the hut without being seen by the watchman. That will renew my prestige.

"You can't save her. You might shoot a few blacks, but there would still be scores left to kill you—and her. But I have a plan—yes, I am a priest of Zambebwei. When I was a boy I ran away from my Arab master and wandered far until I came to the land of Zambebwei. There I grew to manhood and became a priest, dwelling there until the white blood in me drew me out in the world again to learn the ways of the white men. When I came to America I brought a *Zemba* with me—I can not tell you how . . .

"Let me save Constance Brand!" He was clawing at McGrath, shaking as if with an ague. "I love her, even as you love her. I will play fair with you both, I swear it! Let me save her! We can fight for her later, and I'll kill you if I can."

The frankness of that statement swayed McGrath more than anything else the octoroon could have said. It was a desperate gamble—but after all, Constance would be no worse off with John De Albor alive than she was already. She would be dead before midnight unless something was done swiftly.

"Where is the place of sacrifice?" asked McGrath.

"Three miles away, in an open glade," answered De Albor. "South, on the trail that runs past my cabin. All the blacks are gathered there except my guard and some others who are watching the trail below the cabin. They are scattered out along it, the nearest out of sight of my cabin, but within sound of the loud, shrill whistle with which these people signal one another.

"This is my plan. You wait here in my cabin, or in the woods, as you choose. I'll avoid the watchers on the trail, and appear suddenly before the blacks at the House of Zemba. A sudden appearance will impress them deeply, as I said. I know I cannot persuade them to abandon their plan, but I will make them postpone the sacrifice until just before dawn. And before that time I will manage to steal the girl and flee with her. I'll return to your hiding place, and we'll fight our way out together."

McGrath laughed. "Do you think I'm an utter fool? You'd send your blacks to murder me, while you carried Constance away as you planned. I'm going with you. I'll hide at the edge of the clearing, to help you if you need help. And if you make a false move, I'll get you, if I don't get anybody else."

The octoroon's murky eyes glittered, but he nodded acquiescence.

"Help me bring your guard into the cabin," said McGrath. "He'll be coming to soon. We'll tie and gag him and leave him here."

The sun was setting and twilight was stealing over the pinelands as McGrath and his strange companion stole through the shadowy woods. They had circled to the west to avoid the watchers on the trail, and were now following one of the many narrow footpaths which traced their way through the forest. Silence reigned ahead of them, and McGrath mentioned this.

"Zemba is a god of silence," muttered De Albor. "From sunset to sunrise on the night of the full moon, no drum is beaten. If a dog barks, it must be slain; if a baby cries, it must be killed. Silence locks the jaws of the people until Zemba roars. Only *his* voice is lifted on the night of the Moon of Zemba."

McGrath shuddered. The foul deity was an intangible spirit, of course, embodied only in legend; but De Albor spoke of it as a living thing.

A few stars were blinking out, and shadows crept through the thick woods, blurring the trunks of the trees that melted together in darkness, McGrath knew they could not be far from the House of Zemba. He sensed the close presence of a throng of people, though he heard nothing.

De Albor, ahead of him, halted suddenly, crouching. McGrath stopped, trying to pierce the surrounding mask of interlacing branches. The octoroon's face turned toward him, a dusky oval in the gathering dusk.

"What is it?" muttered the white man, reaching for his pistol.

De Albor shook his head, straightening. McGrath could not see the stone in his hand, caught up from the earth as he stooped.

"Do you hear something?" demanded McGrath. De Albor motioned him to lean forward, as if to whisper in his ear. Caught off his guard, McGrath bent toward him—even so he divined the treacherous African's intention, but it was too late. The stone in De Albor's hand crashed sickeningly against the white man's temple. McGrath went down like a slaughtered ox, and De Albor sped away down the path to vanish like a ghost in the gloom.

5. The Voice of Zemba

In the darkness of the woodland path McGrath stirred at last, and staggered groggily to his feet. That desperate blow might have crushed the skull of a man whose physique and vitality were not that of a bull. His head throbbed and there was dried blood on his temple; but his strongest sensation was burning scorn at himself for having again fallen victim to John De Albor. And yet, who would have suspected that move? He knew De Albor would kill him if he could, but he had not expected an attack *before* the rescue of Constance. The fellow was dangerous and unpredictable as a cobra. Had his pleas to be allowed to attempt Constance's rescue been but a ruse to escape death at the hands of McGrath?

McGrath stared dizzily at the stars that gleamed through the ebon branches, and sighed with relief to see that the moon had not yet risen. The pinewoods were black as only pinelands can be—with a darkness that was almost tangible, like a substance that could be cut with a knife.

McGrath had reason to be grateful for his rugged constitution. Twice that day had John De Albor outwitted him, and twice the white man's iron frame had survived the attack. His gun was in his scabbard, his knife in its sheath. De Albor had not paused to search, had not paused for a second stroke to make sure. Perhaps there had been a tinge of panic in the African's actions.

Well, this did not change matters a great deal. He believed that De Albor would make an effort to save the girl. And McGrath intended to be on hand, whether to play a lone hand, or to aid the octoroon. This was no time to hold grudges, with the girl's life at stake. He groped down the path, spurred by a rising glow in the east.

He came upon the glade almost before he knew it. The moon hung in the low branches, blood red, high enough to illumine it and the throng of black people who squatted in a vast semicircle about it, facing the moon. Their rolling eyes gleamed milkily in the shadows, their features were grotesque masks. They were all stark naked, men and women. None spoke. No head turned toward the bushes behind which he crouched.

He had vaguely expected blazing fires, a bloodstained altar, drums and the chant of maddened worshippers; that would be voodoo. But this was not voodoo, and there was a vast gulf between the two cults. There were no fires, no altars. But the breath hissed through his locked teeth. In a far land he had sought in vain for the rituals of Zambebwei; now he looked upon them within forty miles of the spot where he was born.

In the center of the glade the ground rose slightly to a flat level. On this stood a heavy iron-bound stake that was indeed but the sharpened trunk of a good-sized pine driven deep into the ground. And there was something living chained to that stake—something which caused McGrath to catch his breath in horrified unbelief.

He was looking upon a god of Zambebwei. Stories had told of such creatures, wild tales drifting down from the borders of the forbidden country, repeated by shivering natives about jungle fires, passed along until they reached the ears of skeptical white traders. McGrath had never really believed the stories, though he had gone searching for the being they described. For they spoke of a beast that was a blasphemy against nature—a beast that sought food strange to its natural species.

The thing chained to the stake was an ape, but such an ape as the world at large never dreamed of, even in nightmares. Its shaggy gray hair was shot with silver that shone in the rising moon; it looked gigantic as it squatted ghoulishly on its haunches. Upright, on its bent, gnarled legs, it would be as tall as a man, and much broader and thicker. But its prehensile fingers were armed with talons like those of a tiger—not the heavy blunt nails of the natural anthropoid, but the cruel scimitar-curved claws of the great carnivore. Its face was like that of a gorilla, low browed, flaring nostriled, chinless; but when it snarled, its wide flat nose wrinkled like that of a great cat, and the cavernous mouth disclosed saberlike fangs, the fangs of a beast of prey. This was Zemba, the creature sacred to the people of the land of Zambebwei— a monstrosity, a violation of an accepted law of nature—a carnivorous ape. Men had laughed at the story, hunters and zoologists and traders.

But now McGrath knew that such creatures dwelt in black Zambebwei and were worshipped, as primitive man is prone to worship an obscenity or perversion of nature. Or a survival of past eons: that was what the flesh-eating apes of Zambebwei were—survivors of a forgotten epoch, remnants of a vanished prehistoric age, when nature was experimenting with matter, and life took many monstrous forms.

The sight of the monstrosity filled McGrath with revulsion; it was abysmal, a reminder of that brutish and horror-shadowed past out of which mankind crawled so painfully, eons ago. This thing was an affront to sanity; it belonged in the dust of oblivion with the dinosaur, the mastodon, and the saber-toothed tiger.

It looked massive beyond the stature of modern beasts—shaped on the plan of another age, when all things were cast in a mightier mold. He wondered if the revolver at his hip would have any effect on it. Wondered by what dark and subtle means John De Albor had brought the monster from Zambebwei to the pinelands.

But something was happening in the glade, heralded by the shaking of the brute's chain as it thrust forward its nightmare head.

From the shadows of the trees came a file of black men and women, young, naked except for a mantle of monkey skins and parrot feathers thrown over the shoulders of each. More regalia brought by John De Albor, undoubtedly. They formed a semicircle at a safe distance from the chained brute, and sank to their knees, bending their heads to the ground before him. Thrice this motion was repeated. Then, rising, they formed two lines, men and women facing one another, and began to dance. At least it might by courtesy be called a dance. They hardly moved their feet at all, but all other parts of their bodies were in constant motion, twisting, rotating, writhing. The measured, rhythmical movements had no connection at all with the Voodoo dances McGrath had witnessed. This dance was disquietingly archaic in its suggestion, though even more depraved and bestial—naked primitive passions framed in a cynical debauchery of motion.

No sound came from the dancers, or from the votaries squatting about the ring of trees. But the ape, apparently infuriated by the continued movements, lifted his head and sent into the night the frightful shriek McGrath had heard once before that day—that he had heard it in the hills that border black Zambebwei. The brute plunged to the end of his heavy chain, foaming and gnashing his fangs, and the dancers fled like spume blown before a gust of wind. They scattered in all directions—and then McGrath started up in his covert, barely stifling a cry.

From the deep shadows had come a figure, gleaming tawnily in contrast to the black forms about it. It was John De Albor, naked except for a mantle of bright feathers, and on his head a circlet of gold that might have been forged in Atlantis. In his hand he bore a gold wand that was the scepter of the high priests of Zambebwei.

Behind him came a pitiful figure, at the sight of which the moonlit forest reeled to McGrath's sight.

Constance had been drugged. Her face was that of a sleepwalker; she seemed not aware of her peril, or the fact that she was naked. She walked like a robot, mechanically responding to the urge of the cord tied about her white neck. The other end of that cord was in John De Albor's hand, and he half-led, half-dragged her toward the horror that squatted in the center of the glade. De Albor's face was ashy in the moonlight that now flooded the glade with molten silver. Sweat beaded his skin. His eyes gleamed with fear and ruthless determination. And in a staggering instant McGrath knew that the man had failed— that he had been unable to save Constance, and that now, to save his own life from his suspicious followers, he himself was dragging the girl to the gory sacrifice.

No vocal sound came from the votaries, but hissing intake of breath sucked through thick lips, and the rows of black bodies swayed like reeds in the wind. The great ape leaped up, his face a slavering devil's mask; he howled with frightful eagerness, gnashing his great fangs, that yearned to sink into that soft white flesh, and the hot blood beneath. He surged against his chain, and the stout post quivered. McGrath, in the bushes, stood frozen, paralyzed by the imminence of horror. And then John De Albor stepped behind the unresisting girl and gave her a powerful push that sent her reeling forward to pitch headlong on the ground under the monster's talons.

And simultaneously McGrath moved. His move was instinctive rather than conscious. His .44 jumped into his hand and spoke, and the great ape screamed like a man death stricken and reeled, clapping misshapen hands to his head.

An instant the throng crouched frozen, white eyes bulging, jaws hanging slack. Then before any could move, the ape, blood gushing from his head, wheeled, seized the chain in both hands and snapped it with a wrench that twisted the heavy links apart as if they had been paper.

John De Albor stood directly before the mad brute, paralyzed in his tracks. Zemba roared and leaped, and the octoroon went down under him, disemboweled by the razorlike talons, his head crushed to a crimson pulp by a sweep of the great paw.

Ravening, the monster charged among the votaries, clawing and ripping and smiting, screaming intolerably. Zambebwei spoke, and death was in his bellowing. Screaming, howling, fighting, the black people scrambled over each other in their mad flight. Men and women went down under those shearing talons, were dismembered by those gnashing fangs. It was a red drama of the primitive—destruction amuck and ariot, the primordial embodied in fangs and talons, gone mad and plunging in slaughter. Blood and brains deluged the earth, black bodies and limbs and fragments of bodies littered the moonlighted glade in ghastly heaps before the last of the howling wretches found refuge among the trees. The sounds of their blundering, panic-stricken flight drifted back.

McGrath had leaped from his covert almost as soon as he had fired. Unnoticed by the terrified negroes, and himself scarcely cognizant of the slaughter raging around him, he raced across the glade toward the pitiful white figure that lay limply beside the iron-bound stake.

"Constance!" he cried, gathering her to his breast. Languidly she opened her cloudy eyes. He held her close, heedless of the screams and devastation surging about them. Slowly recognition grew in those lovely eyes.

"Bristol!" she murmured, incoherently. Then she screamed, clung to him, sobbing hysterically. "Bristol! They told me you were dead! The blacks! The horrible blacks! They're going to kill me! They were going to kill De Albor too, but he promised to sacrifice—"

"Don't, girl, don't!" He subdued her frantic tremblings. "It's all right, now—" Abruptly he looked up into the grinning bloodstained face of nightmare and death. The great ape had ceased to rend his dead victims and was slinking toward the living pair in the center of the glade. Blood oozed from the wound in its sloping skull that had maddened it.

McGrath sprang toward it, shielding the prostrate girl; his pistol spurted flame, pouring a stream of lead into the mighty breast as the beast charged.

On it came, and his confidence waned. Bullet after bullet he sent crashing into its vitals, but it did not halt. Now he dashed the empty gun full into the gargoyle face without effect, and with a lurch and a roll it had him in its grasp. As the giant arms closed crushingly about him, he abandoned all hope, but following his fighting instinct to the last, he drove his dagger hilt deep in the shaggy belly.

But even as he struck, he felt a shudder run through the gigantic frame. The great arms fell away—and then he was hurled to the ground in the last death throe of the monster, and the thing was swaying, its face a death mask. Dead on its feet, it crumpled, toppled to the ground, quivered and lay still. Not even a man-eating ape of Zambebwei could survive that close-range volley of mushrooming lead.

As the man staggered up, Constance rose and reeled into his arms, crying hysterically.

"It's all right *now*, Constance," he panted, crushing her to him. "The Zemba's dead; De Albor's dead; Ballville's dead; the negroes have run away. There's nothing to prevent us leaving now. The

Moon of Zambebwei was the end for them. But it's the beginning of life for us."

Black Hound of Death

Chapter .1.

Egyptian darkness! The phrase is too vivid for complete comfort—suggesting not only blackness, but unseen things lurking in that blackness; things that skulk in the deep shadows and shun the light of day. Slinking figures that prowl beyond the edge of normal Life.

Some such thoughts flitted vaguely through my mind that night as I groped along the narrow trail that wound through the deep pinelands. Such thoughts are likely to keep company with any man who dares invade, in the night, that lonely stretch of densely timbered river-country which the black people call Egypt, for some obscurely racial reason.

There is no blackness this side of Hell's unlighted abyss as absolute as the blackness of the pine woods. The trail was but a half-guessed trace winding between walls of solid ebony. I followed it as much by the instincts of the piney-woods' dweller as by the guidance of the external senses. I went as hurriedly as I dared, but stealth was mingled with my haste, and my ears were whetted to knife-edge alertness. This caution did not spring from the uncanny speculations roused by the darkness and silence; I had good, material reason to be wary. Ghosts might roam the pinelands with gaping, bloody throats and cannibalistic hunger as the negroes maintained, but it was no ghost I feared. I listened for the snap of a twig under a great, splay foot, for any sound that would presage Murder striking from the black shadows. The creature which I feared haunted Egypt was more to be dreaded than any gibbering phantom.

That morning the worst negro desperado in that part of the state had broken from the clutches of the law, leaving a ghastly toll of dead behind him. Down along the river, bloodhounds were baying through the brush, and hard-eyed men with rifles were beating up the thickets.

They were seeking him in the fastnesses near the scattered black settlements, knowing that a negro seeks his own kind in his extremity. But I knew Tope Braxton better than they did; I knew he deviated from the general type of his race. He was unbelievably primitive—atavistic enough to plunge into uninhabited wilderness and live like a blood-mad gorilla in solitude that would have terrified and daunted a more normal member of his race.

So while the hunt flowed away in another direction, I rode toward Egypt, alone. But it was not altogether to look for Tope Braxton that I plunged into that isolated fastness. My mission was one of warning, rather than search. Deep in the mazy pine labyrinth, a white man and his servant lived alone, and it was the duty of any man to warn them that a red-handed killer might be skulking about their cabin.

I was foolish, perhaps, to be traveling on foot; but men who wear the name of Garfield are not in the habit of turning back on a task once attempted. When my horse unexpectedly went lame, I left him at one of the negro cabins which fringe the edge of Egypt, and went on afoot. Night overtook me on the path, and I intended remaining until morning with the man I was going to warn—Richard Brent. He was a taciturn recluse, suspicious and peculiar, but he could scarcely refuse to put me up for the night. He was a mysterious figure; why he chose to hide himself in a southern pine forest none knew. He had been living in an old cabin in the heart of Egypt for about six months.

Suddenly, as I forged through the darkness, my speculations regarding the mysterious recluse were cut short—wiped clear out of my mind. I stopped dead, the nerves tangling in the skin on the backs of my hands. A sudden shriek in the dark has that effect—and this scream was edged with agony and terror. It came from somewhere ahead of me. Breathless silence followed that cry, a silence in which the forest seemed to hold its breath and the darkness shut in more blackly yet.

Again the scream was repeated, this time closer. Then I heard the pound of bare feet along the trail, and a form hurled itself at me out of the darkness.

My revolver was in my hand, and I instinctively thrust it out to fend the creature off. The only thing that kept me from pulling the trigger was the noise the object was making—gasping, sobbing noises of fear and pain. It was a man, and direly stricken. He blundered full into me, shrieked again, and fell sprawling, slobbering and yammering.

"Oh, my God save me! Oh, God have mercy on me!"

"What the devil is it?" I demanded, my hair stirring on my scalp at the poignant agony in the gibbering voice.

The wretch recognized my voice; he clawed at my knees.

"Oh, Mas' Kirby, don' let him tetch me! He's done killed my body, and now he wants my soul! It's me—po' Jim Tike. Don' let him git me!"

I struck a match—and stood staring in amazement, while the match burned down to my fingers. A black man groveled in the dust before me, his eyes rolling up whitely. I knew him well—one of the negroes who lived in their tiny log cabins along the fringe of Egypt. He was spotted and splashed with blood, and I believed he was mortally wounded. Only abnormal energy rising from frenzied panic could have enabled him to run as far as he had. Blood jetted from torn veins and arteries in breast, shoulder and neck, and the wounds were ghastly to see, great ragged tears, that were never made by bullet. One ear had been torn from his head, and hung loose, with a great piece of flesh from the angle of his jaw and neck, as if some gigantic beast had ripped it out with his fangs.

"What in God's name did this?" I ejaculated as the match went out, and he became merely an indistinct blob in the darkness below me. "A bear?" Even as I spoke I knew that no bear had been seen in Egypt for thirty years.

"He done it!" The thick, sobbing mumble welled up through the dark. "De white man dat come by my cabin and ask me to guide him to Mistuh Brent's house. He said he had a toothache, so he had his head bandaged—but de bandages slipped and I seen his face—he killed me for seein' him."

"You mean he set dogs on you?" I demanded, for his wounds were such as I have seen on animals worried by vicious hounds.

"No, suh," whimpered the ebbing voice. "He done it hisself—aaaggghhh!"

The mumble broke in a shriek as he twisted his head, barely visible in the gloom, and stared back the way he had come. Death must have struck him in the midst of that scream, for it broke short at the highest note. He flopped convulsively once, like a dog hit by a truck, and then lay still.

I strained my eyes into the darkness, and made out a vague shape a few yards away in the trail. It was erect and tall as a man; it made no sound.

I opened my mouth to challenge the unknown visitant, but no sound came. An indescribable chill flowed over me, freezing my tongue to my palate. It was fear, primitive and unreasoning, and even while I stood paralyzed I could not understand it; could not guess why that silent, motionless figure, sinister as it was, should rouse such instinctive dread.

Then suddenly the figure moved quickly toward me, and I found my voice. "Who comes there?"

No answer; but the form came on in a rush, and as I groped for a match, it was almost upon me. I struck the match—with a ferocious snarl the figure hurled itself against me, the match was struck from my hand and extinguished, and I felt a sharp pain on the side of my neck. My gun exploded almost involuntarily and without aim, and its flash dazzled me, obscuring rather than revealing the tall manlike figure that struck at me—then with a crashing rush through the trees, my assailant was gone, and I staggered alone on the forest trail.

Swearing angrily, I felt for another match. Blood was trickling down my shoulder, soaking through my shirt. When I struck the match and investigated, another chill swept down my spine. My shirt was torn and the flesh beneath slightly cut; the wound was little more than a scratch, but the thing that roused nameless fear in my mind was the fact that the wound was similar to those on poor Jim Tike.

Chapter .2.

Jim Tike was dead, lying face down in a pool of his own blood, his red-dabbled limbs sprawling drunkenly. I stared uneasily at the surrounding forest that hid the thing that had killed him. That it was a man I knew; the outline, in the brief light of the match, had been vague, but unmistakably human. But what sort of a weapon could make a wound like the merciless champing of great bestial teeth? I shook my head, recalling the ingenuity of mankind in the creation of implements of slaughter, and considered a more acute problem. Should I risk my life further by continuing upon my course, or should I return to the outer world and bring in men and dogs, to carry out poor Jim Tike's corpse, and hunt down his murderer?

I did not waste much time in indecision. I had set out to perform a task. If a murderous criminal besides Tope Braxton were abroad in the piney woods, there was all the more reason for warning the men in that lonely cabin. As for my own danger, I was already more than halfway to the cabin. It would scarcely be more danger-ous to advance than to retreat. If I did turn back, and escaped from Egypt alive, before I could rouse a posse, anything might happen in that isolated cabin under the black trees.

So I left Jim Tyke's body there in the trail, and went on, gun in hand, and nerves sharpened by the new peril. That visitant had not been Tope Braxton. I had the dead man's word for it that the attacker was a mysterious white man; the glimpse I had had of the figure had confirmed the fact that he was not Tope Braxton. I would have known that squat, apish body even in the dark. This man was tall and spare, and the mere recollection of that gaunt figure made me shiver, unreasoningly.

It is no pleasant experience to walk along a black forest trail with only the stars glinting through the dense branches, and the knowledge that a ruthless murderer is lurking near, perhaps within arm's length in the concealing darkness. The recollection of the butchered black man burned vividly in my brain. Sweat beaded my face and hands, and I wheeled a score of times, glaring into the blackness where my ears had caught the rustle of leaves or the breaking of a twig—how could I know whether the sounds were but the natural noises of the forest, or the stealthy movements of the killer?

Once I stopped, with an eery crawling of my skin, as far away, through the black trees, I glimpsed a faint, lurid glow. It was not stationary; it moved, but it was too far away for me to make out the source. With my hair prickling unpleasantly I waited, for I knew not what, but presently the mysterious glow vanished, and so keyed up I was to unnatural happenings, that it was only then that I realized the light might well have been made by a man walking with a pine-knot torch. I hurried on, cursing myself for my fears, the more baffling because they were so nebulous. Peril was no stranger to me in that land of feud and violence where century-old hates still smoldered down the generations. Threat of bullet or knife, openly or from ambush, had never shaken my nerves before; but I knew now that I was afraid—afraid of something I could not understand, or explain.

I sighed with relief when I saw Richard Brent's light gleaming through the pines, but I did not relax my vigilance. Many a man, danger dogged, has been struck down at the very threshold of safety. Knocking on the door, I stood sidewise, peering into the shadows that ringed the tiny clearing, and seemed to repel the faint light from the shuttered windows.

"Who there?" came a deep harsh voice from within. "Is that you, Ashley?"

"No, it's me—Kirby Garfield. Open the door."

The upper half of the door swung inward, and Richard Brent's head and shoulders were framed in the opening. The light behind him left most of his face in shadow, but could not obscure the harsh gaunt lines of his features nor the gleam of the bleak grey eyes.

"What do you want, at this time of night?" he demanded, with his usual bruskness. I replied shortly, for I did not like the man; courtesy in our part of the country is an obligation no gentleman thinks of shirking.

"I came to tell you that it's very likely that a dangerous negro is prowling in your vicinity. Tope Braxton killed Constable Joe Sorley and a negro trusty, and broke out of jail this morning. I think he took refuge in Egypt. I thought you ought to be warned."

"Well, you've warned me," he snapped, in his short-clipped Eastern accent. "Why don't you be off?"

"Because I have no intention of going back through those woods tonight," I answered angrily. "I came in here to warn you, not because of any love of you, but simply because you're a white man. The least you can do is to let me put up in your cabin until morning. All I ask is a pallet on the floor; you don't even have to feed me."

That last was an insult I could not withhold, in my resentment; at least in the piney woods it is considered an insult. But Richard Brent ignored my thrust at his penuriousness and discourtesy. He scowled at me. I could not see his hands.

"Did you see Ashley anywhere along the trail?" he asked finally.

Ashley was his servant, a saturnine figure as taciturn as his master, who drove into the distant river village once a month for supplies.

"No; he might have been in town, and left after I did."

"I guess I'll have to let you in," he muttered, grudgingly.

"Well, hurry up," I requested. "I've got a gash in my shoulder I want to wash and dress. Tope Braxton isn't the only killer abroad tonight."

At that he halted in his fumbling at the lower door, and his expression changed.

"What do you mean?"

"There's a dead nigger a mile or so up the trail. The man who killed him tried to kill me. He may be after you, for all I know. The nigger he killed was guiding him here."

Richard Brent started violently, and his face went livid.

"Who—what do you mean?" His voice cracked, unexpectedly falsetto. "What man?"

"I don't know. A fellow who manages to rip his victims like a hound—"

"A hound!" The words burst out in a scream. The change in Brent was hideous. His eyes seemed starting from his head; his hair stood up stiffly on his scalp, and his skin was the hue of ashes. His lips drew back from his teeth in a grin of sheer terror.

He gagged and then found voice.

"Get out!" he choked. "I see it, now! I know why you wanted to get into my house! You bloody devil! *He* sent you! You're his spy! *Go!*" The last was a scream and his hands rose above the lower half of the door at last. I stared into the gaping muzzles of a sawed-off shotgun. "Go, before I kill you!"

I stepped back off the stoop, my skin crawling at the thought of a close-range blast from that murderous implement of destruction. The black muzzles and the livid, convulsed face behind them promised sudden demolition.

"You cursed fool!" I growled, courting disaster in my anger. "Be careful with that thing. I'm going. I'd rather take a chance with a murderer than a madman."

Brent made no reply; panting and shivering like a man smitten with ague, he crouched over his shotgun and watched me as I turned and strode across the clearing. Where the trees began I could have wheeled and shot him down without much danger, for my .45 would outrange his shortened scattergun. But I had come there to warn the fool, not to kill him.

The upper door slammed as I strode in under the trees, and the stream of light was cut abruptly off. I drew my gun and plunged into the shadowy trail, my ears whetted again for sounds under the black branches.

My thoughts reverted to Richard Brent. It was surely no friend who had sought guidance to his cabin! The man's frantic fear had bordered on insanity. I wondered if it had been to escape this man that Brent had exiled himself in this lonely stretch of pinelands and river. Surely it had been to escape *something* that he had come, for he never concealed his hatred of the country nor his contempt for the native people, white and black. But I had never believed that he was a criminal, hiding from the law.

The light fell away behind me, vanished among the black trees. A curious chill sinking feeling obsessed me, as if the disappearance of that light, hostile as was its source, had severed the only link that connected this nightmarish adventure with the world of sanity and humanity. Grimly taking hold of my nerves, I strode on up the trail. But I had not gone far when again I halted.

This time it was the unmistakable sound of horses running; the rumble of wheels mingled with the pounding of hoofs. Who would be coming along that nighted trail in a rig but Ashley? But instantly I realized that the team was headed in the other direction. The sound receded rapidly, and soon became only a distant blur of noise.

I quickened my pace, much puzzled, and presently I heard hurried, stumbling footsteps ahead of me, and a quick, breathless panting that seemed indicative of panic. I distinguished the footsteps of two people, though I could see nothing in the intense darkness. At that point the branches interlaced over the trail, forming a black arch through which not even the stars gleamed.

"Ho, there!" I called cautiously. "Who are you?"

Instantly the sounds ceased, and I could picture two shadowy figures standing tensely still, with bated breath.

"Who's there?" I repeated. "Don't be afraid. It's me—Kirby Garfield."

"Stand where you are!" came a hard voice I recognized as Ashley's. "You sound like Garfield—but I want to be sure. If you move you'll get a slug through you."

There was a scratching sound and a tiny flame leaped up. A human hand was etched in its glow, and behind it the square, hard face of Ashley peering in my direction. A pistol in his other hand caught the glint of the fire; and on that arm rested another hand—a slim, white hand, with a jewel sparkling on one finger. Dimly I made out the slender figure of a woman; her face was like a pale blossom in the gloom.

"Yes, it's you, alright," Ashley grunted. "What are you doing here?"

"I came to warn Brent about Tope Braxton," I answered shortly; I do not relish being called on to account for my actions to anybody. "You've heard about it, naturally. If I'd known you were in town, it would have saved me a trip. What are you-all doing on foot?"

"Our horses ran away a short distance back," he answered. "There was a dead negro in the trail. But that's not what frightened the horses. When we got out to investigate, they snorted and wheeled and bolted with the rig. We had to come on on foot. It's been a pretty nasty experience. From the looks of the negro I judge a pack of wolves killed him, and the scent frightened the horses. We've been expecting an attack any minute."

"Wolves don't hunt in packs and drag down human beings in these woods. It was a man that killed Jim Tike."

In the waning glow of the match Ashley stood staring at me in amazement, and then I saw the astonishment ebb from his countenance and horror grow there. Slowly his color ebbed, leaving his bronzed face as ashy as that of his master had been. The match went out, and we stood silent.

"Well," I said impatiently, "speak up, man! Who's the lady with you?"

"She's Mr. Brent's niece." The answer came tonelessly through dry lips.

"I am Gloria Brent!" she exclaimed in a voice whose cultured accent was not lost in the fear that caused it to tremble. "Uncle Richard wired for me to come to him at once—"

"I've seen the wire," Ashley muttered. "You showed it to me. But I don't know how he sent it. He hasn't been to the village, to my knowledge, in months."

"I came on from New York as fast as I could!" she exclaimed. "I can't understand why the telegram was sent to me, instead of to somebody else in the family—"

"You were always your uncle's favorite, Miss," said Ashley.

"Well, when I got off the boat at the village just before nightfall, I found Ashley just getting ready to drive home. He was surprized to see me, but of course he brought me on out—and then—that—that dead man—"

She seemed considerably shaken by the experience. It was obvious that she had been raised in a very refined and sheltered atmosphere. If she had been born in the piney woods, as I was, the sight of a dead man, white or black, would not have been an uncommon phenomenon to her.

"The—the dead man—" she stammered—and then she was answered most hideously.

From the black woods beside the trail rose a shriek of blood-curdling laughter. Slavering, mouthing sounds followed it, so strange and garbled that at first I did not recognize them as human words. Their unhuman intonations sent a chill down my spine.

"Dead men!" the inhuman voice chanted. "Dead men with torn throats! There will be dead men among the pines before dawn! Dead men! Fools, you are all dead!"

Ashley and I both fired in the direction of the voice, and in the crashing reverberations of our shots, the ghastly chant was drowned. But the weird laugh rang out again, deeper in the woods, and then silence closed down like a black fog, in which I heard the semi-hysterical gasping of the girl. She had released Ashley and was clinging frantically to me. I could feel the quivering of her lithe body against mine. Probably she had merely followed her feminine instinct to seek refuge with the strongest; the light of the match had shown her that I was a bigger man than Ashley.

"Hurry, for God's sake!" Ashley's voice sounded strangled. "It can't be far to the cabin! Hurry! You'll come with us, Mr. Garfield?"

"What was it?" the girl was panting. "Oh, what *was* it?"

"A madman, I think," I answered, tucking her trembling little hand under my left arm. But at the back of my mind was whispering the grisly realization that no madman ever had a voice like that. It sounded—God, it sounded like some bestial creature speaking with human words, but not with a human tongue!

"Get on the other side of Miss Brent, Ashley," I directed. "Keep as far from the trees as you can. If anything moves on that side, shoot first and ask questions later. I'll do the same on this side. Now come on!"

He made no reply as he complied; his fright seemed deeper than that of the girl; his breath came in shuddering gasps. The trail seemed endless, the darkness abysmal. Fear stalked along the trail on either hand, and slunk grinning at our backs. My flesh crawled with the thought of a demoniacal clawed and fanged *thing* hurling itself upon my shoulders.

The girl's little feet scarcely touched the ground, as we almost carried her between us. Ashley was almost as tall as I, though not so heavy, and was strongly made.

Ahead of us a light glimmered between the trees at last, and a gusty sigh of relief burst from his lips. He increased his pace until we were almost running.

"The cabin at last, thank God!" he gasped, as we plunged out of the trees.

"Hail your employer, Ashley," I grunted. "He's driven me off with a gun once tonight. I don't want to be shot by the old—" I stopped, remembering the girl.

"Mr. Brent!" shouted Ashley. "Mr. Brent! Open the door quick! It's me—Ashley!"

Instantly light flooded from the door as the upper half was drawn back, and Brent peered out, shotgun in hand, blinking into the darkness.

"Hurry and get in!" Panic still thrummed in his voice. Then: "Who's that standing beside you?" he shouted furiously.

"Mr. Garfield and your niece, Miss Gloria."

"Uncle Richard!" she cried, her voice catching a sob. Pulling loose from us, she ran forward and threw her lithe body half over the lower door, throwing her arms around his neck. "Uncle Richard, I'm so afraid! What does this all mean?"

He seemed thunderstruck.

"Gloria!" he repeated. "What in heaven's name are you doing here?"

"Why you sent for me!" She fumbled out a crumpled yellow telegraph form. "See? You said for me to come at once!"

He went livid again.

"I never sent that, Gloria! Good God, why should I drag you into my particular Hell? There's something devilish here. Come in—come in quickly!"

He jerked open the door and pulled her inside, never relinquishing the shotgun. He seemed to fumble in a daze. Ashley shouldered in after her, and exclaimed to me: "Come in, Mr. Garfield! Come in—come in!"

I made no move to follow them. At the mention of my name, Brent, who seemed to have forgotten my presence, jerked loose from the girl with a choking cry and wheeled, throwing up the shotgun. But this time I was ready for him. My nerves were too much on edge to let me submit to any more bullying. Before he could bring the gun into position, he was looking in the muzzle of my .45.

"Put it down, Brent," I snapped. "Drop it, before I break your arm. I'm fed up with your idiotic suspicions."

He hesitated, glaring wildly, and behind him the girl shrank away. I suppose that in the full flood of the light from the doorway I was not a figure to inspire confidence in a young girl, with my frame which is built for strength and not looks, and my dark face, scarred by many a brutal river battle.

"He's our friend, Mr. Brent," interposed Ashley. "He helped us, in the woods."

"He's a devil!" raved Brent, clinging to his gun, though not trying to lift it. "He came here to murder us! He lied when he said he came to warn us against a black man. What man would be fool enough to come into Egypt at night, just to warn a stranger? My God, has he got you both fooled? I tell you, *he wears the brand of the hound!*"

"Then you know *he's* here!" cried Ashley.

"Yes; this fiend told me, trying to worm his way into the house. God, Ashley, *he's* tracked us down, in spite of all our cleverness. We have trapped ourselves! In a city, we might buy protection—but here, in this accursed forest, who will hear our cries or come to our aid when the fiend closes in upon us? What fools—what fools we were to think to hide from *him* in this wilderness!"

"I heard him laugh," shuddered Ashley. "He taunted us from the bushes in his beast's voice. I saw the man he killed—ripped and mangled as if by the fangs of Satan himself. What—what are we to do?"

"What can we do except lock ourselves in and fight to the last?" shrieked Brent. His nerves were in frightful shape.

"Please tell me what it is all about?" pleaded the trembling girl.

With a terrible despairing laugh Brent threw out his arm, gesturing toward the black woods beyond the faint light. "A devil in human form is lurking out there!" he exclaimed. "He has tracked me across the world, and has cornered me at last? Do you remember Adam Grimm?"

"The man who went with you to Mongolia five years ago? But he died, you said. You came back without him."

"I thought he was dead," muttered Brent. "Listen, I will tell you. Among the black mountains of Inner Mongolia, where no white man had ever penetrated, our expedition was attacked by fanatical devil-worshipers—the black monks of Erlik who dwell in the forgotten and accursed city of Yahlgan. Our guides and servants were killed, and all our stock driven off but one small camel.

"Grimm and I stood them off all day, firing from behind the rocks when they tried to rush us. That night we planned to make a break for it, on the camel that remained to us. But it was evident to me that the beast could not carry us both to safety. One man might have a chance. When darkness fell, I struck Grimm from behind with my gun butt, knocking him senseless. Then I mounted the camel and fled—"

He did not heed the look of sick amazement and abhorrence growing in the girl's lovely face. Her wide eyes were fixed on her uncle as if she were seeing the real man for the first time, and was stricken by what she saw. He plunged on, too obsessed and engulfed by fear to care or heed what she thought of him. The sight of a soul stripped of its conventional veneer and surface pretense is not always pleasant.

"I broke through the lines of the besiegers and escaped in the night. Grimm, naturally, fell into the hands of the devil worshippers, and for years I supposed that he was dead. They had the reputation of slaying, by torture, every alien that they captured. Years passed, and I had almost forgotten the episode. Then, seven months ago, I learned that he was alive—was, indeed, back in America, thirsting for my life. The monks had not killed him; through their damnable arts they had *altered* him. The man is no longer wholly human, but his whole soul is bent on my destruction. To appeal to the police would have been useless; he would have tricked them and wreaked his vengeance in spite of them. I fled from him up and down across the country for more than a month, like a hunted animal, and finally, when I thought I had thrown him off the track, I took refuge in this God-forsaken wilderness, among these barbarians, of whom that man Kirby Garfield is a typical example."

"*You* can talk of barbarians!" she flamed, and her scorn would have cut the soul of any man who was not so totally engrossed in his own fears.

She turned to me. "Mr. Garfield, please come in. You must not try to traverse this forest at night, with that fiend at large."

"No!" shrieked Brent. "Get back from that door, you little fool! Ashley, hold your tongue. I tell you, he is one of Adam Grimm's creatures! He shall not set foot in this cabin!"

She looked at me, pale, helpless and forlorn, and I pitied her as I despised Richard Brent; she looked so small and bewildered.

"I wouldn't sleep in your cabin if all the wolves of Hell were howling outside," I snarled at Brent. "I'm going, and if you shoot me in the back, I'll kill you before I die. I wouldn't have come back at all, but the young lady needed my protection. She needs it now, but it's your privilege to deny her that. Miss Brent," I said, "if you wish, I'll come back tomorrow with a buckboard and carry you to the village. You'd better go back to New York."

"Ashley will take her to the village," roared Brent. "Damn you, *will* you go?"

With a sneer that brought the blood purpling his countenance, I turned squarely upon him and strode off. The door banged behind me, and I heard his falsetto voice mingled with the tearful accents of his niece. Poor girl, it must have been like a nightmare to her: to have been snatched out of her sheltered urban life and dropped down in a country strange and primitive to her, among people whose ways seemed incredibly savage and violent, and into a bloody episode of wrong and menace and vengeance. The deep pinelands of the Southwest seem strange and alien enough at any time to the average Eastern city-dweller, and added to their gloomy mystery and primordial wildness was this grim phantom out of an unsuspected past, like the figment of a nightmare.

I turned squarely about, stood motionless in the black trail, staring back at the pinpoint of light which still winked through the trees. Peril hovered over the cabin in that tiny clearing, and it was no part of a white man to leave that girl with the protection of none but her half-lunatic uncle and his servant. Ashley looked like a fighter. But Brent was an unpredictable quantity. I believed he was tinged with madness. His insane rages and equally insane suspicions seemed to indicate as much. I had no sympathy for him. A man who would sacrifice his friend to save his own life deserves death.

But evidently Grimm was mad. His slaughter of Jim Tike suggested homicidal insanity. Poor Jim Tike had never wronged him. I would have killed Grimm for that murder, alone, if I had had the opportunity. And I did not intend that the girl should suffer for the sins of her uncle. If Brent had not sent that telegram, as he swore, then it looked much as if she had been summoned for a sinister purpose. Who but Grimm himself would have summoned her, to share the doom he planned for Richard Brent?

Turning, I strode back down the trail. If I could not enter the cabin, I could at least lurk in the shadows ready at hand if my help was needed. A few moments later I was under the fringe of trees that ringed the clearing.

Light still shone through the cracks in the shutters, and at one place a portion of the windowpane was visible. And even as I looked, this pane was shattered, as if something had been hurled through it. Instantly the night was split by a sheet of flame that burst in a blinding flash out of the doors and windows and chimney of the cabin. For one infinitesimal instant I saw the cabin limned blackly against the tongues of flame that flashed from it. With the flash came the thought that the cabin had been blown up—but no sound accompanied the explosion.

Even while the blaze was still in my eyes, another explosion filled the universe with blinding sparks, and this one was accompanied by a thunderous reverberation. Consciousness was blotted out too suddenly for me to know that I had been struck on the head from behind, terrifically and without warning.

Chapter .3.

A flickering light was the first thing that impressed itself upon my awakening faculties. I blinked, shook my head—came suddenly fully awake. I was lying on my back in a small glade, walled by towering black tress which fitfully reflected the uncertain light that emanated from a torch struck upright in the earth near me. My head throbbed, and blood clotted my scalp; my hands were fastened together before me by a pair of handcuffs. My clothes were torn and my skin scratched as if I had been dragged brutally through the brush.

A huge black shape squatted over me—a black man of medium height but of gigantic breadth and thickness, clad only in ragged, muddy breeches—Tope Braxton. He held a gun in each hand, and alternately aimed first one and then the other at me, squinting along the barrel. One pistol was mine; the other had once belonged to that constable Braxton had brained.

I lay silent for a moment, studying the play of the torchlight on the great black torso. His huge body gleamed shiny ebony or dull bronze as the light flickered. He was like a shape from the abyss whence mankind crawled ages ago. His primitive ferocity was reflected in the bulging knots of muscles that corded his long, massive apish arms, his huge sloping shoulders, above all the bullet-shaped head that jutted forward on a column-like neck. The wide, flat nostrils, murky eyes, thick lips that writhed back from tusklike teeth—all proclaimed the man's kinship with the primordial.

"Where the devil do you fit into this nightmare?" I demanded.

He showed his teeth in an apelike grin.

"I thought it was time you was comin' to, Kirby Garfield," he grinned. "I wanted you to come to 'fo' I kill you, so you know *who* kill you. Den I go back and watch Mistuh Grimm kill de ol' man and de gal."

"What do you mean, you black devil?" I demanded harshly. "Grimm? What do you know about Grimm?"

"I meet him in de deep woods, after he kill Jim Tike. I heah a gun fire and come with a torch to see who—thought maybe somebody after me. I meet Mistuh Grimm."

"So you were the man with the torch I saw," I grunted.

"Mistuh Grimm smaht man. He say if I help him kill some folks, he help me git away. He take and throw bomb into de cabin; dat bomb don't kill dem folks, just paralyze 'em. I watchin' de trail, and hit you when you come back. Dat man Ashley ain't plumb paralyze, so Mistuh Grimm, he take and bite out he throat like he done Jim Tike."

"What do you mean, bite out his throat?" I demanded.

"Mistuh Grimm ain't a human bein'. He stan' up and walk like a man, but he part hound, or wolf."

"You mean a werewolf?" I asked, my scalp prickling.

He grinned. "Yeah, dat's it. Dey had 'em in de old country." Then he changed his mood. "I done talk long enough. Gwine blow yo' brains out now!"

His thick lips froze in a killer's mirthless grin as he squinted along the barrel of the pistol in his right hand. My whole body went tense, as I sought desperately for a loophole to save my life. My legs were not tied, but my hands were manacled, and a single movement would bring hot lead crashing through my brain. In my desperation I plumbed the depths of black folklore for a dim, all but forgotten superstition.

"These handcuffs belonged to Joe Sorley, didn't they?" I demanded.

"Uh huh," he grinned, without ceasing to squint along the sights. "I took 'em 'long with his gun after I beat his head in with a window bar. I thought I might need 'em."

"Well," I said, "if you kill me while I'm wearing them, you're eternally damned! Don't you know that if you kill a man who's wearing a cross, his ghost will haunt you forever after?"

He jerked the gun down suddenly, and his grin was replaced by a snarl.

"What you mean, white man?"

"Just what I say. There's a cross scratched on the inside of one of these cuffs. I've seen it a thousand times. Now go ahead and shoot, and I'll haunt you into Hell."

"Which cuff?" he snarled, lifting a gun butt threateningly.

"Find out for yourself," I sneered. "Go ahead; why don't you shoot? I hope you've had plenty of sleep lately, because I'll see to it that you never sleep again. In the night, under the trees, you'll see my face leering at you. You'll hear my voice in the wind that moans through the cypress branches. When you close your eyes in the dark, you'll feel my fingers at your throat."

"Shut up!" he roared, brandishing his pistols. His black skin was tinged with an ashy hue.

"Shut me up—if you dare!" I struggled up to a sitting position, and then fell back cursing. "Damn you, my leg's broken!"

At that the ashy tinge faded from his ebon skin, and purpose rose in his reddish eyes.

"So yo' leg's busted!" He bared his glistening teeth in a beastly grin. "Thought you fell mighty hard, and then I dragged you a right smart piece."

Laying both pistols on the ground, well out of my reach, he rose and leaned over me, dragging a key out of his breeches pocket. His confidence was justified. I was unarmed, helpless with a broken leg. I did not need the manacles. Bending over me he turned the key in the old-fashioned handcuffs and tore them off. And like twin striking snakes my hands shot to his black throat, locked fiercely and dragged him down on top of me.

I had always wondered what would be the outcome of a battle between me and Tope Braxton. One can hardly go about picking fights with black men. But now a fierce joy surged in me, a grim gratification that the question of our relative prowess was to be settled once and for all, with life for the winner and death for the loser.

Even as I gripped him, Braxton realized that I had tricked him into freeing me—that I was no more crippled than he was. Instantly he exploded into a hurricane of ferocity that would have dismembered a lesser man than I. We rolled on the pine needles, rending and tearing.

Were I penning an elegant romance, I should tell how I vanquished Tope Braxton by a combination of higher intelligence, boxing skill and deft science that defeated his brute strength. But I must stick to facts in this chronicle.

Intelligence played little part in that battle. It would have helped me no more than it would help a man in the actual grip of a gorilla. As for artificial skill—Tope would have torn the average boxer or wrestler limb from limb. Man-developed science alone could not have withstood the blinding speed, tigerish ferocity and bone-crushing strength that lurked in Tope Braxton's terrible thews.

It was like fighting a wild beast, and I met him at his own game. I fought Tope Braxton as the rivermen fight, as savages fight, as bull apes fight. Breast to breast, muscle straining against muscle, iron fist crushing against hard skull, knee driven to groin, teeth slashing sinewy flesh, gouging, tearing, smashing. We both forgot the pistols on the ground; we must have \ ed over them half a dozen times. Each of us was aware of only or \ esire, one blind crimson urge to kill with naked hands, to rend an \ ar and maul and trample until the other was a motionless mass of \ ody flesh and splintered bone.

I do not know how long we fou ht; time faded into a blood-shot eternity. His fingers were like iron talons that tore the flesh and bruised the bone beneath. My head was swimming from its impacts against the hard ground, and from the pain in my side I knew at least one rib was broken. My whole body was a solid ache and burn of twisted joints and wrenched thews. My garments hung in ribbons, drenched by the blood that sluiced from an ear that had been ripped loose from my head. But if I was taking terrible punishment, I was dealing it too.

The torch had been knocked down and kicked aside, but it still smoldered fitfully, lending a lurid dim light to that primordial scene. Its light was not so red as the murder lust that clouded my dimming eyes.

In a red haze I saw his white teeth gleaming in a grin of ago-nized effort, his eyes rolling whitely from a mask of blood. I had mauled his face out of all human resemblance; from eyes to waist his black hide was laced with crimson. Sweat slimed us, and our fingers slipped as they gripped. Writhing half-free from his rending clutch, I drove every straining knot of muscle in my body behind my fist that smashed like a mallet against his. There was a crack of bone, an involuntary groan; blood spurted and the broken jaw dropped down. A bloody froth covered the loose lips. Then for the first time those black, tearing fingers faltered; I felt the great body that strained against mine yield and sag. And with a wild beast sob of gratified ferocity ebbing from my pulped lips, my fingers at last met in his throat.

Down on his back he went, with me on his breast. His failing hands clawed at my wrists, weakly and more weakly. And I strangled him, slowly, with no trick of *jiu-jitsu* or wrestling, but with sheer brute strength, bending his head back and back between its shoulders until the thick neck snapped like a rotten branch.

In that drunkenness of ba͞͞ᵈ͞ I did not know when he died, did not know that it was death ᶠᵉ͞ ͞had at last melted the iron thews of the body beneath me. Reeli͞ ͞up numbly, I dazedly stamped on his breast and head until the b͞ ͞es gave way under my heels, before I realized that Tope Braxton͞ ͞as dead.

Then I would have fallen and lapsed into insensibility, but for the dizzy realization that my work was not yet ended. Groping with numb hands I found the pistols, and reeled away drunkenly through the pines, in the direction in which my forest-bred instinct told me the cabin of Richard Brent stood.

Tope had not dragged me far. Following his jungle instincts, he had merely hauled me off the trail into the deeper woods. A few steps brought me to the trail, and I saw again the light of the cabin gleaming through the pines. Braxton had not been lying then, about the nature of that bomb. At least the soundless explosion had not destroyed the cabin, for it stood as I had seen it last, apparently undamaged. Light poured, as before, from the shuttered windows. But from it came a high-pitched inhuman laughter that froze the blood in my veins. It was the same laughter that had mocked us beside the shadowed trail.

Chapter .4.

Crouching in the shadows, I circled the little clearing to reach a side of the cabin which was without a window. In the thick darkness, with no gleam of light to reveal me, I glided out from the trees and approached the building. Near the wall I stumbled over something bulky and yielding, and almost went to my knees, my heart shooting into my throat with the fear of the noise betraying me. But the ghastly laughter still belled horribly from inside the cabin, mingled with the whimpering of a human voice.

It was Ashley I had stumbled over, or rather his body. He lay on his back, staring sightlessly upward, his head lolling back on the red ruin of his neck. His throat had been torn out; from chin to collar it was a great, gaping, ragged wound. His garments were slimy with blood.

Slightly sickened, in spite of my experience with violent deaths, I glided to the cabin wall and sought without success for a crevice between the logs. The laughter had ceased in the cabin and that frightful, unhuman voice was ringing out, making the nerves quiver in the backs of my hands. With the same difficulty that I had experienced before, I made out the words.

"—And so they did not kill me, the black monks of Erlik. They preferred a jest—a delicious jest, from their point of view. Merely to kill me would be too kind; they thought it more humorous to play with me awhile, as cats do a mouse, and then send me back into the world with a mark I could never erase—the brand of the hound. That's what they call it. And they did their job well, indeed. None knows better than they how to *alter* a man. Black magic? Bah! Those devils are the greatest scientists in the world. What little the Western world knows about science has leaked out in little trickles from those black mountains.

"Those devils could conquer the world, if they wanted to. They know things that no modern even dares to guess. They know more about plastic surgery, for instance, than all the scientists of the world put together. They understand glands, as no European or American understands them—know how to retard or exercise them, so as to produce certain results—God, what results! Look at me! Look, damn you, and go mad!"

I glided about the cabin until I reached a window, and peered through a crack in the shutter.

Richard Brent lay on a divan in a room incongruously richly furnished for that primitive setting. He was bound hand and foot; his face was livid and scarcely human. In his starting eyes was the look of a man who has at last come face to face with ultimate horror. Across the room from him the girl, Gloria, was spread-eagled on a table, held helpless with cords on her wrists and ankles. She was stark naked, her clothing lying in scattered confusion on the floor as if they had been brutally ripped from her. Her head was twisted about as she stared in wide-eyed horror at the tall figure which dominated the scene.

He stood with his back toward the window where I crouched, as he faced Richard Brent. To all appearances this figure was human—the figure was human—the figure of a tall, spare man in dark, close-fitting garments, with a sort of cape hanging from his lean, wide shoulders. But at the sight a strange trembling took hold of me, and I recognized at last the dread I had felt since I first glimpsed that gaunt form on the shadowy trail above the body of poor Jim Tike. There was something unnatural about the figure—something not apparent as he stood there with his back to me, yet an unmistakable suggestion of *abnormality*—and my feelings were the dread and loathing the normal naturally feel toward the abnormal.

"They made me the horror I am today, and then drove me forth," he was yammering in his horrible mouthing voice. "But the *change* was not made in a day, or a month, or a year! They played with me, as devils play with a screaming soul on the white-hot grids of Hell! Time and again I would have died, in spite of them—but I was upheld by the thought of vengeance! Through the long black years, shot red with torture and agony, I dreamed of the day when I would pay the debt I owed to you, Richard Brent, you spawn of Satan's vilest gutter!

"So at last the hunt began. When I reached New York I sent you a photograph of my—my face, and a letter detailing what had happened—and what *would* happen. You fool, did you think you could escape me? Do you think I would have warned you, if I were not sure of my prey? I wanted you to suffer with the knowledge of your doom; to live in terror, to flee and hide like a hunted wolf. You fled and I hunted you, from coast to coast. You did temporarily give me the slip when you came here, but it was inevitable that I should smell you out. When the black monks of Yahlgan gave me *this,*" (his hand seemed to stab at his face, and Richard Brent cried out slobberingly) "they also instilled in my nature something of the spirit of the beast they copied.

"To kill you was not enough. I wished to glut my vengeance to the last shuddering ounce. That is why I sent a telegram to your niece, the one person in the world that you cared for. My plans worked out perfectly—with one exception. The bandages I have worn ever since I left Yahlgan were displaced by a branch and I had to kill the fool who was guiding me to your cabin. No man looks upon my face and lives—except Tope Braxton who is more like an ape than a man, anyway. I fell in with him shortly after I was fired at by the man Garfield, and I took him into my confidence, recognizing a valuable ally. He is too brutish to feel the same horror at my appearance that the other negro felt. He thinks I am a demon of some sort, but so long as I am not hostile toward him, he sees no reason why he should not ally himself with me.

"It was fortunate I took him in, for it was he who struck down Garfield as he was returning. I would have already killed Garfield myself, but he was too strong, too handy with his gun. You might have learned a lesson from these people, Richard Brent. They live hardily and violently, and they are tough and dangerous as timber wolves. But you—you are soft and over-civilized. You will die far too easily. I wish you were as hard as Garfield was. I would like to keep you alive for days, to suffer.

"I gave Garfield a chance to get away, but the fool came back and had to be dealt with. That bomb I threw through the window would have had little effect upon him. It contained one of the chemical secrets I managed to learn in Mongolia, but it is effective only in relation to the bodily strength of the victim. It was enough to knock out a girl and a soft, pampered degenerate like you. But Ashley was able to stagger out of the cabin and would quickly have regained his full powers, if I had not come upon him and put him beyond power of harm."

Brent lifted a moaning cry. There was no intelligence in his eyes, only a ghastly fear. Foam flew from his lips. He was mad—mad as the fearful being that posed and yammered in that room of horror. Only the girl, writhing pitifully on that ebony table, was sane. All else was madness and nightmare. And suddenly complete delirium overcame Adam Grimm, and the laboring monotones shattered in a heart-stopping scream.

"First the girl!" shrieked Adam Grimm—or the thing that had been Adam Grimm. "The girl—to be slain as I have seen women slain in Mongolia—to be skinned alive, slowly—oh, so slowly! She shall bleed to make you suffer, Richard Brent—suffer as I suffered in black Yahlgan! She shall not die until there is no longer an inch of skin left on her body below her neck! Watch me flay your beloved niece, Richard Brent!"

I do not believe Richard Brent comprehended. He was beyond understanding anything. He yammered gibberish, tossing his head from side to side, spattering foam from his livid, working lips. I was lifting a revolver, but just then Adam Grimm whirled, and the sight of his face froze me into paralysis. What unguessed masters of nameless science dwell in the black towers of Yahlgan I dare not dream, but surely black sorcery from the pits of Hell went into the remolding of that countenance.

Ears, forehead and eyes were those of an ordinary man; but the nose, mouth and jaws were such as men have not even imagined in nightmares. I find myself unable to find adequate descriptive phrases. They were hideously elongated, like the muzzle of an animal. There was no chin; upper and lower jaws jutted like the jaws of a hound or wolf, and the teeth, bared by the snarling bestial lips, were gleaming fangs. How those jaws managed to frame human words I can not guess.

But the change was deeper than superficial appearance. In his eyes, which blazed like coals of Hell's fire, was a glare that never shone from any human's eyes, sane or mad. When the black devil-monks of Yahlgan altered Adam Grimm's face, they wrought a corresponding change in his soul. He was no longer a human being; he was a veritable werewolf, as terrible as any in medieval legend.

The thing that had been Adam Grimm rushed toward the girl, a curved skinning knife gleaming in his hand, and I shook myself out of my daze of horror, and fired through the hole in the shutter. My aim was unerring; I saw the cape jerk to the impact of the slug, and at the crash of the shot the monster staggered and the knife fell from his hand. Then, instantly, he whirled and dashed back across the room toward Richard Brent. With lightning comprehension he realized what had happened, knew he could take only one victim with him, and made his choice instantly.

I do not believe that I can logically be blamed for what happened. I might have smashed that shutter, leaped into the room and grappled with the thing that the monks of inner Mongolia had made of Adam Grimm. But so swiftly did the monster move that Richard Brent would have died anyway before I could have burst into the room. I did what seemed the only obvious thing—I poured lead through the window into that loping horror as it crossed the room.

That should have halted it—should have crashed it down dead on the floor. But Adam Grimm plunged on, heedless of the slugs ripping into him. His vitality was more than human—more than bestial—there was something demoniac about him, invoked by the black arts that made him what he was. No natural creature could have crossed that room under that raking hail of close-range lead. At that distance I could not miss. He reeled at each impact, but he did not fall until I had smashed home the sixth bullet. Then he crawled on, beastlike, on hand and knees, froth and blood dripping from his grinning jaws. Panic swept me. Frantically I snatched the second gun and emptied it into that body that writhed painfully onward, spattering blood at every movement. But all Hell could not keep Adam Grimm from his prey, and death itself shrank from the ghastly determination in that once-human soul.

With twelve bullets in him, literally shot to pieces, his brains oozing from a great hole in his temple, Adam Grimm reached the man on the divan. The misshapen head dipped; a scream gurgled in Richard Brent's throat as the hideous jaws locked. For a mad instant those two frightful visages seemed to melt together, to my horrified sight—the mad human and the mad inhuman. Then with a wild beast gesture, Grimm threw up his head, ripping out his enemy's jugular, and blood deluged both figures. Grimm lifted his head, with his dripping fangs and bloody muzzle, and his lips writhed back in a last peal of ghastly laughter that choked in a rush of blood, as he crumpled and lay still.

The Devils of Dark Lake

1. The Horror at the Cottage

I remember, as though it were yesterday, the sultry breathlessness of that late afternoon, when a tense stillness seemed to settle over the woods and lake, as if the very forest held its breath in terrified expectation. I found myself affected by this atmosphere; a nameless foreboding filled me with restless uneasiness, as a man may sense the presence of a hidden serpent before he sees or hears it. When the telephone in my lakeshore cottage jangled suddenly and discordantly, I almost jumped out of my skin. I reached it in one bound, for I knew its unusual clangor portended something out of the ordinary. It was a party line, connecting my cottage with that of my neighbors, the Grissoms, whose cottage stood three miles to the south along the lakeshore.

As I lifted the receiver, I was paralyzed to hear Joan Grissom's voice shrieking over the wire, edged with frantic horror and the fear of death.

"Steve! Steve! For God's sake, come to me!"

"What is it, Joan?" I gasped. Faintly I could hear other sounds coming over the wire—sounds that made me tremble with nameless fear.

"*Something!*" she screamed. "Oh, God, it's tearing at the windows! It came out of the woods! It's killed Jack and Harriet! I saw it kill them!"

"Where's Dick?" I croaked through dry lips.

"He went to his fishing shack this morning and hasn't got back!" she shrieked, almost hysterical. "Oh, Steve, it's not human! It's not an animal, either! I shot it—I emptied Dick's pistol into it through the window! It only laughed! Oh, God help me! *It's in!*"

Her voice rose to an awful scream, and mingled with it came a sound as of rending wood and snapping metal. A splintering crash—Joan screamed once more in heartrending horror and despair—her cry was shut off suddenly, and over the wire drifted a ghostly, bestial tittering of laughter that turned the blood to ice in my veins. Then utter silence.

Dropping the telephone, I hurled myself from the house and leaped into my car which stood near the porch. The sun hung low over the sullen pine woods; its slanting reflection turned the surface of the lake to blood. As I hurled the car recklessly out on the road that skirted the beach, the whole scene was suddenly repellant to me, dark and bloody, fit setting for such a deed of horror as had suddenly burst upon the peaceful lives of those who dwelt on the western shore of Dark Lake.

I remember that three-mile drive as a frenzied bit of eternity, the roar of the motor in my ears, the glimmer of the lake flashing by on one hand, on the other the everlasting gloom of the forest. I saw no human being. The east shore of the lake was lined with cottages, but only the Grissoms and I inhabited the lonely western shore. They were young people, three years married, both friends of mine since childhood. The horror that had overtaken them left me stunned and bewildered. If they had human enemies I did not know it; and there were no flesh-eating animals in the woods large enough to attack human beings.

But I wasted no time in vain conjecture. I was less a reasoning organism than a bulk of muscle and quivering nerves, hurtling blindly to the aid of a friend in grim peril. That drive seemed hours, yet it could have been only a few minutes till I slid to a brake-squealing, sand-spattering stop before the white-fenced cottage that, like mine, stood on the shore of the lake.

I leaped out—and stood aghast, momentarily numb with horror.

Jack Richards and Harriet Wilkins were friends who frequently drove out from the city to spend weekends with the Grissoms. Harriet's car was standing nearby. They must have just been entering the yard when the mysterious killer came out of the pine woods. Harriet must have died first. She was stuck on the picket fence, as a butcher bird skewers a smaller bird on a thorn. Her soft, slender body hung across it, impaled by one of the sharp-pointed pickets, whose splintered, blood-drenched tip stood up between her breasts. Her head was drawn back between her shoulders in a last spasm of agony, her beautiful face staring upward, a bloodless mask of sheer terror. *Something* had lifted her and smashed her down bodily on the pickets with terrible force.

"Joan!" I screamed, dashing through the gate. There was no answer from the silent house, but I almost stumbled over another body. I had found Jack Richards. At first I thought he was lying on his back, for his face stared sightlessly up at me, horribly purple, glassy eyed. Then I saw his body lay on its belly. *But the head had been twisted about on its broken neck so that the face looked up from between the shoulders.* My brain reeled at the implication. Jack Richards was a tall, powerful young athlete, almost as strong as I, and far more agile, a football star and a crack college wrestler. Yet *something* with terrible hands had wrung his neck like a chicken's . . . . .

I wheeled and ran toward the cottage, and as I ran my heart came into my throat and wedged there, locked in an icy fist.

Because he frequently had to leave his wife alone in that isolated cottage, Dick Grissom had provided the windows with strong iron bars, far beyond the power of the ordinary man to dislodge. I knew I could not have moved even one, and I am a strong man. But the bars on one window hung apart, bent and twisted as if they had been made of wax. Some had been torn clean out of the sill. The front door too was smashed and splintered—*outward.*

Scarcely daring to breathe, I entered; but I did not see what I feared to see—Joan's mangled body lying on the floor. The telephone lay where she must have dropped it when the horror seized her, and there were evidences of a struggle in the room. A revolver lay near the window and I snatched it up. It was Joan's gun, and it reeked of burnt powder. Each chamber held an empty cartridge case. It had been emptied, at a range too close for even a woman to miss—and Joan was a good shot. What in God's name was it that laughed at bullets? And where was it? And where was Joan? The answer was unmistakable. The visitant had carried Joan off with it. I turned and ran from the room, my brain reeling at the thought.

The front door was burst from within; having torn the bars off the window to effect an entry, the *thing* must have left through the door, smashing it from its hinges. On the jamb, unnaturally high, I found the print of a slender hand in blood, where Joan must pitifully have clutched at the wall while vainly resisting abduction. Its height would seem to indicate that her abductor was carrying her on its shoulder—but that would suggest that it was at least in the *form* of a man. And she had said it was no human.

Abandoning the riddle, I dashed out and leaped into my car. The brute was gone, and it had taken Joan—where, I could not know. My brain was in such a turmoil I could hardly think consecutively. I did not know which way to turn. My only thought was to get to Dick, at his fishing shack four miles to the south, and tell him what had happened. Then, together we must devise some means of tracing the fiend and its victim.

The sun was hung in the upper branches of the pines as I roared into view of Dick's fishing shack, after a drive that must have broken all previous speed records for that particular road. The shack stood almost at the water's edge, but sunk amidst a stand of oaks and cypresses.

But I stopped a few hundred feet from the shack whose roof I saw through the trees, for a strange automobile was parked beside the road, in a straggling grove. And as I slid to a stop, and the engine roar subsided, I was galvanized to hear a low, muffled moan from that car!

In an instant I was out of my car, had leaped across the road and jerked open the door of the strange auto—I looked down on Joan Grissom, bound hand and foot and gagged. Blood was smeared on her shoulders and torn dress, but she was alive and conscious, for her eyes were wide—dilated, in fact, with a fear that sickened me.

"Joan!" I tore the gag from her mouth, began fumbling at her cords.

"Don't stop for me!" she begged hysterically. "Save Dick! *It* went after him! Rackston Bane—when I married Dick, Bane swore to be revenged—he's come back to kill us both—*oh!*"

It was her scream and the sudden flare of her eyes as they looked over my shoulder, that caused me to whirl around. The movement saved my life, for the blackjack that would otherwise have crushed my skull, fell numbingly on my shoulder instead.

Even as I staggered under the blow I recognized the man who had sneaked up behind me and struck it—a swarthy half-caste named Strozza, formerly employed by Dick Grissom as a chauffeur, and discharged only a week before.

But even as I recognized him, I acted. As he lifted the black-jack again I smashed my left under his heart with the impact of a trip-hammer. I felt his ribs give way, and as he gasped and staggered, I crashed my right to his head. Had it connected as I intended, it would have crushed his jawbone. But it smashed into his mouth instead, splattering blood and teeth, and stretching him stunned in the road.

The crack of a twig under a padding foot brought me around—face to face with the horror itself!

At first glance I thought it was an ape, this hairy, hulking monster who stood there with Dick Grissom's limp and senseless body flung carelessly over one gigantic shoulder.

But it was not an ape. I have hunted gorillas in the forests of the Cameroons, and this creature resembled them only little more than it did a man. It stood up straight like a man, and it wore a ragged, muddy pair of trousers. But it was frightfully hairy, not furry like an animal, but shaggy like an incredibly hairy man. The face was hairless, flat, with huge nostrils and wide lips that writhed back to reveal yellow dog-tusks. The monster was as tall as I, and an awesome image of primordial power, with mightily muscled limbs, chest swelling in great arcs, and tremendous shoulders. But it was no beast; in spite of the apelike body and bestial face, intelligence glittered from the red piglike eyes—an evil and monstrous intelligence, but sickeningly human, nevertheless.

At the sight of me he let Dick's body slide limply to the ground and advanced, grinning ghoulishly and lifting hideously long arms which ended in gigantic hands, black with dried blood. But my loathing and fear had vanished in red rage. I was not armed, but this thing was a man of some sort, and I had never yet met my human match in bare-handed battle.

With a fierce cry I rushed to meet him—shifted with the old boxing trick that brought me inside his clutching arms, and smashed my left fist under his heart with every ounce of beef and thew and fury behind it. It was harder than the blow that had caved in Strozza's ribs, and it numbed my left arm to the elbow. But the brute did not fall; he grunted and swayed back on his splay feet. That was all. His ribs were like hoops of heavy iron.

I had thrown my right after my left instantly, rising on my toes with the lifting force of the blow. It caught him full on the jaw, and blood spurted. But the next instant the great arms locked on me with a crushing grip. I had no time to grapple with him, no time to fight for resisting leverage. Before I could move I was swept off my feet, lifted high above the monster's peaked head—one fleeting split second I saw his bloody face leering up at me—then he hurled me headlong to the earth. With the impact came blackness and oblivion.

2. Voodoo Hate

I could not have lain senseless long, for when I opened my eyes, darkness had not yet fallen, though the sun had vanished behind the black trees, and the bloody sheen was fading on the dark surface of the lake. For an instant I lay motionless, trying to gather my scattered wits, and only this saved my life, as I was quickly to learn. Silence wrapped the dark pine woods and somber lake. From where I lay I could see the roof of the fishing shack, and my car. But the other car was gone. Neither the Grissoms, Strozza, nor the monster were in sight. Then, before I could move a muscle to rise, I was aware of a curious weight on my breast, and bent my glance to see what it was. And when I saw a chill froze my spine and my tongue clung to my palate.

There on my breast squatted a shaggy, many-legged horror, black, with fantastic silver markings—a giant spider, broad as my hand.

Fantasy was being piled on fantasy. I had never dreamed of seeing such a thing in America, for it was one of those monstrosities spawned in the reeking jungles of Africa, which was long ago given over to the rule of the Evil One and his ghastly servants. They called it the Shroud-Weaver, because of its grisly habit of spinning its web on dead men. Few white men ever saw one. But as I lay there staring into its red eyes, a grim scene of long ago flashed across my brain—dawn in another land, when I came from the jungle with my terrified black boys, into a village devastated by tribal war, where dead men lay thick in the street, each clad in a glistening sheath, silver in the rising sun, spun by the shaggy monsters which squatted, each on a dead man's breast. The Shroud-Weavers had come from the swamps and woven their shining shrouds, even as this fiend would soon weave mine. And I knew its bite was death.

Now the full horror of my plight rushed upon me. The Shroud-Weaver thought me to be dead; if I moved it would sink its deadly fangs into my flesh and I would die hideously and slowly, with liquid fire racing through my veins, and my flesh turning black and putrefying before my eyes. I lay rigid, hardly daring to breathe. The thing squatted, staring at me. How could it suppose me dead, when my eyes were starting from my head with fright, and my limbs were bathed in an icy sweat? I clenched my teeth, fighting to steady my shrieking nerves. Blind instinct screamed to cry out and leap up, to strike the hideous thing aside with my hand. But reason held me in a grip of iron, so tensely motionless that my spine began to ache from the strain. But I could not lie there forever; some time, somehow, I would move, involuntarily—and then the bite and the long agony that would end only in death. And meanwhile Dick and Joan Grissom were being borne away to some nameless fate.

Just when the strain was becoming unbearable, there was a sharp crack behind me, something burned a streak across my breast, and the spider, torn asunder and knocked a dozen feet away, fell in twitching hairy fragments to the earth. In one motion I was on my feet, bewildered, thinking myself bitten, until I realized that the sound had been a pistol shot, and the sharp sting had not been the fangs of the spider, but a bullet that burned my skin, so closely it missed me.

I turned and saw two figures approaching me in the dimming twilight. A man and a woman, yellow of skin—probably quadroons. The man was tall, lean, bony, with a sinister face, rendered more evil by several scars. His long hair was not kinky like a negro's. He was bare footed, and his garments were torn as if by briars, and mud stained. He held in his hand a smoking pistol.

The woman was younger, slender and supple bodied. Her black hair was arranged in a curiously barbaric fashion, and she wore only a single garment, low necked and sleeveless, which did not come to her knees and was belted with a snakeskin girdle that held a wicked-looking dagger. Her features were regular, and she was handsome in a wild, exotic way.

"Who the devil are you?" I growled, swaying on my feet. I was still shaking from my experience, and my bones were bruised from the terrible fall I had got.

"Bartholomew La Tour and his sister Celia," answered the man, with a French accent. "We come from Haiti on the trail of an enemy—your enemy, if you are a friend of Joan Grissom."

"Where have they gone with her?" I demanded. "I must follow—I must find her—Rackston Bane—"

His eyes glittered as he said: "Do you know Rackston Bane?"

"I knew him once," I muttered, caressing my throbbing head. "An elegant young dandy—rich man's son—who wanted Joan. When she threw him over to marry Dick, he took it hard. I didn't know he made threats. I'd lost track of him for three years. Heard he'd gone to China."

"He returned to the land where he was born," said Bartholomew grimly. "He was the son of an American trader who lived in Pekin, and young Bane spent the early years of his life there, where he absorbed more Chinese ideas than is good for a white man. He did not forget them when he came and took up his abode in America.

"When the girl rejected him he returned to Asia, not to seek solace in forgetfulness, but to perfect a devilish scheme of revenge. Simply to shoot the girl and the successful rival, as an American might have done, was not enough for Rackston Bane. His brain had an Oriental warp. So he wandered through the slimy mazes of the East, collecting his troop of horrors and laying his diabolical plan.

"It was in Haiti that he made an enemy of me!" In the dusk his eyes burned red as fire on black water. "My sister and I followed him. We know where his stronghold is—"

"Then lead me to it, in God's name!" I broke in. "His fiends have taken Dick and Joan—both may be dead, while we stand here and talk."

"They drove southward along the lake shore," said Bartholomew, turning toward my car. "Trust us! We have a debt to pay Rackston Bane!"

Without further comment or question I sprang in, and Celia climbed lithely into the seat beside me, while her brother took the back seat. In another moment we were roaring along the now dimly-marked road that led southward. Dusk was gathering swiftly and a few stars were mirrored on the dusky bosom that gave Dark Lake its name.

"His stronghold is on Cannibal Island," Bartholomew said as we swept along. "There he lurks with his servants. Celia discovered it, and was captured by him, but escaped. We have been watching, but afraid to strike, unaided. But Bane's plans have reached perfection. Today he sent his hairy servant Esau, and the Italian-Somali Strozza, to kidnap Grissom and his wife and bring them to him. We were hiding in the woods, not far from Grissom's fishing shack, when they drove up with the woman. We saw Esau fall on Grissom unaware and knock him senseless. We saw Esau fight with you, and we saw Strozza place the spider on your breast as you lay senseless. Strozza was a witch-doctor in East Africa, and he always carried the thing with him in a specially made case. Until they drove away—Strozza groaning with the pain of his broken ribs—we dared not come to your aid; nor even then until they were too far away to hear the shot.

"From Haiti to this lake we have followed Bane. For days we have hidden in the woods, afraid to warn his victims, afraid to strike at him. But with your aid we dare. A man who can face Esau bare-handed and live—"

"What is that monster?" I asked.

"One of a tribe of monster-men who dwell in an unknown country in Mongolia. Bane calls him Esau because he is a hairy man."

"Joan shot at him—" I began.

"Her gun held only blank cartridges. Grissom discharged Strozza because he thought he was a thief when he caught him in his wife's room. But Strozza was obeying Bane's orders, and had emptied the woman's pistol and reloaded it with blanks."

"There was blood on her," I groaned. "She may be dying!"

"The blood came off Esau's hands, from the man and woman he killed," answered Celia. "The white woman has not been wounded."

"What did Bane do to your brother?" I asked her presently.

"Bartholomew was a voodoo priest," she answered frankly. "Bane came to Haiti on his quest for servants, and took the part of a priest with whom my brother had quarreled. Because of Bane's trickery my brother and I were defeated and forced to flee Haiti. If any people of voodoo ever catch us, they will kill us. But first we will kill Rackston Bane. I will not die until I see him dead—I have sworn it to the Great Snake.

"He captured me and would have killed me, but I learned his secrets and escaped. I made one of his Malays love me with a love potion brewed long ago in Haiti. I got away. The Malay did not. Doubtless Bane flayed him alive."

The matter-of-fact tone in which she said it made me realize that, although chance had allied me with these people, they were as devilish as the man we hunted—priest and priestess of a hideous and bloody cult. But no matter; to aid my friends I would have allied myself with the Devil that night.

There is almost as much difference between the two ends of the long, oval lake as there is between modern America and Elder Egypt. The shores of the north end rise to firm ground, forested by pines and oaks, while the southern end is enclosed by an all but impenetrable cypress swamp, a serpent-haunted, alligator-infested wilderness, shunned by all except fugitives from the law. Many have perished miserably there.

The road, a mere path beat out by wandering fishermen from time to time, for awhile showed the tracks of the car we were following. Then these tracks turned toward the lake shore. I started to follow them, but Bartholomew said: "They have taken to a motorboat they had hidden there. Drive on. We too have a boat hidden on the shore, opposite Cannibal Island."

Cannibal Island had a grisly history, whence its name. A few years before a negro, escaping from the chain gang, had taken refuge there and reverted to cannibalism. Several people, both white and black, had fallen prey to the fiend. I was one of the posse which finally tracked him to his abode, and the sight of the human legs and arms hanging in his "smokehouse" was the most sickening sight I ever looked on. But the man himself escaped us, plunging into the swamps on the mainland and vanishing—supposedly devoured by alligators. But the name of Jeg Buckle was still a synonym of horror.

"What will Bane do with his prisoners?" I asked fearfully.

"His vengeance will be slow, bloody and agonizing," answered Celia. "He will wring the last ounce of pain and shame from them before he grants them the favor of death."

The road dwindled out entirely, and I stopped the car. We were already in the edge of the swamp, and pools of black water glimmered under the gloomy arches of the cypresses.

"The boat is hidden not far from here," said Bartholomew, climbing out. "Esau and Strozza must have reached the island already with their prisoners. We must lose no time."

"Why did they use a car at all?" I asked. "Why didn't they use the motorboat all the way through?"

"It might have been noticed by fishers on the other side of the lake. Bane is crafty. He came in the night and none saw him. None but us know of his presence. He will leave as secretly—if he is so allowed."

We were groping along in the shadowy starlight—at least I was groping. My companions seemed to find their way by instinct, or else they could see in the darkness like cats.

We reached the cypress-fringed shore and Celia, groping deep in the reeds, dragged a canoe out of them. Somewhere a bull alligator roared and splashed noisily. We climbed into the canoe and Bartholomew and I took the paddles. Silently we drove the slim craft through the black water toward the dim bulk that was Cannibal Island, lying a few hundred yards offshore.

"There is only one way to approach what Bane calls his Castle," said Celia softly; her eyes shone like a cat's in the gloom. "It is a narrow creek, winding down from the heart of the island between cypress-grown banks. Up and down that creek his servants come and go by boat. Every other side of the island is guarded with traps of all sorts—steel snares, spring-guns, poisoned darts. We must make our way up the creek."

"And if we meet some of his men coming down?"

"Fight!" she answered grimly. I nodded. I had an axe I had brought from Dick's fishing shack. Bartholomew had his pistol. She had her dagger.

Our paddles made less noise than a night bird dipping after a frog as we slid across the broad strip of shining blackness and approached the eastern side of Cannibal Island. I glimpsed the creek, like a vague canyon opening in the solid black wall of the cypresses, which grew out into the water. We drove the canoe into the mouth of it, and there we halted, beside a tiny sandbar, as Bartholomew grasped a projecting root. He craned his long neck, trying to stare into darkness too thick even for his jungle-trained eyes.

"I do not like this silence," he muttered. "Not a night bird cries along this creek. If we all perish, there will be none left to deal with Bane. Better for one to run the first risk. Wait here, while I paddle up the creek and see if the way is clear."

Apparently his word was law to his sister, for she climbed out onto the tiny sandbar without a word. I followed her; in this affair it was the part of wisdom to be guided by these people who were no strangers to dark and uncanny intrigues. It was in the actual fighting that I would be of value.

Standing on the bar and slowly sinking into the spongy sand, we saw Bartholomew fade into the blackness that overhung the narrow creek. He moved silently as a phantom. The creek was narrow, and an almost solid wall of cypresses and oaks grew on either side, their branches forming an arch that shut out the stars. Bartholomew vanished as into a tunnel within a few feet. We stood there, Celia and I, occasionally shifting our position as our feet sank into the ooze, and I murmured: "Your brother is not acting now as if he ever feared Bane!"

"He did not fear death," she whispered. "Only the failure of his vengeance. We needed an ally like yourself. We fear Esau. That brute has a man's brain in an ape's body. He comes of a race neither true beasts nor true men. Their development was somehow arrested thousands of centuries ago—what was that?"

It might have been a faint cry up the black creek. We stood in silence, and I noticed that the sand bar was not connected with the shore, and that it was some distance before the ground grew high and solid enough on either side of the creek to be called a bank. Anyone reaching the bank would either have to scramble over cypress knees for several yards—making a devil of a noise—or else swim up the alligator-haunted creek. It had just occurred to me that if Bartholomew failed to return with the canoe, we would be in a devil of a pickle, when Celia clutched my arm and hissed in my ear: "Bartholomew is coming back!"

Her eyes were better than mine, but presently I saw a blunt snout detach itself from the shadows and slide silently toward us. It was the canoe, drifting downstream, and coming as silently as a ghost craft on the River Styx. I could not then understand why Celia, gripping my arm, began to tremble violently.

"I see the canoe!" she whispered. "But I don't see Bartholomew!"

Now it was near enough even for my duller eyes to make out its contour, but no shape loomed above it. If Bartholomew was in the canoe, he was lying at full length. Now its nose scraped softly against the wet sand, and Celia bent with fierce swiftness and grabbed the gunwale. I caught it too, and as I swung it in to us, I could tell by the weight of it that there was no man in it. But there was something else.

Celia saw it first, and she gave a low, sobbing cry and let go the gunwale and reeled back, her arms outspread as if to ward off some grisly doom. I stared stupidly, and even when I saw the vague object lying in the bottom of the canoe, it did not occur to me what had happened. I reached for it, and the instant my fingers touched it, I knew, and had to clench my teeth against the cry of horror that rose to my lips. In shuddering silence I clutched the grisly thing by the long hair and lifted it up to the faint starlight which glimmered whitely on staring eyes and bared teeth. I held in my hand the severed head of Bartholomew La Tour!

3. Hands That Clutch in the Dark.

As the full horrible realization rushed upon me, the ghastly object slipped from my clammy fingers and splashed into the black water, disappearing instantly. Celia made no move to try and recover it, and I knew it was useless. Bartholomew's head would rot in the slime of the lake bottom until Judgment Day, unless some alligator crunched it up as a tasty morsel—what an end for a high-priest of Haiti!

Then Celia moved with the sudden, fierce decision of a she-panther at bay. She shoved me toward the canoe.

"They sent us his head!" she hissed. "They know we're here! Get in and paddle up the creek. Don't be afraid! I'll be near. I'm going to swim till I find hard land, and then slip ashore—"

"But the alligators!—" I began—but she was already gone. With a supple twist of her body she slid noiselessly into the black water and vanished. She made no more noise swimming than a fish and she was gone so suddenly I stood and blinked after her.

Then, shamed to action, I stepped into the canoe and turned its nose up the black creek. Somewhere up that channel of blackness were lurking fiends in human form—*or were they even human?*—which had just cut a man's head from his body. But somewhere Celia was swimming inexorably up that black creek, risking her life at each stroke, and I, a man who prided himself on his fighting grit, could do no less. So I paddled up that inky creek, with my flesh crawling, and a feeling that each stroke would be my last. What Celia was up to I did not know, though I faintly guessed that she meant to supply the fangs for a trap of which I was the living bait.

Until that night I had conceitedly deemed myself a brave man; but my feelings as I rowed up that ghastly channel told me that I was a coward—unless it is courage to fight down and overcome fear that grinds a man's reason to powder, that melts the marrow in his bones and turns the blood to ice in his veins. On and on I groped in the blackness, only occasionally glimpsing the stars through the thick black roof of branches that bent over the creek, guiding myself by the somewhat blacker bulwark of shadow that stretched away on either hand, marking the banks.

My own noises sounded startlingly loud in the breathless stillness. Then suddenly, in the black darkness, a great misshapen hand caught at my hair from above.

If my hair had been long like that of Bartholomew La Tour, I would have died there that instant, just as he must have died. But my hair was too short for those ape-like fingers to grasp. They slipped from my head as I involuntarily ducked, and something just brushed my hair—a machete or a cane knife, wielded in a swipe that was meant to decapitate me.

Grabbing blindly and instinctively I caught a thick wrist as I started up, treading the canoe under my foot. It rolled from beneath me and as I plunged into the water I carried a man with me. He had been lying on the interwoven branches above me, and my grip on his wrist jerked him headlong down on top of me. And as he fell he cried out in a thick guttural voice I recognized—the voice of a man I thought dead long ago. Jeg Buckle!

I remember little of that ghastly battle with that cannibal in that black, reptile-haunted creek. I know as we went under I gripped his throat and thrust him beneath me, buoying myself above water by the resistance of his thrashing body, and all the power of his fingers tearing at my wrists could not break my grip. Once I went under myself, but an instant later my head emerged, and Jeg's struggles were growing weaker, half-strangled and half-drowned as he was. In a final burst of repulsion I gave his thick neck a wrench that must have snapped the vertebrae, and thrust him down with my elbows, knees and feet, treading him down and under into the very mud of the creek—then there was a rush and a bellow, a thrashing and splashing and the water was suddenly alive about me with heaving, scaly shapes.

Something tore Jeg's body out of my grasp, and in a frenzy of horror I whirled over and swam madly for the nearest shore. The scaly devils of the black swamps had come for their toll—their eyes gleamed like witch-fire coals about me. A pair of giant jaws snapped behind me as I hauled myself up out of the water by a cluster of cypress roots. I hung there, panting and dripping, for a moment. Here the bank was steep and high as a man's head above the water. I was about to climb on up when I heard a stealthy step and saw an object bulk against the dim stars in a space that had been open an instant before, an opening among the growth on the bank above me. Slowly as I clung and stared, that figure took shape—the black figure of a man poised there with a lifted arm. And that arm upraised something that looked like an axe. I was trapped. Below me the slimy cannibals of the swamp were swarming; and above me another killer was waiting for me to climb up within reach of his axe.

Then there came the sound of a blow; a low, gurgling gasp, and the figure vanished from the open space. An instant later something heavy came tumbling down the bank past me to splash into the water which was instantly torn by a rush of slimy shapes. A low voice called: "Steve! Steve Gorman! Climb to the bank. It is Celia La Tour!"

A reaction of trembling seized me so I was scarcely able to obey. But I scrambled up the ladder of roots, and an instant later was standing beside the yellow woman, who was scarcely visible in the shadows under the trees.

"I climbed up on the bank and sneaked along back of the trees," she murmured, with her lips close to my ear. "They were listening for your canoe—never guessing someone might be on the shore behind them. I knifed one dog back there—but I never thought of a man lying on the branches over the water until I heard the splashing. I was creeping up on this other dog when he heard you climbing the bank and changed his position. I followed him. Come!"

It was as black as Egypt around us, but she led me into a narrow path that wound through the black trees, away from the creek. From time to time she stepped wide of some certain spot, indicating that I should do likewise.

"Hollow steel darts filled with rattlesnake venom," she muttered. "Planted in the ground for strangers to step on. The Malay showed them to me."

A few moments later I caught a glimmer among the trees, and then we emerged into a clearing which I knew to be in the center of the island. It was shut in by a wall of brush and trees that would prevent the lights from being seen by anyone on the lake, or even at the edge of the island. On the site where Jeg Buckle's cabin had once stood, there rose a rambling structure of logs. The light streamed through the windows; and there came to our ears the sound of sharp, slashing blows, and the groans a man involuntarily makes when he clenches his jaws to keep back screams of agony. A woman was crying hysterically.

I started for the door, gripping a heavy limb I had picked up for a club, but Celia caught my arm.

"Wait!" she hissed. "We have slain three of his servants, but there are others—and Esau!" She shuddered as she spoke that dread name. Obviously she feared the ape-man more than all the other terrors at Bane's command.

"I see no guards outside the cabin," she whispered. "Let us look in at that window."

An instant later we were crouched by a narrow, barred window, staring at a sight that turned me sick with rage and horror. The structure was one big room, with bare log walls and ceiling beams. At the end opposite the one door a platform was raised three or four feet above the level of the floor. On that, in a curious ebon chair with dragons carved on it, sat a fantastic figure which I knew was Bane, though I would never have recognized him, had I not known it must be he. He wore the silk robes and coral-button cap of a mandarin, and his thin black mustache was trimmed to droop like a Manchu's. But for his white skin and unslanted eyes, it would have been hard to tell him from a Chinese. The man had gone native with a vengeance.

On the smaller chair beside him sat Joan, bound but no longer gagged. Her face was white, her eyes blazing with anger and horror at what she was forced to witness: the naked figure of her husband suspended by his wrists from a beam in the ceiling just before the platform. His feet lacked just a few inches of touching the floor. Near him stood a giant Chinaman, stripped to the waist, with the fierce mustaches, bulging muscles and huge belly that mark the professional executioner caste of China. He wielded an implement I recognized—a scourge made of a dozen strands of thin wire, used in certain parts of Asia by wronged husbands in whipping to death men suspected of making love to their wives. The very use of it in this case was a deadly and foul insult. And the punishment was terrible. The hissing wires wrapped about the naked flesh, cutting the skin like knives. Already Dick's body was crisscrossed with red lines from his neck to his knees, and blood trickled in streams down his legs. But he set his teeth and did not scream, though the blows fell with such savage force that they had him spinning on the rope that held him, and blood dripped from his wrists where the cords cut into the flesh.

In a maze of red rage I saw Strozza, his dark face twisted in pain, sneering cynically, and a stunted, frizzy-headed black man whose tribal scars indicated that he was a cannibal from the Congo.

"Let me at that door!" I panted. "Bane! I'll kill that leering devil—"

But Celia caught my arm in sudden panic.

"Esau! I don't see Esau in there! That means he's out here somewhere! Oh, God, we must be careful—"

A sudden sound brought us around—to face a shambling figure that rose terribly out of the shadows, great arms lifted.

"*Esau!*" It was a scream of terror from Celia, but even as she screamed she lifted her dagger and leaped at him like a wildcat. One great arm brushed her aside, to lie stunned and crumpled on the ground, and Esau lumbered toward me. I leaped to meet him, backing the flailing swing of my club with every nerve of power in my body. Full on his sloping crown I crashed my bludgeon, a blow that would have crushed an ordinary skull like an egg. But again the primordial strength of the brute-man saved him. My club flew into splinters. Esau staggered but did not fall, and before I could recover my balance from that terrific blow, his great fist swung clumsily and crashed against the side of my head. It was like a blow from a sledge-hammer. Again oblivion rolled up in a black wave, engulfing me.

4. Fangs of Madness.

A light in my eyes momentarily dazzled me, an incessant snarling sounded in my ears as I slowly regained consciousness. As the mists lifted from my bruised brain I saw the light came from a candle stuck on a shelf on the log wall. Abruptly I recognized my surroundings. I was sitting on a dirt floor, with my back against a post that upheld the roof; my arms were twisted behind me, around this post, and the wrists bound together.

My prison was a small log hut, and with a shudder I remembered it. It was the hut Jeg Buckle had used for a smokehouse, years ago—the smokehouse wherein he had hanged the severed limbs of the wretches he had murdered and dismembered to glut his damnable appetite. I saw the very nails he had used, still rusting in the walls—with a wave of revulsion I tore at my bonds. Jeg Buckle was dead by my hands, gone into the bellies of the grim saurians he had cheated so long; but the memory of him was like a foul aura filling the hut his bloodstained hands had built. Then the snarling I had first heard drove all thought of the dead cannibal from my mind. With a cry I recoiled against the post, drawing my legs up beneath me.

Before me crouched a dog, a giant greyish mongrel, whose eyes were green coals of fire, and whose jaws were covered with dripping foam. A mad dog! There was a strong but slender chain about his neck, which ran to a contraption of cogwheels fastened to the logs of the wall. And as I stared a full understanding of the hellish mechanism brought beads of perspiration to my face.

The dog was lunging incessantly at me, trying to reach me, and each time he lunged, the wheels turned and the chain was paid out a few inches, no more. A steady pressure would not release the chain; it required a powerful lunge. But with each lunge the chain lengthened, the distance between the rabid brute and me grew shorter. Eventually he would reach me, and—

Frantically I began to twist and jerk at the cords that bound my wrists. I drew my feet under me, tried to pull my bound arms up along the post, so as to rise. Upright I could at least use my feet to defend myself. But within a few inches the cords hung on some-thing—the broken head of a great nail, driven deep in the post. Like a man snatching at a straw I began sawing the cords against the jagged bit of iron.

And the dog lunged—lunged—lunged! Inch by inch he approached me. Frenziedly I worked, my nerves dancing, sweat pouring down my face. From what I had seen of Bane's methods I did not believe the chain was long enough to allow the dog to tear out my throat and give me a swift and comparatively merciful death. No; it would pay out just enough for him to tear and mangle my limbs; then a slow death would be my doom—death by starvation in a cannibal's hut with a mad dog, until the agonies and delirium of rabies descended on me.

The cords were giving, but the dog was close. I shook the sweat out of my eyes and redoubled my efforts. As he lunged, foam spat-tered on my clothing and I shrank from it as from a cobra's venom. I could almost feel his hot, mad breath as I glared into those green-flame eyes that shone weird as the eyes of hell-born ghosts.

The cords were parting, strand by strand; but even if I freed myself I must move with the speed and wariness of a striking snake. Let one of those dripping fangs just break the skin on my hand, and I was doomed to a horrible death. The cords snapped as I expanded my muscles with a desperate effort that brought a groan to my lips—the chain snapped too!

Somebody had miscalculated the strength of that chain or the weight of the dog. Straight at my throat he soared, as my hands came from behind my back. I was starting up from my squatting position as we collided, and my right hand, nerved to more than common strength and sureness, caught him by the throat, behind those dripping jaws, and with the same motion hurled him over backward and against the wall. His head cracked like a dry gourd as he struck and he fell to the floor and lay there quivering, through forever with menace and suffering.

Weak and trembling I staggered back against the post and tore back my sleeves to frantically examine my hands and arms. There was not a scratch. No fang nor claw had touched me. Then came the reaction, and fear was drowned in a wave of red fury—fury often balked that night, but no longer to be resisted.

The door was barred outside, but it gave way before the impact of my hurtling body. The steel bolt held, but the brackets on each side of the door were torn away—as I found when I lurched out into the starlight. I caught up that steel bolt—a three-foot bar thicker than a man's thumb—and glared about me. The hut stood a few hundred feet from the great log house, from which were now coming screams that turned my blood to ice, though they did not cool the red rage that seethed in my brain.

I had not taken a dozen steps when a figure drove at me from the darkness. It was the stunted African and he lifted a hand axe as he ran. I caught his flailing stroke on the bar, and sparks flew as the steel rang together. An instant later my left fist crushed his jawbone and stretched him senseless, and for all I know or care, dying on the ground. I caught up his hand axe and ran toward the nearest window.

Bane still sat on his platform, eyes flaming, nervous hand twitching at his thin mustache, but Joan no longer sat beside him. She was stretched, stark naked, on a sort of altar before the platform. And near her, before her frantic eyes, stood a cage of thick-meshed wire, seven feet long and four wide. It was open at the top, but downward-turning spikes along the edges kept its grisly occupants from crawling out. For it contained a mass of hissing, writhing shapes—blunt-tailed moccasins, more deadly than a rattlesnake. A few feet above them hung Dick Grissom, his body covered with raw cuts from that infernal whip. He hung face and belly down, his arms and legs drawn up behind him and bound together. A rope fastened to his wrists and ankles kept him hanging at an angle that must have nearly snapped his spine and torn his muscles out by the roots. His position was torture enough to bead his quivering flesh with cold sweat. But it was the slimy death that waited below him which brought the wild glare into his distended eyes.

The rope that suspended him was passed through a pulley fastened to a beam, and the other end made fast to an iron ring in a post. Near the post stood Esau, a shaggy horror in the lamplight. What twist of Fate checked the evolution of his lost people so long ago and left them beings neither man nor ape? He was a Neanderthal—a Dawn Man, whose rightful epoch was back in the mists of earth's beginnings.

Bane spoke a word and Esau untied the rope, lowered Dick a few inches and then made it fast again. The snakes in the cage below reared their heads, hissing, and struck upward, repeatedly trying to reach the man still a few feet out of their range. Joan, bound to the altar, was begging for his life in a voice that shook with hysteria.

Then I saw something else—an X-shaped cross stood on the platform behind Bane's chair and on it Celia La Tour hung, crucified, with iron spikes through her hands and feet. She was still conscious, her vivid eyes fixed terribly on Bane.

He held something in his hands—a wire cage, in which a great gray rat ran back and forth, squeaking and gnawing at the wires. Nearby lay a bronze bowl with a leather strap affixed to it—and near that stood a metal brazier full of glowing coals.

Bane was speaking: "You shall live long enough, Dick Grissom, to witness a pretty comedy! That bronze bowl shall be strapped to your wife's beautiful, naked body—with the rat inside! He is hungry and mad with pain. When the bowl glows red hot from coals applied to it, he will gnaw his way out. He cannot gnaw his way through bronze. He *can* gnaw through that lovely pink body you have held so often in your arms!"

Dick cried out in an agony his own suffering had not wrung from him.

"For God's sake, Bane, kill me any way you like, but spare Joan!"

"No!" cried Joan. "Kill me and let Dick go!"

"This is useless," said Bane, like an emperor pronouncing judgment. "I have decided you shall both die together. While the rat is gnawing into your vitals, your last moments shall be the more poignant as you see your husband sinking into that den of reptiles!"

"You can't get away with this, Bane!" panted Dick.

"Who'll stop me?" Bane retorted. "No one knows what I'm doing but you and Gorman. Gorman's dying in Jeg Buckle's smoke-house now—and you'll all be dead soon enough."

"But why?" wailed Joan pitifully. "Why have you done this to us?"

Bane's eyes blazed strangely. "You put me to shame for that base-born dog!" he snarled. "Not lightly does a woman insult a Son of the Sun! When you scorned me it was not me alone you wronged, but all the honored dead of ancient China! The blood of a thousand mandarins!"

I knew then that Bane was mad. Pure white he was, yet some twist in his brain caused him to believe he was a native of the land in which he was born. And with this hallucination, nothing would stop him from acting just as a medieval mandarin would have acted under similar circumstances—nothing but the axe in my hand.

I lifted it to hew at the bars on the window, then hesitated. They were of steel, set deep in the wood. Inside the house Celia La Tour laughed suddenly and terribly.

"Blood? There will be blood on the floor before this night is over! Your blood, Rackston Bane! I have not followed you around the world for naught."

He turned his head and stared enigmatically at her.

"Take her down," he ordered, and Strozza came forward, with a pair of iron pincers in his hand. As all eyes turned toward the girl hanging on the cross, I left the window and ran around the house to the door. I tried it cautiously. It was locked on the inside, but there was a crack in it and I looked through.

Strozza had withdrawn the nails that held the girl to the cross, and she had fallen to the platform where she groveled, unable to stand on her mutilated feet. Bane had risen and stood looking down at her.

"Lift her!" he said suddenly, and Strozza caught her under the arm pits and hauled her upright.

"You will live till you see me dead!" said Bane slowly. "So you have sworn?"

"So I have sworn!" she answered, her magnetic eyes never wavering.

"Liar!" he spat like a cat. "Your god is only a snake—and it cannot prevail over the ancient gods of China! This proves you lie!"

And before I realized what he was about, he snatched a dagger from his robes and sank it in her breast. Strozza released her and she fell limply; but, with that terrible wound in her bosom, she looked up with her terrible smile unchanged, and said: "This will not suffice! The Great Snake has promised that I shall live until I see you dead!"

Berserk, I swung my axe against the door. The panels splintered and through them I crashed into the room, axe first.

Bane whirled, staring wildly. Strozza was near the door. He stood paralyzed until my axe crashed through his treacherous skull and stretched him dead on the floor. Then as I charged toward the platform, Esau rolled to meet me, great arms spread wide.

I leaped to the attack with a fierce snarl of satisfaction, as primitive in that instant as he was. Twice he had defeated me—but this time the odds were on my side. Straight between those closing arms I plunged and brought my axe down on his head with the full swing of arm and shoulder. The splintering crunch of bone under the edge, as the axe split down through his peaked skull, drove a flame of ferocious exultation through my veins. Still, reeling and staggering, blindly clutching at me, though his head was split to his eyes and his brains gushing out, Esau kept to his feet with the horrible vitality of his breed. But it was only the dying spasm of an organism too primordial to die instantly. Even as his mighty arms locked convulsively about me, he went limp. Well for me; for even in that brief instant of grapple, I felt my ribs bend inward.

As Esau's arms relaxed and slid down my body, I saw the Chinaman advancing, swinging a great curved headsman's sword over his right shoulder. With an effort that made my muscles creak, I hurled Esau's squat body full against him. He struck wildly, staggering, missed me by a foot, and before he could recover his balance, I smashed his shaven head with my axe.

Then I wheeled toward Bane and caught the glint of a pistol in his hand. I hurled the axe, missed, and lunged with my bare hands knowing hot lead would be ripping into me before I could reach him. But if I could live long enough to kill that swine with my naked hands—we had both forgotten Celia La Tour.

She had crawled to Bane's feet, and now as he leaped toward the edge of the platform, lifting the pistol, she rose to her knees, threw both arms about his legs and heaved with all her tigerish strength.

The pistol exploded in the air, and a terrible scream rang out as Bane plunged headlong—*full into the serpent-cage!* I got one glimpse of a heaving, writhing mass—of a myriad heads striking again and again—of a convulsed body, almost covered by scaly shapes. Then his shrieking ceased, and Celia La Tour laughed terribly, with blood gushing from her lips.

"The Great Snake promised I would live to see him die!" she gasped, and so, still laughing, she died.

Trembling, I dragged the great cage aside and lowered Dick to the floor. Not until I had released him and Joan and saw them in each other's arms, did I give way to sudden weakness, and sink down on a bench. Dawn was peering grayly through the windows, and I stared at it like a man awakening from a nightmare.

Guests of the Hoodoo Room

Butch Cronin sighed as he looked across his newspaper at the ragged figure of Smoky Slade.

"This is a hell of a time for you to come in with a Stockley Street mystery," quoth Cronin, "just when I was all set to try and collect the dough old man Wiltshaw's offerin' to anybody that can find his missin' daughter."

He waved the paper accusingly under Smoky's rum-hued nose, and the 'bo got a glimpse of the headlines that blared the disappearance of the steamship nabob's daughter.

"Yeah," said Smoky sadly, shoving his grimy hands deep in his sagging pockets. "When a bloated plutocrat turns up missing they call out everybody from the town-clown to the marines. But when a bum drops out of sight, the best his pals can get is a 'So what?' from the cops. Lookit, Butch, you're the only one I could come to. I've been to the bulls; they gimme the horse snicker and tell me to lay off Dago Red.

"I ain't got no dough, but—"

"Skip it, Smoky," sighed Cronin, folding the newspaper and tossing it on his desk, beside his big feet; it was a gesture of renunciation. "You say three men have dropped out of sight from Big Joe Daley's flophouse?"

"I'm telling you, Butch. Out of the same room. Lookit, Butch: you can get a cot in the big room for a jit; but if you're flush and want to blow four bits, you can get a room to yourself—or you and a pal can split it, see. Well. I didn't think much about it when Dusty Miller went. The last time anybody saw him he was going into that four-bit room that opens on the alley. Well, maybe he got a toe-itch in the night and pulled his foot without waiting to panhandle breakfast at his regular stand. But he never came back.

"But when Red Olman went, I began to get jittery. I was holding down a nickel flop-cot that night. I saw him go down the hall to that same room with Big Joe, and I saw Big Joe come back alone. Some time in the night I woke up; thought I heard somebody give a kind of a choking cry. But you know some poor devil's always hollering in his sleep in a dump like that. But the next morning Red was gone. I asked Big Joe if he'd seen him, and he said it wasn't none of his business where a bum went, or when. Red paid his four bits. That's all Big Joe cared about. He said he guessed Red pulled out in the night without saying a word to anybody, like Dusty did.

"But Joe lied. Red was no hand for rambling. He'd been peddling his shoestrings up and down Kirby Street for ten years; he'd be there right now, if he was alive."

"You tryin' to tell me—" began Cronin.

Smoky spread his hands helplessly.

"I'm telling you. What it means I dunno. But listen: I aimed to dodge that hoodoo room, see. But yesterday me and the Clubfoot Kid cleaned up in a crap game down French Alley, and tanked up on Dago red till the world looked green. Well, I got a vague memory of paying for a room somewhere, but I was too soused to know where. But about midnight I woke up with an awful thirst. Clubfoot was snoring on the bed. I groped around and found a door, but it was locked on the other side. Then I found one that wasn't, and the first thing I knew I was out in an alley that looked familiar. I knew what then—Big Joe had shoved me and Clubfoot into the hoodoo room. But I was still so foggy I didn't give a damn. All I wanted was water.

"As I weaved down the alley towards Buckston Street, I heard a car ease up to the mouth of the alley on Stockley, but didn't pay no mind to it. I got into somebody's backyard and found a hydrant and started drowning the damnedest thirst since the Flood. I dunno how long I hung onto that hydrant—maybe ten minutes, drinking and sloshing water over my head. But when my brain began to clear up, I remembered Clubfoot back in that hoodoo room, and hoofed it back there in a hurry. Just as I come into the alley, I heard a car roar off down Stockley. Not much traffic that time of night, so I heard it plain.

"The door into the alley was open—and Clubfoot was gone. But his clothes was hanging on the floor where he left 'em, and my coat on a chair."

"What'd you do?"

"I run out of that room and down the alley like the devil was after me. I didn't stop till I come out into Buckston Street, and the wind off the bay hit me in the face. That cleared the cobwebs a little, and I got to wondering if I was just seeing things. Dago red plays funny tricks with a man's brain. So I crept back up the alley, slow and easy, opened the door, struck a match—" a tinge of pallor crept over Smoky's unshaven face. "I'd seen right the first time. There wasn't nobody in that room; nor no clothes neither, now. Clubfoot was gone; his clothes was gone; so was my coat."

"Then what?"

"What you suppose? I went down that alley again, like a bat out of hell, and this time I didn't stop till I was hiding under a wharf. This morning I went to the cops, and they just gimme the merry ha-ha. They said who the hell'd want to snatch a crummy bum like Dusty, or Red, or Clubfoot? So I came here. I dunno what's the answer. But Butch, some kind of hell's loose in this town!" The derelict shook in unfeigned terror as he grasped the edge of Cronin's desk.

"Somebody lifted Dusty and Red and Clubfoot out of that room. They'd have got me, only for chance. Maybe they will, yet! I tell you, Butch, Big Joe's selling us out to somebody—or something—like so much beef! You suppose medical students—?"

"They get all the cadavers they want these days," grunted Cronin. "They don't have to resort to body-liftin'. Anyway, they never did lift live bums. Oh, all right. I'll see what I can do. Here's four bits. Go and rent that room for the night. After dark I'll sneak in through the alley and stay there with you."

"Not with me!" asserted Smoky, cabbaging the coin with a grimy paw. "I wouldn't spend a night there with the marines. When you duck in, I duck out."

"All right, all right. Now scram."

As the door closed behind Smoky, Cronin picked up the paper again. He was a big man, hard limbed and powerful, with a slight slouch that made him look like a gorilla. His hard face was scarred from battles with the underworld's denizens. Private detective though he was, he was a throwback to the strong-arm cops of a generation ago, to the hard-bitten men he had known in his childhood on the Barbary Coast. Modern cops looked askance on his methods, and he was not popular with them, but they conceded his ability as a fighting man with the revolver, blackjack and bowie knife he always carried in imitation of those Homeric policemen he had admired in his boyhood.

He sighed as he re-read the newspaper account of the fabulous sums that old man Wiltshaw, owner of a line of passenger steamships, was frantically offering to anyone who could find some trace of his missing daughter. Cronin always needed money. But without hesitation he was abandoning the chance of getting it in staggering quantities, in order to help the wretched derelicts of Stockley Street.

The streetlights were just coming on as Cronin slouched into the Buckston Street mouth of a narrow alley, hands thrust deep into his coat pockets, cap pulled low over his eyes. Big Joe's flophouse opened on Stockley Street. The alley was narrow, lined by brick walls which were broken occasionally by a board fence bounding somebody's backyard.

As he knocked on a door not many yards from the Stockley Street entrance, Smoky's apprehensive voice quavered: "That you, Butch?"

At the grunted affirmative he opened the door; he was sweating with fear.

"I was about ready to fly the coop," he whispered. "Somebody locked the hall door, after I blew out the light. It must have been Big Joe. He was as surprized as hell when I came in tonight, but he tried not to let on. I told him I went out to get a drink last night and while I was gone Clubfoot glommed my coat and took it on the lam. Big Joe looked plenty relieved when I said that. Butch, I ain't staying here, not even with you. I'll hide in that backyard where I got my drink, see?"

"All right."

Smoky wouldn't be any help if it came to a fight, anyway. Cronin grinned as he heard the bum stumbling down the alley. Beneath his hard exterior Cronin, Barbary Coast born, had a soft spot for the poor devils of the slums. That's why he was here tonight. Again and again he had come to their aid in one way or another, without any hope or desire for reward. He was, perhaps, the only friend they had.

The room was a small one, with two doors and one window, the latter opening into the alley, as did one of the doors. The other, he knew, opened into a hall which ran to the cot room of the flophouse. But that door was, as Smoky had said, locked on the other side. He then examined the outer door, and found the lock to be broken and useless, the thumb bolt missing. But the knob and hinges had recently been oiled, for the door swung back and forth without sound. He noted that the one chair in the room had its back broken; not surprizing, in a dump like that. But the broken back made it impossible to brace the chair against the doorknob to substitute for the lock. For the rest there was a flimsy washstand and a dingy bed. That was all. There was no lavatory, no water in the broken pitcher, no electric wiring. A candle stub stuck on the washstand supplied all the illumination considered necessary for the human driftwood which occupied the room in moments of comparative prosperity.

Cronin did not light the candle. He snapped off his flashlight and stretched himself on the ramshackle bed. Born and raised in the shadowy mazes of a great city, he was accustomed to fantastic episodes. He knew things he would never tell to the police; weird secrets none would have believed. But this mystery seemed the strangest of all. Who would spirit away three seedy, penniless bums out of a slum flophouse? Yet he could not doubt Smoky's tale.

Presently he slept, but his sleep was light as that of a jungle dweller. Indeed, he dwelt, and was born and raised in a manmade jungle full of predatory beasts fiercer and craftier than any beast of the natural jungle. The silent turn of the knob did not awaken him, but he did wake at the first soft scruff of a shoe sole on the splintery threshold. And he woke instantly and completely, with full realization of where he was, and what he was there for. He saw the door opening slowly, and a bulky form obscuring the widening rift in the darkness. In the faint light filtering in from the alley he saw the figure creep catlike across the room, arm lifted in silent menace. In the fleeting seconds that elapsed before he went into action, Cronin judged the situation and made his choice of weapons. This was a case for the knife.

Another step and the shadowy figure would reach the bed. Cronin heard breath hiss softly through clenched teeth as the intruder gathered himself for the blow, even as he took that last stride. And then Cronin, moving with a quickness that would have shamed a starving wolf, hurled himself from the bed just as the arm came down with a force that sank a blackjack deep into the pillow where the detective's head had just lain.

Cronin hit the floor on his feet, crouching, and as the invader caught his balance and wheeled, lifting the bludgeon again, Cronin lunged upward, under the lifted arm. He felt the long knife sink deep, there was a choking, throaty cry, and then in a convulsion that wrenched the hilt from Cronin's hand, the wounded man spun away and fell heavily. Gasping gurgles welled up from the darkness of the floor, and then there was silence.

Cronin stooped, snapping on his flashlight. He swore softly at the face revealed in the round white pool of light. It was the face of a Chinaman, broad, smooth, full-fed. The light moved over his body. He was built like a wrestler. He wore mechanic's coveralls, but his shoes were shiny patent leathers, and beneath the cheap outer garment were the flashy and costly clothes of a Canton Street dandy. What connection was there between such a man and this dingy Stockley Street joint?

"Yun Kao!" muttered Cronin. "One of Jum Woon's bodyguard. And Jum Woon's head of the Wu San tong. Where does he fit into this picture?"

He reached a hand to the knife hilt which jutted up from the Chinaman's ribs. It was in deep, wedged hard in muscle and bone. Even a jungle beast has his moments of carelessness. Intent on recovering his favorite weapon, Cronin yet heard the light step that sounded outside, but thought it was Smoky returning. An instant later instinct cried out that it was not Smoky's step, and he released the imprisoned knife and sprang up, wheeling, hand shooting to pistol butt. In that flash of an instant he saw a vague monstrous form looming over him. Then the darkness was shattered by a burst of showering flames that were quenched in yet deeper blackness.

Chapter .2.

The first thing Cronin felt was a splitting headache. Then he was dazzled by a light in his eyes. He shook his head, muttering profanely. Mentally he cursed himself for his carelessness. He might have guessed that Yun Kao wasn't alone. Then as his head and sight cleared he froze in speechless incredulity. On the floor near him lay the body of the Chinaman, the knife still imbedded in the ribs. But that body lay on a costly rug, not on the bare, dingy floor of a flophouse room. And he, Cronin, was lying on a velvet couch! He batted his eyes and struggled to a sitting posture.

This wasn't the hoodoo room in Big Joe Daley's flophouse. It looked like a lady's boudoir, with rich rugs, silk hangings, curtained windows and an ornate bed. And then he saw the lady and nearly fell off the couch. She was standing nearby, clutching a silk negligee about her supple figure with one hand, and gripping a heavy, ornamented candlestick in the other. She spoke shrilly: "He's come to! Hurry, Won Chang!"

"Here I am, and an officer, too!" a masculine voice answered, and Cronin gaped as a slim, dress-suited Chinaman hurried through the door, followed by a blue-coated figure who grunted explosively at the sight of the man on the couch.

"Cronin! Well, I'm damned!" It was Harrigan, a patrolman who had no love for Cronin. "This looks like your finish! I arrest you for the murder of—what's the stiff's name?"

"Yun Kao," supplied the young Chinaman.

"For the murder of Yun Kao, and warn you that anything you say—"

"What the howlin' hell are you blattin' about?" demanded Cronin wrathfully, starting to rise, and then settling down again in a hurry as the woman brandished her candlestick threateningly. "Is everybody crazy? How'd I get here?"

"Through that window, you thief!" The woman pointed to a casement where the curtain was blowing inward.

"Thief? Why you—!" Wrath choked him.

"Do you deny that you killed that man?" broke in Harrigan. "Ain't that your knife sticking in his brisket?"

"Sure, I killed him," snarled Cronin. "But—"

"Well, what are you kicking about then?" demanded Harrigan. "I know your breed, you Barbary Coast gorilla. Posing as a private dick! I've always warned the chief you'd go bad someday, but I didn't think it'd be as raw as this."

"What are you ravin' about?" yelled Cronin. "Listen, flatfoot, I—"

"Suppose you tell your side of it, Miss." Harrigan turned to the woman. "I've heard what Won Chang here had to say, but—"

"Gladly!" She shot Cronin a poisonous glance from purple, slanting eyes. Her skin was of the old ivory hue of a Eurasian. "I am Raquel Mendoza. A little while ago this man crawled through that window there—the one that opens on the fire escape, and demanded the jewels I always keep in that wall safe." She indicated it. "He threatened to kill me if I did not tell him the combination. Mr. Yun Kao and Mr. Won Chang, who were returning to their apartments in the building, happened to pass my door and heard me cry for help. They rushed in to my aid, and this man stabbed Mr. Yun Kao.

Then I struck the ruffian with this candlestick—see the smear of blood on it, and the cut on his head? Then Mr. Won Chang ran to get a policeman before he should recover consciousness."

"Well, Cronin, what have you got to say?" inquired Harrigan.

"Say, hell!" bellowed Cronin, lunging to his feet. "It's a blasted frame! I killed Yun Kao—sure! But not here. I killed him in Big Joe Daley's flophouse, over on Stockley Street. It was a clear case of self-defense. He sneaked in and tried to brain me in my sleep. Then somebody came up behind me and knocked me cold—likely Won Chang, there. They must have lugged me over here while I was out, and cooked up this lie!"

"That's the wildest alibi I ever heard," commented Harrigan. "A three-year-old child could think up a better one than that."

"The man is mad!" This from Won Chang. "Yun Kao and I played fan-tan in the house of Jang Yum from six o'clock until midnight. We left there at exactly twelve o'clock. It is now fifteen minutes past twelve. I can produce a dozen men who will swear to the truth of my statement."

"Sure you can!" gritted Cronin. "Every man in your tong would swear to any kind of a lie your boss told him to! You all belong to the Wu San, and Jum Woon's your little tin god! Harrigan, blast it, can't you see this is phoney?"

Harrigan wavered.

"What proof can you show?" he asked. "What were you doing in Daley's joint? I'll call him up and ask him if you were there—"

"No good," muttered Cronin. "He didn't know I was in his house. A fellow rented a room and I slipped into it after dark. But listen, Harrigan, the man who rented that room knows all about it—find Smoky Slade—"

He could have bitten his tongue for speaking the 'bo's name before those alert Orientals. But he saw something that Harrigan missed—a quick, furtive look that flashed between Raquel and Won Chang. Triumph gleamed in the man's slant eyes, and a faint, cruel smile of mockery touched Raquel's full red lips briefly. As well as if they had said so in that many words, Cronin knew that Harrigan would not find Smoky Slade. Cronin felt a web, drawn by Jum Woon, closing about him. These were all Jum's creatures. It was a perfect frame-up. Blindly, he had meddled in the tong leader's mysterious plans, somehow, and he was being framed out of the way. Cronin had no illusions about being able to prove his innocence, without the testimony of Smoky Slade. These smooth-tongued devils would lie him straight to the gallows.

Harrigan stepped toward him, handcuffs dangling.

"Your yarn's too thin," he grumbled. "I'll look for Slade, and check your story as a matter of routine, but I'll see that you're behind the bars while I do it. I'm putting these cuffs on you while I phone for the wagon, and—"

Cronin's big shoulders lurched. His knuckles impacted devastatingly against Harrigan's jaw and the policeman's gat banged wildly into the ceiling as he went down. Cronin headed for the window, smashing the hanging light bulb as he plunged. Flame jetted in the dark, from the corner where Won Chang crouched, and lead hissed by Cronin, splitting the window curtains. A slug was a leaden bee that stung his ear as he lunged through onto the fire escape. In one way at least the plot had boomeranged. In supplying a logical way for his supposed entrance, they had left him an avenue of escape. But Jum Woon might have foreseen such an eventuality, and, believing men would be lurking in the street below, Cronin went up instead of down. He was already on the top floor.

Below him Harrigan was bellowing for a light. As Cronin went over the rim of the roof, a shadowy form sprang at him with a glint of steel. Cronin ducked and felt a keen edge slice his coat sleeve, stinging the flesh beneath. Killed while fleeing from the law; it would be as good as hanging. He hit back, with his shoulder behind the punch, and felt his fist sink mid-wrist deep in a yielding belly. His victim gasped and went down. Cronin fled across the roof, spurred by a babble of Chinese tongues below and behind him, Harrigan's furious roar rising above the tumult. It was a long leap from that roof to the next, but Cronin made it. He teetered dizzily on the parapet for an instant, with his heels over the edge, and then dropped down on the roof.

He had already recognized his surroundings—Davilla Place, a district of ornate apartment houses, shunned by the Anglo-Saxon element of the city because of the exotic predominance of its inhabitants. Wealthy Orientals favored it as a residential section. Cronin ran across the flat roof, looking much like a great baboon as he ran silently, slouching forward. Butch Cronin was at bay; his native jungle had turned on him.

Chapter .3.

Within fifteen minutes after Harrigan had profanely bellowed his news over the nearest phone, men were combing the city for the fugitive, and the chief of police was prying up hell at headquarters.

"It's a kick in the teeth for the whole force!" he raged. "Bring the so-and-so in—and I don't care how! Yes, yes, blast you!" This to a representative of the ubiquitous press. "We'll have him behind bars inside of a dozen hours."

To the district attorney, over the phone, he spoke less confidentially.

"It'll be like hunting a snake in a thicket. Oh, I'll get him all right, but it may take days, or even weeks. There are a thousand places in the slums for a man to hide, and Cronin knows 'em all. But there's one place he won't go, at least—Kirby Street. He's got too many enemies there, who'd jump at the chance to rub him out. They'll be after him like a pack of wolves, now that he's outside the law."

And, naturally, that's precisely where Butch Cronin was. At the very moment the chief was speaking, Cronin was talking to one Jake Ziegler, in the loft of a little second-hand clothing store in Kirby Street's toughest district.

"Nobody saw me sneak in here, Jake, and I'm not stayin' long enough to get your neck in a sling on my account. I've got to find Smoky Slade. He's the only man who can prove I killed Yun Kao in self defense. The men that slugged me must have grabbed him. Otherwise he'd have made a bee-line to the cops, and this time they'd have listened to him. They may have bumped him off, of course. But if he's alive, I believe I'll find him in Jum Woon's house."

"Better you be careful," remarked Jake. "Jum's a big shot on Canton Street."

"Don't I know it? Somehow he's behind the snatchin' of these bums. And he didn't want me musclin' in."

"Why didn't they bump you off right there?" wondered Jake.

"They must have recognized me," growled Cronin. "Probably Won Chang knew me. But it wasn't him that slugged me. I got a glimpse of the fellow, and he was too big for Won Chang—damned near too big to be a human! Looked like a monstrosity. Anyway, Won Chang must have been there. Probably had a car parked in the mouth of the alley, ready to skip with the bum they caught. They recognized me and maybe thought I knew more than I really did. Anyway, I'd killed a tong brother, and I had to be rubbed out, accordin' to their code. But leavin' me there with my throat cut, or just havin' me dropped out of sight, like the bums, was too risky, even for Jum Woon. Bound to be some kind of an investigation if a dick disappears, even a private dick. And I've got plenty of friends—outside the force. So they ribbed up a cast-iron frame. And it's foolproof, if I can't find Smoky. That Eurasian hussy and that slippery tongued Won Chang'll swear me right into a noose. If they ain't enough, Jum Woon could produce plenty more.

"Blast the luck, this is a pretty scuttle of fish—yesterday I was plannin' how to go after the Wiltshaw flapper, and here I am duckin' from the law myself. I'd even begun my investigations, private, but hadn't had time to learn anything."

"It ever occur to you this might be a frame-up from the beginning?" asked Jake suddenly. "How do you know three bums dropped out of Daley's flop-joint? You only got Smoky's word for it. What if Smoky lied, just to get you into a trap? Maybe somebody didn't want you looking for Joan Wiltshaw."

"What are you talkin' about, Jake?" growled Cronin. "You hintin' that Jum Woon snatched Joan Wiltshaw?"

"I don't know. But you couldn't never tell. He's a devil. Nobody knows why he does things. You laugh at me many times when I tell you he's a devil. But it's the truth."

Cronin snorted. "Every unexplained crime that happens in town—and there's plenty, with our present chief of police runnin' things in his dumb way—you claim Jum Woon's behind it. You think he's a mastermind workin' behind the screens and pullin' strings all over the city. Well, he ain't; he ain't nothin' but a rich Chinee with a finger in some crooked deals. He's got plenty of dough and pull, and he can frame a lone wolf like me into the pen, all right, but he's no super-criminal."

"Maybe not," said Jake, unconvinced. "But he's bigger than you think. You'll find out, now he's after you. You ain't never bucked him before. I tell you, he's king of Canton Street. And always he wants more power—more power! He'll rule this whole State someday, if somebody don't trip him."

"Well, maybe I'm the man to trip him. But you're all wet about Smoky lyin' for him; he wouldn't—not to me."

"What you going to do?"

"Take Jum Woon's house apart if necessary, and find Smoky."

"You're crazy, Butch! That house is full of armed Chinese. They'll kill you!"

"I've got to take the chance. Maybe I can get the drop on 'em."

"Better you should go to the police and give up, and let dem hunt for Smoky. You're in terrible danger, all the time. Right here on this street, there are men who would cut your throat—"

"I know. But I fool them as well as the police by comin' here. They're dumb oxes. I can sneak right under their noses and they'll never see me. As for givin' up, I might as well stick my head in a noose. The cops never could find Smoky. I'm the only man who can do that, and that's why I broke away from Harrigan. Give me some arms, Jake. I'm pullin' out."

Jake knew his guest's preferences. He produced a big blue Colt six-shooter, a slung-shot of plaited leather with a loop on the handle, and a murderous-looking knife, and in a few minutes, with his private arsenal snugly stowed on various parts of his person, Cronin was heading for Canton Street. He went by devious ways, not known to all men—by winding alleys, across shadowy backyards and enclosed courts, and occasionally over a roof. From time to time he heard the screaming sirens of the police cars, and grinned hardly. The jungle had turned on him; those sirens were the howls of the pack that hunted him.

Jum Woon's house was a large, mysterious building rising in a district of small shops. Few white men had ever been in that house, except for the set of screwy faddists, of the sort which exist in every city. Jum Woon had been suspected of being an occult fakir, but no evidence had ever come to light that he had victimized anyone. He was immensely wealthy, and the real head of the powerful Wu San tong. Cronin knew he was behind plenty of shady deals on Canton Street, but he had never been able to prove anything. Nobody had ever offered him money to prove anything on Jum Woon. And Cronin, in spite of his charity work for the Stockley Street bums, wasn't in the detective business for his health.

An alley ran along the right of Jum Woon's house, which stood dark and silent as Cronin approached it, at about forty minutes past one. A door opened into that alley, and a light usually burned over the door. But not this time. Cronin left the alley and slid over a brick wall which enclosed a small court at the back of the house. He knew he was taking his life in his hands. Jum Woon would be justified, in the sight of the law, in shooting him as a housebreaker. But his case could be no more desperate than it was already.

If Smoky were a prisoner in the house, he would most likely be somewhere in the basement. Cautiously Cronin made his way along the rear of the house, searching for basement windows. He heard no sound, only the faint shrilling of a distant police siren that lifted the short hairs on his neck. A few moments' investigation showed him that it was impossible to break in through the basement; the windows were far too small to admit his bulky frame.

A small shop shouldering the big house proved easy to scale from the brick wall. From its roof he could reach an upstairs window. Crouching on the broad ledge he bought his jimmy into play. A lock broke startlingly loud in the stillness and the window slid up. Nerves tingling at the thought of what might be lurking within, he slid over the sill into the darkness.

He stood motionless for a moment, straining his ears. No sound in all the house. Not a board creaked as he stole across the floor, feeling his feet sink deep in the nap of a thick rug. From room to room he stole, nerves taut as banjo strings, gun and knife ready. Doors opened silently to his touch. His light fingers felt chairs, tables, beds and couches. Yet the house had an empty feel. Bewilderment grew in him. He had explored every room on the upper floor, and they were all empty. Yet most of them were bedrooms. Why should the people be on the lower floor, at this time of night, with no lights on? He began to believe the house was deserted.

He found a stair and descended into the broad hall. More boldly now he made his tours of the lower rooms, with the same result. In the back part of the house he found a stair leading into the basement. It was, he found, divided up into a number of rooms, all empty. One was locked, but cautious rapping, and the wary calling of Smoky's name evoked no response. Anyway, it was incredible to think that they would have left their prisoner unguarded in an empty house. And for some reason Jum Woon had deserted his house, with his family and retainers.

Cronin made his way back up the basement stair, and as he came into the broad hall on the lower floor, the sudden whir of a doorbell made him jump. It came from the side of the house that gave on the alley.

On impulse, he made his way toward the insistent sound, found a narrow hallway and came to a door at the end of it. The bell was ringing at that door, which was the one over which the alley-light had always burned before tonight. His fingers, groping over the panels, found an ornamented metal disk, and he turned it, knowing what it hid. A vague finger of grey light filtered in through the peephole it had covered. Cronin peered through. The alley was faintly lighted by a distant streetlamp, enough for him to make out the slender figure posing impatiently on the stoop. It was a young man in evening clothes. He rapped on the door with his cane and spoke something unintelligible to Cronin, as if it were a password. Possessed with a desire to know who came to Jum Woon's house at this hour, Cronin opened the door and snapped his flashlight in the stranger's face.

It was a pale young face, lined by dissipation and vicious living; a face Cronin had seen pictured on the society pages of the newspapers. The man was Richard Van Ritten, a wealthy young sportsman. As he blinked and swore petulantly, Cronin snapped off the light. Van Ritten did not know him.

But the young man seemed to see something unfamiliar about the bulk framed dimly in the unlighted doorway.

"Who are you?" he demanded. "Am I in time? Why don't you let me in?"

"Why do you want in?" grunted Cronin. "There's nobody here."

"Where's Jum Woon?" demanded the young man.

"Gone," growled Cronin. His ears were cocked back into the interior of the dark house. Was that the stealthy opening of a door somewhere? Yet he had proved beyond doubt that the house was empty.

Van Ritten seemed much agitated. He fumbled with his cane.

"But this was the night!" he said nervously. "I missed the last one. I've just returned from Tijuana. I had to go, but I took the fastest plane back. I haven't been informed of any change in time or place. I came directly here, though, without going to my apartment. Perhaps your master did try to communicate with me. Didn't he leave any word?"

"Not with me," answered Cronin.

"But it can't be!" exclaimed Van Ritten, growing frantic. "Jum Woon knows how necessary it is for me to attend the—"

The soft scruff of a foot behind Cronin made him duck instinctively. A gun cracked in the shadows down the hall and Van Ritten gasped and fell heavily on the stoop. Cronin fired at the flash and heard a man yelp in staccato Chinese. But the quick pad of soft-shod feet out in the big hall told of reinforcements. Cronin wheeled and lunged into the alley, hurdling the shape that sprawled on the stoop. Van Ritten had stopped the slug meant for Cronin.

As he ran up the alley he glanced back over his shoulder. A shadowy group clustered about the stoop. There were more than he could tackle alone, and not one was tall enough to be Jum Woon. As several of them detached themselves from the cluster and started after him, he turned aside, scaled a board fence and melted into a maze of crooked ways which he threaded with the certainty of a tiger treading the tangled paths of his native jungle.

A few salient facts stood out obviously. Jum Woon had abandoned his house for some reason or other, but he had sent men back there. They must have come in at the front door while he was talking to Van Ritten. Cronin knew Smoky was not in that house, and he did not believe Jum Woon had returned. He believed that he would find Smoky wherever he found Jum Woon. The Chinaman would take that vital witness with him wherever he went, supposing that Smoky still lived. Van Ritten's appearance had put another mysterious angle in the affair. Van Ritten had never shown any interest in the occult, which had drawn other members of the idle wealthy set to Jum Woon's house. And the man had been on the verge of a collapse. Why should he come in such evident fear and eagerness to the Chinaman's house at that hour of the morning?

Anyway, Cronin had failed in his search. At the moment he was at a standstill. He didn't know where to look for Jum Woon, and, consequently, Smoky Slade. His time was short. He couldn't elude the police forever. Any moment they might stumble on him by skill or chance. If he could just get his hands on one of Jum Woon's creatures, and make him talk—suddenly he swore. Big Joe Daley! Why hadn't he thought of him before? Daley must be in on this deal with Jum Woon. It was impossible that the Chinaman should have kidnapped men out of his house without his knowledge.

In the darkness that precedes dawn Cronin headed for Stockley Street.

Chapter .4.

Cronin entered Big Joe's flophouse by the alley, as he had done once before that night. No one was in the hoodoo room, nor was the inner door locked. He tiptoed along the dim-lit hall, pushed open a door and looked out into the big room with its lines of cots, dimly lighted by a small hanging bulb that burned all night. All the cots seemed to be occupied, and snores of varying keys reverberated through the broad room. As he crossed it, skirting the wall, he did not see the snaky, slanting eyes that watched him from beneath a fold of the pulled-up blankets on one of the cots.

Cronin knocked softly at a door which he knew opened into Big Joe's private bedroom. He could hear Big Joe snoring. He tried the door. It was locked, but the rattle of the knob stopped the snoring. He rapped again. A sleepy voice growled: "Beat it! I ain't got no empty cots."

"Open up," grunted Cronin, disguising his voice. "It's the police."

There was a creaking of bedsprings, the snap of a light switch and then the door swung open and Big Joe, in his drawers and hairy as a gorilla, blinked out. Before he could slam the door Cronin grabbed his throat, strangling his yell, and pushed him back into the bedroom and shut the door.

"I'm lettin' go your gullet, Daley," muttered Cronin. "But you make one yap outside of answerin' my questions, and I'll gut you like a fish."

The dim electric light glinting on the broad blade of the bowie lent emphasis to the threat. Big Joe was livid.

"Where's Smoky Slade?" Cronin asked softly.

"How the hell should I know—ow! For God's sake, Cronin, easy with that knife! I rented him a room last night. I suppose he's sleeping in it. Why don't you look and see if he ain't in there?"

"You know damn well he ain't!"

"Well, what do you care?" demanded Big Joe, obviously puzzled. "Where do you fit into the picture?"

"I killed a man tonight in that room," Cronin said softly. "Didn't you know?"

Big Joe's face was a study in fear and bewilderment.

"I'll swear I didn't! Who—who was it?"

"A Chinaman, named Yun Kao!"

Big Joe started convulsively. Cronin grabbed him and jammed him back down on the bed. He loomed over him, knife hovering near the flophouse keeper's bull-throat.

"Joe, I've got your neck in a sling! Jum Woon's been snatchin' men out of that room, and you've been helpin' him. Yun Kao came after Smoky Slade tonight, but I was in there instead. Yun Kao tried to brain me, and I knifed him. Don't try to act like you didn't know what was goin' on in there."

"I swear to God I didn't!" whimpered Big Joe, his face the color of a catfish's belly. "My God, Jum Woon will think I double-crossed him!"

"Sure, he will!" Cronin agreed heartily. "In fact, I'll tell him that you helped me sneak into that room, to spoil his racket. The cops won't get a chance to send you up the river. His highbinders will bump you off before they can get you to the police station."

"What'll I do?" moaned Big Joe, completely demoralized. The more a slums denizen knew about Jum Woon, the worse he feared him. And Daley knew plenty about the Chinaman's methods—more than Cronin did.

"Spill everything you know," advised Cronin. "It's your only chance."

"I'll talk!" Daley was sweating with fear. He looked like a big, unclean animal as he sat in hairy semi-nakedness on the edge of the bed. There was something anthropoidal about him. "Jum Woon's paid me a hundred dollars for every bum he took out of that room. He wanted bums, because nobody gives a damn when one of them drops out of sight. He's snatched a few out of parks at night, but this was easier and safer. I'd put a man in that room on the alley, and lock the inside door. I kept the lock busted on the door to the alley, so the Chinese could get in. Yun Kao and some other fellows would come in some time in the night and make away with him. I never saw them come or go. Along towards morning I'd go in and get the bum's clothes and burn 'em. They got the Clubfoot Kid night before last—would have got Smoky Slade then, but for an accident. I thought they had got him, till he showed up tonight.

"I didn't think he was wise to me. I rented the room to him again, just like I said. After midnight I went in to get his clothes—to do away with the evidence, see—but they wasn't there, and there was blood on the floor. I thought it was Smoky's. I cleaned it up. You killed Yun Kao—but what about the men with him? What'd you do with the body? Why'd you wait so long before you came to me about this?" His eyes narrowed with sudden suspicion. "Say, I just remembered something! What are the cops hunting you for? They were in here about one o'clock, asking if you'd been in here. They didn't say why they were after you—"

"Never mind that," growled Cronin. "I'm askin' the questions. You do the answerin'. I'm lookin' for Jum Woon, right now. He's left his house on Canton Street. Do you know where he's gone?"

"No—ow! Cronin, I swear I'm telling the truth. If he ain't at his house on Canton Street, I dunno where he is."

There was sincerity in Daley's fright. Cronin pulled the knife back, and asked: "What the hell did Jum Woon want with those bums?"

Daley turned a shade paler and his eyes avoided Cronin's.

"I dunno," he muttered, and there was a strange gleam in his eyes, compounded of horror and fear—repellent and altogether bestial.

Cronin felt his flesh crawl as he sensed a mystery here blacker and fouler than even his conceptions reached. In a sort of cold frenzy he grabbed Daley's throat and lifted the bowie.

"You know, blast you! Tell me, or I'll cut the gizzard out of you—!"

Daley tore vainly at the relentless fingers as he tried chokingly to speak, and Cronin let go of him and lowered the knife. Then Daley's distended eyes looked past Cronin, and at the stark horror in their flare, Cronin wheeled toward the window. He was in time to see a yellow hand smash through that window, tearing the dingy shade away. A black muzzle gaped in the aperture and spat fire and smoke. Big Joe grunted like a stuck hog and lopped soddenly to the floor. Cronin rolled aside as the gun cracked again. His own six-shooter was out, blazing red, and his first shot smashed the light bulb. Lead combed the shadows, but he shifted position again. Now the advantage was on his side. The room was dark and that lean figure outside the window was limned, though faintly enough, against the streetlight. As he shifted he thumbed back the fanged hammer and let it fall. A gurgling gasp mingled with the roar of the report, and the shadowy form fell away from the window.

Outside a clamor of startled voices rose as the occupants of the cots sprang from their beds, awakened by the gunfire.

Cronin took a stride toward the window—and checked, with an oath. It was too small to admit his bulk. The room had but one door, the one by which he had entered. The skirl of a police whistle galvanized him. His only way of escape was back through the cot room, now thronged with wide-awake men, and with a curse, he took it. Men yelled and sprayed out in flight as he came through the door. Shirt tails flapped as the bums knocked over cots and trampled each other in their stampede to get out of the way of that bulky, gun-gripping figure. He heard his name bawled by a dozen terrified voices as he ran. One more stride and he was out of the door and on the pavement of Stockley Street.

Down it a cop came on the run, shrilling on his whistle. He recognized Cronin, yelled, fired and raced toward him. Cronin sprinted, ducked into the mouth of the alley. Daylight was paling the streetlamps, but it was dark in the alley—too dark for the patrolman, charging recklessly in, to see the garbage can that had been rolled across his path until he took a thundering fall over it. When he rose, raving, with skinned hands and torn pants, and had found his gun and whistle, he had the alley to himself. He had not seen Cronin melt through a backyard gate and fade out of sight down a twisting side street.

Nor did anyone see Cronin slip into Jake Ziegler's back door, as Cronin was presently assuring Jake, as he stretched himself out on a heap of old clothes in the Ziegler loft. There were several peculiarities about Jake's store, not the least that of its location, adjacent to a narrow, winding alley by which one could enter or leave the establishment unobtrusively.

"Jake, bring me some grub and the mornin' paper as soon as it's on the street. I'm goin' to have to hide here today. Nothin' I can do in the broad open daylight. If the cops come—"

"Let dem come," grunted Jake. "If they want to search the loft, I'll step on the button behind mine counter. The buzzer hid under that shelf by your head will wake you up, and you duck into the secret closet. Why should they look for you here? They don't know I'd do anything for you—they don't know you kept me out of prison one time, because you was sorry for a old feller with no friends, and—"

"Never mind that," broke in Cronin. "Rustle me some breakfast, will you."

He was asleep when Jake came up into the loft with a platter of ham and eggs and a morning paper still damp from the press. But what he read there woke him up quick enough. The amount of publicity he was getting gave him a feeling of panic.

Last night's happenings were scare-headed in letters you could read a city block away. A ravening man-eater was loose on the defenseless populace!, screamed the headlines. Butch Cronin, notorious Barbary Coast character, once a member of the police force, and later posing as a private detective, had gone berserk. An atrocious photograph of himself leered sinfully up from the front page—in uniform, ironically. It was the only picture of him they'd been able to get hold of.

The accompanying story was a masterpiece in hysterics. This jungle killer had attempted to rob a respectable young lady named Raquel Mendoza, had brutally murdered Yun Kao, prominent young Chinese merchant, and had heinously assaulted police officer Harrigan. But that was not all! In the early hours of morning the brute had murdered Big Joe Daley, keeper of a rooming house on Stockley Street. Cronin had been seen to run from the building immediately after a burst of gunfire had awakened the occupants of the establishment. Many of them had recognized him, and so had a patrolman who had heroically given chase, failing to capture the desperado because of reasons concerning which the account was vague. To further complicate matters, an unidentified Chinaman had been found shot to death just outside the smashed window of the room in which Big Joe Daley lay dead. An empty pistol was found in his hand, and one of the derelicts swore that the man had occupied a cot near him that night—that he had come in some time after midnight and taken a cot near the door of Big Joe's bedroom.

"That fellow must have been sent there to spy on Daley," mused Cronin. "They suspected that Big Joe did double-cross them, and put me in that room himself. So they didn't say anything to Daley about Yun Kao gettin' killed; just sent a man to watch him. He was awake and saw me go into Daley's room and concluded that Daley had betrayed Jum Woon to me. So he got up and sneaked around the house and shot Daley through the window. He couldn't have overheard me threatenin' Daley—couldn't have seen or heard anything that was goin' on in the room till he busted the window, and he shot as soon as he smashed it. He killed Daley thinkin' Big Joe had double-crossed Jum Woon. That's why he shot Daley first before he tried to get me—traitor first, enemies later, accordin' to the tong code."

"They got enough to hang you three times over," Jake pointed out, unnecessarily. "Look how the papers are panning the cops because they are not catching you. They'll be very mad and chase you harder than ever."

"And I can't dodge 'em much longer," admitted Cronin. "I've got to find Smoky. And to find him I've got to find Jum Woon—hell's fire!"

He had run head-on into another jolt in the newspaper story. Yet another murder was credited to the inhuman monster, Cronin. Young Richard Van Ritten, prominent young sportsman, had been found shot to death in the alley back of his palatial apartment house. Near him lay a pistol with Cronin's fingerprints on the butt.

"Blitherin' hell!" ejaculated Cronin aghast. "They lugged him there after they killed him by accident outside of Jum Woon's house on Canton."

"Never," raved the newspaper narrative, "has this city been shocked by such a saturnalia of slaughter, such a red carnival of murder as raged unchecked last night. Cronin is more than a criminal—he is a madman, a homicidal maniac! What are the police doing?"

Cronin could imagine what the cops were doing. He felt sorry for them.

"But it's a great break for the reporters," he remarked. "This story has crowded the Wiltshaw girl clean off the front page. Just a small item sayin' that the police are still huntin' for some clue as to her whereabouts, urged on by her frantic parents."

"No wonder the old man should be frantic," said Jake Ziegler. "He ran his son off, a year ago, did you hear? Some sort of a college scrape. A scandal! He disinherited the boy, and I have heard it that he went to the gutter finally, and was seen in Seattle, panhandling on the streets like any bum. His sister loved the young rascal. Now she is gone, too. Maybe it is the old man, the old devil, is remorseful, yes?"

"Maybe," grunted Cronin, folding the paper. "I believe the girl walked out of her own free will. If she was snatched, why didn't the old man get a letter demandin' ransom?"

"He would be able to pay," mused Jake. "With all the steamships he owns, running across the Pacific Ocean. But tell me this, Butch: if the girl ran away, herself, why did she go at night, with no more clothes than she wore on her back, and no money but a few dollars maybe in her purse? The taxi driver that took her from home to the corner of Canton and Richards Streets, where she left him, he said she had only a light wrap thrown over her evening gown, and when she paid him, she had only a dollar or so left. The corner of Canton and Richards is a funny place to start running away from home from, ain't it now?"

"Hell, I dunno," grunted Cronin. "I got enough worries of my own. I'm goin' to sleep the rest of the day, Jake. You pump all the Chinese you know and try to learn where Jum Woon's hidin'."

The streetlights had begun to glint when Jake brought Cronin his supper and an evening paper.

"They ain't going to hang you for Daley," Jake volunteered. "It stands by the paper, the police have decided the Chinaman killed Big Joe. They found the bullets in Daley came out of the gun in the Chinaman's hand, and your fingerprints wasn't on that gun. So all the murders you got to hang for now is Yun Kao, and Van Kitten, and maybe the Chinaman that killed Daley. His name was Wang Chow. A Chinaman whispered it to me. But the cops don't know, and they won't know. He was one of Jum Woon's highbinders. Nobody is going to identify him, so the cops won't tie up Jum Woon in this business."

"I don't reckon you found out where Jum Woon is."

"As well try to make iron cats talk. Old Kang Su, who runs the antique shop in the next block, he belongs to the Wu San. I bet he knows, but he wouldn't tell nobody. You could tear his tongue out but he wouldn't talk."

"I bet he tells me!" Cronin bolted his food and rose. "Peek out and see if the coast is clear. I'm callin' on Kang Su."

Through a tiny, shadowy backyard littered with trash and cans, Cronin reached the door of the room behind the shop, where Kang Su lived. The door was bolted, but the brittle metal snapped under the drive of Cronin's heavy shoulder. Kang Su sprang up with a choking cry, then froze dumb at the gleam of steel in Cronin's hand.

"Don't yell, Kang Su," said Cronin softly, shoving the door shut with his heel. "You old devil, you've got enough sins on your soul to stain the Sacramento. You remember all the girls you've kidnapped out of China to sell as slaves to big-bellied merchants? I'd as soon cut your skinny old throat as to look at you. I've always wanted to, but couldn't figure how to do it by law. But now I'm outside the law anyway. Another killin' won't matter. If you want to live, you better talk. Where's Jum Woon?"

Kang Su grinned toothily and folded his yellow hands; he looked like a hypocritical old cobra.

"Kill me, white devil! I am a man of Wu San! I do not betray my chief, and I am not afraid to die!"

"I know you don't mind dyin'," conceded Cronin. "But I know somethin' you do mind—what have you saved your dough for the past five years for? I know. To pay for sendin' your bones back to China when you die. Well, Kang Su, if you don't talk, you'll never rest with the bones of your ancestors. I'll set fire to the dump after I've slit your gullet. Your bones'll turn to ashes that nobody'll bother to collect."

Kang Su turned livid, his black eyes burning into Cronin's stormy blue ones. Had another white man spoken thus, Kang Su would have smiled, knowing he was bluffing. But with Cronin he did not know. He knew the man was desperate; he knew the untamed ferocity that lurked in him. Kang Su could not take the chance that he was bluffing. There was too much at stake. His life did not matter, but the thought of his bones doomed to mix forever with the polluted soil of a barbaric, foreign land turned Kang Su's marrow cold.

He spoke, and he dared not lie, with Cronin's fierce gaze fixed on his withered face.

"Jum Woon is in Chin Ong's house on River Street."

"I know the place. Is Smoky Slade there?"

"Yes."

"Why did Jum Woon leave his house and hide?"

"When he heard you had escaped from the police, he knew you would come to his house, for vengeance, or in search of Smoky Slade. He was not afraid of you, but he had business at hand which required secrecy. If you came, you would be killed, but there would be confusion, and perhaps the police would come and learn matters which were none of their business. So he left in haste, with all his people, and went to the house of Chin Ong. Then he sent men of his boo how doy back to the house to kill you when you came, but you had come more swiftly than they had expected."

"How is it that Van Ritten was killed with my gun?"

"He was not. But he was shot with a gun of the same caliber, and the bullet lodged under the skin of his back. It was cut out and thrown away, and the pistol which was taken from you when you were captured by Wen Chang was left beside him, with one chamber fired. It will be enough to hang you."

"Maybe," growled Cronin. "Why was Daley killed?"

"A traitor is always killed. Wang Chow was sent to spy on Daley. If you came secretly to him, it would prove that the man was a traitor."

"Why did Van Ritten come to Jum Woon's house?"

"He had business there. He did not know it had been postponed."

Cronin meditated a moment and then asked: "What does Jum Woon want with those men he snatched?"

"Do not ask me that!" Kang Su's face was grey. "Even if my bones must lie forever in a heathen land, I cannot answer. Some secrets must be kept at all costs."

There was sincerity in his terror. Cronin scowled, recognizing that he had reached the limits to which the Chinaman would go. After all, he had learned more than he had come expecting to learn.

"You said Smoky is at Chin Ong's house. Is he alive?"

"He dies between midnight and dawn."

"Why the hell didn't you say so?" ejaculated Cronin, starting up. "I ought to gut you, anyhow—but I'll fix you so you won't spread any alarms about me."

When Cronin stepped out of the back door and closed it behind him, he left Kang Su bound and gagged on his dingy bunk. Cronin had blown out the candle that lighted the little room. He felt there was small chance of Kang Su being found and released before morning. By that time he would either have failed or succeeded at the task he had before him.

But the door had scarcely closed behind Cronin before the old Chinaman was at work. He made no attempt to free his wrists and ankles. But it is hard to tie a gag that will stay in place, especially on a man versed in all the tricks the Chinese know. In a few moments of writhing, twisting, and scraping the knots of the cloth against the wall, Kang Su's mouth was free. Then he began hitching himself up to a sitting posture, writhing and twisting his bound body like a snake. It was slow work, but presently he was sitting upright, leaning against the wall against which his bunk was built. He pressed his head against what looked like a big-headed peg stuck in the wall, and pushed hard. A square aperture opened in the wall, revealing a telephone set in the shallow niche. He butted at it with his head until he dislodged the receiver from the hook. A sibilant Chinese voice drifted inquiringly over the wire.

"Beware!" panted Kang Su, twisting his neck to get his lips as close to the mouthpiece as possible. "Kang Su, the miserable, speaks. Cronin, the white devil, is on his way to the house of Chin Ong! He knows that Jum Woon and the beggar, Smoky Slade, are there."

"And how did he learn this?" The voice was silky.

"He forced the information from this debased insect. I do not ask for mercy. Only that my bones be taken back to the Celestial Kingdom when the judgment has been executed. The money I have saved for that purpose is in the hands of the treasurer of the tong."

"Your life is forfeit," came back the voice of authority. "But you have redeemed a little by your warning and admission of guilt. The white devil comes to his doom. Your ancient bones shall rest in the holy country of your honorable ancestors."

"I am content!" And the old scoundrel was sincere when he said it.

Chapter .5.

River Street, once an important section of the waterfront, had long fallen into disuse and decay. It was a stretch of rotting wharves, walled by rows of abandoned warehouses, some housing only rats and cobwebs, some occupied by swarms of poverty-stricken Mongolians. It was one of the mysteries of the Oriental nature that Chin Ong, one of the richest of the Chinese merchants, should choose to live in such a squalid quarter. His big house sat back from the waterfront, separated by a narrow alley from the biggest warehouse in the row, and fronting a fairly respectable street. Its sober exterior gave no promise of the luxuriousness said to be spread so lavishly within.

Cronin approached the house by way of the waterfront, stealing over the shadowy, rotting wharves beneath which the black water lapped at the toppling piles. By day this district teemed with life, odorous, clamorous and Oriental; by night it might have been one with the dead cities of the past. Tonight the quarter seemed abnormally quiet. Not a baby wailed; not a gleam of light showed through the tenement windows. The only sounds were the lapping of the water and the sputtering of a motorboat that seemed to be running without lights.

Cronin crouched back in the shadows as the noise grew louder. A police boat would be showing lights. Whoever was at the wheel was taking a big chance of wrecking his craft. Just ahead of him was the big warehouse which stood behind Chin Ong's residence. It had not been made into a tenement; it was supposed to be empty. Cronin saw the speed boat now, a long shadowy shape sliding dimly out of the deeper blackness. He made out a vague cluster of figures on board. It was heading straight for the ruined wharf in front of the warehouse. He grunted and batted his eyes. It had vanished, apparently under the wharf. The sputter of the motor ceased. He crouched, burning with impatience, but fearful of being seen by a landing party.

But time dragged by and no one appeared on the wharf. He determined to wait no longer. A boatload of people had gone under that rotting wharf and apparently were still there, for what reason he could not guess. But it was probably no concern of his; his business was to get into Chin Ong's house and get hold of Smoky Slade, somehow, while the 'bo was still in the land of the living. If Smoky was killed, there went his last chance of dodging the gallows.

He darted quickly across the wharf, turned and glided along the side of the warehouse until he came to the mouth of the alley which separated it from the back of Chin Ong's house. No lights showed in the latter, though he knew the front of it, facing on semi-respectable Richards Street, might be ablaze.

He groped his way along the alley, holding his breath for fear he might stumble over a loose can with a resultant clangor. But when his foot did hit something, it was not a can. It was something soft and yielding, and a low moan floated up from the blackness about his feet. A faint perfume mingled with the alley smells, as unmistakable as the faint cry. A woman was lying there in the dark!

He stooped and his groping hands encountered soft flesh and silky garments. The woman whimpered at his touch, and he felt his hand smeared with something warm and sticky. He recognized the feel of the stuff. Taking a chance, he snapped on his tiny flashlight, sheltering the glow with his broad hand. In the small circle of light he saw a woman's face, hideously splotched with blood. It was the Eurasian, Raquel Mendoza.

Her eyes were closed and low whimpering moans escaped her red lips. He snapped off the light and crouched there, in indecision. Not even with his own hide at stake could he leave a woman lying wounded, maybe dying, in a waterfront alley. There was only one thing he could do with her—carry her to the back door of some nearby tenement or residence, ring the bell and slip away before anyone could get to the door.

Cursing the necessity, he gathered her in his arms and braced his legs to rise with her limp weight. Suddenly she stiffened—her hands clawed at his wrist. Even as he sensed the trick and tried to hurl her from him, he felt the sting of the needle in his wrist.

The girl twisted from his grasp and slipped away in the dark. He staggered drunkenly, a sluggish iciness coursing through his veins. He clawed at his belt, dragging out knife and pistol that suddenly seemed weighted with lead. Somewhere feet were pattering purposefully toward him in the dark. The Colt seemed incredibly heavy in his hand; he groaned with the effort of lifting it and thumbing back the hammer. He heard the crack of the shot like a distant echo, saw a ring of wild, bestial faces blurred in the flash. Then as the dark closed in again they were on him, a dozen hands clawing at him, beating down his arm, wrenching at the smoking pistol. His legs were dead and the rest of him was dying. But as he went down he ripped upward once, murderously, with a knife that seemed to weigh a ton, felt it meet resistance and heard somebody scream. And then he neither felt nor heard anything more.

Cronin did not regain his senses suddenly as he had the night before. He came to slowly, groggily, as a man does who has been drugged. A yellow mist that enveloped him thinned and cleared gradually. A face grew out of the mist—a yellow face with slant eyes and thin drooping mustaches. This, Cronin realized in a detached sort of way, was Jum Woon. He had at last run the tong chief to earth. Or had he?

Then his sight cleared enough for him to get a sane idea of his surroundings. He was in a small bare room and Jum Woon was standing over him, just out of reach of his hands which were, unaccountably, free. The Chinaman was clad, not in his usual conventional Occidental garb, but in dark velvet robes worked with curious gilt designs. When Cronin tried to get up and kill Jum Woon, something checked his lunge. Then he discovered that a length of thin, strong chain was looped closely about his waist and made fast with a padlock. The other end of the chain was fastened to a ring set in the wall.

"So you have searched me out at last," said Jum Woon reflectively. "Strange how a man may rush headlong on doom! If you had slipped out of the city, you might have escaped your stupid police."

"You framed me, you yellow baboon!" snarled Cronin.

"So I did," Jum Woon admitted. "Won Chang recognized you after one of his companions knocked you senseless in the house of Big Joe Daley. He acted with discretion and brought you to me instead of killing you. I instantly saw an opportunity to get you out of my way by process of law—always safer, regardless of the complications and elaborations necessary to accomplish such an end."

"Why did you have Daley killed?"

"I had my doubts about him. I feared he was growing timorous and had betrayed me to you. Yet I gave him the benefit of the doubt and sent Wang Chow to spy on him—and to kill him at the first evidence of treachery."

"But I told Harrigan in Won Chang's presence that Daley didn't know I was in his flophouse."

"True, but you might have been trying to shield him. Were you?"

"No. Daley knew nothin' about me bein' there."

"I believe you. Well, it's no matter. He had served his purpose. As for you, you have walked into a trap. You have put yourself outside the law. Any man, white or yellow, is justified in killing you, especially to defend himself. I have not time to dispose of you now, so you have a few more hours of life. Then you will be shot, cleanly and efficiently, 'while trying to break into Chin Ong's house.' I will call the police and show them your body, in the alley near a broken window. The papers will headline the killing, in self-defense, of the blood-mad slayer of Yun Kao, of Richard Van Ritten, and of the unidentified Chinaman who slew Big Joe Daley. The case will be closed."

"What are you delayin' for?" muttered Cronin, his eyes blue fire, his big fists clenched till the knuckles showed white.

"There is business I can postpone no longer. Already I have postponed it one night because of you. I should have attended to it last night. But I feared an interruption from you.

"I am sorry my reception of you was so crude tonight, but I had not time to prepare anything more elaborate. My faithful servants, hastily put on guard when I received warning of your approach, saw you creeping toward the alley, and I had only a matter of moments to prepare for you. They could have shot or stabbed you, but I feared the noise of a melee might frighten my guests, who were just arriving, or even bring the police, prematurely. A little fresh chicken blood on Raquel's face, your natural Western sympathy for a woman in apparent distress, a little hypodermic needle in the girl's hand—even so you managed to fire one shot and to disembowel one of my men before the injection overcame you. Your bull-like vitality is greater even than I had realized. However your one shot did not cause any panic."

"Who the hell are your guests?" demanded Cronin.

The flicker of a grim smile touched the Chinaman's lips.

"People of your own race who seek the next best thing to immortality. I meant to entertain them at my humble house last night, but your escape caused me to change the time and place."

Cronin did not relish the faint, but bitter contempt with which Jum Woon spoke of his Caucasian "guests." He asked: "What have you done with Smoky Slade?"

"He is at the moment a guest of the gods."

"Dead?"

"Not yet."

Cronin fell silent, staring slit-eyed at the tranquil Chinaman; his scarred face was immobile, but the veins swelled purple on his temples and Jum Woon involuntarily drew back from the savagery shining bluely in his eyes.

"This game ain't played out yet, you yellow skunk," said Cronin thickly. "I'll get you yet."

"That invincible egotism is the dominant characteristic of your race," shrugged Jum Woon and, turning, stalked from the room. The opened door revealed a lamp-lit corridor and a stolid-faced coolie standing on guard. Cronin got a glimpse of Jum Woon handing him a bunch of keys, and then the door shut.

Cronin braced his feet against the baseboard and tried to tear the ring out of the wall. The effort bunched the muscles in writhing knots on his arms and shoulders, but evidently the bolt that held the ring was clinched on the other side of the wall. He tried to twist the chain and break it, but with no better result. He was still trying when he heard a mutter of voices outside, a high-pitched feminine voice demanding and a guttural masculine voice refusing. The altercation ended startlingly in the sound of a blow, the fall of a heavy body, and then the door burst open to admit Raquel Mendoza. She had a knife in one hand and a blackjack in the other and she looked like an enraged tigress.

And like a tigress she came across the room.

"You dog!" she cried hysterically. "If I had known, when I trapped you in the alley—it would not have been a needle I stuck into your vile flesh. Wang Chow—you killed him! I had not known—only just now I learned. You killed the only man I ever loved!"

Cronin, who had not blenched at Jum Woon's threats, felt a chill crawl along his spine as he looked into the wide, blazing eyes of the maddened Eurasian. They were tinged with insanity. Half-caste mentalities hung on hair triggers, and she was capable of any atrocity at the moment. He tensed himself—his hands were free and she'd have to come close to stab him. She laughed wildly, as if reading his mind.

"You fool! Do you think I'll give you a chance to strangle me? You can't rise from the floor. The chain's not long enough. I'll cut off your fingers when you try to grab me. I'll make mincemeat out of you—I'll take your eyes, your nose, your ears, damn you! Jum Woon would have shot you, but that's too good for you."

"And what do you think he'll do to you for spoilin' his plan?" Cronin demanded. Beyond her he saw the coolie, blood streaming from his scalp, rise drunkenly and begin to creep into the room on noiseless bare feet. "Jum Woon can't give me to the cops all chopped up. They'd know there was somethin' phoney."

Raquel's glare wavered and fear mingled with her fury. But it was washed away by a red wave of madness.

"Damn you! You shan't frighten me with your tongue!" She glided toward him, knife lifted, eyes dilated with ghastly purpose. Then the coolie sprang and caught her from behind in his arms. Her reaction was as instant and deadly as that of a startled cobra.

With a feline scream she twisted about and sank her dagger to the hilt under his heart. He cried out chokingly and sank down and she recoiled, her eyes starting from her head. The madness in them was replaced by stark terror at what she had done. All at once she seemed to realize the enormity of her offense against the wishes of her grim master. She clapped a hand to her mouth and stared wildly at the dead man, then with a wailing cry of despair she fled blindly from the room.

Chapter .6.

Cronin scarcely heeded her going. His eyes were fixed on the bulge in the dead man's girdle—the keys Jum Woon had given him! He strained against his chain, clawing desperately at the corpse. It was just beyond the reach of his fingers. A groan of despair was wrenched from his throat. Then he stretched out his legs as far as he could, clamped his feet about the dead man's head and began slowly, clumsily, to draw the body toward him. It seemed an age until he could grasp the coiled pigtail with his hand. His fingers were clammy with sweat when he tore the keys from the girdle. In an instant he stood up, free of the chain, but not of the house of Jum Woon. Stooping, he picked up the blackjack Raquel had dropped, and drew a broad-bladed knife from the coolie's girdle. Grimly he promised himself that Jum Woon's rats should never again take him alive.

He stepped to the door and looked down a dim-lit hall, lined with closed doors on each side. At the end of the hall there was the head of a stair and suddenly a shadow moved near the landing. What looked like a solid panel of the wall was swinging open. He drew back quietly into the doorway, peering around the jamb. It was risky, but the man who emerged from the secret door did not look in his direction. He was a wiry, dark, muscular man, obviously not a Chinaman. He left the panel partly open and he went stealthily, like a man who had no business being where he was. Half-crouching, he stole across the hall to a certain door, turned a key in the lock and slid inside, closing the door behind him. Almost instantly a woman's muffled voice rose in protest, changing suddenly to a shriek of fright. The cry ceased abruptly as if a hand had been clapped over her mouth. Cronin lunged recklessly down the corridor. She had spoken in English. There was a white woman behind that door.

Inside the room he heard the sounds of a struggle. One of his keys might fit the door, but Cronin did not take time to see. The panels splintered under the impact of his iron-hard shoulder. Over the ruins of the door he saw a white girl writhing in the grasp of a Malay whose eyes were red with bhang. One of Jum Woon's servants had run amok.

The Malay released the girl and whirled, snarling like a wild beast. Then with his dark face convulsed he ripped a kris from his belt and ran at the white man. He moved with the convulsive speed of drug-crazed bloodlust, but Cronin had faced his kind before. A quick shift, a swipe of the blackjack that met the wavy blade and knocked it aside, the lightning-quick lunge of the knife in Cronin's right hand—and the Malay gagged suddenly and went to his knees, blood spurting between the fingers that clawed at his throat. He pitched sidewise and lay twitching.

"Oh!" The girl sank her head in her hands and turned away, sick and shuddering.

Cronin wiped the reeking knife on his pants leg, and observed: "It wasn't nice to see, but it was him or me—and I'd a damn sight rather it was him. Ain't you Joan Wiltshaw?"

"Yes." She lifted her head and looked at him, but avoided the sprawling shape on the floor. Her eyes were haunted, her garments those of a Chinese slave girl. "Who are you?"

"Name's Cronin. Private detective."

"You came looking for me? My father sent you?"

"Not exactly. But it amounts to the same thing. Where's Jum Woon?"

She shook her head, her eyes shadowed by a nameless horror.

"I don't know. I haven't seen him since he locked me in here, an hour ago. From what he said, I think he was going to the warehouse that stands behind this building. There's something hellish going on in there! All of Jum Woon's men must be there, or that Malay wouldn't have dared molest me. Jam Woon had him whipped once for annoying me. I think he must have doped himself up to work up his courage, and sneaked up here, knowing Jum Woon was out of the way."

"Are you here of your own free will?" Cronin asked bluntly.

"Certainly not!" There was pride and anger in her voice. "I'm being held a prisoner by force. Listen: perhaps you've heard that my father disinherited my brother and drove him out of the house a year ago, without a cent or any way of supporting himself. My father's a stern man, inordinately proud of the family name. My brother was weak, though not bad at heart. We lost all touch of Jack, but a week ago, Jum Woon, whom at that time I knew only by reputation, sent me word that my brother was at his house. I went there secretly, by night, fearing my father wouldn't let me go if he knew.

"I found Jack in a daze from a drug I now know to have been hashish. Jum Woon told me that his men had picked him up off the streets, thinking he was a common tramp—for poor Jack had sunk so low that he was begging on the streets. But Jum Woon had recognized him, in spite of his rags, and fed him and clothed him and sent for me. In spite of the hashish Jack knew me, and cursed Jum Woon terribly for bringing me into his house. He ordered Jum Woon to send me home, instantly, and Jum Woon promised to do so. I told Jack I would make arrangements to take him to a hotel and care for him, and that seemed to content him. But Jum Woon didn't send me home. I was brought here, to this house, and I've been a prisoner here ever since.

"He's made me wear these clothes, and continually tried to persuade me to smoke hashish, but otherwise he's offered me no harm or insult. I haven't seen Jack, and I believe he's being held a prisoner in Jum Woon's house. For some reason Jum Woon's made a hashish addict out of him, just as he's trying to do with me. Why, I can't imagine. But I'm afraid he'll finally force me to smoke the vile stuff against my will. Only today he threatened me with physical punishment, for the first time, if I didn't comply."

"Your old man thinks a lot of you, don't he?" Cronin asked.

"Yes, he does," she answered, rather puzzled at the question. "Why?"

"If he had you under his thumb he could might near make the old man ship any cargoes he wanted," mused Cronin. "Well, skip it for the time bein'. Our job right now is to get out of this dump."

There was no window in the room, only a skylight grid-ironed with steel bars, and far out of their reach.

"Down the hall is the only way out for us," he growled. "Nobody alive on this floor but us; but I reckon Chin Ong's family's on the lower floor, and maybe a pack of highbinders. Well, come on."

Out in the hall, at the head of the stair he paused. Below them sounded a low murmur of many voices. Undoubtedly the lower part of the house was occupied. He wondered where Raquel Mendoza had gone. He glanced at the gaping panel in the wall, and saw behind it a flight of narrow steps leading down.

"Where does that go?" he demanded abruptly.

"It leads to a tunnel that connects this house with the warehouse behind it. They brought me in by that way. Oh, let us hurry! Let's get out, somehow. When I think of my brother in the power of that beast—"

"I believe your brother's somewhere in this house," said Cronin. "He's not at Jum Woon's house. There's nobody there. Jum Woon must have brought your brother here when he came."

His mind was racing. It was past midnight. Kang Su had said that Smoky Slade was to die between midnight and dawn. Jum Woon had intimated that the 'bo was to die soon. Jum Woon was in the warehouse; then Smoky must be there too.

"Listen!" In the stress of the moment he grabbed the girl with a grip that made her flinch. "We're in a trap that's likely to snap off our heads any way we turn. We can go down these stairs and try to fight our way to the street. If we make it, you can get the cops and bring them here and maybe get your brother out, but the chances are by the time they get here Jum Woon'll have done away with him. And my goose will be cooked, because the only man in the world who can keep my head out of a noose is in that warehouse ready to be bumped off, right now!

"If we head for the warehouse, we'll run right into Jum Woon's whole pack, maybe. But with a little luck, we might save the fellow that can save my hide, and your brother too, at one swipe. If I can get a knife in Jum Woon's ribs, I'll make him do everything we want him to do. What do you say?"

"The warehouse—as quick as we can get there!" she exclaimed.

"Come on, then!"

When they pulled the panel to behind them the darkness was like that of a well. Cronin's flashlight had been taken from him. In the blackness they groped their way down until, through an unlocked door at the foot, they came into a dim-lit tunnel. Along that they stole, feeling as though they were walking blindly into a snake's den.

Another door ended the tunnel, and as Cronin pulled it cautiously open, revealing a short flight of stone steps leading upward, their blood was congealed by a shriek of awful horror. With a bound Cronin reached the top of the steps and wrenched open yet another door. He froze there, and the girl, peering past his shoulder, moaned in sick horror.

They were looking into a broad, low-ceilinged room, at one end of which giant ovens smoked with the heat of a big fire beneath them. Huge pots stood nearby and the size of those pots made Cronin's flesh crawl. What they suggested could not be real. This was nightmare and phantasy. But what he saw before him changed phantasm into revolting reality.

There was a great table, built solidly as a chopping block, with a huge pan beneath it to catch what ran from it. And on that table a figure writhed—a man, naked but for a sort of loincloth, bound hand and foot. A gargoyle figure out of an Oriental fable loomed above him—a huge, half-naked Mongol, one hand grasping the wretch's tousled hair, the other lifting a great meat-cleaver. A gigantic tub of boiling water steamed nearby.

Cronin choked, gagged, found voice.

"Smoky!"

The imprisoned head twisted frantically as the cleaver hovered in the air. Slade's bloodshot eyes burned agonizedly on Cronin's livid face.

"Oh, my God!" whispered the girl. "They're going to cook him!" And quietly she collapsed in a faint.

The Mongol had wheeled ponderously at the interruption, blinking his little pig-eyes angrily. He let go of Smoky and rolled toward Cronin, like a charging dreadnaught. And Cronin, teeth bared, went to meet him. He ducked the heavy swing of the cleaver and sank his knife deep in the Mongol's groin, ripping venomously upward. The brute's bellow of agony broke as Cronin smashed him savagely with the blackjack. The hideous cook toppled to the floor.

Cronin reached Smoky in a stride and slashed his cords. The 'bo pawed at the detective, almost incoherent with terror.

"He was going to cook me, Butch! Cook me like a pig! My God, I've seen Clubfoot's head! These devils ate him, and all the other bums they've snatched!"

"Nonsense!" But Cronin's blood ran cold as he gazed about that horrible kitchen.

"It's the truth! Jum Woon is head of a cult of cannibals! They grabbed me when I lost my head and ran out of that backyard, after they'd dragged you out into the alley. They took me to Jum Woon's house. They was going to have the feast there, that night. But pretty soon Jum got word you'd busted away from the cops, so he postponed it till tonight and sent out word to all them that was going to be there, that he'd have it tonight, in Chin Ong's warehouse. Then they drugged me, and when I woke up, here I was. Chin Ong already had the warehouse fixed up with rooms and things in it, unbeknownst to white people, and they've been all day rigging this kitchen up!" He gagged slightly. "That devil there is the one that belted you out, last night in Big Joe's place. I'm telling you, Butch, they're cannibals!"

But Cronin was remembering Van Ritten's pale, haggard face.

"Good God!" he muttered, aghast. "Van Ritten was one of them!"

"Van Ritten? Sure. I heard 'em talking about him. A fellow named Gop Jow shot him, accidental."

"You can swear that? The cops blame me for it."

"Sure, I can. I heard 'em talking about leaving your gun beside the stiff. But what's the matter with the girl?"

Only then Cronin noticed that she had fainted. He rubbed her wrists and splashed water from a nearby faucet on her face, and presently she opened her eyes and stared around, then remembering, gagged sickly and put her hands over her eyes.

"Never mind that," snapped Cronin, lifting her to her feet. "I know it's bad—I'm kind of sick myself. But we've got to save our hides. Where does that stair lead to, Smoky?"

"To the banquet room," shuddered Smoky. "That's where I was going—on a platter, with my head on top, to show it was the genuine article. Butch, I'll never be able to eat another piece of meat as long as I live!"

"There's only one way out of here for us," growled Cronin. "We've got to grab Jum Woon and hold him for a hostage. If my guess is right he's in that banquet room alone—alone as far as his men are concerned. We don't have to worry about the poor devils he's giving the banquet to. Come on. We'll have him by the neck before he suspects anything,"

He handed them each a butcher knife, and led the way up the stairs. Presently a low hum of chanting made itself evident, and a vaguely disquieting odor permeated the atmosphere. At the head of the stair, Cronin drew the black velvet hangings slightly aside, and looked into a great, shadowy, weirdly lighted room. A banquet table stood in the midst, and the light came from strange black candles which burned with a ghastly blue light and a faintly foul odor. Cronin recognized them for what they were—corpse candles, made from the fat of human bodies. And the guests were there, a ghastly, silent conclave, pale, haggard men and women, in evening suits and gowns, and all masked, sitting like images in the uncanny glow.

Cronin's gorge rose. He did not recognize any of those masked figures, but he knew that wealthy and prominent people were among them. Men and women of the idle rich, men and women who had drained life to the dregs, who had exhausted their souls and bodies in their mad pursuit of pleasures and who now, prematurely aged, sought false youth in the diabolist witcheries of black magic. Cronin understood Jum Woon's purpose, now. The Chinaman was no cannibal; he was a scheming and cynical devil.

The chanting had ceased. Jum Woon stood before his guests, arms folded on his velvet-clad breast. He looked supernaturally tall as he stood, dark and aloof and mysterious, wisps of smoke from bronze incense bowls curling about him. He spoke tranquilly.

"You have begged me for a renewal of youth. I have shown you the secrets of ancient Asia. I have shown you how the black monks of forbidden Tibet extend the span of their lives beyond common conception. Only human flesh can restore the lost vitality of youth. I have given it to you. You have felt its magic power. Again tonight I give it to you."

Cronin was watching the fiend's guests. The blaze of their eyes through the masks told him that they had been drugged, doubtless without their knowledge, but a drug so subtle and insidious that the victims were not aware of taking it, but which roused strange and perverted appetites and desires, and made them amenable to hypnotic suggestions.

"I don't see my brother!" whispered Joan.

"Hell, he wouldn't be in that crew!" muttered Cronin. "Listen: somewhere in this building there's a corridor or tunnel that leads out under the wharf, and there's a speedboat waiting there. That's the way these poor idiots came. I'm goin' to grab Jum Woon and put a knife to his ribs, and make him produce your brother, and then lead us to that boat. Once there we'll make a quick getaway. They won't dare shoot at us, if we've got Jum Woon. Come on!"

Jum Woon turned and smote a bronze gong, to summon the cook with various necromantic dishes to precede the ghastly piece-de-resistance. And the notes of the gong were still echoing when Cronin broke cover. Jum Woon was so paralyzed by his appearance that the detective was halfway across the room before the Chinaman came to his senses. Then his move was unexpected. He did not spring toward the nearest door, a move for which Cronin was prepared. Instead, he jumped back against the wall. A panel swung inward and he vanished, just as Cronin, sensing the move, hurled his knife. It thudded against the closing panel and stuck there, quivering. The secret door resisted Cronin's hurtling body, though in a frenzy of rage and disappointment he launched himself against it like a human battering ram.

Wrenching the knife from the panel he wheeled on the cowering guests with bitter fury. They had sprung up and now, under the loathing and contemptuous eyes of a man of their own race, they hid their faces and shrank back in awful shame and terror. Before he could voice the scalding denunciation that rose to his lips, a wide door opened behind them. Silk-clad arms grabbed them and hustled them through in the twinkling of an eye. The door slammed in Cronin's face as he sprang, and he stood in the room alone, except for the girl and the derelict.

"Butch, the doors are closing!"

It was a scream from Smoky. With a snarl Cronin sprang from door to door, wrenching vainly. Even the door by which they had entered was closed and locked. They were trapped.

They stood in the center of the room, turning this way and that, like caged animals. Then Cronin noticed the candles were dimmed. A strange, yellowish mist hung in the air, and he was aware of a pungent, not unpleasant odor.

"Drug!" he groaned, clenching his hands desperately. "They're dopin' us through the wall!"

"Certainly, my friends!" It was the impassive voice of Jum Woon. It came from somewhere beyond a carved teak-wood door. "We are watching your interesting antics through hidden loopholes. We could have shot you in your tracks before now, but this is better. The mist will presently overpower you, and when we have dispelled it, we will enter and relegate you to your proper destinies—Miss

Wiltshaw back to her prison room, you, Cronin, to the alley with a bullet through your head, and you, Slade, to the chopping block."

"You don't dare bump us off!" snarled Cronin. "A dozen white people have seen us here tonight!"

Jum Woon's laugh mocked him.

"My friend, those people are my slaves! They will never tell what they saw here tonight. You are a fool to think they would."

"Butch, I'm strangling!" gasped Smoky, clawing at his throat. The girl too was showing signs of distress. Cronin fought off a rising dizziness. He could scarcely see the candles now, in the thickening mist.

He lifted his voice in red rage, rather groggily, in a bull's bellow: "Blast you, Jum Woon, the game ain't played out yet! Smoky, grab a chair! We'll bust down that door!"

Above the impact of the chair he lashed madly against the panels, Cronin heard Jum Woon laugh. Smoky was valiantly floundering after him, trying to swing a chair he could hardly lift. Cronin fought despair as he fought the crawling mist. The door was too thick, too thick—

As he lifted the chair again he heard a new voice beyond the door, a voice that checked him.

"Jum Woon!" It was a petulant, Caucasian voice. "What's all this noise? It woke me up, and there's no more dope in my pipe. I've got to have it. You know I have."

"Jack!" It was a faint cry the girl managed to essay. She was on her knees on the floor now, fighting for her slipping consciousness.

"What's that?" It was a cry from beyond the door. "I heard a woman! There's a woman in there! It sounded like my sister! You said you took her home! You—"

"No!" they heard Jum Woon snap. "It is a hallucination! Your sister is not here. Take him back to his room."

"Jack!" bellowed Cronin, reeling on his feet. Smoky was down and out. The girl was sinking. "He lies! Jack Wiltshaw! Your sister's here! He's made a slave of her—"

"Jack!" screamed the girl, with her last bit of consciousness. "It's me, Joan! Help us, Jack—open the door!"

A wild cry echoed beyond the door. There was the sound of a struggle, the impact of blows, and then the door was torn gustily open. Framed in the opening Cronin saw a wild figure clinging to the door—the wild, white face of the boy—then a pistol cracked and the slim figure crumpled and over the falling body Cronin plunged like a mad bull.

Only his fighting instinct kept him going now. Guns were cracking, splitting jets of red, and he felt lead tearing into him. Though he was out of the drugged room, he was still wading in a mist, but it was red instead of yellow. But he saw Jum Woon's yellow face floating before him, and he plunged through the swirling crimson and drove home his knife, with all the power of his straining shoulder behind it.

Somebody yowled his death-scream. The face was no longer in front of him. Somewhere a door was splintering under heavy blows, and deep Saxon voices were roaring above the howling of the Chinese. He realized vaguely he was on his feet and the knife in his hand was dripping red. Blood was running down his arm. Then other forms loomed before him—bulky, blue-coated figures and among them, strangely, was the contorted face of Raquel Mendoza. She was screaming, and it sounded a long way off.

"That's him! That's him! Jum Woon's partner! Kill him, quick!"

He saw the pistol in her hand as it came up, and then suddenly blackness rolled over him in a flood.

Chapter .7.

In the quiet hospital room Butch Cronin grinned hardly at Jake Ziegler and Smoky Slade, the latter squirming in the unfamiliar contact of a new suit.

"Just like I told Smoky here," quoth Jake. "Even with all that lead in you they couldn't kill you! Didn't I know it?"

"I guess that's why you cried out in the hall while they was gouging the bullets out of Butch," grinned Smoky. "That's the way it was, Butch, just like I been telling you. The cop nearest to Raquel knocked the gun up just as she cut down on you. Good thing. Them Chinees had thrown about as much lead into you as you could stand."

"What about Jum Woon?" demanded Cronin.

"He was a bit too slow that time. You ripped him wide open from his groin to his brisket."

"They shot Jack Wiltshaw," said Cronin. "Did they—"

"Naw, just a slug through the shoulder. Them Chinees are rotten shots. He's going to get well. You oughta seen old man Wiltshaw bawl when they brought him and the girl home. He was worse than the old lady. He's sure trying to make it up for all of them, for what he done to the boy. He even bought me this suit, and gimme a hundred dollar bill. And you're going to get the reward he was offering for the return of the girl, Butch. Everything's jake, now. That Mendoza dame spilled the beans—"

"I've figured out why she went to the cops," muttered Cronin. "She was scared sick when she realized she'd killed one of her master's trusted men, in tryin' to disobey his orders. She knew Jum Woon would do somethin' real bad to her. To save her hide she went to the cops and told them about him havin' the girl and boy prisoners, only she made me out as Jum Woon's partner. She figured on gettin' me and Jum both killed in the raid. Ain't that right?"

"Right! And when she saw it was all up with her plans, me being there to testify you killed Yun Kao in self-defense, and all, she blew up and told everything she knew. Hell, it cleared you right there, without me having to say a word. About—about Jum Woon—"

"I'd already figured him out," said Cronin, his face darkening with a look of distaste. "I'll dream about that swine at night, I reckon. The reason he was makin' dope addicts out of Joan and Jack Wiltshaw was to get a hold over the old man. He wanted to use the old man's steamship line to smuggle opium and wet Chinese into the country.

"He meant to blackmail those poor devils he made cannibals out of. They were all drugged, and didn't know it. It's a drug that ain't got any Western name, but the Chinees know all about it. He'd give it to the poor fools, and they'd be temporarily stimulated, and think it was from eatin' human flesh, like he told 'em. Then they'd come back for more. I doubt if he really fed 'em human flesh. It was probably beef, with some poor devil's head on the platter to make it look real—but I don't know. He was a demon. Did the cops find any—"

"No. They'd all got away in that speedboat they had tied under the wharf. Jum Woon must have rushed them right out."

"Good. This mess is rotten enough as it is. When that drug wears away entirely they'll suffer enough, realizin' what they've done. He counted on that. He meant to blackmail them when he got good and ready. Not for money. He had plenty of that. But every one of those people had some kind of pull with people in high places. Power was what he wanted—the power to pull political and financial strings."

"I told you," murmured Jake.

"I know. You were right. He was on his way to more power than any man ever dreamed anyone could get in this country—with a bunch of prominent people under his thumb who'd do anything to keep him from exposin' them as cannibals—he planned that. And every boat of the Wiltshaw line smugglin' in men and women trained to do his biddin', and floodin' the country with drugs to debauch more people—he planned that, too, and the men behind him. It was more than personal ambition with him. A whole nation was behind him. An alien country that wants this country debauched and ruined. I can't prove it, but I know it. What it couldn't do by propaganda, it tried to do Jum Woon's way. I'll sleep easier at night, knowin' it was him I found with my knife in that red mist."

Black Wind Blowing

Emmett Glanton jammed on the brakes of his old Model T and skidded to a squealing stop within a few feet of the apparition that had materialized out of the black, gusty night.

"What the hell do you mean by jumping in front of my car like that?" he yelled wrathfully, recognizing the figure that posed grotesquely in the glare of the headlights. It was Joshua, the lumbering half-wit who worked for old John Bruckman; but Joshua in a mood such as Glanton had never seen before. In the white glare of the lights the fellow's broad brutish face was convulsed; foam flecked his lips and his eyes were red as those of a rabid wolf's. He brandished his arms and croaked incoherently. Impressed, Glanton opened the door and stepped out of the car. On his feet he was inches taller than Joshua, but his rangy, broad-shouldered frame did not look impressive compared to the stooped, apish bulk of the moron. There was menace in Joshua's bearing. Gone was the dull, apathetic expression he usually wore. He bared his teeth and snarled like a wild beast as he rolled toward Glanton.

"Keep away from me, blast you!" Glanton warned. "What's the matter with you, anyway?"

"You're goin' over there!" mouthed the half-wit, gesturing vaguely southward. "Old John called you over the phone. I heered him!"

"Yes, he did," answered Glanton. "Asked me to come over as quick as I could. Didn't say why. What about it? You want to ride back with me?"

Joshua jumped up and down and battered his hairy breast like an ape with his splay fists. He gnashed his teeth and howled. Glanton's flesh crawled a little. It was black night, with the wind howling under a black sky, whipping the mesquites. And there in that little spot of light that apish figure cavorted and raved like a witch's familiar summoned up from hell.

"I don't want to ride with you!" bellowed Joshua. "You ain't goin' there! I'll kill you if you try to go! I'll twist your head off with my hands!" He spread his great fingers and worked them like the hairy legs of great spiders before Glanton's face. Glanton bristled at the threat.

"What are you raving about?" he demanded. "I don't know why Bruckman called me, but—"

"I know!" howled Joshua, froth flying from his loose, working lips. "I listened outside the winder! You can't have her! I want her!"

"Want who?" Glanton was bewildered. This was mystery piled on mystery: black, howling night, and old John Bruckman's voice shrieking over the party line, edged with frenzy, begging and demanding that his neighbor come to him as quickly as his car could get him there; then the wild drive over the wind-lashed road, and now this lunatic prancing in the glare of the headlights and mouthing bloody threats.

Joshua ignored his question. He seemed to have lost what little sense he had ever had. He was acting like a homicidal maniac. And through the rents in his ragged shirt bulged muscles capable of rending the average man limb from limb.

"I never seen one I wanted before!" he screamed. "But I want her! Old John don't want her! I heered him say so! If you didn't come maybe he'd give her to me! You go on back home or I'll kill you! I'll twist your head off and feed it to the buzzards! You think I'm just a harmless big fool, I bet!"

Grotesquely his bellowing voice rose to a high-pitched squeal.

"Well, if it'll satisfy you," said Glanton, watching him warily, "I've always thought you were dangerous. Bruckman's a fool to keep you on the ranch. I've expected you to go clean crazy and kill him some time."

"I ain't goin' to kill John," howled Joshua. "I'm goin' to kill you. You won't be the first, neither. I killed my brother Jake. He beat me once too often. I beat his head to jelly with a rock and dragged the body down the canyon and throwed it into the pool below the rapids!"

A maniacal glee convulsed his face as he screamed his hideous secret to the night, and his eyes looked like nothing this side of hell.

"So that's what became of Jake! I always wondered why he disappeared and you came to live with old John. Couldn't stay in your shack in that lonely canyon after you killed him, eh?"

A momentary gleam of fear shot the murk of the maniac's eyes.

"He wouldn't stay in the pool," muttered Joshua. "He used to come back and scratch at the winder, with his head all bloody. I'd wake up at night and see him lookin' in at me and gaspin' and gurglin' tryin' to talk through the blood in his throat.

"But you won't come back and ha'nt me!" he shrieked suddenly, beginning to sway from side to side like a bull about to charge. "I'll spike you down with a stake and weight you down with rocks! I'll—" In the midst of his tirade he lunged suddenly at Glanton.

Glanton knew that if those huge arms ever locked about him his spine would snap like a rotten stick. But he knew, too, that nine times out of ten a maniac will try to reach his victim's throat with his teeth. Joshua was no exception. Reverting completely to the beast, he plunged in with his arms groping vaguely, and his jaws thrust out like a wolf's muzzle, slavering teeth bared in the glare of the headlights. Glanton stepped inside those waving arms and smashed his right fist against the out-jutting jaw with all his power. It would have stretched another man senseless. It stopped the half-wit in his tracks, and blood spurted. Before he could recover his balance Glanton struck again and again, raining terrific blows to face and head, driving Joshua reeling and staggering before him. It was like beating a bull, but the ceaseless smashes kept the maniac off-balance, confused and dazed him, kept him on the defensive. But Glanton was beginning to tire, and he wondered desperately what the end would be. The moment his blows began weakening Joshua would shake off his bewilderment and lunge to the attack again—

Abruptly they were out of the range of the car lights, and floundering in darkness. In panic lest the maniac should find his throat in the blackness, Glanton swung blindly and desperately, connected glancingly and felt his man fall away from him. He himself stumbled and went to his all-fours, almost pitching down the slope that fell away beneath him. Crouching there he heard the sounds of Joshua's thundering fall down the slant. Glanton knew where he was now, knew that a few yards from the road the ground fell away in a steep slope a hundred feet long. It was not hard to navigate by daylight, but by night a man might take a nasty tumble and hurt himself badly on the broken rocks at the bottom. And Joshua, knocked over the edge by Glanton's last wild haymaker, was taking that tumble.

It might have been an animal falling down the slope, from the grunts and howls that welled up from below, but presently, when the rattle of pebbles and the sounds of a heavy rolling body had ceased, there was silence, and Glanton wondered if the lunatic lay senseless or dead at the bottom of the slope. He called, but there was no answer. Then a sudden shudder shook him. Joshua might be creeping back up the slope in utter silence, this time maybe with a rock in his hand, such a rock as he had used to batter his brother Jake's head into a crimson pulp—

Glanton's eyes were getting accustomed to the darkness and he could make out the vague forms of black ridges, boulders and trees, but he knew he could not see a human form sneaking after him, and that devil-begotten wind that shrieked through the trees would drown a stealthy footstep. When a man turns his back on peril it assumes an aspect of thousandfold horror. When Glanton started back to the car his flesh crawled cold, and at each step he expected to feel a frightful form land on his back, gnashing and tearing. It was with a gasp of relief that he lunged into the car, eased off the handbrake and clattered off down the dim road. He was leaving Joshua behind him, alive or dead, and such was the grim necromancy of the gusty dark to tinge sane minds with its own madness, that at the moment he feared Joshua dead no less than Joshua living.

He hove another sigh of relief when the red spot that was the light of John Bruckman's house began to glow in the black curtain ahead of him. He disliked Bruckman, but the old skinflint was sane at least, and any sane company was welcome after his experience with a ghoulish maniac in the black heart of this evil night.

A car stood before Bruckman's gate and Glanton recognized it as the one belonging to Lem Richards, justice of the peace in Skurlock, the little village which lay a few miles south of the Bruckman ranch.

Glanton knocked on the door and Bruckman's voice, with a strange, unnatural quaver in it, shouted: "Who's there? Speak quick, or I'll shoot through the door!"

"It's me, Glanton!" called the ranchman in a hurry. "You asked me to come, blast it!"

Chains rattled, a key grated in the lock, and the door swung inward. The black night seemed to flow in after Glanton with the wind that made the lamp flicker and the shadows dance along the walls, and Bruckman moaned and slammed the door in its ebon face. He jammed bolt and chain with trembling hands.

"Your confounded hired hand tried to kill me on the way over," Glanton began angrily. "I've told you that lunatic would go bad some day—"

He stopped short. Two other people were in the room. One was Lem Richards, the J.P., a short, stolid, unimaginative man who sat before the hearth placidly chewing his quid. The other was a girl, and at the sight of her a sort of shock passed over Emmett Glanton, bringing a sudden realization of his work-hardened hands and hickory shirt and rusty boots. She was like a breath of perfume from the world of tinsel and bright lights and evening gowns that he had almost forgotten in his toil to build up his fortune in this primitive country.

Her supple young figure was set off to its best advantage by the neat but costly dress she wore. Her loveliness dazzled Glanton at first glance; then he looked again and was appalled. For she was white and cold as a statue of marble, and her dilated eyes stared at him as though she had just seen a serpent writhe through the door.

"Oh, excuse me!" he said awkwardly, dragging off his battered Stetson. "I wouldn't have come busting in here like this if I'd known there was a lady—"

"Never mind that!" snapped John Bruckman. He faced Glanton across the table, his face limned in the lamplight. It was a haggard face, and in the burning eyes Glanton saw fear, murky bestial fear that made the man repulsive. Bruckman spoke hurriedly, the words tumbling over each other, and from time to time he glanced at the big clock on the mantel, sullenly ticking off the seconds.

"Glanton, I hold a mortgage on your ranch, and it's due in a few days. Do you think you can meet your payment?"

Glanton felt like cursing the man. Had he called him over that windswept road on a night like this to discuss a mortgage? A glance at the white, tense girl told him something else was behind all this.

"I reckon I can," he said shortly. "I'm getting by—or would, if you'd stay off my back long enough for me to get a start."

"I'll do that!" Bruckman's hands were shaking as he fumbled in his coat. "Look here! Here's the mortgage!" He tossed a document on the table. "And a thousand dollars in cash!" A compact bundle of banknotes plopped down on the table before Glanton's astounded eyes. "It's all yours—mortgage and money—if you'll do one thing for me!"

"And what's that?" There must be a catch to this somewhere—John Bruckman giving away money!

Bruckman's bony forefinger stabbed at the cringing girl.

"Marry that woman!"

"What?" Glanton wheeled and stared at her with a new intensity, and she stared wildly back, in evident fright and bewilderment.

"Marry her?" He ran a hand dazedly across his head, vividly aware of the loneliness of the life he had been leading for the past three years. Why, any man who would object to marrying that lovely young thing, even without this princely dowry offered, would be a fool. But—

"What does the young lady think about it?" he asked.

Bruckman snarled impatiently.

"What does it matter what she thinks? She's my niece, and ward. She'll do as I say. She could do worse than marry you. You're no common ridge-runner. You're a gentleman by birth and breeding—"

"Never mind that," growled Glanton, waving him aside. He stepped toward the girl.

"Are you willing to marry me?" he asked directly. She looked full into his eyes for a long moment, with a desperate and pitiful intensity in her own wide gaze. And she must have read kindness and honesty there, for suddenly, impulsively, she sprang forward and caught his brown hand in both of hers, panting: "Yes! Yes! Please marry me! Marry me and take me away from him—" Her gesture toward John Bruckman was one of fear and loathing, but the old man did not heed. He was staring fearfully at the clock again.

He clapped his hands in a spasm of nervousness.

"Quick! Quick! Lem brought the license, according to my instructions. He'll marry you now—now! Stand over here by the table and join hands."

Richards, slow, dull of wit, rose heavily and lumbered over to the table, fingering his worn book. All this drama and mystery meant nothing to his bovine mind except that another couple were to be married. And so Emmett Glanton found himself standing holding the quivering hand of a girl he had never seen before, while the justice of the peace mumbled the ritual which made them husband and wife. And only then did he learn the girl's name—Joan Zukor.

"Do you, Emmett, take this woman—" droned on the monotonous voice and Glanton gave his reply mechanically, his fingers involuntarily clenching on the slim fingers they grasped so that the girl glanced questioningly at him. For, pressed briefly against a window, he had seen a face—a white, blood-streaked mask of murder—the face of the half-wit Joshua. The maniac's eyes burned on Glanton with a mad hate, and on the woman at his side with a sickening flame of desire. Then the face was gone and the window framed only the blackness of the night.

None but Glanton had seen the lunatic. Richards, paid by old John, lumbered stolidly forth and the door shut behind him.

Glanton and the girl stood looking at each other speechlessly, in sudden self-consciousness, but old John gave them no pause. He glared at the clock again, which showed ten minutes after eleven, jammed the mortgage and the banknotes into Glanton's hands and pushed him and the girl toward the door. Sweat dripped from his livid face, but a sort of wild triumph mingled with his strange fear.

"Get out! Get off my place! Take your wife and go! I wash my hands of her! I am no longer responsible for her! She's your burden! Go—and go quick!"

In a sort of daze Glanton found himself out on the porch with the girl, and from inside came the sound of drawn bolts and hooked chains. Angrily he took a step toward the door, then noticed the girl shivering beside him, huddling about her a cloak she had snatched as they were evicted.

"Come on, Joan," he said awkwardly, taking her arm. "I think your uncle must be crazy. We'd better go."

He felt her shudder.

"Yes, let us go quickly."

Richards, characteristically, had left the yard gate unfastened. It flapped and banged in the wind which moaned through the junipers. Glanton groped his way toward the sound, sheltering the cowering girl against the gusts that whipped her cloak about her. He shivered at the thick-set, cone-shaped outlines of the junipers along the walk. Either of them might be hiding the maniac who had glared through the window. The creature was no longer human; he was a beast of prey, ranging the night. John Bruckman had given Glanton no chance to warn him of the madman. But Glanton decided he would phone back from his ranch house. They could not loiter there in the darkness, with that skulking fiend abroad.

He half-expected to find Joshua crouching in the car, but it was empty, and a feeling of relief flooded him as he turned on the lights and their twin beams lanced the dark. The girl beside him sighed too, though she knew nothing of the death that lurked near them. But she sensed the evil of the night, the menace of the crowding blackness. Even such a dim illumination as this was comforting, a symbol of man's conquest of primordial darkness.

Wordless, Glanton started the car and they began the bumping, jolting ride. He was consumed with curiosity, but hesitated to put the question that seethed to his tongue. Presently the girl herself spoke.

"You wonder why my uncle sold me like a slave or an animal!"

"Don't say that!" exclaimed Glanton in quick sympathy. "You needn't—"

"Why shouldn't you wonder?" she retorted bitterly. "I can only say—I don't know. He's my only relative, so far as I know. I've seen him only a few times in my life. Ever since I was a small child I've lived in boarding schools—exclusive, expensive places—and I understood he was supplying the money that lodged, dressed and educated me. But he seldom wrote, more seldom visited me.

"I was in a school in Houston when I received a wire from my uncle ordering me to come to him at once. I came on the train to Skurlock, and arrived there about nine o'clock tonight. I was met at the station by Mr. Richards, who told me that my uncle had phoned and asked him to drive me out to his ranch. He also had the license, though I didn't know it at the time.

"When we got here my uncle told me abruptly that I'd have to marry a young man he had sent for. Naturally, I—I was terrified—" She faltered and then laid a timid hand on his arm. "I was afraid—I didn't know what kind of a man it might be."

"I'll be a good husband to you, girl," he said awkwardly, and thrilled with pleasure at the sincerity in her tone as she replied.

"I know it. You have kind eyes and gentle hands. Strong, but gentle."

They were approaching a place where the road had been straightened by a new track which, instead of swinging wide around the sloping edge of a steep, thicket-grown knoll, crossed a shallow ravine by a crude bridge and ran close by the knob on the opposite side where it sheered off in a forty-foot cliff. As the knoll grew dimly out of the windy darkness ahead of them, a grisly premonition rose in Glanton's breast. Joshua, loping through the mesquite like a lobo wolf, could have reached that knob ahead of them, if he had started as soon as he disappeared from the window. It was the most logical place along the road for an ambush. A man crouching on the thicket-clad crest of the cliff could hurl a boulder down on a car passing along the new stretch of road—with sudden decision, Glanton wrenched the car into the old track, now a faint trace grown up in broom-weeds and prickly pears.

Joan caught at him for support as she was thrown from side to side by the jouncing of the auto—and then as they swung around the slope and came back into the plain road again, behind and above them yammered a fiendish howling—the maddened, primordial shrieking of a baffled beast of prey which realizes that his victims have eluded him.

"What's that?" gasped Joan, clutching at Glanton.

"Just a bobcat squalling in the brush on that knob," he assured her, but it was with convulsive haste that he jammed his foot down on the accelerator and sent the car thundering down the road. Tomorrow, he swore, he'd raise a posse and hunt down that slavering human beast like a rabid coyote.

He could imagine the madman loping along the road after them, foam dripping from his bared teeth onto his bare, hairy breast. He was glad the lamp was burning in the parlor of his ranch house. It reached a warm shaft of light to them across the windy reaches of the night.

He did not drive the car into the shed that served as garage. He drove it as close to the porch as he could get it, and opened the car door in the light that streamed from the house as old Juan Sanchez, his Mexican man-of-all-work, opened the front door. Glanton was briefly aware of the bareness of his residence. There had been no time to adorn it in his toil to build his spread. But now he must have a front yard with a fence around it, and some rose bushes and spineless decorative cacti. Women liked things like that.

"This is my wife, Sanchez," he said briefly. "Señora Joan."

The old Mexican hid his astonishment with a low bow, and said with the natural courtliness of his race: "*Buenos noches, señora! Welcome to the hacienda.*"

In the parlor Glanton said: "Sit down by the fire and warm yourself, Joan. It's been a cold drive. Sanchez, stir up the fire and throw on some more mesquite chunks. I'm going to call up John Bruckman. There's something he ought to know—"

But even as he reached for the phone, the bell jangled discordantly. As he lifted the receiver, over the line came John Bruckman's voice, brittle with fear and more than fear—with physical agony: "Emmett! Emmett Glanton! Tell them! In God's name tell them that you've married Joan Zukor! Tell them I'm no longer responsible for her!"

"Tell who?" demanded Glanton, all but speechless with amazement. Joan was on her feet, white-faced; that frantic voice shrieking from the receiver had reached her ears.

"These devils!" squalled the voice of John Bruckman. "The Black Brothers of—aaagh! Mercy!" The voice broke in a loud shriek, and in the brief silence that followed there sounded a low, gurgling, indescribably repellant *laugh*. And Glanton's hair stood up, for he knew it was not John Bruckman who laughed.

"Hello!" he yelled. "John! John Bruckman!" There was no answer. A click told him that the receiver had been hung up at the other end, and a grisly conviction shook him that it had not been John Bruckman's hand which hung it up.

He turned to the girl who stood silent and wide eyed in the middle of the room.

"I've got to go back to Bruckman's ranch," he said. "Something devilish is happening over there, and the old man seems to need help bad." She was speechless. Impulsively he took her hands in his and stroked them reassuringly. "Don't be afraid, kid. Sanchez will take care of you till I get back. And I won't be gone long."

As he drew the old Mexican out onto the porch, a glance back showed her still standing dumbly in the center of the room, her hands pressed childishly to her breasts, an image of youthful fright and bewilderment lost in an unfamiliar world of violence and horror.

"I don't know what the hell's happened over at Bruckman's," he said swiftly and low-voiced to Sanchez. "But be careful. Joshua, the half-wit's gone on the rampage. He tried to kill me tonight, and he laid for us at the knob where the new road passes. Probably meant to brain me with a rock and kidnap Joan. Shoot him like a coyote if he shows his head on this ranch while I'm gone."

"Trust me, *señor!*" Old Sanchez's face was grim as he fondled the worn butt of his old single-action Colt. Men had died before that black muzzle in the wild old days when Sanchez had ridden with Pancho Villa. Sanchez could be depended on. Glanton clapped him on the back, leaped into the Ford and roared away southward.

The road before him was a white crack in a black wall, opening steadily in the glare of the headlights. He drove recklessly, half-expecting each moment to see the shambling figure of the maniac spring out of the blackness. Grimly he touched the butt of the pistol thrust into the waistband of his trousers.

There was no reason to suppose that Joshua was still lurking at the crest of the knoll; he would have no cause for supposing that Glanton would return along that road that night. But aversion to driving under that gloomy cliff was so strong in Glanton that again he swung aside and followed the dimmer, longer road that wound around the opposite side of the knob. And as he did so he was aware of another roar, above that of his own racing motor. He caught the reflection of powerful headlights. Some other car was eating up the road, racing northward and taking the shorter cut. As he drove into the open road beyond the knob he looked back and glimpsed a rapidly receding taillight. A nameless foreboding seized him, urging him to wheel around and race back to his own ranch. But there was not necessarily anything sinister in a car speeding northward even at that hour. It was probably some ranchman who lived north of Glanton returning home from Skurlock, or some traveling salesman bound for one of the little cow towns still further north, and leaving the paved highways to take a short cut.

There was no light in the window of the Bruckman ranch house as Glanton approached it; only the glow of the fire in the fireplace staining the windows with lurid blood, crimsoning without illuminating. There was no sound but the moaning of the ghostly wind through the dark junipers as Glanton went up the walk. But the front door stood open.

Pistol in hand, Glanton peered in. He caught the glimmer of red coals glowing on the hearth. The dry, toneless ticking of the clock made him start nervously. He called: "John! John Bruckman!"

No answer, but somewhere a moan rose in the fire-shadowed darkness, a low, bestial whimpering of anguish, thick and gurgling as if through a gag of welling blood. And a steady drip, drip of something wet and sticky on the floor.

Panic clawed at Glanton's spine as he moved toward the smoldering hearth, instinct drawing him toward the one spot of light in the room. At the moment he did not remember just where stood the table with the oil lamp on it. He must have a moment to gather his wits, to locate it. He groped for a match, then froze in his tracks. A black hand had materialized out of the shadows, faintly revealed in the light of the glowing embers. It cast something on the coals while Glanton stood transfixed. Little tongues of red grew to life; the fire rose and the shadows retreated before the widening pool of wavering light. A face grew out of the darkness before Emmett Glanton—a grinning face that was like a carven mask somehow imbued with evil life. White pointed teeth reflected the firelight, eyes red as the eyes of an owl burned at him.

With a choking cry Glanton lifted his gun and fired full at the face. At that range he could not miss. The face vanished with a shattering crash and Glanton was showered with tiny particles that stung his hand. But a low laugh rang through the room—the laugh he had heard over the phone! Whence it came he could not be sure, but in the flash of intuition that came to him, as it often comes to men in desperate straits, he realized the trick that had been played upon him, and wheeled with a gasp of pure terror. Pointblank he fired, with the muzzle jammed against the bulk that was almost on him—the bulk of the fiend that had crept up *behind* him while he was staring at its reflection in front of him.

There was an agonized grunt and something that swished venomously ripped away the front of his shirt. And then the creature was down and floundering in its death throes in the shadows at his feet, and in a panic Glanton fired down at it again and again, until its thrashing ceased and in the deafening silence that followed the booming of the shots he heard only the dry tick-tock of the clock, the drip-drip on the floor and the moaning that rose in the dark.

His hands were clammy with sweat when he found the oil lamp and lighted it. As the flame sprang up, sending the shadows slinking back to the corners, he glared fearfully at the thing sprawled before the hearth. At least it was a man—a tall, powerful man, naked to the waist, his shoulders and arching chest gigantic, his arms thick with knotting muscles. Blood oozed from three wounds in that massive torso. He was black, but he was not a negro. He seemed to be stained with some sort of paint from his shaven crown to his fingertips. And the fingers of one hand were frightfully armed, with steel hooks that were hollow nearly to the points and slipped over the fingers, curving and razor sharp, making terrible, tiger-like talons. The thick lips, drawn back, revealed teeth filed to points, and then Glanton saw that he was not painted all over, after all. In the center of the breast a circle of white skin showed, and inside that circle there was a strange black symbol; it looked like a blind, black face. An arrangement of mirrors fastened at right angles to the mantel and to the wall, one shattered by his bullet, revealed the trick by which he meant to take Glanton off guard. He must have made his arrangements, simple and easy enough, when he heard the car driving up. But it was diabolical, betraying a twisted mind. From where he had been standing, Glanton could not see his own reflection in the mirror on the mantel, but only the reflection of the black man behind and to one side of him, like a spectral face floating in the shadows.

What takes long in the telling flashed lightning-like through Glanton's mind as he looked down at the black man; and then he saw something else. He saw John Bruckman.

The old man lay naked on a table, on his back, arms and legs spread wide, so that his body formed a St. Andrew's cross. Through each hand, nailing it to the wood, and through each ankle, a black spike had been driven. His tongue had been pulled out of his mouth and a steel skewer was driven through it. A ghastly raw, red patch showed on his breast, where a portion of skin as big as a man's palm had been savagely sliced away. And that piece of skin lay on the table beside him and Glanton gasped at the sight of it. For it bore the same unholy symbol that showed on the breast of the dead man by the hearth. Blood trickled along the table, dripped on the floor.

Nauseated, Glanton drew forth the skewer from John Bruckman's tongue. Bruckman gagged, spat forth a great mouthful of blood and made incoherent sounds.

"Take it easy, John," said Glanton. "I'll get some pliers and pull these spikes out—"

"Let them be!" gurgled Bruckman, scarcely intelligible with his butchered tongue. "They're barbed—you'll tear my hands off. I'm dying—they hurt me in ways that don't show so plainly. Let me die in as little pain as possible. Sorry—would have warned you *he* was waiting for you in the dark—but this accursed skewer—couldn't even scream. He heard your car and made ready—mirrors—always carry their paraphernalia with them—paraphernalia of illusion—deception and murder! Whiskey, quick! On that shelf!"

Though he winced at the sting of the fiery liquid on his mangled tongue, Bruckman's voice grew stronger, and a blaze rose in his bloodshot eyes.

"I'm going to tell you everything," he panted. "I'll live that long—then you set the law on them—blast them off the earth! I've kept the oath until now, even with the threat of death hanging over me, but I thought I could avert it. Curse their black souls, I'll keep it no longer! Don't talk or ask questions—listen!"

Strange the tales that dying lips have gasped, from the days of witches down to the mad dreamers of today, but never a stranger tale than that Emmett Glanton heard in the bloodstained room, where a dead black face grinned by a smoldering hearth, and a dying man, spiked to a table, mouthed grisly secrets with a mangled tongue in the smoky light of the guttering lamp, while the black wind moaned and crawled at the rattling windows.

"When I was young, in another land," panted John Bruckman, "I was a fool. I joined a cult of devil worshippers—the Black Brothers of Ahriman. I need not speak of their aims and purposes—they were foul beyond ordinary conception. Yet they had one characteristic lacking in many such cults—they were sincere. More, they were fanatics. They worshipped the fiend Ahriman as zealously as their heathen ancestors did. And they practiced human sacrifice. Once each year, on this very night, between midnight and dawn, a young girl was offered up on the burning altar of Ahriman, Lord of Fire. On that glowing altar her body was consumed to ashes and the ashes scattered to the night wind by the black-painted priests.

"I was one of the Black Brothers. On my breast was tattooed indelibly the symbol of Ahriman, which is the symbol of Night—a blind, black face. But at last I sickened of the revolting practices of the cult and fled from it. I came to America and changed my name. Some of my people were already here—the branch of which Joan's an offspring.

"With the passing of nineteen years I thought the Black Brothers had forgotten me. I didn't know there were branches in America, in the teeming foreign quarters of the great cities. But I might have known they never forget. And one day I received a cryptic message that shattered my illusions. They had remembered, had traced me, found me—knew all about me. And in punishment for my desertion, they had chosen my niece, Joan, for the yearly sacrifice.

"That was bad enough, but what nearly drove me mad with terror was knowledge of the custom that attends the sacrifice—since time immemorial it's been the habit of the Black Brothers to kill the man nearest the girl chosen for sacrifice—father, brother, husband—her 'master' according to their ritual. This is partly because of a dim phallic superstition, partly a practical way of eliminating an enemy, for the girl's protector would certainly seek vengeance.

"I knew I couldn't save Joan. She was marked for doom, but I might save myself by shifting her responsibility onto somebody else's shoulders. So I brought her here and married her to you."

"You swine!" whispered Glanton.

"It did me little good!" gasped Bruckman, his tortured head tossing from side to side. His eyes were glazing and a bloody froth rose to his livid lips. "They came shortly after you drove away. I was fool enough to let them in—told them I was no longer responsible for the chosen maiden. They laughed at me—tortured me. I broke away—got to the phone—but they were set on my doom, as a renegade. They drove away, leaving one of them here to attend to me. You can see he did his work well!"

"Where—where did they go?" Glanton spoke with dry lips, remembering the big automobile roaring northward.

"To your ranch—to get Joan—I told them where she was—before they started torturing me—!"

"My God, and you're just now telling me this!" yelled Glanton, springing frantically to his feet.

But John Bruckman did not hear for, with a convulsion that spattered foam from his purple lips and tore one of the bloody spikes out of the wood, the life went out of the renegade in one great cry.

Like a drunken man, Emmitt Glanton stumbled from that lamp-lit room where a black face on the floor grinned blindly at a blind white face lolling on the table. The black wind ripped at him with a thousand invisible fingers as he ran to his car.

The drive through the screaming darkness was nightmare, with the black wall splitting before him, and closing behind him, horror loping like a werewolf on his trail, and the wind howling awful secrets in his ears.

He did not turn aside for the somber knoll this time, but plunged straight on, thundered over the bridge and rushed past the black cliff. No boulder fell from above. Joshua must have left his ambush long ago.

Three more miles and his heart leaped into his throat and stuck there, a choking chunk of ice. He should be able to see the light in the ranch house window by now—but only the glare of his own headlights knifed the black curtain before him.

Then the ranch house bulked out of the night and on the porch he saw a strange pale spot of radiance glowing. There was no sign of the automobile that had come northward. But he checked his own car suddenly to avoid running over a shape that sprawled in the fenceless yard. It was the mad Joshua, lying face down, one side of his head a mass of blood. He had come, as Glanton had feared he would, only to meet death.

Glanton slid out of the car and ran toward the house, shouting Sanchez's name. His cries died away in the stormy clamor of the wind and an icy hand gripped his heart. His dilated eyes were fixed on the pale spot that grew in size and shape as he approached—a man's face stared at him—the face of Sanchez, weirdly illuminated. Glanton stole closer, holding his breath. Why should the face of Sanchez glow so in the darkness? Why should he stand so still, unanswering, eyes fixed and glassy? *Why should his face be looking down from such a height?*

Then Glanton knew; he was looking at Sanchez's severed head, fastened by the long hair to a pillar of the porch. Some sort of phosphorus had been rubbed on the dead face to make that eerie glow.

"Joan!" It was a cry of agony as Glanton flung himself into the darkened house. Only the wind outside answered him, mocked him. His foot struck something heavy and yielding just inside the door. Sick with horror he found a match and struck it. Near the door lay a headless body, riddled with bullets. It was the body of Sanchez. And but for the corpse the house was empty. The match burned down to Glanton's fingers and he stumbled out of the house.

Out in the yard he fought down hysteria and forced himself to look at the matter rationally. Joshua must have been shot by Sanchez, while trying to sneak up on the house. Then it would have been easy for strangers to catch the old Mexican off-guard. He had not expected an attack from anyone except the half-wit, nor would he have been expecting enemies to come in a motor car. He would have come to the door at a hail from a stopping auto, unsuspectingly showing himself in the lighted doorway. A sudden hail of bullets would have done the rest. And then—beads of perspiration broke out on his body. Joan, alone and undefended, with those fiends!

He whirled, gun in hand, as he thought he heard a noise like something moving in the bushes north of the house. It diminished, ceased as he went in that direction. It might have been a steer, or some smaller beast. It might—suddenly he turned and strode toward the car. The body that had lain there before it was gone. What diabolism was this? Had dead Joshua risen and stalked away in the shadows, and was that him Glanton had heard stealing northward through the bushes? Glanton did not greatly care. At that moment he was ready to believe any grisliness was possible, and he had no interest in Joshua, dead or alive.

He walked around the house, wiping the sweat from his face with clammy hands. The house stood on a rise. From it he could see the lights of any car fleeing northward, for several miles. He strained his eyes but saw no distant shaft splitting the dark. The raiders must have already put many miles between them and the scene of their crimes. He must follow—but where? Northward, yes—but a few miles north of his ranch the road split into three forks, each leading eventually into a highway, one of which ran to New Mexico, one to Oklahoma, and one north into the Panhandle. He twisted his fingers together in an agony of indecision. Then he stiffened.

He had seen a light—yet not a distinct shaft like a car light. This was more like a blur in the dark—like the glow of embers not yet extinguished. It seemed to emanate from a spot somewhat east of the road which ran north, and this side of the forks. Night made sight and judgment deceptive, but tracing out that eerie glow was better than sitting in racking inaction.

Fixing the spot in his mind as well as he could, he ran to his car and drove northward. As soon as he had descended the rise on which his house stood he could no longer see the glare, but he drove on until he reached a spot which he believed was the point where the road most closely approached the spot where he had seen the glow. A long, wooded ridge stood east of the road at that spot.

He left the car and toiled up the western slope of the ridge, scratching his hands and tearing his clothing on rocks and bushes. And nearly to the crest he heard something that stopped him in his tracks. The wind had dwindled to a fitful moaning, and somewhere ahead of him there rose a weird sound that set his flesh crawling. Chanting! Beyond that black ridge men were chanting in an evil monotone that brought up shuddersome racial memories, old as Time and dim as nightmares, of grim black temples where clouds of foul incense smoke rolled about the feet of bowing worshippers before a bloodstained altar—in a frenzy Glanton charged to the crest, tearing through the thickets by sheer force. Crouching there he looked down on a scene that wrenched his horrified mind back a thousand years into the black night of the medieval when madness stalked the earth in the guise of men.

At the foot of the ridge, in a wide, natural basin glowed a ring of fire. He saw its apparent source—boulders had been rolled to form a solid circle and these boulders glowed with a blue-white light that was like an icy heat beyond human comprehension. From them rose a glow that hung like an unholy halo above the shallow basin. It was this light he had seen from his ranch. It might have been a glow from the slagheaps of hell. And devils were not lacking. He saw them, three of them, inside the circle—tall, muscular men, naked, black as the night that surrounded them, their heads hidden by grinning golden masks made like the faces of beasts. They stood about a heap of stones which glowed with a dull blue radiance, and on that crude improvised altar lay a slender white figure—

Glanton almost screamed aloud at the sight, though he had expected it. Joan lay there, stark naked, spread-eagled in the form of a St. Andrew's cross, her wrists and ankles strapped securely. In that instant Glanton knew what it would mean to him to lose that girl—realized how much she had come to mean to him in the few hours he had known her. His wife! Even at this moment the phrase brought a strange, warm thrill. And now those devils down there were preparing, by some hellish art, to reduce that lovely body into ashes—

Madly he hurled himself down the slope, pistol in hand. As he went he heard the chanting cease, and was aware of a strange, yet curiously familiar humming in the air. Whence it came he could not tell, but it sounded like the pulsing of a giant dynamo. Joan cried out, more in fear than in pain, but an edge of pain vibrated through her voice. The halo over the circle mounted, grew more intensely blue. The rocks glowed with a fiercer light; pale tongues of flame licked up from them. The hue of the altar under the girl was changing. The blue was growing more pronounced, less dull. That the change in its color was accompanied by painful sensations was evident from Joan's cries and the writhings of her bound body.

Glanton yelled incoherently as his feet hit level ground, and the black men turned quickly toward him. His lips drew back in a wolfish snarl and the old single-action gun went up in a menacing arc as he thumbed back the fanged hammer. He meant to shoot these devils down in their tracks, like so many mad dogs—then his out-thrust left hand touched one of the glowing boulders. Merely touched it, but the contact was like the jolt of a fork of lightning. Glanton was knocked backward off his feet and rolled, blind and dizzy with brief but stunning agony. As he staggered up, snarling and still gripping his gun, he recognized the truth.

Somehow those boulders had been made conductors of electricity. They were charged with a voltage terrific beyond his understanding. And so was the altar, though as yet the full force had not been turned on in its case. The rising hum that now filled the air told its own grisly tale. Joan was to die by electricity, not swiftly, shocked to death as in an electric chair, but slowly, agonizedly—burned to a crisp—to white ashes to be scattered to the night wind.

With an inhuman yell he threw up his gun and fired. One of the masked men spun on his heel and fell sprawling, but the taller of the remaining two bent quickly and laid a hand on some sort of a contraption at his feet. Instantly the hum grew to a shriek. White fire danced around the ring, blinding and dazzling the man outside. He saw the tall black forms within vaguely, through a dizzying blue-white curtain of flame. Shielding his eyes from the glare, panic tugging at his soul, he fired again and again until the hammer fell with an empty snap. He could not hit them. The noise, the glare bewildered him; everything was thrown out of its proper proportions; vision and perspective were distorted.

He hurled the empty gun at them and reeled toward the blazing barricade with his bare hands, knowing that to touch it would be death, yet choosing death rather than standing by and watching the girl die. But before he reached it a black shape hurtled past him, out of the darkness. Joshua! Blood clotted his scalp, but his primitive fury, his mad desire for the white body on that glowing altar were undimmed. Like a charging bull he came out of the dark, headlong at the barrier. Running hard and low he bent, gathered his thews and leaped! Only a beast or a madman could have made that leap. He cleared the barrier with a foot to spare; one instant he was etched in midair, black against the glare, arms wide and fingers spread like talons, then he hit catlike on his feet within the ring of death.

And as he struck he lunged. The priests were naked and weaponless. The taller let go the lever he held, sprang aside, stooped and snatched up some object, even as Joshua struck his companion. It might have been a bull that smote and tossed the black priest. Plain above the lessening hum and crackle of blue flame sounded the snap of splintering bones, the shriek of the priest. He was whirled from his feet, a broken, dangling doll, lifted high in apelike arms above the bullet head and dashed headfirst to the earth with such fury that the broken corpse rebounded before it lay still. Head down, the killer plunged at the taller priest's throat.

It had been a pistol this man had snatched up, and a raking blast of lead met the charging madman—met, but did not stop him. With bullets smacking into his body at close range, Joshua bellowed with pain and swayed on his feet, but came on in an irresistible surge of fury and threw his arms about the black body of his foe. He must have been dying on his feet, but the blind force of his rush was enough to carry the priest off his feet. Together they hurtled on—to crash full against the blazing ring of boulders!

A crack like a clap of thunder, a blinding spray of blue fire, one awful scream—then the reek of burnt flesh filled the air and in the swiftly dying glare, Emmett Glanton saw two hideous figures—both black now—crumpled in a fused, indistinguishable mass against the dulling rocks.

Something had happened to the generator of that terrible power. The hum had ceased; the demon halo was dying. Already the stones of the altar had assumed their natural tint. But on it the girl lay limp and motionless. As Glanton crawled over the barrier his heart was in his mouth. Tenderly he freed her and lifted her, grateful to feel warm, living flesh under his hands, but setting his teeth against what he might find—but her tender back and limbs showed none of the ghastly burns he feared. Obviously no great amount of electricity had been turned into the altar. He saw wires running in all directions from the amazingly small, compact, black case-like thing that stood near the altar, with its many levers and buttons. Before he carried Joan out of the ring he smashed the thing with a heavy rock. The Black Brothers knew secrets better kept from the world at large. Even a clean science became a hurtful black magic in their hands. That tiny dynamo, of a type undreamed of by the world, contained more energy than sane men conceived of—power to turn naked rocks into live wires. Such a secret could only be evil in its sources and results.

He whipped off his torn shirt and wrapped the girl in it, as carefully he carried her over the ridge and down to the road. As he went, he thought of Joshua, and the only logical explanation offered itself. The bullet that had struck the madman had not killed him, but only creased him and knocked him out. When he came to himself, he started on the trail of the woman his crazed brain desired, drawn either by the same glimpse of the distant fire that had drawn Glanton, or by the dark, psychic instinct that only the mad possess.

Glanton had almost reached the car when Joan opened her eyes, stared about her wildly, then clung to him, crying out pitifully.

"It's all right, kid," he soothed her. "You're not hurt. You just fainted. Everything's all right now. Joshua paid his debt, without meaning to, poor devil. Look, it's getting daylight. The night's past and dawn's coming."

He meant it in more than its literal sense.

"Take me home, Emmett," she whimpered, nestling deep into his arms. Then, irrelevantly: "Kiss me, Emmett!"

And Emmett Glanton kissed his wife for the first time, just as dawn touched the eastern hills with its white mist.

Miscellanea

Taverel Manor

(unfinished)

Chapter .1.

Sir Haldred Taverel sat up in bed, conscious only of a bewildered, crawling horror. He raised his hands to his head, trying to collect his scattered faculties, as a man will do when wakened suddenly out of a deep slumber.

He had dreamed—or was it a dream, that hideous yellow face which had floated before him? Sir Haldred shuddered. The memory of those glaring inhuman eyes and the loose bestial mouth was startlingly vivid. But he could not tell if the memory were that of a dream or—

He began piecing the fragments of jumbled memory together, while his eyes wandered about the great room with its costly and somber furnishings. While his eyes sought for stealthy movements among the antique hangings he recalled the events of the last few months.

The death of a distant relative had lifted the young lord from the position of a small country nobleman whose family fortune had gone to seed, to one of comparative affluence. Within a short week, Sir Haldred had found himself snatched out of his boyhood environment and the transition had left him dizzy and not altogether pleased, after the novelty had worn off. From pleasant south England he had come to this wild and desolate northern Coast to be the sole occupant of this grim old castle which tradition proclaimed was haunted by the ghosts of past crimes.

Not the sole occupant either—there was Lo Kung, the one servant the place boasted, left there by the previous owner. Lo Kung, Sir Haldred reflected, was a suitable attachment to the castle, for he was thin, silent and ghostly—though the young man could not rid himself of a feeling of familiarity about the man which he could not place—a tantalizing something in the stooped shoulders or in the soft sibilant voice of the Oriental.

But Lo Kung had assured him that they had never met before; had firmly maintained it, in that courteous, impersonal manner of his. And yet why had he acted so strangely the day Sir Haldred arrived? He had opened the door in response to the bell, had stepped aside and motioned the young man in, then had suddenly stopped short as if struck, standing perfectly motionless for an instant. His eyes had seemed to burn Sir Haldred through the heavy colored spectacles the Chinaman always wore, but his immobile face, with its queer thin pointed beard, had given no sign.

Sir Haldred's shoulder twitched under his thin silk pajamas as he recalled his life at Taverel Manor—short, to date, but far from merry. He had had few visitors; had spent most of his time wandering about the grim old castle trying to get used to the silence, the air of unseen watchers, the feeling of stealthy footprints—

Suddenly he sprang from bed with an exclamation of impatience. Either he had dreamed it, or there had been a man in his room a few minutes before—a man? Perhaps not a man but some creature with a hideous yellow face, that no more resembled Lo Kung or any other Chinaman he had ever seen, than he resembled Sir Haldred himself. Imagine a hairless ape, with parchment-hued skin—Sir Haldred crossed the room hurriedly and opened the door, feeling a little shiver of apprehension as the knob yielded to his efforts. He had left the door locked, or had intended to.

He hurried on down the darkened corridor, dimly lit by the moonlight which managed to filter through some of the curtained windows, and descended the stairs, into the utter blackness of the first floor. There was no sound, but he was angered at himself to find himself holding his breath. He wished that he had a weapon; this old house was getting on his nerves. Only that morning Lo Kung had mentioned the fact that he seemed pale, and had urged him to run down to London for a few days. Lo Kung had been urgent in his advice and now Sir Haldred, remembering, found time to wonder at the feeling that had vibrated in his tone. He wished he had taken that advice, as he groped his way down the darkened stairs. He had no torchlight and the house boasted no electrical connection with the village power plant.

Now he had reached the foot of the stairs, which let into the lower hallway. Not a sound in the house—he fell heavily over something which lay sprawled near the foot of the stairs.

He sprang up, struck a match. He stared in open-mouthed bewildered horror while the match burned down to his fingers. Lo Kung lay at his feet and a glance sufficed to show that he was dead. The Chinaman had been frightfully mauled as if by some huge animal. Sir Haldred struck another match and bent closer. The spectacles had been knocked off and the dead eyes stared wide open. The young man's breath caught in a quick intake. He grasped the thin pointed beard; it came away in his hand. For a moment he stared unbelievingly, then a sudden sound brought him round.

Down at the end of the hall something had moved—there had sounded the stealthy pad of unshod feet—human or otherwise. Sir Haldred snatched up a heavy poker and strode down the hall, his face set in grim lines. The horrid drama for which that dark and silent house had formed a stage that night, was not yet over.

At the end of the hall there was a curious relic of a former owner's wanderings in strange lands—a grim pagan shrine. A tall, grotesquely carven pedestal stood behind a low stained altar; the pedestal set firmly against the end wall of the hall. On this pedestal sat a great idol, loathsome and horrific, a frightful caricature of mankind.

Here Sir Haldred halted, puzzled. His gaze was fixed on this idol. Suddenly his eyes flared with horror and unbelief; then the poker dropped from his nerveless hand and one terrible, brain-shattering scream burst from him, splitting the grisly stillness. Then silence fell again like a black fog, broken only by the nervous scampering of a rat who stole from his covert to view the dead man who lay by the stairs.

Chapter .2.
The Haunted Manor.

"But, my dear girl, how am I to aid you, if all Scotland Yard has failed?"

The girl addressed twined her white hands helplessly and her eyes wandered nervously about the bizarrely furnished room. Besides herself there were four persons in this room—another girl and a young man, her companions; the other two sat facing her and it was to them that she had just made her appeal. One of these men was a tall, broad-shouldered man, lean and sun-bronzed, with piercing grey eyes. The other was not so tall, but heavier, a powerfully built man, whose dark features were as immobile as an Indian's.

"You see, my dear," the taller man was saying gently, "I'm not really a detective; I'm connected with the British Secret Service in a way, it's true. But my proper field of endeavor is in the Orient—"

"That's one reason why I came to you!" the girl broke in. "The main reason was I had nowhere else to turn after the police gave it up—then because of the circumstances—"

"Sir Haldred Taverel meant a great deal to you, did he not?"

"We were engaged to be married," her voice broke in a dry sob. "Then this terrible affair came up—"

"Let me tell the full details, sis," interrupted the young man at her side. "They've read about it, of course, but there may be some points—

"You see, Mr. Gordon, Haldred Taverel was born and raised in our parish; we all grew up together and I know him like a brother. If it had been anybody else I might have thought he'd gotten into a jam and skipped, but not he! If he had he'd face the music. That's why I know something's rotten somewhere.

"I've been making inquirement around the neighborhood of the castle where he vanished and find it has a long and unsavory history. Up to a hundred years ago, that branch of the Taverel family was a bad lot—nothing like our south country Taverels. They gradually died off and finally the castle was left vacant. Sir Rupert Taverel, the last of the direct line, roved around over the world most of his life, but a few months before his death, decided he'd repair the ancestral estate. He moved in with one servant, a Chinaman, and he hadn't been there but a few months when he fell from an upstairs window—or was thrown—and died instantly. There was some dark talk about it, but nothing that could be proved. There was no one else in the house at the time—the Chinese servant proved that he had been down at the tavern in the village. It seems pretty conclusive that Sir Rupert fell from his bedroom window while drunk or walking in his sleep. He was a hard bitter man, with a black past and he left neither friends nor will.

"In the absence of a will, the estate reverted to Sir Haldred, a distant relative, but the next in line. He moved there, for that was the custom—the heir of the estate always lived at Taverel Manor, up to Sir Rupert, and he eventually came back.

"Then one night it happened. Haldred Taverel and his Chinese servant, the same man who had worked for Sir Rupert, vanished completely as if from the face of the earth!"

"There was no clue?" Gordon's keen brown face showed interest. "No trace to show if they had been murdered or had fled alive?"

"There were stains of blood on the floor near the stairs, in the lower hallway—the evidence of a struggle; a heavy poker lay across the altar of a peculiar shrine at the other end of the hall. Otherwise—nothing!

"Up in Haldred's bedroom, the clothing he had presumably worn the day before lay as carefully arranged as when he had removed them to go to bed. None of his belongings were missing, not even his watch or pocketbook. If he fled, he must have done so in his night clothes!

"The local police were baffled and Scotland Yard sent down a man who had no better result. That was nearly a month ago. The police have given it up; they ransacked the castle from cellar to attic and found exactly nothing."

"Is the house occupied by anyone now?"

"Yes, a fellow named Hammerby turned up—staid, clerical-looking chap, with a sort of bill of sale from Joseph Taverel. Joseph is next in line and by Haldred's death—or disappearance—the estate fell to him. But Joseph can't come back to England without looking up a rope, for he fled the country some years ago after the brutal murder of a girl with whom he'd had an affair—pretty sordid case.

"The police were naturally interested, but Hammerby swore he didn't know where Joseph was, and knew nothing about the crime. Hammerby is an Englishman, but he's lived in America for about twenty years. He said he had business dealings with Joseph there, though he said the fellow went under a different name then.

"Joseph stole a lot of money from him in a business deal and when he was going to send him to the pen, Taverel told him—and proved to him—that he was one of the heirs of a large estate in England, and as he had just heard of his cousin's disappearance, he made over his rights in the Taverel estate to Hammerby. That is, in case it was proven Haldred was dead. Hammerby had a letter signed by Joseph in which he stated that Hammerby represented him and was to have full charge of the estate until it was proven absolutely that Haldred was alive. If he chanced to be alive, of course Hammerby was out. If dead, the estate went to Hammerby in payment of debts. Hammerby was taking a heavy chance, but somehow Joseph seemed pretty certain that Haldred was dead.

"Rather irregular, but of course Joseph couldn't come to attend to it himself, with the shadow of the gallows hanging over him. And the letter wasn't a forgery; comparison with examples of Joseph's handwriting showed the signature on Hammerby's letter to be genuine. As no one wanted to have anything to do with the house, Hammerby was allowed to move in, which he's done. He's to occupy the house, rent free, for the time being. If Haldred shows up, Hammerby has agreed to pay back rent and get out. If it's proved Haldred is dead, the house and money goes to Hammerby. Rather irregular, but stranger things have happened."

"And what sort of a man is this Hammerby?" asked Gordon curiously.

"Oh, a prim, middle-aged chap, rather pedantic. The sort of middle-class Englishman who has money himself but would trade his eyebrows for a title or anything approaching it. You know the sort; good chap but dry and tedious."

"Oh, we're getting off the main subject," cried the girl who had first spoken. "Mr. Gordon, you've been a friend of my family's longer than I can remember! You'll do this for me, won't you? Just run up to Taverel Manor with us and have one look around! Please! I'm going to go insane if something isn't done!"

"To be sure I'll go, Marjory," said Gordon gently. "I'll be glad to help you all I can; though I fear I can do nothing. If the case has baffled the best minds of Scotland Yard, I'm afraid you need hope of nothing from a man who is used to working in the open. But run along now; Costigan and I have a good deal to do to get ready for the journey."

Marjory Harper silently held out her hands to him, tears coming into her soft grey eyes. Gordon patted her shoulder gently, and her brother and the other girl rising, he escorted them to the door. Costigan made no move to rise, and the boy, Harry Harper, glanced back at the dark somber figure where he sat cramming a pipe with tobacco.

"Queer sort of fellow, your friend?" he murmured in a low voice to Gordon, as he stepped into the hallway.

Gordon nodded. "Silent, moody chap to those who don't know him. But a marvelous friend. Shot up and shell shocked in the war— took to dope and spent years in the Limehouse—underworld. Take all night to tell you his story, how I helped him break the habit and how he helped me break up a gang of desperate criminals. Run along now; Costigan and I will meet you at that antique shop downstairs in two hours. We're to motor up to Taverel Manor, I take it?"

John Gordon turned back into his apartments and shut the door.

"Rotten luck in a way," he said with a slight frown. "I've known Marjory Harper and her brother ever since I used to dandle them on my knee. Fine kids and this piece of business is a shame. I can't refuse them—but what can I do? And this smuggling job taking up all my time."

Costigan puffed at his pipe before replying:

"Looks like we haven't done much on that job, Gordon."

"I know," the other cried, pacing the room like a great tiger. "It's the most baffling case I've ever worked on. Here we trace a ring of opium smugglers out of China and clear across Europe, only to be brought up short here! There's a leak somewhere, but I can't find where. It's like chasing a rat up to a fence, seeing him get through and then be unable to find the hole. Oh, p'shaw! Let's forget it for a few days. I don't know in which direction to look—I'll probably accomplish just as much looking for smugglers up on the northern coast as I'm accomplishing here in London. It's infuriating—knowing the stuff's flooding the country through some loophole, and yet we can't discover the loophole."

"What do you think about Sir Haldred Taverel's disappearance?" he whirled suddenly on his companion with that sudden shift of subjects which characterized John Gordon's conversation.

"I think he got into a bad spot and took it on the lam," answered Costigan, unconsciously slipping into the patois of the underworld. "Or maybe the slant eye put the kibosh on him and got out from under."

"Then where's the corpse? And what became of the Chinaman?"

"Don't ask me," Costigan's indifferent manner masked all but his eyes which were beginning to burn with a feral light.

Chapter .3.

Mr. Thomas Hammerby blinked mildly at his visitors. Mr. Hammerby was a rather stout man of medium height, and would have appeared only about early middle life, had it not been for his snow-white locks which lent him a benevolent air, an appearance heightened by a pair of bright friendly eyes which gleamed from behind his spectacles.

"I hope," he said apologetically, "that Sir Haldred's friends do not look on me as an interloper—an intruder who has taken advantage of circumstances to obtain possession of the ancestral estate?"

"Not at all, Mr. Hammerby," he was assured by Marjory Harper. "We have come to make one more investigation of the premises, in hopes—"

Her voice faltered. Mr. Hammerby bowed, sympathetically.

"Please do not feel at all constrained by my presence, and no don't hesitate to call on me if I can be of assistance. I need not tell you how I regret this lamentable occurrence, nor how I hope that Sir Haldred will turn up safely, though it would mean the loss of the estate to me."

Gordon did not conduct investigations after the popularly conceived idea of detectives. In the first place, he knew that any possible clues would have been discovered long ago by the regular police. In the second, he was secretly convinced that for some reason or other, Sir Haldred Taverel had fled secretly.

He looked at the faint reddish stains on the floor near the foot of the stairs and examined the strange shrine at the other end of the hall. This occupied his attention for some time.

"What do you make of it, Costigan?"

"Thibetan," said the taciturn one briefly. "Hill country—devil worshippers, eh?"

"I think so," Gordon nodded. He was engrossed with the obscene idol which squatted upon the black carven pedestal. This idol was manlike in form, but with the face of a simian devil. It was cunningly fashioned of some yellow ancient stone, and was as large as a large man. Two semi-precious stones leered down for eyes.

"Human sacrifice," murmured Gordon, glancing down at the ancient stains on the low altar before the pedestal.

"Undoubtedly." It was Hammerby speaking in his pedantic schoolmaster fashion at the detective's elbow. "I think you are right, sir, in naming it Thibetan in origin—the work of some obscure mountain people, I should say, judging from my study of anthropology. It was brought from India by Captain Hilton Taverel in 1849, the villagers say, and has set here ever since. It must have taken a vast amount of labor and money to transport such a huge thing so far. But the Taverels never considered expense or trouble when they wanted something—or so I hear."

"It was on this altar that the poker was found," said Harry. "And Haldred's fingerprints were on it. That meant little, though. He might have had occasion to lay it on the altar and then forget about it, a day or a week before his disappearance."

Gordon nodded shortly; his interest appeared to have waned. He glanced at his watch.

"Getting late," he said. "We'd better be getting back to the village."

"I should be glad if you would spend the night here," said Hammerby.

Gordon shook his head before any of the others could speak.

"Thanks. I think it best to return to the inn. There's nothing we could do tonight—yet, wait a moment. I believe Costigan and I will take advantage of your offer, after all."

After Harry, Marjory and Joan had left, Gordon turned to his host.

"You knew this Joseph Taverel; what sort of a man was he?"

"A scoundrel, sir!" Hammerby's eyes flashed and his mild countenance became suffused with anger. "A rascal of the first water! A fraud and a cheat in his business relations, he did not hesitate to dupe his partners and swindle those who trusted him.

"Only threats of the penitentiary induced him to settle with me. At the time I accosted him I had no idea of his relationship to any title or estate; I knew him only as John Walshire, contractor. He swore he was without funds, which was very likely, because of his dissipated habits and spendthrift ways, and he himself suggested that I take the estate as settlement."

"The debt must have been considerable," remarked Gordon.

"It was, I assure you!" exclaimed Hammerby.

"Isn't it rather lonely out here?"

"Why, not to a man of my tastes. Here I have leisure for study and meditation, and then," he flushed and smiled with a naive embarrassment, "I have always wanted to live in a castle! I was raised in a hovel, I am not ashamed to say it, and in my childhood I often dreamed of the day when, having risen to prosperity by my own efforts, I should live in a castle as fine as any.

"Sometimes our childhood dreams are strongest of all ambitions, Mr. Gordon; mine has been realized, I am happy to say, though I regret deeply the circumstances by which it has come to pass.

"Then, as to loneliness, there is the village in case I feel the need of human companionship, and though none of the villagers ever comes here, there is nothing to prevent me from going there. Then here are Mrs. Drake, my housekeeper, and Hanson, my man of all work.

"No, I assure you, Mr. Gordon, my days here are full of work and study and even if I am ousted within a few weeks, I shall always look back upon the time spent here with the greatest of pleasure.

"It is such a pity that Sir Haldred had to come to woe in order for me to acquire this place! But that is the way of the world, whether we wish to or not, we gain by others' losses."

"How far is it to the coast?" asked Gordon abruptly.

"About a half mile. You can hear the breakers against the rocks at high tide."

"Let's take a stroll to the shore, Costigan," Gordon rose. "I have a peculiar penchant for walking in the mist, and the thunder of these northern coasts attracts me."

"As you like, sir," said Hammerby. "You must pardon me for not accompanying you, but neither the cold night air nor the exertion is good for one in my condition. I will send Hanson to guide you, if you like."

"Oh, no need of that. It's a straightaway course to the cliffs, isn't it? We will make it all right. And you needn't wait up for us, because we may be some little time."

Not until the black bulk of Taverel Manor lay starkly in the fog behind them did either of the men speak. They strode stolidly forward through the heavy dank mist, their pipes glowing in unison to their strides. Far ahead they heard the faint booming of the sea. All about them the moors lay barren and desolate for as far as they could see in the fog.

"Joseph Taverel must have owed an enormous amount of money to our friend Hammerby," mused Gordon.

Costigan laughed. "I think so, myself. All that estate taken on a debt? Bah! Hammerby put the screws on Taverel and shook him down for his whole wad, if you ask me."

"Meaning that he blackmailed him—threatened him with prison? Like enough; I don't believe that Taverel proposed deeding the estate to Hammerby—I believe that was Hammerby's idea. He'd always wanted an estate in England; he saw where he could get one for perhaps half the value. He's ashamed to admit that he forced Taverel—oh, I don't have any sympathy for that murderer. He was probably glad to exchange his birthright for his freedom."

"What's the idea of staying in the Manor tonight?" asked Costigan abruptly.

"Oh, no particular idea. There's nowhere to take hold to work, in this case—if you could call it a case. I've got to do my best for Marjory's sake, but I can't see anything to it. I pity the girl, from the bottom of my heart, and more because I can't keep from believing that Sir Haldred must have had reason for running away."

"The villagers say he was snatched away by the ghosts of the long dead Taverels."

"Bosh—there's the shore."

Wild, bare and rugged rose the cliffs, at the foot of which the grey waters tossed endlessly. The droning grey waste spread out before them to vanish in the fog, and the men, struck by a sense of loneliness and futility of human endeavor, were silent. Then Gordon started.

"Look! What's that?"

Through the fog there winked and flickered a faint light far out at sea.

"Look! The flickering is too regular to be by chance! They're signaling somebody ashore!"

"A fellow at the village told me a foreign-looking ship had been hanging off and on for a couple of days," muttered Costigan. "He said he figured she had a passenger to put ashore here and was waiting for favorable weather to work inland. Bad place along this coast for a ship to come inshore. Likely to be thrown on the rocks."

Gordon wheeled with a sudden intuition and looked back the way they had come. In the thick fog the stark bulk of Taverel Manor could be but vaguely seen, but from the highest tower on the castle a pinpoint of light began to wink.

"Something here!" rapped Gordon. "Good thing we decided to stay! Here, let's leg it back to the Manor! Maybe we can catch whoever is signaling!"

They hurried along in silence, the fog growing denser.

"By Jove," said Gordon suddenly as they brushed past a clump of stunted shrubbery, "I wonder—"

At that moment Costigan cried a sharp harsh warning, but it was too late. Beneath the sudden vicious blow of the figure which rose from the shrubbery, Gordon went to his knees. In an instant Costigan was the center of a whirlwind attack; dark figures seemed to materialize from the earth to leap at him.

But in the first instant of attack, the unknown assailants found that they had essayed no easy task. With a snarl of battle fury the powerful American went into swift and deadly action. He met the first attacker with a smashing straight arm blow that dropped him writhing, flung off another who had leaped on his mighty shoulders, and whirling with catlike speed for all his weight, met the charge of a sinister form who bounded in with a shimmer of cold steel.

Costigan felt a keen edge slice along his upflung arm, then his iron-hard right hand crashed against the attacker's jaw and the other shot backward, to fall in a grotesque heap, ten feet away.

At that moment a pistol cracked and someone yelled and cursed. Gordon was on his knees, firing. Like ghosts the unknown thugs faded away in the fog, leaving behind them only the crumpled form of the last man Costigan had struck.

The American was at his friend's side in an instant.

"Hurt?"

"No, just a trifle dizzy, thanks to this heavy cap. But you're bleeding!"

"Nothing to it," Costigan impatiently put his arm behind him. "Just a scratch. Let's see about the fellow that did it. He's still out."

Gordon bent over the fallen foe, and then with a sharp exclamation, tore a thick strip from his shirt and swiftly bound it about the man's leg, above the knee.

"Tourniquet," he explained hurriedly. "The beggar's bleeding to death; he may die anyway. He's fallen on his own knife and it's apparently severed that great artery behind the knee. Gad, he's lost a raft of blood!"

Costigan was leaning over the unconscious man, frowning.

"That fellow's a Malay!" he said suddenly. "Look at his knife—a crooked-bladed kreese—if his face wasn't evidence enough!"

"Thunder!" Gordon ejaculated as the man opened his eyes. "Malay? I should say! And what's more, he's Ali Massar, wanted in both Burma and Siam for a score of crimes! I've seen the rascal before! What are you doing here?"

The Malay was fully conscious now, though the white tinge about his lips showed that he was in a bad way. His evil eyes gleamed with recognition, but he said nothing.

"Talk!" snarled Gordon. "Or we will leave you here to die."

The steady snakelike eyes of the Oriental never wavered.

"No," said the detective calmly, "you won't die; you'll live to expiate your crimes on the gallows."

The Malay's eyes flickered. No true Moslem can face the thought of hanging without flinching.

"You will hang me?" he spoke for the first time; his voice was very weak, almost a whisper.

"If you tell me what you are doing here, and what this mystery means, it may go easier with you."

The Malay's eyes brooded in the faint moonlight which filtered through the fog. Then he moved and his action was unexpected and horrifying. With a fierce wrench he tore loose from Gordon's clutching arms, whirled on his side, and tore the tourniquet from his leg. An incredible burst of blood followed; the body of Ali Massar shuddered once and then lay limply, but the dead eyes stared upward with a seeming malignant triumph.

"Gad!" John Gordon whispered, shaken.

Costigan looked on unmoved; his grim life in the underworld had hardened him more than the average man, even more than Gordon who was used to scenes of violence.

"Scarcely looks possible that a man could bleed to death so quickly from a stab in the leg," said he.

"He'd lost a terrific amount of blood before I bound his leg up," said Gordon. "That artery is a large one and connects directly with the great aorta of the abdomen."

"What are we going to do with the corpse?" asked Costigan, touching the dead man with his foot, as impersonally as if he had been a dead snake.

"Have to leave him here," Gordon decided. "Looks a trifle cold blooded, but we can't carry him across these moors with the expectation of another attack on us any minute. We will get a cart and come back after the body. Just now, we're in a hurry. They're still signaling from the castle, see? But the ship no longer shows a light."

As they hastened toward the Manor, Gordon mused: "Suppose that ship might be waiting to take someone on, instead of putting someone off? What if there was someone in the Manor who had been lying low, waiting for a chance to escape without being seen? Someone who'd been hiding there a month or more!"

"You mean Sir Haldred? Do you think Sir Haldred is up there signaling?"

"There's no telling."

After what seemed an endless time, they stood at the door of Taverel Manor and were admitted by Hanson, the man of all work—a stocky, heavily built man with heavy unintelligent features.

"You're hurt, sir; your arm's bloody!"

"Mr. Costigan fell and cut his arm on a sharp rock," Gordon cut in. "Hanson, is your master in bed?"

"Yes, sir."

"Very good. Lead us to the highest tower in this building."

"Very good, sir," the man turned and led the way without question. The detectives followed him up innumerable flights of winding stairs, and through dark corridors coming at last to the top room in the tower which rose above the west wing. This tower Gordon knew to be the one from which the signal light had flashed. Now it was empty of human occupants; a small barely furnished chamber, the dust and cobwebs bearing out Hanson's statement that it was never used.

Gordon moved to the window that faced seaward, and on an impulse took from Hanson the single candle which formed their only means of illumination. He believed that some other mode must have been used, since it seemed impossible that a mere candlelight could be seen that far through the fog, but on impulse he began to move the flickering candle back and forth in regular motion.

Scarcely had he done so, when Hanson, glancing toward the door into the darkness of the outer corridor cried out wildly and springing backward, caromed full into Gordon, knocking the candle from his hand and plunging the room into darkness.

Chapter .4.

On the instant Gordon wheeled toward the door which he could not see, drawing his pistol. He heard the quick gasping intake of Hanson's breath beside him and Costigan's measured untroubled breathing in the silence that followed.

"Blast it, Hanson!" he asked irritably, "What's all the bally row?"

"A face, sir," gasped the man clutching in the darkness for the detective's arm. "A face outside the doorway! A fearful, yellowish face it was, with loose hanging lips!"

Costigan laughed grimly in the dark. "I'll go out and see if it's still there."

"Stay where you are!" Gordon ordered sharply. "Hanson, here's a match. Strike it, find the candle and light it while I watch the door."

A flicker of light followed, framing the black opening of the door in momentary radiance but revealing nothing of what might be lurking just outside.

"Too bad, sir," said Hanson presently. "I don't know what we're going to do, but the candle's gone!"

"Nonsense! It must have dropped close to my feet when you blundered into me."

"You can see for yourself, sir." Hanson held a lighted match close to the floor. Gordon's eyes took in the whole dusty surface. There was the mark in the dust where the candle had fallen but of the candle there was no sign.

"Somethin' darted in and snatched it!" babbled Hanson, shaking with apparent fright. "I know it did! Nor it ain't the first time either. I've warned the master but he wouldn't heed me! I've told him about the footfalls after night through the empty chambers, and the rustling of the hangings—aye, and the foul yellow face that peeps through the dark at you! Twice I've seen it!"

"Indeed!" Gordon rapped. "And why have you said nothing about it?"

"The master ordered me to keep shut," the man said sullenly. "Hints I been drinking. It's little I care; I'm leaving this terrible place tomorrow, I wouldn't stay, not for no amount of money."

"Are you going to stay here all night?" Costigan broke in impatiently.

"Come on," Gordon answered shortly and strode through the door, pistol ready. It was uncanny work, groping their way down those dark stairs but nothing attacked them; not a sound disturbed the grisly silence.

Once in the great lower hallway Gordon said, "Hanson, unless I'm much mistaken there is a man hurt out on the moors. Have you a cart that we can use to get him in?"

Hanson seemed to have recovered from his fright and to have lapsed back into his usual stupidity.

"I have, sir."

"Harness a pony to it and bring it around to the front at once."

"Very good, sir."

The order was obeyed with commendable promptness and as they jogged through the fog which seemed to be growing ever thicker, Costigan said: "Stupid fellow."

"Stupid or unusually shrewd. Do you believe that guff about a yellow face? I scarcely do. What if Hanson didn't want me to be waving a candle in the window where it might be construed as a signal? What if he lurched against me on purpose and pretended the rest? He could easily have secured the candle and put it in his pocket while we were waiting from some hobgoblin to burst through the door on us."

"But if it's Sir Haldred whose hiding in that tower, how is Hanson connected with him? And how could Sir Haldred hide without being found by the police who ransacked the house?"

"I can't say as to Hanson's possible connections with Sir Haldred. From what I can learn, the man came here with Hammerby. As for the vanished nobleman's hiding—most of these old castles are full of secret passages, hidden rooms and such like."

"No one knows of them, then. The police were unable to find any trace of hidden passages."

"They would be cunningly concealed, of course. Here's the place where we left the body—and no body! I half-expected as much."

The corpse of the Malay had vanished.

"Friends in the offing!" muttered Gordon turning the horse about and starting back for the castle. "Looks like we've run into a thicker mystery than we bargained for. I came out to please Marjory Harper who thought I could help her find her vanished lover. We've found no clue of him, but we've seen a mysterious ship signaling to the castle, discovered that a gang of murderous thugs are lurking about for some unknown reason, and—unless we choose to discount Hanson's tale—we've been haunted by a yellow-faced ghost."

"The men who attacked us are connected with the ship out there, some way."

"I believe so. And the ship is connected with someone in the castle—who?"

They drew up at the gate, hitched the horse. No sign of Hanson. They went up the long driveway and knocked at the door. No one answered.

"Shove in, Costigan," said Gordon impatiently. "It's getting along toward morning and Hanson must be asleep. We will rouse him up and send him out to take care of the horse, and—"

He broke off suddenly. From somewhere inside the unlighted building there came a sudden scream, horrifying in its intensity and volume.

"Help! Help! Oh God, help!"

"Hammerby!" exclaimed Gordon, electrified. "In with you, Costigan, wait—let me go first!'"

The screaming broke off in a sudden hideous gasp and silence fell like a black fog.

Chapter .5.

Harry Harper woke from a sleep full of chaotic and disordered visions. Someone was knocking softly on his door. He sat up in bed and called: "Who is it?" There was no answer but he heard a stealthy sound outside his door, then the noise of light footfalls retreating. He rose, donned his bathrobe and turned on the light. The white corner of a note protruded under the door, but when he looked out, the corridor was empty.

The note read as follows: "Bring Marjory and Joan and come at once to Taverel Manor. This is imperative. Speak to no one, but come at once." It was signed John Gordon.

Why the detective should desire his presence at this time of night, Harry could not understand, but he prepared to obey. He crossed the hall to the girl's room, knocked lightly at the door, and soon the three of them were speeding across the moors through the light rain which had begun to fall.

They drove up the shadowed driveway and alighted. The great castle rose about them, dark, gloomy and forbidding. Harry felt the silent fear of the girls and he himself was guilty of a tremor or two. Where were the detectives? He made for the door, his sister and his fiancé clinging close to either arm. He lifted the knocker and the hollow reverberations which echoed through the house in a ghostly, muzzled manner, filled him with a crawling fear. He waited for the door to open but there was no movement inside. At last he drew forth a flashlight in one hand and a pistol in the other, and pushed the door open. Utter darkness met his eyes.

The girls, fearful of entering that black building, but more afraid of being left alone, crowded in after him. Harry was cursing under his breath, berating the folly of the men who had caused him to bring two frightened girls into such a place. And where in the name of heaven were Gordon and Costigan? Where, for that matter, was Hammerby—and Hanson—and Mrs. Drake? A sudden ghastly panic took hold of him. He felt as if they were all in the grip of some inhuman sorcerer of another world. He turned on his torchlight and the white shaft lit up the furnishings, making the rest of the room seem darker by comparison. The circle of light hovered on the dark stain near the stairs, wavered a moment as the wrist that directed it shook slightly, then shot down the hall.

The ghastly face of the idol of the shrine was illumined, the uncertain light adding tenfold to its diabolical appearance. And Joan screamed wildly; Harry, shocked and horrified, fired wildly and without conscious thought. The same motion jerked the thumb off the switch and utter darkness fell over the terrified group. In the darkness there came a stealthy sound at the other end of the hall but Harry did not find the courage to press the switch and bring that ghastly image into life again. He stood there in the dark, speechless and sweating blood while Marjory clung to him and Joan, who had fallen at his feet in a near faint, clutched his knees and whimpered wildly.

"Joan!" How husky and unnatural his voice was. "Brace up!"

"Don't turn on the light again, Harry," the girl whimpered. "If I see it again, I'll die! Oh, Harry, Harry, I SAW ITS EYES BLINK!"

"Nonsense." Harry desperately refused to believe what his senses told him but his reason denied—that he had seen the same phenomenon. "It's just the light fell on the face. I'm going to turn it on again."

Joan promptly hid her face in his trousers leg and refused to even breathe.

Harry turned a beam of light again down the hall, bracing himself against the shock of bringing that frightful face out of the dark again.

"There, Joan," he said with a gusty sigh of relief. "It's not winking now; it's real—I mean it's stone."

Joan looked fearfully; Marjory begged: "Harry, lets be going. There's no one here; otherwise your shot would have brought them. There must have been a mistake."

"There must have been." Harry lifted Joan to her feet and turned towards the door. He had let the light go out while lifting the frightened girl; now he turned it on once more. Even as he did, both girls screamed terribly. Harry was aware of a dim bulk looming up beside him, of a shadowy arm which shot down with a cold shimmer of steel.

Chapter .6.

"Gordon!" Costigan's low-pitched voice cut the stillness. "The idol's gone!"

The two secret service men stood in the shadowed hallway of the great Taverel mansion. Utter silence reigned, yet the ghastly screams which had but an instant ago reverberated through the house, still seemed to re-echo in their ears.

Gordon's torchlight played down the hall and halted on the shrine. He swore under his breath. The great carven pedestal was bare. All along there had lurked in the detective's brain the feeling that somehow all this mystery centered on that silent grim shrine. The screams which had brought them bursting into the house had seemed to come from the end of the hall. He strode down the hall to the shrine and narrowly examined the pedestal. He had supposed that the idol had been fastened to it in some way, but he now saw the surface was perfectly smooth. He began to tap the walls behind the shrine.

Costigan grunted; a narrow panel had swung inward.

"This was hidden by the idol," whispered Gordon, playing his light into the dark aperture. A narrow passage, walled with stone, was disclosed.

"Stay here," the Englishman ordered. "I'm going to explore this; I think it's the answer to our questions."

"So do I," answered Costigan. "And that's why I'm going with you."

Gordon knew the futility of arguing with his companion. He shrugged his shoulders, climbed over the pedestal and dropped into the passage on the other side. Costigan followed him, leaving the secret door open. (Here they found the idol and spoke of Hammerby.) A flight of rough stone steps went down and the two men followed them, to come down into another, wider passage. The walls, ceiling and floor were of rough stone, beaded with dank moisture.

"Must be pretty far underground," muttered Gordon. "These were built by Sir Haldred's pirate bandit-baron ancestors, no doubt. Regular catacombs," he added, noting the dark openings on either side, which evidently marked other passages leading away from the main one. The torchlight flung a faint wavering radiance which seemed stifled by the surrounding gloom.

"Listen!"

From one of the dark doorways there sounded the faint clink of chains and a low groan. Gordon snapped off the light and the companions stood in the darkness. The groaning voice became audible and intelligible.

"Gordon! Help! Help! For God's sake! They're torturing me!"

"It's Hammerby!" hissed Gordon gliding toward the opening from which the racked gasps seemed to emanate. Suddenly he snapped on the light and sprang through the doorway, pistol in his hand and Costigan close beside him. The light, flashing swiftly from corner to corner revealed only a bare cell-like chamber, with a smaller doorway in the opposite wall. Hammerby was nowhere to be seen and the groaning voice ceased. Suddenly Costigan, long blood brother to the underworld rats, with sudden intuition struck the light from Gordon's hand and jerked him to the floor. Even as he did so, a sudden crackle of pistol fire split the darkness and half a dozen bullets sang viciously above the heads of the crouching men. Above all there rang a hideous insane laugh.

A silence painful in its intensity followed the volley. Moving with infinite caution, the two trapped men crawled to opposite sides of the cell and crouching against the walls, waited, pistols in hand for what might next chance.

"Gordon!" a voice suddenly broke the silence, a voice sardonic, mocking and with a strange foreign inflection. "This is an unexpected pleasure! I had not thought to have you for my guest at this time."

Gordon, crouching in grim silence, made no move to give away his position to the unseen sniper.

"Is it that I must give you credit for more intelligence than I had thought for," the mocking, illusive voice went on. "Or is it a mere train of circumstances that led you here? I had though—ah, well—after tonight, Mr. Gordon, you will no longer interfere in my affairs—"

Gordon's pistol spat viciously as he fired in the direction of the voice; a low, mocking laugh answered him and another volley from the outer corridor rattled against the wall above him.

Again the voice spoke, this time from another quarter. "I am sorry I cannot remain to watch your demise, Mr. Gordon, and yours, Mr. Costigan, but time presses and I must leave you to the watchful care of my faithful friends."

Again stillness closed down like a pall. Gordon heard the faint drip of water from the dank walls. Then far back up the corridors in the direction from which they had come, there sounded a shot. Instantly the corridors were filled with sound, strident and confused. From both doorways pistols cracked and the cell hummed with the passage of the leaden pellets. Gordon felt his sleeve jerked as if by an invisible hand and something stung his cheek sharply. Above a medley of unknown tongues, a harsh voice was shouting savagely in English, but the detective could not understand the words.

Gordon fired at the flashes in the doorway through which they had come, and someone howled like a stricken wolf. Another storm of lead pelted across the cell, then there sounded a pattering of feet which dwindled away down the corridors. Gordon ventured a low call: "What now, Costigan? Do you think they have gone or is it a trap?"

"Lie low," growled the American. "Wait—did you recognize that fellow that was talking to us?"

"I think I did," snapped Gordon. "But what—"

A light glimmered outside. People were coming down the corridor.

"Oh Gordon!"

The detective swore. "It's Harry Harper!" He sprang erect and ran recklessly out into the passageway, stumbling over a form which sprawled there. The light which illumined the place showed him that the man was a Chinaman. Now a strange scene presented itself. Harry Harper was marching down the passage, flashlight in one hand, pistol in the other. Close behind him came Marjory and Joan, clinging together; in front of the boy, hands bound fast behind him, walked a short sullen-faced man.

"Hanson!" ejaculated Gordon.

"Gordon!" cried Harry sharply. "Your face is bleeding!"

"Just a slight cut." Gordon passed his hand over his cheek. "A bullet grazed me."

"Thank God you're not hurt!"

"But what are you doing here?"

"Well," said Harry, "when I got your note at the tavern—"

"Note? I never wrote you a note!"

"Well, someone did, telling me to come here and bring the girls. We got here but there was no one here. Then in the hall, somebody jumped me with a knife. I knocked him silly with my pistol barrel and behold when I turned the light on him, it was this fellow—Hanson.

"He came to in a moment but not before I'd tied him up well. He seemed pretty desperate and told me he'd spill the whole thing if I'd promise to speak for him later. About that time we heard shots, faintly, and he said it was you and Mr. Costigan, trapped underground somewhere. So—"

"You young imbecile," broke in Gordon. "You mean to say you came barging along through these tunnels with the girls?"

"Well, I couldn't stand by and let you be butchered, you know. As for the girls, I thought they'd be in as much danger in the house as they would with me. And anyway, I made Hanson walk in front. Didn't figure they dare shoot at us for fear of hitting him. And he must have thought so too; he's been shaky to no end. He told me to push on the idol and I did and a door opened. But I guess you know about it—we came through and at the bottom of the stairs I caught a glimpse of something that looked like a big bat. But it was human, because it fired at me and I fired back. A fellow with a curious kind of disguise on, no doubt. I don't think I hit him, but he legged it down the passage as fast as he could and we followed."

[. . .]

The Return of the Sorcerer

(unfinished)

Chapter .1.
Mihiragula's seal.

I moved my stiff limbs in the dank darkness, cursing at the clank of the chains that weighted me. How long I had lain in that subterranean dungeon I did not know; the drab monotone of unchanging darkness, days and nights merged indistinguishably and were one. Even when my scanty sup of water and moldy food were brought me, only a small opening gaped into the slimy stone wall, letting in a faint grey mockery of light, wherein I saw only the yellow, black-nailed hand that fed me. Could I have reached that hand with my jaws, I would have sunk in my teeth until they met in that foul flesh and hung on, bulldog-like, as long as a breath of life remained in me.

Trapped like sheep! That was what stung—the fact that we had blundered into a snare, John Ladeau and I, like a couple of green fools—we who had tramped the length and breadth of the Orient, carrying our lives in our hands, boasting that we knew the depths and trickery of the Eastern mind.

Again I reviewed the sequences of events which had brought me to this pass. It was in Nanking that we heard a tale in a native quarter that clinched vague rumors at which we had laughed—rumors of hills in the Gobi where no hills should be, and a strange black lamasery whose mysterious monks guarded a secret thing. What could that secret thing be but treasure? Gold, or rare jewels? So we reasoned, John Ladeau and I, and laid our plans with the recklessness of hard-bitten wanderers who have left both fears and scruples behind the door that locks the Past.

With a small band of renegade Chinese we had plunged boldly into the Gobi. But wind of our venture had been wafted abroad somehow and on the wings of a terrific dust storm, wild riders, squat, broad-faced men on shaggy horses, had struck our camp. Our ruffianly followers were wiped out to a man, and John Ladeau and I, shooting our way through and fleeing that slaughter, somehow gave our pursuers the slip in that blinding swirl of flying sand. We might have turned back, but we would not. Every cent we had had, we had sunk in the venture; we tossed the dice of Chance—our lives against the dream of a fortune. And with the defiance of desperate men, we pushed on alone into the desert.

Of the hardships of that terrific journey, of our battles with thirst and hunger and sandstorms and howling nomads, there is scant use to repeat. But at last we saw, in the first blaze of a white desert dawn, gaunt bare hills looming on the horizon and a grim castle black against the morning sky.

It was our intention to go boldly up to the gates and demand shelter, as lost and hungry travelers. Once inside our plans would be laid according to the number and disposition of the inhabitants. If there were not many of them, we intended making an attempt to catch them off their guard and hold them up. I scorn hypocrisy; we intended to ruthlessly shoot them down if they resisted. A mad plan, perhaps, but no more mad than the plan Cortez carried out. We were powerful men, hard and quick as wolves, well armed and well versed in the use of our weapons.

We rode up to the gates and shouted. There was no answer. No sign of life showed anywhere about the building. The gate swung idly open. We entered warily. We saw no one. The lamasery showed signs of occupancy but though we went through the courtyard and the chambers, we saw no one. And we were forced to the conclusion that for some inexplicable reason the place was temporarily deserted. Then, opening a door, we came upon the treasure room of the lamas—a small cell, with tiers of brass-bound chests. We broke open one of these chests and found it full of gold and silver coins and trinkets—English, French, German, Russian, Chinese coins;

coins that had been minted in Rome during the days of the latter empire; coins with the head of Alexander the Great stamped upon them; Epthalite coins; ancient Persian and Turkish coins; mintage of India and Japan.

And while our eyes were dazzled and our souls maddened by this riot of wealth, our fate overtook us. The floor of the treasure chamber gave way beneath our feet, plunging us into a pitch-black cell below. The fall knocked Ladeau senseless and I was beaten unconscious by a swarm of vile-smelling assailants that I could not see, before I had time but for a single blow in my defense. That one blow I gloated over ferociously in my mind, as the one soothing touch to my rage and stung vanity. I had taken toll of one at least, for I had felt my blindly lunging knife shear through sheepskin coat and camel-hair shirt to disembowel the wearer.

I regained my senses in the utter darkness of that dank and slimy cell, on the vile floor of which I lay chained hand and neck, so closely I could scarcely reach a hand to the food and water they gave me irregularly. Where my companion was, or if he still lived, I had no idea, nor could I understand why they kept me alive. For I well knew that word had come to them somehow that Ladeau and I had meant to steal their treasure.

And now as I cursed my plight beneath my breath, there was a creaking of rusty bolts or hinges, and grey light streamed into my dungeon. Looking up I saw that a sort of window had been opened in the wall, and framed in the grey light of the aperture was the head of one I instinctively knew to be the head lama of the monastery. In the shadow of the hood he wore, his lean ascetic face seemed more somber, more remote from humanity, than any face I ever looked upon—except one. His features were not particularly Mongolian in cast, nor did his bleak grey eyes slant; I believed him to belong to that strange, nameless tribe which dwells in the Neketoya region and is neither Tataric nor Slavic.

"You have lost the game, man from the West," said the lama in his own tongue—a branch of Mongoloid. "You have forfeited your life—can you tell me why we should not take it?"

"Let me loose for a few minutes and I'll show you plenty of good reasons," I snarled. "What have you done with Ladeau—my companion?"

"He has been as well used as you," answered the lama. "And we have to be merciful; if you wish, both of you may go free."

"If I wish!" I said sardonically. "Is it likely I would wish otherwise?"

"It remains with you," the monotoned voice droned on. "Certain conditions are attached—agree to them and you shall both go forth from the Black Lamasery unharmed."

"What are these conditions?" I asked.

"You must perform a certain feat for us."

"I'll do it," I answered. "Get us out of here and give us some decent food and I'll do what you want, if it's within the range of human possibilities."

"We ask naught beyond human power," answered the Black Lama.

I heard a rattling of chains and bolts as the window closed, then a huge Tibetan entered and busied himself with my shackles. Those on my feet and neck he removed, replacing the chains on my wrists with a sort of handcuff affair, between the cuffs of which hung a long thin chain. One end of this he held in his left hand, while in the right he held a wicked Luger pistol with the safety off. With a grunt he motioned me to follow him and we went out of the cell into a dank, narrow tunnel, along the tunnel to a winding stone staircase, up the stair to another corridor, wider and lighter than the lower passage, up another stair and through an arched door into a spacious chamber. I was astonished; the rooms and corridors we had explored before our capture had been fitted with the bareness and Spartan simplicity of the usual monastery. But this room resembled the cell of an ascetic monk less than the chamber of some voluptuary of an exotic Indian court. The floor was of polished teak, the domed ceiling of lapis lazuli, the walls hidden with richly worked tapestries, behind which, I had a curious sensation, someone was lurking.

Silver-worked divans and silken cushions littered the floor in careless profusion, and sitting cross-legged on a coarse, camel-hair mat, an incongruous image of somber drabness amid all that luxury, sat the Black Lama.

I sat down on a cushion opposite him, and the big Tibetan squatted just behind me, still holding the chain that secured my wrists, and keeping the muzzle of his pistol pressed against the back of my head. Evidently the Black Lama was a personage of much importance and no chance was being taken on a sudden vengeful move on my part.

"We knew of your thievish plans," said the Lama suddenly. "Eastern walls have ears and tongues, and my spies sent word of you before you crossed the Great Wall. Your efforts at secrecy were amusing. The Black Lamasery is the heart of Mongolia and all things are known to us, for like a spider we reach our tentacles into all lands of the East.

"You escaped the children of the desert, but we were well warned. We left the treasure room open to trap you. We were well concealed in secret rooms and corridors. Have you any claim to clemency?"

"Stow the guff," I snapped, curling my lip in an ugly manner. "We lost the toss and I'm not kicking. We came here to loot you and you were too smooth—that's all. Don't moralize—you're just as crooked as we are, in your own way. You've a use for me, somehow, or you'd have snapped me off long ago. Spill it."

"Exactly," the hooded one nodded, as if in meditative reflection. "We have a use for you; we will send you to England on a certain mission. That accomplished, you and your friend go free."

I was somewhat thrown off my guard by this unexpected proposition.

"How can I trust you, or you, me?"

"We keep our word," he answered. "You have no choice but to trust us—and we will trust you, because we will keep your friend as a hostage against your return."

"What is this mission?" I asked, more and more curious.

"It is to recover something holy, that was stolen from us long ago," the Lama answered. "Look." He took from his robes a piece of parchment and held it up before me; thereon was a curious sketch. The thing depicted appeared to be a twig with seven buds upon it, and was about five inches long.

"The twig broken from the Tree of Dreams by the Master, long ago," droned the Black Lama. "Stolen from us by unbelievers. You must buy your life with its return. You will know it when you see it, for there is no other relic in the world like it—it was transfigured when it was taken from the Tree of Dreams; its stem is black jade, its buds are crimson jewels.

"It is in the possession of Professor James Dornley, who lives by a village called Drackly, in Yorkshire, England."

"Wait a minute," I broke in. "If your spy system is so perfect, why haven't you had it stolen by one of your own men?"

"There are difficulties of which you know nothing as yet," the Lama answered. "Dornley is eccentric and suspicious; he fears our vengeance and his greed for the holy emblem is great. He allows no one within his walls, but Abner Brill will succeed where others have not."

I did not even bother to ask how he knew my name. I had heard enough to convince me that I had stumbled onto something bigger than I had guessed. That the lamas constituted a vast and mysterious secret society I had already known, but that they controlled such a vast spiderweb of underground information, I had not guessed.

"Take the parchment," said the Lama, "but be careful to show it to no one except such as I name. You agree?"

"Wait," I growled. "How do I know that John Ladeau is even alive?"

He rose and, walking over to a side of the wall, beckoned me. I got up and walked over, my huge guard keeping pace with every movement I made and still holding his pistol ready. The Lama drew back a hanging and, sliding back a narrow panel, I was able to look into another chamber. This room was wide, airy and well furnished, and on a comfortable divan sat Ladeau, smoking a cigarette and reading what appeared to be a novel. He did not notice the opening of the panel, and the Lama quickly closed the opening and replaced the hanging.

"You are satisfied?"

"Can't I see him a few minutes and explain that I'm not deserting him?" I asked. "Better still, why not send him and let me stay as hostage?"

The Lama shook his head. "You are better fitted for the task; it will require a man of more education than your friend possesses. It has been explained to him and he is quite content; but you cannot talk together. You are both crafty; you might plot to cheat us. We will give you a year to procure us the Twig. During that time Ladeau will be well treated and not too closely confined. Return within a year with the Twig and he is a free man; fail, and he dies. You must not fail!"

I nodded slowly, understandingly.

"Do not underestimate the difficulty of your task," the Lama warned me. "Had it been easy, we had not called on you. The Twig is well hidden and closely guarded; you will be in constant danger of your life from they who guard it. It is now close upon midnight. You will start just before dawn—"

"But I have no money," I broke in. "And the Mongols will cut my throat before I ever see the Great Wall."

"Money will be given you; one will ride with you to shield you from the children of the desert. Your way to England will be made smooth. You will go directly to Suchau and call upon the Mandarin Yotai Lao, who will fit you up for an ocean voyage and give you your final instructions.

"Once in England, you must win the confidence of Professor Dornley. To his friendship, I give you the key." And opening a small chest he took therefrom a heavy signet ring of curious make; it was of heavy gold, set with a large jade symbol, curiously wrought.

"The bauble for which James Dornley squandered his youth," said the Black Lama rather grimly. "Thirty years he searched the mazes of the East for the thing—the seal of Mihiragula!"

I gave an exclamation of surprize.

"Aye—the seal-ring of the mad conqueror, whose White Huns swept down from the plains of the Oxus to flood India with fire and gore. It was an obsession to the English professor, who in his youth had rumors of its existence. He combed all India—but when the Turks stamped out the Epthalite nation on the Oxus, the seal went into the hands of a wild Moslem chieftain and by devious ways came to rest in the Black Lamasery. Go now; Bugra will take you to a chamber where you will be fed and may sleep a few hours before your departure."

As I followed the big Tibetan out of the chamber I glanced back and could have sworn that I saw the hangings behind the Black Lama move as if someone stood there. And for no reason at all, I shuddered; the slight undulation somehow suggested the presence of an enormous serpent rather than a man.

Bugra led me into a barely fitted but clean chamber, where he removed my handcuffs and shouted some order. A slant-eyed Mongol in the camel-hair robes of a lesser lama brought me aplenty of food and native wine—kumiss—and after I had eaten ravenously, I lay down on the fur-covered bunk and slept soundly.

I was awakened by Bugra in the darkness before dawn. He was dressed as if for a journey and I gathered that he was to accompany me as far as the Great Wall. He gave me a heavy sheepskin coat against the chill of the desert night, and I followed him, yawning, through the courtyard and out of the lamasery. The great vague black bulk loomed darkly and evilly, like an ogre's castle, against the dim stars which blinked vaguely in the thick dark. A keen wind blew across the desert sands, as sharp as a knife; I made out the dim bulks of two riding camels—rather unusual transportation for that part of the world. The Black Lama stood near, and behind him I made out a vague, shadowy shape; I could not tell what sort of man it was, but I got an impression of thinness and great height, and straining my eyes saw that the figure was masked.

Bugra and I swung to our mounts, tapped them under the jaw with the sticks given us, and the Black Lama came close to me and lifted his hand: "Do not fail!" was all he said; then grunting and snorting, our camels swung away in their long rocking gait and the shadowy shapes by the gate of the Black Lamasery merged with the darkness.

Chapter .2.

We made good time across the great Gobi, that silent, surly Tibetan and I. We stopped only to sleep a few hours at a time and to eat and brew some of the nondescript stuff they call tea in that part of the world. We were not molested by the nomads—evidently word had gone out ahead of us. We occasionally saw their wandering herds and felt yurtas in the distance, but none ventured near us. The Black Lama's word was law, apparently.

I do not believe that Bugra spoke a dozen words to me between the time we mounted our camels in the dawn before the Black Lamasery's gate, and the moment that he pointed silently to the long undulating line on the horizon that marked the Great Wall, and silently swung his mount back into the desert.

When I had almost reached the Wall, I glanced again into the leather pouch the Hooded Lama had given me. It was almost full of coins, all gold, and mostly English or French minting. But among them I found one I could not classify; the head stamped in the metal had features strongly Semitic, but I could not decipher the worn characters. Evidently the masters of the Black Lamasery had dipped their hands deeply into the money bags of all nations, and I could not but wonder at the enormous amount of wealth lying idle and apparently useless in that treasure chamber.

My journey to Suchau was uneventful and I had no trouble getting in touch with the Mandarin Yotai Lao—a prominent and powerful merchant king, and one whom I would not have suspected of any connection with the mysterious lamas of Mongolia.

[. . .]

"From the black, bandit-haunted mountains . . ."

(untitled and unfinished)

From the black, bandit-haunted mountains of Kang to the swarming, reeking streets of Canton, the word had gone forth: "Black John O'Donnel must die." Coolies whispered it to each other as they pattered along the dust swirling hot streets like human horses; sedate merchants murmured to each other over their amber cups of tea; sinister figures that slunk through the darkness before dawn in the winding mysterious alleys hissed the word as they thumbed their curved knives. Aye—the word was on the wind and Black John O'Donnel was marked for the black doom of vengeance.

And in a hidden room Yuen Yin looked at me obliquely across the wine-stained table. And I swore for I was restless as a trapped wolf.

"I'll slink here like a scared rat no longer," I growled. "Three days I've hidden here—"

"And danger is but yet begun," said Yuen Yin. "You know who your foe is."

Aye, right well I knew, and in my mind's eye formed a picture—

It was in the little mountain town of Kao Sung. Suddenly brief chaos burst; rifles spat death, knives flashed, men died howling. Bandits swept down from the black hills like a sudden devastating whirlwind. There were sufficient soldiers quartered in the town to beat off the attack, but the bandits struck on the opposite side. Before the soldiers could arrive, they expected to be gone with their loot. Their objective was an old monastery used then for a dwelling place of the few foreigners—castle and dwelling at once. There were women there, and children.

They rode up and burst the antique gates, while scattered fire from the defenders emptied a few saddles. Springing from their shaggy ponies, they swarmed over the ruins of the gates and ran firing across the compound. And there were but a handful of men to face them, among them myself, unarmed, and Yuen Yin, but newly returned to his native land from England.

He was using a German automatic. A lean giant wielding a four-foot scimitar he shot through the head, then the gun jammed. A clump of attackers charged him, knives clicking like castanets, headed by a tall youth dressed in [. . .]

A heavy oxen yoke—too heavy for the average man to wield—leaned against a nearby wall. As death loomed above my Chinese friend, I caught up the yoke and smote the foremost attacker a terrible blow. His head caved in like an eggshell and he fell face down in the dust, his red silk suit horridly [. . .]

The Red Stone

(unfinished)

Chapter 1. Red horror.

It is my custom, and has been for years, to go for a stroll just after sundown, every day. This habit is not altered by the place where I may be, or the conditions which I may be among, though as a preference I prefer city streets and a cloudless sky. Still, as is often the case, this special habit has such a hold on me that I cannot often sleep unless I have walked at least a quarter of a mile, no matter how inclement the weather may be.

It was this custom that introduced me into a series of the strangest, fantastic, and may I say, gruesome, experiences, that it has ever fallen my lot to participate in.

In the early spring of 1921, I was in London, as a visitor of a friend, whose name was James Oldwick. He was a man of rare ability, keen insight and was not wholly unconnected with Scotland Yard. On the evening of the 15th day of March, I found myself practically alone as Oldwick had been called away to Liverpool on some important business. So I was obliged to take my daily stroll alone.

It had sprinkled all day and when the sun set, a slow drizzle set in, which bade fair to last all night.

As I walked along the streets, which were almost deserted notwithstanding the earliness of the hour, I felt a depression of spirits, a foreboding which I attributed to the dismal weather.

I bent my steps in no certain direction and presently found myself in a wealthy residence district.

[. . .]

"The night was damp..."

(untitled and unfinished)

The night was damp, misty, the air possessing a certain disagreeable quality of penetration despite the fact that the season was summer. Fogs billowing in from the sea drifted down the streets and made dim apparitions of the few who walked late.

The setting was certainly not of a sort usually associated with happenings of the weird and dramatic, yet—

My room opened upon a side street. The door was shut. As I sat in the darkness half-drowsing, there came to my hearing the sound of flying feet—as if someone ran for life itself. The sound came from the side street and as they grew closer and more distinct, the footfalls merged with quick panting breathing. Then my door was flung open, a vague shape showed in the greyness for an instant, then the door was as swiftly shut—but now the runner was on my side. I sat bewildered, stupidly straining my eyes through the darkness, seeing nothing, hearing nothing but the short, swift breathing. Something crouched like a hunted thing in that dark room with me and I admit my hair prickled slightly.

I reached out hurriedly and flooded the room with light. An involuntary sigh of relief escaped me. The phantom resolved itself into a girl. She was shrinking back against the door, eyes wide and staring, and fixed on my face with a startling intensity. Yet though she was looking at me, her back was pressed hard against the door, feet and elbows braced as though she were holding back some terrific force upon the other side.

I sat and she stood for a matter of seconds, neither speaking. She was of slim but supple build—even then she reminded me of a leopardess—and at the time the whiteness of her face was intensified by her dark, staring eyes, her disheveled black hair and the vivid scarlet of her full lips. So much I saw before she opened those lips—then she spoke and cold shivers trickled down my spine.

"He's here! Oh God! He's just behind me! Don't let him get me, please, please! Keep him away from me!"

These words sound melodramatic on paper, but spoken with the terrible intensity she gave them, backed by her terrified appearance, they were enough to convince me that either the girl was insane or else that she fled from some horror.

I had risen precipitately as she spoke and now as I advanced toward her, she cowered back, arms flung out as if to ward off a blow.

"No, no!" she whispered. "Don't put me out in the street, for God's sake! Let me stay here—I'll be your slave—" her words became incoherent.

I laid my hands on her arms and as gently as I could, I said, "There's no need of being afraid. Nothing will harm you here."

She gave a wild haggard look for an instant then threw her arms about me and clung close to me, her whole body trembling in a very frenzy of fright.

"Come and sit down," I said soothingly. "You are safe here."

"Lock the door!" she whispered in a manner that again made me shiver. I complied and then she allowed me to lead her to a chair. She seated herself nervously and kept glancing fearfully at the windows—she seemed to be listening.

I sat silent, consumed with curiosity but not caring to bluntly ask her the cause of her flight. Suddenly she started.

"Listen! HE'S HERE!" her slender fingers sank like claws into my arm. I heard nothing. She cowered against me, shuddering.

"Girl, what is the thing you fear?"

"A snake!" she whispered, her eyes smoldering strangely.

"A snake!" I admit she gave me a frightful start—I was almost sure now that she was insane. "Nonsense—a snake in London?"

"Listen!" she hissed fiercely. A tense silence reigned as I strained every faculty—then—gods, did my imagination trick me or did I in truth hear a faint, slithery sound beyond the door?

I would have risen, but the girl clung tighter to me—a vague repulsive scent seemed to pervade the dank atmosphere—I began to doubt my own sanity.

Then just as I was about to put the frightened girl aside by force and go to investigate, another factor took its place in the event. Footsteps again sounded, this time in the house. They crossed the hall and ceased just outside my door—which was just opposite to the door by which the girl entered. Coincident to the approach of these second footfalls the strange sounds—if sounds they were— seemed to grow even vaguer, the scent became less apparent, and both vanished entirely as the door opened.

I doubt if I had seen my neighbor across the hall three times before. I had been vaguely aware of his presence—aware of the fact that he kept ungodly hours, that he was a tall dark man with little leaning toward geniality, but my knowledge went no further than these facts and his name.

Now he stood in my door, his hand still on the knob, foot lifted as if hesitant to enter.

"You seem to have a visitor, Gordon. May I come in your room?"

"Ah, that you, Falcon? Certainly, come in, certainly."

He entered, his immobile face giving no sign of his thoughts. He was a tall, lean man, almost gaunt, yet he gave the impression of great physical power. His features were dark and inscrutable, his eyes a cold grey, like ice or steel; his forehead was high and broad, topped by incredibly black hair, while a great beak of a nose gave his face a certain predatory look.

The girl stared at him as I disengaged myself from her arms and rose. Somehow it did not occur to me that his conduct was rather presumptuous, considering the fact that we were comparative strangers.

"I might be of aid to you," he said suddenly, and the girl started.

"You aid me? Would you?" she was leaning forward in desperate eagerness, then she slumped, "No, nobody can help me—"

"Tell us just what you fear," suggested he. I wondered if he had been listening at my door.

She shook her head slowly, chin resting on her hand in a peculiarly discouraged posture. "No, you'd think I was crazy. I can't say any more than

[. . .]

This was too much for me. I had been growing more perplexed each moment, but had kept silent. Now I felt it was time for me to interfere.

Falcon glanced at me, evidently masking the irritation he must have felt.

"Pardon me, Gordon, but this matter lies between the young lady and myself."

There was a menace in his eyes, but my Irish blood was up and my eyes clashed with his.

"I don't know what this is all about," I said, "but it looks to me as if this child was being victimized by a clever mesmerist and it isn't going any further. I don't know what your game is, Falcon, but I don't like the looks of it."

I had an uncomfortable feeling that, in spite of my athletic build, he could crush me easily if the matter came to physical conflict, but I did not flinch from his gaze. Then with a shrug of his lean shoulders, he turned to the girl.

"I will leave it to the young lady."

The girl put out her hand timidly and laid it on my arm. "He means me no harm, I am sure; please let him do as he wishes."

I looked searchingly into her eyes, still half-convinced that she was under some mesmeric delusion, but her clear and unwavering stare made me doubt. I stepped back, bewildered, and Falcon again placed his hand on the girl, this time turning her so that she faced the east. Then from his clothes he took a small straight dagger with a curiously chased hilt. This he passed seven times in front of her face, then with a swift motion set the point against her bosom. I sprang forward with an involuntary exclamation, but the dagger was already concealed again and Falcon was fastening the girl's clothing again;

but not before I saw, gleaming redly upon her white skin, a small, fantastic emblem or symbol that the dagger point had left upon her breast. My previous bewilderment was as nothing compared to this; without the door came the roar and rumble of London, but here in this room had just taken place a deed savoring of the ritual of some lost age. Visions of sorcery, foul magic and devil worship thronged my mind as I looked at the two.

[. . .]

The Ivory Camel

(unfinished)

Karnes McHenry whistled softly as he tugged rhythmically at the teats of the patient Guernsey; under his practiced hands twin streams of rich liquid drummed into the bucket he gripped between his knees, churning the contents into creamy foam. From the trough into which the Guernsey's head was thrust came a contented crunching. Fat hens waddled about the milking shed, clucking importantly. One jumped to the top of the feed bin, spread her wings and hopped and flapped her way to the top of the hay bales piled high behind the slats which partitioned off one side of the shed. She landed on the hay, then instantly, with an outraged squawk and a wild fluttering of wings she took to the air again, soared over Karnes' head and the cow's back, and struck the earth hysterically just outside the open door.

Karnes' gaze wandered idly to the spot just vacated by the hen, his fingers never losing their stroke. His eyes were caught by a gleam of steel in the hay, almost over his head. As he stared idly, it took shape—the head of a hatchet. Karnes McHenry knew every tool and implement on the place, and where each was ordinarily kept. Absently he wondered what he had been doing with a hatchet up there in the hay, and why he had left it there. He kept on looking idly and milking, and his gaze wandered down the head, down the handle; and slowly something else took shape, half-seen, and the rest of the outline guessed out among the wisps of hay; a human hand, gripping the handle.

Karnes' soft whistling did not cease. It merely became discordant for a fleet instant, and then renewed its accustomed note, a trifle softer and more measured. His eyes wandered away from the hay, indifferently. He shifted slightly on the nail keg that was his milking stool, in order to set down the filled bucket. His left hand made a reaching motion toward another, empty bucket standing nearby, and his right casually scratched his ribs, near the place where his shirt gaped a little because of a missing button.

And then there was a .45 roaring flame and smoke in his hand, and the heavy slugs were ripping through the planks and the hay bales, and through the thing that lay upon them. The cow made a blundering and frantic plunge headlong through the door, kicking the pail winding and knocking over the trough. The chickens squawked and scattered, and up on the hay something flopped convulsively, gurgled in a way that was not nice to hear, and then lay still.

McHenry stood for a moment staring upward, his gun smoking in his hand, and no particular expression on his sun-burnt face except perhaps a slight narrowing of his blue eyes, and then he stuck his toe between a couple of the slats, grasped a higher one with his left hand and swung up so his head was level with the top of the hay bales. He stood there for an instant without moving; then he reached and secured something, laying his pistol on the hay in order to do it. Presently he dropped to the ground, picked up the buckets, stuck his gun back in its hidden holster, and went swiftly to the house, straightening the bucket the cow had kicked as he went.

He entered the back door, set down the pails, and went on into the front part of the house. His sister, a lithe, handsome girl some years younger than himself, inquired: "Shootin' at rats?"

He made no answer, but took down the receiver of the telephone, and ground the crank.

"This you, Miz White?" he inquired into the mouthpiece. "Well, say, do you see Jim anywhere around there? Oh, he is? Well, call him to the phone, will you?"

"What do you want with Jim?" asked the girl in the interim in which Karnes stood silently at the phone. Just at that moment her brother spoke.

"That you, Jim? Well, listen, I just shot a man in the barn— shut up, will you! No, not you; I was talkin' to Alice. Yes, he's dead, alright. No, nobody I know. Looks like some kind of a nigger."

"Thank goodness!" came the ghost of a whisper from Alice.

"How should I know? He was layin' up there on the hay with a hatchet. I don't know whether he was intendin' to hit me with it or not. I didn't take any chances. All right, I'll be here."

He hung the receiver on its hook, and turned from the phone staring absently at Alice. She was accustomed to his faraway look at times, and did not suppose he even saw her, especially as he did not seem to heed her questions. But presently he spoke.

"Alice," he said, "how would you like to have a coat trimmed with ermine?"

"Ah, don't kid me!" she laughed.

"I may not be kidding you," he answered.

Three days later Karnes McHenry sat on the back porch, his powerful legs thrust out in front of him, while he lazily whittled on a piece of wood with a knife that was more weapon than implement. On a chair beside him sat a slender man of early middle life, a keen-faced man, whose erect posture, and quick curt speech contrasted with the drawling slouchiness of his host, just as his clothes marked him as an alien in the post-oak country.

"I traced him to the state line," said this man. "Somewhere just south of it I lost him again. I thought perhaps he had turned back into Oklahoma. But I came on south, on a sort of hunch, and when I heard, through the papers, of the man you killed, I came on to investigate. One of the papers said it was a negro, but—"

"I knew he wasn't a nigger all the time," said McHenry. "No niggers allowed in this county. Of course, one might have been driftin' through. But any dark-skinned human is a nigger to these hillbillies."

"I saw the body at the county seat where they had it on display, trying to find someone who could identify him. As you know, there was nothing on him to give a hint of who he was.

"But I knew, of course. That's why I came on to you. You couldn't know he was a fugitive from the law, of course—"

"I figured it out that way," answered McHenry. "When I first saw him layin' up there on that straw, all I could see was his hand, and I thought it was somebody hidin' up there to get me. He could easy have split my head when I got up off the stool. There's plenty of men in these hills that might try something like that. So I let him have it. Afterwards I figured he was just runnin' through the country and hidin' out, ready to fight if anybody caught him, but not layin' for me, anyhow."

"That's right!" snapped the other. "The man was desperate. He was running not only from the law, but from something worse than the law. Look here, McHenry, I'm laying my cards on the table. You know I'm a detective. I've told you I was after that man.

"His name was Ahmed Ali, and he was a mixed breed—Arab and Indian. He stole a piece of jewelry from a secret cult in the Eastern part of the United States, and they were after him—a gang of Orientals. That's not what I was chasing him for; he murdered one of them. I can't prove he stole anything at the same time, but I know he did: an ivory camel, set with precious gems; it's worth a fortune.

"I said I was laying my cards on the table. If you took that trinket off him, I'm advising you to give it to me. I'll return it to the right parties, and there'll be no more harm done."

McHenry shifted slightly on his seat and spat at a grasshopper crawling along the edge of the porch.

"See that critter?' he said conversationally. "They're worse than boll-weevils in this country. They've played hell with the cotton. Drouth ruined the corn, too; no water out for the stock, either. I'm glad I left the farm, even if I haven't done so well for myself. This your first visit to Texas?"

The detective moved restlessly on his chair. His expression betokened impatience, but his voice was even, proving his next statement.

"No; but this is the first time I've ever been west of Fort Worth. I've been in the state enough to know that a Texan doesn't always tell everything he knows."

"Especially on these post-oak ridges," agreed McHenry genially. "Biggest liars on earth."

"Listen, McHenry," exclaimed the detective, "I'm asking this for your own good. You don't realize what you're up against, if you really have that ivory camel and intend keeping it. The law can't take it from you, because the law doesn't recognize its existence; nobody but me knows about it. But the man who tries to keep the thing will be in deadly danger. The cult that owns it will stop at nothing. You can be sure they've traced Ahmed Ali as far as I did. They may be somewhere in these hills now—may even be hiding about Lost Knob. If you have the ivory camel, you'd better give it to me."

McHenry glanced out across the lots and pastures at the edge of the town, where the post oaks and mesquites drooped under the dust and heat. He fingered his patched trousers idly and absently let his gaze wander along his faded and broken shoes.

"I've been out of work for nearly a year," he said irrelevantly. "The Depression hit this country hard."

The detective sighed and rose.

"If you won't think of yourself," he said, "at least think of your sister. Those devils wouldn't be above burning your house and shooting into it."

"Don't rush off, Mr. Ord," urged McHenry. "Stay and have dinner with us. Alice'll fry a chicken, and I've got a keg of cold beer—"

"I'm going," answered Ord impatiently. "I'll be at the Lost Knob Hotel, in case you change your mind."

McHenry sat motionless until the sound of the detective's automobile had faded down the street, and then he bestirred himself. He rose and pocketed his knife and strode into the house.

"Alice," he addressed his sister, "I want you to pack your bag and go spend a few days with Joan Grimes' folks. You can take my car."

"But what for?" she demanded.

"Never mind. You skin out. I'll phone you when you can come home."

[. . .]

Yellow Laughter

(fragment)

(Some words missing or illegible in the typescript, guesses at the words are marked with a [ ].)

[. . .]

used to sling it a lot. I remembered one of his poems and I chanted it over and over, just a snatch of it.

"I'm more than a man and less than a god;
I've traveled the ways that the sea-[winds trod].
I've ridden the stars the ages long;
I've swept up the wind on the wings of song.
I'm old, I'm old with years untold,
But I laugh as I snatch at the [eons'] gold."

Crazed? Wasn't it? But a man does crazed things when he has a big idea. And I had. It wasn't yellow colored like the other thoughts I'd been thinking but more like the thoughts I'd had when I was a man.

I waited till night. I despised night because the sky was so filled with blinking yellow stars—millions of 'em. I toiled nearly all night and when I was through, there was a hole in the floor big enough for me to shove my arm through. The cargo was stacked so high that I easily reached the stuff I wanted. Then after awhile a faint, yellow light began to steal through the rattan porthole and I knew that the yellow dawn was gliding over the saffron waves. Then the torturer came into my cabin. Ao Fong was yellow, all except his black eyes. The torturer's eyes were yellow too.

As he stepped through the cabin door, from the deck, with yellow eyes glittering like a cat's, I sprang and slammed a straight right to his body. His yellow ribs broke like dry twigs. I held him with his head in the brazier until he stopped struggling.

Then I slipped out on deck. The big yellow sun was just coming up. There [was] no one on deck. The ship seemed deserted. It was uncanny. I ran to the [aft] rail and looked over. There was a small skiff floating aft. There [were] oars in it but nothing else. I wondered how it came to be there. I [got] up on the rail. Then I heard Ao Fong laugh behind me and I jumped. [I hit] the boat, all right, and something cracked like a dry stick. I cut [the line in] frantic haste. Ao Fong was leaning over the rail but he made no [move to] stop me. As I pulled away, the rails were lined with yellow [faces]. They all laughed. They pointed at me and shouted with fiendish mirth

[. . .]

The Jade God

(unfinished)

I started up from a sound sleep, shaken with a nameless horror. The moonlight illumined my room, lending ghostliness to familiar objects, and as I wondered what had awakened me, I remembered—and even as I remembered, I froze as again the ghastly scream which had rent my slumber burst horridly on the midnight stillness. It seemed to come from the house of my eccentric and taciturn neighbor, William Dormouth. I did not wait to dress; catching up a heavy blackthorn I raced down the stairs and out across the lawn, toward the dark house which loomed starkly against the stars. As I approached the porch, another figure detached itself from the shadows of the hedge and I saw it was another neighbor, John Conrad.

"What's the row, Kirowan?" he asked, rather breathlessly, and I saw the gleam of a revolver in his hand.

"I don't know, I answered. "Somebody cried out."

"The front door's locked," he said, fumbling.

"Listen!" From somewhere inside the house there came faint sounds of a struggling—a ghastly moaning cry and an indescribable tearing noise.

"Break the door!" shouted Conrad. "Dormouth's being murdered while we stand here!"

With no more ado I launched my full weight against the portal and with a rending and snapping of wood and hinges, it crashed inward. I catapulted into a darkened hallway and Conrad sprang over me in his rush for the stair.

"This way!" he called. "Dormouth sleeps upstairs—"

I was already after him, and we raced up the winding stairs, still hearing the dim sinister sounds of some kind of struggle. Dormouth's bedroom door was locked, but under the impact of our combined weight, it gave way and we sprang into the moonlit room. As we did I heard a strange rushing noise at one of the windows and Conrad cried out and fired. But no foe met our eyes—only the ghastly, blood-splotched figure which writhed on the floor, hideous in the moonlight.

"Dormouth!" Conrad cried out, and we sprang forward to bend in horror above the man. It was evident he was going fast; he lifted glazed eyes in the moonlight and tried to speak, but a rush of blood strangled him.

"Dormouth!" Conrad cried again. "Who did this thing?"

With a mighty effort the dying man reared himself on his elbow and pointed shakingly at the open window. He tried again to speak, but his eyes went glassy, and he sank back.

"The jade god!" he muttered, as in delirium. "The—jade—god—" His head fell back limply, blood gushed horridly from his torn lips, and his lank body went limp.

Conrad eased him down, mechanically cleansing his hands. The gaze he turned upon me was fraught with horror.

"Dead!" he whispered. "It's the work of a maniac! Strike a light, in God's name!"

All over the plantation hounds were howling dolefully. I heard their dirge as with sweating hands I found and lighted a lamp. Together we gazed fearfully at the tattered ruin that had been William Dormouth. And we shuddered anew at what we saw. The man's light pajamas had been shredded, and the tatters were soaked with blood. The man himself had been rended as a hawk rends a lesser bird. His body and limbs were gashed and torn, half a dozen deep cuts showed on his head, but it was evident that death had been caused by a deep triangular-shaped stab directly beneath his heart. At this stab we gazed in incredulous horror.

"No knife ever made a wound like that!" I muttered.

"It might have been made by a bayonet, or a three-edged spike of some sort," Conrad answered. "No, don't try to lift him onto the bed. We must leave him just as he lies until the coming of the proper authorities."

"How are we to get word into the village?" I asked. "The telephone lines, washed away by the recent flood, haven't been replaced."

"We'll send one of the boys," answered Conrad. "Listen—there's Joe now!"

"Massa John!" came a quavering call from outside the house. Conrad beckoned me and we went down the stairs to the porch, where a frightened young negro was waiting.

"Ah heah shot, Massa John," he said nervously. "Anything wrong?"

"Yes, Joe," answered Conrad, speaking rapidly. "Mr. Dormouth has been murdered."

"Murdered?" Joe recoiled. "Oh, golly, suh, who done it?"

"We don't know," answered Conrad. "Are any of the other darkies awake?"

"No, suh, dey all asleep in deir cabins."

"Good," rapped Conrad. "Don't waken them. There's no use to frighten them. I want you to saddle a horse and ride to the village for the sheriff."

Joe visibly blenched at the prospect of riding the ten miles through the cypress swamps and forests, but he manfully replied, "Yassuh, Massa John," and departed.

With unspoken mutual consent, Conrad and I returned to the upper room where Dormouth lay. We spread a sheet over him, for the sight of the mutilated corpse was too much for our nerves, and I said, "Conrad, what was it you shot at as we broke into the room?"

He shook his head. "It was only a shadow—a fleeting glimpse I caught of something at the window. I have no doubt that it was the murderer escaping."

We went to the window and looked out. Several feet away stood a tall tree, its spreading lower branches about level with the window. The light from the window shone full on the tree, showing that whoever might have recently occupied its branches, they were empty now.

"He could have leaped from the sill to the tree," said Conrad. "Then while we were occupied with Dormouth, could have easily slid to the ground and made good his escape."

I demurred, after studying the distance between window and tree.

"Conrad, I don't believe a man could jump that far. I'm something of an athlete, and I know I'd fall short by at least three feet."

"But the murderer escaped from this room," Conrad answered. "The door was locked from the inside, and from the sounds we know that he was here when we ascended the stairs. He did not escape by way of the door, and there is no other exit. Look!" He recoiled involuntarily, pointing to the sill from whence the screen had been torn away. There were flecks of blood upon the polished wood.

"The killer clambered across the sill," said Conrad. "Up, he could not go; to drop to the ground would have broken the legs of any man. So he must have leaped across to the tree. Had we not been so overwhelmed with horror, and had gone to the window, we had surely seen him descending the tree trunk."

I was silenced; Conrad's arguments were unanswerable, yet when I looked at the gulf which lay between window sill and the nearest branches, I felt a strange chill of fear—a hint of something abnormal and unnatural.

"What did he mean by his dying words—'the jade god'?" I asked uneasily.

"He could have meant only the idol he gave today into my keeping," Conrad answered. "I have a feeling that it is tied up in some way with this murder—though why anyone should commit a crime for it is more than I can see, for it is of little monetary value. Besides, Dormouth swore that no one knew of its existence besides myself."

"Get the image," I suggested. "I'd like to see it myself. Meanwhile, I'm going down and look for tracks under the tree."

"Good enough," he replied. "Only don't tramp about too much and spoil the spoor for the bloodhounds—as I have an idea the sheriff will bring them. And be careful; we don't know that the murderer's left the grounds."

I descended the stair and soon stood, with a slight shudder, directly beneath the great tree. I had an uncomfortable feeling that something might suddenly descend upon me, but repeated glances showed me the tree was empty of human or animal life. The hard, close-cropped sward beneath gave no trace of a track. I looked about in the starlight, across the broad lawns toward the silent barns and stables, beyond them to the wide fields and beyond these again to the silent black forest, mysterious and sinister. An owl called sleepily from the depths, and a faint breeze rustled the black leaves. Certainly such a night and such a setting were fitting background for grisly deeds of horror. It was with a certain alacrity that I rejoined Conrad in the library.

[…]

Spectres in the Dark

(unfinished)

The following item appeared in a Los Angeles paper, one morning in late summer:

"A murder of the most appalling and surprizing kind occurred at 333 —— Street late yesterday evening. The victim was Hildred Falrath, 77, a retired professor of psychology, formerly connected with the University of California. The slayer was a pupil of his, Clement Van Dorn, 33, who has, for the last few months, been in the habit of coming to Falrath's apartment at 333 —— Street for private instruction. The affair was particularly heinous, the aged victim having been stabbed through the arm and the breast with a dagger, while his features were terribly battered. Van Dorn, who appears to be in a dazed condition, admits the slaying but claims that the professor attacked him and that he acted only in self defense. This plea is regarded as the height of assumption, in view of the fact that Falrath has for many years been confined to a wheelchair. Van Dorn gave bail and is under surveillance."

I had settled myself comfortably with a volume of Fraser's *Golden Bough* when a loud and positive rap on my door told me that I was not to enjoy an evening alone. However, I laid the book down with no very great reluctance, for as all raps have their peculiarities, I knew that Michael Costigan craved a few hours chat and Michael was always an interesting study.

He lumbered in, filling the room in his elephantine way, as out of place among the books, painting and statues as a gorilla in a tearoom. He snarled something in reply to my greeting and seated himself on the edge of the largest chair he could find. There he sat silent for a moment, chafing his mallet-like hands together, his head bent between his huge shoulders. I watched him, unspeaking, taking in again the immensity of him, the primitive aura which he exuded; admiring again the great fists with their knotty, battered knuckles, the low, sloping forehead topped by a rough mass of unkempt hair, the narrow, glinting eyes, the craggy features marked by many a heavy glove. I sat, intrigued by the workings of his heavy features as the clumsy brain sought to shape words to suit the thought.

"Say," he spoke suddenly but gropingly as he always spoke at first. "Say, lissen, do youse believe in ghosts?"

"Ghosts?" I looked at him a moment without replying, lost in a sudden reverie—ghosts; why this man himself was a ghost of mine, a spectre of my old, degenerate days, always bringing up the years of wandering and carousal and drifting.

"Ghosts?" I repeated. "Why do you ask?"

He seemed not entirely at ease. He twined his heavy fingers together and kept his gaze concentrated on his feet.

"Youse know," he said bluntly. "Youse know dat I killed Battlin' Roike a long time ago."

I did. I had heard the story before and I wondered at the evident connection of his remarks about ghosts, and about the long dead Rourke. I had heard him before disclaim any feelings of remorse or fear of after judgment.

"De breaks uh de game," he expressed it. Yet now:

"Ev'body knows," he went on slowly, "dat I had nuttin' agin him. Roike knows dat himself."

I wondered to hear him speak of the man in the present tense.

"No, it wuz all in de game. We had bad luck, dat wuz all, bad fer Roike an' bad fer me. We wuz White Hopes—dat wuz de jinx—youse know."

I tapped a fingernail on the chair arm and nodded, thinking of Stanley Ketchel, Luther McCarty, James Barry and Al Palzer, all White Hopes, touted to wrest the heavyweight title from the great negro, Jack Johnson, and all of whom died violent deaths, at the height of their fame.

"Yeh, dat wuz it. I come up in Jeffries' time but after I beat some good men dey began to build me fer a title match, as uh White

Hope. I wuz matched wid Battlin' Roike, another comer an' de winner wuz tuh fight Johnson. For nineteen rounds it wuz even," his great hands were clenched, a steely glint in his eyes as if he were again living through that terrible battle—"we wuz bot takin' a lotta punishment—den we bot went down in de twentieth round at de same time. I got on me feet just as the referee wuz sayin' 'Ten!' but Roike died dere in de ring. De breaks uh de game, dat's wot it wuz and dat's all. Bat Roike knows I had nuttin' agin him and he ain't got no reason tuh be down on me."

The last sentence was spoken in a strangely querulous manner.

"Why should you care?" I asked in the callous manner of my earlier life. "He's dead, isn't he?"

"Yeh—but say, lissen. I wouldn't say dis to anybody else, see? But you got savvy; you're my kind, under de skin, see? You been in de gutter and you know de ropes. You know a boid like me ain't got no more noives den uh rhino. You know I ain't afraid uh nuttin', don'tcha? Sure yuh do. But lissen. Somethin' damn' queer is goin' on in my rooms. I'm gittin' so's I don't like tuh be in de dark an' de landlady is raisin' Cain 'cause I leave de light on all night. Foist t'ing I saw dat wuzn't on de up an' up wuz several nights ago w'en I come in me room. I tell yuh, somethin' wuz in dere! I toined on de light an' went t'rough de closets an' under de bed but I didn't find a t'ing an' dere wuz no way for a man tuh git out without me seein' him. I fergot it, see, but de next night it wuz de same way. Den I began to *see* things!"

"See things!" I started involuntarily. "You better lay off the booze."

He made an impatient gesture. "Naw, taint de booze; I can't go dis bootleg stuff an' anyway I got outa de habit when I wuz trainin'. Jes' de same, I see t'ings."

"What kind of things?"

"Things," he waved his hand in a vague manner. "I don't jes' see 'um, but I feel 'um."

I regarded him with growing wonder. Hitherto imagination had formed a small part in his makeup.

"Shadows, like," he continued, evidently at a loss to explain his exact sensations. "Stealin' an' slidin' around w'en the light's off. I can't see 'um, but I can see 'um. I know they're there, so I'm bound tuh see 'um, ain't I?

"Yeh, dey—or it—I don't know which. De udder night I nearly saw 'um." His voice sank broodingly, "I come in an' shut de door an' stand dere in de dark a minute, den I *know* dat somethin' is beside me. I let go wid me left but all I do is skin me hand an' knock a panel outta de door. W'en I toin on de light, de room is empty. I tell yuh"—the voice sank yet lower and the wicked eyes avoided mine sullenly—"I tell yuh, either I'm bugs or Bat Roike is hauntin' me!"

"Nonsense," I spoke abruptly but I was conscious of a queer sensation as if a cold wind had blown upon me from a suddenly opened door. "It's neither. You changed your habits too much; from a gregarious, restless adventurer, you've become almost a recluse. The change from the white lights and the clamor of the throng to a second-rate boarding house and a job in a pool hall is too great. You brood too much and think too much about the past. That's the way with you professional athletes; when you quit active competition, you forget the present entirely. Get out and tramp some more; forget Battling Rourke; change boarding places. It isn't good for a man of your nature to think too much. You're too much of an extrovert—if you know what that means. You need lights and crowds and fellowship, too."

"Mebby you're right," he muttered. "Dis is gettin' on me noives, sure. I been talkin' to uh bootlegger wot wants me tuh go in wid him, woikin' outa Mexico; mebbe I'll take him up." Suddenly he rose abruptly.

"Gettin' late," he said shortly. A moment he turned at the door and I could have sworn I saw a gleam in his cold grey eyes—was it fear? A moment later his huge hand shut the door behind him and his footsteps died away in the distance.

The next morning my breakfast room was invaded by my closest friend, Hallworthy and his young wife. This young lady, a slim little twenty-year-old beauty, perched herself on my knee and held up a pair of rosy lips to be kissed. Her husband did not object in the least, however, because his wife happens to be my sister.

"This is a truly remarkable hour for a visit," I remarked. "How did you ever get this Young American up this early, Malcolm?"

"The most terrible thing!" the girl interrupted. "I can't imagine—"

"Let me tell it, Joan," said Hallworthy mildly. "Steve, you knew Clement Van Dorn, didn't you, and Professor Falrath?"

"I know Clement Van Dorn very intimately and have heard him speak of Falrath."

"Look here," Hallworthy laid a Los Angeles paper before me. I read the item he pointed out, attentively.

"Falrath murdered by Van Dorn, his best friend? I am surprised."

"Surprised!" exclaimed Hallworthy, "I am astounded! Nonplused! Dumfounded! Why, outside the fact that they were the best of friends, Clement Van Dorn had the greatest abhorrence of violence that I ever saw in a man! It was almost an obsession with him! He kill a man? I don't believe it!"

I shrugged my shoulders.

"There is but a thin veneer over the savagery of all of us," I said calmly. "I, who have seen life, both at its highest and its lowest, assure you of this. Trivial things can assume monstrous proportions and loose, for an instant, the primal savage, roaring and red-handed. I have seen a man kill his best friend over a checker game. Men are only men and the primitive, monstrous instincts still hold sway in the dim corners of the mind."

"Not among men like Van Dorn," Hallworthy dissented. "Why, Steve, Clement is positively bloodless in his erudition. He was out of his element anywhere but in Greenwich Village, where he was an authority on the most pallid form of *vers libre* and cubist art."

"I agree with Malcolm," said Joan taking his arm, her protective feminism uppermost. "I don't believe Clement killed him."

"We shall soon know," I answered. "We're going to see Clement."

This necessitated a trip to the prison, for Van Dorn's bail had been remanded and he was being held for trial. Van Dorn, a slim, pallid youth with delicate and refined features, paced his cell and gesticulated jerkily with his slender, artistic hands as he talked. His hair was tousled, his eyes bloodshot and he was unshaven. His universe had crashed about him; his standards were upset. He had lost his mental equilibrium. Looking at him, I felt that if he were not already insane, that he was hovering on the verge of insanity.

"No, no, no!" he kept exclaiming. "I don't understand it! It's monstrous, a terrible nightmare! They say I murdered him—that's preposterous! How do they account for the fact that when we were found his body was clear across the room from his wheelchair?"

"Tell us the whole thing, old fellow," Hallworthy's voice came soothing calm. "We're your friends, you know, and we will believe you."

"Yes, tell us, Clement," echoed Joan, her large eyes tender with pity for the wretched youth.

Van Dorn pressed his hands to his temples as if to still their throbbing, his face twisted in mental torment.

"This is the way of it," he said haltingly, "I've told this tale over and over but no one believes me. I've been going up to Professor Falrath's apartment nearly every night for the past week and he was explaining Spencer's principles, the deeper phases of them. I never saw a man who possessed such a store of metaphysical learning, or who had gone deeper into the roots of things in general. Why, there never were two greater friends. That night we were sitting and talking as we had been and I stepped over to a table to get a book. When I turned—" he closed his eyes tightly, shook his head as if to rid himself of some inner vision, then stared fixedly at us, his hands clenched, "when I turned, Professor Falrath was rising out of his chair; that in itself was astonishing, because he hasn't left the chair in years, but his face held me in frozen silence. My God, that face!" he shuddered violently. "There was no likeness of Professor Falrath, no *human* likeness in those frightful features! It was as if Falrath had vanished and in his place sat a horrid Spectre from some other sphere. The Thing leaped from the chair and hurled itself toward me, fingers stretched like claws. I screamed and fled toward the door but it was in front of me; it closed in on me and in desperation I fought back. Violence of any sort has always repelled me; I have always looked upon the exercise of physical force as a return to bestiality. As for killing, the very sight of blood from a cut finger always nauseated me. But now, I was no longer a civilized man, but a wild beast fighting frenziedly for life. Falrath tore my clothing to pieces and his nails left long tears in my skin; I struck him again and again in the face but without effect.

"At last I secured—how I know not for all is a scarlet haze of horror—a dagger which was one of his collection of arms—this I drove through his wrist and the start of the blood weakened and revolted me. Yet, as he still pressed his attack, I steeled myself and thrust it through his bosom. He fell dead and I too, fell in a dead faint."

We were silent for a time following this weird narration.

"We've stayed our limit, Clement," I said presently. "We will have to go, but rest assured that you will receive all the aid possible. The only solution I can see, is that Professor Falrath was the victim of a sudden homicidal insanity, which might have temporarily overcome his physical weaknesses as you say."

Clement nodded but there was no spark of hope in his eyes, only a bleak and baffled despair. He was not suited to cope with the rough phases of life, which until now he had never encountered. A weakling, morally and physically, was learning in a hard school that savage fact of biology—that only the strong survive.

Suddenly Joan held out her arms to him, her mothering instinct which all women have, touched to the quick by his helplessness. Like a lost child he threw himself on his knees before her, laid his head in her lap, his frail body racked with great sobs as she stroked his hair, whispering gently to him—like a mother to her child. His hands sought hers and held them as if they were his hope of salvation. The poor devil; he had no place in this rough world; he was made to be mothered and cared for by women—like so many others of his kind.

There were tears in Joan's eyes as we came out of the cell and Hallworthy's face showed that he too had been deeply touched.

I had learned that a detective had been put to work on the case—rather an unusual procedure since Van Dorn had confessed to the killing, but the object was to find the motive.

The detective working on the case gave his views as follows: "Van Dorn is just bugs, I figure. One of these fellows that was born half-cookoo and completed the job by hanging around such crazy places as Greenwich Village where they're all crazy and liable to kill anybody just for the sensation" (evidently his knowledge of artists and the New Thought was gathered from ten cent movies). "He and the old professor must have had a row and he killed Falrath, dragged his body across the room, tore his own clothes and then lay down and pretended to be in a faint when the people, who had heard the noise, came busting in at the door. That's the way I think it was. Must have been a terrible thing, Falrath's face was twisted all out of shape; didn't scarcely look like a human."

"What do you think?" asked Hallworthy as we were on our way back.

"I think what I said to Van Dorn: that Clement is telling the truth and that Falrath was insane."

"Yet, could even violent insanity cause a man of Falrath's age and disability to spring on and nearly kill a younger man with his bare hands? Could insanity have put strength in those shriveled muscles and bloodless tissues which had refused to even support his frail body for so many years?"

"That—or else Van Dorn is lying or insane himself," I answered and for a time the conversation was dropped. Van Dorn had plenty of money and at the time I could see no way in which we could aid him. At the trial something might come up.

That night as I turned out the light, preparatory to retiring, I had an opportunity to observe the power of thought suggestion. Michael Costigan's tale had been revolving in the back of my mind and as I plunged the room in darkness, I smiled to myself at the hint of movement in the shadows about me, which my vivid imagination created.

"Suicide follows sudden attack of insanity. The people of a boarding house on —— Street were last night roused by a terrific commotion going on in an upstairs room, and upon investigation found Michael Costigan, ex-prizefighter, engaged in a debauchery of destruction, smashing chairs and tables and tearing the doors from their hinges, in the darkness of his room. A light being turned on, Costigan, a man of huge frame and remarkable strength, stopped short in what was apparently a battle with figments of his imagination, stared wildly at the astounded watchers, then suddenly snatched a revolver from the hand of the landlady and placing the muzzle against his breast, fired four shots into his body, dying almost instantly. The theory advanced is that Costigan was a victim of *delirium tremens*, but he was not known to be a drinking man. The landlady maintains that he was insane, and asserts that he had been talking strangely for some time."

Laying down the paper in which I had read the above article, I gave myself over to musing. This indeed was unusual. Had Costigan's obsession of Battling Rourke's ghost driven him to suicide or was this obsession merely one of the incidents of a latent insanity which had finally destroyed him? This seemed more likely; a man like Costigan was not one to kill himself because of a fancied "ghost" even though he had confessed to a partial belief in its existence. Moreover, considering the terrible punishment he had received in his years in the ring, it was likely that his mentality had been affected.

I picked up the paper and idly scanned the columns, glancing over the usual lists of murders and assaults which seemed extraordinarily numerous, somehow.

Later in the day I paid a visit to the Hallworthy's who lived not overly far from my apartments. I could tell that their minds were still running on Van Dorn and deliberately steered all talk into other channels.

I leaned back in my easy chair regarding the two who sat on a lounge before me. Malcolm Hallworthy was such a man as I had always hoped my sister would marry; a kind man, kind almost to a fault, generous and gentle, yet not weak like Van Dorn. He was not many years older than Joan but he seemed so because of his indulgently protecting attitude, yet at times they seemed like happy children together. This attitude was shown in his unconscious posture, an arm about the girl's slim body as she nestled against him. My only doubt was that he was too indulgent. She was a willful reckless sort of a girl, not old enough to have any judgment and she needed, at times, a strong hand to guide her.

"How do you manage this little spitfire, Malcolm?" I asked bluntly.

He smiled and gently caressed her curls.

"Love will tame the wildest, Steve."

"I doubt if love alone will tame a woman," I answered. "Before she married she could be a little wildcat when she wanted to. The first thing you know you'll let her have her way so much that you'll spoil her."

"You talk as if I were a child," Joan pouted.

"You are. I warn you, Malcolm, her mother gave her her last spanking when she was seventeen."

A shadow touched Hallworthy's fine, sensitive features.

"That's never necessary. Punishing a child is simply brutal— that's all. A relic of the Stone Age that should have no place in the twentieth century. Nothing revolts me quite as much as someone coercing a weaker mortal by the ancient tyranny of flogging."

I laughed. Long roaming in the byways of the world had calloused me to many things. I could scarcely get Hallworthy's viewpoint on some subjects; Joan's either, for that matter. Though we were brother and sister, yet our lives, until recent years had been as different as the poles. She had been raised in luxury, but I had wandered forth into the world at the age of eight and some of the things I had seen and the ways I had traveled had not been of the nicest.

"Many things may not be right," I said, "but they are necessary."

"I deny that!" exclaimed Hallworthy. "Wrong is never necessary! The rightness of a thing makes it necessary, just as wrongness makes it unnecessary."

"Wait!" I raised a hand, "You think, then, if a thing is Right, it should be done, no matter if the consequences are bad."

"The consequences of Right are never bad."

"You are a hopeless idealist. According to your theory, all knowledge gained by research should be given to the people, since it is certainly Wrong to keep the race in ignorance?"

"Certainly. You seem to believe that the end makes things right or wrong. I believe that everything is fundamentally right or wrong and that nothing can make for good results but right."

"Wait. You forget that the great host of people cannot even assimilate such knowledge as has been gained through the past centuries. Suppose hypnotism were a proven fact; would it be right to give to all people the power of controlling others?"

"Yes, if it were a proven fact. It is wrong to suppress knowledge, therefore it is right to dispense knowledge and the results would be good."

That evening I visited Professor Falrath's apartments. I had gotten permission to do so, with the intention of going through his papers to see if any light could be thrown on the murder, or his past relations with Van Dorn.

Among them I found the following letter which he had evidently never finished; it was addressed to Professor Hjalmar Nordon, Brooklyn, New York and the part which caught my attention follows:

"For the last few nights I have been the victim of a peculiar hallucination. After I turn out the light, I seem to sense the presence of something in my room. There is a suggestion of movement in the darkness and straining my eyes it sometimes seems as though I can almost see vague and intangible shadows which glide about through the darkness. Yet, I know that I cannot see these things, as one sees a physical object; I feel them, somehow, and the sensation is so realistic that they seem to register themselves on my sight and hearing. I cannot understand this. Can it be that I am losing my mind? As yet I have said nothing to anyone, but tonight when Van Dorn comes here, I shall tell him of this illusion and see if he can offer any logical explanation."

Here the letter ended abruptly. I re-read it, again conscious of that strange feeling of an unknown door opening somewhere and letting in the dank air of outer spaces.

This was monstrously strange. Michael Costigan and Hildred Falrath had been as far apart as the poles, yet here seemed a common thought between them. Costigan, too, had spoken of shadows lurking and gliding about his room and the strange thing, each had spoken of *feeling* the presence of the spectres. Each had impressed the fact that the Things were unseeable and unhearable, yet each spoke vaguely of *seeing* and *hearing*.

I took the letter to my rooms, and composed a letter to Professor Nordon, narrating the whole affair and telling him of the letter, explaining that I did not enclose it for the reason that it might be of use in Van Dorn's trial to prove the friendship existing between him and the late professor.

This done, I went out into the warm starlight of the late summer night for a stroll, feeling fagged somehow, though I had done nothing to justify such a feeling. As I went along the poorly lighted and almost deserted street—for it was late—I was aware of the strange actions of an individual just in front of me. His progress seemed to be measured by the areas of streetlights. He would hesitate beneath the glow of a light, then suddenly dart swiftly along the street until he came to another light, where he would halt as if loath to leave its radiance.

Feeling some interest, I hastened my step and soon overtook him, for in spite of his haste between the lamp posts, his lingering beneath them made his progress very slow. He was standing directly beneath one, staring this way and that when I came up behind him and spoke to him. He whirled, hand clenched and raised and struck wildly at me. I blocked the blow easily and caught his arm, supposing he thought I was a footpad. However, the evident terror on his face seemed abnormal, somehow. His eyes bulged and his mouth gaped while his complexion was as near white as the human skin can become.

Yet before I could explain my honest intentions, he breathed a gusty sigh.

"Ah, you; pardon me, mister. I thought—I thought it—it was somethin' else."

"What's up?" I asked, bluntly curious.

He shuffled his feet and lowered his eyes, in a manner that reminded me of Costigan's attitude.

"Nothin'," he said rather sullenly, then modified the statement. "That is—I dunno. I'll tell you somethin', though," his face took on an air of low cunning, "stay in the light and you'll be alright. They won't come out of the dark, not Them!"

"They? Who are They?"

At this moment, just as his lips were opening to reply, the streetlight beneath which we stood gave a flicker as though about to go out, and with a scream, the man turned and fled up the street, his frantic heels drumming a receding tattoo on the sidewalk.

Completely dumbfounded, I continued my stroll and returned to my apartments, wondering idly at the number of lights burning in so many houses at such a late hour.

Again at my apartments I settled myself for an hour or so of reading. Selecting a work expounding material monism, I made myself comfortable and upon opening the pages, was reminded, by contrast, of Malcolm Hallworthy and his extreme idealism. I smiled and reflected:

"Maybe Joan hasn't a husband who will control her as she needs to be, but at least she is married to a man who will never mistreat her."

At that very instant there sounded a skurry of feminine high heels outside, the door was hurled open and a girl staggered into the room and threw herself panting into my arms.

"Joan! What in Gods name—"

"Steve!" it was the wail of a frightened and abused child. "Malcolm beat me!"

"Nonsense," if she had grown wings and flown before my eyes, I could not have been more dumbfounded. "What are you talking about, child?"

"He did, he did!" she wailed, sobbing and clinging tightly to me. Her curls were disheveled, her clothing disarranged. "I went to sleep on the lounge and when I woke up, he had me bound there by my wrists and was flogging me with a riding whip! Look!" With a whimper she slipped the flimsy fabric from her back and I saw long, ugly red weals across her slim shoulders.

"You see?"

"Yes, but I don't understand; why, he thought it was brutal to spank you."

[. . .]

The Spell of Damballah

(unfinished)

Our young visitor shifted nervously. He was a young man of athletic build and frank, comely countenance.

"It's about my fiancé, Miss Joan Richards, Mr. Kirby," he said. "I came to you because it's a very delicate matter—and, well, you got me out of that scrape when I was in college, you know, when that occult fakir got me in his clutches. And I hoped you could help me now."

"Let me have the details," requested Kirby. He was a rather slight man of medium size, but his every movement betokened the wiry power and quickness that characterized him. His face was clear-cut, his lips thin, his grey eyes cold and inscrutable. He delved in occult matters as some men pursue a hobby and in times past his extensive knowledge of dark magic and the furtive characters that dealt in it, had stood the forces of law and order in good stead.

"Well," said our visitor, one John Ordley, in some embarrassment, "I hardly know how to begin. But the thing of it is this: my fiancé Joan Richards has apparently become infatuated with an outlandish sort of fellow, and I believe he's cast some sort of a spell over her!

"It's like this: not very long ago a fellow came to our town, calling himself Ahmed Bey. He seemed to have plenty of money and he leased a place for the summer. Well, the people were interested of course, but a little slow about recognizing him socially, because he looked like a half-caste of some sort. But he claimed to be some sort of an Arabian nobleman—a shayk's son—sent to America to be educated. He is well educated—well, some of the society women decided it would be a fine thing to have a real romantic Oriental prince in their fold, so they took him to their bosom, and ever since he's been in the way of becoming a social lion. Well, that's all right with me. But Joan seems to have completely lost her head over him.

"Well, I'm not so confoundedly vain that I think nobody could take a girl away from me—but Joan and I—why, we've been in love with each other ever since we were just kids. She hasn't been acting natural lately. She has a faraway look in her eyes, and she looks at this Arab like—well, like a slave might look at her adored master. I tell you, Kirby, it's neither natural nor holy!" Ordley was becoming intensely excited. "There's times when I can hardly keep from knocking the fellow's head off. Of late he's assumed a proprietary air toward her that's extremely offensive—though she doesn't seem to notice it. And another thing—we were always scrapping like kids with each other—she's a scrappy piece, and I liked to stir her up just for fun—but she never questions anything this Oriental says or does. She's too docile with him—I tell you, he's cast a spell on her."

"What does this man look like?" asked Kirby.

"Well," said Ordley, "he's tall and pretty powerfully built—bigger than O'Brien here, I should say. His complexion is a sort of brownish yellow, and his eyes are yellow, too; you get the impression that they'd gleam in the dark like a cat's. He's not unhandsome, I'll admit, and he moves with the ease and suppleness of a big panther. He wears a turban, but that's the only Oriental style garment he does wear. Let me see—oh, yes, the scar."

I saw Kirby stiffen.

"Scar?"

"Yes, on his throat, a white line running from the angle of his jaw down the side of his neck."

Kirby nodded, seemingly sunk in meditation.

"Well, how about it?" demanded the youth. "Do you think I'm a rattle-brained sap—which I probably am—or will you see what you can do?"

Kirby rose and reached for his hat.

"We'll go with you."

On the way to Ordley's town Kirby was as noncommittal as ever, asking only a few questions, not about Ahmed Bey, but about the town and countryside. We arrived at the town in the middle of the warm summer afternoon and Ordley took us directly to his house, an old-fashioned mansion, set, with several others of the same style, somewhat apart from the town, in a rather exclusive section. There were broad lawns, shaded by great oaks, and not far away began the thick tangle of woods which deepened in the distance to stretches of sullen and mysterious swampland. For Ordley's town was located in the very edge of the swamp country.

Ordley said that the house next to his estate was that of the Richards'.

"They're having a party there tonight," he said. "You'll go as my guests. I'll introduce you to Joan—and you'll get a chance to see Ahmed Bey—damn him!"

I detest such affairs, personally. But I went along of course, and met Joan Richards, a slim, dark-eyed beauty and we were introduced to Ahmed Bey. And I instantly knew the man was lying when he called himself an Arab. No Arab—at least no pure-blooded Arab—ever possessed the brownish-yellow complexion of this man. What Kirby thought, I did not know. As usual, he gave no hint of his thoughts. But presently he drew me aside into the library.

"Ordley was right," he said, "the girl's charmed. She's hypnotized. That fellow is no more an Arab than I am. I thought I recognized the description Ordley gave. His real name is Loup, and he's a mulatto from Haiti. Wanted there for murder, too. Who'd have thought to find him masquerading as an Oriental prince in the States! Son of a rich half-caste family in Haiti, he was bad from the beginning. He got a fine education but it only increased his deviltry. There were dark tales told about him in Haiti, and hints that he was a priest of the Snake—a voodooist."

"Ah!" I exclaimed, "that explains those objects on Ordley's porch—the white bones tied up in the red rag."

"Exactly," Kirby snapped. "Loup is not content at stealing a white girl by his hypnotic powers—no doubt he fears and hates Ordley, and means to put him out of the way if he interferes. Well, I don't think Mr. Loup is going to succeed so well with the girl, at least. He had to leave Haiti for the same reason—he worked his spell over a young white girl, and forced her to steal a large sum of money for him from her father. A young negro was accused of the theft, and to clear himself, revealed the whole plot—black people have a way of knowing everything that goes on. Loup fled the island barely in time to save his dirty life—the girl's furious father was hunting him, intending to shoot him on sight. Look!"

As he spoke, Kirby caught my shoulder and drew me back behind some hangings. From where we stood, we looked, unobserved, out onto the wide veranda at the side of the house. Ahmed Bey, or rather Loup, had come upon the veranda with a slim girlish figure I recognized as Joan Richards. The moonlight fell full upon their faces—the beautiful lifted face of the girl, and the dark, gloating, sinister countenance of the man. He was speaking in a low tone that was vibrant with strange power.

"You are mine," he said, tilting her head so that her clear eyes looked full into his. "You are mine," his voice was low and monotone. "None but I am your master."

"None but you are my master," she repeated in a soft mechanical voice.

"We will go away tonight," he said in the same low even tone. "You have no will of your own. You know only obedience to my commands. Go, now, to your father's safe. You know the combination. Open it and take out the money which is there. Go then to your room and change into clothes for travel. Then slip out by the back way and come to the orchard. I will await you there."

"Why, you dirty rat!" Ordley stepped from the shadows and faced the man, his face convulsed with rage, his fists clenched. "I couldn't help but hear what you said," he said, "and I'm glad I did. Joan, are you mad?"

She did not reply but stood, her hands hanging limply at her sides, her head slightly lifted, her eyes unseeing.

"Tell this young man, Joan," intoned Loup, "that you do not wish to see him again."

"I do not wish to see you again, John," intoned Joan.

"Joan!" Ordley caught her wrists. "Girl, what has come over you? What has this scoundrel done to you?"

She pulled away from him and Loup spoke harshly, "Ordley, I will thank you to keep your hands off my property."

"Why, you damned—" roared Ordley, leaping at his enemy. I saw a brief momentary whirl of figures, then Ordley dropped and lay writhing, and Loup stepped back, evil triumph in his eyes.

"Just a little *jiu-jitsu* trick, my friend," he said. "Lie there a little while and reflect on the foolishness of opposing one stronger than yourself. Joan, go and do as I bade you."

She had stood listlessly during the short fight, and I seemed to see a vague hurt look come into her cloudy eyes as if pity for her former lover struggled feebly through the fog of hypnotic illusion; but now she turned obediently away. And then Kirby flung open the French windows and stepped out on the veranda. I followed him, fairly trembling in my eagerness to smash my sledgelike fists against Loup's sneering mouth.

The Haitian whirled and glared at us.

"Well met, Loup," said Kirby coolly. "Perhaps you thought I would not know you with that moustache and the Oriental accoutrements. Loup," he caught the Haitian's arm in a steely grip and his voice grew hard and menacing as a knife edge, "your game's done."

Loup's eyes were those of a mad dog's in the moonlight, but he lowered his head sullenly and muttered, "Very well, I go."

"Not until you free this young lady from your hypnotic spell," snapped Kirby.

"Free her yourself," snarled Loup, in evident fear, but dangerous as a crippled snake.

Kirby smiled, and Loup's dark face turned ashy at the quality of that smile.

"Loup," said Kirby deliberately, "I might take you back to Haiti and hand you over to a certain gentleman there who would give you your desserts quickly. I might give you up to the authorities who would assuredly see that you spent the next twenty years of your life behind bars. But I do not choose to do that. No. I give you your choice—release this girl instantly, or your colored friends shall know about the ruby eye in the Black Snake, and the glass bead you carry about with you."

The blood drained from the half-caste's face, leaving him perfectly ashy. He trembled like a leaf.

"Enough," he muttered. "I will release the woman."

I had lifted Ordley onto a chair. The effects of the vicious trick by which Loup had paralyzed him was wearing away, but he was sick and shaken. Loup turned to the girl and holding out his hands above her head, intoned: "Be ye free! Awake! You are your own mistress. I have no more power over you."

Joan started, the cloudiness vanished from her eyes, and she looked about amazedly. Then seeing Ordley slumped in the chair, she cried out and rushed to him.

"Oh, John, it's been a terrible nightmare! Are you hurt?"

Kirby jerked his head at Loup. "Get out," he said in cold disgust and Loup slunk away like a thievish dog. We helped Ordley to his feet and into the library, where Joan hovered over him, and he quickly recovered his full powers. Kirby was explaining, when the sudden crack of a pistol outside brought us to our feet—except Kirby, who dropped like a log. A high-pitched yell of savage triumph, that seemed to crack on a high note of fear, cut the night, and then silence. We bent at Kirby's side, and discovered the bullet had ploughed through his scalp, knocking him senseless, but not seriously injuring him. As we staunched the blood flow he opened his eyes, and laughed grimly: "I forget even a jackal will strike from behind. He must have found Ordley's pistol. Let me up; I'm all right."

I flung open the French windows.

[. . .]

"James Norris…"
(untitled synopsis)

James Norris
Joe Rogers
Spearman
Mrs. Bond hired the stranger to trail her husband to Woodlawn. He established an alibi because he was afraid of his wife. The stranger was the man that Miss Minsey saw coming from Mary Young's room Saturday night. Mary Young stopped working for Bond because he was too familiar. He made a date with her to meet him at Woodlawn.

Mary Young's secrecy: hiding from some one—a man—her lover—rejected. This man was seen by Miss Minsey, leaving Mary Young's room. James Norris was in the scenic with Mary Young, no.

Joe Rogers and James Norris were connected in some way. That partly explains Joe Rogers' flight and Norris's absence Sunday night. Thursday Norris and Mary Young had a row about Bond. Norris was with Rogers Sunday night.

1. The flight of Joe Rogers.
2. The failure of James Norris to establish an alibi.
3. The man Miss Minsey saw leaving Mary Young's room Sunday evening.
4. The note in Bond's handwriting. Signed with a J.
5. The presence of the cigar lighter with Norris' initials.
6. The presence of the knife in Norris' room.
7. The apparent secrecy of Mary Young.
8. The subway worker, Spearman.

Joe Rogers had been working the stock markets. This accounts for: his flight (feared detection), the rubbish in his room, and the figures.

Some girl of James Norris' acquaintance was in trouble and it was she who had called him that night, and she to whom Rankin heard Norris talking. He could not establish his alibi without involving her in some way.

The man whom Miss Minsey saw leaving Mary Young's room was the man who had followed her from Gary—the man from whom she was hiding—the man who was with her on the scenic and the man who killed her.

Mary Young had had a row with James Norris over Bond and had given Bond to understand that she was through there. Bond wrote her, being infatuated with her, and signed J., either knowing she would come thinking it to be James Norris, or else through fear of his wife.

Mary Young had found Norris' cigar lighter and dropped it in the scenic.

The man who killed her knew Norris and hid the knife in his room to avert suspicion.

Mary Young was hiding from someone, possibly a persistent lover. This man was seen by Miss Minsey leaving her room Sunday night. He took her for the ride and killed her, after which he paid for her second ride, he left the knife in Norris' room to implicate him. Norris had been helping a girl who was in trouble and would not establish an alibi. Rogers fled because he had been working the stock market with the bank's money. Bond wrote the note and his wife had him trailed. He established his alibi because he was afraid of her. Mary Young had found the cigar lighter and was keeping it to give to Norris.

The girl killed was not Mary Young. She was hiding from someone and Mrs. Schmidt and Mrs. Edgecomb were in on the deal to get her away.

Sons of Hate

(partial synopsis 1)

Say it was the 3rd of August. Stalbridge was in England, Kerim Ali was in Cairo. Kerim Ali saw the picture first, but Stalbridge got to the city a day ahead of Kerim Ali. Stalbridge got there the 3rd, located Pembroke's house, and sent him the picture. Watching the house, he saw Pembroke immediately leave for the city, and followed him. That was the morning of the 3rd. That day he made the appointment with Kirby and Gorman. Stalbridge was watching the club, and following him when he drove to the detective's office. In the meantime, Kerim Ali had also arrived and located Pembroke's house, shortly after Pembroke left. He got in touch with Juan and bribed him, and then Juan learned from William that Pembroke intended going to the detective agency. Kerim Ali laid their plans, Juan persuaded them not to capture Pembroke as he arrived.

Sons of Hate

(partial synopsis 2)

Characters: Brent Kirby, Butch Gorman, private detectives; Colonel Pembroke,

Colonel Pembroke made his fortune in the Soudan, in the latter part of the nineteenth century. He was a slave trader until the outbreak of the Mahdi war, when he joined the dervishes and aided in the sack of Khartoum. An Englishman named Ashley had just returned from an expedition up towards the headwaters of the Nile, where he had found a tribe that claimed descent from the ancient Egyptians. He had secured a vast treasure in jewels from them, the most striking of which was a cat carved of green jade, known as the cat of the Pharoah. Pembroke, under the guise of friendship, trapped Ashley and murdered him with the aid of a chief of the Soudanese called Muhammad. They secured the treasure, but Pembroke managed to escape with it; he left Africa, eluded his pursuers and came to America, where he lived safely, with his niece, until a young reporter managed to get a picture of him and the cat and wrote up a highly colored yarn with the aid of the niece, who knew nothing about her uncle's past. The old chief Muhammad saw and recognized the picture, and sent his son and a band of native killers to avenge what he considered a wrong; at the same time the picture of the cat was recognized by a nephew of the murdered Ashley; his uncle had sent his father a picture of the cat awhile before the rise of the Mahdi. He came to seek what he considered his own fortune as a right of relationship.

Sons of Hate

(partial synopsis 3)

Richard Brandon ordered Kirby to call Gorman over the phone and tell him to bring Colonel Pembroke to the office of the detective agency. He leaned close to hear Gorman's voice, which he said he knew. Kirby got Gorman on the phone, and then the wire was cut. Kirby gave a fantastic order, knowing Gorman could not hear, and then slugged Brandon and knocked him down, took his gun, got him in his car and started for Pembroke's house. Just outside the grounds a lead slug was thrown through his windshield, blinding him, and he crashed into a tree. He leaped out and was attacked by a shadowy form, but shot his way through. Gorman came to his rescue and they carried Brandon into the house. There Brandon accused Pembroke of being a renegade and told of the Pharoah's treasure. Pembroke admitted it. Gorman went out to investigate a noise and was knocked senseless on the lawn. The house was rushed by Soudanese fanatics and Brandon and Kirby were knocked out, Brandon senseless, Kirby paralyzed. The Soudanese tortured Pembroke to make him tell them where the treasure was, and he showed them a secret panel. They went into it, carrying him and the girl, and muffled screams issued. A big negro left to execute the white men was about to cut off Brandon's head, when Gorman, who had come to and rolled away in the shadows, appeared and knocked the negro senseless. They then followed into the secret tunnel, found Pembroke had been executed and they were preparing to execute the girl. In a bloody knife fight in the shadowy tunnel, Gorman had the best of it with the leader of the fanatics. Brandon had gone after the police, and Gorman, Kirby and the girl were trapped in a room in the tunnel. While Kirby and the girl held the door, Gorman fought the Soudanese giant with knives and won. Then they fled from the tunnel and the police came and the remaining Soudanese were captured.

The Devils of Dark Lake
(untitled synopsis)

Steve Gorman, late one evening, toward sundown, received a frantic telephone call, on a party line, from Joan Grissom. He was in his cottage on the west shore of Dark Lake, and the Grissom cottage was three miles to the south. Joan screamed that a monstrosity like an ape-man was trying to break into the cottage, that he had already killed her companions, Jack Richards and Harriet Wilkins. Her husband, Dick Grissom, was at his fishing shack, four miles to the south, where there was no telephone.

Joan screamed that she had shot repeatedly at the monster without effect—that he was a fiend out of hell! She shrieked that he was tearing away the window bars, and Gorman, electrified, heard a rending crash, an awful scream and then a mutter of horrible laughter. Racing forth, without a weapon, he sprang into his car and arrived at the Grissom cottage in a few minutes. The west shore of the lake was uninhabited except for himself and the Grissoms, though the east shore was lined with cottages.

Arriving at the Grissom cottage, standing on the shore of the lake, he found the girl Harriet Wilkins impaled on the pickets of the fence, her slender body jammed there by some terrific force. On her white throat were the marks of inhuman fingers. Inside the yard lay Jack Richards, a star football player. His neck had been twisted around so his face grinned between his shoulders as the body lay on its belly.

Entering the house, Gorman found the window bars torn off, and a door ripped from its hinges. Joan Grissom was gone. He found her gun, empty. He rushed forth, sprang in his car and raced for Dick's fishing shack. Arriving there just before sundown, he was startled to see an automobile standing close to the shack. He went up to it and was attacked. He saw Joan lying in it, bound and gagged, and just then was attacked by a dark-faced servant he recognized as a man formerly employed as Joan's chauffeur, and discharged because he had been caught snooping around in the cottage. He struck at Gorman with a blackjack and the next instant was lying bleeding and half-stunned in the road as Gorman smashed a left to his heart and a right to his jaw.

Then Gorman wheeled to be confronted by an ape-like monstrosity carrying a limp senseless form over one shoulder. The thing had captured Dick Grissom. It dropped the captive and sprang at Gorman, whose smashing blows were futile. He was caught up, lifted high in the air and dashed unconscious against the ground.

When he regained consciousness the sun was setting, and on his breast squatted a black and silver hairy horror, the Shroud-Weaver, a huge spider from Africa, so called because of its habit of weaving its web on the bodies of dead men. He remembered the flash of a scene in Africa, a village where dead men lay after a tribal raid, clad in a glistening sheath of web. If he moved it would bite him and kill him.

Then a pistol cracked, the bullet burned across his breast and tore the horror asunder. He sprang up. The car was gone, with it the monster, the furtive servant, and the Grissoms. Before him stood a yellow-skinned man and a woman—brother and sister. They told him their names were Bartholomew and Celia; they were Haitians. They told him that a former suitor of Joan's had struck, in revenge for her rejecting him, three years before.

His name was Rackston Bane; he was born in China, the son of an official, and partly raised there, and had absorbed Oriental ideas. After his rejection by Joan, he had returned to the Orient, and built up a horrible organization, in which he had included Bartholomew and Celia. Or rather, in Haiti he had aided a rival voodoo man to usurp Bartholomew's power and drive him and his sister from the island. Ever since they had followed him, seeking revenge.

He had captured Celia and kept her a captive in his stronghold on Cannibal Island, at the south end of the lake, subjecting her to nameless indignities, and finally releasing her in scorn. Or perhaps she escaped. Bane had established himself on that island, surrounded by his servants. The monster was one of a strange tribe of humans living in a lost country in Mongolia, more like apes than human beings. His master called him Esau, because he was hairy. The servant driving the car was a half-breed called Strozza, Italian-Somali, who had put blanks in Joan's pistol.

They had captured the Grissoms and were taking them to Cannibal Island, for torture. Strozza had left the spider on Gorman. The Haitians and Gorman followed. While the north end of the lake was surrounded by firm ground and open forests, the south end was encircled by swamps. Cannibal Island was so-called because a negro, living there alone, had reverted to cannibalism, and escaping the party sent after him, had fled into the swamps on the mainland. Gorman had been one of the posse and remembered the sickening sight of the smokehouse hung with human limbs.

Leaving their car on the shore, they found a canoe and paddled to the island, through the darkness. Bartholomew had a pistol, Celia a dagger, Gorman an axe. Celia told them there was only one approach to the stronghold, and that was up a narrow creek, winding between over-hanging cypresses. All other approaches were carefully guarded by horrible traps of various kinds.

Bartholomew insisted on paddling up the creek alone, to scout the way. Celia and Gorman waited for him, standing on the cypress knees. Presently the canoe came floating back to them—with Bartholomew's head in it. At that Celia slipped into the water and started swimming up the creek, in spite of the alligators, telling Gorman to follow her in the canoe. She intended slipping ashore and stealing along the bank behind the trees. She was using Gorman as a bait for her trap, though he did not realize it till later. Paddling up the black creek, suddenly a misshapen hand reached down from the overhanging branches and gripped his hair, which was close-cropped. He ducked and the machete-blow aimed at his neck missed. He grabbed a thick wrist and jerked the killer out of the tree, knowing he was a negro by the smell. And when the man cursed he realized he was grappling with the cannibal for which the island was named.

The canoe sank, and fighting in the water, Gorman drowned his man. Then, his flesh crawling in fear of alligators, which tore the corpse from his grasp, he swam ashore. As he climbed up on the bank he got a glimpse of a black form poised with a lifted axe. The next moment Celia stabbed the negro from behind and pushed him into the water.

Gorman came out of the creek, and together they started along a winding path which led to Bane's stronghold. But as they came in sight of a house, Esau appeared before them, a hideous, shambling figure in the shadows. Gorman vainly broke a club over his head and was knocked senseless. Esau snatched up Celia and carried her off.

Gorman came to his senses in a log hut, lighted by a candle. He was sitting with his arms twisted behind him and bound around a post. Before him a mad dog was lunging at a chain which worked on cogwheels, so each lunge would turn a wheel an inch and lengthen his chain. Eventually he would reach the bound man. Frantically Gorman began twisting at his cords, picking with his fingernails. As he worked, the dog lunged. An instant before the brute reached him, his bleeding fingernails did the trick, and seizing the dog by the throat as it leaped, he dashed it to the floor and broke its neck.

Then he burst open the door, and a stunted African ran at him with an axe. He broke the man's neck and took the axe, and strode on toward the house. Looking through a window he saw Joan Grissom stripped naked and stretched on an altar, with Bane standing over her. Grissom, already bleeding from a cruel lashing, was hung by his feet and wrists from a rope and a pulley. This was letting him down slowly into a wire-cage filled with swamp moccasins who struck viciously at him again and again. Celia was there, crucified on an X-shaped cross. There were Esau and three other hideous servants.

Bane was tormenting Dick with descriptions of the torture his wife would be subjected to, holding a cage with a great grey rat, squealing with pain and hunger. He ordered Celia taken from the cross. She could not stand, but fell to the floor, cursing him. In anger he stabbed her, but she reared up with a terrible smile, and told him she would not die until he was dead. While all stared in horror, Gorman burst open the door. Esau plunged at him, and Gorman crushed his skull. One after another he killed the three other servants.

Bane leveled a pistol, dodging the axe Gorman hurled. Then Celia, who had crawled to his feet, threw her arms about him and flung him into the cage with the snakes, who instantly bit him to death. Then Celia died, still smiling vindictively.

The House of Om

(synopsis)

Chapter .1.

Bill Blanton, hearing a cry for help, as he walked along a side street in a certain seaport town, groped into a dark alley and stumbled over the body of a dead man. He recognized the body as that of one Bixby, a man with whom he had exchanged blows earlier in the day, when the fellow became pugnacious over a collision in a hotel lobby. His head was bloody, and he was already rigid, a circumstance which seemed unusual to Blanton. He forgot this, however, when a man appeared, exhibiting a detective's badge, and covering him with a pistol. He recognized the man as Corrigan, right-hand man for Joel Bainbridge, the political boss of the city.

Corrigan accused Blanton of the murder of Bixby, and arrested him. But instead of conducting Blanton to the police station, Corrigan took him to a room in a nearby building, where he handcuffed him in a chair and then began manhandling him to make him confess to the murder. Corrigan produced a confession, already typed out, and told Blanton that if he'd sign it, he'd arrange to have him let off with a suspended sentence.

Blanton accused him of trying to work an unbelievably crude frame-up, and Corrigan answered that he could be as crude as he wished, since he had him, Blanton, in a cleft stick.

While they talked, a mysterious masked man who spoke with a peculiar accent, picked the lock and entered the room, covered Corrigan with a gun and made him free Blanton. Then, as the stranger and Blanton left the room, the former dashed a small glass ball on the floor near Corrigan's feet, which emitted a cloud of yellowish vapour which rendered the detective senseless. Assuring

Blanton that Corrigan would recover in an hour or so, the stranger led Blanton to a mysterious building in the Oriental quarter of the city, where, in a bizarrely furnished chamber, he removed his mask and revealed himself a Mongol. He called himself Togruk Khan, "servant of Mr. Om."

He then told Blanton that he had been framed at the instigation of Joel Bainbridge, the boss of the city. Blanton had a concession from a certain South American republic for the development of certain mineral resources, which had been given him by the bandit which had recently made himself dictator of that republic—a man Blanton had once befriended.

Blanton had come to the States looking for financial backing, and had approached Bainbridge, who had a finger in any number of moneymaking pots. But Bainbridge had demanded an outrageously huge share of the profits, and Blanton had refused. Bainbridge had then had him framed, with the intention of using the signed confession as a club to force Blanton to make any concessions the boss might wish. Bainbridge was a sinister figure who would commit any crime, including murder, to gain his point, and he was anxious to get his fingers into the project Blanton was trying to promote, which was even richer in possibilities than Blanton realized. Bainbridge had appeared mysteriously out of nowhere some ten years before, and, by virtue of his enormous wealth, had made himself practically ruler of the city.

Togruk Khan gave Blanton to understand that he had learned of Bainbridge's plot through spies in the boss's confidence, and he told Blanton that his master, the mysterious Mr. Om, was Bainbridge's enemy, and had chosen that very night for his overthrow. Blanton was a big man, scarred, and of a formidable appearance, which led Togruk Khan to believe that he was a desperate character. He pointed out that Blanton was a fugitive from justice, and that his only security lay in the overthrow of the forces which had framed him.

But Blanton sensed something sinister behind all that, believed that Mr. Om must be the head of some secret Oriental criminal society, and refused to join the Mongol. Togruk did not insist, but offered

Blanton a glass of wine. As the white man lifted the glass to his lips, he recognized the scent of a peculiar Chinese drug, which destroyed willpower and individual initiative, leaving the victim temporarily a mindless robot. He smashed the goblet, and was instantly attacked by a gang of Mongols which came at Togruk's call. Evidently Togruk felt he had told the white man too much. After a vicious battle in the dark, Blanton escaped into a series of subterranean tunnels, and in one of these he saw, to his amazement, Joel Bainbridge, apparently watching the mutilation of his right-hand man, Corrigan, who was strapped down on a table and being worked over by men in masks.

Chapter .2.

Blanton found his way out of the rat dens in which he had taken refuge, emerging in a small court at the back of a tenement house. Scarcely had he reached the street when a riot of unexpected proportions broke out in the Oriental quarter, with fighting in the streets, and fires, which drew practically all of the police and firemen of the city to that section. Blanton sneaked back to his hotel to get the concession which he had hidden there in his rooms, and discovered that the rooms had been ransacked and the papers stolen. He could not understand why Bainbridge should steal it, since it was useless in any hands but his own.

But rendered desperate by this implacable hounding, he determined to go to Bainbridge and recover the concession, or kill the boss. He found Bainbridge alone in his house, and accused him of the frame-up and the theft. Bainbridge cynically admitted the frame, but denied the theft, and while they quarreled, Corrigan entered, to Blanton's surprise, who thought he had been killed or maimed in the tunnel under Togruk Khan's house.

The detective attacked Blanton, and in the struggle Corrigan's gun went off, and an instant later the fighters saw Bainbridge lying dead on the floor, with his brains oozing out, apparently having been hit by the stray bullet. Knowing that Corrigan would try to pin this killing, too, on him, Blanton knocked the detective senseless and bolted from the house.

In the shadows of the shrubbery outside, he encountered a mysterious white man, who said he was Hawksbane, a private investigator, and persuaded Blanton to trust him. Hawksbane said that he had followed Mr. Om from China, had learned that an attack would be made on Bainbridge's life that night, and had hurried to the spot as quickly as he could.

Re-entering the house, they found it deserted. Neither Corrigan nor Bainbridge's body was to be found. Corrigan's gun, with one chamber fired, was found on the floor of the study. Hawksbane found the bullet from the gun embedded in the wall, which it had entered at an angle which showed it could not have struck Bainbridge. They found a bloodstained hatchet of curious make behind the hangings of the door near which Bainbridge had been standing when he was killed. Hawksbane believed that the riot in the Oriental section had been staged by Mr. Om to draw the police into that part of town. The servants of Mr. Om had then invaded Bainbridge's house intending to kill him, and had merely taken advantage of the struggle between Blanton and Corrigan to strike down Bainbridge unaware from behind the hangings. Hawksbane believed that after Blanton had fled from the house, Corrigan had likewise been murdered and the bodies of both men disposed of.

Hawksbane told Blanton that the mysterious Mr. Om, whom no white man had ever seen, was the head of a Mongolian devil-worshipping cult. Om had murdered a friend of Hawksbane, an English official, in China, and Hawksbane, himself an American amateur criminologist, had set out to run him down. He had followed him to America, and there learned, from an eccentric old Chinaman named Yun Wang, that Om had marked down Bainbridge for destruction. Why, Hawksbane did not know, but it had something to do with a former partner of Bainbridge's, John Stark. Ten years before Stark and Bainbridge had gone into inner Mongolia to steal a hoard of jewels from an ancient temple there, a treasure dating from the days of Genghis Khan. They had been discovered by the native priests, but Bainbridge made his escape at the expense of his partner, who fell into the hands of the priests. Bainbridge got away with the jewels and returned to America, to become enormously wealthy as a result. Hawksbane believed that Om had killed Bainbridge because of this theft.

Sensing a crawling peril in the silent house where Bainbridge had died, Hawksbane and Blanton left it hurriedly, and made their way to the house of the old Chinaman, Yun Wang, hoping to learn something that would give a clue as to Om's whereabouts. (Hawksbane had promised to help Blanton out of his jam, if the adventurer would aid him in running down Om.)

They found old Yun Wang dying from the bite of an Oriental spider which had mysteriously been introduced into his house, but before he died, he gasped out the true identity of Om; he was the white man, John Stark. The priests who had captured him, instead of crucifying him, as Bainbridge had thought, had admitted him into their devil-worshipping cult, and for ten years he had dwelt among them, rising to be head of the society. At last he had come to America for revenge on his treacherous friend, but Bainbridge's death was not all he plotted. There was something still more monstrous—but Yun Wang died before he could divulge it.

Chapter .3.

Leaving the house of Yun Wang, Hawksbane and Blanton were arrested by half a dozen policemen. These men made no charge of murder or otherwise, they merely said that Joel Bainbridge had ordered Hawksbane and Blanton to be picked up and brought to his house for questioning. They averred that they had received the order from Bainbridge's own lips, less than half an hour ago, with directions as to the whereabouts of the men wanted. Hawksbane and Blanton knew that someone might have spied on them and followed them from Bainbridge's house, but they were puzzled as to the assertion of the police that they had recently seen Bainbridge alive.

They were more dumbfounded when they came to Bainbridge's house and were confronted by both Bainbridge and Corrigan, neither of whom showed any signs of having gone through a battle. Blanton knew that he had seen Bainbridge lying on the floor with his brains seeping out, but the boss laughed at him, when he said so. The police were dismissed, leaving the four alone in the study, Hawksbane and Blanton covered by Corrigan's pistol.

Bainbridge told them he had a proposition to make, and displayed the concession stolen from Blanton's room. Then he offered them cigars, and at the first whiff, Blanton knew they were doped. But already the drug had taken effect, and he and Hawksbane passed out.

Chapter .4.

Hawksbane came to his senses chained hand and foot in a cell-like chamber, with a hooded figure looking down at him. This was the mysterious Mr. Om.

Om told Hawksbane that he had accomplished his vengeance on Bainbridge, for the latter's treachery, but that this vengeance was merely incidental, a cog in the machinery of his plans. Om said that he was head of the cult of Erlik the Black, a religion dedicated to destruction, of which the cult of the Thugs of India was but a minor branch. This cult found its pleasure in the debauching and destroying of humanity, just as the other religions of the world found gratification in uplifting.

Om plotted a horrible revenge on the city, in which he had been born and raised, and from which he had been sent to serve a prison term when a youngster. The details he told to the horrified Hawksbane. Gaining full control of the city, he would cause dope to be smuggled through by the tons; this dope would be used to debauch the young people, instigated by various faddist cults, such as that of the mystic "Gondai," one of his servants posing as a seer and esoteric teacher. Then, within the next week, he intended starting a deadly plague of infantile paralysis among the schoolchildren. The city health officer would be removed and replaced by one of his minions, who would force each child to be given a special vaccine which he would pretend to be recently discovered, but which would in reality rob the victims of their mentality. A city full of idiot children and degenerate dope-fiends appealed to Om's perverted mind.

Om assured Hawksbane that he and Blanton were cogs also in the wheel. Hawksbane would return to China and tell the British officials that Om was dead. Blanton would go to South America and work out the mining scheme—for Om. Om then revealed to Hawksbane the secret of his power.

(The secret revealed to Hawksbane, which almost unhinged his mind, is not at this point fully revealed to the readers. Om was a plastic surgeon, having learned the art from the Mongolian priests, who had progressed far beyond the western world of science. Coming to America, he had gotten various wretches into his power, and by his science altered them to resemble anyone he pleased. The man Blanton had thought was Joel Bainbridge in the tunnels was one of these creatures, watching while another was made to look like Corrigan, the last touches as to hair, teeth and so forth being done at the time.

Bainbridge had been murdered and Corrigan done away with, and their duplicates simply substituted. No one would know the difference. The city would take the orders of the man they thought Joel Bainbridge, and Om would give his orders to the false Bainbridge.

A man had already been made up to look like Hawksbane, when Om first learned the criminologist was on his track. It was he who would return to China with the news that Om was dead. Another, made over to resemble Blanton, would go to South America with the concession Om had had stolen, and work the mines. Hawksbane and Blanton would be murdered, the real ones. All this is not revealed to the readers until later in the story.)

Chapter .5.

Blanton came to himself, meanwhile, in another chamber, and indeed in another part of the city. He knew nothing of Hawksbane's fate. Togruk Khan was in the room, and took a plaster cast of Blanton's features, which he proceeded to employ to make a wax bust of the white man. (This, of course, was to be used in molding a man to resemble Blanton, though the latter did not know it.)

An interruption came in the form of an attack by a madman who broke from the dungeon where he was being tortured. Blanton was horrified to recognize Corrigan. (Who had been captured by the Mongols when Bainbridge was murdered.) Corrigan was riddled by the Mongols' bullets, but in the confusion Blanton escaped. He found himself in the heart of the Oriental quarter, and making his way back to a more decent part of town, he encountered a man he thought dead—Bixby. The man, seized by Blanton, admitted that he had aided in framing him. He had a peculiar knack of simulating death, through a self-induced catalepsy, and had been used more than once by Bainbridge for such purposes. He swore that the regular police knew nothing about it, were not looking for Blanton for his murder. Only Corrigan and Bainbridge and himself had been in the plot.

In the midst of his confession he was killed by a thrown knife which missed Blanton, for whom it was aimed, and Blanton barely made a getaway from a gang of Mongols who were pursuing him. Getting back into the main part of the city, he was struck dumb to see Corrigan—or a man who looked exactly like Corrigan—pass in an automobile with Joel Bainbridge. (Of course he did not know that these were Om's fakes.)

Blanton was bewildered, thought himself bewitched. He believed that Bainbridge himself was "Mr. Om"; dared not show himself openly, for fear the police would arrest him again and place him once more in Bainbridge's—or Om's—power. He realized the urgent need of finding and rescuing Hawksbane, but had no idea where to start.

Chapter .6.

At last in desperation, penniless, hungry and worn out for sleep, Blanton sought out an acquaintance of his, one Jack Ridley, a wealthy young sportsman. Ridley agreed to let Blanton use his apartments as a hangout, Blanton merely saying that he was in trouble with the police, and saying nothing about Om and Hawksbane.

Ridley, a garrulous youth, told Blanton of a mystic, Gondai, whose magic and esoteric mummery had become quite a fad among the younger society set. It almost amounted to the establishing of a cult, with Gondai as the high priest, and in Ridley's description of the man, Blanton thought he recognized Togruk Khan. Ridley said that a séance would be held that very night, attended by the elite of society, and Blanton determined to accompany Ridley, on the chance that he might discover some clue as to Hawksbane's whereabouts. With Ridley's aid he disguised himself to an extent he believed would fool the police, who would not be expected to scrutinize a companion of Jack Ridley's very closely. He doubted if it would fool Togruk Khan, but that was a risk he would have to take.

As they drove toward the house where the cult gathered, Ridley remarked that a certain young heiress, Constance Reynolds, seemed to have fallen under Gondai's spell more than any of the others.

At this moment the heiress was the subject under discussion in the house of Gondai, between the mystic and an unidentified man. Gondai asserted that Om had given definite orders concerning the girl, and the other, after some argument, agreed to follow Gondai's directions.

Blanton, arriving at the séance, or "mystical demonstration," noted the audience, all young people, sons and daughters of prominent and wealthy families, and visualized a gigantic blackmail plot. Gondai, whom he quickly recognized as Togruk Khan, in another guise, gave demonstrations of magic and hypnotism, in which Blanton recognized characteristics of devil worship. He saw that this "cult" was being used to debauch the misguided youngsters who came there, and introduce degraded practices to them.

The girl Constance was hypnotized, and disappeared in the midst of a demonstration of black magic which included balls of light floating in smoky mists, disembodied heads leering from the fog, and ghostly voices speaking in strange tongues.

Chapter .7.

Just after the disappearance of the girl, someone touched Blanton on the shoulder from behind some hangings, and he was amazed to recognize Hawksbane. The latter motioned for Blanton to follow, and the adventurer did so, greatly puzzled. Constance was lying, still in a hypnotic trance, on a divan in an inner hallway, and Hawksbane lifted her and carried her to an automobile in the driveway, bidding Blanton to accompany him.

He drove out of the city and up into the hills, stopping in a clump of thick woods near a deep pitlike pond, which lay directly behind a cliff on which stood a house, dark, silent and supposedly untenanted.

Hawksbane placed the unconscious girl in a small hunting lodge, almost hidden among the trees, and asked Blanton to accompany him to the shore of the pool. Blanton, puzzled at his manner, went with him, watching him furtively. Suddenly he saw that a scar he had noticed on Hawksbane's hand was missing, and realized that this was not Hawksbane at all, but someone in his guise. He realized Hawksbane was one of Om's men, who meant to shoot him and throw his body into the deep pool. Both men went for their guns, but Blanton was a fraction of a second quicker, and the false Hawksbane tumbled into the water and sank.

A few moments later Blanton saw a door open in the supposedly solid cliff on the other side of the pool, and a body, bound, gagged and weighted, was thrown into the water. Then the door closed, but Blanton had recognized the body as that of Hawksbane—the real one this time, he believed.

Apparently whoever threw the man into the pool kept no watch thereafter. Blanton dived in and brought his friend up, almost dead. Then he learned the full details of Om's ghastly plot against the whole city. The very next day the plague was to be loosed among the children.

Hawksbane decided that Togruk Khan must be double-crossing his master somewhere, by having the girl Constance brought to the old hunting lodge. He reasoned that if Om had ordered her abduction, she would have been placed in the house of Om, which stood on the cliff overlooking the pool, in which he, Hawksbane, had been a prisoner.

Om believed that the real Hawksbane was dead. Hawksbane decided upon a desperate course—to return to Om's house, and acting the part of the false Hawksbane, Om's henchman, accuse Togruk Khan of disobeying orders. He hoped to lure Om out of the house and into the woods where they could capture him. Leaving Blanton hiding in the hunting lodge with the still senseless girl, Hawksbane returned to Om's house. His ruse worked. Om was fooled by his own invention. Thinking he was talking to his henchman, the false Hawksbane, Om went into a fury when he learned that Constance had been abducted by Togruk Khan. He had other plans for the heiress, including a scheme to blackmail her parents.

As Hawksbane had hoped, Om came to the hunting lodge, accompanied only by the man he thought was the false Hawksbane.

Chapter .8.

In the meantime, Togruk Khan had come to the lodge, and brought the girl out of her hypnotic trance. He gave her the choice of living imprisoned as his slave, or of marrying him openly. In the latter case, he swore, he would defy his master Om—of whom she had never even heard—and aid the police in trapping him. He was narrating to her some of Om's plans, and his own importance, when Om entered, with Hawksbane.

Om, in a fury, killed Togruk Khan in a horrible manner, by hypnotizing him and making him believe that the turban coiled about his head was a serpent. Togruk Khan, tearing at it, pierced his hand with the clasp of the brooch, and died, thinking himself bitten by the serpent which the hypnotic powers of Om had created in his mind.

Hawksbane, snatching up a pistol he saw lying on a table, covered Om with it, and ordered him to throw up his hands. The wizard laughed, and Hawksbane was horrified to see the pistol turn to a bit of wood in his hand. Suspicious of Hawksbane, Om had caused him, by hypnosis, to seem to see a weapon lying there.

Holding the criminologist helpless by his hypnotic spell, Om ordered the girl to kill him with Togruk Khan's dagger. Impelled against her will, she was moving to do it, when Blanton, who had been hiding outside the window throughout the affair, shot the wizard through the head, taking no chances with his weird powers. The story ends with Hawksbane telling of his determination to apprehend the servants of Om, posing as Bainbridge and Corrigan, and give the story of Om's incredible plot to the world, as the three of them drive back to the city from the house of Om.

The Black Hound of Death

(synopsis)

Kirby Garfield was going along a path in the pine woods at night, to warn a man that a bad negro had broken prison and taken refuge in the woods—at least it was thought so. The man's name was Richard Brent. He had come into the piney woods a few months before, apparently not a fugitive from justice. He lived with a single servant, a white man, in a cabin far deep in the piney woods. The servant came out once a month for supplies. The servant was called Ashley. The bad negro's name was Tope Braxton. Garfield, going along the dark trail, heard a man screaming and running. A negro stumbled into him and fell, groaning. He struck a match, and saw that it was Jim Tike, a nigger who lived at the edge of the deep pines. Tike was horribly ripped and torn, as if by hounds. Before he died he gasped out that a masked man had hired him to guide him into the deep weeds—called Egypt. This man's mask has slipped, and the man had killed him. Garfield believed the man had set dogs on him. He looked up to see a dark figure looming in the path, unspeaking. It approached and he struck a match. Instantly with a snarl the thing—or man—struck the match from his hand, slashed murderously at his throat, and was off in the pines, as Garfield blasted away at him. Investigating, Garfield was horrified to find that his shirt and shoulder were slashed as was Jim Tike. He hurried on, intent on finding and warning Brent. He found the man alone in his cabin. Ashley had gone after supplies. Brent went into hysteria when told of the affair and drove Garfield from his cabin with a shotgun, firing after him. Believing Brent to be insane, Garfield left the cabin, intending to return to the village and get men to bring in Jim Tike's body. On the way he met Ashley, accompanied by a frightened girl who said she was Brent's niece, Gloria Brent. Garfield determined to return and see her safe to the cabin, despite Brent's former threats and Ashley's hostility. He returned with her, and Ashley tried to murder him, obsessed with the belief that he was a spy for a mysterious enemy he called Grimm, and to escape whom he had hidden in the woods. Garfield gathers, from the remarks dropped by the men, that Brent had been on an expedition in inner Mongolia with Grimm, and that he had deserted the man when they were attacked by fanatical natives. Grimm had somehow escaped and returned to America, and was hunting Brent for vengeance. Brent ordered Garfield from the cabin, and he went in disgust, but returned, thinking of the girl, just in time to see the cabin apparently go up in a burst of flame. Dazzled, he received a blow on the head, and when he regained consciousness, he found himself lying in a glade, lighted by a torch. He was handcuffed with cuffs taken from the deputy sheriff Tope Braxton had murdered, and Tope was squatting over him, holding his revolver. Telling Tope that a cross was scratched on the inside of the cuffs, which would damn utterly the man who killed anyone wearing them, he tricked Tope into taking them off. A savage fight ensued, in which Tope was killed. Garfield then hurried to the cabin. Grimm, the dog-headed man, had tossed a mysterious bomb into the cabin which only worked inside walls, which had rendered Garfield and the girl senseless. Ashley, outside, had had his throat ripped out by Grimm, whose jaws were like those of a dog. The girl was spread-eagled on a table, and Brent lay bound on the floor, apparently insane, as was Grimm. In his raving Grimm disclosed the awful punishment inflict on him by the monks of Mongolia. He started to flay the girl, Garfield shot him, and he killed Richard Brent before he died.

Moon of Zambebwei

(untitled synopsis)

The story opens with Bristol McGrath, wanderer and adventurer, making his way through a pine forest toward the ancient Bellville estate, where lived his one-time friend and later rival and enemy, Richard Bellville, the last of the aristocratic line. He had received a letter from Bellville, who had lived in seclusion for three years, begging him to come to his aid and cryptically naming Constance Brand, the girl they both had loved, and who had mysteriously disappeared three years before. Only because of that McGrath had come. Suddenly, making his way along the dim road, amid almost impenetrable walls of pine trees, he saw a human form hanging from a tree ahead of him. It was Ahmed, Bellville's Arab servant and bodyguard. He had been tortured and his tongue cut out, but he was not yet dead. McGrath lowered him to the ground and the Arab recognized him, and traced Arabic characters in the sand with his finger—his master's name, the name of the girl, a warning that danger lurked, and part of a name that looked like John DeAlbor. Then he went limp. McGrath determined to hasten on without delay. He believed that Constance lived and was in danger. But he felt that peril lurked on the road; he had visited the Bellville mansion in the youth and he remembered an old trail which parallelled the road at a distance of some three or four hundred yards and approached the back of the house. Turning, as if to retrace his steps toward the distant town, he rounded the turn in the road, out of sight, then plunged straight through the woods until he struck the old path. Following it, he presently came to the back of the crumbling old mansion. The scream of a man in agony hastened his steps. Looking through a window, he saw Richard Bellville being tortured by a hideous negro. Leaping into the room he killed the negro with his knife, and released Bellville, who was dying. The man told him that he had kidnapped Constance three yeas ago and had kept her captive in the mansion, trying to force her to marry him. No one lived in that lonely, isolated river country except negroes, descendants of slaves owned by the Bellville family. His power over them had been absolute, until the coming of John DeAlbor, a negro from Haiti. This man had made voodoo worshippers out of the negroes, and he lusted for Constance. He had seized Bellville by force and was torturing him to make him divulge her whereabouts, for Bellville had hidden her in a place no one knew but himself. DeAlbor had gone away to talk to his henchmen, leaving the negro to guard Bellville, and this man had decided to torture the white man himself. While telling, and having revealed that the girl was hidden in a cavern back in the tangled forest, Bellville died. Mcgrath was about to start out to the cave, when a man entered the house, an Oriental in a turban with a beard, who said he was the brother of Ahmed, and that the latter had sent for him. He desired vengeance against the negroes. They made their way to the cavern in the heat. The Arab, Ali, gave McGrath a drink of wine from a flask. They found the cavern, where Constance was concealed, and McGrath opened the massive door as Bellville had told him. Then he was struck down from behind by Ali, who seized the girl. McGath lay helpless, conscious but paralyzed, and Ali taunted him telling him that the wine had been drugged, with a jungle drug which became active through a heavy blow on a nerve center. He tore off his turban and beard, revealing himself as a mulatto negro—John DeAlbor. He said he was leaving with the girl; but a band of negroes rose out of the brush and surrounded him, demanding that she be sacrificed. They all went away except for one negro who remained to behead McGrath. The white man had recovered from his paralysis, however, and killed the negro after a savage fight. Following the band into the deep swamps, he came upon DeAlbor and captured him and was about to kill him when the mulatto said only he could save Constance. McGrath released him, and followed him to the place of Execution, where the girl was to be given to a huge ape. DeAlbor lost his nerve and was about to sacrifice the girl to save his own hide; McGrath shot the ape which went mad and wrought havoc among the negroes, during which McGrath and the girl escaped.

"The Story Thus Far..."
(Skull-Face)

(The November and December 1929 installments of "Skull-Face" in Weird Tales were headed by a short recap of the preceding chapters. Such paragraphs were usually written by the magazine's staff, but because Howard is known to have written the recaps for at least one of his serials, "The People of the Black Circle," we present the following.)

The Story Thus Far.
(Chapters 1-12)

Stephen Costigan, an American hashish addict in London's Limehouse district, is released from the hashish craving by a skull-faced man known to his slaves as the Master, and as Kathulos of Egypt, who gives him an elixir so strong that he is consumed by fiery tortures when he is deprived of it. Costigan is sent by the Master to murder Sir Haldred Frenton, disguised in the hide of a giant ape, but gives himself up to John Gordon of the British secret police, and Gordon raids the Master's retreat in Limehouse, rescuing Costigan, who has been sent ahead as a decoy. The Master and his fanatics escape through a snake-infested tunnel, to continue their plots to overthrow the white race and establish a black empire. With him goes Zuleika, who has given Costigan enough of the elixir to last him four days.

The Story Thus Far.
(Chapters 1-17)

A mummy-case is found floating in the ocean, and taken on board ship. The next day the mummy has disappeared, and the scientist in whose stateroom it was kept is found murdered. Following this, rebellion and unrest seethe throughout Africa and Asia, and rumor says that the old prophecy will soon be fulfilled, that a "Man from the Sea" will overthrow the rule of the whites and establish a black empire. In London's Limehouse district a mummified, leprous-looking man, known to his slaves as the Master, as the Scorpion, and as Kathulos of Egypt, rescues Stephen Costigan (an American dope addict) from his craving for hashing by giving him an elixir so strong that he is racked by fiery tortures when deprived of it. The Master sends Costigan to murder Sir Haldred Frenton, but Costigan gives himself up to John Gordon of the British secret police, and Gordon raids the Master's retreat in Limehouse, but the Master and his fanatics escape through a snake-infested tunnel. Zuleika, one of the Master's slaves, with whom Costigan is in love, has given him enough of the elixir to last him for four days.

ROBERT ERVIN HOWARD (1906-1936) grew up in the boomtowns of early twentieth-century Texas, eventually settling in Cross Plains where he lived for the remainder of his short life. Deciding early on a literary career, he spent the bulk of his time crafting stories and poems for the burgeoning pulp fiction markets: *Weird Tales*, *Action Stories*, *Fight Stories*, *Argosy*, etc. Howard's literary reputation was assured with the publication of "The Shadow Kingdom" in 1929, which featured a unique blend of Fantasy and Adventure which has since been termed Heroic Fantasy. The creation of Conan the Cimmerian in the pages of *Weird Tales* has earned him lasting recognition.

ROB ROEHM has edited more than a dozen Howard-related books for the REH Foundation Press as well as a couple with his own Roehm's Room Press. He has won multiple awards for his research and writings in a variety of Howard-themed publications. He has traveled to every location in the United States that Howard mentions visiting—from New Orleans to Santa Fe, and dozens of Texas towns in between—verifying and expanding our knowledge of Howard's biography. His research has also uncovered lost Howard stories, letters, and poems. He writes about these discoveries, infrequently, at howardhistory.com.

PAUL HERMAN, long-time engineer and intellectual property attorney, began publishing REH in 1999 via his own Hermanthis Press and later, Wildside Press; he has edited well over one million words. His etexts have been the starting material for a significant number of REH books published in the last 17 years. His REH bibliography, *The Neverending Hunt* became the new standard when it was first published in 2006, and is the basis for the HowardWorks website. His wife of 38 years, Denna, continues to tolerate his hobbies. Paul currently resides in Weatherford, Texas, a few miles from Robert E. Howard's birthplace.

MARK WHEATLEY holds the Eisner, Inkpot, Golden Lion, Mucker, Gem and Speakeasy Awards and nominations for the Harvey Award and the Ignatz Award. He is also an inductee to the Overstreet Hall of Fame. His work has often been included in the annual Spectrum selection of fantastic art and has appeared in private gallery shows, the Norman Rockwell Museum, Toledo Museum of Art, Huntington Art Museum, Fitchburg Art Museum, James A. Michener Art Museum and the Library of Congress, where several of his originals are in the LoC permanent collection.

DON HERRON published his now classic defense of Robert E. Howard's Conan stories, "Conan vs. Conantics," in 1976—and the very next year he began leading The Dashiell Hammett Tour in San Francisco, which continues hiking up and down those mean streets to this day. Among other titles he has edited two critical anthologies on Howard, *The Dark Barbarian* (1984) and *The Barbaric Triumph* (2004)—plus *Willeford* (1997), a book about the books written by the cult crime writer Charles Willeford. The first of his "Mr. Hunt" stories, written in homage to Hammett and the Black Mask school of hard-boiled detective fiction, is included in *San Francisco Noir 2: The Classics from Akashic Press*.

STÅLE GISMERVIK has been passionate about REH since discovering Conan in 1990. He established one of the earliest and largest Conan-focused websites, and currently manages the comprehensive REH resource at reh.world. Ståle also administers the Robert E. Howard Foundation website and its Press counterpart, and oversees the curation and editing of Foundation eBooks. He has also taken on the role of preparing the new Ultimate Books for publication. His work contributes to the preservation and promotion of Howard's legacy.

9 781955 446